LO

LARGE

LOVEJOY AT LARGE

An Omnibus

featuring

SPEND GAME
THE VATICAN RIP
THE TARTAN RINGERS

Jonathan Gash

ARROW BOOKS

Arrow Books Limited
20 Vauxhall Bridge Road, London SW1V 2SA

An imprint of Random Century Group

London Melbourne Sydney Auckland
Johannesburg and agencies throughout the world

First published in Great Britain by Arrow Books, 1991

© Jonathan Gash 1991

Incorporating

SPEND GAME
First published in Great Britain by
William Collins (The Crime Club) 1980
Hamlyn Paperbacks edition 1980
Arrow paperback edition 1986
Mysterious Press edition 1988
Reprinted 1989

© Jonathan Gash 1980

THE VATICAN RIP
First published in Great Britain by
Collins (The Crime Club) 1981
Hamlyn Paperback edition 1983
Arrow edition 1986, reprinted 1986
Mysterious Press edition 1989

© Jonathan Gash 1981

THE TARTAN RINGERS
First published by William Collins Sons and Co. Ltd 1986
Arrow edition 1987, reprinted 1987
Mysterous Press edition 1988

© Jonathan Gash 1986

The right of Jonathan Gash to be identified as the author of this work has been asserted by him in accordance with the Copyright, Designs and Patents Act, 1988.

Phototypeset by Input Typesetting Ltd, London
Printed and bound in Great Britain by
Courier International Ltd, Tiptree, Essex

ISBN 0 09 982440X

Contents

SPEND GAME

Chapter One

No matter what people say, you can't help getting into trouble. And the antiques game is nothing *but* trouble – beautiful, lovely trouble all the bloody time.

This story starts where a pretty but terrified woman was holding my hand in a thunderstorm. We were looking down at the dead man in the ditch, and I was frightened too. In fact, I bet I was more scared than she was, because I knew roughly why he'd been killed. She didn't.

The rain was hurtling down in great falling clouds. We were soaked and it was pitch black. Occasional sheets of lightning washed the silent night sky into sudden silver, letting us see his face and our own aghast paleness. It was my friend from the auction, all right. We call him Leckie. The rumble of thunder from the east seemed to shut the light away and Sue and I hung on to each other's hands for dear life. We slithered down the embankment from the road, calling out to see if he gave any sort of answer, though I think we both realized he was killed the moment he was flung clear of his tumbling car.

'A torch, Lovejoy,' Sue said frantically. 'We need a torch.' I was impressed. Women are so much more practical. Often useless, but permanently practical. She kept on about a torch, getting me mad.

'I've not got one.' I was literally shaking.

She sounded snappy. 'Everybody with any sense keeps a torch in their car.'

'I've not got one,' I said back doggedly.

3

'You should always keep – '

'Shut up.' I needed to think.

'Headlights!' Sue exclaimed, tugging at me. 'Lovejoy, your headlights! You can turn your car this way with the lights on – '

' – Then we can see what we already know,' I finished for her. 'That he's already dead.' She was getting me madder, as well as more frightened. What if the big car came back? It had been deliberate, blundering into a lunatic swerve and chucking Leckie's little car into the air like that.

'Have you a lighter?'

'You know I don't smoke.'

'Then feel his pulse.' This sort of thing turns my stomach over, but Sue might be right. You never know till you make sure.

We'd seen his flying body leave the car and hit the roadside tree, to flip brokenly aside towards the ditch. All these unlit country by-roads in East Anglia have ditches lined by hedgerows, though they were no shelter. Sue's blonde hair was straggling across her face from the rain. We couldn't get any wetter. The sheet lightning showed us how poor Leckie lay crookedly in the glistening mud, folded into the spattering ditch water, his left shoulder humped under a grassy overhang and his overcoat crumpled up above his waist. Leaving Sue's hand I slid down towards the muddy bottom and reached along Leckie's arm, thinking, where the hell do you find a pulse? His hand felt warm. Dead, but warm. For a minute I pressed anxiously around his wrist, with no real hope of knowing what I was doing.

'Well?' Sue whispered down.

'Well what?'

'His *pulse*,' she hissed.

'I don't even know what a bloody pulse is,' I hissed back, though why we were whispering in a downpour at the bottom of a ditch with the nearest village six

4

miles away God alone knows. Death does it, makes whispers. Sue clucked from exasperation and slid down beside me with a muddy splash.

'I'd better do it. You're *hopeless*, Lovejoy . . .'

I pressed Leckie's hand towards hers. She gave a small gasp as her fingers touched the cooling skin but gamely stuck to the task. Every so often I listened for an approaching car just in case. There had been two men in the sleek motor that had seen Leckie off. They had seemed casual enough to come driving coolly back with the intention of 'finding' the accident and reporting it to the police. They might have enough nerve, but would they be so stupid? They'd performed a swift, silent search, very businesslike and rather sinister.

'Lovejoy,' Sue whispered.

'What?'

'I can't feel his pulse.' A pause. 'He's dead.'

I pulled her up on to the tall roadside grass. We sloshed back to where my contraption was parked in the muddy gateway of a large field. The lightning was still busy battering the low valley. On the underbelly of the stormclouds to the south you could see the orange glow from our local town's lights, some miles of wet fields and woods away.

'What do we do, Lovejoy?' she asked.

'We go back.'

'Back? To Medham?' I'd attended the antiques auction in Medham that afternoon. It's my game. I'm an antique dealer.

'No, Sue. To the main road.'

'But the police, Lovejoy.'

I opened the door and pushed her in. The trouble with women is they think everybody else is law-abiding and peaceable. Their belief happens to be untrue but I usually go along with them to save bother.

'You *will* phone the ambulance, Lovejoy?' Sue demanded as I climbed in beside her.

I pretended to reflect a split second, then gave her

5

a smile I hoped was reassuring. In that instant, dwelling on the relative usefulness of honesty and untruth, I settled swiftly for falsehood. It's more predictable, especially when you're in adverse circumstances like now. I've found that.

'Of course,' I said. I switched the engine on and gunned my archaic little bullnosed monster into creaking action. I drove for a few hundred yards by memory and the occasional lightning flash, one hand on the wheel and peering out into the driving rain, until Sue could stand it no longer.

'*Lights*, Lovejoy. For heaven's *sake*.'

'Silly me!' I switched them on and notched up to an aggressive twenty, which for me is flat out with a following breeze.

'What is the matter, Lovejoy?' Sue was eyeing me sideways as I drove.

'It's the shock, love,' I said. It was that all right, because I knew something about Leckie. The more I thought, the more I remembered. We'd known each other on and off for some years.

'They didn't even go down to see if he was all right,' Sue said angrily. 'Those two men. Just getting out and walking over like that, looking in the car and on the grass. They didn't even seem to *care*. You should report them.' (Note: not we, nor I. You, Lovejoy. *You* should do the reporting. That's a typical woman for you – essential but woolly-minded.)

'Well . . .'

'You should, darling,' she urged me earnestly. 'Why, they seemed more interested in the poor man's car than – '

I didn't want her dwelling on that aspect too much so I broke in hastily. 'Do you suppose *they* reported the accident?' I asked innocently. After that we drove on in silence. Sue's not daft. She didn't think so either.

I got back to the main road, thankful for the absence

of that powerful car's immense staring lamps and the pair of cold malevolent lunatics that drove it. The storm was still on, but there was plenty of traffic now, switchback lines of headlights undulating in the darkness, buses full of singing football supporters beering their way homewards from the big match, and juggernaut lorries unerringly finding pools to spray over my windscreen.

We drove back to the motorway café. Sue leaves her car there. It is convenient, only a few miles or so from where we live in our respective dwellings in apparent mutual disdain. Her car's one of those long low things the size of a small bungalow, so we mostly use hers for our nocturnal discussions among the hedgerows. This particular night, though, some kind guardian gremlin had nudged me into insisting that we use my own elegant conveyance, a mercifully nondescript little banger I'd painted dark blue to disguise the scrapes. Of course Sue grumbled like mad, but I get these stubborn moods. In summer there's lovely sweet grass to lie on. I could see her point. I telephoned from a booth in the hallway while Sue waited outside. The police station asked my name and address. I obligingly invented the name of a mythical Mr Witherspoon of Solihull, poor chap, and reported finding an overturned car and a man probably dead.

'I stopped four cars for help,' I lied to confuse the issue in case Old Bill got a rush of blood to the head and started filing our footprints. 'They're waiting there for you.'

'Where are you?'

I gave the name of a distant pub at Kelvedon. 'In the taproom,' I told him briskly. It was overdoing it a bit, but I like touches of local colour.

'Wait there, please, Mr Witherspoon,' the constable said, all efficient. 'One of our cars will be with you shortly.'

'Anything to help.'

7

'You didn't mention me, darling?' Sue checked as I returned to the car. I said of course not. When we're together in public she develops that reserved ultra-cool look of the secret sinner, a woman ever so polite but who obviously can't really be bothered with this nerk opposite transparently boring her to death.

It was time to go, Sue being due back home. I raced out with her into the rain. We ran stiff and hunched, holding hands.

'I'm still shaky,' she said in her car.

'Me too.'

'Drive safely, Lovejoy.' The accident was on her mind.

'Don't I always?'

'No, love,' she said. 'Do try.'

We said a protracted farewell. Sue's husband would be home about ten. She had a safe hour to spare when we finally parted, which is our usual safety margin unless passion's particularly rampant. Sometimes we cut it pretty fine.

I waved her off into the streaming traffic and splashed back into the café's brittle glare, but only when I was sure she wasn't going to turn round with some afterthought. I still had some change. The emergency call had cost nothing. Tinker Dill would still be sober so early in the evening, thank God, even at the weekend. I'm so used to phoning him at the White Hart its number's engraved on my cortex.

I got through first time. The public bar sounded crammed and noisy. Some charitable soul amputated Tinker from the bar and dragged him to the blower.

'Whatcher want, Lovejoy?' He was peeved as hell. 'You seen me all bleeding day at the auction.'

'Just listen, Tinker,' I said, putting my threatening voice on. 'And don't radio what I say all round the pub.' I felt his sulks come over, force five.

'Have I to go out?' He hates leaving a pub.

'No. Today's auction. Leckie bought an escritoire, right?'

'Yeah, and – '

'Shut up,' I snarled. 'I told you. Say nothing, just tell me if I missed anything.' The White Hart's one of those rambling old East Anglian pubs where antique dealers congregate in droves. Even the woodworms have ears.

'Don't get shirty, Lovejoy,' Tinker whined. He has a specially humble stoop for whining. I could see him doing it now.

'And a crummy doctor's case, Victorian?'

'Bleeding horrible it was,' Tinker cackled indignantly. 'Bloody prices – '

'And that book.' We paused, thinking. There had been seven hundred items auctioned at Virgil's auction house in Medham that day, a long stint relieved only by ecstasy, beauty, excitement and the scent of profit. A typical country auction in a typical country town. I avoided mentioning Leckie's accident. They would hear at the White Hart soon enough, preferably when I was there. And I'd make certain I looked as astonished as everybody else when the bad news came.

'That's all, Lovejoy.'

'Sure, Tinker?'

'Yeah.' Another pause while his brain swam out of its alcoholic fog. 'Here, Lovejoy,' he croaked in what he imagined was a secret whisper, 'we in trouble again?'

'No, Tinker. See you in a minute or two.'

I left the caff and drove with the rest of the traffic towards the orange sky-glow. The rain was easing now and the cars fewer. I would reach the pub a bit later than usual but the other dealers wouldn't notice because we turn up at all hours. First I had one job to do.

Leckie's one of those people who never seem much

9

while they're knocking about, yet when they depart leave a rather depressing space. We'd been in the army together for a spell, in one of those nasty little wars we used to have going on simultaneously in a dozen places. Leckie and I were in the same artillery unit. He's one of those odd calm Englishmen you get now and then who look great on camels and are naturally full of linguistics whether they come from the slums of Moss Side or a duke's stately home. Leckie always managed to convey the impression that no matter how accurate the desert snipers were the main problem was having sherry trifle properly served when the bishop called for croquet on the lawn. I was posted to a snow-bound war as punishment for getting malaria. I never saw him after till he turned up here.

I found myself smiling as I drove, remembering his arrival. He was a Keswick man, thin and pleasant. He took as naturally to tweeds and hand-sewn leather shoes as a duck to water. It was a noisy Saturday night when he'd sailed in, found me and strolled across. We said hello and chatted. He was out of a job.

'What's the local industry, Lovejoy?' he'd asked, forcing himself to like the gin. It was labelled 'Best London Brands Blended', but only for the sake of appearances.

'Well, we're mostly antique dealers,' I told him. He grinned, shrugged and looked us over, in that order.

'That'll have to do,' he said casually, as if the whole of East Anglia had made him an offer and he hadn't much else on that day.

'Know anything about antiques, Leckie?' Mind you, most antique dealers are utterly clueless about antiques. And the good old public comes a close second.

'No. What does one do?' He watched me grin and shake my head. I told him he hadn't changed. 'I suppose it's buying and selling, something in that line?' he'd gone on, still not batting an eyelid.

10

That was Leckie all over. Didn't care much about difficulties, knowledge and education. He just knew his attitude would carry him through. Most times he'd been right. Like the time our platoon went into a high scrubland plateau where the tribes spoke a weird private language of clicks, hisses and croaks. Within a week he was our official translator, having absorbed the language by a sort of osmosis.

We were never really very close once he started in antiques, just casual competitors in a fierce trade. I don't think I had any special affection for him, even though I'd known him some years. You just don't get many Leckies to the pound, not these days.

I turned off the motorway into town. Our two cinemas and fifty-seven pubs were still hard at it, but the shops had that benign retirement look which all showy glass fronts get after the Saturday rush. A few people strolled, or waited for the buses to take them out into the countryside or down along the estuary to their cold sea-sprayed cottages on the harbour walls. Our town's one official tart was already out, well wrapped, by the furniture shop. I wagged an arm and shouted 'Wotcher, Jo,' to show I wasn't biased, then put my ancient little crate, every erg agog, hard at the slope below the preserved cathedral ruins. It spluttered bravely up towards the garrison.

We're a garrison town; in fact, never have been anything else since Cymbeline did his stuff and Claudius landed. You wouldn't think it, though, because the barracks are now tidied away between the football grounds and encroaching woods, and in any case low terraced houses submerge much of the evidence. You can see the layout of the barracks and spiderhuts from the train, but only if you know where to look. I hurtled at a breathless fifteen into a small street near the barracks and jerked my horseless carriage to a wheezing stop outside a quiet little pub. There were three other cars by the pavement, all innocent. I made sure nobody was in the street as best I could – there are only four or five street lamps there, and they're still those old gas-mantle standards kids can climb up or use for cricket stumps. I hurried round the back street and went into the little stone-flagged yard of the house next to the pub. A knock on the window like a clandestine lover.

'It's Lovejoy,' I said. The light came on over the yard door. Val let me in, her face disapproving.

'You know the time?' she said. I nodded and shook rain all over the carpet.

'I'll not be a minute, love. Has Leckie been?'

'No.'

'Not to leave anything? No messages?'

'No.' She was right to look puzzled. 'Should he have called? You didn't tell me. Is anything wrong?'

She gave me a nip of rum for the cold. Val and I had been friends in the roaring days of youth, learning our adolescent snogging techniques in joint training sessions in school lessons quaintly called 'Agriculture: Methods and Theory.' Education's gone downhill since then. She'd married George, who's the barman at the next-door pub, an arrangement which saves on fares and leaves Val sufficiently free to run an antiques side-line. She does no dealing herself, only guards what's given her until it's collected. Posh London dealers have their own depositories. Lone antique dealers either do without or have a safe lock-up arrangement with some trustworthy soul like Val.

'Can I look?'

'I'll get the key.'

These older terraced houses are admittedly small, but whoever built them had his head screwed on. There's a narrow stone-flagged cellar under each. You enter through a doorway set below a few steps leading down from the yard. There's no window, only a solid wooden door. Val had persuaded the publican to have it metalled with iron strips and linked by a warning bleep in case he ever needed it for extra storage of bottled spirits. When I met up with Val again and incorporated her in my famous arrears system of payment I let Leckie use the same facilities. Antique dealers call this sort of arrangement a 'cran', just as other gangsters call it a drop.

Val and I went down with a flashlight. She always takes time fumbling with the lock because there's no outside light. Only a few weeks before George had rigged up a light bulb on a perilous flex to cast a feeble glimmer on our valuables. My phoney eighteenth-century oak chest was ageing usefully still. Unless my luck changed I'd soon have to auction it, a terrible admission of failure for any self-respecting antique dealer. There was an ebony flute in its case, distinguished by that grim little-finger D-flat key, the size of a small springboard, they had before the Boehm system let the modern instrument makers have some restful nights. Flautists must have had digits a foot long before 1850. And there was my famous non-painting, an oil copy of Il Sodoma's 'tailor' portrait, of that skilled type which abounds in the country areas of England. I'd bought it for a song from a German tourist who had paid the earth. (Tip: never buy a painting without measuring it. If the size of the real thing is well known, and the painting you're considering buying is thirty square inches too small, it follows that the latter is probably a copy – a legitimate copy perhaps, but still a copy.)

Leckie had a few pieces of lustreware on the one shelf we'd rigged up and two of those Lowestoft jugs I hate. But no escritoire, no doctor's bag, and no book. Now there's a thing, I thought. How very odd.

'Lovejoy. Is anything the matter?'

'Eh?'

'What's wrong?' She pulled me round to face her. 'I've never seen you like this, except for that time.' That time was a dust-up everybody ought to have for-

13

gotton by now. Only women remember fights, their own included.

'Nothing, love,' I said jovially.

'Lovejoy?' She kept hold of me. I saw her eyes change. 'Dear God. Is . . . is it Leckie?'

I felt my chest fall a mile. Her face was suddenly white as a sheet. Things clicked horribly into place. I now remembered that holiday she had taken last year with an unnamed friend to the Scillies. Leckie had been away too, by an odd coincidence. After that he'd had more money to buy with. His trade had looked up. Twice he hinted at a silent partner. Christ Almighty, I thought, suddenly weary as hell. It never rains but what it pours crap. Sometimes I'm just stupid. Val and Leckie, for gawd's sake.

'Tell me, Lovejoy.'

'It might have not been him, love,' I said desperately. She drew back and looked at me, up and down and up and down. She shone the flashlight.

'That's mud.'

'There was an accident . . .'

'Leckie?'

'It . . . it looked like him, love, but – '

She walked away towards the wall and stood there a minute.

'It was a car, Val. He got . . . got. . . .'

'Killed,' she said, turning. She fumbled for the key and held the door. 'And the first thing you could think of was what antiques he'd left here, in case there was a chance of making a few pounds.' Her eyes were streaming.

'Not really, Val,' I began, but she wasn't having any and gestured me up the steps.

'Take your stuff out of here first thing tomorrow, Lovejoy,' she said in a monotone. 'You're not nice any more. Don't come here again.'

'Look, love,' I tried desperately. Val and Leckie. How was I to know?

She dropped the key on its string and went into her house, just let the key fall there on to the steps and walked off, leaving the cellar door open and me standing there like a goon. I had to feel around before I could find it, and even then it took a while to lock up. I put the key on the lintel. I knocked a couple of times, half-hearted. She must have heard but didn't come to the door.

The rain had eased off. I cranked my zoomster into feeble bronchiectatic life and rattled back through town towards my own village. It's three miles off to the north-west. Three-quarters of an hour before closing time, the town hall clock said as I trundled past. It would be touch and go, because two miles are uphill. My old crate sounded worn out. It feels these sudden strains, same as me.

Chapter Two

There's nothing so welcoming as a good pub and nothing so forbidding as a bad one. We've some repellent ones, but the White Hart's as kindly as they come. I stood in the porchway pretending to be preoccupied with my coat, but really sussing out who'd got back from the auction. Tinker Dill was there looking like a derelict straight off the kerb in his tattered mittens and rubbishly old greatcoat. He was standing among a group of other thirsty barkers, all runners for us dealers. Tinker might be the shabbiest barker in the known universe, but he's the best by a street. He's also the booziest. He saw me and came weaving through the crowds, not spilling a single drop. A barker only lets go of his glass under anaesthetic.

'Hiyer, Tinker.' I spoke quietly. 'Get my stuff from Val's.'

'Eh?' He goggled.

'You heard.' My eyes were everywhere. 'First thing tomorrow.'

'*Sunday*: Bleeding hell.'

'That's what she said.' We fought to the bar. I chipped out for a refill and snatched at the barman's eye for my usual. Tinker grumbled, but that's nothing new. He hates merely shifting stuff. His job's sniffing out antiques wherever they lurk.

'Where do they go?'

'Tell you later when I've arranged something.' The four people crammed nearest us were dedicated anglers talking about massacring the next bream run on the Ouse. Ted was a mile down the bar and his wife Jenny

16

sprinting between the two bars. It looked safe enough, but I kept my voice down. 'Don't gape about, Tinker,' I said casually, 'but tell me who was here when you arrived.'

Tinker measured the clock and turned round to lean his elbows on the bar. There's never any problem about space round Tinker, not with his pong.

'Helen?' I began, smiling and nodding at the familiar faces in the bar mirrors. I like Helen, long of leg and stylish of manner, shapely of fag-holder and quick of mind. She saw my eyes and nodded a quizzical smile. She does English porcelain mostly, and does it well with profit. Her eyebrows said, Come over here a minute, Lovejoy, but I was busy and frightened.

'She was here,' Tinker growled. 'She's asking for you.'

'Aren't they all?' I looked round some more. 'Jean?' Jean Plunkett's a middle-aged woman who suddenly metamorphosed from a mild housewife into an aggressive dealer about four years back. Continental silver and tooth and nail. Big Frank from Suffolk's been after her for a while now, seeing her as a potential third spouse to add to his bigamous affairs which litter the surrounding countryside. He was busy now, plying her with clever alcoholic combinations. Both Jean and he were smiling happily. He'd bought a copy of a Ravenscroft glass at the auction – unusual, because he's mostly silver and furniture.

'Her and Frank reached the pub before me,' Tinker said jealously. I said to keep calm, we'd buy a helicopter.

We seemed to have the usual crowd, in fact. A score of dealers and barkers, with a couple of tough-looking vanmen to do the lumber in case any dealer infarcted at the thought of having to do any lifting.

'The vannies, Tinker?' I suggested. He grinned a no.

'They came straight here – with Jill.'

Worn out with the worry over Leckie as I was, I just

had to smile. Jill was talking slagware to Brad, a real mismatch if ever there was one. Brad hasn't thought of anything except Regency flintlocks since he learned to read and write, and Jill couldn't tell one from a ballistic missile. She'd been at Medham and bought a good pair of blue saltboats in that odd opaque slag glass which you either hate or crave. Early Victorian furnace workers were allowed to skim off the metalled surface 'slag' at the end of the working day. They used to make what they called 'foreigners', little pieces of art to sell or give. The artistry is often pretty cumbersome and really rather crude, but sometimes varies between the merely natty and the exquisite. It was the only perk glassworkers got in those days besides silicosis. Jill has an eye for such knackery, especially when prices are blasting off as they are at present. She also has an eye for the male of the species. In fact she's known for it. I've never seen her on her own in ten years, nor with the same bloke twice. She carries a poodle the size of a midget mouse, the focus for many a ribald jest.

'She's buying,' Tinker said in a gush of foetid breath from the side of his mouth, still grinning. He nudged me, cackling. 'They've got some shovelling to do later.' One of the vanmen was tickling the poodle's chin. A lot of meaningful eyeballing was going on. I could see Brad was rapidly getting cheesed off. Soon the vannies would have Jill all to themselves, lucky lads.

Good old Tinker, I thought sardonically, still sorting through the crowd. Alfred Duggins was in from down the coast. He's a benign little chap underneath a bowler. Never animated, never interrupts, just incubates thoughts behind his split lenses and sucks on the rim of a quart tankard. He'll do prints and hammered coinage up to the Civil War. He gave me a nod and pulled a comical face at the clock. A laugh. For some reason we haven't yet fathomed he hates going home.

A huddle near the fire caught my attention, gin drinkers all. Two were strangers to me. The man looked a contented sort who had to be a Londoner.

'Was Happiness at Medham?' I asked Tinker, carefully looking away from the extravagant bloke.

'Yeah. You must be blind, Lovejoy.'

'I didn't mean her. I meant him.' The blonde woman had been noticeable in the auction all right. She'd sat on one of the chairs crossing her legs till we were half out of our minds. The auctioneer had even started stuttering and losing control at one point. She happened to glance up as I looked again at her through several layers of pub mirror. Thirty or so, smiling between earrings made of gold-mounted scarabs, original trophies from ancient Egypt. Even without them she'd have been gorgeous. Neat clothes, light fawns and browns. The shoes would match, million to one. Our eyes met. I turned away, but noted the startled air she conveyed. Perhaps it was finding herself lusted at by the peasantry. Maybe I looked as sour as I felt. I liked her. She didn't care much for me. Well, that's the way the Florentine crumbles.

'That grotty escritoire,' Tinker told me. 'Leckie outbid him, remember?'

'So he did,' I said. 'So he did.'

Tinker stared hard over the bar and wagged his eyebrow for another pint. Ted streaked up with it. I watched all this, peeved as hell. I have to wave and scream for service. The slightest gesture from Tinker Dill's like a laser. My eyes got themselves dragged into the mirror by awareness of the woman through the noise and shouts and smoke. She looked carelessly away just in time, back into the huddle of people she was with. Happiness was tapping knees and cracking jokes. The others were falling about obediently with displays of false hilarity. It had to be sham because antique dealers are like a music-hall band – they've heard it all before. Other people in the bar were looking round at them with each gust of laughter and smiling.

'Who is he?'

'Fergus, London. They call him Fergie.'

Fergus, Black Fergus. I'd heard the name. Some trouble a few months back about possession of a silversmith's 'touch', a metal marker for hallmarking. I've heard it's quite legal in the States. Here our magistrates go bananas if you're found with one. The fuss hadn't done Fergus any harm, though. If there'd been any bother he looked well on it.

He was sitting on a fender stool. Facing him was Sven, a Scandinavian originally. Sven was literally washed ashore after one of those terrifying winter storms we have here on the east coast. His ship was a diminutive freighter plying across the North Sea. They put our lifeboats out, and Sven and six others were saved. Sven refused to go home once he was ashore, just simply refused point blank to cross either by air or boat. 'I'll go home when they've built the bridge,' he jokes when people ask what does he think he's playing at. They say he's still got a wife and two kids over there, writing the same sad questions to him in every Monday post. He scratches a living as a freefloating barker, side-trading as a flasher. A flasher's not what you're probably thinking. Nothing genital. He'll go around antique shops sussing out what he supposes to be a bargain – say it's a necklace of carved rose quartz. He agrees to buy it as a present for his girl or wife (note that: a flasher *never* says he's buying for himself). He then gives the least possible deposit, or perhaps 'pays' by a dubious credit card or cheque, and goes into a nearby pub where he tries to sell it at a profit to a tourist or a dealer. If he's successful he returns to settle up, and simply keeps the balance. If not – and it usually is not, especially with Sven – he brings it back complaining the woman doesn't like it or it won't go with her new orange blouse. If necessary he'll break a link and claim he's returning the goods as faulty. That's a typical flasher. It's a hopeless game, operated entirely by useless goons who have even less clue than the rest of us. Sven's the world's worst, but I've a soft spot for him. He got me out of some complicated trouble I was having with a woman once, so I owe him a favour.

Madge was with them, dark-haired, swingly and flouncy in a bluish swingback swagger coat and those shoes that seem nothing but thin straps. She's furniture and porcelain in her shop on East Hill near the Arcade and is probably the wealthiest dealer in town. Her husband has this trout farm to the north of Suffolk. Why he sees so little of her nobody knows. Madge is what we call a 'tea-timer' in the antiques game – she'll take up with a knowledgeable bloke, using any means in her power, until she has assimilated most of his expertise. Then she'll ditch him for a different interest and never again give him the time of day. It's a very novel and worthwhile form of apprenticeship. So I've heard, that is. She currently had Jackson in tow, a rather sad thin elderly man who wears a waistcoat and makes models. He used to do a thriving business in militaria and engineering prototypes, including buying and selling the original designs – now a very profitable line I urge you to buy into as fast as you can. Then he threw himself into Madge's promotions, scattering all caution to the winds. He moved in with her for a spell and the inevitable happened. He was rumoured not to have done a deal in months, at least not on his own account. Madge has thrived.

'They friends?'

'With Sven? No.' Tinker looked about for somewhere to spit but I held up a warning finger just in time. I'd rather him gag than pollute the rest of us. 'I heard Madge introduce him to Blackie at the auction.'

'When did they come?'

'Oh, ten minutes before you.' He lit one of his homemade fags and coughed. The taproom paused respectfully. One of Tinker's specials takes a full ten seconds and starts a mile down the road. He subsided. Conversation picked up again.

'What car?'

'A bleeding great Humber.'

'They know Leckie?'

'Dunno.' Tinker nudged me. 'What's it all about, Lovejoy? You and Leckie had a dust-up over Val?'

Sometimes people amaze me. I stared at Tinker till he grew uncomfortable.

'Well,' he said, all defensive, 'she's got Leckie going because of you and Janie. Everybody knew that.'

Janie and I had our last holocaust three weeks before all this. She stormed back to her husband in her expensive solid-state Lagonda in a livid temper for reasons no longer clear to me. She was always storming somewhere. We'd been together a long time on and off. Very critical of a man, Janie was. She'd found out about Magdalene staying at my cottage for a few days. Wouldn't believe she was only helping me to redecorate. Now how had Tinker Dill spotted the Val-Leckie affair when it had taken a killing to push it into my thick skull?

Suddenly I had a headache. It had been a hard day and tomorrow wouldn't be any easier. There didn't seem to be any clues here, I thought in my stupidity and ignorance. This was all too much to sort out just now. I cast a final glance round and saw Margaret, a cool middle-aged woman who has a neat corner in the town's antiques arcade. I mouthed a request for a lift home. She nodded, smiling to her companion, a tall thin priestly-looking character I'd never seen before, and started to fight her way to the door. I gave the keys to Tinker.

'I don't feel so good, Tinker. Drive my crate back to the cottage, there's a pal.'

Outside, the night air was like a cold flannel on my

face. Margaret came limping out – some childhood injury that, curiously, makes her fortyish roundness more intriguing. She told me I was white as a sheet. In her motor I lay back and closed my eyes as we moved off and the pub noise receded.

'You look terrible, Lovejoy.'

'I've got a bad head.'

'I'll make you a hot drink.' She drove us out of the pub yard into the narrow lane between the hedgerows. 'Come back with me?'

'Yes, please,' I said, astonishing myself, but I couldn't face the Old Bill calling on everybody at all hours asking when we'd last seen Leckie.

'Good heavens!' Margaret cried suddenly. 'Whatever's Patrick doing?'

Patrick's paintings and early Victoriana. He was hanging from his car on the other side of the road, flashing his lights and waving his handbag at us to slow down. We could see him being all dramatic in our headlights. He'd seen us come out of the pub yard and stopped to shout across.

'Carry on, Margaret,' I said. She slowed and started to pull in, winding the window down.

'But Patrick wants to tell us something – '

'Carry on.

'Oh.' She dithered and we jerked a bit, then picked up speed. 'What was all that about, Lovejoy? It might have been important.'

'It would only have been bad news,' I said, and closed my eyes again to shut the horrible world out. The more you remember the more you remember, especially about a bloke like Leckie. Ever noticed that?

Chapter Three

That night was odd, really weird. Margaret made me up a bed in her other bedroom and produced some men's pyjamas. I've more sense than to ask. I hate bathing at night because I never sleep after, so I sat reading Keppel's voyages till Margaret came out all clean and brewed up for us both. She smiled and called me lazy. It's not true that I'm idle – only her coffee's a bit less lousy than mine. She made it plain that our past, er, friendship was not to be regarded as much of a precedent for tonight. We had some cheese on toast to fill odd corners.

'Are you in one of your moods?' she asked me.

'No, love. Tired.'

The phone rang about midnight. Margaret went down to answer it and was kept talking there for a long time. I heard her come up the stairs eventually and heard my door go. I was still into Keppel and didn't look up.

'Lovejoy?' She was in the doorway.

'Mmmh?'

'There's some news,' she said carefully, standing there.

'Go to bed, love,' I told her. 'There's time in the morning.'

'You knew.'

'Good night, Margaret.'

You'll have gathered we antique dealers are a varied bunch. Most of that night I lay awake going over the auction in my mind. Leckie wasn't really a dedicated dealer, not half as good as Patrick, our world-famous

24

pansy, or a tenth as lucky as Helen, or anything like as careful as Margaret. He never had the learning of Big Frank, nor Brad's dedication, Black Fergus's money-backers, or the inside knowledge of the Aldgate mob who are said to bribe half the barkers and auction-eers in the known world. Just a dealer, reasonably good.

I stared at the ceiling, wondering a little about that curious expression. Reasonably good. Leckie is – all right, *was* – a reasonably good antique dealer. Funny, but I'd never thought how very odd it was until now. 'Reasonably good' in the antiques game means really pretty shrewd and very adaptable. Moderate antique dealers go to the wall in a millisec. Hopeless ones never even get off the ground. Now here was the odd thing: I couldn't for the life of me think of a single thing Leckie was *bad* at. How odd. He had even helped Bill and Jean Hassall, friends of mine who deal in furniture and historic maps, to decorate their new house down on the sea marshes at Peldon. Word went round it was a stylish job, though they seemed ordinary colours to me. He was good with engines, too. Thinking about it, with most mechanical gadgets. And his small garden actually grew things, vegetables and flowers and bushes that managed to keep their berries weeks after birds stripped mine clean. He was good at everything.

Dozing sounds easy till you're desperate to do a bit, then it's the hardest thing in the world. Half the trouble was that I was missing Lydia, my enthusiastic and bespectacled trainee. Prim as any nun, she'd finally moved into my thatched cottage for the best of all possible reasons. Like a fool I'd spent my last groat to send her on an antiques course in Chichester, still thirty days to go, so just when I needed her she was missing. See how unreliable women are? I suppose I ought really to have been longing for the wealthy Janie, but I've found that some women creep into your bones.

Funny how things go round and round. I slept fitfully

until the sky turned palish. A car revved distantly. I got up and padded over to draw a curtain. Margaret lives in a flat right in the town centre. You could just see the shops. Yellow street lights were being doused in strings. A bobby stretched an extravagant yawn on the cobbled shopwalk below, probably thinking of a warm bed.

It was the hour when Chandler's private eyes light cigarettes, but I don't smoke. Just my luck. A clatter, suddenly muffled, told me Margaret was up and about. Val's face misted into my mind. Her and Leckie. Tinker said because I'd taken up with Janie that time. Dear God. If I'm good at antiques, how come I am so bad at everything else?

Margaret came in, smiling at my modesty as I hurtled back into bed. She left the light off.

'You've forgotten I'm part of your Dark Past, Lovejoy.'

'I've not,' I said. 'I remember you. Rapist.'

'Cheek.'

She put the tray on a chair and faced me from the bucket seat. Oho, I thought. Here it comes. Coffee and grill.

'Leckie's dead. Tinker phoned to tell you last night.'

'That's terrible,' I said, even-voiced, taking the cup carefully. Margaret goes mad if you spill things.

'A road accident.' Her eyes never left my face.

'Shame.'

'Will the police be round?' she asked, too casual.

'Late as ever, I suppose.' I can be as casual as her any day.

She rose and twitched the curtains back for more light. 'Are you in trouble, Lovejoy?'

That's all people ever say to me. I shrugged.

'How did you know?' she pressed.

'Who says I did?'

'Me.'

26

I slurped her gunge and collared all four biscuits to avoid her challenge.

'Do me a favour, Margaret,' I said. 'If Old Bill calls, act surprised.'

'How did it happen, Lovejoy?'

'When did Leckie leave the auction?' First things first.

'He was still there when I left.'

'Talking to anybody?'

'Loading his stuff, like always.'

I'd forgotten that. Leckie took his purchases with him after auctions, the big stuff strapped under plastic covers on his roof rack. But he hadn't put them in Val's cran, and he didn't have them when he'd crashed. The two tough nuts had gone off empty-handed. So where had Leckie been, between leaving Medham and hitting the tree? Answer: where his escritoire, book and doctor's case now reposed. But where the hell was that? Val's was his only cran.

'Come back, Lovejoy.' Margaret adjusted the curtains and put the lights on.

'If you played your cards right,' I said fluttering my eyelids temptingly, 'you could have me. I'd not tell.'

'Cheek,' she said. 'Breakfast in twenty minutes.'

'Then drive me,' I called after her. She paused to ask where. 'Past a ditch I know,' I said.

Margaret went quiet at that, but finally said all right.

St Osyth village has pretentions to class, but its recent marriages of styles show, so to speak. Bungalows designed in 1930 council meetings, hopeless wartime forgetfulness in architecture and latish 'fifties concrete styles are jumbled about the feet of great Tudor houses and this ancient Priory, making a posh shambles. People go there for holidays, presumably under sentence. There are lovely walls, though, flint and mortar. I got Margaret to take me to Leckie's house. I knew where it was from dropping something off there for him once, but that was all. It's a windmill. It's not as daft as it sounds. It is set back from the road on an ancient mound, looking vaguely like a large dome-topped shed with a rectangular base and steps up to its one door. It only has two sails now, projecting at right angles to the main building. They never go round. Margaret tried dissuading me from going in but I wasn't having any.

'The police, Lovejoy,' she tried soulfully.

'You've missed the point, love,' I said unpleasantly. 'They're not here.'

I swarmed up the struts to the door, to save leaving any signs of me on the steps. Leckie's alarm's the same as mine. I unkeyed it easily and stepped inside the place. I waved Margaret up but she wouldn't come, which was a pity. Women have this instinctive ability to judge if anybody's been in lately, if anything's out of place. I'd have to manage on my own.

Apart from a small Continental clock with a rare platform escapement (you can still pick them up for less than a day's wages) there wasn't an antique in the place. And it hadn't been done over, either. Neat, fairly clean; signs that some resident obsessional woman came in to dissect the joint every morning. There was a note from a daily help explaining something complicated about the groceries and wanting a weighty decision on the fish delivery next Thursday. I read it for background, but got nowhere.

I must have been in there an hour. Margaret was on tenterhooks all this time, and hooted her horn several despairing times. Nothing. I re-set the alarm and swarmed my inelegant way down the windmill's running struts to ground level.

'Ta, doowerlink,' I told her. She was mad at me for taking the risk, but drove us back to the side road where I'd seen Leckie done in last night. We went in silence, me staring politely at the countryside and

Margaret changing gears noisily to show me how mad she was at me.

There was no sign of Leckie's motor. One ugly set of tyre burns marked the camber. A horrible whitish scar showed vividly on the elm trunk. Two bobbies measured and mapped. I told Margaret to stop, and wound the window down. We were the only vehicle except for a police car blinking its blue light for nothing, as usual.

'Good morning,' I called. 'Can I help?'

'What are you doing here, Lovejoy?'

Oh hell. I'd not seen Maslow, lurking behind the car. Burly, aggressive, and being all geriatric macho with a pipe and overcoat.

'No, Maslow.' I stayed pleasant. 'Let's begin again. What are *you* doing here?'

'Leckie had an accident.' He peered in at Margaret and walked round to memorize her number. I seized my opportunity, quickly got out and went over to the ditch. A photographer clicked away in the undergrowth. I was beside him in a flash, trampling about among the white tapes laid carefully along the ditch bottom. He yelped and tried to push me off.

'Keep back there . . . ' A bobby flapped his arms hopelessly.

I tut-tutted and trampled a bit more before climbing out. Maslow was glowering. He does it really well.

'You stupid burke, Lovejoy. We're photographing the footprints.'

'Where is Leckie?' I asked innocently.

'It was last night. Leckie's dead.' He paused, glanced shrewdly at the ditch. I saw it coming. 'Where were you – ?'

'Don't be daft, Maslow,' I said. 'You couldn't sound like a proper detective in a million years.' He's head of our local CID. 'I've alibis even – ' I smirked – 'even for breakfast.'

29

He glanced towards Margaret as she got out of the car.

'You aren't very surprised to hear the news.'

'I'm more than that. I'm astonished. Why is the head goon doing spadework for a routine crash?'

He smiled, bleak. Margaret had joined us nervously.

'I know you, Lovejoy, you bastard,' he said, all ice. 'You're always bother, and I don't like it, lad. I have more trouble with you than all the antique dealers in the kingdom. Tell me what you know.'

I thought a bit. 'No,' I answered calmly. He eyed me.

'Then you're in trouble, Lovejoy. And I'm nasty.'

'I know.' I paused. 'Oh. One thing, Maslow. You must make a real effort to find the baddies. Otherwise . . .'

'Yes, Lovejoy?' Quiet and dangerous. The constables were suddenly still, listening.

'Otherwise keep out of my frigging road,' I said over my shoulder. 'While I do it for you.'

'One day, lad, one day.'

'Don't fret,' I told Margaret loudly. 'He's all talk.' She made a shaky start, but that didn't stop me squeezing my eyes at Maslow in coy friendliness as we passed. He watched us go between the tyre marks.

'Why do you *do* it, Lovejoy?' Margaret was furious, slamming her gears. 'Why?'

'Shut it.' I watched the trees flit past. 'Leckie's not going to be shelved in some crummy office file and forgotten. The poor sod's taxes paid Maslow's wages. It's time Maslow earned some of it.'

'You frighten me.' She was quite pale.

'Then get out and let me drive.'

We coursed into town like tiffed lovers, lips squeezed and not speaking.

Margaret dropped me by the War Memorial. I'd seen Tinker as we passed, waiting outside the Sailor's

Return on East Hill, twenty minutes before opening time. I wonder where he waits if it's raining.

'Wotcher, Lovejoy,' he croaked, a horrible lazaroid spectre so early. It looked touch and go whether he'd last out.

'Get my crate from the cottage, Tinker.'

'Bleeding hell. Right now?' He kicked the pub door in distress.

I relented. 'In half an hour, then. Look. Who told you?'

'About Leckie? Patrick. I phoned Margaret.' He was peeved I'd taken no notice.

'Where'll he be now?' Knowing this sort of thing's a barker's job. He rummaged around in his mind.

'Just left Lily's,' he decided finally. 'You'll catch him at St Nicholas.'

That was odd, but I know better than argue with Tinker's mental radar. I hesitated.

'Black Fergie,' I said. 'Suss him out, eh?'

'And that bird?' He was grinning all over. 'Her with the big knockers?'

'Charmingly put, Tinker. Her too.'

I left him thirsting and cut across by the remains of the Roman Wall. Pneumatic drills were going. Another car park, more progress. St Nicholas is a late-Saxon church, rescued from destruction by conversion into a museum. It specializes in farm crafts and rural occupations. I'd given it a set of three ladies' decorated clay pipes, seventeenth-century, to help get it started. I must have been off my rocker. They're worth a fortune now.

Patrick was there as Tinker said, arguing in the foyer and stamping his foot. I don't know how Tinker does it. I waited impatiently for Patrick's tantrum to subside. Lily was catching it good and proper for buying some old Indian playing-card counters of mother-of-pearl made for some officer in the days of the Raj.

'You won't be told,' Patrick was wailing. He spoiled

the effect by seeing how dramatic he was being in his handbag mirror. 'I said don't pay more than sixty quid.'

'But, darling – '

'Don't.' He closed his eyes and reeled about a bit. Lily gasped and propped him up. 'I can't *bear* it.' They're partners. She's married to this engineer but loves only Patrick – and so does Patrick. I'd explain further but it's too complicated.

I lost patience with all this drama, partly because sixty quid for a complete vintage set of officers' 1878 counters is a gift.

'Look, girls,' I interrupted. 'About Leckie.'

Patrick recovered and shook Lily off.

'Lovejoy.' He glared and shook a finger. 'I've a good mind to smack your wrists. You and that cow Margaret *ignored* me last night. You – you barbarian.'

'Who told you about him?'

'You don't deserve to know,' he pouted. He's like this all the time. Lily thinks he's marvellous. Why women go about looking for a crucifix to carry heaven knows. Life's difficult enough.

'Speak up,' I said, not smiling. 'Or I'll be narked.'

He looked at me. 'Well. It was Bill, Bill Hassall.'

'Where?'

'Lovejoy,' Lily cut in. 'Patrick's emotionally disturbed about Leckie. Couldn't you leave it to some other time?'

'Where?' I said again.

'The King Hal at Medham. I went back for some stuff and popped in for drinkies.' He vapoured again, tottering on to Lily's arm. 'And you're a heartless beast, Lovejoy, so there.'

'Come on, darling. Rest.' Lily gave me a reproachful glance. I left them doing their thing, thinking, well, well. Bill.

Bill Hassall. Now, how did he come into it? He'd been at the auction too but I'd a vague idea he left early. His was the house I told you about that Leckie painted. I crossed to Woody's nosh bar for a cup of his outfall. Tinker would be bringing my zoomster in a few minutes. I decided I'd go to Peldon and maybe see if Leckie's colours had faded.

Tinker was in a flaming temper delivering my old wheezer opposite the post office. The pub had been without him a full half-hour. I gave him a quid. For once he didn't sprint off.

'Here, Lovejoy. Are we in trouble?' That old refrain.

'Not more than usual. Why?' He'd left the engine running so I wouldn't have to wind it up. Rust sprinkled the roadway from the vibrations.

'That bleeding grouser niggled me on Bercolta Road.' Grouser is dealers' slang for a policeman of nasty disposition. He meant Maslow. 'Stopped me and asked where you were last night.'

'*Bon* appetite,' I said, ferreting into the stream of eastbound cars. There was no sense in stopping to explain to Tinker.

Half a mile and I was past the turn-off and heading out into horrible open country where no antique shops exist. Most traffic swings due east there towards the Clacton coast. I settled down at a pacy 18 mph on the switchback rural road due south to Peldon marshes. Driving gives you a chance to think.

I'd been to yesterday's auction because of the Kashan carpets, a lovely pair. The auctioneer – dumber even than us antique dealers, which is mind-boggling – had written them up as Isfahan. The luscious deep red gave the Kashans away, that and the fine knotting, the double borders, the lustrous feel. See the carpet-dealers in Persia price an antique carpet worth its weight in gold. They do it by a cigarette, counting the number of knots per single fag length. The more knots, the greater the price. Kashans will have two, maybe three times as many as Isfahans. And the coarser Isfahans are usually three times the size, often fifteen by twelve feet. These little darlings were six by four. Helen told me I stood no chance. I said who cares and I wasn't interested anyway. Seeing them go to a quiet Manchester dealer broke my heart. He paid a brave price, knowing how exquisite they were.

I swung past the football ground, tears in my eyes at the memory. Other than that the auction had been pretty uneventful. I'd seen Leckie win the escritoire, bidding against Helen, Jill, Patrick, Brad and a couple of others including Fergie. I'd gone out at that point to talk over an alleged Estonian parcel-gilt tankard by Dreyer, 1780 or so. It was a fair copy, modern of course. Nodge, a 'thin' dealer from the antiques Arcade in town, had been trying to unload it for weeks. Thin means holding only low-grade antiques, mostly junk. That must have distracted me because I hadn't seen the rest of the auctioned items close to. I'd eventually got fed up and streaked off for some of Sue's special consolation. I hadn't even seen the things Leckie bought, though I'd heard Helen say she'd tried for all three.

The road to Peldon seems downhill, through woods and receding fields. After a dozen miles the sea glistens and the estuary's before you. Mersea Island's a mile off, with the Strood road straight as a die across sea marshes then climbing the island's dark green shore. It floods with each tide. When that happens you follow the marker posts, but it's safer to wait for low water. Peldon's the village this side.

Bill and Jean Hassall had married, to general astonishment, only a month before. They'd been lovers and antique-dealer partners for six years. Patrick shrilly called them obscene exhibitionists, then insisted on choosing Jean's wedding outfit. He drove us all crackers, phoning everybody at all hours asking if beige clashes with yellow, stuff like that. We'd all gone. A boring business, enlivened only by Big Frank trying to do a deal with the vicar for his sixteenth-century reredos.

Their bungalow stands back from the narrow rutted lane. Bill keeps geese and chickens. Jean does folksy handloom weaving, using invented patterns she says look Gothic. Bill's car was missing when I bowled up. He usually leaves it by the gate. Just my luck to find them out. Timothy sprinted up, barking furiously, then halted sheepishly when he recognized me. He rolled over on his back.

'Look,' I said as I passed, 'Let's come to some arrangement. You don't scratch my belly, and I'll not scratch yours. Okay?'

He followed me round the back, wagging happily. Why these animals are always so pleased at me I don't know. Jean was in, clacking away at her loom. I knocked on the open window.

'Is that supposed to be medieval?'

'Lovejoy.' Her eyes were wet. 'Did you – ?'

'I heard.'

'He decorated our bungalow,' she said, weeping steadily.

'Your woof's a mile out,' I couldn't resist telling her. 'Early English weaving's characterized by –'

She gave me a half-incredulous laugh and shook her head. 'Come in, Lovejoy. You're good for the soul.'

Timothy hurtled ahead of me into the little kitchen, obviously delighted at the digression.

'Bill's gone into town. Inspector Maslow phoned.' She mechanically started to fill a kettle.

'Did Leckie call here last night, Jean?'

She paused, looking tearfully at me. The kettle over-flowed but she took no notice for a moment.

'No.' She suddenly became careful, slow in her actions. I watched, thinking, oho. The match, the stove, the coffee bit. 'How did you find out, Lovejoy?' she asked quietly.

I almost said find out what, but turned it into a shrug

35

just in time. I stirred Timothy absently with my foot to gain a second. My mind blared *What the hell's going on around here*? Suddenly I felt completely out of touch with everything.

'Oh, just two and two,' I said casually.

'Do the rest know?'

'Well, no.' *Know what*?

'It was my fault, not Leckie's.' Jean stared out of the kitchen window, swirling a spoon round and round in the same cup, her eyes fixed on nowhere. 'Bill has no idea, Lovejoy. Please.'

I nodded, avoiding her by playing with Timothy. Now it was Jean and Leckie, as well as Leckie and Val. Gawd, I thought, Leckie put it about. Nearly as bad as me.

'We broke it off a dozen times,' she went on absently. 'I think Bill occasionally suspected. You know how Leckie was – self-sufficient, independent. He never really needed me, not really. I don't know why he bothered. Now this.' Jean wept steadily, stirring away.

I gave her a minute, then interrupted. 'The auction. You saw him at the auction?'

'Yes, but not like that.' She sniffed and dabbed her face. 'Only with the others. We left before him.'

'Why did Maslow phone you?'

'Our address was in Leckie's car.'

Which all seemed fair enough and quite tidy. Now, Bill Hassall's a cheerful pleasant sort of chap. He wasn't the sort to do Leckie in because of Leckie and Jean. At least, so I thought. Anyway, the point didn't arise because Bill hadn't known. Jean said so, and women are famous for being pretty shrewd about this sort of thing.

'Where did Leckie leave his stuff?'

She swung round, ready to accuse me of greed the same way Val had. Then she paused, tilted her head quizzically.

'You clever bastard, Lovejoy. You didn't know.' She examined me some more. 'So I gave myself away. Lovejoy, it – it *was* accidental?'

'What else?' I rolled Timothy about. He was in ecstasy. Dogs never seem to worry like us.

'Leckie takes – took his stuff with him. Isn't it to some place in town?'

The problem seemed clear, yet more obscure. Leckie had loaded his items from yesterday's auction. They'd now vanished. Then Leckie got done, with precision, by two hard lads who'd searched his car and found nothing. Apparently he'd been late leaving Medham.

I decided not to wait for Bill. There was an antiques fair at the King George in town. Everybody would be there sussing out the exhibits, and so would I. Timothy accompanied me reproachfully to my crate. Jean waved me off from her window. I heard the clack-clack of her handloom begin. Some consolation.

As I pulled away I had a sudden curious thought. Forget for a moment the problem of where Leckie had *been*. The mystery then changed into: Where was Leckie *going*? That narrow lane where Sue and I snog leads hardly anywhere, maybe a farm or two. In fact, it's one of these purposeless loop roads the ancient Britons were expert at creating, which is why I invariably choose it for seeing Sue and other birds.

I swung left on to the town road, the estuary behind me, now worried sick. Did Leckie know where I'd be snogging busily in the rain last night? Maybe he did, and came haring that way because the hard lads were after him.

I felt ill. If so, Leckie had been racing to find me. For help. And I'd sat there safely out of the rain contentedly rutting and watching him get done. Not good enough, Lovejoy. Nil out of ten, and no star for effort.

'Do better next time.' I gave myself the stern order in the clattering car. Only there would be no next time for Leckie. I normally feel quite proud of myself, even if nothing happens to justify the feeling. This time I drove miserably on, feeling a louse, I tried eating my reserve pasty which I keep in a cardboard box under the seat, but threw most out of the window. I felt I didn't deserve it.

Chapter Four

Tinker was in the sixth pub I tried. By then I was hot and irritable. He was surrounded by a clique of mournful barkers each sourly trying to avoid buying the next round and whining in unison about the lack of antiques. Finding them's supposed to be their job. They live on commission, which ranges from a single pint to ten per cent of the purchase price. Tinker, the filthy old devil, was swilling and whining with the rest but I knew his instinct was still there, his brain still tuned for the slightest stray hint of an antique. I'd been screaming for a Regency model of any local East Anglian church, but he'd not come up with one. And I had a beautiful delicious buyer – actually an irascible retired colonel, but you know what I mean. These models are often done in real stone, complete with gargoyles and real stained glass, real slate and real lead. And when I say 'often' you'll realize by now that term's relative. Cost? Oh, nowadays you'd have to sell your house and car to bid for a good one. Points to look for: named modellists (especially those who *dated* their creations); named churches; whether the model is of a church now destroyed and (last but certainly not least) the model's provenance – that is, who's had it all this time. Remember you're not looking for something tiny – one will cover the average coffee table, doll's house scale. Exquisite things.

'Tinker. Your wally's in,' somebody called, meaning me. A wally is a barker's dealer. I'm good to Tinker. I'm always a mile behind with my payment but I never default. Other dealers 'slice' their barkers' commissions all the time. That's why I'm poor and other dealers aren't. Honesty's a real drag.

I gave Tinker the bent eye and he carried his pint over.

'Just having me dinner, Lovejoy. No dinkie yet.' For dinkie read antique and authentic scale model.

'Sod it. Sit down.' Normally I'd have gone over and joined them. I made sure nobody could overhear. 'Concentrate. About Leckie, women, and me.'

'Eh?'

'Did Leckie know about Sue?'

Tinker's stubby face opened in a cadaverous toothy grin. 'One day you'll catch it, Lovejoy. Everybody knows you're a randy swine.' I held my breath as his cackle wafted over me in a foetid alcoholic spray. 'Sure he did.'

'Did he know *where*?'

'Not from me, Lovejoy.' He began to get my drift and became wary. 'But they call it your loop. That by-road you park in.' This seemed suddenly hilarious to him and he couldn't resist falling about some more. 'Lovejoy's loop. Leap's more like it, eh?'

'Very witty, Tinker,' I gave back gravely. 'So Leckie knew where Sue and I go?'

He sank back into his whining position. 'I told nobody, Lovejoy. Honest. It weren't me.'

'Calm down,' I said testily. 'I've a job for you – find Leckie's stuff.'

He stared puzzled. 'It's all at Val's. I shifted your stuff. His is – '

'No, lad.' I let the fact sink in. His face unscrewed suddenly.

'Hey! You're right! From the auction – '

'Shut up, you burke,' I hissed, throttling him with a hand. He wheezed as I let go. The barkers were listening hard, pretending to chat still; they go all casual, the only time in their lives they seem off-hand.

'His Medham pickings,' Tinker whispered, as if he'd

thought of them and not me. 'They weren't in Val's cellar. Where are they, Lovejoy?'

I gave him a sour grin. 'Off you go.' I could see the penny drop.

'Oh. How soon, Lovejoy? Next week?' he asked hopefully. My smile dimmed his expression.

'By tonight, Tinker. Come to the cottage. No phoning.'

'Lovejoy.' He flicked the quid I gave him out of sight like a frog does a gnat. 'Why's Maslow sniffing about?'

'We tell him nowt,' I said curtly.

'And Val's all burned up about you,' he warned.

I shrugged and left Tinker to saunter back to his cronies while I set out to walk over to the King George by the cattle market. That didn't mean Tinker was being idle. If anything could be sniffed out between now and midnight about Leckie's secret cran Tinker would find it. More important still, he'd make it seem he wasn't actually looking for anything in particular. That was vital. I didn't want those two heavies coming after me, but I badly needed to find Leckie's stuff before they got their hands on it. After all, you don't go killing somebody for *cheap* antiques, do you? Only for valuable, pricey items. And things hadn't been going too well for me lately. I was uncomfortably near the bread-line. I was mad at myself for having missed spotting the stuff he'd bought. In fact, I couldn't quite understand it because I'm what's known in antiques as a 'divvie'. Put me near a genuine antique and I gong like a fire bell. And the more brilliant the antique, the more I gong. Sometimes I can't hear people speaking for the beautiful clanging of my hidden bell. So I was shaken by all this in more ways than one. If there had been anything at all at Medham yesterday I ought to have sussed it out just by standing there looking daft. As it was I'd only felt a few minor chimes. Leckie couldn't have got blotted for mere junk, could he? Vaguely possible, but a hell of a mistake for somebody

41

to make. I could hear street music up ahead, and went between the narrow gabled houses towards the sound.

The other thing which intrigued me was that the two heavies had not even glanced about in the lane, nor shone a light. Therefore they didn't know it was Lovejoy's famous loop. But Tinker said all our local dealers *did* know, which suggested that the pair weren't locals. Anyhow, I hadn't recognized them. Nor would I, in the dark. They had lacked the feel of familiar figures, which was good enough for me, but I was sure they were men. Could Fergus have been one?

Our brass band was playing tipsily in the old coach-yard of the King George as I walked in. People milled about. I like Sunday antique fairs because only the nicest kinds of people are about. The cold thought clanged somewhat as I went in through the arid saloon bar – only the nicest kinds of people plus two. And if Tinker managed to find Leckie's escritoire, old leather bag and book, those two horrible purposeful killers would come knocking on my door, sure as God built trees.

I waved to a few other dealers, beaming like an ape. There's nothing so unprofitable as gloom in our game. Margaret was there, inevitably at the porcelains. She was wearing a new green dress, simple and fetching. That's why I like older women. They never make mistakes the way younger ones do. She beckoned me across. I pushed into the smoke, elbowing the noisy crowd and giving out big hellos everywhere.

'Brought your cheque-book, Lovejoy?' Sven cracked.

'Mine's empty. I fetched yours instead, Sven.'

A laugh all round. Margaret pointed with her eyes. One porcelain leapt into clear view and suddenly I could hardly breathe. Bustelli's porcelains are always on too shallow a base which is uninterestingly level. His cavaliers and ladies, though, are superb. He modelled them mostly from the Italian stage, gestures and all. After he died in 1763 – he barely reached middle age – the Nymphenburg factory in Bavaria was never the same. The most valuable of his porcelains is the Coffee-Drinkers, a Turkish chap swigging with his bird, all rococo. And this was such a piece, genuine, by the master. I could feel the blood drain from my face.

'No,' I said, pretending away. It took all my strength. 'Did you think it was Bustelli?' I chuckled a shrill badly-acted chuckle at her folly.

'Well . . . ' Margaret hesitated, knowing me.

The thirty or so stalls were set out around the rectangular dance hall, mostly draped trestle tables pushed as far back as they would go. It costs a few quid to rent one for the day. An antiques fair usually brings more dealers than collectors. Today we were here in force. This particular stall was a real miscellany of stuff; Victorian fob-watches, spoons, playing-cards, old embroidery samplers and pottery. And in the middle this luscious piece of Bustelli. You never see his Coffee-Drinkers without their background of delicate scroll-work, invariably beautifully done. It was Nodge's stall, the 'thin' dealer I mentioned.

'Thought you had me there, Nodge?' I said affably, putting it down. I didn't even shake. He looked at me.

'It's Bustelli,' he said doggedly.

'Not even Nymphenburg, lad.'

'Get knotted, Lovejoy.'

'Charming.' I made to turn away, desperately thinking of something to say to keep the chat going, paused. 'Oh. That other copy – parcel – gilt thing. You get rid of it?'

'Which?' He looked suddenly shifty.

'You showed me it. Medham. The auction.' I grinned, my antennae still fixed on the Bustelli porcelain.

'Did I?' He glanced uneasily about the room.

'Not like you to forget, Nodge,' I joked. In fact it's not like any dealer to forget. I gave Margaret that look

43

which meant we'd split the price and profit and she picked the Bustelli up casually.

'Oh, er, yes. I sold it,' Nodge said.

'What's the asking price?' Margaret began the deal.

'Take my tip, love,' I told her, moving off. 'Save your gelt. I could make you six copies by tea-time.'

'But I like it,' Margaret said, on cue.

'Women,' I gave back, shaking my head, and nodded a farewell to Nodge. 'Good luck with your crockery, Nodge.' He said nothing, just watched me go.

I drifted about, wondering. During the next few minutes I occasionally glanced casually back at Nodge, to catch his eyes just averting by a millisec. He was definitely uneasy at seeing me. And reminding him of the Medham auction had made him worse. I was suddenly irritable. No antique dealer ever forgets a deal, for heaven's sake. Not ever. And here was Nodge trying to avoid any mention of that Medham auction. Why?

'Lovejoy.' Helen appeared at my elbow. 'Coins, now?'

'Er, no.'

'They're going up. So they say.' Her joke.

'I wish they'd take me along with them.' I'd been staring at a tray of coins belonging to Chris, a hopeful Saxmundham dealer.

'I've hammered silvers, Lovejoy,' he said.

'You're too dear, Chris.'

I was ready to begin a brief enjoyable heckle, to take my mind off worrying, when Helen said the words which changed everything and caused people to start dying all over the bloody place. And none of it was my fault, honest. Not any part of it. I'll swear to that. Hand on my heart, if ever I find it.

'Lovejoy,' Helen said in my ear.

'Your Norman mints are cheaper in London,' I was saying cheerfully, hoping to nark Chris.

'Lovejoy. I've a message.' Helen.

'Mine are finer,' Chris shot back, successfully narked, to my delight.

'*Lovejoy*.' Helen pulled me away an inch. 'I said I've a message for you'.

I let Chris off the hook a second, still smiling. 'Who from, love?'

Helen put her lovely mouth against my ear to whisper. 'From Leckie,' she said.

'Who?' My face tightened. I felt my scalp prickle and could swear the room turned full circle.

'I tried to give it to you last night.'

Cain Cooper saw us talking and deliberately barged us apart, his idea of fun. He's a big puppy, all action and no sense.

'Stop that, you two,' he yelled. General laughter, with people looking our way and nudging and grinning. 'Lovejoy's at it again, folks.'

I managed a grin, with some effort. I was damned near fainting.

'Don't mind Cain,' I told Helen loudly. 'It's time for his tablet.' More laughs as I pulled Helen aside. Nobody more casual than Lovejoy, as Cain returned to his collection of paintings – some even genuine – and we drifted over to see Alfred Duggins, commercial as ever under his bowler.

'I've some good prints, Lovejoy.'

'Lend me one, then, Alf.' Keeping up the wisecracks was giving me a headache. The room seemed suddenly unbearable, stifling. A message from Leckie, when Leckie's dead?

'Let's get out of here, Helen.'

'I tried to phone you all evening.'

'I'd gone to earth.'

Jill bore down on us with her poodle outstretched like a figurehead. It licked me while she tried to interest me in some loose portabilia.

'See you in the bar in ten minutes,' I lied, shamming

45

interest in the set of household gadgetry. Women used to carry them around the house in a small handbag.

'Lovejoy, you're an angel,' she carolled. 'Take good care of him, Helen. Come along, Charles.'

Charles looked knackered. He's one of the vannies. He trailed her back into the smoky oblivion while Helen and I slipped out. Jean Plunkett was still being propositioned by Big Frank from Suffolk in the foyer. We passed them just as Black Fergus arrived, complete with the luscious bird, with a thin cadaverous bloke in tow, incongruous in a bright check suit. I'd seen him before somewhere. Helen and I got out of their way by stepping aside to examine the books. They always set up a bookstall in the downstairs lobby, new collectors' publications and suchlike. Fergus passed us like a carnival and added to the hullabaloo inside. The blonde woman now had an elderly Wedgwood cameo, her scarab earrings presumably back in the family vault. Her eyes had flicked at me, again with that same startled air, before she gave Helen a cool once-over, the typical critical hatred of any two women passing each other. Women don't like other women. Ever noticed that? When we got outside Helen still had her lips thinned out, recovering from having given the blonde tit for tat.

We crossed the road, dicing with death among the traffic. I bought two ice-creams at the entrance to Castle Park, Helen laughing and shaking her head. 'You're like a big kid.'

'Here.' I collared a spot on the low wall near the rose-garden. People were milling here and there.

'This is hardly my scene, Lovejoy.' She examined the wall distastefully. I can't see what's wrong with sitting on a wall.

'Don't muck about, love.' Women get me down when they go all frosty. 'The message.'

'Couldn't we go into the Volunteer?' There was a

bonny breeze blowing, which always makes a woman think of firesides.

'The message.'

She sighed, nodding and perching reluctantly on the wall beside me.

'He gave it me just as I left the sally.' Dealers' slang for auction.

'What did he say?'

' "Give it Lovejoy," he told me. "Nobody else, Helen." It's written down.' She rummaged in her handbag while I held both ice-creams. 'Here.'

An envelope, and the words, '*In case*' written on in pencil. I felt sick because I'd seen the words before and in the same handwriting.

'Was he okay?'

'A bit preoccupied.' She put her hand on my arm. 'I'm sorry. You look so shocked. But I did try to get you all last night, and I told Tinker –'

'It's all right.' I remembered now. Tinker had said Helen wanted a word with me in the White Hart. But that was before they'd known Leckie was dead.

'Aren't you going to read it?'

'Not yet.'

I made Helen describe what happened at Medham. She'd been among the last to leave Virgil's auction warehouse, hoping to do a cash-adjusted swap with Cain Cooper. He'd got a Pembroke table and she had a Regency snuffbox. It came to nothing. Cain roared off in his Aston-Martin while Helen settled up for the two little Georgian watercolours she'd bid for. Leckie had come over and given her the letter.

'Did you see Leckie leave?'

'No. He just stopped to have a word with the whizzers.' They are the lumber men who set out the items for auction.

'Here. You Lovejoy?' This lad was leaning on the wall, his eyes all over Helen's legs. He wore the clobber

47

of the modern trainee psychopath – studded leather, wedge-heeled boots and a faint sneer between pimples.

I gave him the bent eye. 'Yes.'

'What a crummy name.' He snickered. Two of his mates snickered behind him. I looked them all up and down.

'Your gear's out of date, lads.' I watched the consternation show for a second before he turned sulky and cut his losses.

'Clever, clever. Val says call.' They melted among the people going into the Park gates. Helen gazed at me.

'Word is, Val banished Lovejoy from her cran,' she murmured. Despite my worries I couldn't take my eyes off her tongue as it took the ice-cream in lick by lick.

'Word's right.' So now what makes Val change her mind, I wondered.

'I'm dying to know what's going on, Lovejoy.'

'Me too, love.' I gave her a peck on the cheek and dropped down. She moaned away about gallantry, reminding me to come back and lift her down. I wasted more time waiting while she brushed imaginary contamination from her skirt, though Helen even looks good doing that.

'Here, love,' I said. 'Got any change? I could ring Val now.' There's a phone booth near the path to the High Street. She lent me some and I rushed off. I find borrowing's cheaper.

'Val? It's Lovejoy.' A pause at the other end. 'This lad –'

'I sent him.' She sounded world-weary. 'Young Henry from next door. He's a good boy. Going through one of these phases.'

'What is it, love?'

'Oh.' She summoned nerve and rushed the words out. 'Leckie's cousin Moll phoned. She's got a cupboard. Leckie dropped it off last night.'

Now Val can't tell an escritoire from a circus tent.

They are all cupboards to her. I got her to tell me Moll's address. We then rang off, full of hesitations and politeness. It was Val's way of making up. I find that conversations with women are crammed full of significant pauses. It's a hell of a strain sometimes. I was shivering despite the watery sunshine, and the envelope in my pocket weighed a ton.

I sat in Woody's nosh bar, remembering.

The letter was brief, a few words on a crumpled invoice, the sort of paper that accumulates in pockets in spite of good intentions to clear it out. Leckie's hand had scrawled on it hastily:

Lovejoy, Take care. The side walls are even worse this time, older but of course they couldn't be as deep. No running, though. Keep faith, Leckie.

I struggled not to understand, but I knew right enough what he was referring to. I sat staring sightlessly over my tea out at the crowded pavements. The whole lot vanished. I was in a hot, sweaty, hilly land and frightened out of my skin.

Leckie had been an explosives man in the army. Though I was a gunner – so they told me – I was put on a job with him and four other soldiers.

A railway ran perilously high across this plateau, over two gorges, on spindly trellis bridges made of bamboo. Even to think of it now gives me heartburn. We climbed on to the ridge among the vegetation. It had taken us four days to reach. From there we could see the first gorge and the rickety bridge swooping into the tunnel opposite. We saw a hoop of distant light in the blackness where the railway emerged from the hill on the far side. I'd never been so scared in all my life, but Leckie just gave one glance at the scene and stood up, not even using his field-glasses. 'Should be all right, chaps,' he said, and strolled down.

49

That was Leckie all over. With my scalp prickling I stumbled after him. The corporal carrying the radio transmitter was immediately behind, the three yokels to the rear making more bloody racket than a football match. At least I was always quiet in the jungle, more from terror than training. I never did find out how Leckie's sixth sense worked. Other times he'd give the same quick glance, then signal for us to lay low. I'd never even see the sniper till our riflemen got going. This time he was right again, of course. He strolled across the creaking bridge into the tunnel, while I tried not to look down at the river gorge a trillion miles below.

'We blow the tunnel, chaps,' Leckie informed us as if announcing a rather dull menu. We hadn't known till then.

This we tried to do, only the side walls had some concealed internal buttresses made of concrete. We only saw them after our first small explosive charge revealed them among the settling dust. It was a clear mistake, probably unavoidable, but Leckie felt bad about it, especially as he knew we were all petrified. The echoes were still reverberating round the chasm, and the bridge behind us was creaking like an old floorboard.

'Sorry about that, chaps.' Leckie was casual as ever, always casual. 'It needs a second go.'

We looked at each other. Leckie was amused.

'My turn,' he said apologetically. 'Sorry, but I insist.'

It should have been me, but I could hardly stand upright from fright. I'd have run like hell except they'd have shot me for desertion.

That's when the tunnel began its noises. Our first explosion must have weakened the mountain's innards. Have you ever been _under_ a mountain, especially one that has half a mind to crumple? It complains, whines, groans, even hums and hisses, full of noises. I'd heard one old geezer from our street talk about it when I was a kid. He'd got out of the Pretoria pit disaster as a young miner. Luckily his dad, also a miner, had told him how to listen to the rock on his first day and he'd made it back to the surface. 'The sound of the rock's breathing changed,' this geezer explained to me years later. I'd always thought him daft. Until our first explosion the tunnel had seemed empty, quiet. Now it crackled and twanged as the mountain above shifted uneasily. The lads began to back off, but Leckie only struck a match to light a cigarette. His sudden action made me jump a mile.

'Er, isn't it going to cave in, er, anyway?' I croaked, my voice an octave higher than normal.

'Possibly.' Leckie smiled. 'But possibly is also possibly not.'

We got his point. If the tunnel didn't crumple, a few of their side's diehards could clear the debris and shore it up in a few hours. Risky, but simple.

'What about blowing the bridge instead?' I suggested helpfully. Leckie laughed and wagged a finger.

'That's a different game, Lovejoy.' He was telling me our orders were the tunnel, so the tunnel it had to be.

He sent two of the lads, both riflemen, back to the ridge to hold it for us. The corporal was to wait just below them and to radio independently as soon as the tunnel blew. The spare rifleman was to stay on the safe end of the bridge, watching with Leckie's glasses, to report back should things go awry. I helped Leckie. He wouldn't let me come into the tunnel while he laid the charge up.

'Some other time, perhaps,' he joked, smiling. I'd tried to smile confidently back, but my teeth chattered and he finally had to untangle the wires for me. Thank Christ the other lads hadn't seen my hands shake.

By now the mountain was making incessant noises. It sounded like a distant orchestra tuning up. Cymbals crashed and instruments ravaged scales. Once the rock actually screamed, a real living scream which chilled my spine. Even Leckie looked down the tunnel as that terrible scream echoed and echoed. 'My word,' he murmured. 'Do you think it knows what we're up to?' I was pouring sweat. My fingers were too slippery to be any use. Leckie did it all, occasionally sussing out the surrounding hillsides with a rapid glance. As I scooped the instruments into my pack I dropped the pliers. They hurtled into the void below. For the life of me I couldn't take my horrified eyes off them – until Leckie pulled my arm and jerked me back.

'Off you go, Lovejoy,' he said amicably, as if nothing had happened. 'All set. Oh'. He pulled out a sealed envelope. 'Could you hold this for me?'

I stuffed it into my battledress.

'Er, am I not supposed to stay?' It took three swallows to get the words out. It's the hardest sentence I've ever said in my life.

'Not just now, Lovejoy.' He nodded towards the far side of the bridge. 'Scoot over there. We might need a third go and you'll have to do it.'

There'd be no chance of a third go. We both knew that. I nodded anyway and crossed over, drenched with sweat, trying to walk like Leckie, but all the wrong muscles kept going tight. The blast came as I crouched beside the bridge's five splayed holding struts where our first rifleman was lying beside a small overgrown outcrop of rock.

You could see nothing over there except dust. The narrow-gauge railway lines ran into a haze of suspended dust where the tunnel mouth had been. Leckie's end of the bridge was obscured by a brownish cloud. Rocks tumbled and crashed in the gorge below. The bridge was switching from side to side like a twitched rope under the impact of the blast. To my horror I found myself running and stumbling along between the iron rails across the bridge towards the tunnel, several times having to scramble upright from catching my boots on the sleepers. I must have had some daft idea about seeing what had happened to Leckie, maybe helping him back. Small rocks spattered about me as I ran. It couldn't have taken more than a few seconds. As I reached the cloud Leckie came hurtling out of the dust at me, choking and spluttering as he came. His white eyes peered from his blackened face.

'Get back, Lovejoy!' he yelled, floundering towards me. 'Get back. *The bridge is going!*'

I dithered for a split second, abruptly realized where I was and the lunatic thing I was doing, and tore back the way I had just come, wondering what the hell I was playing at. Leckie was on the safe mountainside nearly as quickly as I was.

'Come on, you two,' he said, waving us. 'Run.' The rifleman was off like a Derby starter, scrabbling up the hillside ahead of me. Leckie brought up the rear. We made the ridge, where the radio man waited with the other pair, having done his stuff. I halted and looked back then. The bridge hadn't gone after all but the tunnel was filled solid and part of the mountain face to one side of it had been stripped clean away in a miniature landslide.

'Settle down, chaps,' Leckie told us, hardly out of breath. 'Let's wait a bit and see what happens. Fag?' He offered them round, and we stretched out on the ridge, watching.

It was an hour later that the bridge wobbled and tottered finally into the gorge. It hit the bottom with hardly a sound. I went quietly off into the undergrowth and was spectacularly sick at the senseless risk I'd taken, running back over the bridge just to get Leckie like that. Sometimes I think I'm off my stupid head.

It was on the trek back that Leckie reminded me. 'One thing, Lovejoy,' he said casually over his shoulder. 'Got that envelope?'

'Eh? Oh, here.' I found it and passed it forward. We were moving in single file.

'Good of you, Lovejoy. Coming back like that, I mean.' He gave me a grin, turning on the narrow track. I can see him now, doing it, as I write. 'Always good to meet a chap who'll keep faith.'

I mumbled something. We got to our base about eight o'clock one morning four days after, only Leckie always called time something hundred hours. And Leckie never mentioned the tunnel or the envelope again. That was the last real soldiering I did, and if I have any say at all it's the last I'll ever do. The reason I've told you all this is that, as I'd passed Leckie his envelope back, I'd noticed the two words scribbled on the front of it. They were *In Case*, same as on the scribble Helen had given me.

I didn't need to be told in case of what.

'Lovejoy.' Tinker Dill was sitting opposite me, already half-way through a revolting mound of egg and chips. 'Why you saying nuffink?'

'Eh? Oh, wotcher, Tinker.' I put the note away. 'Sorry. Miles away.'

'Sauce.'

I passed him the sauce. He cascaded it over his grub. It's not a lovely sight. I wish he'd take his filthy mittens off while he eats. I'd wish the same about his tatty greatcoat and his greasy cap, but God knows what sights lurk underneath. He tore a chunk off a bread roll, one of Woody's special cobbles, and slopped it through his tea. A bit never made it. It plopped into the sauce, but Tinker just scooped it up with his stained fingers and rammed it into his mouth.

'I found out where Leckie's stuff is, Lovejoy,' he said.

'So have I.'

You can see the door of the King George from Woody's. I watched idly through the window. Fergus, the blonde and their thin pal were emerging, chatting and obviously in a festive mood. He must have done a good deal. I guessed Cain Cooper's paintings.

'Here, Tinker. That thin bloke.'

'Him? Jake Pelman. Clacton. Silver and Continental porcelain.' He ate noisily on. 'Just gone partners with Nodge, word is.'

I'd not heard that before.

'Any reason?'

Tinker shrugged. 'Why not?' I realized that Pelman was the bloke I'd seen chatting to Margaret in the White Hart the night before.

A sudden thought struck me. 'One thing. How did you know Leckie left his stuff at his cousin Moll's?' I hadn't even known he'd got a cousin living locally.

He grinned, all brown crags and gaps. 'I didn't because it's not there.' He cackled away, nodding at this fresh evidence of my dependence on his ferreting skills. 'It's still at Medham.'

'*Eh*?' But Val said it was at this cousin's. What the hell?

'Medham.' He wiped his stubbly chin on his sleeve and belched. 'He never took it. Left at the sally. Virgil's.'

'But . . .'

Tinker eyed me pityingly. 'You're losing your touch, Lovejoy. Leckie got an old three-ply post-war piece. Gave that whizzer Wilkinson a quid for it, all of a sudden, and dashed off with it on his car. But the stuff he'd bid for in the auction's still there.'

I gaped. A decoy. Leckie knew they were waiting outside for him to leave. So he'd done the best his gentlemanly soul would allow – message to me via Helen, a decoy piece of grotty furniture strapped to his car to his cousin Moll's, and then coming to find me. Me. The one pal Leckie had who would keep faith and help a friend in need. Who had watched him get done.

'Thanks, Tinker,' I said as normally as I could. 'You did well.'

'Keep your hair on, Lovejoy.'

He watched me go in silence. The trouble with people who are on your side is they always know what's best. They give me heartburn sometimes.

I slammed the door and took no notice when Woody bawled after me. He's always wanting to be paid.

I left town then, and drove to Moll's like a bat out of hell. Well, nearly twenty. But there was bile in my mouth and I've never had indigestion in my life.

Chapter Five

I didn't know it then, but my peaceful days had ended. Looking for Leckie's stuff was, until I drove out of town on the coast road that Sunday, a sort of innocent instinct.

From then on it was war.

Moll turned out to be thirtyish, fair-haired, squeaky and excitable. Plump, as any man in his right mind likes them. The odd thing was that she wanted to draw me, draw as in sketch. She was a watercolour artist, amateur without aspirations. I realized I'd vaguely heard of her but never considered her real. It's like that with people you never expect to meet.

'And you're Lovejoy! I simply must take a sitting.'

'Er – ' I'd only said hello so far.

'Sit!' she commanded, pushing me on a chair and rushing about with a lamp standard.

'The cupboard . . .'

'You're exactly, as I imagined! So positively . . . *lived in!*'

'Look, Moll – '

She shut me up and trotted about the room looking for shadows. It was definitely her room, flowery wallpaper and dazzling curtains, prettily decorative. In other circumstances I'd have reached for her. Paintings hung everywhere, crummy modern stuff. Sitting there like a nerk, I felt how modern her bungalow was. Not an antique in the whole place. Disgusting.

'Stay absolutely motionless!' she cried, tilting her head to see me sideways. 'How atrociously sensual!

How excruciatingly, totally sensitively . . . malign!' I can never understand words artists use.

'I've come about Leckie's cupboard,' I said doggedly.

Her eyes instantly filled with tears. She flopped down on a sofa and wept, lamp flex trailing.

'Poor, poor Leckie. And he'd called only *minutes* before!' She pointed at the door. 'He put a cupboard in the garage – '

I was out of the back door and in the garage before the next breath. It stood there, ashamed and 1948 utility. Pathetic repro door handle, rusting screws. The inside was horrible and cheap.

'You're not even furniture,' I told it critically. 'Never mind antique.'

A voice said, 'No clues there, Lovejoy.'

I turned. What the hell was Maslow doing in Moll's garage? He'd wormed in behind me.

'Get lost, Maslow. You've no business here.'

'Oh, but he has,' this other geezer said. A taller version of Maslow, but smiley and brisk. He looked a good footballer.

I looked from him to Maslow, then back again. Hellfire. Different faces, but very very similar. That's all I needed, Leckie's trail of clues obstructed by a family full of coppers.

'Are you Tom? Moll's husband?'

'That's me.'

'How do. I'm Lovejoy. I . . . I knew Leckie. I came to see his stuff.'

'Come inside.'

And Maslow even followed us in, greeting Moll casually and sitting down without being asked. Tom and him had a stronger resemblance indoors. Moll recovered fast with a flurry of greetings. She called Maslow Jim. My heart sank. Brothers.

'I've been on duty,' Tom explained to me. 'You're the friend I heard about.'

'He's the friend everybody's heard about.' Maslow grinned without humour. 'What you here for, Lovejoy?'

'I'm going to outline his face,' Moll put in eagerly.

'Leckie's cupboard,' I said. Coppers speak of being on duty. So Tom was not only Maslow's brother. He was in the peelers with him. Two coppers and a sketching wife. What a bloody family.

'Typical.' Maslow went colder still. 'Trying to make a bob or two, and Leckie not even stiff.'

I kept my temper. One day I'll rupture Maslow. He knows it, too. Still, it does no harm to mislead the Old Bill. On principle I let it go.

'Maybe,' I said, cool. Moll's eyes filled.

'And I thought you were Leckie's *friend*. How *could* you?'

'His sort's always the same, Moll.'

'If that's all Leckie brought . . . ' I said, rising. It's times like this I wish I'd a hat to fumble with.

Nobody saw me off. I now knew why Maslow had gone to the loop road in person. Leckie was vaguely related through his brother's wife. Not that it made any difference to me, or to Leckie any more.

I took the south road into town. It was time I went home and did a few things. The Medham auction warehouse would be shut on Sundays, or I'd have gone straight over there and searched for the escritoire. It's a miracle I didn't run anybody over, weaving my pre-occupied way through the strolling families on the riverside that links with the village road. All I could think of was Leckie, suddenly aware he was being watched in an emptying warehouse by the bad lads, and with no friends around save Helen, desperately passing her a note and then trying to reach me for help. He'd even tried leaving a dud cupboard at his cousin's as a decoy, probably hoping against hope that her stolid husband Tom the copper was home.

I slammed the gears up and down on the Bercolta

59

road, making some afternoon drivers honk at me, but I didn't care. Leckie was too much of a gentleman to protect himself with women, say by cadging a lift with Helen or staying at Moll's. I'd have sheltered screaming behind the nearest woman quick as a flash. That was typical. Leckie couldn't be a mean bastard if he'd tried.

'But Lovejoy's one already,' I said aloud, full of resolve.

The shadows were already lengthening when my crate gasped clanking into my garden. Sue was in the cottage porch, posting me a message by the looks of things. I cut the engine and shrugged. My crusade would have to wait till tomorrow. I waved to Sue. We went towards one another, smiling. Anyway, I excused myself, Sunday's a day of rest for everybody, even the two killers.

Sometimes I just make one mistake after another.

I knew there was something wrong the minute I clattered into the warehouse yard the next day. Virgil's is one of these ancient auctioneers which litter East Anglia. As the rest of the world evolves, they stay immutable. They may behave all modern and efficient, even to the extent of having computers around the place, but in reality they are Queen Anne, and no nonsense about change.

For a start they have their own night guard. He hadn't done much good last night, judging from the sober faces of the four people standing near the double doors. Nodge was there, funnily enough. My crate fitted neatly between a furniture van and a police car. For the only time in recorded history the bobby wasn't Maslow. Wilkinson, the auctioneer's chief whizzer, gave me a wave. He's one of these long, loping men who can't stop their arms from dangling about. Tinker says whizzers have telescopic arms for taking bribes faster.

'Trouble, Wilkie?'

He came over, smoking a fag. His fingers are black from nicotine. 'Vandals done us over, Lovejoy.'

'Anybody hurt?' I couldn't avoid glancing over at Nodge. I knew what Wilkie was going to say.

'No. Old George didn't hear a sound.'

I thought, oh, didn't he, and crossed the yard to see the broken window, glass crunching underfoot. Whoever it was had split the double doors at the top of the loading ramp as well. All in all a neat crowbar job. Old George was giving his version of the raid to the young red-faced stammering copper, who looked fresh out of the egg. Nodge listened, shaking his head sadly at the deplorable sinfulness of mankind.

'Can I go in, Wilkie?'

He shrugged and glanced at the copper. By the time he had phrased the request I was inside. The warehouse is one large ground-floor rectangle of plank flooring. An auctioneer's stand is positioned against one long wall opposite the doors, and a curtained space shows burglars unerringly where to search for next week's accumulating stock of dubious antiques. I switched on the lights, because an auctioneer's natural preference, like Dracula's, is towards an all-concealing gloom. The light from the two bare bulbs just made it to the far corner, where an Edwardian copy of an escritoire had been split and practically shredded by aggressive but meticulous hands. I crossed over and sorted the bits. A real hatchet job, done in a hurry by people bent on plunder. The only recognizable piece was a Bramah lock still stuck to its wood.

'They came with the right tools,' Wilkie grumbled, which was just what I was thinking.

The quack's bag was a small elongated leather job, very like a bowling bag. Its contents were scattered and the base was slit lengthways.

'Don't touch. The Old Bill's going to look, just as soon as he's ready.'

I grinned at Wilkie's sarcasm. One way and another our local antique whizzers like Wilkie and his merry crew have pulled off more illicit deals than the rest of the world put together. They do it naturally, like breathing. I crouched down and began assembling the doctor's gruesome instruments.

'Here, Lovejoy – '

'Shut up.'

I replaced them in the bag. The clip had been broken, so it couldn't fasten. By the time I straightened up Wilkinson was on tenterhooks, but was wisely keeping watch on the uniformed lad. Nodge was hovering on the ramp and trying to peer in at us while the bobby scrawled away. A book, marked with a sticker to show the same lot number as the bag, lay underneath the pedals of a decaying piano. I scraped it out with my foot. The binding had been expertly split down the spine, whether from spite or as part of a search I couldn't be sure. A name was written on the flyleaf, Doctor Chase of Six Elm Green.

'Wilkie.' I gave him the bag and book, keeping my back to the daylight in case Nodge's bleary vision reached this far. 'Into my crate on the sly.'

'Here, Lovejoy,' he croaked, furtive eyes instantly on the doorway. 'I don't want no trouble – '

'Money,' I interrupted pleasantly, which shut him up. I find that word calms the most troubled seas. 'One other thing. Was anything nicked?'

'That Cruikshank picture.'

'Big deal.'

Some things you can be absolutely sure of in antiques. One is that minor artists will get copied and faked from now till Doomsday. Virgil's chief auctioneer Cecil Franklin had been exhibiting the Cruikshank picture for three weeks, boasting of its authenticity. It was allegedly a Georgian print done by Bob and George Cruikshank, showing two elegant blokes playing a prank on a night watchman in a London street.

The faker had got their clothes wrong – the commonest mistake a forger ever makes in manufacturing this sort of print. The two characters were Tom and Jerry. Not the cartoon creatures, but the originals, Jerry Hawthorn and his cousin Corinthian Tom, who were pranksters widely publicized in Georgian London. Their favourite trick was creeping up on a dozing watchman 'Charley' and up-ending his sentry-box, laying face down so he couldn't get out, and then running like hell. A lovable pair.

'And give me the address of the vendor,' I added. 'Slip it in the book.'

'Watch out,' Wilkie hissed, sensing the policeman's approach. I broke away and went forward, smiling and full of those questions a perturbed member of the public naturally asks when confronting mayhem. Wilkie would get the stuff undetected into my car boot somehow. The fact that it's always locked would be a mere detail to an honest whizzer like him.

I didn't give Wilkie or the warehouse another glance while I asked the bobby and Old George more questions than they asked me. The young peeler finally drew breath and went into the warehouse to defend law and order now the crooks were miles off. Nodge, hands deep in his overcoat pockets, seemed anxious and morose, on the fringes of everything.

'Cheer up, Nodge,' I told him happily. 'You're in the clear.'

He gave a sickly grin. I had a sudden strange idea. Wherever I'd been lately I'd seen Nodge's apprehensive face. And he'd seemed so odd yesterday at the antiques fair. I glanced about. We were all alone in the yard. Old George's quavering lies were still audible from inside the warehouse.

'Look, Nodge.' I tried to keep it casual. 'What the frigging hell's going on?'

'Eh?' He shuffled nervously.

'And what are you doing here?'

'Just passing,' he muttered. 'No law against looking in, is there?'

'You look hunted, comrade. Where's the happy Nodge of yesteryear?'

'Nothing wrong with me, Lovejoy,' he said, still shifty.

'You've got my phone number.' I shrugged and went inside with him to tell the others good morning.

As I pulled out of the yard I saw another familiar face across the road among the early shoppers. Jake Pelman was standing in a butcher's shop opposite, hesitating between the veal and lamb counters while a couple of women offered advice. He swung away abruptly on seeing my crate, but not before I'd made sure it was him.

Medham village is quite big for East Anglia, three thousand people or so. Maybe it's even a town. There was a lucky phone box near the Yew Tree pub. I had to sort a few things out or I'd go bananas. To save my ulcer perforating from worry I phoned Margaret first.

'Lovejoy here, love.'

'Where've you been?' she sounded as though she'd just got up.

'Shush. You were talking to Jake Pelman that night in the pub. What about?'

'Well, honestly . . .'

'*What about?*'

'Don't be so rude, Lovejoy.' She unbent slowly. 'About Leckie. Jake was asking what sort of things Leckie collects.' We politely ignored the wrong tense. I thought, most dealers aren't collectors, otherwise they'd be collectors and not dealers. Right?

'And you replied . . . ' I prompted, knowing Leckie didn't collect anything at all.

'Relics.' Margaret was all patience.

'*Eh?*'

'Relics. Church relics. Saints' bits and bobs.'

'Oh. Right then,' I said lamely. This was all news to

me. Later on I was to wish I'd heard it earlier. And clearer.

'Can I be of any further assistance?' Margaret asked sweetly into the pause. 'Take a message to Sue? Tell Helen you're on your way, perhaps?'

'Er, no thanks. See you, love.'

'Well, really – '

Isn't indignation ridiculous?

I found another coin to ring Helen. She'd be into her second fag of the day. Monday morning's her nightie-and-coffee dreamtime among last week's antique-collecting journals. She answered on the third ring. This is the best luck I've ever had with a phone box, two successes one after the other.

'Lovejoy,' I told her.

'You all right, Lovejoy?'

'Look, Helen. The night Leckie got . . . '

'I remember.'

'You had this message.'

'I gave it you.'

'But you didn't give it me *then*,' I pressed. It was one of these details which were beginning to get on my nerves. Outside I saw Jake Pelman standing on the corner. The blighter must have followed. He was peering uncertainly towards my phone box. All this was making me irritable. What sort of nerk wears a green suit like that, for God's sake? 'Why not, Helen?'

'I gave you the eye,' she complained. 'But you didn't come over.'

'But Leckie told you it was urgent. Why didn't you shout you had an urgent message from him for me?'

'How did I know you'd take off so suddenly with that old bitch?' She meant Margaret, women being like this about each other. 'Anyhow,' she said with finality, 'I couldn't. Not with Leckie's wife there.'

'*Who?*'

'Leckie's wife. With Fergus.'

We read the silence like mad for a minute.

'Leckie's ex-wife, then.' Another pause. 'Didn't you know? That showy blonde, wrong shoes and that ghastly handbag.' She mistook my stunned silence for an invitation to continue her invective. 'She's never had a proper hairstyle in the three years she's lived here. And her make-up's like a midden. I don't know why she bothers – '

Jake Pelman was still at the corner as I clattered past in my zoomster. He'd a parcel of some unspeakable meat under his arm, and was ever so casually inspecting an extinct bus timetable. I honked my horn. He started guiltily, but didn't look round, not even when I shouted, 'Wotcher, Jake!'

Near Medham there's one of King Cymbeline's earth-works, only we call him Cunobelin round here. It's an oval rampart about seven feet high, swelling from the ground of a small forest and curving for half a mile. Normally I'm not one for countryside and trees and bees and all that jazz. I like towns, where people and antiques are. For once I relaxed my rule, which is to get the hell out of the beautiful countryside and back into a smelly noisy town as quick as my beat-up asthmatic cylinders can haul me. This particular morning I parked among the roadside trees and struggled knee-deep in filthy leaves until I reached the crest of the overgrown earthworks. My head was splitting. Since when had Leckie a wife? And she was with Black Fergus and Jake Pelman that night in the pub. And . . . and . . .

I sat there in the silent forest in a patch of sunlight while birds and squirrels aped about like they do. Resting is hard work for a bloke like me, but gradually I calmed down. It was an hour before my headache went. I was no nearer making sense of any of it but at least I was able to drive home. I stopped at the station for a plastic pasty, and this time ate it all.

Chapter Six

Next morning the cottage looked like a battlefield. Living as I do, occasionally without a woman's assistance, I can tolerate most shambles with good grace. It's only when such as Sue are too tired to go home that the fur flies in the dawn. Honestly, I just can't see the point of moving things to a fixed spot for the sake of mere tidiness. Things only wander about again. I find it more sensible just to stay vigilant, simply keep on the lookout for essentials like towels and the odd pan. In fact, I'd say neatness is a time-waster.

My cottage is a thatched reconstruction, the sort modern architects deplore as inefficient. The place is not very spacious. There's a little hall, a bathroom, and a living-room with a kitchen alcove the size of a bookcase. I kip on a folding divan. Sue says it looks suggestive, but she's only joking.

Today was my laundry day. Sheets, pyjamas, towels and shirts. I do socks and underpants in separate bits. They have to come round every day or you get uncontrollable mounds if they're left. I put some wood under the old copper boiler in the back garden and got it lit third go by a fluke. Luckily the cottage is set back from the country lane on its own, so there's nobody nearby to complain about the smoke. Filling it takes ten buckets. I usually feed the birds before breakfast, otherwise they come tapping on the windows and I get no peace. Today they got some of Sue's Battenberg cake. I'd been trying to get rid of it for days. Her marzipan's a foot thick. She has this thing about wholesome food.

That done, I scrambled two eggs and brewed up. On

good days I sit outside, though the birds pester me and hedgehogs are always on the scrounge. Today it looked like rain. Anyway, I had several reasons for noshing indoors. They were laid on the carpet beside the doctor's bag.

Wilkie had got them into my car as I'd asked. I had some daft idea of leaving them a day or two to collect my thoughts, but I'm not strong on resolution. I'd stayed up half the night looking at this crummy book and the contents of the bag, and I was still no wiser.

The doctor's instruments turned my stomach over. Even clean and shiny they'd have been gruesome. Patchily rusted as they were now, I could hardly look. Some of the needles were five inches long. And they weren't your average darning needle for lovely innocent cotton. They were for people, and seemed to be triangular in section, with cutting edges along the length like those frightening short Land Pattern socket bayonets collectors are all after nowadays. Some were curved, others slender and tiny. The old quack also had a mask, rather like a fencer's, covered with gauze. For dropping ether anaesthetic, I guessed. I'd seen one of those before in the medical museum in Euston. A pair of curved forceps big enough to . . . I hate to think what they fitted round. Lancets, all shapes and sizes. And some scissors that curved and others that didn't. A stethoscope like an ear-trumpet. A group of lenses in a leather slot-box, with one spare lens coloured like you see in those children's kaleidoscopes. I tried fitting it into the slots with the others but there was no room for it, so I chucked it into the bag and forgot about it. With instruments like this bagful I'm glad the old doctor was on the side of health.

As I mopped my plate with some bread I read the card Wilkie had slipped in the bag. The same address as inside the doctor's bag. I knew the village, having been on the knocker round Six Elm Green during one of my bad spells. Old Dr Chase's ageing widow, I guessed, had put her late husband's effects up for sale to eke out the groats during her winter years. I'm naturally full of sympathy of these cunning old geezers but I'm usually poorer than they turn out to be.

The book was only twenty years old, privately printed for the author. It was that well-known world-shattering best-seller *Structural Design of Experimental Carriage-Ways in Nineteenth-Century Suffolk*, by none other than that famous quack Dr James Friese Chase, MD, whose medical bag I now possessed. I'd flipped through it last night, but decided I'd wait for the film. No hidden messages, no beautiful marginal notes by the author which might have increased its value, and no handwritten letters from Shakespeare skilfully concealed in the end papers.

I laid it aside and sorrowfully repacked the bag. Nothing. After all that, nothing. So Leckie had been killed for nothing. Some tearaways had believed Leckie had a real find, a priceless antique among the day's items bought at auction. They'd probably asked him to sell. He'd said no, sealing his doom, and for nothing. You can buy old medical instruments for practically a penny a ton. And a tatty copy of the world's worst-seller like Dr Chase's book is even more piteous.

Outside, the boiler was heating up well. A few more bits of wood and it was ready. I stuffed the washing in and swirled it round to get it properly wet. Sometimes I have to do without soap powder because it's so dear. I put the iron lid on with a clang and went in. It was coming on to rain. I sat on my stool inside the doorway listening to the raindrops hissing on the boiler's hot cover. I was supposed to be thinking, but all I could feel was relief. After all, if Leckie had no precious antiques it meant there could be no motive for murder, right? And no motive for killing Leckie meant that Leckie's loyal old pal Lovejoy couldn't possibly be blamed for just sitting doing his washing in his safe old garden when he should have been chasing after Leckie's murderers on his own. Right?

'Right,' I said fervently, congratulating myself.

The rest of the morning was great. I milled about, happily sussing out antiques, reading between bits of washing. I cleaned up the cottage in case Sue came later, and put my decrepit mac on to hang my washing out in the rain. I eyed the dark skies hopefully. If it rained all day the stuff wouldn't dry before tomorrow evening at the latest, with luck. A reprieve from ironing.

Things seemed to be looking up for Lovejoy Antiques, Inc. A reprieve from ironing, and now safely absolved from chasing after Leckie's killers, and therefore immune from risk. I whistled happily as I locked the cottage. I'd celebrate by having nosh in Woody's café, and persuade Erica to let me pay in promises.

My crate made it proudly into town with only one thrombosis, and that was on the railway slope, which I don't count. I parked boldly in the town solicitors' yard because it was pouring.

The antiques Arcade is a glass-roofed alley between two sets of rickety shops. One end is open to wind and weather. The other's full of Woody's obnoxious caff. There's a dozen leaning tables and scattered chairs. Woody spends his life cooking nosh and losing half-smoked fags in the grease. His idea of nourishment's to start off with carbohydrate and protein and simply add congealed fat.

I entered, coughing and spluttering at the first smoggy breath of airborne cholesterol, and signalling for tea. It's the only thing not fried. To my surprise Tinker Dill was absent. That's very odd because, had I been able to see through the solid air between me and Woody's wall clock, it would have confirmed that it wasn't yet opening time for the nation's taverns.

'Over here, Lovejoy.'

'How do, Sven.' I crossed and sat opposite him.

A few other dealers were in, already stoking up for the day's knavery. I gave them my electioneering wave to indicate affluence and ease. Antique dealers can detect poverty in a colleague quick as light, and everybody knows how contagious poverty is.

'And a pasty, Woody,' I yelled, to show them all.

'I got a stool, Lovejoy.' Sven said, grinning. 'Been waiting for you.'

'Date?'

'About 1720, maybe earlier.'

'Great,' I said evenly. The chances of Sven actually flashing a genuine stool that age are remote. 'Sitting on it?' I joked.

He made my heart turn over by saying, 'Yes,' and pulled this stool out from under himself. Lucky I wasn't half-way through my pasty or I'd have choked. Eyes swivelled as the others gazed across like a suspicious herd at grass.

It had everything, a luscious stool weighing heavy in the hand. I stood it reverently on Woody's plastic table.

'Do you mind, Lovejoy?' The waitress stood tapping her foot. 'Take that dirty little stool off our table.'

I gave her one of my special stares and took the tea from her in case of war. 'Not be a minute, Erica.'

'It's an important deal,' Sven boasted to her, ever the born optimist.

'Money, Lovejoy.' Erica tried to keep her voice down, but Sam Denton and his partner Jean overheard and chuckled. I tried not to go red. 'Woody *says*,' Erica told me desperately.

'Okay, love.' I made a show of delving in my pocket. 'What price do you put on it, Sven?' That was a distraction. While everybody hung on Sven's lunatic guess I pressed Erica's hand, giving her a mute glance of appeal. She knew I was broke again, and gave me a tight-lipped glare, but you could tell she'd square it with Woody again somehow. She slammed the pasty down and stalked off. I thought of yelling to keep the change, but decided better of it, and concentrated on the stool.

An ancient stool's practically always worth its weight in gold. A chair isn't, because stools are much rarer. Oh, they weren't once, but whereas chairs tended to be carefully preserved stools were just chucked on the fire. People simply replaced them. It's a modern trick to take a genuine eighteenth-century chair and cut it down to make a stool. The trouble was that my bell was silent. My antennae didn't give a single quiver. If Sven's stool was original and genuine I'd have been ringing like a cathedral at Christmas. As it was, not a single chime. My heart sank. I felt underneath the stool and bent to peer. Sure enough it was covered beneath with two layers of hessian, the old give-away. And Sven was still grinning like a fool.

'The original hessian, too,' he said, nodding. He's no idea.

'It's a fraud, Sven.' I avoided his eyes as I whispered the terrible news. All this truth hurt me more than him, but I knew how he'd feel. I ran my thumb along the little rails of the stool and felt the telltale Roman numeral incised under the bar. The stool had started life as V, fifth of a set of chairs. A cut-down.

'We could do a special price,' he offered eagerly.

'No, thanks.' I can make fakes myself, and cheaper than anybody else.

The door clanged open and in breezed – well, stumbled – Tinker Dill. He homed in on me and Sven and flopped down.

'We buying that, Lovejoy?' he rasped, coughing and wheezing, nodding at the stool.

'Not today, Tinker. Where've you been?'

'Doing as I was told,' he said with feeling. He slurped my tea and filched my pasty. He meant I'd told him to suss out Jake Pelman and Fergus. 'Your pal Maslow's out shopping. I had to come the back way to miss him, the bleeder.' I grinned at this, then had a sudden thought. Now I felt let off the hook I could go out and rile the Old Bill as any rightfully indignant citizen would.

'Back in a minute. Get some grub, Tinker. On the slate.'

I left Tinker and Sven and shot out of the Arcade. There he was, sour and useless as ever, talking to his brother Tom near the post office. People were hurrying along the crowded pavements in the rain. Moll was talking prettily under a coloured umbrella. Pity her bloke was huge, and a copper. I trotted over at the traffic lights, sure I'd surprise him.

'You're supposed to wait till the cars stop.' Maslow had been watching me out of the corner of his beady little eye.

'Morning.' I gave a hearty smile, because his sort likes us gloomy. 'How's the case?'

He actually blushed. I mean it. Honestly, he looked down at his feet and shifted his weight. I had a sudden funny feeling things were going to go wrong. Peelers don't blush easy.

'Er, the case?' He sounded hesitant.

'Yes. The c-a-s-e.' I waited a bit. Like a fool I was still beaming. 'Leckie. Remember?'

He faced me at last, after a quick glance at Tom. 'It's closed, Lovejoy. And before you start – '

I couldn't understand for a minute. You can't close a case without catching the baddie, can you? Everybody knows that, even goons like Maslow.

'Did you catch them, then?' I was asking, still thick, when Moll broke in.

'Oh, how *can* you?' She stamped her foot with a splash, glaring from Tom to Maslow. They hadn't told her.

'Road accident,' Maslow said doggedly. 'It's closed.'

'But he was murdered,' I said. It still wouldn't sink in.

Moll gasped at the word and rounded on them both.

'There! I knew something was wrong when he came – '

'A road accident's a road accident, Lovejoy,' Maslow pronounced. 'Unless you saw something or have firm evidence . . .'

We all stopped. People were staying close to the shop front for dryness. Cars swished by on wet tyres. I looked about, clearing my throat. I could hardly see for the red mist in my vision. How I didn't clock him one I'll never know. I took two goes to speak.

'You've given up? Is that it, Maslow?' I managed finally. 'You've done your very, very best for Leckie?'

'I don't want any lip from you – ' He began a lecture about public co-operation.

If I owned up to seeing the killing Sue would be roped in. And witnesses, even in dear old England, get crisped by tearaways who feel that evidence is often undesirable. So me and Sue would 'accidentally' get done, same as Leckie, soon as I opened my mouth.

'How does it feel to be utterly useless, Maslow?' I said the words politely because my face was tight and my voice shook. Tom looked uncomfortable. Moll was being furious with them both, but pretty women are handicapped in a way.

'One more word out of you . . .' Maslow threatened. I watched a cluster of kids clatter past into a toyshop. Their dad was laughing, trying to keep up and fold his umbrella at the same time. Some hopes.

'It's all right,' I said kindly. The words were out before I could control them. 'I'll do it, Maslow. You just go home and put your feet up. Watch telly football or something.' I leant towards him, my voice just about keeping going. 'I'll see the bastards off. You rest.' And I turned and left them there.

I don't remember much about the next hour, except that I splashed about the town pavements and got wetter still looking in shop windows. There seemed to be so many people about. I kept having to say sorry for bumping into folk going in and out of shop doorways. Once a couple of girls nearly put my eye out with the prongs of their bloody umbrella. They spent a whole giggly minute apologizing. I said I was fine, and we parted friends.

When I came to I was outside the Arcade again, standing at the same traffic lights in the pouring rain and just looking across at the stalls under the glass roof opposite. Twice cars stopped to wave me across, but I wouldn't move. I realized I was on a traffic island halfway across the main road. People were looking. Tinker was bawling at me from near the Arcade. I went over in case he'd accidentally left some of my grub.

'You'll get yourself bleeding run over,' he grumbled as I approached. 'Then what?'

'You'd work for Elsie.' I try to give as good as I get, but I was feeling really down. He cackled, and pushed ahead of me into Woody's. Elsie's rumoured to make most of her antique deals in bed.

'Seen Elsie's thighs?' he was chuckling as we crossed over to where Moll was sitting. 'One of those would drive me in like a tent peg.'

'Charmingly put,' I said, staring. *Moll?*

'At *last!*' she squeaked, rising. Her face was pink. She'd been braving Woody's tea. 'Lovejoy! You're *soaked!* Now just sit right down here and we'll get some lovely hot food – '

'Eh?'

She pulled me into a chair and rushed at the counter. I heard her prattling away to Woody saying not too well done and things women say like that about grub. Tinker shrugged, all bashful.

'We've been talking,' he said. I saw he'd taken one of his mittens off, revealing a row of blackened digits and filthy bitten nails. I've never seen him eat without this horrible woollen mitten before. This was obviously

75

an occasion. 'Talking about what?' I was thinking how I'm always ten moves behind these days.

'You. She keeps on.'

'What have you been telling her?' I grabbed his evil throat.

'Nowt.' He rubbed his neck. 'Chance'd be a fine thing. She's a gabby cow.'

'*Now!*' Moll flounced back and settled her elbows on the table in a conspirator's attitude. She whispered, frowning, 'Is this gentleman to be trusted, Lovejoy? Implicitly?'

I looked about, but she meant Tinker, so I nodded. She squealed jubilantly and clapped her hands.

'Marvellous!' she cried. 'Then we are . . . Three Musketeers! Isn't this deliciously exciting?'

'Er . . . what, exactly?'

'Why!' She gave me a blinding smile. 'You setting out to do battle with Leckie's murd – '

I clapped my hand over her mouth, frantic.

'Here, Lovejoy.' Tinker had that shifty look about him. 'It's not like last time, is it? I don't want any bother.'

'How despicable!' Moll wrenched herself free from my hand to turn on Tinker. 'And you with so many medals! All that brave war experience – '

I gave Tinker one of my sardonics. He had the gall to simper. This is what a pretty bird does for a bloke, saps strength and sense. Look at Samson. Then look at Tinker. I decided on the spot I'd have no allies.

'Shut it,' I hissed, head bent forward. We were like a Dickens tableau. All we needed were striped jerseys and a candle in a bottle and we could have played the Old Vic. 'I don't need help, Missus. And no more noisy chat, for Christ's sake.'

She wasn't at all abashed. Just smiled sweetly and waited for Erica to come. Chips, meat pies, beans, peas, gravy. Tea. Even rolls and margarine. Erica's foot started tapping as Tinker whaled straight into his plateful. Mine steamed reproachfully untouched. I shrugged to Erica. She shrugged coldly back. I get mercy when I'm on my own. With another and showier bird like Moll Maslow sitting opposite I'd get none. I felt the sweat prickle on my shoulders from embarrassment. The rest of the crowd watched, pleased.

'Oh,' Moll said innocently after about a year or so. 'How *foolish* of me. Of *course*.' Her blue eyes stayed on mine as she flicked her handbag and brought out a note. I sensed Tinker's eyes swivel in to the money as Erica took it and flounced off. Talk began again. Moll smiled and patted her hair absently, eyes still holding mine ever so casually. Hello, I thought warily, what have we here?

'Er, I'll owe it,' I said in a croak. The aroma of the nosh was driving me mad.

'No need, Lovejoy.' Moll reached over hesitantly and touched my hand. 'Partners don't owe, do they?'

'Partners?'

'Yes.' No hesitation now. If anything I was being ordered. 'Anyhow,' she continued, 'I don't expect it will be the first expense we shall incur. Do you?' There was a pause while Tinker sloshed and noshed.

'What about Tom?' First things first.

'Tom's just leaving on a course for two weeks.' She split my roll and stirred my tea. 'By then we'll have settled the entire affair. I have adequate funds.'

I tried to reason out a quick way of using her money to keep me going without having to take Leckie's killers on, but her eyes kept getting in the way of my thinking. Women take advantage of people.

'Eat up, Lovejoy.' She did that mysterious bit with a powder compact and glanced across, smiling. 'We have so *much* to do, haven't we?'

I avoided Tinker's gaze and started on my grub, trying not to wolf it. Moll watched me, still smiling. Women like to see appetites, any sort. I have this theory that appetites are the cause of most troubles, especially mine.

Chapter Seven

Entering another person's house is probably quite enjoyable, as long as you're not an antique dealer. You can sit and chat, eye the bird and chat her up and see how cleverly she's arranged the dahlias. For me it's not that easy.

First of all there's suspicion. It strikes straight to your cerebrum: *antiques might be here!* And when coffee's up you find yourself crawling all over the crockery looking for Spode or Rockingham ware. You can't for the life of you focus on anything else. Then there's the skulduggery bit. As soon as she's gone for more milk you hurtle round the room fingering chairs and mauling the sideboard to see if it's vintage. I don't really mean to pry. It's just the way we are, because antiques are everything. It's no wonder I can sense an antique through a brick wall.

Moll turned out to be one of those women who never stops talking – well, almost never. All the way to her house she prattled. I didn't bother to listen to the actual words, just kept an earhole open for the sense. She drove like a scatterbrain, pointing out the sights and occasionally waggling the wheel experimentally for nothing, presumably just to test the universe hurtling erratically past on the other side of the car windows.

'Why do you drive in third gear all the time?' I'd had to ask.

She tutted furiously. 'I *have* to,' she complained. 'So I can hang my handbag on the lever. There's just *nowhere* else. These *designers*!'

Silly me.

But we made it to her home. I could tell she was mentally gauging my face for a sketch while she rushed about brewing up and deciding where I was to sit. Round the room she had other people's art work, which pleased me, though it was all costly modern stuff and therefore of no possible account. Her furniture was flouncy and feminine, the sort you know has been chosen by a high-spirited woman who usually smiles and will always be one jump ahead. Bright colours, lots of windows with pot plants that didn't look trapped. By the time she came in with tea I'd resignedly sussed out the furniture and paintings and was all attention while she poured. We sat opposite, across a modern Chinese rosewood low table like chess players at a match. When I was flat broke I'd cut one down and made a Pembroke table. Another dealer bought it. He advertised it as 'possibly eighteenth-century' and made a mint (which is quite legal because those words also mean 'possibly *not*'). I was innocent in those days. It makes you wonder whether innocence and poverty go together.

'Here you are, Lovejoy.' Moll was patiently holding a cup and saucer out.

'Sorry.'

Being in another bloke's chair makes for difficulty, especially if his wife's bonny and vivacious like Moll. When he's in the CID and she's bent on some daft Robin Hood type of crusade you can't help feeling even more uncomfortable. All along I'd felt this was not my scene.

'Look, Mrs Maslow – '

'You will call me Moll.'

'Moll.' I was a second too long. It sounded uncomfortably like an order again. 'I'm not sure what it is you think we decided, er, but . . .

'Biscuit?' She was smiling.

'Er, thanks.' I cleared my throat and began again, careful as I could. 'Look. I can't afford to rub your old man up the wrong way, Moll. And your brother-in-

80

law's, er, known for putting the elbow on us antique dealers. . . .'

'Go on.'

Her gaze was disconcerting, but I found new resolve from somewhere. 'What I mean is,' I said, more uneasy with every word, 'maybe we should drop the whole thing.'

'What whole thing?' She'd stopped smiling and that exaggerated innocence was back. Talking to women's like watching a kaleidoscope and trying to guess the next pattern.

'Er, well. Looking for Leckie's . . . er . . .'

'I take it you want to welsh on our arrangement.' She rose and crossed to a bureau. I watched her uncertainly. The file she fetched had an awful official look about it.

'Well, yes.'

'Why, Lovejoy?' She lit a cigarette and crossed her legs, suddenly so much calmer and a great deal less innocent. 'Fear?'

I swallowed, nodded. 'Yes.'

'What exactly happened to Leckie?' For all her new assurance her eyes avoided mine.

'Dunno.'

She leaned forward for the ashtray, a modern greenish agate. 'Yes you do, Lovejoy.' She opened the file. 'This is the county CID file.'

'File? On. . . ?' The bloody thing had my name on.

'You.' She nodded, flipping the leaves casually. 'Want to read, Lovejoy? But of course you'll know everything about yourself, won't you?'

'Most of that's – '

Moll closed it and interrupted my indignation skilfully. 'Concocted? Misreported? Biased?'

'Yes. Especially if Maslow's reports are in there.'

'The trouble is, Lovejoy, that it's *there*. Recorded. All about you.'

I rose, angry at letting myself get put on this way. 'That does it. I'm off.'

'Not for a moment, please.'

She sounded so bloody sure of herself I suddenly lost my wool and stood over her blazing. I always finish up doing what everybody else wants.

'Listen here, lady. I admit it – I saw Leckie killed. Two blokes in a black car deliberately crashed him up.'

'I knew it – '

'Shut your teeth and listen for once in your posh smarmy life.' I was shaking with rage. 'I can just see you now, that day. What sort of welcome did you give Leckie? Go on, admit it. You were *bored*. Your cousin turns up, first time for maybe months – '

'How dare you – ' She struggled to rise, her face pale.

I clocked her one. She fell back, hand on her face. I knew she was thinking: This can't be happening. Men don't clout women of my class. It's not done.

'Listen, you smug bitch.' I realized I was wagging my finger at her and folded it away, embarrassed. 'Leckie came here, and I'll bet it was all you could do to give him the time of day. He called at an "inconvenient moment" – isn't that what your kind says when they mean piss off?'

'I'll report you to – '

'Did he ask to stay?'

'I'm not going to continue this discussion – '

I shook her wildly till her hands flopped and her teeth clicked. Hearing her neck-bones rattle fetched me to my senses. I dropped her, frightened I'd done damage, but still wild.

'*Did he?*'

She was a mess now. Tears poured down her face.

'Yes.' She sniffed and did those dry hiccups.

I looked about the room.

'Where did he sit?' Maybe he'd slipped a message into the upholstery.

She huddled in the corner of her sofa, sobbing and jerking. Her eyes didn't meet mine any more.

'He didn't.' She could hardly speak for weeping. 'Please don't. You're right. He knocked at the door. It was practically dark. He'd put his car near the garage. The engine was still running.' She found a hankie.

'I'm waiting,' I said, 'partner.'

'Please.' She was heartbroken, but I'd had enough of all this fencing crap and forced her chin out of her hands, to make her look at me. 'Please, Lovejoy. He – he just said, "Any chance of a sundowner, old girl?" I . . . I was in the middle of a sketch and said could we leave it till another time.'

I let her go, trying not to recoil.

'Please don't look like that, Lovejoy.'

'You didn't even *let him in*?' Dear God, I thought. Dear frigging God. I turned away from the bitch, sick to my soul. It's not just me. Or me and Maslow. It's all of us.

'I'd promised the sketch for the morning – '

'Of course,' I said with vicious politeness. I couldn't help myself. 'An important jumble sale, no doubt?'

'Church charities,' she answered mechanically. 'He never said. Just shrugged and said fine. I suggested he come round next week instead. He said fine again.' That was Leckie, politely saying 'fine' and 'not at all', when condemned to death. I'd have battered my way in screaming for help.

'Did you see – ?'

'Nothing else. No car lights. The lane's visible from the door.'

'And then you shut the door on him?'

She wept again, face in her hands.

'We never had much in common. Cousins aren't always close. I only thought it odd afterwards, coming over without giving me a ring first.'

'You waved him off?'

'No. I wanted – '

' – to finish your sketch,' I capped nastily. 'And now you want me to get rid of your guilt. Well, do your own dirty work.'

I went to the front door. It had stopped raining. You could see four other houses, the village green at the end of the lane, a church spire. Not a busy place, but not the back of beyond, either. I tried to work it out. Moll had shut the door on Leckie. He'd put the crummy bureau in Tom's garage, hoping the watching followers would be misled. Some chance.

Moll was behind me. I felt her arm touch my arm but stepped out on to the little garden. I'd had enough.

'Please, Lovejoy.' She followed me desperately to the lane. 'I know you'll try to catch them on your own. You'll need help. I have money –'

I pushed her back into her garden and shut the low gate on her, suddenly exhausted by all these bastards. Some days there are just too many know-alls.

'Keep it, lady. Keep everything. Just leave me alone.'

'I'll drive you home – '

'I want to walk, or there'll be a bus.'

'Lovejoy.' Her voice made me pause and turn. 'If you do catch them, be careful.'

'Catch?' I spat sour phlegm on to the unpaved lane's stones. 'You've read my file, love. Who said anything about catch?'

'But you can't – ' She hung over the gate, aghast.

'What do your menfolk do when they *catch*?' I grated on, irritated beyond endurance. Two neighbours were out in the next garden, obviously in case Moll needed rescuing from this wild-eyed visiting scruff. 'Two years with remission, isn't it? Colour telly, central heating, good grub, and books on the good old tax-payer?'

I gave a grin and stepped back to face her. She put a hand apprehensively to her face. One neighbour exclaimed, 'I *say!*' I waved nonchalantly and called, 'It's all right, Councillor,' without glancing his way.

'That's . . . anarchy, Lovejoy.' She could only muster a whisper.

'Anarchy's when the Old Bill can't make the rules work, love. You can't blame me.'

I was several yards away when I heard her say in a bewildered voice, 'But people aren't *allowed*, Lovejoy.' The eternal cry of the innocent and the dispossessed. I didn't bother to turn back.

The old neighbour was still bristling busily as I passed. He didn't raise his hat to me, but standards of behaviour are falling everywhere. I've noticed that.

Chapter Eight

Sometimes you wake up ready to conquer the universe. You know that rare feeling: everything seems sunny and easy; women are spectacular, available, and money comes in; genuine antiques glow everywhere you drop your eyes. Other days can appear perfect, yet you wake like a sick refugee. The morning after I'd blacked Moll's eye was one of these; exquisite sunshine with that cool deep crystalline air you only get in East Anglia. I should have been happy as a lark, but I was in a worse state than China.

All night long I'd had nightmares. You know, the sort you can't even bear to go over again even though you're safe noshing breakfast. I'd woken drenched in sweat, with my mind in turmoil. The cottage had seemed full of reproof – but what the hell had I done? An innocent snog – well, almost innocent – in a country lane even with another bloke's missus isn't a capital crime, now, is it? Yet that had accidentally started it all.

I banged and crashed about the place frying breakfast, making myself madder because I only had bread left and I hate fried bread on its own. The milkman had stopped coming before the Jubilee, so I have to use that powdery stuff when I can afford it. The birds were tapping on the window. I suppose it's my fault for trying to train them away from massacring worms.

'Fried bread, lads. Sorry.' I chucked them some pieces. My robin came and defecated unceremoniously on the sleeve of my tatty dressing-gown. Obviously a critic as well as a songster. I told it angrily, 'If snogging with a bloke's wife was the worst we ever got up to, the world wouldn't be in such a bloody mess.' I pushed it off and slammed back inside in a temper.'

Before I was half-way through this young woman with horn-rimmed specs was knocking on the door. Some days it's nothing but people.

'Good morning!' She was past me before I realized, wrinkling her nose at the sordid scene. 'Oh! Still not fully prepared to leap piping into the world, and it's almost nine!' Roguish smiles in the early morning are poisonous.

'Don't misquote Blake to me,' I growled. She had a clip-board. 'We are here on a health visit,' she carolled briskly, making it sound like I'd won a prize.

'We bloody well aren't – '

'Our doctor has put us down for health training.' She checked her neffie list. 'Our name's Lovejoy, isn't it? Two sessions weekly.'

I hate officials. 'Tell Doc Lancaster to sod off.'

She went all hurt. 'He's very concerned at the lack of fitness in his patients in this village,' she informed me soulfully.

I snatched her clip-board and scanned the names furiously. I was listed. Doc wasn't. 'He smokes, and drinks like a fish,' I reminded her. 'Why isn't he down?'

'Doctor,' she informed me distantly, 'has *decided*.' Her aloof tone announced that he was somehow above all this mortality business.

If I hadn't been so tired I'd have just given her the sailor's elbow. As it was I made a fatal mistake, though looking back, how could I have avoided any of the consequences? My mistake was to argue. Never argue with a bird. You start out right and finish up wrong.

'I don't want two sessions of anything.'

She was horrified. 'But you can't refuse! You're part of the test group.'

'Can't I?' I was on the phone in a flash, bullying my way past Doc's snotty receptionist by the simple expedient of pretending I was dying. The specky bird tried verbal disuasion, but since when has that ever succeeded? Doc was his usual poisonous chuckly self.

'Lovejoy,' I snapped. 'This bird you sent. Get her off my back.' She tut-tutted angrily behind me.

Doc tried to sound professional, but I could tell he was falling about laughing on the other end. 'I've scored you as Unfit,' he chuckled. 'We need four hundred of you, and suddenly I'm one short. Don't let us down.'

'Two short,' I corrected icily. 'I'm the second that got away.'

He went all smooth. 'Can't Miss Haverill persuade you?' He was smiling. 'She managed to inveigle several recalcitrants in Chase's control group – '

'*Eh*?' Suddenly I was awake. *Chase?*

'We send her to, er, persuade our male patients – '

'*Whose* control group?'

'Dr Chase. My late partner.' He paused, puzzled. 'We worked this clinical trial out before he died. Miss Haverill's my co-ordinator, though she's based at Six Elm Green. Did you know him?'

'Er, no.' I paused, thinking fast. 'Er, well, Doc.' I cleared my throat, smooth and casual. 'I've reconsidered. Seeing you've explained what an, er, important, er . . .'

'Clinical trial,' he prompted.

'Er, clinical trial it actually *is* . . .'

'What changed your mind?' he was asking suspiciously when I hung up.

I turned back to ask it, full of dread and already knowing the answer. They'd had four hundred active men for their tests. Now Doc was suddenly one short. I cleared my throat, grinning nervously.

'So I'm a replacement for, er, for . . . ?'

'Poor Mr Leckworth,' she said sadly. 'Such a good friend of Dr Chase. A tragic accident. But driving these days . . .'

88

Leckie. I'd known it the instant Doc spoke.

'A *friend?*'

'Yes. Quite casual. Only because Mrs Leckworth was Doctor's receptionist for a while.' I got the feeling things were out of control again. Leckie. Leckie's blonde wife Doc Chase's receptionist. Chase's stuff in the auction. Her and Fergie's lot. Leckie dead, the antiques smashed up. And . . . and . . .

'It's my duty to the nation to stand in for him, I suppose,' I said bravely. 'I'll join your, er, group . . .'

Miss Haverill was looking sceptical. I swept a muddle from a chair and said to sit down. She did, gingerly, as if the place was contaminated.

'What an interesting piece of, er, medical, er – ' I began, smiling through my stubble and wishing I'd shaved. Events were ganging up on me.

'Did Doctor explain what you'll have to do?'

'Er, no.' I covered the ruin of my divan bed with the coverlet. It folds into a smaller thing and pushes back against the wall.

'Wait!' she cried. 'The bed isn't made!'

'Eh?' I'd gone back to my foul nosh when I realized she'd unfolded the bed again and was ripping the bed-clothes off, the maniac. I shrugged and let her get on with it. Whatever turns people on, I always say.

'You really *must* be more hygienic, Lovejoy!'

'About these, er, sessions . . . ?' The quicker I got to hear more about Doc Chase the quicker I'd learn if he'd had any antiques which could be mistaken for his grotty old bureau. After all, Leckie had died for it.

'Two miles and exercises.'

Two miles away, I thought, my mouth full of fried bread. Not far. I could manage that, but I didn't like the sound of those exercises.

'Have you running shoes?' She was really quite attractive without her clip-board. I watched her making the bed, full of thought.

'Er, no. I can do exercises without.' In my innocence I was trying to be helpful.

She smiled. 'You'll need some old shoes for running. The path to Friday Wood's absolutely awful – '

'*Running?*' Friday Wood's at least a mile away. I was gripped by a sudden overwhelming fear. One mile to the wood plus one mile back equals two. She couldn't mean *run* two miles, could she? The lunatic. I haven't run anywhere since I was courting. 'Er – '

'You'll *love* it!' She paused, glowing with crusading fervour. 'The invigorating dawn air! The crush of fallen leaves underfoot! Think how you'll benefit, Lovejoy. Your muscles will ripple and tingle with health as you sprint through the forests at sunrise.' She plumped the cushions.

'Sounds great,' I said miserably. 'Er, if I have a bad leg can I get a doctor's certificate –?'

Miss Haverill smiled a brilliant but knowing smile and wagged a finger. 'Doctor said you'd ask that, Lovejoy.'

I laughed merrily. 'Only my little joke,' I said, thinking, the cunning old swine. Well, if I was in I was in, but I deserved my pound of flesh. 'You work for Dr Chase, Elizabeth?' Her initial was on the clip-board.

She reddened slightly. 'Elspeth, actually.' She finished the bed and started mechanically on the rest of the room, folding things and making piles. I'd never find a bloody thing. It takes days to get back to normal after they tidy me up.

I got her reminiscing about her old boss. She told me how keen he'd been on physique assessments as parameters of health indices predictions, whatever that means. I told her that was really great. He'd hit on this maniacal scheme to compare his patients with his partner's after different sorts of exercises. I was now one of their statistics.

'Wasn't Doc Chase the doctor with that interesting

hobby?' I asked casually, going to wash up. 'I heard about it.'

'Oh, his old history.' She smiled, coming over to help me at the sink. 'He was always pottering about the countryside measuring mounds and things.'

'I'm interested in history.' This is absolutely true. I am. History's where antiques come from.

'You'd have got on well with him. Here, let me.' She swapped us over, me drying instead of washing. I keep meaning to get one of those stick mops. Hot water burns my fingers. I don't know how women do it. They can even drink hot coffee straight down, thermodynamic throats or something.

'Didn't he write some book about the place by, er, over by . . . ?'

'Scratton.' She nodded, smiling. 'I used to pull his leg, say to him why didn't he just read his own book to learn about that silly old tunnel!'

My hands froze. She laughed, then tutted as a plate crashed and broke.

'Oh! Mind the pieces, Lovejoy, you butterfingers!'

I tried to smile at all this drollery but my heart was in a vice. I'd felt my stomach turn over when she'd said tunnel. No wonder I'd been postponing thinking about Leckie's message. Not that a deep dark tunnel's anything to be scared of. I mean to say. And I'm really not frightened of a long tunnel with water trickling down the bricks and the mountain creaking and settling all around you. I'm not, honestly. But I felt a sudden unreasoning violent rage against Leckie. Why the hell couldn't he have just given the heavies what they wanted for Christ's sake, and saved me from being more and more terrified? Getting himself killed like that suddenly seemed the height of inconsideration.

'Tunnel?' I asked in a light croak. I tried to grin but my face wouldn't work. My forehead was cold and damp.

'He even went down into it, so they say.' She was

glancing about for a dustpan. She'd be lucky. I've plenty of dust but no dustpan. 'Mind you don't cut yourself on the bits. You've nothing on your feet.'

'I don't suppose he ever found much treasure trove.' I went and got a broom while my heart hammered and my brow dripped. I felt I was back in a tunnel's mouth near a bamboo bridge over a gorge for an odd minute. It's funny how your mind works.

'Oh, he found some old railway things. Gave them to the Elm Trees.' That's a museum near the Three Cups pub in town. I hadn't been for over a year. 'Lovejoy. Are you all right?' She was looking at me.

'Fine, fine,' I said heartily, staring her straight in the eye and beaming.

'You're not diabetic?' she asked hopefully. 'I *did* interrupt your breakfast . . .'

'Not today, thanks,' I joked.

She left about tennish, not without incident. I went to the front door to see her off. Sue, an expression of pleased anticipation on her face, was on the doorstep just about to knock. Her car was on the gravel. A red Ford stood in the lane, probably Elspeth's.

'Ah,' I said swiftly. 'Er, hello, er, Mrs Vaughan.'

'Oh. Good morning.' Sue's quick at these situations, like all women. 'I called about that antique . . . watch.'

'Very well. I'll pack it for you.' Actually Sue wouldn't know a Tompion timepiece from a sundial. 'Would you mind waiting, please? I'm just seeing, er, Miss Haverill off. She's my health visitor. She called about my exercises. . . .'

'Oh, really?' Sue asked sweetly. From the look on her face I'd gilded the gingerbread. There was that fractional pause while she and Elspeth decided on mutual hatred as today's best social policy. 'Did you perform to her satisfaction?'

Elspeth decided to cut out. 'I'll telephone about your programme, Lovejoy.'

'Er, great.'

'Not *too* strenuous, I hope?' Sue cooed innocently.

I grinned farewell as Elspeth swung down the path, then dragged Sue in and rammed my fist threateningly under her nose.

'Cut out the icicles, Sue, or I'll tan your bum.'

'Promises, promises! I might do it all the more.' She gave me a light kiss, smiling properly now, and walked ahead into the living-room. I trailed after her. I try, but I've never been much good at telling people off. Sue rounded on her heel, fingers suddenly drumming on elbows. 'How tidily you've made your bed!'

'Er, my health visitor . . . ' I tried lamely.

'And breakfast cleared away, too!' she gritted. 'Isn't the Health Service considerate these days!'

'Shut it. Doc Lancaster sent her.'

'A likely tale – '

'I'm glad you called, love. I've been wanting to ask you about the other night.' I went and got my shaver while Sue started rearranging the room on principle. 'Those two people, one tall and the other short.'

She stilled. 'The ones who caused . . . the accident?'

'Yes. Could one have been a woman?'

She thought hard, then nodded.

'Sure?' I pressed.

'*Could* have been. I'm uncertain.'

The door banged again, making me jump a mile. Front the side window I could see Moll's car blocking the gate. My cottage is like Piccadilly sometimes.

'It's Mrs Maslow,' I said. 'Copper's wife.'

'What a lot of visitors you . . . entertain these days.'

She was getting ready for war again, but I hoofed her out, ready again to pretend I was seeing a buyer off. Sue neatly scuppered that act.

'Good morning!' she chirped, stepping past Moll at the door. 'I'm Miss Haverill, Lovejoy's health visitor. I've been deciding which exercises he's best at. He's really very vigorous – '

'Thank you.' I pushed her out on to the gravel.

'I'll phone about your programme, Lovejoy,' Sue called over her shoulder. And she meant it. 'Good morning.'

'Great. Good morning.'

'Good morning,' Moll said, looking doubtfully from me to Sue and back again. She had sun-glasses on.

'Good morning.'

All these good mornings should have made me feel quite calm, but that's what they say before a duel, isn't it?

I sat on my unfinished wall, thinking. It doesn't separate any particular bit of garden from anything, just a wall. But my best guesses come when I'm sitting on it.

Moll had only stayed a couple of minutes. Behind her sunglasses she had a real shiner, left eye. There was a graze under the lower lid. I went red when I saw it, but from her attitude we might have been simply renewing an old friendship.

'Er, shall I brew up?' I felt I had to offer something. I didn't tell her it was either that or fried bread.

'No thanks, Lovejoy.'

I didn't care much for that quiet voice.

'Are you all right?'

'Yes, thank you.' She wouldn't sit down.

When you've blacked a bird's eye you can't look straight at them like you normally do. I mean head on with your gaze evenly distributed, so many watts per eye as it were. You find your stare somehow concentrates itself into the injured eye while your mind squirms and you wait for the lawyers' eerie politeness to come cascading through the letterbox.

'Er, I suppose you called the Old Bill?'

'No.' Still quiet.

'Phoned your Tom instead?'

'That neither.'

We watched each other in silence. Any woman can achieve a look. Moll was dressed for spring, small white gloves and everything different colours but matching. I wished now I'd not belted her one.

'A summons?' One of our local magistrates is a right cow. She's got it in for me, through no fault of mine.

'No.'

I thought a bit. 'Look, Moll. I've not a groat – '

She shook her head impatiently. 'I'm not here to take it out on you,' she said at last. 'You were quite right to – to be angry, Lovejoy.'

'*Eh?*'

'I deserved it.' She gazed dispassionately round at the cottage's insides, taking in the general level of wealth. I waited uneasily for my sentence. Birds can be very odd, especially where blokes are concerned. 'Leckie should be alive today, Lovejoy. And it's my fault.'

She pulled out an envelope. It crackled slightly, a beautiful and melodious sound. I felt dizzy. I always do when money raises its exquisite head.

'For your expenses, Lovejoy.'

I couldn't take my eyes off it. 'Expenses?'

'Yes.' She dropped it on the table. She watched me and I watched the envelope. 'I've read your file – ' She stopped me with a gesture when I drew breath. 'Let me finish. You're a violent man. Some of the things – '

'Not my fault,' I got in quickly, hating all this. Women are easier when they're mad at you.

'Of course not.' Moll gave me that level agreement which means just the opposite. 'I know you'll try to kill them, Lovejoy. You'll do it for Leckie, for you, for all of us. I know it. Take the money. It'll help.'

'Rubbish,' I said cagily. 'Anyway, you're a cop's wife.'

'It's not a trick, Lovejoy.' She half-smiled as I backed off. 'Don't worry. I'm not going to weep all over you, though I suppose I ought to. I've been very stupid. Just take it. I realize now I was only wanting to play cops and robbers.'

'No.' Saying it took a bit of nerve and a lot of idiocy.

She waited, thinking. 'I expected that.'

She walked about, looking and occasionally touching what passes for furniture. I suddenly wished I hadn't had to sell my last good piece, a small mutton-fat finger jade, early Ch'ien Lung. It was the only thing I'd had in living memory worth looking at. She'd have been really impressed if I'd had that to show her. As it was my cottage looks like a doss-house.

'Lovejoy. You first come to my place looking for some precious antiques Leckie had just bought.'

'I got them, but they're duff.'

'Duff?'

'Wrong. Not worth anything. Maybe they're not even the ones he started out with.'

'Very well.' She walked past me to the front door, pausing to pat her hair at the mirror. 'Find them, then. Find the real ones. That money's the commission.'

'It can't be,' I explained. 'Commission's – '

'Don't be obtuse, Lovejoy.' She opened the door herself. For once there was no woman on the doorstep. 'Find the – the unduff antiques. I'll buy them, or it. Whichever it turns out to be.'

Unduff, for gawd's sake.

'But how can you buy them, if we don't know what it is?'

'I collect unidentified objects,' she said serenely. 'I've just begun, today. And I'm employing you. Get on with it.' She clicked down to where the gravel begins.

'What if it's too dear?' I called after her, wondering what was going on.

'I'll make the price up to you somehow,' she said over her shoulder but not looking.

And that was that. Her car weaved its way back to the main road in second gear, the blackthorn hedges scraping her paint all the way. I stood, listening. Sure enough, it changed up to third by the chapel. Satisfied she now had her handbag dangling correctly from the gear lever, I went in to go over the evidence. I decided to look up obtuse in the dictionary. I'd get mad with her again if it turned out to be an insult.

In the bath I did some thinking. Not really cerebral stuff, but feeling my way outwards into the bloody mix-up. I'd honestly tried to keep out of it, hadn't I? But Maslow was going to do sod all, and there wasn't anybody else but me to keep faith with fairness in this mad tangled world. I'd have to do it – yet where the hell do you start?

Leckie's lovely blonde missus kept forcing her way into my mind, but why? All these events were all somehow connected. And the connection was through Leckie, now deceased by violence. I splashed my toes against the taps, though it always makes a mess over the side. Sue does her nut and moans about having to mop the floor.

So Leckie and Doc Chase were friends. My mind went: first Doc Chase dies (but when and how? Maybe I ought to ask). Then some of his rubbishy odds and ends are disposed of in a tatty local auction, Virgil's dump in Medham. They're always scouring the villages for stuff to sell on commission, so no mystery there. Then Leckie bids and wins it. Maybe his blonde wife learned somehow from Leckie that Chase's effects contained something precious. She then disclosed it to, say, Black Fergus or Jake Pelman or the jittery Nodge – or all three? Maybe they then tried to 'chop' (this is dealers' slang: to share profit and risk) with Leckie, and he refused. They then decide on hard aggro. Leckie's killed. They realize the stuff's still at Virgil's. They go back during the night hours, tell old George to get lost and break in. They rummage about and whistle Chase's stuff up, but did they find whatever was precious hidden in it? If I'd guessed right they hadn't found a bloody thing, judging from Nodge's nervous face and Jake Pelman's clumsy shadowing – always assuming they were the baddies.

I sighed and stood up, dripping water. The best thing about having a bath is getting out of it, except when Sue's in it too. It seemed I couldn't escape from Leckie's last request no matter how hard I tried. There seemed nothing for it. I decided to start by breaking a couple of fingers, one on Nodge and then one on old George. I whistled absently as I dried, pleased now that matters were out of my hands.

Start as you mean to go on, I always say.

Chapter Nine

Nodge is one of those antique dealers who are called 'caley' men in our part of this lunatic game. Somebody once told me it started out as ceilidh, Celtic for ding-dong, a spree. Nodge goes along for months nervous as a trout, never buying without agonies of indecision and worried about selling. Then he'll buy everything in sight, good and bad, spending like a drunken sailor and plunging into debt.

Once every six months he ends up with a ton of pseudo-antiques nobody in his right mind would look at twice. It's all hit or miss. You'd be surprised which world-famous collectors – I include museums – are run on the caley principle. Why people go along like this, hoping that ignorance might in fact actually turnout to be bliss in the end, nobody knows.

It took me an hour to find Tinker. He was in our local bookie's with his mate Lemuel (not 'Lem', except at your peril). Lemuel's an asthmatic and grubby old soldier who breathes like my car. He gambles his – and possibly others' – social security money as long as it lasts, then cadges the rest of the week. Social workers are good to him, though. They bought him a wheel-chair last Lady Day. He sold it after an instantaneous and miraculous recovery from his limp. He wears an old forage cap without badges.

The bookie's was just crowding up before the afternoon races. I caught them both there in the planning stage.

'Nodge?' Tinker thought a second. He always offers

to roll me a corrupt cigarette on one of those little pocket machines.

'He comes in here sometimes, Lovejoy,' Lemuel wheezed. He took the first fag off Tinker's assembly line.

'Nodge isn't in town yet.' Tinker's verdict.

'How long will he be?' You can ask Tinker things like this. He always knows.

'Not long. Ten minutes. In here.'

'I'll wait.'

They lit up, spluttering and wheezing on the ends of their respective Tinker-made monstrosities. Tinker's fags are better-looking after being smoked than when they start off. I watched, marvelling. Never had so many lungs managed so little.

While Tinker and Lemuel unerringly sussed out today's losers I gazed round at the maelstrom. Our town's gambling fraternity is an assorted bunch. I don't often come in except for the Derby and the Grand National, maybe the St Leger. There are housewives, layabouts, neatly dressed blokes fresh from selling insurance confident hard-faced ladies with Jags left running at the kerb, the whole gamut. They all seem to smoke. My eyes run after a few minutes. I listened, bored to death, seeing those mysterious numbers being chalked up on the boards. Lemuel, advised by Tinker, was filling in papers with a pencil stub. It was a real drag. So one horse runs faster than another. Who cares? And yet water-colours of Georgian and early William IV racehorses, not to mention the Victorian, are soaring in value. The prints as well, so be on the look-out. Always go for fame: Eclipse, Hermit, Hyperion, even as late as Airborne. For heaven's sake, though, make sure the print you buy is *named* (horse, owner, the race and jockey if possible). The rule is: the more factual detail the better. If you merely want to invest and you don't care about real antiques much, go for the best such paintings or prints you can buy at

100

a good dealer's. Anything up to and including even the Brown Jack era should reap rewards. When buying originals, demand certificates of provenance – that is, what the painting's been up to since it left the artist's lilywhites. Don't worry so much about provenance if it's a print, because they're not being forged yet. I mean so far. It won't be long.

Nodge came in hunched and forlorn. He was startled to see me among the muttering, obsessed crowd. I was across in a flash, pulling him in and smiling. I didn't let go.

'Over here.'

Tinker and Lemuel were huddled in a corner. There aren't any tables or chairs in these dumps, only mounds of fag-ends and possibly a shelf to write on. Tinker gave me a bleary glance then carefully took no notice. I could say what I like. He's on my side. Lemuel's not, but he's not daft.

'Nodge,' I said in an affable undertone. 'You heard Leckie got done?'

'I heard.'

I smiled at him. 'I think it was Fergie, Jake Pelman and you.'

'Me?' His yelp made a few heads turn for a second. 'Me?' he hissed, white.

'Any two of the three of you.'

'I wasn't even in the bleeding car, Lovejoy.'

'What car, Nodge?' I saw the penny drop. We were muttering in the corner like punters, buffeted by pre-occupied people pushing all around.

'Er – it was a car accident, wasn't it?'

'Don't try covering up, Nodge.'

'Let me go, Lovejoy.' He was desperate now, lips trembling and sweaty. A punter tried elbowing past to reach the betting slips on the shelf, but Tinker got in the way with studied absent-mindedness. The punter swore and moved off. Tinker never even looked my way. A good lad.

'You did Virgil's warehouse, right?'

Nodge's eyes widened. It warned me he was going to try it on so I snapped his finger. His attempted rush for the door halted before it was begun. He squawked and doubled up.

'Here, you lot.' The bouncer started out from behind his false grille. I gave him one of my looks through the smoke and he hesitated. 'Less of that. We want no trouble.'

'Just going.' I called, smiling over the heads. The bouncer dithered.

'*Christ.*' Nodge was nearly fainting. There's nothing so painful as a broken digit. It matters which digit, of course.

'Yes or no, Nodge?' I helped him into the vestibule and stood between him and the street door.

'They'll kill me.'

'You did the warehouse?'

'Yeah.'

'What were you looking for?' I helped him a little. 'Come on, Nodge. I know all about Doc Chase.'

That let him off the hook of conscience, such as it was. 'They weren't sure what. Summat hidden in his things. Fergus said it would tell us where the stuff was hidden in Scratton.'

'Come on.' I indicated the door.

'I'd better go out on my own, Lovejoy – '

'No, Nodge,' I said contentedly. 'I want you in trouble with Jake and Fergie.'

'Please, Lovejoy – '

I nodded to Tinker and Lemuel and we barged slowly towards the door in a mob. 'Out, Nodge,' I told him. We left Tinker and Lemuel in the smoke and babble. I pushed Nodge out on to the pavement but kept hold. We had to be seen together. The smog of the market square seemed fresh as milk.

Jake Pelman was across the way, coming forward among the stalls. He saw us and stared.

'Jake's always out shopping these days,' I said pleasantly to Nodge. He groaned, more from seeing Jake than his finger.

'You bastard, Lovejoy. They'll do for me.'

'We can but hope, lad. See you.' I stepped away, still smiling for Jake's sake and waving casually to Nodge. 'It's a deal, Nodge,' I said loudly, nodding.

'Jake!' Nodge shouted urgently, beckoning.

I felt rather than saw them come together among the shoppers. Nodge would have to do some quick explaining or go the way of all flesh. Jake would assume we'd done a private deal. Nodge was for it. I went whistling towards the pub. Happiness makes you peckish.

I called in at the Three Cups for a drink and a pasty, happy that things had started moving. I'd learned not only who'd killed Leckie, but that they were no nearer finding the valuable item than I was.

Jean was in the saloon bar. I was glad. When one thing cheers you up lots of other things join in the jollity, don't they? I've often noticed that. Here was Leckie's mystery practically solving itself, me with a wodge of gelt in my pocket and Jean buying me a drink. She had a rare piece of 'toy' porcelain from the Girl-in-a-Swing Factory – look for *tiny* figurines with streaky brown hair, minuscule mottoes with atrocious spelling, and you're half-way there.

I perched on a stool, elbows on the bar and gazed at the lovely piece. Sit down when you meet a genuine antique. I do. Don't rush. It wants friendship. It needs company. Hang about for a few minutes and listen to its viewpoint, because it's got civil rights just like you. Take your time and acquaint yourself with its exquisite truth. Just as women are the living instruments of the sacrament of love, so are antiques their counterpart, only a little more inanimate at first sight. I sometimes wonder if antiques are really a vigil between different women. Or maybe vice versa. Anyhow, you get the idea.

To get the price down I told Jean it wasn't genuine, but she could see how breathless and quivering I was, and only laughed.

'Yeah, yeah.' She doesn't actually know much, so we had a good chat. I told her how Charlie Gouyn had slammed out of Lawrence Street full of Huguenot temper in 1749, leaving his partner Nicholas Sprimont in the lurch, and started up the Girl-in-a-Swing Factory. We don't know its proper name. We dealers actually call it that nowadays from a little piece in the Victoria and Albert. The funny thing is that Gouyn was a superb silversmith, yet often put gold mounts on his tiny scent-bottles, figurines or chain-seals. My own trick is to see if the lassies' dresses (usually whitish with a red rose pattern) are lined with deep rose or yellow, and see if the base has a rose on patterned leaves. You can't really go wrong because they're so exquisite. Jean's delicious piece was three luscious ladies leaning against a tree stump. Charlie Gouyn's buxom wenches often do that. I wonder about the symbolism sometimes. I bought it off her there and then with the expenses money Moll had given me. Well, I'd tell Moll I used a lot of petrol.

By the time I left town on the Medham road I was chirpy as a cricket and singing that Tallis madrigal which changes key a million times in the first bar. I was in good voice. When a crisis comes to the crunch I'm full of this alert feeling. I think it's a sort of realization that honesty's the best policy.

Something like that.

The damaged doors were repaired. New frosted glass glittered in the windows. Old George and Wilkinson were busy supervising the unloading of some stuff in the cobbled yard. A few people milled about, an early viewer and a dealer or two. I put my crate facing down the yard's slope in case of possible engine non-cooperation and strolled inside.

'Out of it, Lovejoy,' Wilkie called bossily, arms a-dangle.

'Get stuffed, Wilkie.'

I was up the ramp and inside as the vannies sniggered. Wilkie came after me. I shook him off. There was only the office girl Brenda there, and she was behind the glass partition near the posh entrance. For once she seemed to be engaged in work.

'I said, out.'

'Wilkie,' I said in my business voice. He shuffled a bit at that. 'What did you do with the escritoire?'

He shrugged. 'It got smashed up. You saw it.'

'Where are the bits?'

'Chucked out at the back. We'll burn it.'

I got him to show me the heap. They'd piled it among other broken bits against the yard wall out of the way of the traders' cars. There are some old sheds for storing stuff they can't sell. The escritoire still looked a cheap Edwardian copy smashed up, yet something was niggling me. The wood was honestly fairly new when looked at closely. The Bramah lock was obviously nicked from an old piece and screwed into this feeble reproduction furniture to make it seem older. It had been only recently done judging from the scratches, and inexpertly done at that. This is a common trick to make a relatively modern piece of furniture seem old. It shouldn't deceive an infant. The lock was hardly worth taking, because lock-and-key collectors are rare and the items are many.

I let Wilkie go and stayed in the warehouse yard an hour, scrutinizing every splinter and handling it all inch by inch.

No good. I rose at last, stiff as hell, and wandered out to watch them loading. After a few minutes I gave George the bent eye. He came over after a glance at Wilkie, who nodded at him once. Wilkie must have warned him I was around and being critical. I took him to see the heap.

'Nobody to see us or hear us, George,' I began. He looked about. I shook my head warningly.

'Look here, Lovejoy . . .'

'You're an old geezer, George. And you know me, tough and nasty with it. Old geezers fall and break legs, right?' We both analysed the situation. Charitably I gave him an extra minute.

'I don't know – '

' – Nuffink?' I capped cheerfully for him. 'But you do, George.'

'Don't touch me, Lovejoy. I'll shout out.' If he hadn't helped to kill Leckie I'd have felt quite sorry for him, a shaky old sweat scraping a meagre living. The way I felt, though, I wouldn't piss on him in hell to cool him down. He takes a few quid to tip dealers off when good items are coming in for auction. That's all he's good for. And it got Leckie crashed.

'What's it to be, George?' I gripped his arm. He winced and finally nodded. 'Nodge did the place over, right? He told me.'

'Then what're you asking me for? It's bleeding killing me – '

'Who else?'

'Him with the fancy whistle.' Whistle-and-flute, suit. Only Jake wears fancy bright green gear.

'Jake. And Fergie?'

'No.'

It had the ring of extorted truth. I let go. Nodge and Jake had known Old George dossed in the warehouse when there was stuff passing through. That meant any day before or after an auction. They'd probably just knocked on the door and barged in past him. A few threats probably shut him up.

'Here, Lovejoy,' he quavered. 'Don't tell them it was me grassed, eh?'

'Cross my heart, George.' And, I prayed kindly,

106

God help you, because that's the first thing I would do.

The funny feeling was there still as I watched him shuffle off down the yard to the corner where the vans were standing. I turned the shattered wood pieces over with my foot. It was simply modernish wood, poor quality with horrible varnish and wrong staining. So what was there to worry about? And why was I dithering like this? I decided to get back to town at the finish. Maybe I should go over to the late Dr Chase's surgery and suss it out.

I was actually in my crate fumbling for my keys when the light came on and I froze. *Keys.* Keys have locks. Locks are in escritoires. But who on earth takes a genuine Bramah lock *recently* from a genuine piece of antique furniture and plonks it in a piece of trashy reproduction furniture? I dropped my keys and hurtled back up the yard. A dealer called, grinning, 'What's the hurry, Lovejoy?' the burke. The lock was still there, still screwed on its piece of backing wood among the rubbish. I'd been right. It had only recently been put on. You can always tell from the screw lines and the lock edges, especially if it's been done by somebody who has never done it before. And it looked a botch job, done by somebody with no skill but a lot of determination. Somebody maybe like Dr Chase?

The crowd by the loading ramp was still watching the new items coming in for auction. I went inside the warehouse. Wilkie was talking to Brenda in her illuminated glass cell. He quickly looked away from me. On my hands and knees I crawled about the floor, feeling along each board as I went. I crisscrossed the site where the escritoire had stood. Every yard I got a new splinter but the weight of the Bramah lock in my pocket goaded me. The key was in a corner, a cylindrical rod on a fixed ring.

The key probably didn't matter, though, only the lock. I just had to have both because there were endless possibilities. I slotted the key in. It fitted. Tired now, I went out to my crate the back way.

Wilkie called, 'Here, Lovejoy. Did you pinch anything . . . ?' but only when he knew I'd not bother to turn back.

I ignored his shout, smiling to myself. Aren't people odd? We work like dogs to trick ourselves. Maybe we all know we don't admire the real bits of our own personalities. I'll bet I'm the only person on earth who's really honest about myself, honest and fair minded.

It took a real effort to switch the engine on. I knew most of the story now. Who killed Leckie was obvious – Jake, Nodge and/or Blackie. Possibly Mrs Leckie egged them on. Motive: greed. For what? Well, that would be revealed once I got the lock home and took it to bits.

My chirpiness had gone. I didn't sing a note this time as I clattered along the main village street towards the exit road.

I'd better explain at this stage how I killed him. It's clear in my mind still, and nothing trains your mind to be retentive like antiques. Of course, some antique dealers have better memories than others. Patrick, for example. He can even tell you if a single Staffordshire figure had been seen in the district during the past ten years. And Tinker's like that with auctions. I once asked him about a silver-topped walking-stick, plain as a pikestaff and monogrammed 1881 in Cheltenham. Somebody had auctioned it locally six years ago. I only had the vaguest recollection. If it had been an eighteenth-century cane swordstick with a gold-mounted ivory or porcelain figurine handle – worth a year's wages – well, anybody can remember gems like that. But this particular stick even nowadays would only bring in a week's wages. They're still common. Tinker just wrinkled his gnarled face and said, 'Top-angled, straited, monogram not edged, ebony with horn-based tip? Thirty-quid, Easter auction six years back. Elsie. She sold it to Brad. He's still got it.' Margaret's good too, but keeps careful files and clippings on everything she sees, same as me. It's good observation. So I remember killing him in some detail.

I told you I was subdued driving homewards from Virgil's that day. There was trouble ahead, but Fergie and Jake seemed not too much of a threat, not as threats go these days. Nodge would be no bother. My only worry was if Fergus fetched a couple of London lads up to put the elbow on me. Or if he got the Item before I did and reaped all the benefit.

You might be wondering why I instinctively believed in the Doc Chase story, discovering a vital and precious 'find'. On the face of it, an elderly quack isn't much of a Hawkeyes when blundering round East Anglia's scenery. But this old island creaks under the weight of its history. Within literally a ten-mile radius of my crummy thatched cottage there are thirty buried temples, over a hundred pre-Christian burial mounds of tributary kings, numerous sunken treasure ships in the estuaries and graveyards of famous Roman legions. And, in the same area, two hundred important 'finds' of rare and precious valuable antiques have been made this year alone – none by Lovejoy Antiques, Inc, worse luck.

As I said, minds are funny things. When you hear of a find, you tend only to think of the great bronze head of Claudius being fished up intact from our riverbed. Your mind lingers on the treasure troves found in the craziest places, like the Ardquin Treasure in that bloody fishpond or the Winterslow Trove in that chalk pit. Like that gravedigger business in that churchyard, now famous as the Hickleton Hoard. But you don't have to go digging for antiques. After all, that Vlaminck daub 'by an unknown artist' was merely hanging on the wall. People saw it every day for ages.

Yet once it was identified Sotheby's sold it for a fortune.

What I mean is, it's only natural in these circumstances to believe old Chase had come across a valuable find, something worth killing for. And if you think people won't kill for antiques my tip is stay innocent. But I was on about how I killed him.

Our roads in East Anglia are only two kinds. One's the newly built dash-track several maniacs wide. The other's the ancient and narrow switchback blundering between hedges and round sudden unnecessary blind corners. Both are as daft. Like many motorists, including drivers of the long distance double-trailer wagons, I keep off the new roads because they're a waste of all the places in between.

Leaving Virgil's I took the small side road which, signposts promise, will eventually head vaguely in the direction of Norwich should you live that long. I didn't mind because I had to have time to think. Once I got back to the town the other dealers would be sussing me out as usual and antiques would take over.

Presumably the Bramah lock would tell me somehow where the old doctor had found the Item. Or maybe where he'd hidden it. Perhaps, I thought excitedly, it was even hidden inside the lock. If it was. . . .

My reverie was interrupted by a sharp nudge. The crate gave a sudden jump. My neck nearly dislocated as the car jerked forward. I have to look round because I have no proper mirrors. An enormous black humped car was practically stuck to my tail. It looked horribly familiar. I quickly tried to use that glance to see who was driving but the sun was coming from behind. It nosed forward and belted my feeble old crate, whiplashing my neck dangerously. I remember yelping with fear and swearing. The bend in the road allowed me to struggle my motor on line again, but the huge black car came alongside and pushed me sideways.

'Get over! Get over!' I shouted. I tried accelerating,

but it had me for speed and was there again, coming on my right side and slewing my stern round again. My crate only just kept going.

'Sodding murderer!' I screamed, foot down. I'd never heard the cylinders so loud. I tried desperately thinking where we were. The nearest village was about five miles. I could only remember a farmhouse a couple of miles ahead, and even that stands back from the road behind hedges. They'd chosen well. A long, narrow, tortuous and undulating road, with no witnesses.

I tried leaving my brakes off going down the next hill, but my nerves gave out. The old banger can't take the stress of sudden turns any more and I could see the sharp oblique climb up the other side of the slope. We were rushing downhill towards the small stone bridge at the bottom. I was going as fast as I could.

He took me again at the turn. The massive sinister black bulge came on the inside and was forcing my stern across the road as we tore down to the bridge. It was all happening so bloody quick and sudden. I got free this time by risking everything, letting my brakes free and stamping on the throttle. Better to get crisped trying to escape than meekly submit by driving carefully. The extra speed and the bend saved me for a brief instant.

The stone bridge is an ancient medieval span they built with recesses for people keeping out of the way of horse-drawn carts. The humped roadway was too narrow for the big saloon and it braked, suddenly, revving high with a boom. I made a lunatic ninety-degree screech and clattered on up the hill.

My old crate was gasping now, climbing the macadam between the thick hawthorn hedges with diminishing speed. Every third beat was missing, and something was whining steadily between my back wheels. It wasn't used to all this. I swear it was as terrified as I was. The black car came thundering close

111

and with a crash belted me again. My head nearly flew off my shoulders. It took a few seconds for my vision to clear.

Then, in respite, my crate gave that giveaway juddering sound, warning me. Something big was coming the opposite way. It always makes my little motor shake. Maybe one of the juggernauts, I prayed, with a bloody great trailer. They're always in a hurry and come on fast, confident in their smooth air brakes and high-seated power. Frantically I smashed into second gear, sacrificing a few yards for better control. My engine caught up again and sounded healthy for several beats as the bronchitic cylinders strained easier.

The saloon hammered me again but I'd guessed their timing and corrected early enough for once. I realized I was alternately screaming with terror and babbling abuse. They were going to do me like they did Leckie. I'd end up crushed in a ditch, battered and emptied of life.

The narrow climb had forty yards to go when I took the sudden decision. They wouldn't kill me. Not Lovejoy Antiques, Inc. If anybody had to go it would be them, the evil bastards. I went stone cold. My foot lifted once then forced itself down hard. At first I'd determined to go as slowly as I dared on the hill, hoping to save time while frantically praying for somebody to come along to be a safe witness. Now it was time for killing.

The road banked left at the top. I could see it easily. Hedges stood close to the left verge but on the right there was a small grassy space with a few trees. Any juggernaut hurtling our way, suddenly coming across an obstruction, would instinctively straighten for a few yards in a desperate attempt to avoid a crash by using the meagre verge, then try to correct for the rest of the curve and continue its downward rush – and all in an instant. Even the best driver would jack-knife his two linked wagons. I'd seen it happen.

Please God, I prayed, as the crest loomed. A sudden crashing blow from behind came again. I felt the crate's floor judder with the rumbling approach of the unseen vehicle. The black car's engine notched up half an octave getting ready for the kill. They'd changed gear for even more power. So they were going to take me on the inside at the top, force me to slide to the right and leave me only the tree-crowded space to drive into. All because I hadn't the power to cut clear. If the tree trunks didn't get me I'd slam into the high bank beyond. The best I could hope for was having to stop and be at their mercy.

The juddering told me the oncoming juggernaut was almost on us. The booming saloon rammed against my tail with another crash. My engine cut, recovered, howled once, and just as suddenly steadied. Glass tinkled as a side window went. And abruptly I was at the crest. The black shape swelled darkly on my inside. I saw it out of the corner of my eye.

I wrenched the wheel to the right and stamped on the brakes, wishing to God I'd had the money to get them mended properly. I remember yelling one final insult at the bastards. I heard the saloon's engine mute. My tyres slithered, gripped, squealed as the crate slid across the narrow road sideways on towards the crowded trees. The trunks thickened horribly towards me. And a beautiful immense juggernaut came hissing on to the hill, its radiator tall as a church surmounted by windows like a liner's bridge. All in a millisec I banged the throttle pedal down, whining with fright. The juggernaut saw me across its path and bucked. Its engine shrilled. For one second I thought it wouldn't see the space, but its impetus was just too colossal. Its front heaved to my right. The sky darkened above me as the gigantic vehicle poised fractionally at the top. Then it jack-knifed. The trailing half clattered loudly into the leading part and swung across towards me, shuddering crazily. I hadn't the power to get clear.

It caught my offside rear wheel. Glass exploded and spattered my neck and scalp like a million needles. I saw twigs and grass. My windscreen went and the steering-wheel crashed against my chest. The world suddenly seemed full of noises and fire and rubbery stenches. I heard somebody screaming and another voice saying Dear God, Dear God, over and over. All the hedgerows on earth seemed to be full of flames. Then the sky was streaming blood, but at least things were steady and trying to stay still.

My vision cleared about fifteen minutes later. I inspected the mad scene from a lady's lap a few yards from the crest of the hill. She was dabbing my forehead with a scented hankie and kept telling me how long it was since the accident and that I was going to be all right. Her frock was powder-blue. For a mad moment I thought I was in Paradise, because all I could see at first were five strands of baroque pearls, alternate white and rose. Strung thus they shrieked of Italy before this century. The woman moved. She told me she was on her way to a play rehearsal when they saw the crash. Her husband had phoned for ambulances and police from the farmhouse I mentioned, and now was trying to help to get the poor man out of his car. It was burning, hopeless.

'I hope nobody's hurt,' I said, for the record.

'Lie still, dear. Don't you worry.' She kept dabbing at me.

'A car tried to overtake on the wrong side . . . ' I let my voice dwindle wearily. It didn't take much acting.

'Lie still. Everything's all right.'

We stayed like this for some time. I saw the police arrive, with Maslow coming in the second wave. Spectators gradually accumulated. Ambulances came and went. I refused to go in one, and struggled erect after a team of tired emergency people tinkered with me a

114

bit. They covered one of my eyes up and turbanned my head. The Bramah lock had been driven into my side. A young quack put six bloody stitches in, but I got the lock back. They padded me up and wound strapping round my middle.

I got the lady's name and address before they continued to the rehearsal. Her lap deserved better than a half-conscious bloke in it, and her Italian pearl necklace was gold-clasped. I waved them off, wobbling somewhat.

Maslow took a statement from me, a constable doing the heavy paper labour. I reported faithfully how this car had simply tried to overtake on the wrong side, to my astonishment.

'A juggernaut came round the bend just then,' I explained. 'That's all I remember.'

'Look at me, Lovejoy.' Maslow's voice cold as a frog.

'I'm trying,' I said. 'With my one good eye. Will I still be able to play the piano?'

'If I thought . . .'

'Good heavens!' I sounded really quite good, properly horrified. 'You're surely not suggesting – '

He flapped a hand wearily. 'Go home, Lovejoy.'

'Wait.'

I went to look at my crate. It was a hell of a mess, but maybe rescuable. On the other side of the road the juggernaut stood, its driver still dictating trembling answers to a woman copper, poor bloke. The black saloon was still burning. A fire engine was there, a few helmeted firemen standing about. There wasn't much more for them to do now. I felt Maslow join me.

'Reported stolen,' he said morosely. I didn't look at him.

'From anybody in particular?'

'Chap called Fergus, London. An antique dealer.'

'How terrible.' I shook my head sadly, then had

115

a theatrical after-thought. 'Oh, Inspector. Who was driving?'

'Your friend Nodge.

I gazed back at him then with my one eye steady as a laser. 'Tut fucking tut,' I said evenly. 'The things people do.'

I stepped closer to the smouldering motor and its unspeakable inner mass. 'God rest, Nodge.' I'd broken more than his finger, as it turned out, but what else could I have done? It hadn't been my fault, not really.

They got a police car to run me home. On the way I asked the copper to stop a minute. We pulled in. I reeled out and vomited spectacularly in the hedge. I retched and retched. The peeler asked if I was all right. After a few minutes I wiped my mouth on a handful of grass and got back in.

'You'll be fine,' the lad said kindly. 'It's just reaction.'

'Thanks,' I said back.

But fear isn't got rid of as easily as that. I should know.

Chapter Ten

The spectacular sunrise surprised me. A mist covered our valley so densely I could have walked across to Lexton on it. Trees close to my cottage projected through it like small mountains. It was a gentle, unassuming and blissful picture. Then the sun bounced up quite suddenly. The valley mist showed red. Gold tinted the world's edges. I'd never seen such a sight. And in this lovely daylight I was black and blue. My face was bloated. The skin bulged green and purple. I was sore as hell. I could hardly stand up from the wall where I'd been sitting most of the night. But I was alive, solid and breathing and beating. Even aching was pleasant.

Last night before going the bobby had asked if I needed help. I'd said I was great. They'd come back today. They always do. Good old Fergus must have lent Nodge his car then reported his car stolen to keep himself in the clear. Maybe they'd made some telephone arrangement before Nodge was sent off to do me. I didn't blame myself for not sleeping much, because the Girl-in-a-Swing piece was ground to powder in my jacket pocket. I'd only found out when I tried to get undressed. I won't admit whether or not I wept at odd times behind my darkened cottage thinking of Nodge, or maybe the porcelain. Once anything's gone it's gone for good, but the passing is too much to take sometimes. I mean, in one go, as it were.

Once I'd got the sun properly up I went in and got in a blazing temper trying to brew up. I needed help. Things were starting to move and I had to move with

117

them. But who to ask? Tinker's not on the phone, which narrowed the choice. He'd be caylied until opening time anyway. Sue's tough husband probably wouldn't prove co-operative if I tried to borrow her for a few days, selfish sod. Helen only wakes slow – pretty, but slow. Margaret was up in the Smoke for her weekly spending spree on the Belly, Portobello Road street market. I can't really rely on Jill, Jean or Lily like I can the rest, so they were out of it. And Miss Haverill would have me sprinting to Friday Wood and back when I couldn't raise a trot. I couldn't even think that far.

Painfully I dialled Moll. She lifted third ring.

'Lovejoy here,' I told her, trying to speak through split oedematous lips.

'Oh, Lovejoy!' she cried. 'I've just heard about your accident from – '

I cut in. 'Busy?'

'No. I was just about to ring you.'

'Get your coat on and come over.'

'This instant. Don't move.'

'I promise. Oh,' I added. 'One thing. Bring some grub, partner. I'm starving.'

She paused, then said of course, partner, politely.

I set to on the Bramah lock in my shed. You're sure to see a genuine one if you go to any antique shop, but don't write them off just because lock-and-key collectors are pretty rare folk. The Bramah lock is a delightful piece of wondrous engineering in lovely warm brass. Its precision and delicacy are exhilarating. They are the only honestly important antiques *you can still get for nothing*. Junk shops round here still chuck them out, like this one at Virgil's, but the time will come . . .

Joseph Bramah was a Yorkie, and a genius at that. His legendary lock patent is dated 1784. Nowadays we can only imagine what a sensation his new design caused in Georgian London. A real furore. He thought up some radial sliders, with the key pin pushing in against a spring. In his description he claims it is infallible, but even the addition of a metal 'curtain' inside it failed to protect it against the breathtaking (and quite legitimate) lockpicking skills of that quiet American A.C. Hobbs. Knightsbridge was in uproar for half a century in lockpicking contests, as locksmiths battled night and day to keep one step ahead of burglars and people who claimed they could pick any old lock any time. Groups of gentlemen assembled to referee claims. There were even lawsuits. Public competitions were arranged, with multitudes gasping and applauding every flick of the wrist.

In those early days locksmithing was centred in Willenhall. People still call the place 'Humpshire' because the Staffordshire men were practically deformed from filing locks on the bench. They walked the streets with their hands frozen around an imaginary file and their shoulders hunched. Nowadays the manufacturing is spread around a bit, especially since young Linus Yale gave up portrait painting and set about explaining how good his dad's lock design really was.

The Bramah lock's simplicity is so stylish you tend to forget that Joe's innovation was the first major step forward since the locks of Ancient Egypt.

I made myself stop admiring the masterpiece and get myself going. I got the key in. It turned with a succulent click. No sign of anything hidden, though. The key emerged with traces of carbon which smudged my fingertip. Somebody, presumably Chase, had seen to it that the lock was properly cared for. No stupid dollops of oil to harden with the passing years, but careful gusts of powdered graphite blown into the lock aperture once every ten years.

Even though the escritoire itself was gone I had to summon all my nerve to damage the wood sliver on which the lock was fixed. I finally fixed the wood in a

119

vice and lifted the lock's brass plate off after a struggle. It took half an hour to get it away undamaged. I'd have done it quicker but for my one eye and getting the shakes from the bruising. The plate came away. I was quivering with eagerness. I'd put a folded car blanket underneath the vice to catch the precious clue I knew would undoubtedly be concealed behind the lock. Gingerly I lifted the plate away. A small disc fell on to the blanket. That was all.

I peered at the back of the plate with a lens and along the wooden recess. Nothing. Disappointed, I found the coin and examined it slowly. Even there any hopes were dashed. It wasn't gold, or even silver. It wasn't even a Roman copper denarius. Not even a coin. I took it to the shed door and peered at it in direct daylight. It was a measly train pass, a grotty Victorian common-as-muck passenger chit. You can find even the rarest ones for a few quid. They're often in what we call the tuppeny tray, that little box you see set outside junk-shops, filled with duff buttons, jettons, tokens and neffie modern foreign coins. An interesting collecting field if you like that sort of thing, but even a hundred of these cheap little tokens won't make your fortune. It was blank on one side. The other bore the words 'The Rt Worthy Jn⁰ Case – No 1 – Mt St Mary Rlwy Grand Opening.' Not even a date, either. Mount St Mary is not far. I knew for a fact there was no railway there. It was probably just some sentimental child's play by old Doc Chase, him concealing his ancestor's train pass and playing secrets. Some people do this sort of thing for a giggle. Or maybe another decoy? If so, it had worked.

'Big deal,' I told the little disc in disgust.

I'd just finished tidying the shed as Moll bowled in. You can imagine the scene we had, Moll doing her nut at the state I was in and me saying oh leave off for gawd's sake. She unloaded a ton of stuff and made us breakfast. I'm always amazed at how little grub women eat. Beats me how they keep going. Anyhow, we became more or less friends. By the time she'd washed up and I'd put the things away we'd stopped jumping a mile whenever the other spoke. I told her about the accident and kept very few details back.

'Was Nodge trying to . . . ?' She had two attempts at it.

'We'll never know,' I said gravely. I couldn't forget she was a peeler's wife.

'You poor man.' Her eyes filled. 'And he was your friend.'

'Well, er, yes.' I was uncomfortable. She kept on about this for some time, saying things like the tragic ironies with which life abounds and all that, and drawing unrealistic parallels from her own family's humdrum experiences. I said, isn't life astounding.

About elevenish, Miss Haverill phoned in. I was due at Chase's surgery for the first exercise pattern in the health scheme at noon. I told her I would toe the line.

Moll was aghast. 'You can't possibly do exercises – '

But I was already locking up, and told her it was where the next clues were coming from. She nodded determinedly then, and helped me with my jacket. In the interests of morale I didn't dare admit what a useless trail I'd found so far.

'Six Elm Green,' I said. 'Then Scratton. Where the tunnel is.'

As Moll drove us over to Six Elm Green I couldn't help glancing at her. It wasn't just the knees going up and down in that alluring way as she managed the pedals. She definitely had something, an extra erg of attraction. Of course all women have it, but in some it can't be avoided. They glow with a chemotactic radiation. You can't keep your eyes off. I suppose being admired must get on their wick much of the time. She caught my one-eyed awareness and decided to fix me good and proper.

121

'Who is Mrs Markham, Lovejoy?'

That was Janie. 'Er, a . . . a sort of cousin.'

'And Lydia?'

'Oh. She's, er, another cousin.' I cleared my throat. 'Used to visit me now and again.'

'Lisa?' Her tone was very critical. 'Another cousin, I suppose?'

'Er . . . yes.' I said brightly. She bit her lip. Her face was starting to colour up.

You can go off people. She must have found their names in my file. Trust women to be bitter about other women, even when a relationship's innocent. Well, almost innocent. The peelers should be catching tearaways, instead of keeping tabs on innocent law-abiding members of the public like me. She pulled us into a layby. An overtaking lorry honked joyously, predicting a snogging session. If only they knew.

'Listen to me, Lovejoy.' She had one of those chiffon scarves. It only needed a Georgian cameo brooch to be dazzling. 'I've read your file from cover to cover. Your record is one of utter degradation. Your behaviour is loose, completely improper.'

I wasn't having that. 'The police never check properly – '

'Let me finish.' She was furious at me, but why? I hadn't done anything. 'These episodes of . . . of carnal practices, and these terrible so-called accidents which keep happening. And always you're involved.'

'It's antiques,' I explained.

'It's *you*! One woman after another. And the deaths – '

I took her hand gently and let her rhyme on for a bit before I interrupted.

'Moll, love. It's antiques. It's not me, not ever.' She clearly didn't believe me so I tried to explain. 'All we ever want on earth, any of us, is love. There's nothing else worth breathing for. Antiques *are* love, but in a material form. They're just inert matter carved or

shaped with love. That's why they're valuable to everyone. We see the love in them. Wanting them so badly
is only natural. Get it?'

'But Nodge's death. It follows the pattern you
create – '

I wasn't having that either. 'Nodge only lusted after
Chase's precious item, same as the rest of us.' I
shrugged. 'He wasn't careful enough, that's all.'

She wouldn't be mollified. 'What I started to say,'
she announced primly, 'is that you're not to presume
on our . . . relationship, such as it is. Our partnership
is entirely . . . entirely . . .'

'Judicial?'

'Judicial.' She caught at the word with relief. 'A
judicial working arrangement.'

'Agreed.' We shook hands soberly. She got us out
on to the road again. We carried on, chatting of the
possible meaning of the tin disc and the Bramah lock.
We both stared studiously ahead, me not seeing Moll's
knees out of the corner of my eye and her not seeing
me not looking.

The trouble is you see more when you're deliberately
not looking. Ever noticed that?

Dr Chase's surgery stands among neat houses and
bungalows. The village is a scattered affair with an
ancient church and three pubs. It's not as big as ours,
maybe a thousand people served by two small grocery
shops. The surgery's just a converted house, with no
place to park. All I ever see in Six Elm Green is little
lawns.

The house lies back from the pavement. Beyond the
line of dwellings is a row of gardens. Then the dreadful
countryside starts, rolling fields, woods, streams, trees.
Really horrible, not an antique shop anywhere. I hate
the bloody stuff.

And there was Miss Haverill, keen as mustard for
us all to run round it. She was still chained to her

123

clip-board. If only she'd wear a ton more make-up, I couldn't help thinking. Five assorted blokes stood about in their idea of athletic garb, all red faces and white hairy knees. They looked a sight.

'Lovejoy! What a terrible mess!' Elspeth came rushing at me as soon as I stepped out of Moll's car.

I glanced sardonically at her track team. 'I'm the best you've got, love.'

'But you can't run in your condition!' she squeaked, horrified. I thought bitterly, I can hardly bloody *walk*.

'I had to come,' I said nobly. 'You stressed how important it is.'

'How very . . . fine of you, Lovejoy.' She went all misty. I limped a bit more, obviously biting on the bullet.

'Oh. You've met Mrs Maslow? Miss Haverill.'

Elspeth said hello, but Moll looked puzzled. Oh, hell. I'd forgotten Sue's little game. I'd have to think up some tale for later. I pressed matters on hastily.

'I've some stitches and dressings needing attention, if Nurse Patmore's free.'

'Very well.' Elspeth looked harassed. 'An accident, I suppose? Do go through, please. I'll start my group off and be with you in a moment.'

I saw a familiar face and grinned. 'How do, Bernard.' I gave him a wink. Bern's a machinist in a local factory. He glowered threateningly, a terrifying figure of bulbous middle age in his thin podgy vest and flappy running shorts. Like two tents tied together wrong.

'You supposed to be in our group, Lovejoy?'

'Yes, lads.' I beamed encouragingly. 'Good luck. Can't make it today, I'm afraid.'

One or two made cracks back at me, grinning. Bernard looked miserable as sin. I had to laugh. He was probably having to waste his day off doing this maniac stunt. His idea of fun's sitting on the railway bridge across the valley photographing signals and talking with the level-crossing gatekeeper.

'Are you ready?' Elspeth cried, horn-rims poised in her hand. 'Now remember. No *undue* exertion. Are we all agreed?' She got a few dejected mumbles.

'Only *due* exertion, Bern,' I reminded him cheerfully. Then I had a sudden thought and stepped across. They were lined up doing nervous practice flexings. 'Here, Bern. Know anybody who collects passenger passes?'

'For railways? Me. Got one?'

'Mount St Mary.' I didn't need to explain there's no such railway.

He shook his head doubtfully. 'None struck that I know of. It never opened, not after the disaster.' I didn't like the sound of that. I thought I knew Mount St Mary well. There just isn't a railway. 'Got it with you? I'd like to see it.'

Elspeth was glaring and tutting. They had to be off.

'I'll wait,' I told him. 'How long will you be?'

'They'll be back in thirty minutes,' said Elspeth, all keen still. She naturally would be. She didn't have to go.

'We'll be back next Thursday,' Bern grinned, and trotted off with the rest. Elspeth clicked a watch and made notes.

'Need England Tremble,' I quoted loudly after them, receiving a chorus of abuse.

The next hour I had Nurse Patmore all to myself. And vice versa. She ripped the dressings off my stitches and put new ones on. She tore the bandages off my head and covered me in yellow fluid. My two eyes had a bad time working out distances for some time.

I was bullied and thoroughly chastised. She went on and on about careless driving, though I tried telling her it wasn't my fault. She had me on one of those gruesome steel tables with tubes and tins everywhere.

125

Makes you think of Frankenstein. 'You're supposed to be full of sympathy,' I moaned.

'No I'm not, Lovejoy,' she slammed back, doing things with hideous instruments. 'I'm here to patch you up so you can go and do it again, stupid man.'

'I'll complain about your manner to Dr Lancaster,' I said sternly. 'That'll sort you out.'

'Do,' she said sweetly. 'Shall I dial for you? He'll be *so* interested to hear you've had a crash. Keep still.'

I glared at her. If only my eyes would agree on where she was. 'Er, not just yet.' Doc's berserk on accident prevention. And I'd messed up his physique panto-mime by making his first group one short.

'He'll see your clinical card this afternoon, Lovejoy,' she persisted triumphantly. Women love rubbing it in. 'He'll go mental. I'd keep out of his way if I were you.'

Until then I'd had visions of dropping in on him for a light chat about Doc Chase's hobby. I decided she was right.

On the other hand Nurse Patmore must have known almost as much as the old chap. It was worth the risk. 'How did Doc Chase die, Pat?' I tried a casual air.

'Nurse Patmore while on duty, if you please.' She clashed tins together. I always want to look what they're doing to me but I'm too scared. 'A stroke, poor man. He didn't linger.'

'Elspeth said he was interested in history.'

'Miss Haverill has no business disclosing Doctor's private affairs.'

I ducked these arrows. 'Didn't he write a book?'

'Yes.' She started reminiscing. 'He was a lovely old man. Very keen on exercise. Every single day off he'd cycle to Scratton, then back to Mount St Mary for an hour's fishing by the river. Always the same spot. We miss him.'

She prattled on a bit more, then let me go. I was bulky round my middle from dressings. Moll was out-side on a garden seat watching her heroes totter back

126

across the fields. They looked knackered. Elspeth was with her, jubilant.

'Aren't they perfectly *splendid*, Lovejoy?' she cried.

'Great,' I said as they straggled in. I've seen better retreats.

Bern was in no fit state to discuss Victorian passes and tokens. In fact I doubted if he'd last the day. They sprawled on the grass, huge bellies heaving with every gasp.

'I'll call round, Bern,' I called. 'I'm off.'

He managed to raise an arm but couldn't speak.

'Scratton, Moll.' I got in the car and reached for her maps in the glove compartment. 'Then Mount St Mary.'

She sat beside me a moment, then glanced back at Elspeth. 'What was all that, Lovejoy?' Her fingers were drumming on the steering wheel. 'I thought I'd already met Miss Haverill at your cottage. It was a different woman altogether.'

'Ah,' I said. I'd forgotten to think up a story. 'Ah, well, you see, it's like this. By a strange coincidence there are these two health visitors with identical names . . .'

By the time we were in Scratton village I could tell Moll hadn't believed a word. I was in the dog-house again. That's the trouble with women. They always think you're lying when you're actually trying hard to tell them only what's good for them, put things in the best light. It must be terrible to be like that, suspicious as hell all day long. I'm glad I'm not that way. Innocence makes you a better person.

Chapter Eleven

This tunnel.

Ever seriously thought what a crime a tunnel must be? It's not just a horizontal hole. To the mountain it must be a deadly insult, vicious as a knife thrust. And let's face it – the motive's greed. Gain. Money. You gang up and dig a hole for good old gelt, not for art or adventure or somewhere to live, not any more. Modern Man digs for shekels and nothing else. That's how far civilization's got. Cavemen knew better.

And even before Leckie blew those charges that day, doing my job, I'd felt this way. If you were a hill you wouldn't want anybody strolling about your insides. It's not natural. That's why I stared from the deep railway culvert from among the dog daisies, and didn't go in.

'Maybe there's a train coming,' I told Moll airily. 'Best to be careful.'

'It looks disused.' Moll pointed at the train lines. 'There are weeds everywhere.'

'It isn't.' I gave a light laugh, casual and off-hand. 'I, er, telephoned from the surgery. The railway people said it's still used.'

Moll glanced at me. 'Are you all right, Lovejoy?'

That's all stupid women ever say to me. 'Right as rain,' I snapped.

We were peering from the side of the cutting. I slid down to the granite chippings from bravado and stood on a sleeper. My heart was thumping. I felt my hands go cold and thrust them in my pockets. My shoulders went damp.

I knew the Scratton tunnel wasn't used these five years. It looked it, too, with elderberry and hawthorns already enroaching on the tunnel's mouth. I shuddered. Moll saw me and linked her arm through mine. It's an evil thought. No sooner does Man abandon anything than seeds blow along and settle in cracks and the greenery snakes in to strangle every sign that Man's enterprise ever existed. You could see a dark smudge against the tunnel's parapet. Steam trains had run through it for well over a century, each adding slightly to the grime, year after year. Now derelict.

'Do we walk through?' Moll asked. 'Isn't that what we came for?'

I shrugged, abandoning all pretence that an express was due any second among the undergrowth. 'No need, really.' But I was desperate to see if there was any sign of Chase's activities in there. 'Well, er, maybe.'

'Look, Lovejoy,' Moll said suddenly, far too brightly. 'I wonder if you'd do something? Could you drive the car round to the other side? First left, I think. I'll go through and have a quick search.'

'You've no torch,' I said feebly.

'I always carry a pencil light.' She rummaged in her handbag. 'For finding keyholes when it's dark.'

'That's not fair, though.' Feebler.

'I don't want you falling down in there.' Moll showed me her little torch was working. 'Nurse would come after me.'

'Well, if you insist . . .'

Sometimes I think I'm pathetic. I watched her trek along the lines and vanish down a tunnel. I climbed slowly to the top of the embankment. The car seemed friendly, safe. Funny how you get these anthropomorphisms.

I was waiting for her when she came out at the far side. She was slightly breathless and indignant.

'There are *creatures* in there, Lovejoy!'

'What kind?' My voice must have sounded strangled.

'Oh. Only scuttly ones, little things. Bats, I suppose. The squeaky sort.'

Her natural sciences were on a par with mine.

'No sign of any digging? No bricks loose?'

'I didn't see any. Nothing recent, anyhow.'

That was Scratton tunnel. A disused old railway structure with no signs of tampering. So why did Doc Chase come all this way so often to look at a tunnel, and do nothing?

Moll did her face with lipstick and all that. I drove the car the three miles or so to Mount St Mary. The motor seemed to stop outside the Three Tiles of its own accord. Even now I don't know if it was a mistake, but I told Moll about Leckie and the time he blew the bridge. She kept her gaze on me as I drove.

'Why didn't you say you were frightened?' she asked as we got out in the pub's coachyard. 'It's nothing to be ashamed of.'

That irked me. 'Who said I'm frightened?' I demanded. 'What's there to be scared of in a rotten old tunnel?'

'Sorry, Lovejoy.' She caught the keys I threw her.

'I'm just careful,' I said, in a huff. 'Careful's not frightened.'

'Sorry, dear.' We went into the pub, marching frostily side by side. 'I didn't actually mean frightened,' she said, 'I really meant careful.'

The usual midday rural mob was in, a score of workers tanking up for the afternoon's assault on the land. I ordered for us and started my patter instantly with an agile geriatric in hobnails.

'Bet it doesn't seem the same round here without old Doc Chase fishing, eh?' I said, grimacing ruefully. I jerked my head towards the road. The curve follows the bend of the river. Sane friends and spouses watch their loved ones from beside the bar's fire during fishing contests in winter.

'Who?' He looked blank. A couple of others pricked up their ears.

'Doc Chase. My old pal,' I lied easily. 'Always seemed to be fishing when I drove through.'

'He means the Champ,' an old geezer cackled. They fell about at that, even the barman laughing.

'We called him that, God rest him,' I was told.

'Was he that great?'

That was the signal for convulsive hilarity. The old gaffer practically had apoplexy and spilled his pint. Moll had to bang his back to get him breathing again. He wiped his eyes.

'Lord love ye, young feller,' he gasped. (They really talk like this. I'm not putting you on.) 'Never caught a fish all the time we seed him at it.'

'Aye,' another chipped in. 'Forgot the frigging worm, often as not.'

'Never remembered his maggots!'

They rolled on the aisles while I tried hard to grin.

'Forgetful old bugger,' the first old cock rasped. 'Knew no better than to sit among those nettles on the wrong side!' I had his glass topped up while we laughed at Doc Chase's hopelessly bad angling technique.

We chatted some more before leaving. I learned that Chase's favourite place was on the opposite bank. 'The same spot,' Nurse Patmore had told me. I gave Moll the eye. We drank up and were waved off.

Moll drove. A few hundred yards homeward I told her to stop. We were on the upward slope, where the road turns away from the river to run towards our distant town.

This river has three bends. The first lies between barley fields, and straightens before the Mount itself is reached. The third is further inland, beyond the actual village, and consists of a gentle curve with woods crowding densely along both banks. It was the second that interested me.

It is double. The river courses across the small plain

131

where the village houses cluster. There is the inevitable gaggle of thatched roofs, the flintstone church with its impressive spire, and the ornate Early English stone bridge. It all speaks of the wealth of the mediaeval wool trade and commerce channelled by the dour Christian zeal of those days. The Three Tiles pub is at the crossroads near the bridge, lying snugly on the outside bank of the curve. Doc Chase's favourite fishing spot was almost directly opposite the tavern. I could see birds flashing into the sandy patch.

'Sand martins.' Moll pointed. 'Maybe he liked to watch them.'

'Maybe,' I said. But you can see them better from the other bank. If you sit on the same side of the river as the sandy mounds you have your back to them all the time.

The Mount stands on the pub side of the river. It's tall, as East Anglian hills go, but nobody else would think so, except perhaps a Dutchman. From where we stood, though, it seemed spectacularly large, maybe because there are no other hills thereabouts. A house or two shows on the inland side of its lower slopes. On this side, however, there is only a dense low scrub of broom and grass with humps of small hillocky bushes here and there. People put the odd sheep out on it sometimes but that's about all.

A cloud darkened the sky as we stared at it. The sunshine was slowly caressed from the Mount's face in a gradual sweep. I couldn't help thinking what a bloody place to stare at for day after day, month after month, as Chase must have done from his vantage point across the river. Had he fished from the tavern bank he'd have had plenty to look at – the village, the road, the downstream flow of the river and the lovely old church. As it was, he'd only faced the empty hill.

'I hope they didn't pull his leg too much in the tavern,' Moll said, smiling. 'He must have been the world's worst fisherman.'

'So he must,' I said. It makes you think. Too bad, in fact. Even a hopeless angler will catch something sooner or later.

I got her to pull in as soon as we saw a phone box. I pretended my arm was stiff so she came pressing in with me and did the dialling. She was a bit mistrustful, but it was very pleasant.

'Hello, Pat darling!'

'Get off the line, Lovejoy,' Nurse Patmore snapped. 'Medical calls only.'

'About Dr Chase,' I said. 'Tell me how many fish he caught on his days off. On average.'

'Well, it was a bit of a joke with us, actually.' She sounded on the defensive. 'He wasn't very lucky.'

'You mean none,' I said.

'It's not a very good river.' She was smiling. Isn't loyalty wonderful? 'I think he had rather a soft spot for the fish. He used to say "Lucky again!" meaning they'd all got away.' She paused. 'Why are you asking all this, Lovejoy?'

'Thank you,' I told her. 'Keep taking the tablets.'

Moll and I drove back to the cottage. She told me my hands were quite cold when we got there and our fingers accidentally touched. I blamed her motor, said it was full of draughts.

Chapter Twelve

Moll left at about eight that evening, but I have to tell you about something that happened after she'd gone. It was unexpected. I'd not planned for anything so frank, which only shows how stupid I can be most of the time. The trouble is that when you start finding things out and events finally go your way you start assuming that you're driving the bus. In fact you might only be a passenger on the wretched thing.

Moll got ready to go. We were in one of our epidemics of politeness. She kept asking if I'd got her phone number in case I wanted anything and I kept checking it was written down right.

'You're all alone here,' she explained. 'You can't shout out for help if anything happens.'

'It's quite safe,' I assured her, like an idiot.

'Do lock your door, won't you?'

That nettled me. 'I'll be all right. I'm not scared.'

'I know,' she said swiftly. 'Of course you're not. But I'm worried your crash was deliberate.'

She thought Jake and Fergus sounded bad people just from their names. That's just typical of the sort of illogical allies I usually get. Efficiency's always on the side of the wrong people. I finally waved her off, dishing out profuse thanks for a day's help.

The story pieced neatly together. Neat, but disturbing. An old village quack, interested in local history most of his life, stumbles across a valuable rare find. It's near Mount St Mary. Aware that maybe others would not only become interested but could nick his precious Item before he could get his own clutching hands on it, he starts some evasive tactics. He zooms over to the Scratton tunnel to mislead followers. Then he goes to Mount St Mary where he sits working out where his Item is buried, or maybe just merely keeping an eye on it. Being a kindly old geezer, he hates the idea of hooking fish for nothing so he pretends to be the universe's most forgetful and useless angler, to everybody's merriment.

You couldn't help but admire him. He remained true to his collector's instincts and stuck to his act. It worked. He deceived everybody, including Black Fergus and his crew. Nodge had said that whatever was hidden in the auctioned items would explain where in Scratton the precious thing was hidden. Nodge had said Scratton, not Mount St Mary. So they must have followed him yet still been misled by Doc Chase's feint. The clever old sod. Nothing in the tunnel at all, thank God.

But I knew something they didn't. The little disc-shaped railway pass did not refer to the Scratton tunnel at all. Moll had examined it and found nothing. So the disc was a pass for a non-existent line to Mount St Mary. Doc Chase had hidden it to prevent his gem of worthless information falling into the wrong hands. Being wise he'd concealed it behind a Bramah lock in a cheap old piece of crummy furniture, knowing no true collector would miss that. Maybe he'd actually told Leckie about it. Either way, Leckie had success-fully bid for the stuff.

I took out the pass and examined it again. It looked the same, and I was no wiser. Yet there was something making me uneasy. You get these feelings.

For the next hour I pondered the problem, trying to look up auction catalogues and filing notes away. I stared at maps of the area. It was hopeless. I finished up having a glass of cider and doing nothing. I was on the wall in the garden, ruminating, about nine with dusk coming on. That was how they caught me.

135

I heard the car stop in the lane. A door slammed. I never thought it would be Fergus and Jake. I especially never thought they would have two tearaways with them. They came crunching up the gravel. Fergus was beaming.

'Convalescing, Lovejoy?'

'I'm better.' I hadn't the sense to run in and slam the door.

'You don't look it.' He puffed up and plonked himself down beside me. 'Nasty accident, I heard.'

'Nasty.'

'Nodge bought it,' he said sadly. His grin never left him. Jake and the goons stood silently by, listening. Their eyes were on me.

'Shame,' I said.

'You did it, didn't you, Lovejoy?'

I looked about, realizing I was caught. 'If you say so Fergie.'

'Save yourself, Lovejoy.' His persistent bloody cheerfulness was sickening. 'Give me Chase's thing.'

'Thing?' I decided to be dim.

'Wilkie told us how you went back for some wood. Give it us.'

I'd have to have a word with Wilkie. 'I don't know what you mean, Fergie.'

'Do him,' Jake said.

One of the goons kicked my leg, right against my shin. I yelped and stood up to hop. That brought the end goon between me and the one who kicked me. I cracked my cider glass on the wall and scagged his face open, all in a single sweep of an arm.

'*Jesus!*' The goon stepped back, dabbing his face and looking at his bloodstained hands in horror.

'Mind your new suit, Jake,' I told him. It was maroon, today's fashionable colour. I held the shattered glass lightly by the handle.

'Lads, lads,' Fergus reproved, sorrowfully shaking

his head. The bastard was still sitting down. 'This is no way to behave.'

'They the best you can do, Fergie?' I tried my best to sound scornful but I felt shaky. 'Where I come from they'd starve.'

Jake and the healthy goon were separating, watching me. They had knuckledusters on now. Even if I set off running I'd not get far.

Then, mercifully, Moll's car pulled in.

'Hello, Moll,' I yelled, drenched in a sudden sweat of relief.

'Get rid of her, Lovejoy.' Fergus gave his bleeding nerk the bent eye. He stepped back, hands and handkerchiefs to his face.

'No. She's a copper's wife.'

'Hello, Lovejoy.' Moll saw the blood and my broken mug. 'I came back to . . .' She glanced at Fergus, me, the two men. Jake was softly giving instructions to the undamaged goon.

'It's time for tea, love,' I said brightly.

'Go away, lady.' Fergus rose and nodded to Jake. 'Put a match to it, Jake.'

'Eh?' The goon had a petrol tin. The bastards were going to fire my cottage. He was moving towards my open doorway.

Jake gave an unlikely yelp of glee. 'We'll warm your beer, Lovejoy.'

I was stepping forward with my puny glass to do the best I could when Moll sorted it all out.

'Stop that!' Her voice cut through the dusk like a ray. We all stopped where we were, more surprised than anything. 'I shall phone the constable.'

'Leave off, lady.' Fergus chuckled. 'I've a dozen witnesses who'll say we're miles away.'

'Very well, then. If that's your attitude.' Moll rummaged in her handbag. Believe it or not she handed me a small purse and then a powder compact while she searched feverishly. I stood there holding them, feeling a right lemon. We all waited from curiosity, wondering what the hell she was going to bring out.

'Get on with it, Jake,' Fergus was just saying, when we learned what Moll had brought.

The goon with the petrol tin was starting forward as Moll finally gave a satisfied murmur. She pulled out a blued Smith and Webley. There was a sharp sound like silk tearing. One of my windows crashed and my eyes were momentarily blinded by the explosion. The nerk howled with fright and Fergus swore.

'There!' Moll said breathlessly. She was holding this howitzer out as if offering somebody dessert. 'There now. You must stop,' she instructed, 'or take the consequences. I won't have this kind of behaviour.'

'Christ.' Jake was stuck. The goon with the petrol put it down and nervously backed away from it. I knew how he felt.

'Now, lady,' Fergus said. He was less cocky now.

'Please stand still.' She was hardly the fastest draw in the West, but it's wise to do as you are told when being pointed at.

He was moving forward at her, beaming, when she hit him. The ripping sound and the flash set us diving for cover. Moll pulled the trigger three times, swinging wildly. I was screaming for her to stop. I heard this crack and a dull thud but didn't think at the time. Moll stilled. Jake and the injured goon were lying down. The healthy nerk had scarpered, leaving his petrol tin. I could hear him crashing gears trying to reverse the car in the lane. Fergus was on the ground. It looked like his leg. He was shouting for Moll to stop.

'Give it here, love.' I took the pistol.

'It's Tom's,' she explained.

Even police aren't allowed to keep guns at home. I knew that. I decided to report Tom Maslow when all this was over. He's no right evading the law.

'Off you go, Fergie,' I said cheerfully.

'She fucking well shot me.' He moaned and rolled over to get up. He really was bleeding badly.

'Sue her.'

'I'm so sorry,' Moll told me penitently. 'I only meant to make them nervous.'

'You did that all right. You frightened us all to death.' I waggled the weapon uneasily at the three. I'm as useless with these murderous things as Moll. Now, if it had been a lovely Mortimer dueller of Regency days, or a delectable flintlock holster pistol by Sandwell or James Freeman of London, with that luscious browning and perfect balance . . .

We stood there while Jake Pelman and his uninjured tearaway carried Fergus to their car.

'Take your petrol, lads,' I called.

Jake came back for it, keeping his eyes on us. For some reason he seemed angry with me.

'There'll be another time, Lovejoy,' he said.

'Wait a minute, Jake.' I went over and booted him on the shins, right and left. He yelled and hobbled about. 'Off home, now.' I grinned and saw him safely down the path.

'You wait, Lovejoy.' Fergus was sprawled across the back seat. The others were crammed in the front, one goon holding his face together still. 'One day your tame tart won't be here to hide behind, lad.'

I stuck my head in the open window and we looked eye to eye for a minute.

'What's the antique, Fergie?' I asked him straight out.

'Dunno. And neither do you, Lovejoy.'

'True.'

He gritted his teeth because I tapped his shot leg hard with the pistol barrel. 'The minute you step outside your gate, Lovejoy, we'll be here.' He managed a beam, a rudiment of his usual expression. 'And we'll take Chase's clue off you like toffee off a brat.'

'I'd make it easy for you, Fergus,' I said. 'But I can't forget you killed Leckie.'

The thought made me clout his leg in earnest. He screamed so loudly I reflexly started back. The combination of that scream and this terrible persistent grin was horrifying. I stood there while the motor rode up the slope. Moll came and stood beside me. We listened to the sound. A pause at the chapel, a rev-up on to the main road. Turn right, then descend a few notes as they set off out of the village into town.

The sound faded. I looked about. It was quite dusky now. I saw that Moll had happened to park her car inside the garden half-way up the gravel path, almost as if somebody intended to stay. We walked slowly to the cottage.

'Did I do right?'

'More than that, love.'

'Are you pleased I came back?'

'Delighted.'

We paused in the doorway.

'I just wondered about your being safe,' she explained.

'Good judgement,' I said. 'That's what it was.'

'I'd leave you Tom's pistol,' she said carefully. 'Except it's his licence, you see. So I can't let it out of my possession.'

'I, see,' I said.

'But I suppose . . .'

'Yes?'

'Have you a spare room? If I were to stay, just overnight perhaps, until you get on your feet properly again . . .'

'Then we could keep the gun here,' I concluded brightly.

'Well, yes. It would be . . . legal, then, wouldn't it?'

'Why, so it would.' I switched the hall light on.

'I'll just get my things from the car. I usually have a

suitcase with me.' She hesitated. 'Are you sure this will be all right?'

'Certain,' I assured her gravely. 'Anyhow, my granny always said to share.'

Chapter Thirteen

Next morning Moll answered the phone twice before I could get to it. Both times the other end rang off before speaking.

'Can't think what's got into people,' Moll announced sweetly.

'Er, I'd better answer.' I was thinking of Val, Helen, or Elspeth Haverill with some fresh Olympic programme and, last but by no means least, good old Sue.

Apart from this tiff we adjusted fairly well. I reclined grandly on my unfolding divan because of 'my condition', as Moll called it, like I was seven months gone. Naturally we went through a stage of typically English hesitancy, worrying sick about using our knives and forks properly, no elbows on the table and being desperately silent on the loo. In spite of it all we finished up quite well attuned. I was narked at her flashing to the phone first, but what can you do?

I sent her to the Corporal's on East Hill about nine.

'I have to pay for services rendered,' I explained. 'To you.'

'There's no need – '

'Do as you're told. Got some money?'

'Some. I have my cheque-book. Will that do?'

'Almost certainly,' I answered, straight-faced, thinking, the poor innocent.

'What are we going to buy?'

'You,' I corrected. '*You* are going to buy for yourself a small collection of treen.'

'What's treen? Is it a kind of antique?' She got all interested. 'I do hope so. I'm fascinated.'

I pushed her into a chair. 'Sit and listen.'

'I once bought a teapot with a decorated spout. They said it was ever so valuable.'

I put my fingers in my ears to keep out this rubbish. People will keep on talking gibberish. She shut up, and I started to explain. There are fashions in antiques. If you want a tip about profit it's this: try to *anticipate* the next fashions, and you'll be well away. I'll give you some guidance. Firstly, unless you are loaded, go for fairly recent first editions. They aren't real antiques, but dealers pretend they are for sordid gain. Secondly I'd go for Victorian jewellery of the semi-precious kind – sombre jet brooches, garnets and so on. Thirdly I'd go for 'fringe' household items that are seriously underpriced: pewter, polescreens, soapstone ornaments, decorative glass table bells, that sort of thing. And treen. Treen is dealers' slang for any wooden kitchenware. You can still, believe it or not, find even the rarest genuine Tudor treen for a few quid. Any old town has a stock of it. I defy any collector with half an eye for antiques to fail to find it, and cheap. You buy it in junk shops, or even these travelling antique fairs which abound everywhere at weekends these days.

The commonest treen is the old family bread-board, with or without knife slots and decoration to match. That and little peppermills, salt-boxes (made for hanging by the fireside to keep the deliquescent impure salt mixtures dried out), platters, decorative butter moulds and carved cheese paddles, wooden cups, scissor-shaped glove-stretchers, anything from lovely sycamore cooking mortars to ingenious wooden washing tallies for checking that the serfs were hard at it. If you don't believe me, try it. I did a favour once for Taffy, a local dealer I owed for a lovely illuminated parchment manuscript Book of Devotional Hours. He was getting after me for the price and I hadn't managed to bring myself to sell it. He was broke and had a buyer. I staved him off by borrowing a hundred quid and taking him round about twenty antique shops in two days. It knackered us both, but he finished up believing me. We bought a luscious little Welsh oak herb chest, an Elizabethan spice grinder, three seventeenth-century lemon squeezers, a basting stick inscribed 1647, ginger-bread boards galore, and six square platters with handles and salt 'sinkings' (smoothly hollowed recesses). We got a lot more for the same money, but I'll lose the thread if I go on. Taffy sold the lot as a 'collection' of historic treen at an auction by the following week. He made plenty and shut up whining for his gelt. It's still that easy.

'Get it?' I concluded.

Moll was wide-eyed. 'But what if I buy the wrong things?'

I described the layout of Corporal's crummy dump on East Hill. He isn't bad as antique dealers go. Rough-mannered and a bit greedy, but quite fair on those rare occasions when he's not sloshed on pale ale. He believes he is a major world authority on Norwich School and Dutch oil paintings, though Christie's are rumoured not to have lost any sleep over this claim. Corporal's thick as a plank.

'Can't I just ask Mr Corporal for them?' Moll was saying.

I closed my eyes. Women like Moll give me a head-ache. 'It isn't done that way, love.'

'Why not?'

'He'll know what you've come for. And he'll increase his price. See?'

She was instantly indignant. 'How very unfair!'

'True, true,' I said with deep feeling. 'But look for the money code. That'll tell you if he's hiked the mark-up.'

Women are good listeners when you mention money, and Moll for once listened intently. We have no 'fixed' prices in the world of antiques. Whether we're dealing for the fabulous Eureka Gem or a mundane Edwardian inkwell *there is no fixed price* except the one the dealer himself puts on. Always remember that. So every dealer above the junk-shop level invents his own code, or uses somebody else's. Even famous firms do it. You simply take any word or words totalling ten (or possibly nine) letters, and they become the numbers from 1 to 9 plus 0.

'Am I allowed to look at each sticker?' Moll asked.

'Look?' I tapped the air vehemently. 'You must crawl all over the bloody things.'

'But the code – '

'Every dealer's code's easy to break, simply because no letter can ever recur. Get it? By asking the price of about three items you can deduce the code in practically every shop you come to.' She looked blank so I made it easy. 'Corporal uses *Come and Buy*,' I told her. 'Copied from a famous firm in St James's.' I didn't tell her which one, because I'm sure Spink's of London would prefer to remain anonymous. Continental dealers have their own codes but most of the ones I know use *Goldschmit*, like Münzen & Medaillen secretly used to in Basel.

'How many do I have to buy?'

'As many as you can without an overdraft.'

'Really?' I could tell she was becoming excited at the thought of a spending spree.

She was gone in a few more minutes. I gave her a wave and streaked to the phone. There was no chance of raising Tinker this early, so I rang Margaret. She was just opening her place in the Arcade. I made her promise to catch Tinker as he reeled past towards breakfast at opening time, and get him to phone in for instructions. In case she missed him among the shoppers I rang Woody's and told Erica the same thing. She was all set for telling me off but I put the receiver down because women always get necessity in the wrong order. Finally I rang Bern's and told his missus I'd be calling round in his dinner hour. Rosie said one o'clock, but earlier if I wanted veal and two veg.

Moll returned so late I was sure we would miss Bern. I was in something of a temper, worried what nasty facts about my railway pass Bern was going to cough up. I told her off, but she was too flushed and excited to notice.

'Don't be angry, Lovejoy!' she cried, rushing in while I said where the hell have you been. 'I've had a lovely time. Done exactly as you said!'

'Hurry up.'

'One second.'

I waited, fuming, in the car while she hurtled crashing about the cottage. Bathroom going, her case under the divan, a door slamming, and out she zoomed. I had to drive because she was breathlessly eating bread and honey. She forgot to set the burglar alarm – all antique dealers have burglar alarms – and had to dash back while I turned the car round.

'Where is it?'

'The treen? Coming this afternoon,' she applauded herself with delight. 'You'll be thrilled!'

That seemed odd, but I said nothing. I didn't see why she couldn't have fetched it. The phone started up as I got in gear, but then it always does. I ignored it.

'Did Tinker catch you?' He'd eventually phoned in, sounding bleary. I'd sent him to find Moll and stay with her in case Corporal got delusions of grandeur at the sight of a genuine customer.

'Yes, Lovejoy. He's a perfect dear, isn't he?'

'Er, yes . . . ' Nobody's called Tinker that before. 'Putting up with so much from his assistants, and being paid so little.' She slipped her arm through mine, but only friendly. 'I do wish he had an easier life, poor soul. Having to go off and do the shopping for his old Mum. Aren't some people marvellous?' She prattled on about how Tinker, that noble pillar of virtue, also cared for an old and feeble comrade-in-arms named Lemuel, whose terrible leg condition had caused the Minister of Health mercilessly to write him off, leaving him unprotected in a changing world. 'Poor Lemuel,' she said, practically tearful. 'He waited so patiently while Tinker advised me. Such a bad limp.'

A terrible suspicion was forming. 'You didn't give him any money, Moll?'

'Of *course*. He hadn't a penny. I gave him the money for his dinner, and a taxi to see his sister's child in Lexton. The poor mite's ill with a terrible disease they can't – '

I sighed wearily. One day I really will cripple Lemuel. 'Love,' I told her. 'Lemuel's fit as a flea. And his sister's lad is our local champion swimmer. Lemuel's a dirty old devil who gambles and boozes every farthing he can cadge. He does odd jobs for Tinker, who's as bad.'

'How dare you, Lovejoy!' She pulled her arm away. 'Typical, just typical!'

I drove doggedly on. 'And Tinker's old Mum's an evil old cow worse than he is. They're the worst scroungers in the whole of East Anglia, love.'

'You're horrid, Lovejoy. They're two lovely old men who need *care*.' I gave up arguing. She raved at me then, as I drove out on the Wormham road north out of our village. She kept it up for bloody miles, going on about cynicism and selfishness. I even learned a new word, gravamen. She said the gravamen of our differences were so enormous as to make us irreconcilable. I didn't like the sound of gravamen, whatever it was.

I just shut up and held the wheel. Anyway, I had plenty to think of. While Moll was out I'd gone over the Ordnance Survey map of the Mount St Mary and Scratton areas, inch by painstaking inch. In fact, that's partly why I'd got her out of the way. There was no tunnel, not even a viaduct, in or on or even near the Mount St Mary hillside. And the river bridges are so narrow, being medieval, that even I wasn't scared of them.

But all morning I'd fretted uneasily. Maybe that's why I had shelved the idea of seeing Bern or some other local historian for so long, subconsciously knowing there was something unpleasant and even frightening at the end of it. And, as it turned out, there was.

We came to Wormham's erratic main street. Moll was still going on. 'How could you be so – '

'Shut it, Moll.'

' – positively callous and unfeeling – '

'*Shut it.*' She took a sidelong look at my face and shut up. I pulled into this small estate of uniform semi-detached houses and stopped us opposite the eighth house. A garden sign read '*The Junction*'. Good old Bern. 'We're here,' I told her.

My palms were damp. If Bern told me there really was a frigging tunnel under that frigging hill then I for one wasn't going down into its horrible deep slimy cobwebby blackness for all the tea in China. And, I thought with feeling, there's a hell of a lot of tea in China.

'Lovejoy,' Moll said as I started to get out. 'I think you should rest for a few days – '

I reached back in and got a handful of her blouse at the neck. 'One more word from you,' I said. 'Just one more word.'

'Yes, Lovejoy,' she said after a pause.

Bern was at the door, smiling. 'Thought you were never coming, Lovejoy. We've finished nosh.'

'Sorry, Bern.' I walked up the little garden path, Moll trailing. 'I have help these days. Always makes me late.'

I heard Moll snort and draw breath to make some retort, then wisely say nothing.

Train enthusiasts go in gaggles, like geese. If you

find one wandering lone he's lost. There's another characteristic: no matter how amateur they are, they are very, very expert. It's true of the entire breed. I know one chap who can tell you the whole yearly timetable of the Maltese railways, and there hasn't been a railway there for decades. See what I mean? So I wasn't surprised to find Bern had another historian with him.

'I got Gordon along,' Bern told me as the young blond lad rose and said hello. 'He's our local branch-line expert.' That's another thing. You learn to expect all ages of expert. This lad was about fifteen, thin and tall as a house, as they all seem to be these days. I think it's school dinners.

'How do.' I explained Moll to them both, and we settled round the table. Rosie cleared the meal away with the practised alacrity of a wife escaping from a hobby.

Gordon and Bern began fetching maps and books. I watched uneasily. It seemed a big pile of fact for what I was hoping would be a legend. I contributed my disc, to Bert's excitement.

They did their mysterious bit with magnifying glasses and catalogues. Rosie hurried a table-lamp in, pretending to share in the thrills. I waited for the verdict.

'I never believed they'd struck one,' Bern concluded, marvelling.

'Me, neither,' from Gordon.

'Who's they?' I asked nervously.

'The railway company.'

'*Which* railway company?' I persisted. I wanted negatives, not vague replies that suggested there were horrible positives just around the corner.

Bern deferred to Gordon with a nod. 'This railway company tried to build a branch line through here,' the lad said earnestly. 'From town, on up the valley. One arm out through Scratton going inland. The other through Wormham to Mount St Mary.'

'They wanted to run it coastwards,' Bern put in, still goggling at the disc with a glass at his eye.

I said, 'But the old railway station here in Wormham's – '

' – the end of the line,' Gordon finished for me, reaching to show me its course on a 1930 Ordnance Survey map. 'Of course it was.'

'So it never actually ran to Mount St Mary?' There was no dotted line going north from Wormham station, thank God.

'No.'

I sighed with relief and rose smiling but trying to look disappointed. 'Well, that's that,' I said cheerfully.

'Is that all you want to know, Lovejoy?' The lad was obviously downcast.

'I've taken an extra hour off,' Bern complained.

'Good of you, Bern,' I countered happily. 'But another time. Come on, love.'

Gordon was puzzled, as well as sad he was going to lose his audience. As I started for the door he turned to Bern and said accusingly, 'You told me he'd want to know all about the Mount's railway disaster.'

I stopped. Moll bumped into me. 'Disaster?' My voice seemed miles away. Bern had mentioned a disaster when we'd met at Elspeth's medical centre.

'Why, yes. At Mount St Mary.'

I felt my hands chill with sudden cold. Surely you can't have a railway disaster without a railway, can you? 'You said it never reached there.'

'It didn't.' He held up a book which seemed familiar. '*Because* of the disaster.' It was a copy of Chase's book with the town library's gilded stamp on its spine.

I cleared my throat. 'Er, what happened?'

'The tunnel,' he said.

'Tunnel,' I repeated faintly. 'In Mount St Mary?'

Bern chuckled, the lunatic. 'Well it couldn't be on *top*, could it?'

I didn't smile. My eyes were riveted on Gordon.

150

'It was awful,' Gordon said. 'The tunnel caved in.'

Tunnel, I thought, keeping tight control. The deep dark tunnel. It caved in. Dark and deep and it caved in.

I felt Moll's hand clamp hard on my arm. She propelled me to a chair. Gordon's enthusiastic voice and Bern's cosy little front room receded into a mist as all cares vanished.

'There now.' Rosie was bullying us all, but mostly me. 'That's what comes of going back to work too soon after an accident.'

'He insisted.' Moll was defending herself, not me.

'You don't need to tell me, my dear.' Rosie had the table cleared of Bern and Gordon's clobber, which showed how narked she was. 'Men are born stupid and stay so.'

She had a bowl of water and some towels.

Bern's concerned face came close. 'Are you all right, Lovejoy?' I wish people would stop saying that.

'You almost keeled right over.' Gordon sounded quite pleased.

Moll was holding me, her hands cool on my forehead. 'I'd better get him home.'

Rosie wasn't going to be thwarted. 'Drink this herb tea, Lovejoy.'

I drank a ghoulish mess of unspeakable green liquid. It stripped my mucosa down to my boots. I thought I'd finished with all this when my granny went.

'He needs some thick gruel,' Rosie pronounced.

'Jesus, Rosie!' from me in a whine.

'Don't argue, Lovejoy. He does.'

I hate the way women talk all around you, as if you either aren't there or are imbecilic.

'And,' Rosie battled on, glaring at Bern and Gordon, 'if you ask me, he needs less of your ridiculous stories about people being buried alive and screaming for help – '

'You're perfectly correct,' Moll cut in swiftly, yanking me to my feet. She practically hauled me to the door.

Gordon and Bern, both now properly in Rosie's bad books for reasons beyond me, followed us meekly to the car. Gordon reached in and put a brown folder on the back seat.

'That's my stuff on it,' he said, worried. 'You can give it to Bern when you've done.'

'Thanks, Gordon. Sorry about that, folks.'

'Get better soon, Lovejoy,' Bern said, giving a thumbs-up. 'Pop over when you want – '

'Not for at least a week, Bern,' Moll said firmly. 'He's to rest.'

'But look, Moll . . . ' I started. She gunned the engine.

'People who are too stubborn,' Rosie said with satisfaction, 'have to be *told*.' She was still rabbiting on at them when we drove off. And one look at Moll's face told me I was in trouble with her as well. That's women. Just when they should be sympathetic they get mad as hell.

I decided to break the ice with some merry chatter. 'Sorry, Moll,' I said brightly. 'I – '

'Shut it.' She snapped it out just like me, so I did.

It was probably just as well we didn't speak on the way home. I never know what women mean half the bloody time anyhow.

In my garden a vannie called Doug was sitting on the grass. Tinker was there. They were part-way through a crate of brown ale, bottles everywhere. Two other vannies were smoking and swilling. A right party. They'd parked two vans on my gravel.

'What's going on?' I was all ready for a dust-up.

'Wotcher, Lovejoy.' Tinker gave me a wave.

'It's my treens,' Moll exclaimed, pleased.

'Treen,' I corrected mechanically. 'Collective noun.'

'You'll be so thrilled, darling.'

I hesitated at that 'darling', but as long as our tiff was forgotten I'd bear it.

'It's all here, Moll.' Tinker handed me a brown ale. He took Doug's bottle off him, wiped it on his filthy sleeve and gave it to Moll. His idea of gallantry.

'Oh,' she said faintly, taking it like something ticking. 'How kind.'

'Cheers.'

We all said cheers and drank, some more enthusiastically than others. My eyes were on the two covered vans.

'Right, lads.' I questioned Tinker with a nod. 'What's the game?'

He looked at me, puzzled. 'Should I have taken it to Val's?'

'I told you, Lovejoy,' Moll said. 'My treen.'

I stepped across and flicked the canvas aside. It was crammed with antiques from floor to ceiling. I'd never seen so many antiques on the road all at once. I thought, Moll hasn't bought two lorryloads in one morning, that's for sure. She came beside me, smiling eagerly and pointing.

'That was from Corporal. And that from Big Frank. And Jenny Bateman on North Hill sold us that table – '

'Wait,' I told her. I went to the other van. It was packed, too.

It was definitely one of those days. I took her to one side while the blokes loafed and swilled on the grass.

'You *bought* all this, Moll?'

'Yes.' She searched my face. 'You said.'

'*All* of it?'

'You told me, Lovejoy. Until I ran out of cheques.'

I closed my eyes and leant on the van's nearside.

'You know how much this lot'll cost?'

'Oh yes.' She rummaged in her handbag and brought out the stubby remains of a cheque-book. I nearly fainted again. 'I've kept a list.'

'You'll be paying till you're ninety, love.'

She laughed at that. 'Oh, Lovejoy. Don't worry. I'm really quite wealthy. Now. What are we going to do with it?'

An ache was splitting my forehead. 'It's yours, Moll.'

I explained I'd wanted her to make a profit. 'The expenses money you gave me, well, I spent on a porcelain. The accident smashed it. So I really owed it you back.'

She stared at me, her eyes filling.

'Oh, Lovejoy. How absolutely sweet. I thought it was for your ordinary business.'

As if my ordinary business came in lorryloads, I thought sardonically. There was nothing for it. Taking it all to Val's cran would set tongues – and worse – wagging. So it had to be here. I unlocked the door and waved to Tinker. He came up, sensing some uncertainty.

'It's all right, isn't it, Lovejoy?'

'Sure, Tinker.'

He shrugged. 'She said you'd given her two hours to buy all the wooden antiques in town. Here.' He plucked at my sleeve and whispered. 'Where the hell did we get the gelt?'

'That's taken care of,' I said.

'Thank gawd for that.' He took my bottle absently and emptied it down his throat. 'Did we get everything on your list?'

'Oh.' I made my reply in a studied voice. 'I think so. I'll have to check.'

'Great.' He whistled to the vannies. 'Shell it inside, lads.'

The vannies rose and did their stuff, all three eyeing Moll with unconcealed lust as they carried the things in. Tinker supervised, sitting contentedly on the beer crate. I got hold of Moll.

'What list?' I demanded softly.

She giggled. I'd never seen anybody so pleased with

154

herself. 'I got confused about the codes and forgot the passwords. I pretended I was your partner. So they would bring the prices down.'

I wouldn't let go. '*What* list?'

'I had an old shopping list. I made them think you'd given me a list. We went into twelve shops. I knew they might cheat me, but all the dealers seemed very careful when I mentioned you.'

I'd never heard of anything like this in my life. And a bloody novice at that.

'Why the furniture? Treen's small kitchen stuff.'

She said brightly, 'But it's *wood*, Lovejoy. You said wood.'

And then I forgave her everything. Because a vannie carried past into the cottage a brilliant scintillating pre-Empire carver chair of genuine Sheraton design. I gasped. It was from Jason's place in the Arcade.

'That was very expensive,' Moll chatted happily. 'The stupid man took *such* a long time making up his mind to sell. I really had to act quite cross . . .'

The vannies unloaded piece after piece. She must have gone through town like a vacuum cleaner. There were walking sticks, minute stamp boxes, carved Bible rests, tobacco jars, pipes and racks galore, letter cases, drinking-glass cups, Pembroke tables, Sven's crummy fake stool, Chinese screens and lacquered trays, a serpentine silver-table with a pierced gallery (a sort of raised rim) unbelievably intact and at least eighteenth-century mahogany, wall plaques, polescreens, a sixteenth-century egg-tempera religious painting on a wood panel, a Canterbury . . . They were finished in an hour. Moll asked me how much to give them. Tinker told her that traditionally it's two pints each. She said how much is that, please? We waved them off a few minutes later.

'Let's go and look at it all, darling.'

Oho, I thought. Darling's back. She was delighted.

I went inside gingerly. There was hardly room left to swing a cat. We'd be lucky to find the sink.

'Wasn't it fortunate, Tinker knowing the price of two pints?' she said.

'A real fluke,' I agreed gravely.

We'd hardly started making a genuine list when Maslow's bulk filled the doorway. You can imagine how I felt.

I won't go into details about his suspicions, or what he said. His reason for calling was to ask where I'd suddenly got enough money to drain our town of antiques, and so quickly after Nodge died at my hands. Just shows what a nasty-minded bloke he is.

Worse, he was not pleased finding Moll in my cottage. I guessed that his sinister little eyes would be sure to spot indications of her residence. He took Moll outside. I didn't interfere. They talked in the garden for nearly an hour while I got on with the job.

Eventually I heard his car go. Moll came in and paused on the threshold. I waited, not looking up but pretending to be examining a dumb-waiter. (Tip: these started about 1750 and genuine early ones *must* have three trays. If the bottom one is fretworked it will be invariably three-ply wood.) I spun it out, waiting for her to say she was going home and start packing. Then I heard her fill a kettle in the kitchen alcove. I relaxed and carried on.

'We'd better have a meal, Lovejoy,' she said in a quiet voice. 'I rather think it's been one of those days.'

Chapter Fourteen

We went to sleep that night thinking different things but in the same sort of way. I'd said yet again I wanted no bother with Tom. Moll pointed out there's strength in numbers. I said, fine, but would the Maslow brood see our relationship in those practical terms? Moll asked innocently what kind of relationship did I have in mind exactly, which made us both go quiet. Women are always one one move ahead.

She told me the next morning I'd talked a lot in my sleep. Twice I'd seemed to be having nightmares. I answered lightly it was probably something I ate. She said sharply it was nothing of the kind.

The whole valley of the Bures river was layered in mist. It was still early, before seven. A watery sun managed to throw straight slivers of shadows through the erect elms and beeches of the northern end. Some cowbells tinkled nearby. Now and again a splash came from the river. The birds seemed late today, for some reason. Probably all gathered at my cottage shrieking their silly heads off for their cheese. Well, they could wait. Moll and I had driven as far as the village church and doubled back on the unpopulated bank. The mist filled the river hollow between its rims of trees so we could only vaguely see the roofs opposite, not the houses themselves. One car started up. Otherwise the only noise was Moll and me walking the bankside in the long grass.

We headed downstream. The river has low patches of reeds and some overhangs of trees and bushes. Here and there anglers had spread reeds to fish from. A big swan rose once nearby, frightening us as it held its wings and hissed. Moll said it had a nest on some low muddy recess next to the river. I used to think swans were placid.

I spotted the tavern first. We got ourselves orientated, lining up opposite the chimneys which poked from the mist and working out where the patch of nettles and that small sand hill would be. We found Chase's fishing spot with no trouble.

Moll had fetched a flask and some nosh. I sat dangling my bare feet in the water reading Gordon's file. Moll said we should keep an eye out for the shape of the hill as it became visible when the mist cleared. 'First impressions are always best,' she instructed.

I drew breath to say, oho, are they, but didn't. Gordon's file held some diagrams of a tunnel, section by section. They were labelled 'Scratton/Mount St Mary.' His own notes on lined paper in a round schoolboyish hand filled about eight pages. Then there was this newspaper cutting.

In 1847 the railway boom was on. Steam power had come to propel the Industrial Revolution as vigorously as watermill power had brought the world hurtling out of the Dark Ages a millennium previously. And even dozy East Anglia was caught up in the great drive to communicate and join in the motion. Any centre of population or industry had to have a railway. Profits at first promised to be enormous. The only thing needed was a pair of iron rails and a few wooden sleepers. And men.

The newspaper cutting was of the grand opening ceremony of the Mount St Mary tunnel. They had dug it out before the railway progressed this far. Even the Romans did this, having construction units begin viaducts or aqueducts in bits along their length rather than simply having the road or canal extend from its

158

growing tip as a twig does. The tunnel was completed ahead of time. A ceremony was planned at which two engineers would crank a small decorated bogie northwards. On it, seated in elegant style, would be one of our esteemed local councillors in his regalia. Jonathan Chase, no less. As the town's mayor-elect he would wear the ancient seal and important chain of office and be the first official traveller through the tunnel. To symbolize the occasion, some artistic enthusiast hit on the idea of levelling contributions from the railway companies and having this dignitary carry an appropriate gift to the small hamlet of Mount St Mary. So this is what they did, on a terrible rainy day. I read on while Moll sketched the river bank.

A band played. Crowds attended for the festive occasion. Morris dancers danced. Schools were unleashed. Speeches were made about the prosperity to come, about joining the great onward concourse of Mankind and suchlike jazz. Then the decorated carriage rolled up, pumped by two workmen, and Chase's ancestor stepped up to claim his mobile throne to enormous acclaim and the waving of streamers. The band played 'See the Conquering Hero Comes', and (I hated this bit) the little iron carriage trundled into the long tunnel.

It had rained for days. The river was higher than it had ever been in recorded memory. Farmers were grumbling about harvests. The brave tunnellers had had to cope with landslips, soaks, springing waters. Several times extra shoring was needed. The local clays were given to unpredictable shifts when the water-table rose, and four men died in the bricking alone. One had died of drowning when the tunnel was about halfway and was being driven through the course of an old lined well. It had been easily blocked and covered in, of course, but it served as yet another bad omen. The newspaper report said labourers had spoken for weeks about the running slurries which had necessitated sleepers being relaid several times during the finishing phase. Another ominous hint of coming tragedy was a monstrous crack which had appeared the Saturday before the ceremony.

Anybody but the Victorians would have chucked it in. But this much-maligned race was made of sterner stuff. Dangers existed to be faced down. Tragedy was there simply to be endured. Whether from a horde of charging fiends or a mountain cracking over you, the Victorian's task was merely to do one's duty, preferably with a casual smile playing around one's lips and a touch to the hat in farewell. You'll have guessed it's not my scene.

The year before, 1846, was the Great Railway Panic when 272 Acts zipped through Parliament and the iron horses really hit the road. Everybody on earth seemed to be inventing patented gadgets to do with railways, from Footwarmers For Ladies in Railway Coaches While Travelling to winches for raising counterweighted engines up inclines. A company whose tunnel opened late or – worse – not at all was utterly doomed in the scramble. And those stoic Victorians knew Duty when they saw it. Example had to be given to the lower social orders. Courage was the main necessity of life. Inevitably the omens were written off. Mankind was omnipotent, after all. There was no question of postponement, in some namby-pamby manner. God so clearly was an Englishman, especially if you sorted other upstart contenders out first.

So the iron carriage rumbled fatefully into the hill. The tunnel walls dripped. The echoes beat and reverberated. The two workmen's steady breathing was the only other sound. Behind, the band's playing faded. The cheering was cut off. Up ahead the hoop of daylight showed where the assembled crowds were waiting. Chase probably kept his gaze on the distant light. Maybe he mouthed the words of his forthcoming speech.

People afterwards estimated the carriage was at about the midpoint of the tunnel when the hill slipped. Just slipped. Maybe it was the weight of hillside waters held from drainage by the clay subsoil. Maybe some fault in building. Or maybe the bands and the crowds set up a growing flux of sound waves which established a tremor in the tunnel. But the hill slid sideways, slowly and with a fearsome whooing sound which quietened the spectators and the music.

The people ran, clutching children and heading away from the sight of trees and mounds of earth slithering down towards the river below. A small group was trapped and almost asphyxiated. Bandsmen dug with bare hands and clawed them free of the muddy deluge. Not a life was lost; except that deep in the earth three men were entombed.

Teams of workmen attacked the hill within minutes. Strings of paniered horses were fetched. The men worked with that berserk fury rescuers always find, spurred on by feeble tapping signals from deep inside the Mount. The trouble seemed to be that nobody knew precisely which way the mountain had slipped. The tapping sounds emerged at a vent-hole, a cylindrical aperture tunnellers drive upwards to give themselves air while digging deeper into a hillside. Mercifully the vent-holes had not been covered in before the ceremony, but the landslip had either deformed them or severed them across. Rescuers hacking their way in along these vent-holes were obstructed by solid walls of dark clay. They had no means of guessing how long the new geological fault was.

A day passed. Then the now indescribable figure of the Right Honourable Jonathan Chase was seen clambering up the hillside towards the clusters of rescuers. He was identified as the dignitary only after being washed, and he was demented. Half out of his mind, he babbled how it was his duty to try to climb the nearest vent-hole and lead the rescuers in. He remembered starting struggling up some vent-hole but got lost. Everywhere there seemed solid clay and seas of mud. Twice he found himself drowning when the mud level rose sharply. He could remember nothing further until suddenly he was rolling downhill in the open air and two waiting children had screamed at the macabre sight.

Teams tried to backtrack for three days, led by the desperate Chase. They opened up all seven vent-holes and started tunnelling through the clay obstructing each one, though no clear place was detected where Chase could have escaped from. The conclusion was that the land had made several further surreptitious slips in the meantime. There was no clue to the route he took and he, poor man, was too overwrought to remember.

'Coffee?'

I jumped a mile at Moll's words. My feet were wrinkled from being immersed in the river too long. The Mount was just coming through the mist above us.

'Thanks.'

'Interesting?'

'You can read it after.'

The tunnel simply was no more. Eventually, after the inquest, the terrain around Mount St Mary was regarded as unsuitable for tunnelling. A different coastwards route would be sought at a later date, and that was that. The tunnel mouths were covered in, and traces of the disaster vanished with age.

Sipping Moll's hot coffee, I went back to the beginning. Chase had been presented with a cased gift from the Mount St Mary officials. The cutting stated that it was a 'munificent mechanical device' manufactured with 'consummate artistry' by George Adams and Francis Higgins. The company had contributed a sum equal to one full day's wage for every labouring man employed on the tunnel. The object, the reporter said, was a mechanical contrivance 'moving in all its parts and being of precious metal much admired'. As a 'humorous counterpoint', he narrated, certain workmen had donated with much improvised ceremonial a railway passenger's 'permissive token or pass' to Jonathan Chase. The listening spectators had been considerably amused by this levity. Chase took it in good part, announcing he was thereby legitimately entitled to travel as the very first passenger.

I took out the disc. The account explained the 'No 1' and the existence of a pass for a non-existent railway.

We watched the hillside emerge across the river into the pale morning sun. Moll took the clipping and started to read.

She asked questions here and there, but all I could think of was George W. Adams, maker of silver spoons. He worked from 1840 onwards in partnership with a wealthy lady called Mary Chawner. Francis Higgins was more famous. He was always at international exhibitions. You have to go a long way before you find more beautiful floral decorative cutlery than his. How odd that two spoonmakers were asked to make a 'mechanical contrivance', in precious metal. Maybe they were closer to the booming centre of industry and more familiar with engines. My eyes were fixed on the hill. The thought of a unique creation in silver lying preserved in pristine condition in there was breathtaking. It was miraculous. And made by two of the most fashionable silversmiths in an age of silversmithing brilliance. Preserved in a presentation casket in all its perfect loveliness. And priceless, almost.

Now, I'm no railway enthusiast. And modellers like Bert and Gordon really give me a bit of a pain when they're on about their subject. But even the most humdrum of clockwork models brings heady prices at famous London auctions nowadays. It's an area of neo-antiques you can't ignore, not any more. My mouth watered, but my heart screamed fear from my boots.

Somebody had to go into the hill to find the contrivance. Deep inside.

'More coffee, Lovejoy?'

I jumped again. 'I wish you'd stop that,' I snapped irritably.

'Sorry, dear. Penny for your thoughts.'

'How many men does it take to build a tunnel, by hand?'

'Won't Gordon know?'

I already knew roughly the price of silver, but only for mid-1850s when it stuck at 61 pence an ounce, say five old shillings. At a rough guess a labourer got twice this a week. So translated into ounces of silver one man got equivalent to maybe a third of an ounce of silver a day. How wonderful it must have been when money was real. And how strange. I made a quick calculation. Ten labourers meant the Contrivance was three ounces. If they employed a hundred men it weighed thirty ounces. On the other hand, if they meant all the men on their bit of the nation's railways . . . I realized I was moaning softly and tried to turn it into a cough.

'Lovejoy. We must tell the police.' Moll had finished the article. She spoke full of determination. We were both sitting dangling our bare feet in the water now.

'Eh?'

'About the tunnel in there.'

'What have the police to do with it? The newspaper's nearly a century and a half old.'

'Well,' she said breathlessly, 'it's what police are for. Keeping order. That sort of thing.'

'No, love.'

'Tom says the police give us a code to live by.'

There's only one way to stop this kind of crap, so I said, 'Like they did for Leckie?'

She said nothing else. We sat side by side in silence, staring at the hillside. The big swan came and looked

164

us over angrily from time to time. As if anybody would want to pinch any of its little grey ducks.

I think Moll knew then that we were going to try to find the way into the hill. How else to get back at Fergus and Jake? Getting the Contrivance when they wanted it was the only means I had of striking at them. And I'd laugh in their faces when I sold it for a fortune. It would be known as the Lovejoy Contrivance. Or maybe the Lovejoy Trove? The Lovejoy Treasure? *At Claridge's Reception today, in the presence of the Keeper of the Royal Museums, London Society paid glowing tribute to Lovejoy's bravery and ingenuity. The Coroner, in handing over a cheque, stated –*

'Can't we hire a potholer to dig it up for us?' Moll demanded.

'No. Whoever finds it first gets its full market value.' I shrugged. 'That's got to be me.'

'Us, darling.'

Oh, well. 'Us, then,' I said after a pause.

There was no point in putting it off. The mist had cleared. The hill stood mild and benign above the small hamlet. It was so bloody pastoral and innocent.

'Come on, love,' I said. We dried each other's feet on a towel and set off for the bridge.

Chapter Fifteen

You can *smell* precious antiques. I swear it. All that day as Moll and I climbed the hillside I could feel that lovely sexy exquisite Contrivance beneath us, inside the living breast of the Mount. I felt its glowing strength radiate up through the rock and the hill's bones into my chest. There it set up a chiming and a clanging lovelier to me than any peal of cathedral bells. Antiques are life. They are everything.

Allow me a digression, folks.

There are more stolen antiques than there are straight ones. And there are more lying buried, waiting to be found, than both those put together. I can show you the precise spot in a sandbank off our coast here – you can stand on it at low tide – where it is known for certain that scores of ships lie sunken in the sands. Their cargoes were merely valuable centuries ago, but now they're beyond utterance. There's no word beyond priceless, is there?

The trouble is we all want these precious things. So we buy what's available. And think a moment: what *is* available, to be exact? Well, stuff for sale, as in antique shops or auctions, and stuff we dig up ourselves. And that's all.

The main difference is that stuff we dig up – should we be so lucky – is free. And nothing else in this life ever is, nothing else at all. Think, therefore, how wonderful it would be actually to dig up a ship like the Viking King's tomb in Sutton Hoo, and claim the lot. Naturally, it goes into the national museums, but you get the gelt and the prestige.

But hold hard. Before you rush out with bucket and spade, ponder how much *more* wonderful it would be not to do any digging at all, yet *still* finish up owning real genuine priceless (or even pricey will do) antiques. This equation has preoccupied Mankind since Adam dressed. It has been solved by two kinds of people. They are the crooks, and the rich unscrupulous collectors.

In countries with a wealth of archaelogical remains – Italy, Greece, Turkey, the Latin Americas, India, Egypt, Iraq, *et cetera* – there's a thriving criminality. There are diggers who locate, say, a tomb and dig up the stuff to sell. They're called *tombaroli* in Italy, *tymborychoi* in ancient Macedonia, and 'scavvies' around here. The trick is to loot genuine antiques from their place of rest and sell to the highest bidder who'll keep his mouth shut. Don't tell me it's illegal and dangerous – it's been that since Emperor Vespasian passed his famous law against it. But people still do it. And it doesn't have to be an ancient building such as a Celtic ring-grave or a buried temple. Nowadays the biggest boom in this kind of illegal knavery is 'industrial archaeology'. This daft term means prototype engines, whole buildings, clothes, models working and otherwise, engineering drawings, architectural mock-ups, patent copies, navvies' diaries, sociological records, expense books, legal records, instruments, medical devices, commercial samples, and hundreds of kinds of artifacts. If you don't believe me, look at the latest price catalogue from your local auction. You'll find somebody just paid a sum equal to your entire year's wages for some little clockwork sundry, and maybe ten times that for a big one.

Theft therefore raises its ugly head. Nowadays people will steal rushlight holders from outside your house. Your old street gas-lamps. Your elderly car. Your fascinating old garden gate with those quaint old hinges, and Grandad's old watch and his pincenez while he dozes at the seaside. Theft, and forgery. The only risk is getting caught.

A legitimately lost antique, though, is different. It's quite legal to find it. And that's exactly what is so exciting. And that's what was exciting me now. Somewhere in the hill was *my* precious discovery.

Normally I'm not very patient. You can imagine how I was on that bloody hillside. I was almost frantic, hurrying to and fro over the ground and scratching myself to blazes on the gorse. Moll kept on stopping for a rest but I got her up each time. We quartered the ground and walked in waggles, six paces one side and six the other. I knew the contours, very roughly. The hill is a sort of skew-shaped mound, with the river cutting its way round the steeper slope and a road following it until the houses begin almost as soon as the bend is complete. A Roman road runs straight as a die northwards through there, maybe two miles off. But even from the very top there seemed to be no sign of the vent-holes. The notes Gordon gave me said seven. It didn't seem enough to draw air in for a gang of men slogging away knee deep in mud. Maybe they had some kind of wind engine to funnel air down on to the labouring teams.

There was a line of gorse bushes running obliquely across the steeper face of the hill. The growth was interrupted by a small hollow, after which the line began again further down. We sat in the dip and had another glug of Moll's brew.

'I'm tired, Lovejoy.' And she looked it.

'So am I,' I said mercilessly. You can't go stopping for a doze when you're so near, can you? 'The problem as I see it is old Chase.'

All we knew about Doc Chase was that he stuck to a routine on his day off. Zip to Scratton's archaic tunnel for a few minutes, then down to the river. There, pretending to fish, he would sit on the opposite bank *which meant he was facing this way*. I scrambled to the downhill margin of the dip and looked out. You could just see the swan's big flat nest. The sand hill was in clear view but the gorse bushes near me partly obscured Doc's fishing spot.

I slid down and explained to Moll. She was unimpressed. 'What's so marvellous? If you sit opposite a hill of *course* you can see it,' she said heartlessly, 'you can't miss it.'

'But it explains why he sat *there*, Moll.'

She shrugged. 'An angler needs a river or he can't fish.'

'He only *pretended* to.'

'Lovejoy,' she said with maddening reason, 'if the old man wanted to find what's inside this hill, why didn't he come up and search like we're doing?'

Women are exasperating. 'He was old. Maybe he knew he was close to a stroke.'

'Then he should have been more sensible,' Moll said calmly. 'Leckie would have helped him.'

'Maybe he tried to tell Leckie, through Leckie's wife?'

'I never liked Julia. Mean little eyes. More coffee?'

We rested for a few more minutes, then started on the summit and worked downwards, heading towards the southern slope. It took a long time but I reached the end of my area before Moll did, and whistled to her. She looked up and waved. I pointed to show I was coming up. That was another quarter of an hour. We met on the lip of our hollow. I looked around to see where the cigarette smoke was coming from.

'Found anything, Lovejoy?'

Jake Pelman and his nerk were lounging in the dip. They had Moll's hamper open.

'Caught you,' I said lightly.

'You didn't leave us much,' he complained, grinning.

'Next time you'll get less, Jake.'

Moll was furious. 'How dare you! You've eaten the

salmon!' she blazed. 'Lovejoy, I had some lovely salmon – '

The nerk kept his eyes on me. They rose as Moll and I came down slowly. I'd quickly scanned the rest of the hillside. They seemed to be all the enemy there was. For the moment. I had to hold Moll back. She was all for taking a swing at them.

'You'll get yourselves in trouble,' I told Jake.

'That's what Fergus sent us to say, Lovejoy.' Jake blew fag smoke at us. 'Trouble. You're in it.' He nudged his goon to share the joke. 'Somebody's just paged a certain CID man. Passed word his wife's shagging Lovejoy in the long grass.'

'You – ' Moll started for Jake but I yanked her still.

'I'll ask you again, Lovejoy.' I'd never seen Jake smile properly before. 'Found anything?'

'No,' I admitted candidly. 'But I know what I'm looking for.'

I hit the goon with a stone. I'd picked it up on the edge of the hollow on the pretence of helping Moll down. His teeth splintered and he staggered on his heels. Splashes of red radiated over his countenance and blood drooled down his chin. He fell back with a gratifying thump, dazed. Jake was instantly ten feet off. He had one of those knives. I just had to laugh. He looked like a staid amateur dramatics showing of a Parisian apache.

'Put it away, Jake,' I told him, still amused. 'You'll frighten the life out of me.'

He stayed where he was, eyeing me warily while his mate groaned. 'Fergie's getting mad, Lovejoy.'

'Message received, Jake.' I still held my stone. The nerk was spitting and feeling his teeth.

Jake gave his pal a nod. They made their way out of the dip. For a second they stood looking down at us both. I could tell what they were thinking, and smiled nastily.

'You dare,' I chided, all friendly.

They glanced at each other and went. We gave them a few minutes to get clear, collected our stuff and then cut through the zigzag line of gorse bushes towards the Three Tiles. As we walked through the cobbled yard Fergus merrily raised a glass to us from the window. He was still beaming.

That night Moll phone Tom from my cottage while I went out and sat on my unfinished wall, thinking. It was a long conversation.

And that night, too, a crowd of blokes disrupted the usual gaiety of the pub in town where Val's husband George works. They injured George and the two other barmen, but not too much. There was a good old-fashioned rumble. Several customers were hurt. By all accounts the public bar and the taproom were left in an absolute shambles. And all the windows in Val's house were broken, front and back. Not one other house in the street was touched. Margaret phoned me to tell me all this about midnight. Tinker had just got the news to her. Maybe he had been trying to get through when Moll and Tom were speaking. I asked if Val was hurt. Margaret said no, just frightened. Inspector Maslow was there now, and asking questions. I wonder he doesn't get a job and go to work like everybody else.

Moll drowsily asked what's the matter when I got back to bed.

'Nothing,' I told her. 'Go to sleep.'

Chapter Sixteen

The next few days were hard work. I combed the library for maps of the Mount. I plagued the history department in a local college. I kept on at the Folklore Club, which meets every Sunday in the Hole-in-the-Wall, our oldest pub for miles. I even got on to the University, but finally wrote them off. I finished up knowing more about the geology of our district than anybody I know. And I was no wiser.

Of course, what was narking me was that I knew precisely what the precious Item was. It was almost certainly a working model of the first engine due to come along the new railway line. And I knew precisely what it was made of because silversmiths work in silver, right? And even who made it. And I knew where it was – somewhere inside one of East Anglia's very few definite hills. When you say it quick it sounds easy. If you know where and what and that it's free . . . The galling thing was getting my claws on it.

Gordon and Bern came over to the cottage twice. I had to keep up the pretence of developing an interest in their hobby. It's very difficult, especially when a train to me is just a long box on wheels. And *real* antiques only start from 1836, backwards of course. Which means that railways and their gadgetry should properly be called modern, apart from the short run from 1813 when first William Hedley courageously replaced a pit pony by a travelling thing called a steaming engine in Wylam Colliery.

Still, I pretended enthusiasm as much as I could, and tried not to nod off or yawn too obviously. I kept trying to get us round to the structure of that horrible tunnel. They kept trying to tell me where I could travel on our few remaining steam trains. There was another problem. If Jake and his nerks were watching out for my movements I'd not be doing Bern and young Gordon any favours by associating with them. Jake's thick, but with application and a bit of luck even he might work out about two and two being four.

The gorgeous Nurse Patmore took my stitches out the following Friday. Moll dropped me off at the surgery while she went shopping for us. Pat hurt me like hell, but told me with breezy determination that it didn't hurt at all and that I'd soon be as bad as new again. I called her heartless. Elspeth poked her clipboard in then and asked if Lovejoy was able to run yet. Pat ignored my frantic eyebrow signals. She said, smiling with sadistic glee, that I could run tomorrow, exercises as well.

One of Elspeth Haverill's teams was already lumbering across the countryside. I sat with her on a form waiting for any chance survivors to return. During my unstitching I'd pumped Pat for more information, until she got worried. They both knew I was asking too much, too often, but I wouldn't say why.

A local historian like Chase would naturally be fascinated by his ancestor Jonathan Chase's gruesome experience on that terrible day. Maybe tales had been passed down through the family. But the old doctor's trick of hiding his little railway pass, and his determinedly hopeless fishing, told me a great deal about the man. He was a thinker, a clever and quiet man. He wasn't the sort to go babbling to Mrs Leckworth, his clerical assistant. There was some obvious clue here, a clue as big as a barn. And I couldn't see the bloody thing for looking. I got to work, skilfully nudging Elspeth's attention off her list of atherosclerotics.

'Is that somebody?' I pointed, smiling and eager.

'Not yet.' Elspeth had a stopwatch. It was, I noticed

173

with disgust, modern, accurate, and dull as ditchwater. 'Say five more minutes.'

'I'm looking forward to joining in,' I lied cheerfully.

She was pleased. 'I'm so glad you've come round to our way of thinking, Lovejoy. Such a *benefit*.'

'Were you working with old Chase when Mrs Leckworth was here?' It was too sudden a switch. Elspeth shot me through with a glance.

'No.' She said it primly, with dislike. 'And I'm quite glad.'

'Isn't, er, wasn't she very nice?' I was all innocence, peering towards the distant wood for her runners.

'She didn't have a very good reputation. Nurse Patmore found her bossy and . . . unprofessional.' Elspeth's eyes were on her lists, but her mind wasn't. 'Look, Lovejoy. I'm not stupid. Don't treat me as if I am.'

'Eh?'

She doodled idly on her paper. 'I *know* you're not really interested in our health scheme. I can feel it.' I tried to start an indignant denial but she got in first. 'There's something wrong, isn't there? To do with Doctor and Mr Leckworth. I sensed it in your cottage.'

I gave in, shrugged. 'Maybe, love.'

She turned her eyes full on me. 'Is Moll a policewoman?'

It was a horrible thought. See how devious women's minds are, deep down? That possibility hadn't even crossed my mind. I swallowed uneasily. Dear God. Moll a peeler. And in my divan, earlier and earlier every dusk.

'No. I hope not.'

A tubby runner trundled flabbily into view from the edge of the wood. Another tottered feebly after him. We watched without speaking for a second.

'You're in trouble with the police, aren't you, Lovejoy?'

So many people kept asking me this I was beginning to wonder. I made a face. 'Dunno.'

She put her hand on my arm. 'Inspector Maslow came here yesterday. He asked a lot about you. We aren't supposed to tell you. He said . . . he said criminal charges were pending.'

And Nurse Patmore hadn't so much as said a word to tip me off. The cow. I felt like asking for my stitches back.

'That's Maslow all over, Elspeth. Don't worry.'

'Is what you're doing . . . *good*, Lovejoy?'

The stragglers were all out of the wood now, the leader a few hundred yards off. She would have to start scribbling soon.

'How the hell do I answer that?'

'Well, would Dr Chase approve?'

I thought hard. He had gone to a lot of trouble to switch the Bramah lock. But why not simply *tell* Leckie about the principal clue, which was that simple little tin disc? Unless Leckie knew already, and Doc's decision to switch the Bramah lock was for somebody else.

'What happened to the rest of his furniture?' I asked her this as the sweating runners came reeling up, knackered.

'Given to the children's home in town.'

'And those three things? The old bag, the book, the escritoire?'

'I sent them to the local auction. He was most particular. Made Nurse Patmore and myself promise.' She smiled. 'Said it was part of some game.'

'Game?' The six men had flopped on the grass now, legs in the air like dead flies.

'The divvie game, he called it. I think he meant – '

'*He said that*?'

'Why, yes.'

Elspeth got started on the exhausted men. She got the back markers strapped into a transparent set of gear like a frogman's and set them breathing into a bag full of tubes. I watched nervously while she made the poor bastards pedal like the clappers on fixed bicycles. They looked in a state of collapse. If that's health, I thought, give me 'flu any time. Within minutes the men were calling over to Elspeth, demanding to be released. I kept out of the way while she checked them off. They went inside the house one by one to change.

Doc Chase had known that some divvie would sooner or later tune in to this Bramah lock, wherever it lay, and wonder what it concealed. It was a fail-safe, in case they got Leckie.

'Still here, Lovejoy?' Nurse Patmore, looking ominously at Elspeth and propping her bike against the wall.

'Er, waiting for Moll.'

'She's in her car out front.'

We said cheerios too cautiously for old friends, and I shouted to Elspeth to get a new hourglass for tomorrow's record-breaking run and I'd show the lot of them.

I got in beside Moll. 'Town, love,' I told her. 'Here, one thing. Are you a bobby?'

'No.' She looked a bit puzzled but let it go. She took us off, definitely peaky. 'I've had a message, Lovejoy. Tom's coming back for the weekend. I think I'd better . . .'

'Right,' I said, feeling rotten. 'Look. Can you lend me enough to get my car mended?' Sooner or later I'd make a start on our antique furniture and that treen.

'Send me the bill.' She added quickly, 'By post would be best.'

'Thanks,' I said. 'Er, I'll owe it you. All right?'

'If you insist.' She only said that after we'd gone another mile. I couldn't tell if she was mad at me again or not.

I said nothing else till we reached the High Street and she put me down outside the library. She said she would leave a meal ready and a load of groceries indoors, and to look out for Jake and his horrid assistants. I said I would. She already had a key to collect

176

her things. I watched her motor off into the traffic. Funny how you can feel alone in a crowded street. I waited for her to wave, but she reached third gear for her handbag's sake and simply carried on going.

Because of my brief Elspeth-Nurse-Patmore-stitches-Moll drama at Six Elm Green, I was late for the auction. There was very little to interest me, but you can never tell. You can't ever trust a catalogue. You have to see for yourself.

By the time I made it down East Hill the cafés were bulging. Dealers' vans were neatly blocking the main sea road out of town. Pubs were fuming and slurping, pie-shops were roaring. This end of town was humming with life and interest. By the time I clinked open the glass doors and slid into the mob Tinker was mad as hell. Not a face turned from the auctioneer, but they all sensed a new rival had just walked in.

'Where the bleeding hell you been, Lovejoy?'

'Why's it Jive?'

Jive's the apprentice auctioneer, a pimply mirthless youth who gets all the rotten jobs. He was struggling to make sense of the bids. The lads were mucking him about, waving and pointing to each other to confuse an inexperienced auctioneer. If enough of you do it he'll knock valuable items down for a song, just from frustrated bewilderment. It's called 'flagging' in the trade, but it's only worth doing if you've a lot of friends in, otherwise you take a fearsome risk.

'Gaffer's ill.'

Lemuel was seated on a chaise-longue sucking on a dripping meat pie and picking losers again. It was the most horrible sight I've ever seen. Tinker saw me recoil and nudged me.

'Lemuel's found out so don't knock him.'

'Eh?'

'Black Fergus and Jake. They've got two blokes to nobble you.'

'Two?' I thought I'd got rid of one.

'Two. They're Brummie lads.'

I went cold. I should explain there's a sort of hierarchy of goons. There's always a lot of aggro where you get antiques and often goons are hired to see somebody off or to straighten a dealer up. But there are goons and goons. You can talk your way out of trouble with hard lads from Blackpool, and I assure you it is well worth the vocal effort. Brighton shells up a very rag-taggle mob – noisy, thick as planks, lots of wind and water. London's goons are so direct it's painful. Their idea of 'correction', as it's often termed, is to arrive like Fred Karno's army and simply flail about. Mancunians stay at home, so outside Manchester you are quite safe. Same with Newcastle. But Tinker's mention of two Birmingham nerks made my flesh crawl. They are real aggro men who'll marmalize anybody for a few quid.

I said, 'Keep calm, Tinker,' though my throat constricted. 'Are they the ones who did Val's gaff?'

'People say so.'

'Mine next, I suppose. How is she?'

'Val? Gone to her auntie's.'

'Thank God for that.'

We stood in the packed hall watching the bidding. Jive was quavering away, hopeless. Some dealers were grinning. The relatively few honest customers were unaware of anything amiss. They are easily spotted, having come to the auction merely for one item, rarely two. Antique dealers give these innocent genuine bidders a funny nickname: 'women'. For every wally and barker there's maybe one 'woman', in most auctions.

'Seen Helen?'

'No.' Tinker thought a moment, tuning his mental radar. 'She'll be at Patrick's place in a few minutes.'

Unlikely, but I knew better than to argue. I scanned the items on display. There was a dull mixture of Victorian furniture. One unidentified Norwich School oil was alluring, though it needed a lot of care. And there was a delectable silver cruet set by the two Fenton brothers of Sheffield. I could see Big Frank from Suffolk ogling it. Jean was in, and Madge. Brad was at the tea bar chatting up the lady. He would be waiting for a small percussion pepperbox pistol, low down in the lot numbers. Alfred's bowler hat was prominent down by the locked porcelain cabinet. He felt my gaze, looked across between the sea of shoulders, and raised comical eyebrows. He's a right one for remembering how cheap everything was before the Great War. I grinned and nodded. Sven was drifting about purpose-lessly. I had mixed feelings about Sven. He seemed cheerful, but I couldn't quite forget how servile he had looked that day in the White Hart with Fergus and Jake. Margaret was going over some pewter, so I slid through the mob and tackled her about Nodge's Bustelli.

'I got it,' she said, after helloing and quizzing me about my decrepit health. 'Lucky. Seeing,' she added quietly, 'seeing Nodge died so soon after.'

'Wasn't it just!' I shook my head sadly.

'Your lady friend's back at the cottage basting the duck, I suppose?'

'Shut it, love. Have you a buyer?'

'I think so. If it falls through, can I use Tinker to find one?'

'Mmmm. Look, love.' I pulled her away from the pewters. 'How safe is Bill Hassall?' She looked uncomfortable. I had to help because women are usually reticent about the other women who run around, especially when it's a man asking. 'I mean about his missus and Leckie.'

'I don't think he knew.'

'Is he anything to do with Jake Pelman? Fergus?' She gave me an immediate headshake, but hesitated after I added, 'Anything between Julia Leckworth and Bill Hassall, for instance?'

'No,' she said finally. 'But they say Julia's daft on Fergus. They're together now.'

'Thanks.'

I nodded to Tinker and pushed my way to the door. Those few minutes Tinker had predicted were up. Helen would be at Patrick's.

And she was, having a cigarette and going over some early Bilston enamels. Patrick screamed at me down the Arcade as soon as I came in view.

'Lovejoy! You perfect poppet!' He struck a theatrical pose of welcome in his doorway. He was wearing a maroon and orange caftan. 'Come in, dearie! Home,' he misquoted grandly in his shrillest voice, 'home is the sailor, home from the sea!'

'How do.' I always go red when he does this act. I could see Helen smiling inside his main display room. These places are only small, one room and an alcove. Helen had managed to find a tall stool again, her favourite pose to show off her shiny curved legs.

Patrick dragged me in. There were four or five customers looking about. He pushed them rudely aside and whispered to me, 'Don't notice Helen's impossible hairstyle, Lovejoy! Just *bear* it!' I went redder, because Patrick's penetrating whispers are made to be heard. Helen only laughed. It's odd, really, because if anybody else criticizes her she goes mad.

'Hello, Lovejoy.'

'Wotcher, love.'

'The brave young man!' Patrick swept aside a customer and did a grand gesture. 'So narrowly plucked from the jaws of death!' He meant the car accident.

The customers were as embarrassed as me. Lily came in from the alcove. She seemed pleased to see me and said how marvellous it was I'd managed to buy so many antiques. She said she liked Moll.

'She's perfectly sweet, Lovejoy,' Patrick agreed silkily. 'And when she *learns* about those off-the-peg pleated skirts with those *crippling* decorated belts from Haythorn's she'll be sweeter still. *Do* tell her.'

'Er, well.' I'd only come to see Helen.

'Helen's full of the joys of spring, Lovejoy.' Patrick sat on a chair to do his eyes. 'She's talked non-stop about you. Watch out. She'll go for your ankles.'

I took advantage of Patrick's preoccupation to pull Helen into the alcove. She guessed I was not so concerned about the lovely Bilston enamels this time.

'What is it, Lovejoy? You look desperate.'

'I am. Is there *anything* you haven't told me?'

'No, love. Except how much I dislike coppers' wives. She's too pretty-pretty sweet-little-Alice by far.'

'It's over.'

'That's good.'

'Nothing about Leckie?' I pressed her. 'Nothing he might have said?'

She flicked her cigarette. I told her not to smoke, because Patrick had coins, watercolours and a display of copper medallions but Helen never takes much notice of what I say.

'Why ask, Lovejoy?' She put down the Bilston carefully. 'You knew Leckie better than anybody. Do you seriously think he would send you a useless message?' She pursed her lips and told me that wasn't her idea of Leckie. 'He was cool as a cucumber when he scribbled it. He paused a bit, even smiled.' Her eyes were damp. 'The fault's in you, Lovejoy. Whatever it is you're looking for you probably already have in your pocket.'

'But this message didn't say much – '

'It will be enough.' She leant across and bussed me lightly on the face. 'Lovejoy. I don't know what's going on, why the CID are everywhere asking about you. Why everybody you know seems to be dying in road accidents. But don't let Leckie have done it for nothing.'

Before I knew it I'd flung myself into the Arcade in

a blazing temper. Patrick shrilled some cutting remark after me, but I didn't pause until I was through the back street and into the old pub yard. Some buskers were playing away there for the pedestrians. I stalked through the crowd, got a pint and sat at a table. The bloody cheek of it. I must have been white with rage.

Helen could have saved Leckie, the grumbling useless bitch. Yet all she did was carry a message, too late to do any good. Couldn't be bothered to lift a finger. Simply criticizes me the minute I want some help. That's the trouble with women. Full of useless bloody advice while they do absolutely sod all. Everybody knows that. I marched in for another glass, fuming.

By closing time I was sloshed. I got a taxi from the stand outside the corn-market and got myself driven back to the cottage. It took practically my last groat.

I paid him off and staggered up the gravel path. I remember even now how quiet the garden was, how the afternoon seemed one for dozing through. Soporific, I think the word is. I started singing, but what I don't know. I must have taken a year to unlock the door.

For an instant I thought it was Moll who had followed me in. When I looked around the woman was standing there, blonde and fetching. I gaped and tried to keep upright.

'We've never really met, Lovejoy,' she said. 'May I come in?'

'You're Julia,' I said foolishly. It was Leckie's wife.

She walked past me and went inside. I shrugged, followed her in and closed the door.

Chapter Seventeen

I'm not so proud of that Friday night that I want to tell everything that went on, even if I remembered blow by blow, which I don't. Julia seemed to expect it, so I fetched out my reserve bottle of dubious sherry. We talked about Leckie. She seemed really rather sad, genuinely so. I was sure she wasn't putting it on. I remember consoling her. We had some more sherry. I decided we ought to have a party to cheer ourselves up. She vanished, came back with more bottles.

By dusk we were in the garden. It came on to rain which drove us indoors. I insisted on making her some grub and shared a meal some friendly elves had kindly left out for me. I vaguely remember singing her a song, and her watching me but not joining in. After that it gets vaguely woozy. I told her about me and Leckie in the army, the bridge of bamboo and that bloody tunnel. At least, I think I did. I can recollect doing something with matchsticks on the table to show how illogical it is to be scared of tunnels falling on you when they are built on mathematical principles. In my hazy memory of this particular night Julia doesn't say much, just seems to be watching steadily. Then dusk fell and I had to put the lights on. I fell over a few things and I can remember laughing like a lunatic at not being able to get up. Then I tried to demonstrate how a savage karate chop would decapitate any Brummie goon that lurched in. Things seemed so funny. I laughed and laughed.

I woke next morning with the light still on. Julia was

gone. The room showed that a lot of activity had taken place. My divan bed, for instance, was a shambles. There was no note. I had a splitting headache. It took me an hour to put the bedclothes out on the line to air. The grass was still wet, but the rain had stopped. I brewed up and sat miserably in the cool air, wondering how much I had told her. It's no good thinking I'm a crude vulgar layabout. I admit it. Julia and I had gone at each other like animals.

What worried me was a map, spread across the foot of the bed when I woke. I should have been more careful. It was the Ordnance Survey map of the Mount St Mary area. Worse still, I couldn't find the little railway pass. Maybe I had dropped it somewhere in town, though. Had Julia, I wondered, said *why* she'd called round in the first place? If so, I couldn't remember. I felt miserably that I ought to assume the worst. Maybe Julia simply knew I'd be easy, came and did her stuff and learned everything I knew about Leckie's and Chase's plan to recover the precious silver Contrivance, and simply find out from me whereabouts it was. I could have kicked myself. I had been ahead of Jake and Fergus in the race, and chucked all my advantage away for a mess of pottage, so to speak. That's the trouble with will-power. Everybody else's is so much better quality.

I showered and cleaned up. I shaved ferociously. I even swept the cottage out, as penance. I fed the birds and washed the windows aggressively. I washed crockery, re-made the bed and folded it away. By noon I'd recovered, with some aspirin. I was still mad at myself, but some determination had crept back into my actions.

The pasties I hotted up for dinner were iron hard. Normally I sling them out, but this time I ground my way through them inch by inch in atonement. I had a cold bath after that. Two pints of tea, and I was ready to face my responsibilities.

From now on I had to assume two things. First, that I'd told Julia all I knew, and that Fergus knew as much as I did. All it meant was that I was now in a flaming hurry, whereas before I'd been ambling along like a fool just hoping things would solve themselves. Second, I had to assume that Helen had been right, that I was mentally shirking truths *that I already knew*. I'd have to face up to it all. If she was right about my self-trickery, I could easily guess why I was evading the issue. I was probably scared of the tunnel I might find deep inside that hill. It was high time I went over all the events leading up to this morning, especially those concerning Leckie. I might make up part of the leeway I'd just lost.

I walked up to the post hut and borrowed Rose's local contour maps from her door. She'd be as mad as hell, but it was time other folk besides myself made a few sacrifices. I went back and sat on my wall. Listing all the things you know about a person isn't all that easy. Try it. You tend to miss things out simply *because* you know them so well. Despite my reluctance, I forced myself to go over every single detail of our relationship, from the moment Leckie took my first parade to the instant I saw him hurtle against the tree in that thunderstorm. There seemed nothing there, so I forced my mind on into the events of his death, right up to finding Jake and his nerk in that hollow on Mount St Mary in the severed line of gorse. I forced myself to go over what Gordon and Bert told me.

It took me three hours. By then I was bushed. I broke for a brew-up, knowing I was coming closer and closer. By four o'clock I was focused clearly and resolutely on the niggly bit that had rankled for so long. I'd found it. It was one of the things Margaret had said that day I phoned her from calling at Virgil's in Medham. She'd said Leckie was a collector of religious relics. I hadn't known that. I remembered how surprised I was.

I got the map out. A small circle was inscribed on a contour line. It would be just about where the hollow is on the Mount. My spine tingled. On the larger scale map there it was again, inscribed as well. My chin was suddenly stinging with sweat and my elbow flexures became sticky. And abruptly I knew it. I said, 'God Almighty.' The birds took no notice but the robin on my arm looked shocked for a minute. The well. The tunnel had pierced an old well.

Now I knew how Leckie and Doc Chase had come together, how Leckie knew of Chase's quest. I knew why Leckie considered himself the legitimate discoverer once Chase had passed on. I knew how old Jonathan Chase, that brave Victorian dignitary, had got out of the hill. And I knew exactly why he and the rescue workers hadn't managed to get back despite the desperate labour of several hundreds of them. I knew why Doc Chase sat for hours just staring at a hillside instead of wandering about on it. And why he went to Scratton to look briefly at a dull old tunnel before going 'fishing'. *And I knew that the tunnel deep inside Mount St Mary could be reached.*

But worst of all, I knew the way in. My teeth were chattering as I set the robin down and brushed the remaining bits off the paving with a broom. I'd have to go. Elspeth came in her car about then to take me to her training programme. I'd forgotten she was coming, but I went with her for company's sake. You can imagine the state I was in afterwards; bad enough before.

We had supper in a pub that evening. She told me which drinks and grub had least calories. I said, great, and borrowed from her because I happened to be a bit short at the time.

I was up at the ungodly hour of five o'clock. I'd tried the night before to phone Tinker at the White Hart, but failed. No mates, no car, no money and no bird.

She hates being called Marlene. 'Mr Scotchman! Mr Scotchman!'

She ran off for the librarian in a flurry while I dug out Attwater's book on Saints and a couple of local histories. They tried to prise me out twice until I lost my temper and pointed a finger, smiling one of my special smiles, at Scotchman; without a word. After that they left me alone, but Marlene banged the books about as they restocked. There was only her and the uniformed watchman left by the time I'd found what I wanted.

In Speed's map of the area the well was marked 'St Osyth's Well'. That was good enough for me. The little coastal resort town of St Osyth is where Leckie lived. What more natural than him taking an interest in the reliquaries and place-names associated with his own village? I stood up and stretched, weary as hell. After all, I'd been on the go since an early hour. And, thinking of Julia, the previous day had been tiring as well. Marlene was still slamming piles of books about as I left. She's a shapely thirtyish. She believes in Good Works, like not letting the public touch her books except as humble supplicants.

'See you, Marlene.' I clicked out through the turnstile. 'Think of me in bed.'

She ran a hand exasperatedly through her hair. 'Lovejoy. Why do you . . . why do you take no *notice* of anybody?'

What an extraordinary question. I stared at her. I take notice of other people all the bloody time. 'It's other people make me bad, love,' I said with conviction. 'Like you. I start out holy every single morning.'

I went out into the brightening day.

Chapter Eighteen

Yonks ago the chances of holiness were largely confined to eccentric nuts, warriors (of the right sort) and
royalty. It's no surprise to learn that St Osyth was not
only a raving beauty, but also sexy queen to Sighere,
king of hereabouts in the seventh century. Eventually
she decided to go straight, and founded a nunnery at
the tiny coastal village of Chich. After some sea rovers
massacred the lot we beatified her as a martyr and
Chich village became St Osyth. The place where she
built her convent's still there. Leckie's windmill is only
a stone's throw.

You might think it sacrilegious, but there's a thriving
trade in religious relics. Not as frank as in the Middle
Ages, when the faithful would slice a finger off a dead
– and even a dying – saint for luck. I believe our
approach is a lot healthier. The trouble is finding *genuine* relics. Some are well authenticated. Others, like
those paintings of the Blessed Virgin allegedly done by
St Luke the Evangelist, are a bit dicey or even outright
frauds. Yet Leckie only *studied*. Margaret didn't say
he *collected* – did she? I was sure she was right. Tinker
or maybe Lemuel would have sussed that out before
long, or maybe I'd have learned of it through auctions.

So Leckie, interestedly examining St Osyth's Well in
the course of his hobby, encountered Dr Chase. Maybe
they'd got talking. Perhaps they'd agree to try for the
discovery together. Things were falling into place.

Crossing the main London road, going out towards
the village, I became aware of Jake Pelman. He was
driving a natty little Japanese car. He gave me a sour

nod, smiling. I didn't like that. It isn't often Jake cracks his ugly face. I gaped at all the cars that passed after that. Nobody looking like two Brummies full of aggro, thank God.

I stopped to use the phone at the village shop. Elspeth was in the surgery, presumably lashing a huddle of sweating slaves to a distant drumbeat.

'Lovejoy!' she exclaimed. 'I'm so pleased you rang! I tried to wake you this morning as I passed but you were so soundly asleep – '

'Look, love,' I interrupted. 'One thing. About Doc Chase.'

Her voice suddenly went all smooth and professional. 'Yes, sir,' she cooed. 'I'll arrange another appointment. Just one second while I shut the door . . . ' She came back a little breathlessly. I guessed Nurse Patmore had popped her head in. 'Go on, Lovejoy.'

'*When* did Doc go, er, fishing?'

'I told you,' she replied, puzzled. 'Every day he possibly could.'

'No, love. I mean *when*. Morning? Afternoon?'

'Oh, always as early as he could. Early morning.'

'Did he ever say why?'

'Something to do with the light, I think. I vaguely remember he said something about the light once.'

'Elspeth,' I said. 'If I come out of this alive, you can have me for a whole week. I promise.'

I rang off before she could draw breath. The last link was in the chain.

The clever old man. He wasn't working out how to get into the hillside. He hadn't been puzzling over a mystery at all. Because to him there just wasn't any mystery. He'd known everything all along, that the entrance to the tunnel was through St Osyth's Well. You can see the small hollow easiest in the morning light, so you could tell if it had been tampered with. By late afternoon it is in shadow. It was all that simple.

He'd not been searching for anything. He'd just been keeping watch. He was a guardian.

The rest of the day I planned with obsessional detail. If my onslaught on the tunnel was going to fail it wouldn't be because I'd forgotten some obvious and essential tool. I determined to take everything but the kitchen sink. And I'd take that, too, if I thought it would improve my chances.

That afternoon I thought of ringing people to explain my plan of action, at least roughly where I would be, but gave up. Tinker would be as petrified as me. Lemuel's known usefulness is a flat zero. Patrick would only have hysterics. All the others would try to beat me to it.

Helen and Margaret would dissuade me as much as possible. Moll had abandoned ship. Pat would tell Maslow. Sue was house-bound, and in view of her suspicions about me and every other woman in the known universe she'd more probably chuck me down the bloody well than help. I was on my own.

It's easy to be brave on an afternoon with the post-girl calling and bright daylight everywhere. People came and went along the lane. One or two waved. I waved back. All innocence and peace.

By four I had a heap of things on my divan. It was still difficult getting about the interior of the cottage. Moll's treen and furniture kept catching my knees. I'm no mountaineer, but I assumed the job would call for some climbing. I fetched in my clothesline to add to the pile. It looked strong, and felt in good nick. I have a few tools and I picked the best. My hammer's pretty worn but looks tough. I included that, and got as many eight-inch nails as I could find. I use those when I'm making heavy picture frames, and managed ten of them. I tied them up with string and put them in a polythene bag.

Torch. I wish I was the sort of bloke that worries

about batteries and always has spare bulbs, but it's no good. I'm not, and I had no money for any, so it had to go on the pile as it was. I included a ball of fine string. In the days when I could afford to collect flintlocks I'd have had a choice of several luscious miracles of firepower. I had one last look for Moll's frightening pistol in case she'd left it for me in some secret hideyhole. No luck. To this day I don't know whether I'd have taken it if I'd come across it in some drawer. Maybe it's a mistake to look back and quiz yourself about motives, because they're a waste of time. I found a small hand fork and a hand shovel that goes with it. On to the pile.

I'd heard it tends to be cold in caves. I laid out two singlets, underpants, socks and my worsted suit. It's the only one I have, and hardly looked typical climbing gear, but it's made of the proper stuff. On impulse I added three unused hankies. Shoes bothered me. The plimsolls from this morning's jaunt were still wet through. I lit a fire and put them on the hearth, deciding to travel in shoes and change when climbing down to the tunnel. I added a box of matches. Funny how your mind works. I brought a propelling pencil with some spare leads and a few squares of white card, maybe thinking of floating a message out on some chance subterranean stream should that ghastly need ever arise. Which, of course, it would bloody well not. I was going to make sure of that, come what may.

There comes a time in planning when you find you are planning too hard. Your brain never leaves off. I found myself getting in this state. I started sweating for nothing and kept rearranging my heap of stuff senselessly, so I got control of myself and made a meal. Then I went out for a walk while there was some daylight still left.

I watched television for a bit. Then switched it off and listened to the radio. Then I watched a play I couldn't make head nor tail of. Then I tried to read, but found I was reading the same page over. Then I sang some madrigals, but my heart wasn't in it. I listened to a radio argument about the soaring costs of new bedding plants, and then watched the Wanderers get thrashed three-nil in a floodlit game, the duckeggs. I thought of candles, and added my only two to the heap.

Then it was dark, and I forced myself into bed.

I woke with the alarm clock going berserk. Three-thirty. For a moment I wondered what the hell I was playing at, setting it for that ridiculous time. Then I remembered. I had to go down a well.

My crate makes a racket at the best of times. I mean, even during the day in noisy traffic people turn, wondering what's coming. Nearly four on a pitchy morning it sounded like a helicopter. I keep meaning to get it seen to, but the cost's terrible.

I decided against the bike. On the grounds that I'd probably need every muscle fascicle doing its absolute thing today, I settled for the car despite its row. The trouble was, they'd recognize my motor anywhere. I'd have stood a better chance if Elspeth had lent me hers. Or Moll hers, or Sue . . .

I wasn't long reaching the Mount, cruising easily on to the down-slope towards the river. Most of our villages have no street lights, so I was relying on a vague, rather shifty-looking moonglow as I cut the engine. With only wind noise and some wheel-swishing I coasted her down to the pub. Luckily, pub yards are traditionally open at the front. No gates or hedges. We rolled on to the forecourt, and I reached the side of the tavern wall before stopping.

I got out, pushing her slowly forwards until she was as far off the road as she would go. People might assume some early devoted angler had put it there, intending to return for a midday break from boredom. Most of my stuff was in a small satchel I used for

carrying my materials as a lad, when I went out painting. The torch was in my pocket, and the pencil and
some of the card squares. I sat on the car seat with the
door open and changed my shoes for plimsolls. If there
was any mud down there my feet would get wet
anyway, and rubber soles are easier to climb in. I was
shaking like a leaf. The cold night mist seeped into my
bones. Sometimes you can talk yourself into a shiver,
can't you?

Ready. I simply turned towards the hill and started
up it straight from the tavern yard. There were a few
obstructions, mostly large flint-stones and large tuss-
ocks of grass. A couple of times I walked straight into
a gorse bush, but got off lightly. It was the line of gorse
bushes that had tipped me off and gave me the final
clue. They followed an obvious contour line as far as
the hollow. There they ended abruptly, to recommence
about a hundred feet down the hillside. Something had
slipped them out of true: the magic landslip of 1847.
What else?

No wonder there was a hollow. The uppermost half
of the well was tilted. It couldn't be any other way. I
imagined a nail, bent almost to right angles by some
powerful force after it had been driven half into a piece
of wood. The uppermost half now lay for the finding.
And the well-head would be located exactly where the
gorse-bushes began again lower down the hill.

I blundered into a gorse bush again. The moonglow
was too feeble but I guessed I was at the lower half of
the gorse line. Which meant that following it left would
bring me to its abrupt end. And the well-head would
be there. I felt with my hands, touching the spiky
fronds at every step.

I wasn't spooked when I reached the end of the gorse
line. Not really. But wells are funny things. In honest
and kindly old Britain wells and springs have always
been slightly magic. And, often as not, the old folk
would protect the magic of their own particular well

197

by some rather odd – and quite evil – practices. It's no accident that our wells are often adorned with stone faces and completely sculpted Celtic stone heads. Don't dwell too long on how the fashion actually started. It isn't very happy reading. These stone heads, incidentally, are worth a fortune nowadays – if you dare risk the spooky vibes. Like most people, I don't admit to being superstitious. It's always somebody else.

I was at the end of the line, feeling on my hands and knees round the tallest of the gorse bushes. I parted the grass on the down-side of the bush and reached underneath. There was a cold stone under my hands. I tried to be scientific, pushed my hands back under and felt around. There was another to its right. There was one a few inches displaced inwards to its left. And a third. And a fourth. They seemed heaped, rather than set in a circle. But wells are always circular. It took me a few more minutes of groping to fathom what had happened. The well had not been shifted sideways, as I'd guessed. It had just been laid down. Naturally, the stones had piled in the form of a small cairn. It was simply an earth-covered, stone-blocked cavern now.

I started picking at the first stone with my minute border fork. It was like trying to extract a tusk with a pin. I started being stealthy and silent. Within five minutes I was swearing and smashing at the bloody stone, probably making enough noise to wake the dead. I paused, wishing I hadn't thought of it in exactly those terms. That made me work things out more intelligently.

If the well-head had been toppled sideways by the sliding hill, then the surest means of gaining entrance would be through the great heap of stones at its mouth. Stones fall down, not up, I lectured myself severely. At this rate I'd be exhausted before I even found a route into the wretched well-head, let alone climbed down into the tunnel.

I walked round until I was standing overlooking the

gorse bushes, then slid down, hanging on to the grass like grim death. I located the marker stone and wriggled back upwards until I was somewhere over the middle of the well's outline. There I started digging, using only the hand shovel. I was shattered when my blade struck something hard and it turned out to be a brick. I worked harder then, after the first moment of amazement.

I had the sense to splay myself to one side so that if the well caved in I wouldn't go tumbling in and get myself crushed to death by falling masonry; one foot was hooked round the stem of a gorse bush as an extra precaution.

It took me the best part of two hours or so. Then, when I was telling myself I'd perhaps made enough of a hole to get through, I was helped by the incaving I had feared. The well side gave way with a rumbling sound, and the bricks I had exposed simply folded in. I only just saved myself from the falling in after the bloody things by grabbing for the grass and holding on. I lost the shovel, which was tough. That didn't matter much for the moment, because I was the jubilant owner of a hole some three feet in diameter into a medieval well which led straight to a valuable possession any antique dealer would give his limbs to own. I found my satchel and the torch. Now I was able to direct the beam downwards into the hole. Nobody could see it from the road.

I wasn't prepared for the filth which confronted me. There were deposits from wildlife several inches deep along the brickwork which now formed the floor of the well's lumen, possibly from badgers or foxes. I'd heard tales of the fury with which dog badgers attack an intruder. Maybe they'd be afraid of the torch-light. I tied a handkerchief round my face against the dirt, slipped over, and clung to the lip of brickwork with one hand, while shining the torch with the other.

The well descended in a slow curve into the hill,

down and in. I let the torch rove and found small recesses with a single brick lip. Some form of primitive handhold? They seemed to be spaced about right for a climbing man. As long as there were plenty, and as long as they went all the way down, otherwise I'd have to risk the rope. I let my satchel fall. It hit the layer of filth and set up a smog of dung. I made sure that I could reach upwards again from the floor of the well before letting go. Careful old Lovejoy. Now nothing could stop me from getting out once I'd completed the task.

From above it had looked miles long. Once down there, it seemed that I'd only taken three or four steps before I was having to hold on to stop myself from slithering forward. A few more paces still, and I found myself actually climbing downwards, holding on to the projecting bricks in the shallow recesses and fiddling about with my spare foot to catch the next slot. It's easier said than done. I never know why people go climbing, anyway. After about ten steps on my brick-work ladder I thought maybe it was time I shone the torch to see in which direction I was now heading. Confident now, I turned from my position and shone the light down. Down.

Down, down it went.

Down into the bowels of the planet.

I whined feebly. There seemed to be nothing, nothing but a great hole whizzing vertically into the earth. And I was dangling from the merest foothold, one – *one* – single brick wide. I whimpered, and froze. Sweat poured down my face and prickled between my shoulders. I felt my hands ice up. My thighs quivered horribly. I even made a move to start up again, heading for fresh air and safety. Then I felt it. A glow began in my chest. From down below, deep in the hole, a radiance emanated. It warmed my chest and set my mind clicking again. My hands eased without being told. I felt the beauty of whatever was down there set

200

up vibrations, with me in the very track of the waves. I found that my foot had begun to search for the next foothold almost of its own accord. I began breathing again, slowly at first but with regularity. I realized I'd gone down another step. Then another. Then again another.

I developed a rhythm, moving five careful, well-tested rungs, then shining the torch. Later, I realized I ought to have had the sense to count while going along, to estimate the distance. You can't think of everything. In fact, when you're terrified you can think of nothing.

I suppose I'd been slowly climbing down for about a quarter of an hour when I shone the torch and saw something there. It was a straight line going from side to side across the well's black base. Another three rungs and I could see there was another line, also dark and somewhat mottled, but parallel to it. At a rough guess I was about thirty feet above the lines when the rungs ran out. I saw the reason for the mottling. They were steel railway tracks, and bricks had fallen, partly covering them here and there.

The trouble is that common sense leaves you when you're near to what you want. It hadn't penetrated my thick skull that I would enter the tunnel at the top of the vault and probably break my neck the instant I forgot this elementary fact. Yet I nearly did.

It was only the vague worry of how to climb up again that stopped me literally letting go. I remembered the care with which I'd entered the well-head, and mercifully paused to wonder the same thing. I realized how close I'd been to falling. I got the shakes again and had to hang on for a minute.

I held on with my left hand and got the hammer out, clenching the haft in my teeth. I decided to bang in all the nails I had.

It took several attempts to get even one in. I dropped two, which left me seven. Some elementary mathematics took over. I spaced five more out in twos, one above the other, and wrapped the clothesline round each pair in turn. It would be less of a strain on them if my weight was shared by three pairs instead of one single long vertical column. God knows how long it took me, but in the end I was gasping and spluttering in the brick dust. And I'd had to hold the torch in my teeth while starting each fresh nail off. Worse still, every stroke of the hammer echoed and hummed up and down the well-shaft. Like being the clapper in a bell. My mind reeled from the racket. The hammer fell when I was clouting the last nail in, and thudded into something soft at the bottom. I gave up then, just turned the rope round as I'd planned and tied it in a million knots for safety.

In the descent I misjudged the rate of sliding and got a couple of rope burns. Added to that, I found myself wheezing from something musty in the air when I finally crashed down on the lines. As long as I stayed on the iron rails I would be all right. If they could bear the weight of a train they could carry me. I got my gear together and shone the torch about.

I was in a space, a bubble in the earth. It was no longer than ten feet and didn't reach quite to the tunnel walls. The brickwork of the tunnel vault disappeared behind an upslope of desiccated mud. Only the rails were exposed; it was rather odd. I remember thinking that at the time. Mud doesn't get flung upwards, does it? It lies there just being mud. The lines ran under the roof fore and aft. I was stuck. There was no sign of the little decorated carriage that I'd read about.

I shone and looked, shone and looked. There was an odd feel about the whole thing. I felt as if I'd come across a stage set with no play. I stayed straddling the rails, though the flooring of the tunnel seemed intact. I prodded it once or twice experimentally. It seemed just a tunnel floor. Then I noticed the rope.

It had rotted, but in its day it had been a good

enough rope. Parts still felt waxy. It was coiled unevenly among the dust and the fallen bricks on the floor as if it had fallen after hanging down. Yet it must have been there a hell of a time to have rotted like that. I picked it up and noticed the iron stanchion ring still attached to a small length of it. Somebody had been here before me, but a century and a half ago. And he had come to a prepared spot, where a rope waited for him inside an old sealed well – a well with climb-holds. And, having escaped by hacking his way through into the well-shaft, he could pull across some odd bush or other, and from there it would be easy in the confusion to appear as if by a miracle near the nearest vent-hole. *And misdirect the rescuers*?

I sat down, my skin prickling with revulsion. Jonathan Chase had escaped according to plan, babbled of vent-holes, and deliberately directed the rescue teams away from his two entombed men. And he had lived a hero's life, even been decorated for his services and his bravery.

But if the Right Honourable had made his honourable way through this chamber, I reasoned in the darkness, and out through the well-shaft, then he must have entered it by some route that should still be visible. I shone the torch round again. From the angle of illumination the mud-caked bricks seemed indented near one rail. As if somebody had shoved anything he could find to fill a hole. It was on the inward direction of the rails, which meant that the carriage might be on that side. The shaft above me seemed to be at a slight angle to the vertical. That suggested the deeper part of the well lay on the incoming side too.

I cast about for my hammer, but couldn't find it. I took my satchel off. Holding my torch in my mouth was making me gag, and I started coughing and coughing again. For a moment I remembered firedamp, the silent odourless gas of the mines, and the terrible tales I had heard about it as a lad. There was only speed to counter that, speed in escaping. And I would be out of this hole like a bat in another instant. I made myself a fervent promise, and set to clawing the earth and bricks away from the indented spot. There was a space behind, a long hole just wide enough for a man. I took my jacket off and rolled it into a sausage shape. I wasn't going to leave it behind, and it would be impossible to push ahead or I wouldn't be able to see a thing. I noticed how cold it had become now that I had stopped really moving.

The small crawl-way Jonathan Chase had made for himself through the mud sloped up through the fall for a couple of feet then levelled off. With the torch I could see a space at the end of it. The whole course could not be more than twelve feet. I didn't like it, but twelve feet didn't seem for ever, or so I thought.

I ducked my head in and crawled forward with the torch leading the way. Easy. Not roomy, but easy. I reached the lip of the inner chamber. From the bobbing rays of the torch I could see by squinting ahead that it seemed at least as spacious as the one I'd just left. I caught hold of the crumbly lip to pull myself forward – and nearly fell into the lower half of the well. I screamed like a stuck pig, squealing and yipping with terror and dangling in space from a crumbling mass of rubble with my feet flailing in empty air. The torch was lodged in the aperture at one side where I'd just emerged, but I was in a mad scramble to get back. My leg caught on something hard. I felt the skin give down my calf. The other leg scagged on projecting iron and the skin tore. I had to do something quickly or my limbs would be shredded. My right leg flung wildly sideways. It struck iron, a firm rod of some sort. I rested it carefully on the metal, pressed, and let it gradually take my weight, or part of it. My fingers relaxed. I stood like a deformed acrobat, at a weird angle. I reached shakily for the torch. I seemed to be standing precariously on a single rail. The other had gone heaven knows where. Beneath me was the well. It wasn't bottomless. The light descended about sixty feet before water caught the beam and reflected it against the sides. Floating in the water, or stuck there on a muddy sediment, were the remains of two men. Presumably men, though now they were skeletal fragments crumpled under a dark brown slime.

My moan echoed hollowly. I fixed my position so I wouldn't slip and turned my head, holding the torch with my arm flexed underneath. I saw the carriage. Had I been facing the other way I could have reached out and touched it. As it was, I dared not let go or I'd fall.

The decorated bogie had stopped right on the edge of the well. It rested on two rails. The left one was shorn away and couldn't be seen. It was a small version of the hand-cranked wagon which plate-layers sometimes use for carrying their tools and metal supplies. A chair was rigged to the front part. It was almost macabre to see the elegant chair in such a position. And on the chair was a glass case ribbed with dark wood. Even in the state I was, my heart gave a lurch. I looked at my right foot. The rail seemed continuous. If it held it could be a way across the well's five or six-foot gap to reach the carriage. Surely it would take my weight? You sometimes hear of several landslips, one after another. Well, everything's a risk.

I got myself upright, pushing carefully on the lip of the narrow aperture through which I'd just wriggled. I drew several deep breaths for reserve and stuck the torch back in my mouth. No daft nonsense about balancing. I crouched down and dangled my legs over the rail, straddling it. Then I shuffled along, swinging my legs and using my hands. It took twelve shuffles. Then I actually touched the glass case. It was beautiful. A feeling rose up inside warming the whole universe. I knew the Contrivance was in there. And, praise God, it was mine. I vowed a forest of candles to St Osyth in thanks and swarmed off the rail on to the wagon. There was hardly room to move between the side of the carriage and the sloping wall of dried mud, but I got there. A huge wooden sleeper, torn somehow from its bed and projecting from the mass of earth, almost slammed me backwards towards the gaping well by wobbling on to the carriage as I disturbed it. It fell with an almighty thump alongside the carriage, projecting over the horrid dark space below as if waiting for somebody to walk the plank.

Breathless, I reached for the glass case. I think the torch gave a flicker, but I couldn't have cared less. I'd actually lifted it from the seat when I suddenly knew I felt wrong. The place felt wrong too. Everybody can feel another's presence. You don't have to hear them or see them or be touched. You can tell. Just as you can tell if there's one person in a crowd staring at you without you looking. You just feel it. And I felt it now.

'Lovejoy.' Such a soft voice, almost a whisper.

The word boomed softly and reverberated around the chamber. I yelped and dropped the torch. At least, it rolled and fell. I can't remember. But a sudden thick dull splash put my light out and I was in there with nothing. Trembling, I replaced the case, with my scalp crawling, felt around where I was standing on the edge of the carriage. Nothing. I hadn't even my jacket, with its matches and candles.

'Lovejoy.' Softly again, wheedling. They'd followed somehow. And now they were in the outer chamber through which I'd passed. It was my only way out.

It was a man's voice. Brummie. Somebody laughed. My skin prickled. I would have fainted if I hadn't been so frightened of falling into the bloody water deep down there and dying, alone but for two skeletons.

'We've come to help you, Lovejoy.'

I thought of trying to explain, offer, bargain, promise, anything to stop them leaving me entombed down here. I couldn't have got further from help if I'd tried. I swallowed, third go.

'Time to pass it over, Lovejoy.'

Two voices chuckled, comfortably and at ease. They had a nasal quality. Hell-fire. Both Brummies were in the outer chamber. They'd probably brought more weapons than the Tower of London. I felt the sweat start down from my armpits and sting my chin. They seemed to have no light, but they weren't daft.

'I'm stuck,' I said. It seemed a voice from light-years off. It whined feebly, a real cringing Tinker-type voice. I vowed never again to criticize Tinker, if ever I got out.

'Balls, Lovejoy.' One of them chuckled again. 'They said you'd try all sorts. Just chuck the stuff out and we'll call it quits.'

That was a laugh. They were going to do for me. I knew it. They knew it. All the rest was chit-chat.

'I'm stuck under this rail. You heard it go, you bastards.'

More muttering. There were only two. I couldn't imagine Fergus doing any of his own dirty work, especially with his leg, and Jake always stays behind the army.

'Under what, Lovejoy?'

'A bloody railway line, you stupid berk.'

'We're not sorry.'

They seemed to be biting, though what good it would do me . . . I thought hard, seeing in my mind's eye the interior of this chamber as it had looked from the aperture when I had a light. I hadn't known there was a well. Surely they didn't, either?

'Look, lads. A deal, eh?'

'That's more like it, Lovejoy.' Mutter, mutter. 'No tricks, mind. We've heard you're a leery bastard.'

There was only one way to handle this, I thought, fear tightening my throat and making it hard to breathe. If I showed anything less than absolute terror, even the slightest glimmer of hope, I'd give the show away. My only ally was a hole. But one from two equals one any way you look.

'Don't be stupid. How the hell can I?' I muttered to myself, complaining loudly of their idiocy the way I knew was realistic. God knows, I was scared enough. 'I've no light or anything.'

'Careless lad.'

'What do you want me to do?'

'Hand the thing out.'

'I can't. I *could* see it. Before my light went.'

'What is it?'

'I don't know,' I lied. 'Some sort of box. My lamp fell before I . . . before I got trapped. This bloody sleeper fell on me from the side.' Well, it nearly had.

'Stay there.'

Bloody fool. It just shows what sort of people are in antiques these days, doesn't it? I was narked even though they were going to crawl through the hole and kill me, the burkes.

I whimpered, 'If one of you just reached through you can take it. It's on the floor.'

'How far inside is it?'

'About eight feet.'

'Stay where you are.' Mutter, mutter. 'You go, Jim. Watch it,' I heard. 'He might have something.'

'We found all his gear,' the first voice said confidently.

A light blinded me for a second as a torch lit with a smart click. I glanced about swiftly. By standing balanced on the bent rail sagging its lunatic way across the deep well I could maybe create an impression of being on solid ground, though it would be difficult. Any time I could slip and fall . . .

'I can't move, you burke,' I snapped with a mixture of a Tinkerish cringe and anger. It was the best I could do. One seemed doubtful, muttering cautions. The other was perky and belligerent.

The light was abruptly blocked. It came through in one or two darts, equally swiftly doused. Somebody was in the crawl-way's aperture. I slid like I'd seen acrobats do on their rope, one foot before the other. My mouth was dry as a bone. I tried to blink but couldn't even do that. I felt the rail dip fractionally under my weight. I crouched for a second, but what if he had a torch and shone it downwards to look at me? He would see the well gaping beneath me and guess I'd tried to mislead him. And I'd be a goner.

'Pass it out, Lovejoy.'

The voice was so near I almost overbalanced and fell from fright.

'How the hell can I?' I snarled. 'I'm under this girder. It's my hand, trapped.' I wanted him to concentrate on the roof, the walls, the fall behind me. Anything but down.

'Stay there.' The light came in and blinded me, shining straight into my face. I swayed, my hand outstretched as if stuck somewhere out of his direct line of vision.

'I promise I won't move,' I quavered. It needed no acting skills. 'But promise you'll let me go if I pass it to you, eh, lads?'

'I promise,' his voice said again. I heard the second bloke chuckle.

His bulk blocked the light again. He called to his mate to shine his torch through. Small dashes of light struck into my chamber, but most was impeded by the first goon's bulk.

'Got you, Lovejoy.' I heard him come wriggling nearer.

The beam traversed my face and the walls behind me. They roved the ceiling and the carriage. I was only three feet from him. He wriggled out like a woodworm, head first. He carefully kept his eyes on me as he gripped the edge of the aperture, just as I had done, and swung lightly downwards. He dropped down, letting go. There was one slight difference. He simply kept on going. He went down and down. It was like a slow motion play. His expression changed, gradually turning from a domineering smile to one of horror. He simply sank without a sound, descending into the well. There came a ghastly wet thud. Something stirred sluggishly for a few seconds in the slime among the skeletons. I scrabbled back along the line babbling with terror and clung to the carriage. The image came of him rising covered with a terrifying macabre slime from the well's filthy mud and embracing me in a horrifying grip. I imagined his smiling face upturned, still smiling, as I scrabbled for brick after brick and dropped them down the well. I finished up hurling them down with all the force I could manage, mentally screaming abuse and hatred. The other nerk in the outer chamber must have thought the world had gone mad.

'Jim? Jim?' he was shouting. 'Are you okay?'

I paused, exhausted. 'He says stop there,' I bawled.

'Jim? Answer, Jim.'

'He says stop there.'

It was an inspired thing to say. I tried for utter weariness in my voice. Trying to say come on in would have tipped him off. He would go back for Jake or even Fergus. Or a hand-grenade. Or some foul thing to smoke me out. But telling him not to come in meant not only that Jim was boss in here, but was playing his mate off. Jim might have found something precious and was having it away. And leaving his mate with nothing.

I waited almost smugly while the poison worked. Then I was more terrified than ever. A goon thinking himself whittled would come in full of aggro. If he had a shooter he would shoot before anything else. And I knew he had a torch. Jim's lamp was down in the well with him, its light dying fast.

I cringed beside the bogie, chattering with fear. If he came in I could chuck a brick but the force would be too weak. And the angle wrong. And bricks have corners, to catch on the sides and lose their force. Anyway, he'd see me move.

'Jim?'

'He says stop there. I surrender, honest.'

'Jim! Pass it out. The thing Fergie wants.'

'I'm trapped. Honest.' I sounded at the end of my tether, which was about right.

'I'll come through,' he threatened. He was narked Jim was saying nothing. And concerned. 'I have a shooter, Lovejoy.'

'Jim says stay there,' I told him desperately.

He called, 'Watch out, Jim.'

There was a sudden flash. For an instant I was puzzled. Then I heard myself screaming and screaming. The bastard had shot through the aperture and my shoulder was burning and smarting.

I fell down, probably a reflex. The torch-light was jerking about. Either he was trying to see what was going on in here or he was already slithering his evil way in, the bastard.

'Get the message, Lovejoy?' he said through the mud-lined hole.

I thought of hiding, but where? I even thought of suicide, but the only place was the terrifying black well. The huge sleeper nearly overbalanced as I tried to shuffle away from the aperture. I lodged myself across the end near the carriage, and it held. I felt it with my palms, splinters ripping into my hands. It was a massive piece of wood balancing on the edge of a great hole. I pushed it gently. It rocked. It only needed the slightest extra weight on that far end for it to tilt downwards into the well. And maybe the whole chamber would go in with it.

'Jim!' He was becoming impatient. 'You all right? What the hell you doing?'

'He says I'm to wait here,' I yelled, thinking like mad: a heavy piece of wood rocking. If one end falls sharply, the other rises. A lever? 'He's gone to find the other way out.' I needed him to come through but not yet.

The goon was puzzled and suspicious. 'The fiddle still there?' He meant the casket.

'Yes.'

'Right, Lovejoy. I'm coming in.' Christ.

The torch flickered again. I crouched on the carriage end of the sleeper and tore my trousers off. Sweat was pouring down me, tickling and irritating. My hair kept guiding rivulets into my eyes. I zipped the empty trousers up and tied the leather belt round their waist, making a bag with two holes.

I clawed every loose brick in reach and stuffed them into the trouser leg.

'What's going on?'

'I'm trying to get free,' I yelled. I was as terrified as I sounded. 'I can't. Jim left me here. There's another tunnel, a way out.'

A shuffling began and the light blocked in fits and starts. He was coming. Oh God. I ran out of bricks. The weight was crippling. My shaking hands managed to tie the trouser legs in a loop. I spread myself over the inward end of the sleeper and began pushing my ungainly bag along it until I ran out of distance. Frantically I turned round and pushed it further with my feet. At one point my heart stopped. The bloody bag nearly tumbled over but I got it balanced again. A flicker of light came. I could just see the bag almost at the limit of the sleeper and I felt my end trying to lift under me as the bag of bricks weighted the other end of the wood. As soon as I rolled off, the weight of the bricks should swivel the sleeper. Its own immense weight would add to the speed and it would flip like a giant seesaw but with one horrible difference. It wouldn't stop and rock back the other way. It would go on, down and down. It was a crude non-stop ballista.

I rose, shaking. So I had a pivoting wood sleeper,

212

but now no missile. The exertion had been too great for my flabby body. My hands were uncontrollable. I retched a couple of times. I wobbled upright on my end of the home-made seesaw. Don't lose your balance and step off, Lovejoy, I begged myself. Please. But the missile?

There were no bricks left. Even if there had been, in the frightened state I was in I'd have piled them up wrong. There was only one heavy, dense projectile available. It had to be. With a groan of utter misery I groped back, touched the chair. The casket lid was gritty with dust and dried mud, but it opened easily.

I lifted the heavy metal object out gently, still balancing. The thrill of feeling it made my fingers tingle and steady. The goon was breathing stertorously, shuffling towards me along the crawl-way. He'd had the wit to bundle a jacket. He was pushing it ahead of him, probably as a shield in case I chucked anything, suspicious sod. I felt my precious object's contours. It was a silky model of an early engine. I didn't look, in the faint glow now coming from the aperture, just crouched and placed the silver miracle at my feet on the sleeper. We waited, both of us. Me practically naked, like a springboard diver waiting his turn at the back end of a diving board, and the precious diminutive gleaming silver machine, throbbing with the life instilled in it so long ago, on the wood between my feet. Standing there I was the trigger of my vast and clumsy home-made weapon.

The torch-light touched my eyes. I raised both hands, squinting towards the aperture.

'Don't shoot, don't shoot!' I squawked. 'Please, mate. Your pal's gone through there.' I pointed to my right. 'I'm stuck.'

The bastard held me like that for what seemed an hour. Of course, he could only see my top half from his position along the crawl-way, but that didn't make me feel any easier.

'Stay like that.' There was a pause. The swine was wondering whether it would be wiser to shoot me now.

'Jim told me to show you the other exit.' Pretty feeble, but it was the best lie I could invent to increase my paltry value.

He thought another minute. 'Pass it out first, Lovejoy.'

'How the hell can I? My leg's stuck fast.'

'You said it was your arm.'

'Jim got that out.'

Another pause. 'Just stand still, Lovejoy. I don't trust you.'

He squirmed nearer, slower and more careful.

There was enough light now from the jerking torch for me to look at the sleeper. The gruesome sights in the deep well kept trying to drag my eyes past the wood and down to the horribly fascinating mess at the bottom. I made myself judge the distance from the well's crumbly edge to my silver missile. The length that would lash upwards was about the same as the aperture's exit was high, more or less. But any more or any less and the beautiful model would smash into the chamber wall. And he'd hear it go, and guess something was wrong. He'd see me move, anyway, and let fly. The torch went out. I had to remember the distances. Maybe the distance was too small? Maybe I'd misjudged . . . I almost bent down to move the silver piece back an inch. My mouth was dry as a rasp.

The torch came on suddenly, so near I felt I could have reached out and touched it. Too late. I stood with my trembling arms raised, blinded. I'd forgotten. How can you judge if a goon's in position if you're blinded? Oh Christ. I closed my eyes. I'd have to listen. But if his head actually projected into the chamber he would be able to look down and see his mate Jim decomposing below. Then he'd kill me. Never mind then what happened to the silver or to the goon. I'd be gone. So

I had to step off and let the sleeper tilt upwards when he was all but within reach.

'Keep like that, Lovejoy.' Shuffle, shuffle.

I opened my eyes. The torch blinded me. It looked near yet no nearer. I couldn't gauge distances any more from dazzle. Then I heard a faint splash from the well below. A fragment of the aperture lip must have fallen. So it must have been pushed, by the goon framed in the aperture. *Now*. I simply stepped back off the huge wooden beam.

All hell seemed let loose. Wood tore my left shin with enormous force. The well quivered and shook. A brick clattered on the carriage. All in a second, dust filled the chamber and a terrible rushing noise came from somewhere far below. A deep thud came instantaneously, and a thick sucking sound. The torch went out. I opened my eyes, squinting and terrified, and crouched clinging to the iron rail in case the whole bloody floor fell away from under me. My mind screeched, stay still, stay *still*. Maybe the silver had somehow missed him and crashed into the dried mud and he was just waiting me out. A stand-off. I tried not to choke on the dust, but I had to breathe. That set me spluttering and coughing, giving myself away. Then I fell silent. The mud below stopped popping and sucking. The sleeper was probably sinking into it forever. I felt sick. There was no sound.

Silently I inched my way along the rail. The gap beneath felt like outer space. If the swine was still there . . . I touched the mud wall ahead and used it to support my forward weight balancing on the rail. I wobbled up straight shakily and stretched out into the blackness. The lip of the aperture felt covered by a folded coat. My touch produced no movement. Nothing. I carefully pulled at the coat. It came free, and I let it fall, making sure no precious silver object went into the well with it. That left only a long hole with a goon in it. I could hear nothing breathing. I reached out.

My hand touched my luscious silver, the cold, beautiful metal. It was embedded in something sticky and running with warm slime. Relief and nausea made me momentarily dizzy. Hard warm splinters of shattered skull-bone pricked at me. I pulled the silver free with difficulty. Still balancing on the rail and leaning on the mud-wall I tore off my shirt and singlet to wrap the silver in. I slithered back and regained the carriage, cautiously clutching the bundle and sat exhausted, my hands sticky with congealing mess, on the carriage chair as the Right Honourable Jonathan Chase had so many years ago. I'm not sure, but I think I blacked out for a while, even though all I wanted was to get the hell out.

The funny thing is it never occurred to me that I'd actually made it. All I could think of was that I was entombed deep in a hill and sick of trying to get myself not killed by everybody. Getting the goon out of the crawl-way was a nightmare of ugliness. I don't know what happened to the torch or his gun because I never found them. It must have taken me hours to pull him free. I stopped a million times to be sick. Hell can't be as bad, that's for sure. The silver had pierced his face, rammed through the facial structure and created a terrible porridge of bone slivers and tissue. His shoulders kept sticking as I pulled and pulled. When he finally tumbled, like a cork from a bottle, I was nearly carried down into the frigging well with him. He seemed all limbs. I just managed to get both arms wound round the rail when his falling body made me overbalance. The metal sagged but held, creaking and bouncing slightly. As his body glugged and squelched, far down, I thought a weary prayer for him. People have to do whatever lights their candle. I admit that. Pity that his had snuffed out, but that wasn't my fault, was it?

The way out was open and free.

Chapter Nineteen

The only difference in the outer chamber was that I could see the bottom of the well-shaft down which I'd climbed. Very vaguely, but definitely. My eyes must have become accustomed to the faint washes of light, such as they were. I could see the rail lines in the grey-black on the ground under the shaft. I never glanced back once I came out through the aperture. My clothes-line lay in a heap, but there was a natty rope ladder dangling, twice as long as needed. They'd come better prepared than I had. I fell over it from trying to go easy, frightening myself because I still couldn't bring myself to trust the floor. They'd brought a pick and shovel. There was a spare torch, but I didn't need extra weight any more. And I wasn't too keen on inspecting myself, either, 1 knew I'd come through smeared with blood, brains, caked with dried mud. And some of the blood was mine. My feet felt swollen. To my surprise I was limping.

I unwrapped the silver engine and used the only legitimate water I owned. I peed on the object to wash it, then dried it on my socks. My singlets and shirt I left there. The engine just fitted into my underpants. I held one hem in my teeth, making sure it was evenly contained and wouldn't slip out of the leg holes. There was no question of resting. When you're in a tomb the first thing is to get out.

The distance between each brick foothold felt enormous at the start of the upward climb. My heart was banging like a train. I had to pause and hold on every second reach, and it wasn't just that I was going up this time, not down. I was simply done for. Time had gone, yet without me knowing how. In fact, I was so useless that I almost nodded off in mid-climb from weariness as the shaft curved towards the horizontal. The silver piece nearly slid out of the cloth, but I held it between my chest and the brickwork until I got myself straight again. I could see light ahead. Lovely, dazzling, glaring light. I crawled forward on my hands and knees, grinning, weary but jubilant.

Astonishing, it was still daylight. I caught on the edge of the hole, blinded by the brilliance of the grey overcast sky. One last haul got me up and sprawled panting on the stubby grass under the gorse bush. I could have wept with relief.

'It's Lovejoy. The bastard's naked.'

Fergus and Jake were smoking cigarettes further up the hill, and staring incredulously down at me. They appeared set for a long wait, judging from the scattered fag-ends and the sandwich wrappings blowing about. Both rose, Fergus on a stick. I almost fell back in the hole.

'You're in a fucking mess, Lovejoy.' Fergus wasn't beaming any more.

Jake asked, bewildered, 'Where's Jim and Cooney?'

With a squeal I turned and staggered at a low run as he moved at me, and plunged down-hill through the gorse line. If I could reach the pub ahead of them I'd survive. People would be on the road by now, surely to God. I heard Jake give a shout. Then they were after me, shouting and swearing at each other. Down on the road a car crawled by. I tried waving, but nearly dropped my prize. Anyhow, stopping to help a filthy blood-smeared maniac sprinting down a hillside is nobody's idea of a tea-time tryst. So I just ran and ran down, really only falling forwards and forcing my legs to be there to catch me. This way I kept going, but only just.

With two hundred yards to go to the pub car park I

glanced back. Jake was nearer. I found myself slowing, though I tried to keep going. Weariness enveloped me. I'd not make it. I was gasping this to myself when Elspeth Haverill suddenly rose in my way, just rose out of the ground, her eyes wide. She gave a faint scream. I collided with her and we rolled over, down in the tussocky grass. I cut myself yet again, this time on her frigging clip-board.

'Fergus.' Jake had halted uncertainly when I looked at them. Fergie was limping after, eyes hard. Elspeth was trying to compose herself. She was frightened stiff.

'Lovejoy!' She gazed at me, open-mouthed. There were small piles of clothing laid out in a row in front of her.

Fergus waved to his mate. 'Get it, Jake.'

I sat down, bone weary. I'd had enough. I thought of throwing Elspeth the silver, but she was winded by our collision.

'Right.'

They were moving down towards us slowly, Jake first, when I heard it. It was lovely. A beautiful sound of footsteps plodding and flopping along the hillside, and the rasping sound of middle-age in the torment of exercise. Round the hill, flabby and rotund, trundled six of Elspeth's runners. They were dishevelled and looked pathetic, but I'd never seen a lovelier sight.

I couldn't even rise to watch them come. They were on us in a few weak strides. They slowed to a stop and stood panting, staring. One pointed at me in astonishment, his belly heaving, and his sweating face a mottled purple. I must have looked in a hell of a state. The others edged closer. One, brighter than the rest, glanced at Jake and Fergus, back to Elspeth and me. Then he stepped closer and picked up a stone. Two others did the same. It wasn't much of an army, but for the first time in my life my side outnumbered everybody else's. Jake looked at Fergus. Fergus looked at Jake.

'Here,' I wheezed suddenly. 'What are you doing?'

Elspeth was fiddling with my middle.

'Putting this towel round you, Lovejoy.' Of course. I was naked.

I let her. We all watched Jake and Fergus turn and go. Their car was parked across the rear of mine. I couldn't have got it out unless they shifted theirs first, anyway. We saw Jake heave a cobblestone through my windscreen. He looked back at us defiantly. I bowed to annoy them as they pulled out.

'What's all this about, Miss Haverill?' the front runner asked.

'This gentleman fell down a crevice in the hillside,' Elspeth said glibly. In the forecourt below the car started. One or two of them thought to ask more but Elspeth wasn't having any. She clicked a stopwatch.

'I would remind you that it's *twice* round,' she instructed. 'Starting now.'

The team plodded off, some casting glances back at me. I watched Fergie's car out of sight, going towards town along the river road.

'I owe you, love,' I told Elspeth.

'What happened up there, Lovejoy?'

'Tell you later. Look. What do I do?' If I set off in my crate in this state I'd be arrested at the first traffic lights.

'Sit here and rest,' she commanded. 'You're exhausted. When the others come back I'll take you home. We'll pretend you're one of my exercise team, and that you fell and hurt yourself. I have a sponge bag and towel. We can get some of that filth off in the meantime. What *is* it? Maybe my men can lend you some spare clothes, if they have any.'

'Why are you here?' I lay on the grass, clutching the silver still wrapped in my underpants. 'I thought the run was from the surgery.'

'Oh, I fancied a change.' She got a cold wet sponge and started on my legs. 'I knew you'd come here, you

221

see. From your questions. I went to your cottage, then drove here and saw your old motor. So I fetched my runners along.'

'What if I hadn't showed up?' I asked from curiosity. 'What would you have done?'

'Mind your own business.' She squeezed the sponge over my middle and made me gasp. She tapped my silver. 'Is that toy train what you were looking for?'

I looked at the exquisite silver engine properly for the first time, holding it up against the sky from my supine position. Quite like an offering to a world full of beautiful space and air and light.

'Yes. Isn't it beautiful?'

'Quite nice,' she said critically. 'But it's bent.'

I said, 'So it is. Wonder how that happened?'

Elspeth got me home. One of the runners promised to drop my crate off at the White Hart for Tinker to collect. A sweaty tracksuit was provided from somewhere.

'You know,' I explained as she drove, 'Poor old Jonathan Chase must have had a nerve.'

'Can't you put that toy on the back seat, Lovejoy?'

I was holding it in my lap. I trusted her, but said, 'It's too valuable.'

I wondered about the respectable Right Honourable gentleman. He had obviously arranged for an explosion to take place and cause a landslip. Of course, his plan was a risk. I felt a twinge of my subterranean fear return momentarily, and wound the window down for air. In fact, it nearly killed him outright. The plan was to halt the little carriage at the one fixed reinforced spot of the tunnel that had withstood the earth's subtle shifts from time immemorial. That was where the tunnel bisected the well-shaft.

The carriage had stopped. On cue, the explosion had caused the landslip. Chase had dug his way through to the well, pulled the bricks out and climbed up. At the top he had simply pulled gorse in the hole, to cover it up. And there it grew, year after year.

He'd had to have some luck, because his plans had gone slightly askew. I could tell that. The landslip had gone faster and further than predicted. But he'd made it, done his act, and successfully lived to finance the rival route. The clever, wicked old devil.

His two engineers would have been in on the plan. They had to be. But why those two tough men had ended up at the bottom of the well when the Right Honourable had managed to escape probably didn't bear thinking about. They probably got a percussion ball in each earhole, from one of those folding trigger pistols we antique dealers are always after. The truth was obvious. Jonathan Chase, pillar of Victorian society, was a scoundrel. And old Doc Chase, maybe not realizing how valuable the silver piece would be, and anyway fearful for his family's reputation – as if that ever matters – kept watch over what he knew to be the terrible evidence of his ancestor's perfidy. You couldn't blame an old bloke of his generation, though. It was only natural. I suppose it needs a scrounger like me to ignore reputations.

'What will you do with it?'

'Eh? Oh.' I thought for a minute and cleared my throat for a lie. 'Give it to the museum, I suppose.'

'Will you? Honestly?'

She looked so moved I was moved too. 'Hand on my heart,' I promised with sincerity.

She smiled radiantly. 'I'm so pleased, Lovejoy.' She squeezed my arm. 'He would have loved that.'

'In memory of him,' I said piously. Being praised is quite pleasant.

'Will there be a formal presentation?' She was already planning a new frock.

'Er, no,' I said, all modest. 'I wouldn't like people to think I was blowing my own trumpet.'

'You're really sweet, Lovejoy.' She turned to me mistily.

'Stop a second. ı actually felt sweet, grotesquely smug.

There was a phone-box at a cross-roads. I dialled emergency. The operator clicked me breathlessly through to a narky policewoman who wanted to start filling in forms.

'Hark,' I interrupted her questions. 'You've got a grouser called Maslow on your books. Tell him Lovejoy rang.'

'We don't pass on personal messages through this telephone exchange,' she told me with asperity. 'This is for emergencies.'

'This is for murder,' I continued. 'Say I'm prepared to make a statement of evidence.' Now I need not say anything about Sue being the other witness. When Fergie and Jake got their ugly mugs in the papers the Brummie mob would start asking nasty questions about their missing pair of nerks. Jake and Fergie would be for it either way. Poor lads, I thought, smiling.

Elspeth chatted happily all the way home. She assumed I had phoned my decision to the museum, and was so pleased. I didn't disillusion her.

The cottage felt as if I had been away for years. Elspeth gasped at the sight of all the furniture and the treens everywhere, but I ran a bath and didn't explain. We decided to go out and celebrate. Elspeth had enough money for us to have a real splash.

I was drying myself when this car came screaming down the lane in third gear. It stopped in the gateway, and Moll emerged, dressed in a smart new green suit. She knows I like green. See what I mean about women? There's no letting up, minds always on the go.

I honestly wasn't trying to keep out of the way, but it didn't seem my sort of scene. I'd had the silver model in the bath with me, soaping it. None of your scraping and sanding for precious silver, please. Mild soap and ordinary water is about the limit, followed by a cold but gentle towel. Having to leave the presentation case was a pity, but I wasn't going back for it at any price. I'd knock up a quick fake instead. That would really set it off, pretty as a picture. Imagine the millions of people who'd get pleasure from seeing it beautifully displayed in our Castle Museum. I finished wiping the silver surface dry while Moll and Elspeth nattered at the door.

'Lovejoy's rather busy,' Elspeth's voice announced, frosty.

'Not to me he isn't, dear.' Moll sounded confident and oversweet.

'For everyone. *Dear*.' Elspeth was obviously going to stand her ground. I made no noise.

'I'm in a somewhat different category,' from Moll.

'That's quite possible, *Mrs* Maslow,' Elspeth shot back.

I slipped on my clothes and wrapped the silver in a dry towel. Time for Tinker to bowl up. The idle swine was still swigging ale somewhere, though I'd phoned him almost an hour ago on the way back. I'll cripple him, I thought furiously.

'Tell Lovejoy I'm here,' Moll ordered.

'If this is in the course of police investigations . . . ' Elspeth's voice turned the sugar on.

'Lovejoy is my *partner*.'

I gasped from behind the bathroom door. *Partner* was beginning to have a nasty permanent ring about it. She must have read more into buying all that bloody treen than I had.

'He hasn't a partner.'

'Where do you think he acquired this houseful?'

It was time I left, even if it was on foot. I ducked and crawled between the furniture. There is a back door, but the hedge is thick and there's no way

225

through. I'd have to make it round the side and some-how cut out of my gate.

The sound came when I was crawling round my little unfinished wall at the rear of the cottage. The beautiful, melodious clattering of my sewing-machine engine. Tinker, with my crate, bless him. I was still blazing, but if I was quick . . . Get down there before they saw me. And before he turned into the garden.

A rapid sidle round the cottage wall, ducking beneath the sill to avoid being seen through the kitchen window, worse than any gangster in a shoot-out. Flat-tened against the side wall I peered round. The splutt-ering sounded nearer and nearer.

'It isn't a question of being obstructive, Mrs Maslow.' They were still at it, with Elspeth gaining the upper hand. She didn't seem to have let Moll in yet.

'Don't you think you are rather misunderstanding your functions?' Moll's voice. The chips were down. 'You're behaving rather like a wardress – '

It was warming up. I knew from the sudden easing of the engine's chug that Tinker had reached the chapel. Only one place to turn, about a hundred yards up. *Now.*

I clutched the silver in the towel and ran. On tiptoe, like a bloody fool, as if grass echoes. I drew breath and ran straight into the hedge as gently as I could. Luckily Moll's car blocked the gateway. I was round it in a flash and scarpering up the lane as my crate rum-bled into view. Tinker was driving, and he had Lemuel with him. He knows I hate Lemuel in the crate, because he always leaves a liberal sprinkling of fleas behind. I spend a fortune on those sprays.

Tinker saw me waving frantically and screeched – well, creaked – to a stop. I hurtled up, signalling him to turn. He was already backing when I undid the door and fell in.

'Get going, Tinker,' I gasped.

'I fetched Lemuel for the aggro,' Tinker explained,

desperately wobbling the gear stick. It's a bit loose. I'll have it mended when I get a minute. Luckily, we dealers always carry blankets. I wriggled under one and lay still, pleading, 'Hurry, for gawd's sake, Tinker.'

We rumbled forward.

'No scrapping, Lovejoy?' Lemuel quavered thankfully.

'It's all done, Lemuel.' Already I was beginning to itch.

Another car sounded ahead of us. A horn tooted. 'Sod it,' from Tinker. We stopped.

'Tinker.' Sue's voice. 'Is Lovejoy home?'

'Er, just dropped him off there, lady.'

'Thank you.'

And she was gone. 'Great, Tinker,' I told him, still muffled under the blanket.

'That all right, Lovejoy?' Tinker asked as we pulled away again. 'Here. What happened to the Brummies?'

'What Brummies?' I said under my blanket. 'There aren't any Brummies.' It was hellish uncomfortable bumping on the motor's tin floor. If only the springs hadn't gone. Sue usually brings cushions.

'Course there are, Lovejoy,' Lemuel croaked earnestly. 'That Fergie's got two frigging big hard nuts to do you – '

His voice was nudged to a thoughtful silence, probably by Tinker's elbow.

I could tell we'd reached the chapel. Tinker was just going to turn right when another motor came close to the van's side and throbbed in my lughole.

'*Stop*, Dill.' Maslow's voice, the bastard.

'Where's Lovejoy?' Oh, hell. *Tom* Maslow's voice now.

'He's, er, at the cottage, Mr Maslow,' Tinker said suddenly. We all hate talking to the Old Bill.

'With that bird with the big knockers,' Lemuel said, cackling evilly.

'That's enough from you.' The engine boomed and went off in smooth top gear, burning my taxes.

Lemuel fell about laughing. He and Tinker would be on about having tricked Maslow for months now. 'They couldn't find a bottle in a brewery.'

'Where to, Lovejoy?'

I stayed silent as we trundled towards the main road. The cottage would be like a carnival, what with Maslow wanting my evidence, and Sue charging in on the existing war between Moll and Elspeth. And from the Maslows' manner they had harsh words for Moll. Maybe Elspeth would catch it, as well, for not informing on me the way Maslow wanted. And Elspeth would fly at Sue for wrongly giving Moll her name that time . . . It was a right mess. The trouble is that absolutely none of it was my fault. Not one bit. I honestly don't know who gets me in these shambles, but it's not me, that's for sure.

'Where to, Lovejoy?' Tinker said again.

I was suddenly happy. I held one of the most valuable pieces of post-Georgian silver probably ever made. Me. I was here with it, embracing it. In my very own motor.

But then I remembered my promise to give it to a museum, the promise which had moved Elspeth so deeply. I'd been really magnanimous, maybe too magnanimous. After all, who'd been sick with terror deep in the earth, down a well full of unspeakable horrors, risking his life hour after hour? Yet I'd promised.

On the other hand, was my promise spontaneous? Given of my own free will and accord? Or had it been extorted from me? Wrung out of my unwilling soul by Elspeth's cunning playing on my emotions? Under the blanket I seethed with indignation.

'Lovejoy. Where the frigging hell are we going?'

Jill's place is a haven full of hardworking vannies, so that was out. Margaret's was too near the cop-shop. Lily would instantly phone Patrick, who would be so excited at helping to conceal me for a few days I'd not last an hour. Lemuel's is a doss-house full of fleas. Tinker's place is so grotty it's indescribable. Big Frank has so many bigamous wives that he's always being followed by divorce agents. I ran my mind down the list of friends. And suddenly Helen came to mind. I could see her now in the White Hart, smiling and smoking and stretching her lovely long legs towards the carpet.

'Eh?' Tinker was asking. 'You all right?'

I must have moaned. Helen could be trusted, if I owned up to escaping from Sue and the others. And Helen always had a good string of buyers for precious silver. Well, the bloody museum would want me to *give* it to them, as a totally free gift. Cheek. After all I'd done. And as for Elspeth, worming that ridiculous promise out of me so treacherously . . . I decided I'd go back to the cottage in a week or so. I like surprises.

'Drop me at Helen's, Tinker,' I said, and smiled under the blankets as we took off.

THE VATICAN RIP

Chapter One

The trouble with life is, you start off worse and go downhill. I'd bought the rip in winter, two days before my Italian lessons with the delectable Maria were to begin – though I didn't know that then.

I'm an antique dealer. The antiques game is always at a lowish ebb in January, probably because everybody's spent up after Christmas and is knackered by the weather anyway, so I was on the scrounge and feeling very sorry for myself. It hadn't been too easy of late, what with inflation and all that. And the scanty tourists who knock about East Anglia in deep midwinter tend to be holy, on their way to carol services in our ancient little chapels. They aren't so keen on our priceless (or indeed worthless) antiques.

On this particular day the roads out of my village were bad. There had been one of those heavy snowfalls the previous night after a solid weekend of sustained gales. Typically, the buses never even started out from the nearby town, and as far as civilization was concerned our village might have been on Mars. A couple of lads from Hall Farm managed to shift the worst snowdrifts using tractors and got the south road partially cleared by noon. I was lucky – so I thought – and got a lift in from Ann Scott, the cheerful and pretty lace-mad wife of an insurance assessor. She tried telling me that the famous nineteenth-century torchon lace was superior to Honiton if properly made. We argued all the way. She was wrong, of course. 'Torchon' means dishcloth, but she wouldn't be told. She has a valuable collection of lace samplers I'd been trying to buy from her on tick for years. We'd had several intimate after-noon negotiations. I'd lost every one on a pinfall.

'You can show me the error of my ways, Lovejoy,' she said, straight-faced and careful as she dropped me off in front of the town hall. 'Before five, this after-noon.'

'Any chance of you selling?'

She smiled, not looking. The traffic swished slowly past through the mush. 'Come and find out.'

'When is Henry back?' I'm always worried about new risks because there are so many old ones knocking about.

'Six. Come early.'

'Right. Thanks.'

She checked the traffic in her driving mirror and pulled out with a cool disregard for the road code. I winced at the squealing tyres and the honks of protest and observed her serene passage off down the High Street. That's women for you. All the breaks and none of the breakages.

The auction was well under way when I finally made it out of the cold and into the fug.

Seddon's Auction Rooms is basically a long derelict shed with alleged antiques crammed into every avail-able bit of space. I saw that today's auctioneer was Millon, a florid-faced, waistcoated know-all who believes the world owes him a living. My spirits rose. He was a newcomer and therefore by definition dimmer even than the regular auctioneers, which is to say beyond belief. Fewer dealers than ever had turned up today on account of the snow. I offered up a prayer of thanks, because fewer bidders means cheaper prices, even among this load of crooks. Still, the one thing you can say about crooks is they're honest, not like the good old law-abiding public. And speaking of crooks, the auctioneer was gavelling again.

'Lot Forty-One. A small genuine antique silver bookmark. Who'll give me fifty to start?'

A hand touched my elbow. Even before looking round I knew from the pong it was Tinker. Bleary as ever, a crumpled alcoholic old reject in a stained army greatcoat, greasy of mitten and threadbare of gear. A stub of a person, but my one and only employee. He's my barker, a sniffer-out of antiques. The greatest.

'Hiyer, Lovejoy. Your crowd from the Arcade have gone for a bite.'

I knew better than to argue. Tinker locates dealers and antiques by some kind of mental beam. Somebody morosely bid a fiver for Lot Forty-One and the bidding was off, to the auctioneer's relief. He didn't deserve such good fortune. Instead he should have been gaoled, because he had deliberately called a false description, an offence punishable by law. The 'genuine antique silver bookmark' was no such thing. Genuine and silver, yes. Antique and a bookmark, no. It was late Victorian and thus not 'antique' by honest definition (and here I exclude the Customs Office which, being unable to count above double figures, has reluctantly pretended for years that antiques begin at a hundred years of age). And it was a *page* marker. These delectable little objects are very collectable, being usually silver or even gold. Most have a split blade to slide over a page's edge leaving the decorated handle protruding. About two-and-a-half inches and all sorts of shapes-scissors, carving knives, pipes, swords, leaves and the like. Lovely. My mouth watered. If I hadn't been broke . . .

'Jane Felsham with them?'

'Aye.'

I cheered up even more. She would be back for the paintings which I saw began about Lot Ninety in today's heap of gunge.

'Jason?'

'Him too.' My spirits fell again. Lately Jason had been seeing Jane more than he deserved. Only I deserved to see Jane Felsham that much, but seeing I was broke and Jason wealthy . . .

Tinker cleared his throat, warming up for one of his famous rasping coughs. I drew a deep breath to last me through the droplet haze. Tinker's cough started as a deep rumble full of such powerful reverberations that several of the crowd glanced idly towards the windows, wondering what kind of monster vehicle could possibly be making that racket on East Hill. It then intensified, growling and lifting in tone and bubbling as the phlegm in Tinker's stringlike windpipe churned. The volume intensified and swelled sending shudders through the brickwork. Finally out it came, a great explosion in a slamming din of sound, a noise so cacophonous it rapped your eardrums. Tinker's wiry little frame jerked double and bobbed with the effort. It's a pity they don't give Olympic coughers' medals. The Russians wouldn't stand a chance. Tinker would walk it.

I opened my eyes in relief as the appalling noise dwindled, Tinker rejoined the human race, wiping his nose on the back of his filthy mitten, his rheumy old eyes streaming from the relief of having coughed and survived. The entire auction room was stunned into an appalled silence.

Tinker was contentedly rolling himself a fresh cigarette when he noticed the ominous stillness.

'Pardon,' he croaked.

A few of the dealers chuckled and nudged each other. And even Helen from the Arcade, the loveliest dealer in East Anglia, smiled at Tinker. The trouble was that Millon chose to be offended, which led to his downfall. Antiques are dear, but there's nothing so costly as pride.

'Who made that awful noise?' he parped. He knew very well who.

The place stilled. Tinker stopped rolling his fag.

'That corf? Me.' Tinker was indignant. 'I said me pardon.'

Millon lost his rag. 'Get *out*! I will not have this auction interrupted by any old doss-house lounger!'

Poor old Tinker was stricken. He glanced apprehensively at me, knowing I needed him for a Kwangtung temple-door carving I had my eye on among the high numbers. A couple of the local dealers, suddenly nervous, shot glances at me. I saw Alfred Duggins, an elderly bowler-hatted collector of hammered coins, roll his eyes in alarm. He'd known me since I was a callow youth and guessed what was coming.

Mortified, Tinker shuffled sideways towards the door. 'Sorry, Lovejoy. I'll see me quack, get something for me chest. Honest.' He thought I was mad at him for one lousy cough.

I said nothing. I was looking at the floor, planks in a row and worn to the nails by generations of people coming in this crummy auction just because they wanted an antique, a piece of the loving past to cherish them against the shoddy crapology of our modern world. In this generation those ordinary people just happen to be Tinker and me. And you.

'Do-you-*hear*-me?' bleated this nerk on the rostrum.

'I'm going, mate,' Tinker muttered.

'Tinker.' I gave him a quid. My voice sounded funny. 'Wait in the pub. I'll only be ten minutes.'

'Ta. But the auction won't be over till – '

He peered at my face and then quickly went, his old boots clumping until the door pinged shut behind him. By now old Alfred was at the door, nervously measuring distances for a quick getaway. Trust him to suss me out before the rest.

Millon announced, pompously tugging his waistcoat neater, 'Now we can get *on*! Lot Forty-One. The bid's with you, sir.' He pointed to a tall neat gabardine-suited bloke, who had bid last in a foreign accent. 'It was fifty pounds. Who'll give fifty-five?'

I found Helen's hand on my arm. '*Please* no, Lovejoy,' her voice begged. But it was miles off and I shrugged her away.

Millon was chanting, 'Fifty-five anywhere?' when I coughed. The place stilled again. It was nothing like a Tinker special, but I did the best I could.

'Who'll give me fifty-five for this – ?'

I coughed again, a non-cough phoney enough to gall anyone. Millon glared in my direction. 'Sir. Please control your noise or I shall have to ask you to leave also.'

So I was a sir and Tinker was a doss-house lounger. I coughed again, looking deliberately at Millon. He reddened and for the first time noticed that the other bidders had silently begun to recede, leaving a clear space around me. I heard Alfred mutter, 'Oh Gawd!' The door pinged once as he slid out. Wise old bird.

Millon's voice wavered but he gamely went on, 'In view of the interruptions we will leave Lot Forty-One in abeyance and go on to Lot Forty-Two, which is Chippendale – '

'No.' That was me, trying for a normal voice but it came out like a whipcrack.

He stared. I smiled back. In that moment one of the strangers next to the big bloke started to say something but he was pulled up by a kindly friend, which saved him a lot of trouble, whoever he was. I heard another voice murmur, 'Watch it, mate. That's Lovejoy.'

Millon's gaze wobbled. For confidence, he stared belligerently to where his three miffs were standing. Miffs are auctioneers' callers who hump stuff about and make sure potential bidders get the barest glimpse of the lots next on offer. They were looking anywhere else. You have to smile. Sometimes they behave like real people.

'What do you mean, *no*?' Millon snapped, which only goes to show how dumb auctioneers can be.

'I mean your "Chippendale" bureau is a fake.'

There was a babble of alarmed chatter, quickly fading.

Millon practically went berserk.

'This is outrageous! I'm putting you out this instant! *And* I'm having you sued for – '

That old familiar white heat glow came in my head. I gave up trying to be patient and found myself walking forward, the mob parting like a bow wave. Everybody gave me their attention, especially when I told them to.

'All of you listen,' I said. 'Lift his Chippendale bureau up. It's the wrong weight for its size. Look at the righthand drawer – you'll find a pattern of old filled-in screw holes. It's oak all right, but nicked from a World War One vintage bedroom cupboard. And the ageing stain's phoney. Invert the drawers and you'll see the paler shrinkage lines round the edges.' I looked up at Millon, now looking considerably less assured. I added, 'It's not Chippendale, chum. It's a bodged mock-up.'

An angry murmur rose from the crowd. Millon paled. I felt so happy.

Blithely I sailed on, 'Like that old sextant.' It had been proudly displayed in the window all week. 'Did you tell them it isn't really seventeenth-century, Millon?' I explained how even with a small handlens you can spot modern high-rev lathe work.

Millon was going green. The ugly groundswell of muttering intensified. He bleated, 'These allegations are quite unfounded – '

'And that old Dutch microscope, Millon,' I announced with jubilation. 'You catalogued it as a mint original. The lenses are whittled-down spectacle lenses from a three-penny stall. Any optician will tell you how it's done.'

Somebody shouted, 'Well, Millon? What about it, eh?' Another dealer yelled, 'I bought that ivory, Millon – '

'Taiwan,' I put in before the dazed auctioneer could draw breath. 'They simulate the grain.' With a wax coating pitted by a kitchen cheese-shredder and a dilute solution of phosphoric acid you can give almost any plastic a detailed texture of ivory. Unscrupulous forgers of antiques can mass-produce them if you make a template, though I've found (er, I mean I've *heard*) the moulds don't really last very long.

'Please, gentlemen.' The nerk tried to gavel but it only irritated everyone still more.

'What about this miniature?' That was the big Continental bloke. He was looking not at Millon but directly at me, which I thought odd. Nor did he seem worried at having risked his money on a load of tat. The man next to him, obviously one of his many serfs, was holding up a small filthy medallion-sized disc covered by a dirty piece of glass. Even across the angry crowd in that dingy hall I felt that luscious shudder deep inside my chest. My breathing went funny, and I shook to the chime of heavenly bells.

For me all strife momentarily ceased, and I was in Paradise. I was in the presence of a genuine sixteenth-century miniature, possibly even done by the great Hilliard himself. I groaned audibly and felt tears start in my eyes.

The big geezer laughed, a strange noise like a cat's cough. I didn't need to explain my jealousy because it must have showed on my face. He had made himself an absolute fortune and suddenly I hated him more than fried liver, the bastard.

I turned away and raised my voice over the babble. 'Pay attention, troops. That bobbin tree catalogued as late Hanoverian is actually brand new, and imported pinewood at that.' I could have gone into details of how fruitwood and laburnum can be simulated in these delectable household necessities of Regency days, but you can't educate antique dealers so it's no use bothering.

'Please. You're ruining – '

'That Civil War cavalry pistol's a fake,' I continued, pointing. 'A cut-down Eastern jezail with a Turkish barrel. Note the – '

I would have gone on because I was just getting into my stride, but with a howl the dam broke. A beefy gorilla in from the Smoke shouldered me out of the way. The furious dealers grabbed for Millon, the poor goon shrieking for help but of course his three miffs had vanished and he disappeared in a mound of flying limbs. I spent the next few seconds eeling my way from the pandemonium, smiling blissfully. The place was in uproar as I pinged out into the cold.

Happier now, I plodded the few snowy yards to the Ship. I could still hear the racket from the auction rooms as I pushed open the tavern door. Tinker was hunched over a pint at the bar. He started at the sight of me. 'Look, Lovejoy. I could get old Lemuel to help instead.'

'Shut it.' I gave him the bent eye and he subsided into silence but still managed to drain his pint. His gnarled countenance led me to understand a refill was a matter of survival, so I paid up. It was in that split second while Tinker's pint glass remained miraculously full that I felt the most horrid sense of foreboding. I started to slurp at my own glass in an attempt to shake it off just as a hand tapped my shoulder.

'*Lovejoy.*'

Chris Anders was normally a taciturn geezer but now his face was puce with fury. He is domestic pre-Victorian furniture – that treacherous shifting sand of the antiques world – and late Victorian jewellery, and good at both. I quite like him but at the moment I wasn't exactly in the mood to have my shoulder tapped. I sighed and put my glass down. It was one of those days.

'You bastard! You shambled the whole bloody auction!'

'Me?' I said innocently.

'*You*! I wanted one of the lots and you stopped me, you – '

I tried to calm him. 'Sorry, old pal. Anyway that Chinese funereal terracotta bird shouldn't be glazed, Chris.' I was only trying to be reasonable, because he's famous for coating with polyurethanes any antique that stands still long enough, the maniac. The object Chris was after shrieked authenticity. It was one of the terracotta figures from Fu Hao's tomb, excavated at Anyang in China during the mid–1970s. Anyway, I have a soft spot for that tempestuous empress Fu Hao who lived such a stormy life. Wife of the Emperor Wu Ding, 1300 BC or thereabouts, and not above leading his armies into battle if the need arose. A real woman.

'I have a right – ' Chris was storming.

'You're thick as a brick, Chris,' I said, honestly trying to be kind.

His eyes glazed and he grabbed me by the throat – or would have done if his rib hadn't cracked on the stool I slammed up under his ribcage. The broken glass suddenly in my hand opened a slit down his sleeve and forearm through which blood squirted.

'You should only *dust* terracotta figures,' I told him as he reeled back aghast and squealing. I heard Sal the barmaid shriek. 'And use a sable paintbrush. Okay?'

The pub was silent, except for the quiet jingle of the door behind old Alfred. The poor bloke was like a refugee today. Chris clutched at his arm as the blood refused to stop and moaned, 'What's Lovejoy done to me? Get an ambulance.'

'Oh Gawd,' Tinker muttered. 'Scarper, Lovejoy.'

The scattered drinkers were simply looking. That is, all except one. And he was smiling, clapping his hands together gently in applause. Pigskin gloves, London-made. Clap-clap-clap, standing by the door. His two goons were there but simply watching.

I slid past Chris and out of the side door. Tinker's

hunched form was just shuffling round the side of the pub on to the snowy slope of East Hill. I wisely took the other direction, slushing past the small timber yard and the Saxon church into the little square where the Three Cups pub stood. I took my time, stopping in the bookshop to price an Irish leather binding, but their prices read nowadays like light years.

Alfred Duggins wasn't in the Cups when finally I reached there. He'd probably given up. But the big stranger was waiting for me just inside the taproom.

'Look, mate,' I said to him. 'If you're narked about the auction, say so and let's get on with it.'

'Drink?' His voice was man-sized, cool and full of confidence.

'What's the catch?'

'Catch?' He gave a lopsided grin. 'No catch. I just thought you deserved one, that's all.'

Without thinking, I said, 'Well, ta,' and we pushed in to the fug.

Arcellano was instantly at home in the Three Cups, exactly as he'd been at home in Seddon's crummy auction rooms, and just as he had seemed in the spit-and-sawdust Ship. While he ordered at the bar I glanced at him. This bloke was a hard nut and no mistake.

Jason and the delectable Jane were just settling down in one snug corner, which failed to cheer me. I glimpsed Big Frank over among a huddle of barkers, all of whom glowered my way. Nobody waved. I guessed my popularity was lower than ever because of spoiling the auction.

'Here, sir.' The stranger passed me my pint. I crossed to the fireplace to dry my shoes. I noticed we were out of earshot of the others. A careful geezer too.

'My name's Lovejoy, Mr Arcellano,' I told him.

243

Oddly, my name caused no screech of merriment. It always had before.

He said slowly, 'You know my name?'

'You bought at Seddon's, remember.' That was the name he had given Millon. Too late now to wonder if he'd made the name up. 'You a collector?'

He shrugged my question off and cautiously he tasted the beer before drinking properly. 'You're pretty definite about antiques, Lovejoy. Other dealers aren't.'

'Most dealers are like Chris, can't tell an antique from a plastic duck.'

'You're famous hereabouts.' He smiled as he spoke but with no warmth. I began to see why his tame goons did as they were told. 'Lots of people gave me your name.'

I didn't like the sound of that and said, all innocence, 'Me? Oh, you know how people are.'

'Yes, I know.' He said it with utter conviction. 'And people say if there's an antique to be got, Lovejoy's the man to get it.'

'Do they indeed?'

'Sure do. In fact,' he added, 'they seem to talk pretty guarded when I asked about you.'

I didn't like the sound of that, either. In fact, I wasn't at all sure I liked the man, but he seemed like a customer with money and I was sick of living on fried tomatoes and what I could scrounge from bored housewives when I was forced to go on the knocker. Things had been really terrible lately. So I smiled affably. 'Take no notice.'

'Oh, but I have, Lovejoy. You're hired.'

'I am?'

He smiled at the irritation in my voice. 'For lots and lots of money.'

The dull world exploded in a blaze of gold fireworks. The muted mutter of the taproom soared into heavenly cadences. The entire universe was once again a magnificent carousel of dazzling lights and brilliant music. I was suddenly aware of how pleasant a bloke he actually was. I cleared my throat and squeaked, 'Have another, Mr Arcellano?'

I reeled back to the bar and gave Jean a weak grin. She's the barmaid, sometimes co-operative. 'Trust me, love. Stick it on the slate. I've a deal on. Pay you back tonight.'

She drew the pints and slid them over, holding my stare. 'I'll hold you to that, Lovejoy. I finish at eleven.'

'You're wonderful, Jean. I'll come, love.'

She smiled mischievously. 'I might hold you to *that*, too, Lovejoy.'

The big man was lighting a cigarette when I rejoined him. I'd never seen so much gold in my life. There were rings, the lighter, watch, tiepin and collar clips, teeth. He didn't offer me a smoke. So I was already one more minion. I'm no smoker, anyway, but the message was there.

'Hired for what?'

'To get me an antique.'

He probably meant for me to bid for him in an auction. 'You want it valued?'

'I already know what it's worth. And where it is. I just need it collecting. You see, I own it.'

My brow cleared. A simple vannie's removal job. Well, in my state I wasn't proud. 'That's easy.' For some reason I'd been getting anxious.

'It isn't, Lovejoy.' That horrid smile was worrying me. The more I saw of it the less I liked it. 'But I saw the way you broke the auctioneer's arm –'

That got me mad, because people have no right to go suspecting things people don't want suspected. 'I did no such thing!'

'You did,' he said flatly. 'I've used the same trick myself. Pretend to help somebody in a brawl and put their elbow backward over the edge of a desk. It never fails.' His face was expressionless now. I noticed his eyes were always on the go, flicking glances here and there as we talked. My brow cleared and I thought, oh Christ. What have I got into?

He continued, 'And that dealer in the pub. Big and tough. But you sorted him out. Never seen anybody move so fast in my life. You're the man I've been looking for.'

'To do a vannie's job?' He looked puzzled till I explained. Vannies are the humpers of our trade, mere shifters. A right mob of brainless old boozers they are too.

He heard me out and shook his head. 'Nothing that simple. You see, Lovejoy, somebody else has got my antique. And I want you to get it back.' His voice chilled me, and I'm not easily chilled.

He'd said 'get'. Not buy, not bid, not collect. Get. As in rob?

'Why can't you, erm get it, Mr Arcellano?'

'Because it's risky. I might get caught.'

I thought, bloody hell. It's a rip. The bastard actually wants *me* to do a rip. Not him, note, because it's frigging risky. I rose, full of bitterness. It had all been too good to be true. Back to the cold snow and a quick rape over Ann's lace in the village. Maybe there was a slender chance of fitting in a quick hot nosh, though other times I'd called round I'd had to nick what I could from her fridge while she went to the loo.

'Sod off, mate.'

'Sit down, Lovejoy.' His face lifted. His smile was there again. I'd never seen such an unhappy smile. 'You just risked gaol for that old man –'

'Tinker's my barker,' I said. My chest felt tight. I was in some sort of scrap and losing fast. 'I'm responsible for him.'

'And Margaret?'

How the hell did he know about Margaret Dainty? She and I have been close friends a long time. She's not young, yet despite her limp she has that elusive style some older women carry like blossom. I glanced around. Arcellano's two serfs were now sitting at a table by the door.

I subsided slowly. 'What is this?'

He blew a perfect smoke ring. 'Do the job and no harm comes to any of your friends – or you. You'll not cry when you hear the fee.'

I swallowed. 'To nick an antique?'

He looked pained. 'Not *steal*, Lovejoy. I did say I already own it. Think of it as returning it to me, its rightful owner.'

'Who has it?' I said.

'The Pope,' he said.

'The *who*?' I said.

'You heard.'

'Fucking hell,' I said. 'You're asking *me* to . . . ?'

'Another drink?' he said. He was still smiling.

Chapter Two

I've always found that youth's no deterrent to age. The ultimate proof was the Pinnacle Peak Language Academy, a big, modern but old-looking house on the outskirts of town. Arcellano had instructed me to report there, making all heads turn by snapping his fingers that snowy January day in the pub and passing me the card one of his goons whisked over. The card read *Specialists in Modern European Languages*.

'You're going to school, Lovejoy,' he'd said. 'To learn Italian.'

'I'm hell as like.' I'd hated school.

'You register tomorrow.'

This was beginning to look too organized for my liking. 'Can't I just buy a phrase-book?'

'Not for this job.' He rose then, a gentle picture of threatening behaviour but still smiling. 'Your wages will be delivered every Friday.'

'Oh.' I cheered up. These language schools are all the same – a convenience for foreign students to get a visa and for our own students to go on the scive. Simply register, attend the first couple of lessons to show willing, then it's off to the boozer with a part-time job on the side for extras. I thought what a nice simple bloke this bloke was. And a charming nature. 'Right,' I said, keeping the card and carefully not yelping with delight as Arcellano and his grovellers made to depart. Money for jam at last. He paused.

'One thing, Lovejoy. About your wage.'

'Oh, that.' I tried to sound only casually interested,

but was pleased he'd remembered the details, like how much.

'It depends on how you do.'

'Eh?'

His blank smile was beginning to get me down. 'Good progress, you get good money. Little progress, little money.'

I thought, what bloody cheek. 'Then you can stuff your schooling.'

' – And no attendance,' he said quietly, 'no Lovejoy. *Arrivederci*.'

I watched the unpleasant bastard go. Thoughts of Margaret, Tinker, Jane and the rest rose within me and stayed. Antiques is a rough game. Antiques plus Arcellano was unthinkable. I thought for an hour before leaving the pub.

There was no doubt left in me. Some failures were just not worth having. Back to school for Lovejoy.

I have to tell you this next bit because it's where I met Maria. And she became more of the rip than ever I wanted, and in a way I hate to remember even yet.

The next morning was bright with that dazzling winter brilliance you get living near the cold North Sea. To the east the sea-marshes glistened, trees standing in spectacular white silhouette against the blue. Even the thought of schooling didn't put me down. I'd wangled my unlearned way through childhood. A day or two more would be peanuts. And maybe they included dinner.

I got a lift into town on a horse-drawn wagon, since there had again been snow during the night and all the modern mechanical wonder-gadgets were frozen under drifts. At such times East Anglia's one useful vehicle is Jacko's cart. He is a smelly, cheerful old devil, much addicted to light opera, who runs a ramshackle removal van in summer and Terence in winter. Terence is his gigantic shire horse, ancient as a church and about twice as big, and he pulls this wooden farmyard cart which Jacko, a born comedian, rigs up with nailed planks he calls passenger seats.

'Is it true you're going to school, Lovejoy?' Jacko called as I climbed up. He was falling about at the notion.

'Shut it, Jacko.' I hate the way word gets round our village.

But he choked with laughter all the way down to the brook and across the water-splash where the town road begins. I had to grin weakly and put up with him because he lets me on for nothing. It was a lot kinder than it sounds – I still owe him for six journeys from last winter when the black ice had blocked us in for three days.

Jacko put us all down at the Albert tavern, from where we could walk up the slushy hill into town. I ploshed my way out to the Pinnacle Peak Language Academy, my chirpiness dwindling with every wet step.

The lowering sky to the south-west was leaden, promising yet more snow. The wind was rising, the air dank and chill. I was hungry as hell, perishing cold and imprisoned in a trap of utter misery by that lunatic Arcellano. My antiques trade would vanish. My life was a wreck.

So I went to school – and met Maria.

From then on things went downhill.

The so-called Academy was heaving. I'd never seen so many shapes and sizes and ages. Somehow a motley mob of people had battled their way to this emporium of learning and were noisily finding acquaintances among the press. There were kids, geriatrics, housewives, workmen, and elegant ladies obviously bolting from boredom. The Pinnacle Peak's idea of welcome was a handshake in the form of grievous bodily harm from a bluff language instructor called Hardy ('everybody calls me Jingo'), a sermon full of veiled threats

250

from a geriatric grammarian headmistress, Miss McKim, and a gentle reproof from old Fotheringay. He was heartbroken because I'd never done classics at Balliol. I sympathized, because so was I.

Jingo Hardy enrolled me in a dusty side room. I nearly fainted at the fees printed on the form. One week's worth would have kept me six months.

He boomed a laugh. 'Don't worry, Lovejoy. Yours have been paid. Ten weeks of special instruction.'

He told me to wait in the hall so I sat on one of the radiator pipes and watched Jingo Hardy, in the thick of things, inform a small disorderly bunch that they were intellectuals about to tackle Russian literature. With poisonous cheerfulness he bullied them off into a side room, leaving only a moderately-sized horde milling blindly to and fro.

What with the warmth and the comfort I must have nodded off or something because the next thing I knew I was being criticized and prodded with a shoe, which proved I was awake again. The hallway was empty. This woman's voice was saying sharply, 'And what do you think *you* are doing?'

'Waiting.'

I blinked up at her. She was one of the loveliest women I had ever seen. Dark, slender, bright and stylish with a warm tweed-and-cardigan look. Pearl stud earrings. I fell for her. She toed me again. The crowd had vanished. A faint hum arose from the rooms all about, school now in session.

'You're a tramp, aren't you?'

'Not yet.' I said. The irony was lost on her.

'Please leave, or I shall call the police.'

I said, 'Lady. Prod me again with your toe and I'll break it. *Off*.'

She withdrew a yard. 'Why have you no socks on?'

'Drying.' I got them off the radiator and felt. Still damp, but I started to put them on. All I could do now

251

was tell Arcellano I'd tried and they'd threatened to have me run in.

'And shoes?'

'Give me a sec.' I'd sloped them on the pipe, heels down, in an attempt to dry the cardboard which covered the holes.

She was watching. 'Do you have far to go?'

You can't help staring at some people. There ought to be Oscars or something for hypocrisy. Today's message from this luscious bird: piss off or I'll call the police, and have a pleasant journey strolling through the blizzard. People amaze me.

'Yes.'

'Oh. Well. Where's your overcoat?'

'Still at my tailor's.'

She flushed then and developed the injured look of a woman wanting some man to take up this particularly cumbersome crucifix. I didn't help by spinning out my dressing process. She stood her ground, though.

'One thing, love.' I stood and stamped my cardboard inners flat. 'Swap that painting to the other wall.'

'I beg your pardon?'

I stepped across and lifted the watercolour down. '*Never* over a radiator. *Never* in a centrally heated hallway if you can help it. *Never* facing what sun we get. And *never* where people smoke.'

The little watercolour sketch was a Thomas Robins, the sort of thing he did before doing the proper Dutch fishing-boat scene. He liked storms in harbours. I'm not all that old, but I can remember the time four years ago when his best paintings could be got for an average monthly wage.

'Take your hands off our property – '

She came at me so I cuffed her and yelled, 'You could have made me drop it, you silly bitch! Look.' I dragged her near to the modern photorepro of 'The Stag at Bay' which I'd just taken down. '*That*,' I explained into her stunned eyes, 'will stand anything.

This original watercolour is vulnerable.' I spelled the word to give her cortex time to adjust to the learning process. 'So we put your repro picture anywhere, see? It'll not warp, change or fade in the sun. On the other hand, love, original paintings by Thomas Sewell Robins need care.' I spelled that too, mounted the watercolour, then walked to the door.

'You hit me.' She was still preoccupied with being annoyed.

'I'll come back next week, love, to check you've not swapped the pictures back. And I'll accept no crappy excuses about your painting being school property.' I wagged a finger to emphasize the threat. 'A genuine antique is everybody's, no matter who owns it. Remember, now.'

She suddenly said, 'You're Lovejoy.'

'True,' I said, opening the door to the kinder world of winter. 'And goodbye.'

She suddenly became a supplicant. The abrupt transformation was really weird. 'Please. Don't go.' She even tried a winning smile. I'd never see a quicker – or more desperate – conversion. 'I'm – I'm your special instruction counsellor assignment.'

'You're my what?' Nowadays everything sounds like the UN.

She gave in and used language. 'Teacher. Please come back in.'

I hesitated between the blizzard and the deep blue sea. Normally I'd have stormed out in a temper, though I'm usually very mild. The reason I didn't was the sheer desperation in her eyes. Somehow I'd annoyed her at first, but now there she was full of frantic appeasement. I could have sworn she was afraid. Maybe she needed the money or lived in terror of mighty Miss McKim.

'Can I dry my shoes on your radiator?'

'If you wish.'

'And socks?' I added shrewdly.

253

'Of course.' She moved past me and pushed the door to.

'And I'm not in trouble for, erm, telling you about the pictures?'

'You mean hitting me,' she said evenly. 'No.'

It seemed there was no way out. Time for a truce. 'All right.'

'Thank you,' she said, and meant it, which was odder still. She extended a hand. 'I'm Maria Peck.'

We went all Regency. 'Pleased to make your acquaintance. Lovejoy.'

She didn't look local, not with those lustrous Italian-ate features and that complexion, but Peck is unshak-ably East Anglian and I commented on it while we shook.

'So I'm told,' she said, and added sweetly, 'Nothing like as unusual as Lovejoy, is it?'

Smarting, I thought okay. Truce, not submission.

'This way, please.'

I followed her lissom form. Whatever lissom means, it's the right word.

Most women have an inherent grace, don't they, with awareness sort of built in. Well, the ultimate was Maria. I swear I was demented for her by the time we reached the classroom, though her attitude seemed to be one of instant aloofness once she'd got me to stay.

But why the terror when I was making my sullen exit? Last time I'd been at school they were glad to get rid of me. Fool that I was, I shelved the little mystery and forgot it.

Late Friday of that week it happened. I was in my cottage frying some pieces of apple. It's supposed to be a country-man's delicacy, but was proving a failure. For a start you need oil for the pan, and I'd got none. Then you need a good stove, and the bastards had cut my electricity off in the midweek. The methylated spirit lamp, which I use for wax modelling, was going full blast – an erg an hour – and the sliced apples were barely warm.

The knock on the door surprised me. My cottage is fairly remote, on the outskirts of a small village. The lane leading to it is narrow and long and goes hardly anywhere else. The daylight had faded an hour since. I cheered up as I went into the little hallway. My first week's wages were due for having attended that punk language school. Apart from having the opportunity to gape at the delectable Maria it had been a real drag, so I deserved every penny.

It was Arcellano and his two nerks all right, but not with my wages. The three of them were crammed into the tiny vestibule, blocking out the vague haze of snow light.

'Mr Arcellano!' I yelped with false delight, thinking of money, and hot pasties and beer at the White Hart. Hunger makes crawlers of us all. 'Good of you to call! Come in!' Nobody moved.

'Where's the lights?'

'Erm, well, I've had the electricity cut off,' I said smoothly. 'Temporary repairs, you understand. This wretched weather brought down a cable – '

'What's the stink?'

'Stink?' I swallowed my irritation. The bastard was speaking of my staple diet. 'Ah. Delicious country recipe. Fried apple. Actually takes hours to make. I haven't done the flaky pastry yet, or I'd offer you supper – '

A flashlight blinded me. With the beam flickering into every corner the two goons bore me backwards and slammed me down in a chair. Heavy hands pressed on my shoulders when I tried to rise. It's horrible to discover you are suddenly out of breath for no known cause. In that instant all I could think of was that quick glimpse of terror on Maria's face when I had started to cut out from the school.

'Is this how you live, Lovejoy?'

'Only temporarily,' I answered, narked. 'I'm having an extension built – '

'Hold him.'

A flashlight was beamed at my face so I could see nothing. With my eyes screwed up against the beam I sat and listened while somebody, probably Arcellano himself, shook out drawers and emptied cupboards and slammed doors and tore things in the darkness beyond the light. I knew better than to hope for neighbours or the police to arrive. The former wisely leave me alone, and the latter are only more trouble and I'd enough to be going on with.

Quite ten minutes later I heard Arcellano return. He sounded slightly winded from all his exertions. I felt the same and I'd done nothing but sit.

A lighter flared, showing his face full of unpleasant shadows. The light snapped off and a cigarette glowed.

'Why do you live here like a pig, Lovejoy?' He sounded surprised but honestly interested.

I tried to shrug but his burkes were still pressing me down. 'I'm a bit short. I've done a few good deals, though – '

'You've not, Lovejoy.' Even when smoke came into my eyes making me cough and blink I knew the sod was smiling. 'You are penniless.'

'Only temporarily,' I shot back. 'If I hadn't wasted the week on your frigging school I'd have –'

'How *was* school?'

That gentle query pulled me up. 'Oh. Horrible as ever.' I tried a chuckle. It sounded like a trapped wasp.

'Make much progress, Lovejoy?'

I swallowed. This didn't make sense. He sounded too gentle for somebody who had come in like Attila the Hun and wrecked the place.

'Quite a lot,' I lied cheerfully. My mouth was dry.

A paper rustled. 'Your report says different.' A silence. 'That's bad news, Lovejoy. Not for me. For you. Light.'

I found I couldn't swallow any more. The beam moved to show his gloved hands and the crested school paper.

'Inattentive,' he quoted. 'Six reprimands daily for reading journals on antiques during lessons.'

Had it been that many? 'Rubbish.'

'Homework: nil per cent.'

I'd done none. 'I've been a bit pushed lately – '

He read on relentlessly, 'Altogether a hopeless start.'

I protested weakly, 'Most of the others are young, still in school. They're naturals – '

'That's not true. There are only four children in your class. The rest are adults. One is fifty and did better than you, Lovejoy.'

I seethed in silent fury. The bastard had checked up. What kind of employer checks up? Where's trust gone?

'The others distract me.'

'But your afternoon teaching is individual. I should know. I paid for it. And your teacher says: "Total lack of motivation." Well, Lovejoy?'

That sounded Maria all over. She and I had wasted every afternoon in a soundproofed room, if you can believe it. I took three goes to start my voice up. 'I suppose this means no wage this week, eh, Mr Arcellano?'

He rose and I got the light back in my eyes. 'True, Lovejoy. But I have to go away for ten whole weeks. I can't leave you here without motivation, can I?' There was some shuffling nearby. One of the goons was getting ready for something. Arcellano's voice hardened. 'Our deal's on, Lovejoy. It's on because I said so. Play dim if you like, but you suffer the consequences. Understand?'

'Well, yes,' I was saying when somebody clouted me.

'Hold him.'

Gloved hands gripped my head while Arcellano extinguished his cigarette on the point of my chin. I whimpered but they held me fast. I was going to bring up some very convincing excuse when they started on me. Even now I can't for the life of me remember what it was, but I know it would have been a cracker. I'm good at excuses.

There's a knack in cooking. I've not got it, but I once had a bird who was really great. Sally used to make these fantastic meals, never the same twice and so many different flavours you never knew what you were eating half the time under all that taste, which is quite an achievement because eating's a right drag. We parted when she developed suspicions – almost quite unjustified – about a rich widow who used to call sometimes when Sally was out at work. I've found that women always want to believe the worst, when it's so much simpler to believe what's easiest.

I had stopped being sick about eight o'clock or thereabouts. By a fluke no bones were broken and the bleeding had stopped on its own while I was flat out. In the light of my spirit lamp I could see my face puffy and battered, with a prodigious blister the size of an igloo bulging from my stubble where the bastard had burned me with his fag. No cuts, but dried blood down my neck from one ear, one eye black and bulging, and my right shoulder sprained. The cottage was a hell of a mess.

For some reason I was tired, even after such a long enforced slumber, so I dozed on my divan for a while. Then my hunger returned and I started warming the pan again. The cold slices of apple stared reproachfully up at me in the gloom. What with the state I was in, she must have been knocking donkey's years before I heard and let her in. My favourite teacher.

I need not say much about the rest of that evening, or of that night. Maria shot a handful of terse questions at me, to which I gave terse unfriendly answers, seeing she was to blame for the battering Arcellano's serfs gave me. She looked closely at me with the aid of the spirit lamp's watery blue flame. Then she did a quick reconnaissance while I glowered sullenly at my pan through my one good eye. Eventually she said she'd be back and went. I heard her tyres skittering and crunching on the snow.

Ever the optimist, I was trying to raise a brew-up when I realized she was back. She must have nicked my key somehow, or maybe I'd given it her. I forget which. She lit a candle and stuck it on a plate. Then another. The lovely golden light bathed the cottage's shambled interior. It looked in a worse state than me. I wondered where she'd managed to buy candles at this hour.

She took the saucer of apple off me and scraped it into the bin in my kitchen alcove. That was the start. She must have made them work – an all-time first – at the Treble Tile because she'd fetched some hot nosh as well. Chips, fish, sausages, a pot of soupy stuff, and bags of cheese, bread, a cake and milk and tea and, among the rest, apples by mistake. I didn't grumble. I'd run out of Ann's grub two days before. Playing at being an angel of mercy was obviously doing Maria a power of good because she was silent for the first time ever. Until then I thought I'd never met such a talkative bird in my life.

I ate her nosh slowly and slurpily while she tidied, always a bad sign in a woman. The more racket they make the more you're for it. Not saying a word, I whittled my way across two platefuls while her slamming and rattling went remorselessly on, a sort of creeping barrage. She was watching me by that sort of feminine feel which requires tight lips and no actual stare. I could tell because the instant I finished she swept the dishes aside and sat washing my face in a cupful of lukewarm water. The sensible lass had used eight whole candles brewing tea.

We reached midnight in total silence, sitting primly

side by side on my folding divan, knees together and politely clearing throats and watching candles glow. I always feel at a disadvantage when women tidy me up. Maybe that's why they do it. The battle started.

'Lovejoy,' she said carefully. 'What happened here is none of my business.'

How true. 'A disagreement with a customer.'

'Be that as it may.' She spoke the words exactly like she taught in pronunciation class, with gaps a mile long. 'But I'm not so stupid that I fail to see the connection between your bad first week's report, and this beating you have suffered.'

I told her rubbish. She fumbled in her handbag and brought out the crumpled report. Arcellano must have left it.

'Then how did this get here?'

'It was posted to me by mistake.'

'Miss McKim *never* makes mistakes.' She read through it quickly, folding it after seeing her own hand-writing. 'These reports are sent only to the sponsors.' She rose and paced, obviously going to put the boot in. 'Tell me the truth, Lovejoy. You've got to do well or suffer. Isn't that right?'

'Yes.'

'Very well.' She turned to face me. Two candles shone from behind her, casting a subtle corona round her from the shadows. I'd never seen such beauty in a woman in all my life, not since Helen, or maybe Lydia or maybe Sally the nosh queen.

Entranced, I mumbled weakly, 'Very well what?'

'We must knuckle down.' She spoke so full of sad-ness that for an instant I misunderstood and thought she'd spotted a way out for me. Then it dawned she meant working, and my bitterness returned. I was trapped between Arcellano, that non-smiling smiler, and this gloomy optimist. 'You sold your Italian gram-mar text – '

'I did no such thing!'

260

'I saw you,' she said calmly. 'In the junk shop on the Hythe. So I bought it back.' And she brought it out of her handbag, the treacherous bitch. 'It's no good glaring, Lovejoy. Your signature's on the flyleaf.'

'You have no right following me – '

She smiled over my protest. 'And on the rare occasions you *do* pay attention in open class, Lovejoy, it's to Joan Culpepper.'

I asked innocently. 'Is she one of our group?'

'She's the lady next to whom you sit, Lovejoy. You started the week in the opposite corner.'

'Oh, *her*!' I'd obviously hardly noticed her, but Maria was not dissuaded, as usual suspicious without a single cause. 'The one with the Justinian period Roman quartz intaglio ring, modern setting in garnets on gold with raised platinum shoulder mounts?'

'Yes, *her*.' She tapped my knee with a finger, not knowing Arcellano's lunatic serfs had kicked it to a balloon size. I nearly screamed. 'From now on, Lovejoy, your Friday reports will be superb.'

'They will?' I brightened. Not only was this luscious woman delectable, but she'd obviously fallen head over heels for me. With Arcellano away for weeks and my bonus money rolling in . . . It was my trillionth mistake of the week. I asked, 'How'll we fiddle Miss McKim's reports?'

'You mean *cheat*?'

I saw her face. 'Well, er, no. Not exactly – '

She went cold as charity. 'There's only one way, Lovejoy, and that's to *earn* a good report.' She collected her coat and gloves. 'Don't worry, I'll see you'll get the right sort of help.'

'Erm. . . .'

She walked towards the small hallway, rabbitting on. I had the idea she was smiling deep down. 'From now on, Lovejoy, you eat regularly. None of this heroic starving for the sake of old pots and ramshackle furniture – ' I gasped, outraged at this heresy. It only goes to show how boneheaded women actually are. 'And from tomorrow your electricity bill will be paid. Light *and* warmth.' She smiled, adding sweetly, 'And distractions will be minimized. I shall see to that first thing tomorrow.'

She meant Mrs Culpepper. My head was spinning with all this. Or maybe it was the unusual sensation of not being hungry.

'Er, look,' I mumbled, 'can't we discuss this?'

'Yes. In Italian.'

'*Eh?*'

'You heard, Lovejoy.' Now her smile was open and visible, a beautiful warm silent laughter. 'From now on, ask for anything in English and the answer's no. But ask in Italian and the answer's . . .'

' . . . And the answer's yes?'

For one instant her smile intensified to a dazzling radiance. 'The answer's . . . quite possibly.' She stepped into the darkness, leaving me in the candlelight. I heard the cottage door go.

'Good night, Lovejoy,' she called from the winter midnight.

'Good night.' I was trying to say thanks as well but the latch went and she had gone.

You can't teach women anything about timing an exit. I've always noticed that.

Chapter Three

From then on it was hell – but a peculiar kind of hell, with torment interspersed with a haunting promise of ecstasy. For a time. Under the white-hot attentions of Maria, I quite forgot about Arcellano.

Unaccountably, the attractive Joan Culpepper attended no further classes, apart from one hour's collective conjugation, so to speak, I got the full teaching blast. 'Incentive teaching,' she often reminded me with hardly a trace of her secret hilarity.

By Tuesday of the following week I was showing withdrawal symptoms which caused a bit of upset. Maria had kept me at it twelve and fifteen hours at a stretch. Apart from that glimpse of Mrs Culpepper's 'tassie', as we call such incised semi-precious carvings, the only antique I'd seen was a Newhall painted cream jug with a 'clip' handle – these are always pre–1790 and still a bargain. It had somehow crept from its place of honour in the little dining-room and was found on our table. I honestly had nothing to do with it, but a poisonous epsilon-minus cretin called Hyacinth reckoned I'd moved it nearer and blew the gaff on me. A tight-lipped Maria came across and restored it to its place on the sideboard. I was heartbroken. Newhall porcelain's enough to melt the hardest heart – Maria's excepted.

I was really peeved. 'Why d'you believe Hyacinth and not me?' Hyacinth's only twelve but she always came top in Italian at the end-of-day test.

Maria let the tea-lady pass with a loaded tray before accusing, 'It's antiques, isn't it, Lovejoy?'

'I'm fine.'

'You're not.' She was eyeing me as if for the first time, in serious puzzlement. 'You're a wreck and going downhill like a pining child.' That was a real laugh. At my age.

'It's just I'm used to one way of doing things – '

'Wait here,' she said suddenly. 'Learn the past perfect of *essere*. I'll not be a minute.'

I shrugged. She hared off, obviously in the grip of some vital decision, while I wheedled a ton of cake from one of the tea-women and sat noshing it while admiring the clip-handled jug. You can still get these little polychrome beauties for a song – almost. And when you think they are *always* older than two whole centuries, made with love and elegance by potters with all the gifts of God in their gnarled fingers, and less than a day's average wage . . . I had tears in my eyes when finally Maria returned and jerked me back to reality.

She was dressed to go out. 'Get your coat, Lovejoy.'

'I've got none.'

'Sorry. I meant get ready.'

'I'm always ready. Where are we going?'

'Round the art galleries, antique shops and ruins of this fair town. Folk Museum. Minories.'

My eyes misted and I reached for her, ignoring the delighted gaze of the canteen women. 'Darling,' I said. She was seeing things my way at last.

'Yes, darling,' she murmured, misty too. 'There's only one thing, Lovejoy.'

'Eh?' I drew back full of apprehension.

'Everything in Italian, please. You know the rules.'

Breathlessly but angrily I raced upstairs for my dictionary and the grammar, thinking of that sly bitch falling about laughing down in the porch. As I hurried I raged at myself, I'll kill her one of these days, just see if I don't.

I wish I hadn't thought that terrible thought now,

264

but you can't look into the future, can you? And honest to God none of this was my fault. None of it.

That day was sheer torture. There was I, frantically trying to tell Maria about the engravings on the Jacobite drinking glasses in the town museum, and of the really serious need for ultraviolet light to distinguish between the fluorescence that demonstrates a glass's origin, and there she was nodding encouragement as I ballsed up my declensions time and again. At the finish we both knew it was hopeless. I was the only known language learner with zero vocabulary, which is some handicap. I lost half a ton in sweat that afternoon.

Maria dropped me off in the village at the end of a harrowing day. I had an idea she lived somewhere down on the estuary but didn't dare ask. During the somewhat uncontrolled journey out of town – the snow was still about with the roads pretty grim – she hit on the idea of one particular item per day.

'It'll work, Lovejoy,' she asserted confidently. 'Pick a card.'

'Illuminated manuscripts,' I said. 'I've a real love for those.

She glanced at me, oddly amused. 'Fine. See you after midmorning break. We might as well go together in the car.'

That night I worked in a maniacal fever, slogging like a mad thing to scrape together enough language to tell the stupid woman about the purity and complexity of style in the mediaeval illuminator's work. Our town museum can only afford this one mediaeval Psalter, but there was so much to say. I was desperate to convert Maria's moronic mind from materialism to a proper appreciation of love in human skills. The trouble is, nothing shuts you up like having no words.

By dawn I was knackered, but capable of bleating a few short sentences about the most beautiful things on earth.

Five weeks later I had worn out my first pocket dictionary and I kept going in grammar only by the neat trick of nicking Hyacinth's text. I'm good at swapping flyleaves without trace so I could prove the book I'd pinched out of her satchel was mine. Anyhow, by then I was streets ahead of the rest. They were even leaving me out of the end-of-day tests. I out-smirked Hyacinth by miles, which served her right.

It was that day too that Maria came to me for the first time. We were speaking in her language all the time now. Admittedly, I had to pause every minute or so for a feverish fumble through the book, but basically it was all progress. I'd discovered the most curious thing: learn one word and use it, and before long it somehow grows into two. Also, by then I wasn't hungry any more and had started filling out. Maria bought me a second-hand overcoat and my wages were already sparkling with bonus gelt. Likewise Tinker had prospered, the parasitic old devil. Maria and I had taken to using our pub hour for revision, and Tinker would bob up in the Cups to cadge enough for five pasties and get paralytic drunk. I didn't mind – though Maria presumably found him hard going – because when he's sloshed his mental radar works best and he starts to find antiques.

Just before everything closed one day Tinker found a small piece of *pietra dura* in Jeff Archer's shop in the antiques arcade. We shot over, me blathering halting explanations to Maria. Jeff's a pleasant bloke who lives with a young blind woman in Arlesford. He has the most phenomenal luck. I don't actually believe in luck, but there's a lot of it about.

'Wotcher, Lovejoy.' Jeff shoved a small gold box on the counter. Tinker took the quid I slipped him and faded like grinning mist, duty done. 'Genuine Florentine, seventeenth century.'

'*Petra dura.*' The lovely pictorial stone was beautifully laid on the box lid. 'But Derbyshire, early nine-teenth.'

'Sure?'

In raptures, I began to explain how the Duke of Devonshire's fluospar mines actually made a continuous profit but the resultant craftsmanship never quite matched Italian work. You can't help being enthusiastic.

I came to feeling my smile dying on my face. Maria was looking at me. Shoppers were dwindling all around, pausing only for a glance on their way through the Arcade to the bus station. Nothing seemed wrong, but there again was that wrong feel. As if she was comparing me with . . . with . . . ?

I guessed, 'Wrong declension?'

'No, Lovejoy.' She was holding my arm. 'But I just can't see it.' She sounded helpless. 'You have such potential. You could be doing so much – '

I dragged her to one side. I've had all this before and you can't let it get a hold of you. All this reasonable criticism can be very corrosive if it isn't soldered shut. Fast. Jeff hastily busied himself in a corner.

'You ever heard of love, Maria?'

'Love?'

'Yes. That stuff two people occasionally make.' I saw her almost imperceptible nod. 'Antiques *are* it. Love's not a feeling, or a mystic dream. And sometimes,' I finished brutally, 'antiques are the only true pieces of love some people can ever find. So don't knock them. Okay?'

'But – '

'Shut it,' I said savagely. I drew back then, looking at the ground because I could feel people staring, thinking we'd had a row. An elderly couple were going tut-tut.

Maria thought. 'I hope you're wrong, Lovejoy.'

'Women always do.'

She was glancing round Jeff's antiques with new eyes. 'Which antique do you like best, Lovejoy?'

'The next, love.'

She looked back at me then, and asked sadly, 'And is there no stopping?'

I had the strange notion she was asking me something about herself. I hadn't a notion what. Not then.

'You mean relax?' I snorted. 'Sooner or later we relax for ever. What's the point of starting early?' My answer did not please her.

She said abruptly, 'I think that's enough for today, Lovejoy.' Jeff was relieved it hadn't come to blows and took my promissory note for a deposit on the lovely box. He was glad to see the back of us.

Maria walked with me through the churchyard to her car. She seemed morose, withdrawn for some reason though I could have sworn I'd got the grammar more or less right. Her skin looked drawn and tired, her eyelids developing a faint crinkled texture as if she had begun to age. Normally she'd have been gunning verbs or rattling off sentences for me to construe, but she drove in silence right to my cottage garden. I got out in a bit of a huff because guilt makes you feel bad, especially if it's someone else's. I've always been able to get rid of my own pretty quick.

'Look,' I said miserably. 'If it's another bad report – '

She averted her head and started to reverse. 'Just put the kettle on, Lovejoy,' she ordered wearily. 'While I bring my things.'

I said, 'Eh?' but she simply drove off up the lane leaving me standing there feeling a pillock and wondering if I'd heard right.

Then I went in with the dusk falling round the cottage like a huge coverlet, and frantically began tidying up before she came.

That was how Maria and I really began. And I really loved her. I honestly mean that. We lasted until they gave me my final examination. I've already said how I screwed (I mean obtained) the result from Maria.

Six next evening Arcellano came, dead on time.

Chapter Four

After the previous day's examination Miss McKim had given a little teaparty. All eighty of us stood about with little fingers hooking air, and trying to look as though we were in a rave-up. Miss McKim made a tearful little speech. We gave her a bunch of flowers and a book token. Hyacinth shook me by giving me a ruler which she had decorated in oils. In return I gave her a hair slide of brilliants in a bow-shaped setting, only 1870-ish but quite bonny. In the final farewells she whispered to me that she quite understood about Mrs Peck and me because after all it was Only Natural These Days, though I should be On My Guard Against Duplicity. I wish now I'd listened to her warning. She kissed my ear, her specs practically gouging my right eye out. Everybody shook hands with everybody while Jingo Hardy boomed a last speech full of jokes in bits of Everybody's languages so we all understood two per cent. Old Fotheringay creaked out a farewell poem in Latin modelled on Catullus, while we applauded at the wrong place. We'd all clubbed for theatre tickets to give all our teachers. Then it was break up and goodbye.

Next day with Maria gone by eleven the cottage felt bare. It only looked the same. For a while I hung about and walked the garden, gave the robin his cheese and all that. There was no trace of her anywhere. She might simply never have been there at all, never crooked her fingers in midair when we made love, never called exhortations against my neck, never uttered hoarse cries for the light to be switched on . . . Finally I couldn't stand it and walked through the drizzle to the pub.

Tinker brought the suitcase to the Queen's Head about one o'clock. It was there that I was called to the phone in the saloon bar and heard Arcellano's voice telling me he would be at the cottage by six. From the background noise I guessed he was at some airport or other.

My money used to come in an envelope simply marked 'Lovejoy'. I still had my final envelope, and shared the gelt with Tinker. I told him I'd be away a few days.

'With that bird with the big bristols, Lovejoy?' He nearly fell into his pint at this witticism, his only joke.

'Very droll, Tinker,' I said. 'Remember. While I'm away buy nothing. Just look out for musical boxes, William IV jewellery and anything that even smells of Nabeshima porcelain.'

'Christ.'

'And try for commemorative plaques, especially any with town names. There's word of some being unloaded in Coggeshall soon. And dancing automata. You'll find two already at Southwold, but don't touch them because they're crap. Somebody's subbed them.'

'Bastards.' Tinker spoke with feeling. 'Subbing' means to replace a few parts of an antique with modern bits. Do it often enough and you have all the spare bits for a genuine original. It is done most often – for this read always – in the field of watches and clocks, automata, early scientific instruments, and early printed books where it's done by dissecting pages. Dealers call this illegal process 'twinning', though that's illogical because you finish up with 'antiques' of different ages.

I drew breath to tell Tinker to keep an eye out for a rumoured Brescian miquelet-flint pistol but that made me think of modern weapons which made me think of revolvers which made me think of Arcellano so I shut up.

Tinker got the vibes. 'Want me to come wiv yer, Lovejoy?'

'No,' I said. 'I'm in enough trouble.'

He would have, though, if I said yes. What he didn't know was that he and the rest – and maybe Maria too by now – were hostages.

'It's in the Vatican,' Arcellano told me, tilting back on the chair legs. He looked bigger than ever. His two animals were outside in his car. I'd insisted on that and to my astonishment he had agreed. It didn't make me feel any more secure.

'Whereabouts?'

'No idea. Finding out's your job. Listen, Lovejoy – '

'No,' I told him wearily. '*You* listen, Mr Arcellano. You want me to pull a rip. You'll blame my friends if I don't. Okay, I'll do it. But what if I rip the wrong antique?'

'You got a photo.'

'It's useless. There might be ten, a dozen tables like this.'

The photograph had been taken by an instant camera, by someone riding a camel to judge from the blur. The lighting was abysmal, the angle atrocious. I'm no photographer but I could still have done better with a cardboard shoebox and a pin. The table had the look of a rent table, standing against a wall by a window. It could have been anywhere on earth.

'What do I do when I nick it?'

He did his smile thing. 'You'll have a contact. Marcello. And you will obey the orders to the letter.' He was smoking a cigarette and gazed reflectively at the glowing tip with his humourless smile. 'And you will never use names. Not mine, not yours. I'll hold you to that, Lovejoy.'

He narked me. Threats are all very well, but it was

272

me taking the risks. This vagueness just would not do. 'Do I get *any* help?'

He raised his eyebrows in mock surprise. 'Not much. Remember you were carefully selected for the task because of your undoubted talents.'

Well, I'd tried. 'Which leaves the small matter of payment. I've no money to fly there.'

'So it does.' He rose and stubbed out his cigarette right on the surface of my wobbly table, the pig. Still, it wasn't on me this time. He took back the photo, careful man that he was. 'The travel agent in town has your tickets and flight bookings. You go tomorrow night.' He dropped a bundle of notes on the table. 'That will give you luxury for five days, or survival for twenty. Choose.'

'What if – ?'

'No more questions, Lovejoy.' He moved to the hall. Mechanically he raised a hand to stop me switching the light on. A very cautious man, every gesture the subject of detailed planning. 'You have a job to do. Do it.'

'And this Marcello pays me?'

'You get ten times the going commercial value of the antique in question, plus expenses. And a basic weekly rate averaged on your past four weeks.'

I worked that out. As far as I was concerned it was a relative fortune. Once I'd pulled the rip I'd be able to eat until Christmas and still have enough left to give a turkey the fright of its life.

I stood at the door of the cottage and watched his big Merc leave. One of his nerks, a gross unpleasing man with the pockmarked face of a lunar landscape and bad teeth, wound down his window and bawled, 'Good luck – you'll need it!' I said nothing back because I could hear somebody laughing. The laughter continued until the closing windows sliced it off. Idly I wondered what the joke was. It couldn't have been

Arcellano laughing because clearly he'd never learned how.

I went inside to pack.

Chapter Five

On the whole I never like travelling much. It always seems to me a waste of all those places in between. No, for me a little distance goes a long, long way.

Absence is great therapy, but during the journey to Heathrow Maria kept coming to mind. Her rather weary acceptance of me as a lover, those occasional remote silences like that time in the Arcade with the Derbyshire *pietra dura*. And most of all those vivid flashes of apprehension – practically wild terror – so soon suppressed yet memorable as a gleam of gold in a lake. Twice I'd asked her outright if she knew Arcellano, describing him, and she said no. I believed her. Even though I can't fathom women I think I know them pretty well. At least, I think I think.

The previous night I'd tried contacting her, but realized I didn't even know her address. She once told me she lodged somewhere down the estuary, but that was as far as I got. The phone people were unable to help. The school was closed.

By a fluke Joan Culpepper was in when I'd phoned, and was able to get away to meet me that evening. We went back to the cottage for a farewell chat, which helped me to forget my worries. A little sublimation does you a power of good. The silly bitch laughingly refused to sell me her tassie ring, though – 'to keep you interested, Lovejoy'. She asked with a great show of sweet innocence what I had done with Maria (' . . . somewhere in the garden, I hope, Lovejoy . . . ') but I put a stop to that. One war's enough.

The flight to Rome wasn't so bad, two hours ten

minutes stuck in a reclining seat and fed to bursting by those girls who always look sterile. I may have missed Maria yesterday but would definitely see her once I got back. That notion pleased me so much I became quite eager to land and get on with the rip. It was bound to be dead simple. 'Easy as stealing from a church' is a saying in the antiques trade. As the plane banked in from the Mediterranean stack over Ostia I was even smiling. Maria would give me a hero's welcome. I knew that.

Then the Customs bit, and Rome.

Marcello was the least likely crook I'd ever seen, and, knowing as many dealers as I do, I must have notched up four figures by now. He was fairly tall, dark-haired, fairly well dressed and youngish. He took me aback somewhat because I suppose I must have been expecting to meet a mini-Arcellano. So when a voice said, 'Lovejoy?' as I hung around the exit concourse among mobs disgorging from the Customs, I was surprised to turn to see this pleasant bloke smiling a realish smile. 'Welcome to Roma. I'm Marcello.'

We shook hands, him quite keen to get on with the chat and me thinking Arcellano was playing a very mixed game.

'I've borrowed a friend's car to take you into the city.'

'That's very kind.'

'Good journey?'

'There's no such thing.'

He gave me an appraising glance and asked, 'Didn't you want to come?'

'Yes.' My own answer seemed to satisfy him but it shook me rigid. Surely I couldn't have meant that? All the way into the city I wondered, but stared politely at the novel scene.

Marcello's car turned out to be a microscopic gadget which had room only on its roof for my suitcase. I'd somehow had the idea everybody in Rome had enormous Ferraris.

It was dark outside. I'd never seen so many cars driven at such speed and with such noise. Marcello entered into the spirit of things, occasionally raising his hands heavenwards and parping the hooter angrily on any excuse. Later he told me quite calmly he enjoyed driving. He could have fooled me.

An hour later we were finishing a bottle of wine in a trattoria somewhere in the centre of Rome. I'd no precise idea where we were. The place was quiet, only two or three tables occupied and music covering everybody's conversation.

I couldn't get over how good the grub was. I told Marcello this. He was delighted and insisted that this particular trattoria was really below average and that he'd only chosen it on account of its central position and quietness.

Until then we had sparred around the main subject. We'd talked of all sorts. I'd mentioned the weather. Marcello had mentioned a shopkeepers' strike of the previous week. I said how pleasant Rome seemed. He praised my Italian, which was a bit effusive. I was relieved it worked with him as well as Maria. And Arcellano. There was very little wine left when I decided to open up.

'Did you book me into a hotel?'

Marcello was surprised. 'I'd instructions not to. I can tell you the names of some you could try.'

'Thanks.' I paused, weighing him up. 'Look, Marcello. How much help are you supposed to be giving me?'

'Whatever you ask, with two exceptions.' He ticked his fingers. 'Money.'

'Great,' I said bitterly. 'And women, I suppose?'

He grinned. 'I'm a married man with two young children. I can't give a bad example.' He shook his head. 'No. Number two is the Vatican.'

'Jesus.'

'We're to be casual acquaintances, Lovejoy. I gave you a lift, a typical stranger at the airport confused on his first visit to the Big R. I showed you a good cheap trattoria. You,' he explained with a flash of wry humour, 'are to express your gratitude by paying for the meal.'

'*Grazie*,' I said.

'*Prego*,' he answered politely.

So everybody was to be protected, except good old Lovejoy. Marcello was to be shielded from the arriving thief – me – and Arcellano was nowhere to be seen. He was therefore immune. Only Lovejoy was to remain exposed like a spare tool, having come to Rome for no obvious legitimate reason. I felt a twinge – well, actually a wholesome cramp – of unease.

'Can I not contact you?'

He hesitated, obviously feeling sympathy. 'If necessary. Learn my home phone number. If you're desperate, you can leave a message. My wife is usually there. Just say you'll be at the trattoria. I'll know you'll mean here.'

'That casual?'

'Why not?' He seemed genuinely surprised but I'll bet I was more surprised than him by a mile. I'd never heard anything like this in my life. Normally crooks never divulge anything about their families. I tried to look as if I understood what the hell was going on.

'No reason. Just a bit more open than I'm used to.'

Piously he put his hand over his heart. 'Us honest Italians.'

We both laughed and I paid the bill.

At the third go I found a room in a fair-sized hotel about an hour later. Marcello had gone home, leaving me walking between the hotels and muttering his phone number to keep it in my thick skull.

My clothes I left in my suitcase. In my innocence I

didn't expect to be staying very long. I lay on the bed and thought of the rip.

Arcellano's story was somewhat porous. Of course, he'd no need to give me any story at all. Most crooks don't – and I'd no doubt Arcellano was a hood of the first order. His family had owned this enormous suite of antique furniture, made by the great Chippendale himself as an entire household set, alcoves built for every single wall piece and suchlike. I'd been fascinated, half wanting to believe his account of an aristocratic family, a heritage in a mansion . . . I'd asked him where.

'Mind your own business,' he'd said straight back, which was fair enough.

Came the war and all hell broke loose, belongings scattered, families in ruins. Afterwards, Arcellano's family set about recovering the various pieces. All eighty pieces were found, except one. I quite understood his eagerness. Remember that most so-called 'Chippendale' pieces are conjectural, and in any case were made only by his workmen. A vast historic genuine documented set was worth a king's ransom. A vast but incomplete set was immeasureably diminished in value.

'My cousin,' he explained, 'visited the Vatican Museum last year. Recognized the missing table, the very one at which his uncle – my father – had been made a papal count.'

'Didn't you write and ask for it back?'

He let his wintry smile loose. 'You mean, simply walk in and say I want your priceless antique, please, Your Holiness?'

'Well,' I said lamely, 'you could explain.'

'Would you give it up?'

Indignantly I burst out, 'Would I hell!' before I realized. Of course, nobody would. 'Are you certain it's the missing piece?'

279

'Positive.' He held up his gloved fist. 'Like I know my own hand.' That too was fair enough. The rent table made the difference between a mindboggling fortune and a more ordinary fortune.

I lay in my hotel room listening to Rome closing for the night. All the usual sounds: voices in the hotel corridors, cars going, somebody speaking to a friend on the pavement outside, an elevator whirring, a woman calling to a neighbour.

My trouble was I was beginning to feel lost and threatened, maybe even set up. This Marcello, for instance. Nice as pie. Trusting, even. I wondered if he had only given me an accomplice's phone number instead. It was all wrong, so bloody unlike any carry-on I'd ever known.

Okay, I admit it. Over the years I've done the odd rip, though honestly every time was a deserving case and none had done anybody any harm. I mean, nobody had starved or gone broke, nothing like that. Looking up at the ceiling of my room, I cheerfully absolved myself of any blame. You see, I'm not big on motive. To me there's simply no sense in sussing out why people do things. There's altogether too much talk about psychology and suchlike crap. It's all rubbish. What matters is what a person actually *does*, not what he thinks or dreams. Consequently I was happy to accept more or less everything Arcellano had told me, except it was pathetically obvious that Lovejoy Antiques, Inc – all one of me – were the entire rip. I was the whole sodding army of villains, including the man driving the getaway Jaguar and piloting the Boeing out to a Bermuda haven. Still, nothing could be easier than knocking a single piece off, and from a church at that. I'd done much, much harder things. And here all around was beautiful Rome, a place I had only read of in awe.

Ignorant nerk that I am, I went to sleep full of optimism.

Chapter Six

Rome *is* beautiful. Seen in the cool daylight of early spring it was exhilarating. Oh, the traffic and the noise were same as everywhere these days, but the place has a definite quality. From my hotel window you could see only the apartments opposite and a bit of the main road to the right with a shop or two, but new is interesting.

Breakfast proved two things: Maria's language also worked in the mornings, and breakfast was unlimited coffee and rolls and jam, not the ponderous eggs-and-bacon slammer I'd never been able to afford. All my life I'd been making horrible coffee. Here in Rome there were real flavours in the cup you'd never dream of. Coffee will catch on.

Only a few people were down for breakfast early as me. We all watched each other with that surreptitious scrutiny of new acquaintances reluctant to become committed. I finally plucked up the courage to ask a woman and her daughter, poring over a tourist map of the city, where they'd bought it. They lent it me for a quick glance. The street and our hotel were marked with an inked cross.

'Very near the Vatican,' I remarked with delight.

'This is why we stay here. Ten minutes' walk.'

'Are people allowed in?' Subtle old Lovejoy starting reconnaissance.

They laughed. 'Of course! It's usually quite crowded.'

'Is it best to go early?'

'You get to see the Sistine Chapel before it fills up with visitors.'

That sounded promising. Caroline, the daughter, was a solemn lass, Elsie the mother a good deal chirpier and eager to chat. I deflected their kind offer to show me round on my first day, saying perhaps another time when I'd found my feet. Two women could be useful camouflage.

The conversation cheered me. I was ecstatic at the thought of all those crowds because crowds are concealment. When a rip is on your mind it is space which is the enemy.

I knew nothing of the Vatican beyond the travel agents' window pictures of St Peter's great church, and vaguely supposed the Vatican and the church must be one and the same thing. Elsie prattled that of course the Vatican, being nominally an internationally recognized city state, had its own everything. Post office, stamps, currency and –

'Police?' I joked.

That threw Elsie. Her face wrinkled in doubt. 'They have the Swiss Guards,' Caroline offered. 'They wear a special uniform.'

I scraped up a dim memory of the fancifully-garbed elderly blokes somewhat resembling the yeoman warders, the so-called 'Beefeaters', of the Tower of London. Well, I've been in the Tower often enough without paying, so a couple of geriatrics in fancy dress would hardly cause me to break step. They were probably failed cardinals.

I smiled. 'How quaint.'

Caroline touched my arm as we left the dining-room. 'You'll *love* Rome,' she informed me earnestly. 'Everything about it is positively *rapturous*.'

'I believe you, love.'

'*Do* ask us,' Elsie trilled, 'if we can be of any assistance. We'll keep looking for you.'

'And I'll do the same,' I promised with poisonous heartiness, thinking, you see if I don't.

We parted and I hit the road.

The city was a-bustle. Cars were everywhere, including on the pavement in the slant-parked way I quickly came to expect. People pleased with their eagerness to talk. I had a great few minutes with a tiny elderly woman standing by a street kiosk, to the amusement of the kiosk man. She was drably dressed, hunch-backed and wistful behind her specs. She somehow provoked me into bargaining for the tourist map I wanted, and argued I had made a terrible choice. We went at it hammer and tongs, both of us laughing and threatening each other. She offered to show me round for a few lire but I couldn't afford a passenger. We parted friends.

It was all happening by then. School children, house-wives, and cars, cars, cars. Green buses, the gliding trams and the shops. I knew the essentials from Maria. For weeks now we had been over things like currency, the newly-opened Metro's Linea A, the coins you must have ready, that kind of thing, so I was not too taken aback.

Not knowing what was coming, I really enjoyed myself for an hour. I tried out the buses for a couple of stops. I had a go on the trams, and even went one stop on the cleanest Metro in the world and was appropriately confused to find nobody at the other end wanting to check my ticket. Badly shaken by this assumption of honesty, I walked into the Piazza del Risorgimento bus terminus for the best cup of coffee since breakfast. I remembered Maria's warning in the nick of time: stand and it's cheaper; sitting costs extra. I thought, let's live, sat and got the map out.

Wherever I had gone so far I had come up against the most enormous brickwork wall. Its foot sloped outwards from a point several feet above the pavement. It could not have been less than a good eighty feet high. Presumably the rear end of St Peter's church was in some churchyard behind it.

I drank my coffee feeling decidedly less full of myself. If *that* was the wall of the Vatican, there was no way of climbing it, for sure. Still, a church is a church is a church. There was bound to be a proper way in. And out. Nicking an antique from a church would be child's play. Always is.

Despite the early time of year, numerous tourists had begun to troop about when finally I left the café. I thought, follow the wall and you will come to the entrance. Nothing could be simpler. Full of resolution, I crossed by the tourist shops crammed with mementoes and religious statuary. A group of Germans, superbly organized, were already photographing a small gateway up ahead. I headed for them and mingled. I disliked what I saw.

The gateway was one car wide. It had everything except size. Its traffic lights worked. It had businesslike gates folded back, but worst of all it had a group of vigilant blokes. They wore the navy-blue attire of tidy artists, slanted berets, cloaks with arm-holes, black stockings. That didn't paralyse me so much as their air of diligence. No car was allowed to enter but these chaps scrutinized each car's occupants and the passes. Worse still, an imposing-looking car earned itself the sailor's elbow.

'Excuse me, signor,' I asked a man nearby. 'What is this place?'

He did not understand and anyway saw his guide raise her folded multicoloured umbrella – the signal of the Roman guide – and was off with the rest. A hand tugged my elbow.

'You never heard of the Vatican, son?'

My drab old lady who had ribbed me so mercilessly at the kiosk, her hat still with its ludicrous black cherries.

'*That's* the Vatican?' I said weakly. 'What's the wall for?'

'To keep bad people out.' She chuckled at my face. 'We Romans have this joke – it's to keep the good people in.'

'What are those men doing?'

'In the gateway? They're the Swiss Guard.'

I looked again, this time harder. Young, tough, vigilant and very fleet of foot should it come to a sprint. My heart sank. That bastard Arcellano.

'How many of them are there?'

A slyness had crept into her voice. She tilted her head up at me, birdlike, her spectacles glinting. 'Enough. You want to go in? There's a museum, but the entrance – '

Irritably I shook her off and walked dejectedly along the wall pavement. People were drifting like a football crowd. Ahead were the pillars of the Colonnade rimming St Peter's square. A toffee-maker and a trinket-seller were doing a roaring business, blocking one of the arches leading into the square with tourists mobbing the stalls. The square itself was crammed. A pop group was singing somewhere on the Colonnade steps. There was a caravan shop selling Vatican City stamps, obviously an improvised post office. Ahead, between the fountains, rose the great basilica of St Peter's. It was a real ball, everybody agog and full of good cheer, but I drifted into the throng feeling a right yeti.

Until then I had really felt quite confident. Idiot that I was, I had assumed the Vatican to be a church – okay, a big one, but still a church, with perhaps one or two elderly vergers pottering among the churchyard flowers. Now I was sure Arcellano had bitten off more than I could chew. It was like a frigging castle. Those calm diligent guards . . .

The mob of us moved like a slow tide, across the great circle and up the steps. The sheer scale of everything was awesome, doors a mile high and the basilica unbelievable in size and splendour. The last thing I expected was to find the place used, but there it was with people praying and milling and a Mass being said. I joined the crowd round Michelangelo's exquisite *Pietà*, now behind protective glass, then wandered down to the main altar. The little birdlike lady happened to be standing near the great Bernini cupola, so I ducked in to see the Papal treasures, a mind-blowing session of rococo exotics. An hour later I reeled out exhausted in a state of unrequited greed. For somebody else to own all that wealth was criminal. And no sign of anything resembling Arcellano's piece of furniture.

That familiar little figure was now flitting among some Japanese tourists. She seemed everywhere, I thought irritably. Anyway I was getting peckish. No good could possibly come of hunger when I had to suss out the Vatican, so I left St Peter's in search of a nosh bar.

That bloody great wall was beginning to get me down. For one thing, it seemed formidably intact. For another, it emitted those chiming vibes which an antiques-sensitive soul like mine hears louder than any foghorn. This wall, I thought uneasily, is not only massive and intact. It is *old*. A couple of corners and a few hundred yards and the wall turned left up the Viale Vaticano.

Half way along there was a grand doorway complete with police-like guards and ice-cream-sellers and tourists trailing in and out of a few coaches. A notice announced that this was the Vatican Museum. I sussed it out for a few minutes, dithering and generally getting in everybody's way until one of the guards started to notice. I found a pizzeria, a neat clean little place near the market. You choose a hunk of different pizzas cooked on trays, have your particular slice weighed and pay up. It's everything grub should be – fast, satisfying and cheap – but I was coming to recognize that, like all things Italian, this famous type of nosh has style, even a kind of grace. So there I stood, oozing tomato sauce and miserable as sin.

What little I'd seen told me the worst. The Vatican was no peaceful East Anglian church, as I had fondly imagined. I had so far done it all properly. Exactly according to the old antiques thieves' adage: *suss the outside, and the inside will take care of itself.* Only, the outside of this particular rip was a real downer.

Irritably I noticed I was being observed. My old woman was peering in at the window. Her face was sad, her gaze fixed wistfully on the hot food through the glass, a right Orphan of the Storm. This pest was getting on my nerves. I fidgeted and ate determinedly, but her stare bored into my shoulders. I finally surrendered and gave her a jerk of my head. She came in like Jesse Owens.

I asked grudgingly, 'Which?'

'*Con funghi*,' she said, really quivering with delight.

Wise in the ways of the world, the pretty serving lass gave her a chunk big enough to feed a regiment. Blissfully the old lady tore into it, while I paid up and left. I was narked to find the irksome old biddy trotting beside me, gnawing her pizza plank.

'*Grazie*,' she burbled. 'The Vatican now?'

I started to cut across the Andrea Doria among the market stalls. 'Mind your own business.' We risked life and limb reaching the other side unscathed. That vast dark brown wall was in clear view down the side streets.

'The Vatican makes you so sad.'

'What's that supposed to mean?'

She cackled a laugh. The market was already showing signs of winding up for the day. Stallholders were beginning to box up their unsold stuff for loading. It was all so pleasant and good-humoured I almost forgot how bitter I felt. I took no notice and tried to shake her off by walking quicker. The old biddy simply trotted faster.

I'll say this for her, she was a spry old bird. She seemed to know a lot of the market people and sprayed greetings right and left as we hurried through to the flight of steps where the street ended. I sat for breath. She sat beside me, still chewing gummily on the shredded remains of her pizza slab.

'Going in this time?'

I eyed her. 'Maybe.'

'You didn't before. You walked round the walls to study the entrances. Never seen a stranger do that before. Except once.' She smiled at me. I had to smile back. The old dear was nothing more than a fly little chiseller, a wheeler scavenging on the fringes of the tourist crowds. Harmless. She went on, 'Three years ago.' Her eyes were merry as a fairground. 'They caught him before he'd got a mile.'

My throat dried. 'Caught him? You mean – ?'

'*Si*, signor. A robber. A bad man.'

'What's that got to do with me?'

She nudged me. 'What's your game, signor? Tourist clipping? A con? A hideout?'

'Just looking,' I told her offhandedly, but worrying like mad. Was I that obvious?

'So young and foolish,' she said mischievously.

I rose in earnest then. I wasn't going to take that from anyone, the stupid old bag. Anyway she was too shrewd for my liking. 'No.' I wagged a finger at her as she made ready to bustle after me. 'No more. You go your way. I go mine. Goodbye, old lady.'

'Anna.' She was enjoying herself.

'Goodbye, Anna.'

'*Arrivederci*.'

She was looking after me, smiling and shaking her head. The pizza was gone.

Chapter Seven

Sickened, I stood looking at it.

The Chippendale rent table, for such it was, stood almost half way down an immensely long gallery upstairs in the Vatican Museum. I checked its appearance against my memory of Arcellano's photo. It was the one all right. That didn't worry me, but its position worried me sick.

On its flat top stood a glass case containing a present from President Nixon to one of the Popes, a horrible ornithological Thing of white birds and ghastly synthetic grass. I reflected that President Nixon had a lot to answer for. Still, with any luck the Thing might get damaged when I did the rip, which would clearly be a major contribution to the world of art.

Hundreds of visitors were ambling about the Museum by now, a good sign. There were plenty of uniformed guards, which was really grotty, one at each angle and in every secluded room. This particular gallery was about twice as wide as the average living-room. It couldn't have been situated worse. No exit near by, no doors. The white library near one end of the gallery was a good hundred feet off. Okay, wall-cupboards stood against part of the opposite wall, and the protrusion of a rectangular wallpillar created an open recess here and there, but that was all the cover there was. And the bloody windows gave me heartburn the instant I clapped eyes on them. Wherever you stood in this long corridor-gallery you felt like a tomato in a greenhouse. I'd never seen windows so wide and tall before, great rectangular things, beautiful but full of the chances of being seen exactly at the wrong time. To one side the windows overlooked a raised terrace, landscaped gardens, lawns and walks. To the other, one could see a small macadam road with a line of parked cars. Each car displayed an official-looking sticker on its windscreen. More open grassy swards, and that was it. Not a place to hide.

The gardens ran off to include a lovely villa and a spectacular little grotto complete with miniature water-fall, but too far away to be any use. The entire place was a miracle of design. Lovely, but ruinous to any rip, at least in the safe old Lovejoy style.

As I hung about pretending to be overawed by the Nixon gift – as indeed I was – parties of visitors came along the gallery. I'd never seen people move so fast in all my life. Everybody simply stomped hurriedly past all the delectable antiques, for all the world as if on a route march. Most gave only a sweeping glance at the cased displays, further along, of early Christian burial artefacts and miniature votive statuary. Of course, this speed was very cheering. Except they would certainly notice, if that lovely antique table were missing and that Thing was left sitting there on the floor. You could hardly miss an aquarium full of white birds, especially if you fell over the damned thing. Simply nicking the rent table was definitely out.

A mixed party of Italians and Germans raced through. I could feel the floor vibrate and felt sad. Sad because the vibrations were small in amplitude, which meant a very substantial solid flooring. You feel these by rocking back on your heels as somebody walks past. And the lovely ceiling was an arched miracle of paint-ing. Note that: the most difficult kind to penetrate from above. So no way in from above, through the windows, the walls, or through the floor. Gawd.

Miserably I tagged on to a group of Americans and plodded downstairs leaving Arcellano's beautiful table standing there.

The rip was impossible. Arcellano had had it. Now I had to tell him.

I phoned the number Marcello had given me. A young woman's voice came on, to the background of an infant's loud abuse. Pausing breathlessly to admonish the infant, which only made another sprog burst into discordant song, she told me Marcello was still on duty, and could she give him a message.

'On duty,' I said pleasantly, but not liking the phrase. 'Please tell him Lovejoy rang.'

'Right. I'll phone him at the station. Where can he reach you if he can't get away?'

That was a bit difficult. 'May I ring you again, in, say, an hour?'

'Yes. That will be fine.'

I kept listening after we said our goodbyes. I didn't like that word 'station', either. Her receiver went down without any special clicks full of ominous implications to an antique dealer like me. No special significance in the woman's voice, either, obviously just a young housewife doing multihanded domestic battle with her two riotous offspring. Which in its way was as ominous as anything I had yet encountered since arriving in Rome.

I had bad news for Marcello. This rip needed Murph the Surf, not me. I cheered up and went out for a gander at the streets. It was high time other people started getting bad news, as well as me. Share and share alike, I always say.

You've never seen such neat shops as there are in Rome. I knew from Maria's relentless teaching that the shops shut for the afternoon and open again about four-thirty. They were just opening for their second rush.

I went down the Andrea Doria, a wide and pleasant street. You have to be an olympic pole vaulter to get across safely but I made it. Two cups of *caffè-latte* with a cake *columbe* the size of a tram and I felt full of myself. Within one hour I'd be free of the rip, the whole bloody thing. I'd simply tell Marcello the Vatican was a fortress, protected by vigilant guards who were obviously wise in the ways of the horrible old world. Then, duty done, I would spend a few happy nights in this lovely city's museums and art galleries until my money ran out, then off home. What was impossible was impossible. No two ways about it. I wandered on in a welter of relief. Even Arcellano would have to accept the obvious.

It was coming up to Easter. I'd never seen so many Easter things in my life. Shop interiors were hung all about with chocolate Easter eggs done in scintillating coloured papers, each egg decorated in a spray effect for all the world like a grenadier's badge. And windows with a zillion chocolate shapes, chocolate baskets full of tiny eggs and little creatures doing their thing. You couldn't help but be fascinated. I saw one that I don't know to this day how it stayed upright, a giant floating dove cake in creams and puff pastry. Marvellous.

Marvellous, that is, until I saw old Anna struggling in the grip of the proprietor, her hand pointing imploringly at me and screaming blue murder.

'Nephew! Nephew! Enrico! He'll tell you the truth!'

I looked round. The old bat meant me.

Shoppers gathered instantly, volubly joining in and having a whale of a time explaining opinions.

'Are you her nephew?' the proprietor demanded.

'Yes! Yes!' Anna screamed, yelling it was all a misunderstanding which her nephew would account for. 'Enrico! Tell them!' *Enrico*, for Christ's sake?

'It's your auntie!' people informed me. I was pushed at Anna. Faces were everywhere. A million voices were raised in tangled explanation as I looked about desperately for escape. And Anna was screeching and

292

pleading, with the weary proprietor accusing Anna of stealing the things in her basket.

'Poor old woman!' people cried.

'Let my nephew explain!' Anna was bawling. She reached over and clutched at me. I could have strangled her.

'Hush! Let the nephew explain!' everybody babbled.

There was no way out. A horde of faces turned expectantly. I drew breath, trapped. The trouble was, every body looked so bloody nice and interested. If they hadn't I'd have scarpered in a flash – and I'd have got away, too. Nobody scarpers like Lovejoy Antiques, Inc.

'Yes?' the proprietor demanded.

Italy abhors a silence, so I started. 'I'm so sorry,' I said to the proprietor, casting a loving glance on Anna. There was no doubt in my mind the sinful old devil had half the shop in her basket and, seeing me contentedly sipping coffee, had hit on the notion of using me for cover. 'Yes. I'm her nephew. Hello, Auntie,' I smiled.

'*There* you are!' everybody exclaimed triumphantly. 'He *is* her nephew!' They told Anna I *was* her nephew, after all.

'I've been looking for you, Auntie,' I announced loudly, quickly beginning to get the hang of Rome talk. This was one thing Maria hadn't taught me: use gestures and keep going. If everybody else talks louder, use a few more decibels yourself. The system of alternates used where I came from – saying your bit in turn – is regarded hereabouts as surrender.

'You *have*?' Anna said, amazed despite herself.

'For two whole days,' I lied, embracing her. 'And here you are!'

'Yes! She is here!' the shoppers chorused.

'My poor auntie,' I bawled into the din, eyes misty, 'has been expecting me for Easter and wanted to give me a present, but she is poor – '

'Ah, how *loving*!'

' – but,' I thundered, '*proud*!'

'Ah! How human!'

I had some of them in tears. The proprietor was glancing exasperatedly about. A strolling policeman across the street was looking across. One more problem I could do without.

'If there's any misunderstanding, I'll pay!' My yell gained instant approval, even scattered applause on the crowd fringes.

'She stole – ' the proprietor tried loudly.

'How much?' I bawled louder over the hubbub. 'I'll pay, this very second!'

The place was a riot of chatter. A couple of tearful old ladies and a well-dressed elderly man pressed forward offering bank notes.

'Here! Take this, signor! For the old *povera*!'

'No!' I carolled. 'This lady is my responsibility! My honour demands – '

'Such honesty!'

The proprietor named a sum beyond my resources. Thankful for the racket, I flourished my handful of notes and, howling explanations that my dear old auntie was in any case slightly loony, grandly miscounted out a complicated sequence of notes. Old Anna looked murderous. The pandemonium reached deafening proportions as I wrung the proprietor's hand. Several of the shoppers embraced me tearfully.

I left the shop a hero, with my dear old auntie clinging to my arm. We walked, smiling and reunited, round the corner to a small alley and paused, carefully looking right and left to check we were unobserved. Then she clobbered me on the side of my head, hissing abuse.

'*Cretino*!' she spat. 'Stopping them from giving us money – '

All for equality, I clocked her back hard enough to glaze her eyes. She leaned against the wall, moaning.

'You beast!' She was obviously at death's door from my criminal assault.

'Yeah, yeah,' I said calmly.

Her basket was crammed with chocolate delicacies under the cover cloth. No wonder the proprietor was narked. Old Anna had practically nicked his entire shop, the evil old witch. I found her purse and riffled inside. Two hundred grotty lire.

I flung the basket down. The old sod was falling about laughing at the expression on my face. I chucked the chocolate figures back, keeping a merry Easter rabbit out of spite.

'Here,' she said, sobering up long enough. 'Got any further on your Vatican job?'

'What Vatican job?'

'I understand,' she said slyly. 'But I could help you.'

'How?' I asked levelly, hating the old crab.

'You're new to Rome. Your Italian's good but raw. Learned too fast, see? Come and live with me.'

The old lunatic was off her nut. 'With you?'

'Not like that, cretin. We'd be a good team. Do that shop act all over Rome.' She went all coy. 'I've extra space. My daughter's away studying. We'd be a great team, Enrico.'

This was getting out of hand. Anyway, I had to phone Marcello to get myself off the hook. I unlatched her arm but I couldn't help smiling.

'You're a scream,' I told her. 'Get lost, Granny.'

She weighed me up. 'You're too dumb to be a good thief.'

'*I'm* not a thief,' I corrected with asperity. 'That's you, remember?'

'Better than you'll ever be,' she said, rather sad. 'I'm in the open market eight every morning if you need me.'

I felt myself warm to the stupid old creature. In her own way she was courageous and vital, and for a senile geriatric she had startling eyes. I shook myself. When you get feelings like that it's time to cut out, so I did.

Smiling to myself I thought, *me*? Need *her*? That was rich. 'Good luck, Anna.'

'Keep it. You'll need it, Enrico,' she called after me. '*Arrivederci*.'

I was still smiling when I looked back from the intersection. She was trotting beside a small group of tourists, chattering eagerly and obviously in her element. I could hardly keep from laughing outright.

With considerable relief I got through to an anxious Marcello from a payphone near the Julius Caesar Theatre.

'Is everything all right, Lovejoy?'

'Look, Marcello. The job's off. It can't be done.'

Marcello sounded astonished. Gawd knows what kind of a build-up Arcellano had given me. He exclaimed, 'But there's no question of backing out, Lovejoy – '

'Oh yes there is.' I was getting narked. The whole thing had gone wrong from the start. It was all based on misconception. And, for Christ's sake, I fumed to myself, one antique's not the whole world. 'I'm backing out right now. So Arcellano has a bee in his bonnet about an antique. Haven't we all?'

Marcello's voice went funny. 'Arcellano?'

'Yes. Tell him I can't do it. Nobody can.' I sailed on. 'Just pass the message on that Lovejoy resigns. Tell him to ask the SAS instead.'

'Lovejoy! *You* know Arcellano?'

I was too mad and too despondent to chat about things that were pathetically obvious. 'See you, Marcello.'

'*Lovejoy*!' He shouted so desperately loud the phone crackled. 'Lovejoy! Tomorrow morning! Six o'clock! The Colosseum! See me there – '

'Nice knowing you,' I said, and put the receiver

down. Everybody else has a thousand excellent ideas about your work. Ever noticed that?

It was only when I was actually on the point of going for a quiet glass of wine that I realized my money was missing. Then I recollected how close Anna tended to walk with one, how trustingly she'd taken my arm – on the wallet side. The old bitch had dipped me, the evil old cow.

Apart from a few coins I was broke.

Chapter Eight

Next morning I escaped from the hotel – into the worst day of my life.

Usually I'm a night owl. I'm up early too, which is just another way of saying I'm hardly a ball of fire once the day is actually under way. With the extra stimulus of wanting to escape without paying I was tiptoeing out by five o'clock.

The previous evening I had laughingly made several deliberate errors of direction down the corridors. This way I learned there was a separate exit, a kind of alleyway leading to a subterranean car park. Once out of the hotel it would be simple to hitch-hike to the airport. With luck I'd be in the air by late afternoon.

I left my crummy suitcase and my few frayed belongings. The spring weather was not overpowering, so I wore two shirts and carried spare socks in my pocket. My small canvas satchel thing came too. This I stuffed with other belongings – a dictionary, an antiques notebook, passport, air ticket, underpants and singlet – and glided out into the corridor.

There is always noise in hotels, but until five that morning I'd no idea how much. It's a wonder anybody kips at all. Flitting down the stairs, I nearly infarcted whenever the lift banged or hotel staff conversed on the landings. In fact at one stage, pausing in the lift alcove while my heart hammered and my breathing wouldn't start up again, I seriously contemplated nipping down to Elsie's room on the third floor, and throwing myself on her mercy, so to speak, but common sense won. A woman finding a man at a disadvantage can be very friendly company. Be destitute, and that same woman becomes utterly merciless. So I crept on and made it safely out into the street after only seven or eight more infarcts.

Left across the Via Campanella. The great somnolent Vatican stared reproachfully down at me as I marched along the quiet streets. Cheerfully I gave it two fingers, meaning Arcellano and his daft scheme.

The bus I caught from the Piazza del Risorgimento was one of the first out. Rome was waking sleepily. A few cars were already abroad, their drivers wearing the non-toxic air of the early motorist rediscovering the freedom of the roads. In an hour they knew it would be hell. Smiling, I got off the bus as soon as I saw an open nosh bar, and with my last groat had coffee. I'd escaped from the hotel, possibly from Arcellano and his rip. I felt really great.

It's funny how your mind plays tricks. I was honestly listening to two blokes conversing about last night's football match and noshing away when I noticed where I was. I was astonished. No, I mean it. Until then I honestly thought I'd chosen a bus at random, simply got the first one leaving the bus station in order to get clear away. But there, illuminated by the slanting sunlight against the blue sky, was the great silent mass of the Colosseum, the early sun slit by its cavities into beams that stencilled its darkness and only made its prodigious stony bulk loom even more. Almost across the blinking road, for heaven's sake. Can you imagine?

I swallowed nervously. Ever since I'd arrived in Rome events had ganged up on me. You must have had that same feeling, when no matter how you plan you finish up having no real choice. There was a girl serving.

'Have you the time, please?' I asked.

'Nearly six, signor.'

Six. Marcello's hour, the time he said to meet him at the Colosseum. I hadn't taken all that much notice of what he'd said – being more concerned with getting my own resignation in. Until this chance bus journey, I honestly hadn't the slightest intention of meeting Marcello. That is God's truth. And if old Anna had not pinched my money . . . See what I mean, about events? I want to get this clearly understood, because the deaths weren't my doing – well, anyhow not my responsibility. If I'd had my way I would have been back in my crummy East Anglian cottage instead of walking towards the curved stone storeys of the Colosseum.

There was hardly anyone about. An ice-cream van arriving, a police car dozing, an almost empty bus wheeling round and a couple of little kids waiting for the day's tourist action to begin. One early car half-heartedly tried to run me down. The city had hardly begun to wake.

The Colosseum's real name is the Teatro Flaviano. It stands at a big intersection of the San Gregorio and the road leading to the Forum. From the outside it has the appearance of a huge gutted edifice still in its undressed fawn-coloured stone. In its heyday it held as many as fifty thousand spectators and is beautifully planned. Believe it or not, it had enough exits and enough room for its audience – an architectural miracle. Find a modern building that has decent doorways and isn't hell to be in. Lovely.

I stood listening a moment between the pillars of the entrance. There was no sign of Marcello, just a great horde of cats insolently giving me their sneery stare. None bothered to move, and I even had to step over two as I entered between the scagged stones.

An empty ruin can be quite spooky, even in the centre of a bustling city in the bright cold sunlight of morning with the occasional car door slamming and noise of a passing bus. I called Marcello's name. It came out a bleat, for no reason because I wasn't scared or anything. I shook myself and called his name a bit

300

louder. No luck. I trod inside, under the stretching stone.

The actual floor of the amphitheatre itself has long since gone. You come out looking up the length of the Colosseum's open space, with the huge slabbed divisions of the cells below now occupying all that is left of the vast arena. All round and climbing upwards are stone galleries for the spectators of long ago. I went to the right along one of the contoured terraces. A sprinkling of cats yawned and prowled after me.

I called softly, 'Marcello?'

A pebble dislodging somewhere practically made me leap out of my skin. There was a light echoing thud, probably some moggie nudging a piece of crumbling mortar off a stone buttress. For some reason I had the jitters, but then I'm like that, always on edge over something that isn't there. Cats are nice, yet when you are in a place like that you can't help thinking of their bigger relatives noshing Christians by the hundred, and spectators howling for blood.

Like a fool I found myself going on tiptoe round the terrace, and this with an ice-cream-seller whistling outside as he put out his awning and in clear shout of that splendid police car out by the pavement and, and . . .

The terrace ended about half way round the great ellipse. An iron railing barred my way. To the right lay the outer wall and its splendid arched fenestrations showing the city of Rome slugging out of her kip. To the left, the central cavity of the arena. If I hadn't been in such a state I'd have found time to marvel at the construction. As it was, I barely had the inclination to glance ahead and down to where the buttressing was being restored. The new giant blocks of stone were symmetrically arranged on the sand to either side of . . . of Marcello.

He lay in the ungainliest attitude twenty feet below, one arm folded behind his back and his head turned

301

at an impossible angle as if he were listening hard. Blood from his nostrils and mouth spattered the pale fawn dust. Pathetically, an ankle was exposed where the fall had rucked up his trouser leg. A moist stain was still gradually extending down his trousers. His bladder had voided under the impact when his body had struck. There was no question of life. An early fly was already at his lips.

I looked about, frightened out of my wits. Dithering like a nerk, I put my satchel down with some daft idea of climbing down, but finally thought better of things. Near by a cat licked its paw with complete disdain. The vast terraces were still empty. Nobody was yet photographing Pope Pius IX's wooden crucifix across the other side. No talk, no other sounds. I whipped round nervously, but was still alone.

The Colosseum was fast becoming no place to be. People would be here soon, and that meant the police. I looked over the edge of the terracing into the recess. My instincts were right – get the hell out. I was sweating and prickling. If Marcello had only just fallen – the sound of that thud came back to mind – his pushers were still here.

The sun was warming the vast bowl as I flitted from pillar to pillar in a feeble attempt to leave undetected. I was disgusted with myself. Some people would be sensible, brave it out. It's called being responsible. Others, like me, chicken out. I bulleted into the main thoroughfare.

The two little lads were still hunched over their game. Neither looked up. The ice-cream-seller had successfully manoeuvred his van into position a good fifty yards away and was smoking over his morning paper. I was mainly interested in the police car, though, which had gone. I had a vague idea I just glimpsed it leaving down the San Gregorio but wasn't going to press the issue.

The streets looked a bit more built up towards St

John Lateran so I strolled that way, my heart in my mouth. A couple of cars took turns trying to get me, hooting noisily as they screeched round the Colosseum. Somehow nearly losing my life crossing the road made me feel better, even when I realized I'd no longer got my satchel. I thought, oh Gawd, and half-started to go back for it, but cowardice won out.

Rome was almost fully wakened now. I was still shaking, but improving. At least I had a great living city to be broke in, and a whole living day before me. Better still, I was alive in it. Marcello wasn't.

I watched Anna. Grudgingly I had to admit she was bloody good.

By ten past eight I'd picked Anna up in the market on the Andrea Doria. She first worked a crowd of tourists from a coach in the Conciliazione, the long broad avenue between the River Tiber and St Peter's. At first I was a bit slow guessing what was going on. She bumped into people and tripped up, always getting in everybody's way. Her profuse apologies were so sincere. She picked two tourists' pockets, and following her down the little intersecting street towards the Borgo San Spirito I was almost certain I saw her discard an extra handbag in the box of a passing pick-up truck, slick as you please. If you've ever seen the traffic hurtle down the narrow Borgo you'll understand my admiration. There is hardly an inch of pavement.

Poor old decrepit Anna was obviously fit as a flea despite the pronounced limp which returned when she was back in the growing crowd. In fact it was all I could do to keep up with the crummy old devil. I had seen enough to have no worries when an hour later she was spectacularly run down by a tourist coach at the corner of the Mascherino. She lay moaning and twitching with her few pieces of fruit scattered in all directions. I waited patiently while she gradually recovered and the sympathetic tourists had a whip-round for her, then followed her back towards St Peter's.

For the next couple of hours she worked the crowds brilliantly, leaving no scam unturned. It was as good a sustained lurk as anything I'd ever seen and I was glad – she was my one possible helper. For her age she was beyond belief. All in one dazzling hour-long spell she did three phoney fetches (you nick something, then 'find' and return it, absolutely brimming with honesty). She even did the fetch gig with a kid and got away with it. You can imagine the father's demented relief. She was unbelievably fast, smoother than any I'd seen for years. The old bag even managed to get *on* a coach as everybody else was getting off, to emerge carrying two cameras and a lady's handbag through the coach's emergency exit and zoom down a side street. I never did see how she got rid of them, but by the time I headed her off she was tottering and being helped by some sympathetic Americans near the Angelica. I decided the young nerk who'd started following me was no more than a stray pickpocket and could be safely discounted for the moment.

By one o'clock the pace hotted up. A pattern was becoming evident. Anna kept strictly to one area, roughly bounded by St Peter's Square, the Borgo and the river, and she only did a fixed number of scams. The dip seemed to be her thing, that and a careful selection of cons of which the spectacular 'accident', the faint and the phoney fetch were her favourites. I followed, marvelling, and stuck to her like glue.

It was about two o'clock when it happened. I was reeling bewilderedly after her hunched, limping, amorphous form when I realized the old bag was pausing. She was by Bernini's fountain in St Peter's Square, with me thankfully trying to get my breath and her sprightly as ever. She did something extraordinary. Quite openly, she deliberately placed a postcard in the water of the fountain. Just layered it with great precision so it floated. I stared as she moved off at a sedate limp towards the great Colonnade pillars among the tourists.

Fascinated, I approached the fountain. There it was, a postcard, still floating. I glanced about. People were clicking cameras, gazing at the great architecture, chatting and strolling or simply staring up at the Holy Father's narrow window in hopes he might show. Nobody noticed the old lady's odd action.

It was barely soggy. I got it and turned the picture over. Her writing was large, decisive and brisk.

Enrico,
The Ponte Sant' Angelo, about six-thirty.
Wait if I'm late. Love, Anna.

I thought blankly, Enrico? Who the hell – ? Then I remembered. Enrico was me, her 'nephew'.

I put the card in my pocket and set off in the direction she had taken. Within two minutes I realized the old sod had slipped me. Furiously I searched for her high and low but finally chucked in the sponge. She had vanished.

I slumped exhausted on the Colonnade steps to wait till six-thirty. The old bag had shown an oddly consistent interest in me – particularly *me* – ever since I'd showed up. There was something odd here. I felt pushed, manoeuvred. The same feeling, in fact, I'd had since first meeting Arcellano that day in the auction. Surely Anna had nothing to do with Arcellano?

I put my head on my knees and pretended to doze. The showy idiot who had been following me since about nine o'clock was now leaning against a pillar forty feet away. He was on his umpteenth bottle of red wine and looked like a villain from bad rep theatre. He was about eighteen and had seen too many cheap movies. He terrified me so much I nodded off.

Chapter Nine

'I saved your life, Enrico,' Anna said, wading into ninety square yards of pizza, a horrible sight. 'From Carlo.'

'Who the hell's Carlo?'

'Look back.'

We were walking at a slow pace away from the Angelo, the great circular castle by the Tiber. We had crossed the bridge and just turned left down the Coronari. A tangle of narrow streets was beginning, the kind I had yet to see in Rome. Anna was clearly at home here, never needing to check direction.

Behind us the youngish bloke was leaning against the wall of a barber's shop, cleaning his nails with a stiletto.

'That 1951 Bogart is yours, I take it?'

Anna cackled. 'That's Carlo. He wanted to spit you.'

'Good gracious,' I said politely.

'He's armed,' she said mischievously.

'His sort always is.'

She fell about at that. 'You're great. This way, Enrico.'

We dived to the right and started going slightly uphill. The streets were no more than alleys hereabouts. A lovely aroma pervaded my nostrils and I started to quiver. Furniture varnish. Several small antique shops, of remarkable elegance for such a crummy-looking district, were dotted in the nooks and crannies of the cobbley labyrinth. Carlo was following, three parts sloshed and weaving from side to side. You have to laugh.

'Visit the Vatican again?' she croaked as we trotted up the alley.

'Me? No. Why should I?'

She rolled in the aisles at this as well. I found myself getting narked at the old jessie. And the spectacle of her ravaged senile face smeared with grease did nothing for me, except make me heave.

'That's no answer.' She laughed so much I had to bang her shoulders to get her breathing again. As soon as her colour came back she assaulted her pizza again. It was horrible. All she needed was some knitting and a guillotine. 'And you've been following me all day.'

The old gamp had me there. 'Actually, I'm strapped.'

'Broke, eh? Get dipped?'

I waited coldly for her paroxysm of hilarity to end. She had to hold on to the doorway of a small antiques shop to recover.

'Yes. By you, you old bitch. I want it back.'

'*Me*? What a terrible accusation!'

Her eyes were gleaming behind her specs. I turned for half a look.

Carlo was closing slowly, every inch real menace. Doubtless Anna had given him some signal because he held his knife hand at that loose angle which did not alter as he moved, a real giveaway.

Other than us the alley was empty. There was a small boozer further along and a couple of antique furniture shops and some place crammed with ecclesiastical vestments. I could see a preoccupied browser or two in one of the antique shops. Somewhere nearby an electrical sander hummed. Maybe this was the right time and place.

I said, 'Hand it over, Anna. My money.'

'You try to riddle me? On my own doorstep? *Brutto*!'

I fetched her one then, only lightly because of her age, but enough to shut her mouth while I lifted her handbag from the basket. This goon Carlo was a real comic, hissing dramatically and narrowing his eyes as he came with his knife weaving sinister patterns in front of him. By then I was just too tired to bugger about. You can't blame me. I'd had a rotten two days.

I slid my left arm into the basket for a shield and gave him a double prod – the shield at his knife and my instep in his balls. My right knee caught under his chin as he oofed forward, then it was only a matter of kicking a couple of his ribs in while he slumbered gently on the cobbles.

Anna was staring in astonishment, holding her cheek as I teased out her money. I tossed her the handbag.

'Here, love. Buy a pizza.'

'You bastard. That's my money.'

So much for Carlo, I thought. 'It's not. It's mine.'

'Have you killed him?'

'Carlo? No. He'll just not play the tuba for a week or two.'

She was just drawing breath for a scream when I grabbed her and stifled it.

'Listen, you octogenarian conner,' I gritted. I'm as hard as nails with geriatrics. 'I've lost my passport and air ticket, been dipped by you, been forced from my comfortable hotel, had a friend killed, got stranded, and get jumped by your threepenny nerk who's too cackhanded to blow his own nose. I've had enough, hear? Enough.'

I released her and took off. I'd reached the end of the alley by the time she started screaming. Like a fool, I had assumed the old devil would only be able to manage a senile mumble but she put up a wail like the QE 2. Bloody hell, I thought, and in sudden panic hurtled along a few zigzaggy alleys until I came out into the Piazza Navona, a place I recognized from the famous pictures in the little guidebook I'd owned until this morning. I subsided in a chair on the pavement outside a restaurant to get my breath.

Well, somehow I'd messed up the chances of having

Anna as a potential ally, but at least I had a bit of my own money back. In any case she was a doubtful quantity, and her sidekick Carlo scored a definite minus. I hoped I was better off, but didn't feel it.

I celebrated my recovered wealth with a quick nosh and a glass or two of white wine, and felt much better. It was that which gave me courage to ring Marcello's number. My hand was shaking.

'Hello?' A man's voice, with that practised flintiness from a lifetime of encountering misery. A copper.

In the background a woman's awful keening was just audible, some bird realizing she was alone now with two kids in a hostile world. I put the receiver down quickly in case calls were being traced. I desperately needed to ask who Marcello had contacted between the last time we'd spoken and six o'clock this morning when he'd been flung to his death in the Colosseum.

I could guess, though. The one person Marcello and I had in common was Arcellano, the hoodlum with enough aggro to waste a bloke like Marcello simply as a warning to me. Well, I felt warned all right.

Settling up with the waiter, there was no longer any doubt in my mind. Arcellano wanted the rip attempted. And by me. After what I'd seen of the Vatican I knew bloody well there was no way anybody on earth could pull it off. A million to one I'd be collared in the act, which must also be what Arcellano wanted – seeing he'd done me over, threatened murder and then finally committed that ultimate atrocity. God knows what I'd done to deserve all this.

But deep within me as I waited for my change there smouldered the small beginnings of a fire which I recognized with dismay.

If I tried the rip and got nicked, at least I'd know what the hell Arcellano really was up to. *But what if I pulled it off?* I'd not only know – I'd have Arcellano nailed. I'd have the priceless antique he wanted. Either way I could call the tune and make the bastard dance. The only way to reach Arcellano was pull the Vatican rip.

It was the thought of nailing Arcellano that did it, made me walk on air. I couldn't think of nailing a nicer bloke.

I'd do the rip all right.

Chapter Ten

To stay in Rome I needed to immerse myself safely among a mob of workers. What better work than antiques?

I found myself drifting instinctively among the narrow alleys not far from the Corso Vittorio Emanuele II, near where I'd had the dust-up with Carlo, and sniffing appreciatively at the luscious pong of mahogany being planed, mixed with the glues and varnishes which antique restorers use.

By now it was getting on for eight o'clock. Most shops were shutting along the Corso – so named by reason of the horse races held down those streets in ancient days. Lovely shops, handsome people, and antique shops every few yards. I felt good. My spirits were soaring under the influence of the grub and the wine. In my innocence I believed I'd seen the last of that ridiculous old woman. Vaguely at the back of my mind was the problem of where she'd intended leading me when I'd met her at the Ponte Sant' Angelo, but I suppressed the worry. Antiques do that – leave me senseless.

So, when I saw a small mixed gaggle of tourists trooping into a small antique shop near the Vecchio I was in among them like a flash. It looked just about right for me. The tourists seemed a pleasant, talkative crew. They were being impressed by the elegant proprietress who was holding forth on the merits of her abundant antiques. She was gorgeous in her stylish fawn twin-set and pearl choker, and knowledgeable with it. I listened with some interest but more amusement as she delivered her spiel. With luck I'd be in here.

'Silver,' she was saying about a lovely tray. 'Even after the Bunker Hunt fiasco, genuine hallmarked silver is the greatest investment you could hope for.'

Well, yes, I thought, but be careful, folks.

'It's really beautiful,' an attractive blue-rinsed woman exclaimed.

'What period?' her husband asked. He was a benign portly gent in executive rimless specs and looked worth a groat or two.

'George the Third. A London maker called Edward Jay.' The woman noticed me. She obviously hated me on sight. Well, I'm no sartorial model. I never look well dressed, and what with the recent carry-ons I suppose she thought me a right scruff. As long as the other customers were there she could hardly sling me out.

'It weighs heavy, George,' the tourist said. 'And so *old*.'

'Over two hundred and twenty six ounces, madam.'

'Is that right!'

'And absolutely original, I assure you. Worth – '

Calmly I said, 'Half.'

The proprietress maintained her pleasant smile at my casual interruption. Two goons instantly appeared, one definitely limp of wrist and highly perfumed, the other a handsome gorilla. They came smiling hard and stood to either side of me. I felt like a nut in a cracker. The Americans turned on me, still benign but with financial antennae quivering.

'You say half, sir?'

'Half. Look.' I took the tray – a genuine, lovely job with applied reeded borders, handles and four panel supports – and tilted it at the strip-light. 'See the centre? The reflection's fine until you get to the middle.'

'A forgery?' the American woman said breathlessly.

312

'Not really. It's original all right. But the one thing which cuts the value of a beautiful tray like this is central engraving – coats of arms, monograms – done later.'

'There *is* none,' the proprietress snapped. Her smile wasn't slipping, but it had definitely tightened.

'Not now.' I squinted along the tray. A definite margin showed around the centre. 'Somebody's machined it off. It's visible from an angle, like oil on water.'

'Wouldn't it be thinner there, sir?' asked the elderly American.

I was impressed. Politeness and common sense come rare.

'Not if you electroplate it time after time in the centre with silver. Still genuine, you see. Still legal. But devalued.'

'Ahem, this early saxophone,' the dainty assistant crooned, sharp as floss, trying to distract attention.

'Basset horn,' I put in. It's a weird looker, detachable spout and all.

His mouth was a pale slit of fury. 'I know it's a horn, stupid!'

'Wrong.' I was enjoying myself. 'It's not a horn at all. It's a woodwind. Basset as in hound, but horn after a bloke. Mister Horn made them in the Strand.'

The dealer was a woman after my own heart. To my astonishment she suddenly smiled and took the tray from me. 'Well done,' she pronounced smoothly, turning casually to her tourists. 'Signor Giuseppe is a member of my staff, ladies and gentlemen. Our little ruse worked, as usual.'

'Erm – ' I said uneasily, wondering what the hell. I hadn't liked being Enrico for old Anna. I definitely hated the idea of being Giuseppe for this luscious bird.

She coursed over my hesitation. 'Ladies and gentlemen, we arrange this demonstration to show our customers that antiques are fraught with risks. Now, with

313

our warning in your mind, please allow me to give you a conducted tour of our excellent stock of antiques. . .'

The two blokes closed on me. I really wanted to cut out and try somewhere else, late as it was, but oozed along with the Americans for protection.

Once or twice I was drawing breath to point out the odd fact – that the *crystallo ceramico* she mentioned as being by the great Apsley Pellat was probably by a contemporary copier (his favourite best-selling trick was a porcelain medallion of some grand personage, set in glass), and that the pair of peasant love-spoons she claimed were Welsh had probably never been further north than Basle. It was no use. Her two goons were breathing hard in what can only be called a threatening manner. Anyhow, the bird was in full flight, posing thoughtfully at every painting, casually arresting everybody's eye. And I'll be frank about it. She had me as mesmerized as the Yanks, though I suppose after smelly old Anna any bird would have looked like Miss World.

She sold a cut-card silver sauceboat (the silver decoration is fretted on a silver slice which is then applied to the silverware. It's not been done well for a good century). Knowing I was there, she wisely glossed over a piece of so-called Rafaello ware (in fact Raphael did none of these; they're simply forged nineteenth-century tin-enamel porcelain maiolicas) and instead sold a little harlequin table of about 1790.

The tourists made to leave after half an hour. Uneasily I realized her two blokes were between me and the exit.

'I'll walk part of the way – ' I was saying with a sickly smile, but the bird was too quick.

'Signor Giuseppe,' she crooned. 'Would you mind waiting a moment, please? Good night, ladies and gentlemen! And thank you!'

The door closed. I kept my smile up but my hands were wet and my heart was thumping. I couldn't help thinking what a bastard of a day it had been. I wanted a job, not a float in the Tiber.

The proprietress stood, hands on her elbows. Her foot tapped. 'Well? What's the game?'

She snapped her fingers and her bigger ape gave her a cigarette. She was bending forward to accept his light, her gaze on me, when I saw her eyes widen in astonishment. That was because I had taken her cigarette and crumbled it into an ashtray.

'No smoking where you've pewter or paintings, love.'

'*Wait!*'

The ape was coming for me when her command froze him. It was just as well because the Stangengläser 'pole' glass I was innocently holding was worth about ten times the lot of us. Their long cylindrical form isn't to my liking, but I'd have crowned him with it if I had to.

'Look, folks,' I said as reasonably as I could. 'You've a choice. I'll bring you a fortune, or you can simply go on in your old ignorant way.'

'Explain,' the bird commanded.

I drew breath. This was my pitch. 'If I hadn't been here you'd maybe have sold that tray.'

She smiled like a moving glacier. 'But thanks to you, I didn't.'

'No,' I said affably. 'Thanks to me you sold a hell of a lot more. That tray dodge can be repeated ten times a day. You need somebody here who knows the difference between an antique and a telly.'

'No, Piero!' Her voice was like a whiplash. The ape halted and smouldered silently. 'Go on.'

'A third of your stock's labelled wrong.'

'And you could do it right?'

'Without a single reference book.'

She was eyeing me up and down, I felt to let. 'It's not a bad idea . . .'

'He's repellent!' the petulant nerk hissed, stamping his foot.

I admit I wasn't looking very affluent, but I thought that was a bit much. She ignored the three of us, simply speculated away behind her hazel eyes.

'Are you in trouble with the police?'

'No, but you would have been if you'd sold that crappy piece of carpet as a genuine Khilim.' I nodded to indicate the labelled rug placed centrally on the floor. A real Khilim is too light to put on the floor. It's properly used for divans or as a wall decoration. 'Khilims have no pile. That things a foot thick. Who made it for you?'

There was a pause, also a foot thick. Finally she nodded as if reaching some inner agreement.

'Come back tomorrow morning,' she said. 'I'll consider you. Nine o'clock. And be presentable.'

I left, backing out nervously. Not much of a promise, but I was becoming used to very little. So long as I hung on in Rome some way, any way at all.

Chapter Eleven

I slept that night in the park near the great Castel Sant' Angelo. Edgy as hell, I kept imagining there was somebody standing watching me under the trees but when I crept over to see who it was I found nobody. I didn't sleep well. The castle's brooding bulk added nothing to my slumber, but at least it didn't rain. Most of the night I thought about popes.

Now, popes have a very chequered history. They haven't always been sweetness and light. If you crossed them – and sometimes even if you didn't – you finished up stabbed, poisoned, burned, garotted, buried, castrated, starved, or if you were lucky simply ignored to death. Even an innocent joke could earn a horrible joke in return.

I couldn't get out of my mind that whizz-kid Sixtus V. His sister had once been a washerwoman, and he considered himself ridiculed when some wag pointedly stuck a dirty shirt on one of Rome's many battered statues. Cunning as a fox, Sixtus pretended great hilarity and offered a reward to the anonymous wag – and cut off the joker's hand when he came to claim it. 'I never said I wouldn't,' the Pope calmly pronounced afterwards, the ultimate infallible theological argument. Well, my worried mind went, if a laugh gets you maimed for life, ripping the Vatican off won't exactly go over as a comedy act. And don't try telling me we don't live in the Dark Ages any more – poor old mankind is *always* in the Dark Ages, and that includes today. No mistake about that. If you don't believe me, walk around any city at nightfall, or just read

317

tomorrow's morning newspaper. And I had even better evidence than that. I'd met Arcellano.

Twice during that long night I had to shuffle down into a small grove while police cars cruised past and their nasty beams probed the darkness searching for layabouts. I'm hardly ever cold but by dawn I felt perished and was certain I looked a wreck. Anybody that's ever been unwashed and unshaven and unfed knows the feeling, especially when the rest of the world looks poisonously bright and contented. Rome's favourite knack is appearing elegant. On this particular morning its elegance got right up my nose.

I was supposed to be at the antiques place by nine so I scrambled about, had a prolonged breakfast, a barbershop shave and a wash and brush up. Naturally I walked everywhere to harbour my dwindling gelt. Even so, I was early and stood among passing pedestrians at the window of the Albanese Antiques Emporium.

Piero the ape was first to arrive and unlocked the shop's glass door with a proprietary flourish. Adriana herself arrived a minute later, coolly stepping out of a mile long purple Rolls-Royce and doubtless stopping a few pacemakers among the peasants as she did so. She was blindingly beautiful. The only person blissfully unaffected by her sleek attractiveness was her other assistant, outrageous in a silver chiffon scarf and earrings, who came rushing in after her, complaining about the traffic on the Corso.

' 'Morning, *tout le monde!*' he crooned. 'Like my new hairdo?'

He introduced himself as Fabio – 'Fab as in fabulous, dearie!' – but I wasn't taken in. I'd once seen a really vicious knife artist with all Fabio's exotic mannerisms.

'Good morning, Signora Albanese,' I said politely.

'Come through.' She swept past into the rear office.

Humbly I stood while she ripped through a couple of letters and checked the phone recorder. Seven messages out of hours, I noted with interest. A thriving business. As she settled herself I wondered about that chauffeur-driven Rolls. There had been a stoutish bloke with her, riffling paperwork in his briefcase. He had barely bothered to look up as she descended. I'd never seen such a distant goodbye. Presumably Signor Albanese.

She looked up at last. 'Your story, please.'

'Oh, er, I was on a tourist trip – '

'Name and occupation?'

She appraised me, her eyes level and cold. First fag of the day lit for effect and radiating aggro. She really was something, stylish to a fault and straight in the *bella figura* tradition. Her smart pastel suit was set off by matching gold bracelets and a sickeningly priceless platinum mounted intaglio that had seen Alexander the Great embark to conquer the world. I wanted her and her belongings so badly I was one tortured mass of cramp.

'Lovejoy. Antique dealer.'

'And you are in a mess.'

'Temporarily, signora.'

She indulged in a bleak smile to show she thought my mess very permanent indeed.

'Money problems?'

'Yes, signora. I was dipped. I have to earn my fare home.'

'So last night's performance was a tactic?'

'I admitted that, Signora.'

She nodded and with balletic grace tapped ash into a rectangular porcelain ash trough. 'What's your speciality?'

'Speciality?' It was years since anybody had asked me this sort of stuff.

'In antiques,' she said as if explaining to a cretin.

'None.' And that was the truth.

She purred, about to strike. 'Then let me put it another way, Lovejoy. Which of my antiques do you prefer? Even an imbecile like you must have *some* preference.'

I could be as vindictive as her any day of the week. 'The genuine ones.'

'*All* my antiques are genuine!' She even stood up in her fury.

'Balls,' I said calmly into her face. 'Half your stuff is crap, love. I'm a divvie.'

That shut her up. She made to speak a couple of times but only finished up standing and smoking. Behind me Piero cleared his throat. I heard Fabio whisper something. Both had evidently been attracted by Adriana's outburst and come in to see the blood.

'*Ask* him!' I heard Fabio hiss.

She judged me then in a different way, blinking away from me, then glancing back several times. I knew the syndrome. Before, it was merely a question of using a scruffy bloke who seemed to possess a limited skill. Now it was a different question entirely. The problem was how much I'd want, because as far as her and her little antiques emporium were concerned I was the best windfall since penicillin. She drew a long breath and fumigated me with carcinogens.

'You two get out,' she said at last. Then to me, 'Do sit down. Cigarette?'

Everybody's a born dazzler – at something. You, me, the tramps padding among the dustbins, and that funny woman down the street. We are all the world's greatest. The only question for each of us is the world's greatest *what*.

I once knew a bloke who was the world's worst everything – well, almost everything. If he drove a car it crashed. If he wound his watch up its hands fell off. If he dialled a friend the phone electrocuted somebody at the other end. He was a menace at work. Finally, in despair, his boss wrote him off and begged him, tears in his eyes, to get the hell off and out into premature

320

retirement. Honestly, they actually paid him to do nothing. He was a brand new kind of national debt.

Then, doodling one day in the public library – which incidentally he'd accidentally set on fire the week before – he realized the singular pleasure he was deriving from simply copying the stylized scrawl of an early manuscript which was framed on the wall. I won't tell you his name, but he is now the greatest mediaevalist calligrapher in Northern Europe, and official master copyist of manuscripts for universities the world over. Get the message? Even the worst of us is the best mankind has got – for something.

A 'divvie' is a nickname for somebody with the special knack of knowing an antique when he sees one. Some divvies are infallible only for genuine oil paintings, or sculpture, or first editions, or porcelain, or Han dynasty funereal pottery. Others like me – rarest of all – are divvies for practically any antiques going. Don't ask me how it's done, why a divvie's breathing goes funny when he confronts that da Vinci painting, or why his whole body quivers to the clang of an inner bell when near that ancient pewter dish or Chippendale table. Like the old water diviners – from whom we derive our nickname – who go all of a do when that hazel twig detects a subterranean river, there's very little accounting for these things.

If people ask me to explain, I say it's just that the antiques' love comes through and reaches out to touch me. And, since everything modern is rubbish, that's QED as far as I'm concerned.

She was staring. 'For *everything* antique?'

'Yes. Except when it's mauled into a pathetic travesty, like your mahogany occasional table out there.'

She flared briefly. 'That's genuine Georgian!'

'Its wood is that old,' I conceded. 'But it's a hybrid made up of a pole screen's base and a remade top.'

She was badly shaken. I wondered how much she'd

been taken for. 'Is that true, Lovejoy? I bought it as Cuban mahogany.'

'The bit you are looking at is veneer.' It's one of the oldest tricks in the book: get an original piece of the right date, and simply remould it. Most commonly done with tables, bureaux, cabinets and chairs. Some of these hybrids have to be seen – or bought – to be believed. I hate them, because some beautiful original has been devastated just for greed. Greed, that horrible emotion which makes hookers of us all.

'And you'll divvie for me?'

I prompted, 'For . . . ?'

'You mean payment.' Meeting an antiques man better than herself had rocked her, but money was home ground. She became brisk, her old poised and perfect self again. 'How will I verify your accuracy? Of course, I can always give you a knowledge test.'

'I might fail it.' They always ask the same things. 'Then where would you be?'

She blew a spume of smoke into the air, getting the point. Knowledge is only knowledge. I was on about the actual business of knowing, which is light years ahead. 'Have you any suggestions?'

'For proof? Yes. Stick your own price on any genuine antique, picked at random. I'll work for it.'

She bowed like the Gainsborough lady but her eyes were focused on distant gold. 'Instead of money? No other pay?'

I smiled at the caution in her tone. People are always stunned by somebody who backs his judgement to the hilt. I said, 'There is no higher price than time, love. It's all a person has.'

'You're hired.'

'Lend me enough to see the week out, please.'

Her eyes narrowed. 'I thought – '

'There's no future in starving to death, love.'

'That bad?' She drummed her fingers on her desk,

shook her head. 'No. You might take off. If you are a genuine divvie, I need you here. Fabio!'

Fabio was into the office instantly, waving a notebook and agog with inquisitiveness. He'd been listening, of course.

'Yes, Adriana.' He struck an exasperated pose. 'What's the verdict? Hitch him to our star, or under a passing bus?'

'Hitch.'

'Ooooh, fantabulation!' he squealed excitedly. 'I wonder what he'll say about that ebony *thing* you keep saying is an eighteenth-century Benin ceremonial mask prototype!' He winked at me with grotesque roguishness. 'She paid a fortune for it, dearie, been on tenterhooks ever since!'

I thought, oh dear. They make them near Dakar and have fooled the best of us. My expression must have changed because his eyes ignited with delighted malice. Adriana sensed the bad news and nipped it swiftly in the bud.

'Fabio. See that Lovejoy receives *no* money, no expenses of any kind.'

Fabio fingered his amber beads and beamed. 'Is it to be *entirely* a labour of love?'

'And you can stop that. We've come to an arrangement. Lovejoy will be paid in antiques of *our* choosing – after he's divvied them for us.'

'I'll book it in as payment in kind,' Fabio whispered confidentially to me. Adriana's lips thinned even more. I could see how Fabio could get on the calmest nerves.

'His food will be provided by me,' she coursed on tonelessly.

'Must I book a table, dear?' Fabio asked innocently, eyes on the ceiling.

She iced him with a look. 'By that I mean under my supervision.'

He pencilled an ostentatious note, murmuring to

himself, 'Lovejoy to feed under Adriana,' then asked briskly, 'Anything else, dear?'

She gave up and turned to me. 'Have you a place to live?'

I thought swiftly. If she was this careful and I was fool enough to admit that I dossed in the park she'd probably stick me in some garret over her stables, with that businessman of hers counting the teaspoons every time I went for a pee.

'Yes, thanks,' I said. 'I'm fixed up.'

They both looked dubious at that but said nothing, and we went to work.

I'd found a nook. I was in with a chance of doing the rip. And doing Arcellano.

Chapter Twelve

The Vatican walls seemed more impenetrable than ever when I photographed them that afternoon. Every gateway, the enormous doors in St Peter's, the Museum entrance, every Swiss Guard in sight and the Angelica gateway, with me grinning and clicking away among droves of tourists all doing the same thing. I went about like someone demented. There wasn't a lot of time.

Adriana had objected when I asked to use the camera. All known antiques firms – except Lovejoy Antiques, Inc, that is – have cameras of various sorts, though most dealers are too bone idle to use them much. She had finally let me borrow a cheap box camera that was hanging on hoping to become an antique, a century still to go.

'Thanks, Adriana,' I said. My last money would go on a film.

'Signora Albanese to you.'

I grovelled. 'Thank you, Signora Albanese.'

'And that's enough for a *rustica*.' That meant eating on the hoof.

I asked what about food this evening. 'That requirement will be met, Lovejoy,' she intoned mercilessly.

The giant purple Rolls called for her just before two. We shut shop with Piero sourly giving me the once over in case I'd nicked a valuable Isfahan carpet or two, and with Fabio taking an age doing his eyes in a French early Georgian period swivel mirror.

Signora Albanese refused to allow the car to drive off until she saw me enter the pizzeria at the street corner and emerge with two chunks of scalding pizza in my hands. Only then did the Rolls glide away, with her businessman still doing his executive bit. He'd hardly looked up when Adriana got in, and I'd taken particular pains to notice, because . . . I wondered *why* I'd been so sly. I hardly notice anything except antiques, except when I'm scared, and then I behave like . . . like I was doing now, moving casually but watching Fabio and Piero and the Rolls reflected in every possible shop window.

I decided I was merely going through a paranoid phase, brought on by Marcello's death and loneliness maybe mixed with apprehension at the thought of the rip. After all I'd done all the choosing, picked Adriana's place at random.

The final agonizing choice came about half past three. To buy a tiny booklet on the contents of the Vatican Museum, or to enter the place to suss it out? I decided on the latter course and spent my last on a ticket. I hurtled up the wonderful ancient staircase (a double helical spiral that curiously is a better model of nucleic acid even than that flashy Watson-Crick mock-up in Cambridge). Adriana had said to be back by five, and the Emporium was a good half-hour's walk from the Vatican. There were seven photographs left in my camera, and I would need to shove the film in for developing on the way. It didn't leave long.

The precious Chippendale piece was still there, sulk-ily supporting the weight of that horrible nature tab-leau. A museum guard was being bored stiff at the end of the gallery when I nipped behind a display case and clicked the view from the nearest window. Then the other way, with a complete disregard of lighting con-ditions. Then the length of the gallery. A couple of times I had to pause for small crowds of visitors – still sprinting as if they got paid mileage. But by the finish of my reel (who can ever work out when a film's ended?) I guessed I had at least six good shots of the gallery.

Then I crossed to feel again those lovely vibes of the true Chippendale, drawn like iron filings to a magnet.

That table really was something to see. I mean that most sincerely, and I've loved antiques all my life.

Genuine ones, of course.

It was on the way out that I realized I was being observed. There is a small glass-covered cloister between two divisions of the Museum galleries. Walk along it and quite suddenly you leave that antechamber where they sell replicas of Michelangelo's *Pietà*, and emerge on a curved terrace. You can sit in the sunshine and look out over the Vatican grounds. They look accessible, but aren't. There's no way for the public to reach either the grounds or the lovely villa situated in them, because although the terrace looks spacious it is very, very restricted. There's no way of climbing off, either up or down. It's a swine of a design.

Look away from the greenery and the Museum buildings loom above you. I guessed the windows high above – and some distance away laterally, too, worse luck still – were those of my gallery. Near, and practically begging you to enter, was the splendid cafeteria they've recently installed. The grub even looks good enough to eat. The place is spotless and – coming as a dizzy novelty to a bloke like me, raised on a diet of enteric from Woody's Nosh Bar – the tables are laminates and tubular steel, and clean. Mindboggling.

The people noshing there were the usual cross-section of modern tourists: denim-geared youngsters with birds and blokes indistinguishable, family clusters with infants laying the law down, intense schoolish couples scoring Items Seen in guide books. Nobody sinister. But that prickling was still there. My shoulders felt on fire with burning unease. I had this notion Adriana might have set Piero or Fabio on to me in case I scarpered with her mouldy old camera, stingy bitch.

It was well after four when I made the exit and set

off down the wide Viale Vaticano. Funny what tricks your mind plays when you feel on edge. I had this odd idea I'd just glimpsed Maria. It turned out to be a woman at least as beautiful and very like her. I first caught sight of her near the ancient Roma section and had almost exclaimed aloud. She even seemed to stand the same, one foot tilted alluringly while posing casually on the other. But when she turned and strolled away among the mediaeval paintings I could see she was very different – smaller, not so full in the figure. She seemed quieter and much, much calmer than Maria. A gentle young soul, possibly a convent novice out on parole.

The odd thing was, I felt she was as aware of me as I was of her. At the corner I looked back but the woman was not in sight. There, I told myself in satisfaction. There, see? Letting yourself get spooked for nothing. And Maria was hundreds of miles away, bollocking a new class for getting its verbs wrong.

I made the Emporium with one minute to go.

That first day was a real success. We fell into a pattern, the four of us. Piero was not much help, except as a removals man; the shop muscle. Fabio on the other hand turned out to be quite good on porcelain and ethnographical items, but useless on anything else. Because of some unmentionable disaster to do with a sale of commemorative medallions he had been demoted from doing any independent buying, and had been relegated to the accounts. Like many of his kind he had a real flare for display, and I very quickly came to trust his judgement when laying stuff out. Adriana of course was our vigilant boss. All cheques had to receive her signature. All sales were pitched round her mark (ie, price) and she had veto over every single tag. What she was trying to prove I don't know, but supposed it was merely competition with that podgy businessman of hers. Women can be very odd.

Calling the place an emporium makes it sound grander than it actually was. The main showroom was about forty feet deep and a smaller room led off to one side, which Adriana called the 'specials' room. There she put anything she considered to be of high value, or which was small enough to be easily nicked by the customers – a right load of light-fingered dippers they are, too. Don't think Adriana was being horrid. The average antique shop loses one per cent of its costed stock per fortnight from thievery by decent members of the public who stop by 'just to look'.

We did our tray trick only once that first day, but it was a bonanza when it came off and I swear Adriana almost smiled with delight. Nearly. This time it was with a painting which a German lady was admiring. I was being a casual browser, strolling and looking at furniture, and only getting drawn in when I heard Adriana doing a lyrical exposition of a sentimental mid-Victorian scene, quite a good painting with very little restoration.

'I'm sorry, signora,' I interrupted. 'But do please advise this lady about the medium.'

'The medium?' Adriana was nonplussed for a second because we had planned to use her vaunted 'solid' Cuban mahogany hybrid. 'But oil paints are the most durable – '

'Not on bitumen.'

At one time bitumen was regarded as a splendid permanent ground matrix for oil painting, and reached a high vogue during the early nineteenth century. The only trouble is that nothing cracks or disintegrates like bitumen does. So whether you buy for love or investment, check that the painting doesn't contain it. I explained this to the fascinated customer. The crowd she was with took great interest and one or two were even eager that I should accompany them back to their hotel and pronounce on some antiques they had bought earlier. The lady wrote me her name and room number.

'Come for supper,' she cooed. 'We could have a really good chat.'

Adriana's expression said over her dead body so I hastily said I might give them a ring. I went on to pick out a good painting for the customer, a little-known Spanish artist's work in egg tempera on laid parchment showing an early scene in industrial Milan. Adriana invented a solid price for it and the lady paid up on my say-so. It was a bargain but I wasn't too happy because I'd had my eye on it for my wages.

As soon as they'd gone Adriana yanked me into her office. Unluckily there was no innocent browser I could use for protection.

'What do you mean by that asinine display, Lovejoy?' she rasped, slamming the door.

'We made a sale – '

'Don't give me *that*! Do you think I'm an absolute fool?'

'That painting's solid bitumen – '

She stormed round the desk at me. 'I'm talking about you ogling that German cow out there in *my* shop! And I saw you collect her hotel number from her *and* I heard you promise you'd deliver the painting personally – '

I reeled under the salvo. 'Look. She insisted – '

'I won't have it! Do you hear? Making a brothel out of my Emporium! Any one of the crowd could have taken offence! I'm employing you to provide – '

I bleated, 'You heard her invite me to supper – '

She practically took a swing at me as I cringed towards the door. 'You were practically down her cleavage – '

'Now, Adriana – '

'And don't Adriana me!' she yelled, heaving up her porcelain ashtray.

I ducked out fast to get that expensive glass door

between us and streaked into the yard to help Piero load up the painting for delivery to the German lady's hotel. He gazed at me sardonically but said nothing. Fabio came out to watch us, his arms folded and an ecstatic smile on his face.

'Lovejoy.'

'Mmmmh?' I was preoccupied knocking up a plywood crate for the tempera. Always remember that tempera painting antedated oils by several centuries, and that to use egg tempera properly you need a relatively inflexible support – hence it is done on copper sheeting or board. You can do it on semi-rigid supports such as parchment paging but the technique is very special. Piero, a right neanderthal, was all for trying to roll the bloody thing up. I ask you.

'You really bother our dear Signora,' Fabio was saying.

'It isn't my fault she hadn't priced it,' I grumbled defensively. 'I haven't stopped since I came this morning.'

'She wants you. Now.'

He didn't move out of the way to let me pass, just raised his eyebrows and winked as I hurried in. Adriana had a small card ready. She held it out without looking up from her desk. I took it gingerly.

'This is the name of a restaurant, Lovejoy. You will dine there at eight-thirty this evening. The bill will be taken care of.'

'I could eat somewhere cheaper and keep the difference – '

Her voice went low and murderous. 'Lovejoy.'

I shut up and stuffed the card away thinking, ah well, I might be able to do a deal with the waiter.

During the rest of the time until we closed at eight there was only one notable moment – notable for me, I mean. There was a small object, solid bronze, of a kind I'd never seen before. It stood only a couple or so inches high and, apart from a small flattening of

331

its upper and lower surfaces, was almost completely ellipsoidal. It emitted strong secret chimes, so it had lived for generations in that fond symbiosis which makes genuine antiques the most wonderful things on earth. I gaped. I don't often feel an ignoramus among antiques.

She asked me, 'Well, Lovejoy? Is it genuine?'

'It feels so. But what the hell?' I was puzzled and turned the bronze solid over and over in my hands. A simple bronze solid.

She glanced oddly at me and took it, twisting its ends and pulling. 'Two pieces,' she said. 'There?'

She set down on the display case a beautiful tiny anvil. I'd heard of these rare Continental jewellers' anvils but had never seen a collapsible one in my life. There it sat, solid bronze, even engraved with vine leaves and small florets on its side. One simple twist and it had become a functional, highly specialized instrument, a positive godsend to any aspiring Benvenuto Cellini. I stared and stared until my eyes misted over.

'Lovejoy?' her voice said from far away. 'Are you all right?'

I looked at her. Ratty as hell, but staggeringly beautiful. 'I'm indebted.' My voice was a croak.

'I beg your pardon?'

'For showing me an antique I've never seen before.'

She gave me one of those eloquent shrugs. 'Don't make too much of it, Lovejoy.'

'Impossible,' I said. 'Thank you, signora.'

She moved on. For just a moment her cheeks coloured. Maybe I'd revealed too much intensity all of a sudden. I know people don't understand, and I'd seen enough to realize that Adriana was an out-and-out pragmatist. I followed meekly.

For teaching me that antique I was in love with her for life.

That evening was memorable for two things. First, I planned the rip – suddenly knew exactly how it could be done, starting right in Adriana's Emporium. Second, I dined lonelier than Shackleton on his ice floe.

I was given a small table by a casual waiter. Not the slightest chance of any deal with him either, because at the other end of the restaurant in grander circumstances dined Signor and Signora Albanese. Not a word passed between them except pass the salt and suchlike. And no friendly wave across the tables to lonely old Lovejoy.

The grub was great. I wasn't told what I could have or what wine the bill ran to. I just kept a wary eye on the waiter's expression and pointed interrogatively. He swiftly got the idea.

'*Fritto misto alla romana*,' he decided, sizing me up. It was a cracking fry-up, and I waded merrily in. We'd decided on *Zuppa inglese* for pud, because I'd remembered the name from one of Maria's test runs back home, and anyway who can resist trifle in hooch?

Every so often I checked that Adriana and her wealthy businessman weren't hoofing off leaving an unpaid bill and me to lifelong dishwashing, but they stayed. He was preoccupied. As far as I could tell she hardly ate enough to last the night.

Even when I got up to make my way out into the dark Roman night I kept my cool. Partly sloshed and replete with my lovely grub, I plodded solemnly past their table and said nothing. But what was driving me demented was the bird from the Museum, the one I thought had a look of Maria. During my meal she had sat at a table near the door, dined sparsely in quiet solitude and never once appeared to notice me.

Now, Rome's not the biggest city in the world. That's a fact. Plenty of cities are far more crowded. But it isn't so small that you bump into the same person in every nook and cranny. I already knew that Arcellano had plenty of minions. And if one of Marcello's killers was a delectable female, it was tough luck on her because tomorrow I was due to start preparing to rip off His Holiness the Pope. I was in no mood to muck about.

I'd never mugged a bird before, but I went out into the darkness prepared for business.

Chapter Thirteen

Befuddled but determined, I waited in the gloom of the church doorway. The petite woman emerged, looking from side to side and obviously puzzled. The minute the restaurant door had swung to I dived to the left and raced across the street. The great façade of the Sant' Andrea della Valle gave only little cover and the main street was well lit but I trusted the sudden switch from a cosy interior to a place of pedestrians and cars would momentarily disconcert her. I pressed back in the doorway, trying to seem casual because a cluster of people opposite were waiting for the 64 bus.

She dithered for a second, half-heartedly made to start one way, then hesitated and finally gave up. She wasn't daft, though. She pretended to stroll one way, then suddenly turned down the Corso del Rinascimento, walking at a hell of a lick. All this was in case somebody was following, which of course I was. Some instinct made me dart across the road and into the zigzag alley which leads off the main street. I ran into the dark and emerged a few seconds later in the Navona. By lounging against the corner shop and looking as though I'd been there for days I could see into the Corso with little chance of her seeing me.

Sure enough she turned into the square within minutes, starting down it past the first of the two splendid fountains. This was a problem, because apart from the great central obelisk and the fountains there was no shelter for me if she suddenly looked back, and I already knew she was suspicious-minded. The square is racetrack-shaped. Popes and suchlike used to flood it in the old days for water pageants, and indeed it used to be a racetrack, but now it has a couple of good café's and a load of artists and drifters. Indeed, some were still drifting. She was halfway down when I finally made up my mind and streaked off left into the parallel street to wait, breathless now and still woozy from the grub and the wine, by the alley corner.

I was almost level with the second fountain, Bernini's great and spectacular Nile figure with its hand to its eyes. As I waited, listening to her footsteps approaching down the square, I had to smile. Bernini's friends used to joke that the statue was hiding its gaze from the sight of Borromini's church across the square. Gianlorenzo Bernini was Borromini's boss, and probably the greatest religious architect of all time. He was everybody's darling – except Borromini's, who was a sullen, withdrawn, paranoiac genius and who hated his witty, eloquent, talented gaffer. Borromini's supporters retorted that in any case Borromini's beautiful church was designed to support Bernini's obelisk should its base crack, like that ghastly fiasco at St Peter's when Bernini's proposed south tower cracked its wonderful Maderno base. There was no love lost between these two geniuses, such opposites of temperament. I always wonder if Bernini actually cracked the base deliberately – Maderno being Borromini's close relative and all that. Anyhow, their hatred died only when Francesco Borromini, that great sour and brooding genius, committed suicide during a fit of despair in 1667 leaving the field clear for Bernini. I'm actually on Borromini's side, though I'm completely unbiased –

'Lovejoy?'

I nearly leapt a mile. The woman was standing a couple of yards behind me. I cursed myself for a fool. The vicinity of such lovely statuary had distracted me. Daft to lurk so near antiques of such quality.

'Yes. Erm . . . ' My heart was thumping. She'd scared me out of my wits.

'Why are you following me?'

'Erm, no, miss. Erm . . . I was thinking, God Almighty. What if she screamed for the police? 'I thought you were following me.' It sounded lame. 'How do you know my name?'

'I have a message for you.'

I was getting a headache. It was all too complicated. I realized I was dog tired. 'From whom?'

'An old lady. A friend of yours. She says she has a proposition.'

'I don't know any old . . . wait!' It wasn't far from here that I'd done Carlo over and recovered some of my money from the old cow. 'Anna?'

Anna had mentioned a spare room, suggested I lodge with her, in fact. And there'd been something about a daughter . . . I asked what was the proposition.

'You'll have to come.'

A passing couple sniggered across the alley in the darkness. They were assuming the worst, that we were making a proposition of a different kind under concealment of night. I shivered suddenly as the glamour of the Navona faded in the chill night wind. Abruptly I was washed in the cold realization that it was here poor Giordano Bruno had been burned alive. Original and brave thinker, he had walked this very spot, been led on to the wood pile simply to provide a spectacle for the nerks of this world. Even when the poor bloke came to London to try to scratch a living by teaching bored young ladies, we'd been so offhand he'd been driven away. And tonight was the first night Marcello would spend in his grave, the first of eternity. And the first night of widowhood for his wife. And the first night as orphans for his two infants. I swear my teeth chattered from the cold.

There was sweat on my face and my forehead was burning. I leant back against the wall, bushed.

'Are you all right?' the bird was asking.

'Will she help me?'

I felt her smile. 'She offered once before.'

I walked with her then among the narrow streets. It was only when she pulled a door open and stepped inside that I realized we were in the alley where Carlo and I had had our disagreement.

Gingerly I followed into the passageway. The minuscule light just about reached the floor from its furry flex. Plaster was off the walls. It looked unswept.

'Er, one thing, miss.' I didn't want knifing.

'What is it?' She paused, key in a door by the stairs.

'Erm, where's Carlo these days?'

'Recovering in hospital,' she said pointedly. 'At considerable expense. Come in.'

'Erm, wish him better.'

The room was tidy but small with a couple of curtained alcoves. A dressing-table with hooped lights of the sort you see in theatre dressing-rooms occupied one end. A divan, two small armchairs and a vase of flowers. A radio. A curtained window. A faded photograph of a man and a woman smiling. A table lamp.

'This is it, Lovejoy.' It wasn't a lot, but I'd have settled for anything. She motioned me to a chair.

I asked anxiously, 'I suppose Anna's gone to bed?' I somehow had the idea I'd get a better deal from the old devil than this quiet young bird.

She made no reply, just looked at me as if I'd come from Mars.

I floundered on, 'Look. The trouble is I have no money for rent. Not yet.'

'Until after you do the job?'

'That's right,' I said before I could stop myself, then I thought, oh what the hell if she knew. I was exhausted, unutterably weary. 'How much is the rent?'

'We'll decide tomorrow. You sleep there.' She indicated the divan.

I was too tired to argue. I'd hardly slept for the past two nights. And the days had been hell. She discarded her swagger jacket and started putting things away. I waited foolishly.

'Erm . . . are you upstairs, then?' Old Anna must already be snoring her stupid head off.

'No. There's another divan behind the curtain.'

I cleared my throat. Well, if she said so. 'Was this Carlo's?' I noticed a man's coat hanging behind the door. Tired as I was, I didn't want there to be any misunderstandings that might cause old Anna to come creeping in with an axe to defend her gorgeous daughter's honour.

She was getting out a couple of blankets. 'Use this cushion for a pillow. You're hardly conscious. There's a loo second door under the stairs. The hall light's always on. If you're shy you can undress under the blankets.'

I got my shirt off while she wiped her face with some white cream stuff at her giant illuminated mirror. She was beautiful sitting there. 'Incidentally,' I told her, thinking I was being all incisive and knowing. 'Tell your mum Carlo's a drunk. He drank umpteen bottles of wine when he was supposed to be following. I knew he was there all the time.'

She was quite unperturbed, creaming away. 'You evidently pride yourself on your powers of observation, Lovejoy.'

'I'm not bad,' I confessed, chucking my trousers out and hauling the blankets up. I decided to take my socks off the minute I got warm.

'You're not all that good,' the luscious creature said. By turning my head on the cushion I could watch her wiping her lips with a tissue. It was so lovely I had to swallow. She looked good enough to eat.

'No?'

'No,' she said. '*I'm* Anna.'

There was a century pause, give or take a year. I cleared my throat. Anna's decrepit clothes hung by the alcove. And on that dressing-table stood boxes and tubes and sprays and paints and cylinders – enough make-up to service the Old Vic in season.

'You're who?'

'*Cretino*!' she said scornfully. 'Go to sleep.'

My head was splitting. This bird had just said she was old Anna. Sometimes things get too much. It's always women's fault.

My cortex groped for its one remaining synapse and switched to oblivion.

Chapter Fourteen

A clamouring alarm clock shot me awake at ten past eight. I was relieved because I'd had a hideous dream in which Maria became the bird and old Anna became Adriana, and Carlo and Piero advanced towards me with knives while Arcellano stood by lighting cigarettes. I sweated into consciousness.

Anna had gone. Presumably she was already out on the streets conning the tourists. Quite a worker. Old Anna's black dress had gone from its hanger. The old bird was nicer than this young one. For the life of me I couldn't think of them as one person.

On her dressing-table stood a paper bag with rolls and jam. One of the curtained alcoves turned out to be a tiny kitchen with an unbelievably complicated kettle that defeated me. Outside I found a shower by the loo but no telephone, which was a setback because I badly wanted to phone Maria. It was at least worth a try.

I washed and ate. Anna had left a battery shaver in clear view, and a note on her chair. It read:

Lovejoy,
Be here at three.
Anna.

Another woman giving me orders. That's all I needed.

Fabio was in a hell of a mood when I reached the Albanese Emporium dead on nine.

'Walk round him, Lovejoy,' Piero advised me laconically. 'He's had a tiff with his boy-friend.'

'Shut up, you great buffoon!' Fabio squealed.

341

Adriana arrived in time to prevent bloodshed and got us all working, me on a collection of prints she had purchased a week before.

That morning my main intention was to work out the details of the rip. Instead I had two successes and one failure. All three came through Adriana. By elevenish I had picked out the spoiled prints and the forgeries and took them in to the boss. She was ploughing through a catalogue from Sotheby's Rome office – only a stone's throw from us. She pulled a face when she saw how many there were in the dud pile.

'Put them back in an auction,' I advised.

'Brick them?'

'Why throw away good prints after bad?'

To 'brick' a group of sale items offered at auction is to include something really quite good or valuable – or a forgery which appears so – in among the dross. This makes for a better price. The risk you take is that the bidders will be too thick to recognize the valuable antique and you'll finish up having thrown it away for a song. I never brick my stuff. It's an insult to a superb genuine antique to make it live among a load of tat.

I told her, 'Think how you'd feel.'

She actually did begin to smile but throttled it at birth. 'Very well. Into next week's auction.'

I said, 'Erm, thank you for the supper last evening.'

She looked down at her catalogue. 'Not at all. I'm glad you dined well.'

As I made to go I pretended to notice a small stand on her desk, a simple circular base with a neatly turned stem not quite ten inches tall. She kept appointment cards in the slot at its top. It still had its screw. 'Excuse me, please, signora. Do you still have the embroidery fans?'

'The what?' She saw I was holding the stand. I knew she didn't know what it was. Fabio had its partner on his desk.

'There is a crenellated embroidered fan-shaped piece

of material which goes with this.' The penny still hadn't dropped. 'It's a rare American candle screen. Ladies used them to shield their eyes from direct glare when sewing. Seeing you have the pair . . . Look, signora,' I suggested. 'Why don't I restore these in the workshop? I could clean them up and maybe we can find the screens. They're really very valuable . . .'

That was my first success, gaining access to the workshop. My second came when Adriana, passing for the umpteenth time to check I was still hard at it, actually came in and commented, 'You seem at home here.'

I was concentrating on milking the screw out. 'I am. Why is it such a shambles?'

She gazed about and did her shrug. 'The business can't run to a craftsman.'

'Because *that's* tragic.' I indicated a small table in the corner. I'd not had time to have a look at it, but it looked a good early nineteenth-century French occasional table. Some goon had stuck its broken leg with sticking plaster. A couple of planks lay across its precious surface. 'The poor little sod,' I said. 'I'll do it for you.'

'Can you? Having them mended costs the earth.'

'I can do better. I'll make you a reproduction piece, something really splendid.'

'The true wood will be expensive.'

'I'll make it pay.' I'd nearly said worth your while. Adriana got the switch and went all prim.

'Do you have a piece in mind, Lovejoy?'

'I think so.' I had a piece in mind all right. 'A Chippendale rent table.'

She thought a second, weighing time against lire. 'All right. Go ahead. But don't botch it. It's a highly specialized – '

That word again. 'I've heard,' I said drily.

Curtly she told me to get on with my work and left me to it, not quite slamming the door.

My failure was my phone call to the Pinnacle Peak

343

Language Academy in East Anglia. Adriana took some persuading to let me use the blower and even had Fabio, full of sly satisfaction, to sit and time my call. Even the few browsers bulldozing their way through our porcelains could hear as Jingo Hardy came on the other end.

'Maria Peck?' he bawled. 'No, Lovejoy, old fruit. She left the day you did.'

I felt sick. 'Why? Where did she go?'

'Dunno, old boy. I'll try and find out if you like.'

'Please.' I gave him the Emporium's number and explained it was in Rome. He fell about.

'Got the language bug, eh?' he chortled. Only people like Jingo chortle. I'd never heard anyone chortle before.

'Er, sure. Listen Jingo. Could you find out the address of the bloke who paid my fees? It's rather imp – '

'Impossible, old thing. Maria did her own tuition-fee acceptances.'

That sickened me even more.

'Hey!' he exclaimed. 'Would you count Albanian loan-words in the Brindisi dialect for us, seeing you're there – ?'

I cut off. I was in enough trouble without linguistics ballsing things up.

Back in the workshop I set about the candle screens again, but started thinking. Until now I'd been like a leaf in a gale, at everybody's whim. And my dithering had helped – all right, all right: had *caused* – Marcello to die. And made my friends hostages to Arcellano. It was time to mend my ways and set my sights on the rip. And on killing Arcellano. The kindly affable old Lovejoy image would have to go.

'Lovejoy! Will you stop that *riot*?' from Fabio in his mini-office up in the showroom. 'My *head*!'

'Sorry, Fabio.'

I'd been whistling cheerfully. First time for days.

Watching Anna take off her make-up was one of the worst experiences I'd ever had. I mean to say. I'm normally attracted by women who wear a lot of cosmetics. The more the merrier, as far as I'm concerned, even if the headshrinkers these days are always on about how it shows you're full of primitive urges and all that. In fact I wish women would wear a lot more mascara and lipstick and jewellery. But seeing Old Anna become young again was unnerving. Fascinating, but weird.

'What's the matter with you, Lovejoy? Don't nudge.'

I must have got too near. 'Only looking.'

She started to peel some crinkled plasticy stuff off her forehead with little ripping movements. It came like chewing-gum. Lovely smooth skin began to appear. I felt ill.

'Tell me about the Vatican, Anna.'

'Right. Sit and listen.' She started to tell me in an excited rush. 'Nine-tenths of Rome's tourists don't know what the Vatican actually is. That's a proven fact. Like you, dunce. It is a private city. It has a helicopter pad, railway station, twenty-four galleries and museums, radio studios, a supermarket, bank, barracks, garages for ninety-eight cars, newspaper printers, motor workshop, a fire station, a population – everything.' Calmly she dissected an eyebrow. I hate things to do with eyes and was dreading seeing her start on those stubby eyelashes but couldn't look away.

'You're lucky, Lovejoy, in one way. Ten years ago the Vatican also had its own gendarmerie, Noble and Palatine Guards. They were disbanded. Now there's only the Swiss Guard, but there's a hundred of them and they're good.'

'Don't people just go in to the bank or the shop? Or get the train?'

Anna laughed then, really fell about. '*Cretino*! Listen: the bank – called the "Institute for Pious Works" – is guarded inside and out. The railway station accepts no passenger trains, only goods. And as for the Anona supermarket, you have to be SCV.'

'Eh?'

'One of the 450 citizens of the *Stato della Città del Vaticano*. All except sixty are in Holy Orders – and you obviously are not, Lovejoy. There are nearly fifteen hundred Vatican employees, and nearly two thousand functionaries and diplomatic hangers-on. They can go in to shop at the Anona supermarket and the liquor store – as long as they remember to bring their ration cards and special personal passes. There was once a black market, you see!' She pulled small slivers from her mouth. Immediately her face filled out. Years dropped off her. It was miraculous. 'We Romans joke that SCV means "Se *Cristo Vedesse*"!' If Christ were to see . . .

This catalogue of security was getting me down. A bigger shock was seeing her catch at her temple and simply sweep off her wispy hair, shaking out dark lustrous waves almost to her shoulders. I hand it to her: she was a real artist. The pads and teeth caps she placed in a coloured solution. The wig was instantly brushed and hung on a wicker stand. Her eyes caught mine mischievously.

'There are four ways in, Lovejoy. The main Museum entrance, from the street. Museum guards. Then the Cancello di Sant' Anna, St Anne's gate where we met – leading into the walled-in courtyards for the barracks, the *Osservatore Romano* offices, the whole service area. Swiss Guards, there. Then the two entrances near the front of St Peter's itself, the Portone di Bronzo for papal audiences, also Swiss Guard. And last the Arco delle Campane.'

I knew the giant bronze door. The Arch of Bells has two flamboyantly dressed Guards with halberds. Anna caught me drawing breath.

'No, Lovejoy. There are two more Swiss Guards just inside. Marksmen with guns.' She started creaming her face, a mask of slithery white. Jesus, but Max Factor has a lot to answer for. 'You look put down.' Only her eyes and mouth were showing as she turned on me. 'Look, Lovejoy. I saw you case the Vatican. I've seen it done by experts – *real* experts, not a bum like you, wet behind the ears. And they all missed out.'

'What's it to you?'

She swung on me then, youthful eyes shining. 'It's never been done – that's what it is to me, Lovejoy! Never. Oh, an army or two have pillaged Rome now and then. But no one living man.'

Light dawned. I stared at her. 'And *you*. . . ?'

'Why do you think I've worked the Vatican geese for two years?' Her blazing eyes softened into rapture and she gave me a blasphemous blessing. 'I dream of the rip, Lovejoy,' she purred, looking past me into some paradise of her own creation. 'I've schemed and waited. And now you've come, Lovejoy. A man with the same dream. We can do it. I know we can.'

'Me . . . ' wishing I didn't have to say it ' . . . and you?'

'Don't make me sound like a penance, *cretino*!' She began smoothing cream off with tissues. 'You need me. Together we succeed. Alone, you sleep in the Castel Sant' Angelo garden.'

So she knew about that, too. She rose abruptly and flung a leg on to the chair, peeling a stretch stocking. Varicosities were clearly painted on the inside. I'd already seen her black buttonstrap shoes and their crafted supports, real works of art. She donned a shabby dressing-gown. 'Don't overestimate me, Lovejoy. I've no private army. Fine, I make a living, though the Mafia don't lose any sleep. But I'm good. You've seen me. We're ideal.'

She went to shower while I lay back and looked at the ceiling. I now had a job which provided sufficient cover, and an ally whose only fault was that she happened to be the best con artist on the streets. And a place to stay, providing I accepted her as a partner. And a workshop where I could make the Chippendale replica, which I desperately needed for the rip.

As a lurk it wasn't so bad. Maybe it was as good as any I could hope for. And the rip was my one sure way of getting to Arcellano. I should have been quite content, but I don't like coincidences. And for the only two people in the world planning separate Vatican rips to finish up living in the same room was too much of a coincidence for me. By a mile.

Chapter Fifteen

The next three days I worked like a dog, had a terrible row with Fabio and a worse one with Anna, and nearly killed the bloke who was following me. At least, I *think* I nearly killed him. I may have done worse, but I'm not going back to find out.

I explained the barest essentials.

'Just a single table?' she had asked incredulously.

I'd told her yes, then lied like a trooper. 'I go for systems, not singles.'

'Explain, Lovejoy,' she demanded.

A gleam in Anna's eye told me she'd developed that basic mistrust so natural to all womankind. I tried to speak with a sneer. 'Tell me this.' I strode about the room belligerently, Marlborough on campaign. 'What *is* the perfect rip, eh? Ever thought?'

'Where you get clean away.' She was fascinated, but doubtful.

I was emphatic. 'No, love. The perfect rip's the *undetected* rip. And why?' I paused to poke a finger towards her. She was all gleaming from the shower and sat mesmerized by my act. 'Because you can do it again. And again. And – '

' – And again!' she breathed.

'Right! You have a system. See?'

'System, not singles!' She was radiant. 'Lovejoy,' she murmured, 'that's beautiful.'

We shook on it. I saw from her manner that she had taken a deep decision.

'Now we're partners, Lovejoy,' she said, primly sitting opposite me, 'who's the man following you?'

'Eh?'

'He's outside now. To and from the Emporium. He watches from the *pizzeria rustica* opposite Albanese's.'

'Oh, I'll look into it,' I said airily. 'I know of him. Spotted him within the hour.'

I hadn't and was badly shook up, but I didn't dare let Anna think her new partner was a complete imbecile. She gave me a look, said nothing.

That was our deal. Me to run the rip, Anna to suss plans and teach me all she knew about the Vatican, the tourist trade, the guides and couriers and hawkers which abounded in its vicinity.

At the Emporium Adriana and I did the tray dodge a couple of times. Rested and fed as I was – and blissfully back in my natural element at last – I was on top form. Not only that, but on the way there I'd spotted a genuine Jacobean hanging bread-hutch in the side window of a small antique shop called Gallinari's, did a promising deal for a song and raced the last few hundred yards to catch Fabio just reopening. Twenty minutes later I had it safe in Adriana's.

I crowed like a mad thing as I wiped the lovely thing down with a dry cloth. 'Look, folks! We're in the presence of a genuine Jacobean period refrigerator!' Untrue really, but it was the nearest they had to it. The whole thing is a cunning wooden bread-airing device, and positively mouse-proof. It's pierced everywhere, cornices and straights. Lovely. 'And,' I sailed on, 'it's not a modern mock-up.' No nasty pale edges to show where the staining's worn off and exposed for the horrible trick it always is. They make them from old church pews. My babbling left them unaffected. There were tears in my eyes from trying to get them to understand the immensity of the find, but there's no telling some people.

'About money, Lovejoy,' Adriana said.

'Oh, no!' I shook my head vigorously. This kind of crappy talk gets me.

'No what?'

'Look. Signor Gallinari made a deal. It's his expertise against mine. Don't dare suggest giving him a higher price. That'd insult this antique.'

I don't go for this rubbish about sharing profit, or owning up before you buy. Remember the antique has feelings too. That's what *caveat emptor* means.

A few times, as I prepared the lovely thing for sale, I caught Adriana's quizzical gaze on me. She never would meet my eye, glancing away whenever I looked up. And Fabio was sulking, earning himself a rebuke from Adriana for rudeness to customers. And Piero was in on it, pursing his lips and doing his silent-screen act. All we needed was a set of eyebrows and we'd have been music-hall naturals. Their attitudes were beyond me. As if I cared.

The row with Fabio erupted just before we closed. Adriana had this ritual which required each of us to come before her, report we'd locked up, and list our completed jobs. I went last.

'There's one point,' I said pointedly to her. 'If anybody damages that Jacobean bread-hutch like they did that early American candle screen – '

'Damaged?' she asked quickly.

I held the candle screen up to show the circular fruit-wood base was scored in several places. The scratches were new.

' – I'll break their hands.' I smiled at Fabio. '*Off.* Okay, Fabio?'

His eyes were bright with venom. 'Thinking to take over here, Lovejoy?'

'Stop it!' Adriana pointed. 'Did you do that, Fabio?'

'Maybe Lovejoy was careless.'

'I see.' Adriana appraised him. 'You resent our new assistant.' That was a step up. I'd always been called a handy-man before.

He said sweetly, 'Of course I'm aware Lovejoy can do no *wrong*, Adriana – '

'Good night,' I put in, and left them to sort it out. Through it all Piero had said nothing, just watched. But I knew I'd made an enemy of Fabio, and that Piero always went about armed from the way he stood and positioned himself when storm clouds threatened. As I left I wondered if Piero was the follower Anna had spotted. There was only one way to find out.

That night on Adriana's instructions I was seated at the restaurant by twenty to nine. The staff fawned over the Albaneses the minute they arrived. I was stuck on a corner table near the kitchen entrance but by now I was so hungry I was past caring. I hadn't spotted my tail on the way, which only proved how valuable Anna might actually turn out to be.

I only had half a bottle of wine, and ate carefully but well, keeping one vigilant eye on the exits and the other on the lovely Adriana. I'll remember her all my life, if I live that long. Her clothes were different again, I noticed, which was a real feat. She'd had less than an hour. She wore pearls – a short chain of baroques, which shows taste, restraint, and something called style because each one is deformed and relatively inexpensive. And her dress was an improbable combination of bodiced looseknit and bishop sleeves. The obsessional slob opposite her might have been a trillionaire for all I know, but he was too thick even to notice her loveliness, the bum. Most of the time he dabbled with his food and referred to his paper. Adriana again ate like a sparrow, hardly a mouthful.

The bill was collected from me and taken to Signor Albanese who was too busy reading and picking his teeth even to notice it had numbers on. I left like a stray, without even a friendly serf to hold the doorhandle.

Dusk was settling swiftly on the streets as I sauntered out to be followed. Last night Anna, tonight one of Arcellano's creeps.

The Via Arenula leads down to the River Tiber at one end of the Tiberina, a small island. Over nosh I'd worked it all out. I took my time because I knew exactly where I was going and I didn't want the tail to get lost.

This ship-shaped island's supposed to be where Aesculapius the God of Medicine landed when introducing doctors to the civilized world. He has a lot to answer for. There's a small sloping square on the island and a lovely old church at the downward side where the old Aesculapius temple used to be. I'd already been inside to see the woodwork on its confessional. The island has a few cramped buildings, including a pizzeria and a shop.

By the time I ambled on to the central bridge it was all very quiet. Over in the city cars were flowing in relentless streams. Buses were making their last runs. Here on the dark island an occasional car bounced over the bridge, lights on now. The Fatebene-fratelli Hospital windows were shining, and a light mist was beginning to envelope the island. Three cars remained parked on the piazza's slope. Nobody walking, and the tourists all gone home.

Still slowly, stopping every so often to look idly at the water, I wandered across the top of the square and picked up one of those polythene bags that blow about streets everywhere these days. Then I waited for him to come into view. My heart was belting along in spite of my outward calm, and my blasted hands were damp and cold. He was there, being at least as casual as I was, strolling over towards me.

My cue. I drifted down to the San Bartolomeo with its Romanesque tower, glancing in the artificial light into two of the cars. One was a French thing with a gear lever like a cistern's ballcock, the other a Fiat. I ignored the vintage Talbot over by the wall. I was in enough trouble.

At first I'd had some lunatic notion of hiding behind

one of the ancient columns in the church's candle-lit gloom. There's a veritable avenue of them leading to the great tomb at the high altar. The trouble is he might be armed and what could I do then? He *knew* I knew he was following me, and even had the bloody gall to light a fag on the bridge. That's nerve. The worrying thing was, he looked vaguely familiar.

Finally I could stand it no longer and strolled in. The second I was inside the doors I slid along the left side of the nave towards the north transept. There were steps up at the chancel, which baffled me for a horrible second. Luckily there was the priest's door on my left, leading outside as I had guessed into that crummy little priest's garden you can see from across the river, with the world's worst statue of Christ looking utterly lost. Emerging, I felt exposed, really prominent. The lights of all Rome were visible, the Palatine and the Capitolino looming over there in the gloom and the great floodlit avenue of the Marcello Theatre sweeping down to the water. Rome was about its busy nocturnal business – and I was about mine.

Doubling back sounds easy. On the side of an ancient church, with inhabited multistoreyed dwellings stuck on the side, it's not so easy as all that. I guessed the bastard would wait outside in the Piazza. Short of swimming in the river there was no way out. I clambered over the wall to the church stonework and groped upwards. There was some guttering, but I'd never wanted Protestant Gothic so badly in my life – the easiest churches to rob by a mile, incidentally. I swung on the crumbling stuff for five interminable yards before managing to clutch hold of a luscious slab of stonework and pull myself onto the ledges. After that it was less of a problem, but you can't help blaspheming a bit at the thoughtlessness of some ancient architects.

There's an archway to the left of the square, where lovers can stroll down and inspect the travertine marble of which the island's 'ship' prow is made. Nobody there on a chilly night with a watermist helping the honest do-gooders of this world, people like me. I dropped off the arch like a thunderclap and stood shaking in case he'd heard, but no. He was still there when I peered round. Smoking, every so often looking at the San Bartolomeo to see I'd not emerged. I was out, and he still thought I was in. The distance to the two cars on the uphill side of the Piazza was only about thirty or forty yards. I waited until he'd just glanced round, then slipped silently along the wall into the shelter of the Renault.

My polythene bag was easy to twist into a string. I pushed it between the rubber join of the driver's side window. Make sure it's doubled as you do it, then push in a bit more, and drop the loop over the button lock. A simple pull, and the door's unlocked. Why they make them so easy to burgle I don't know.

I eeled in. My keys and bendable comb were good enough to unlock the steering. Another minute. Gingerly, I raised my head. He was still there, silhouetted against the reflections from the water. He turned again to glance at San Bartolomeo, looked at a watch – doubtless the sort which gives the winter equinoxes and tidal times in Kyoto – and I undid the handbrake.

There's something horrible in setting forward to kill. I honestly meant only to scare him, show Arcellano I was no pushover. Something like that. But once I got the car rolling silently down the Piazza's slope I swear something – *somebody*, maybe, for all I know – took over. Perhaps Marcello, to be fanciful about the whole business. The wheel seemed to settle in a position, hard over. It was still unlocked, but wouldn't straighten up. And I tried, honest to God.

Anyhow it was too late to think any more. The car rolled down and he was in the way. Simple as that. Only when the bumper was a few feet from him did he realize something was wrong. He whipped round, mechanically throwing away his cigarette. Then his face appeared, puzzled at all this sudden motion and the mass heaving out of the dark mist. The silence was broken by a screech as the grille ground him against the parapet, sliding along the stonework and leaving a blackish stain. I can see his open mouth as reflex slammed his face down against the bonnet with a faint clang. Once the car connected my common sense evaporated and I sat in total stupefaction as the car scraped and bumped with that poor sod getting life smeared out of him against the stone. The metal screeched again. The car shuddered to a stop. I got out shakily, looked about. Not a soul in the little square. Not a sound from the church. Then I looked at him.

I made certain my polythene 'string' was uncoiled and dropped it into the river, of course not looking at the car. Then I carefully shut the door and walked away.

Any alibi in a storm, I always say. The German lady was in her hotel when I rang from the main railway station, just back from a play. I wasn't exactly at my chattiest, but she didn't seem to mind when I said I'd like to call round.

As it turned out she was one of the best alibis I've ever had. I got back to Anna's at three in the morning. Anna was in her alcove with the curtains drawn back. She clicked the light on and told me to wipe that smile off my face. It was a nasty little scene, straight out of marriage. She played merry hell, wanting to know where I'd been. I said for a walk, and like a fool said down by the river not knowing that one of the riverside walks is a knocking-shop, and had to endure an hour's unrelenting abuse while she reminded me I was in Rome to do the Vatican rip, not to whore about the city all night, which was a bit unfair seeing what I'd gone through. Her invective was a lot worse than I've managed to make it sound. She was a world expert.

What I didn't know was a worse eruption was impending.

I undressed as usual beneath my blanket, as usual. And as usual she didn't rape me during the dark hours.

Next morning she'd got a paper at breakfast and looked at me in silence while I cleared a whole bag of fresh rolls. The news was of a fantastic accident which had occurred the previous night. A man innocently standing on the Tiberina had been crushed by a car. Its handbrake had unaccountably slipped.

I'd honestly have felt sorry for him if he hadn't been one of Arcellano's goons, the one who had pressed me down in the chair when Arcellano did me over. And it honestly was an accident, almost completely one hundred per cent accidental. That's the truth. I hadn't realized the wheel would lock that way once I'd released the car and set it rolling. Hand on my heart.

What gave me heartburn was the headline. The newspaper described him as a Vatican guard. Museum detail.

Chapter Sixteen

The football magazine was engrossing, especially as it told me the date of the Vatican rip. No drawing back now.

'I'm going to need a van, Anna. Something the size and shape of a closed ambulance.' It had to hold two tables.

'Ambulances have windows.'

'Make them opaque, then. And a good engine. If it breaks down I've had it.'

'Right.' She was quite assured. 'Can it be a copy?'

'Yes.' I looked speculatively at her. 'Who can copy an ambulance for heaven's sake?'

'Carlo.' I pulled a face. She said cryptically. 'You've been in Rome less than a week and Carlo's in hospital, a Vatican Museum guard is probably dead by now, and you've lost a friend.'

She waited but I said nothing. 'Who was he, Lovejoy?'

'A bloke I met, er, accidentally. He has – had – a wife and two kiddies.'

'Are you in love with her?'

It was an unlikely question. I was coming to the notion that Old Anna was infinitely preferable. 'Never even met her.

'How was he lost?'

'Killed. In the Colosseum.'

Her eyes wrinkled as she thought. 'Funny I didn't hear. It wasn't even in the papers.'

We stared at each other for quite some time.

'How odd,' I said at last. And it was.

The workshop was in some sort of order now. You can't start anything worthwhile till you get a place straight. The shelving was mended and in position. I'd gone at the toolracks baldheaded. The electric hand drill was on the blink, so I'd knocked up an old-fashioned foot-treadle spindle out of a bicycle wheel from somebody's dustbin. The one-third horsepower single-phase motor on the wood-turning lathe was crudded up to extinction. I had it off and sawed into the bench to get a foot-powered band through. Adriana graciously allowed Piero, my silent watcher, to collect a derelict Singer sewing-machine from a junk dealer.

I slogged a whole day, tidying and sorting. Some-body ambitious had once bought in a few lengths of various woods including walnut, small pieces only, but at least a start. Nowadays, when an old walnut tree is worth twice the value of the house in whose garden it grows, any piece is worth a fortune. Adriana and Piero came to look at the workshop when I'd rigged up the last toolrack.

Adriana exclaimed. 'You've created so much space, Lovejoy!'

'It was there all the time, signora.'

'Isn't this marvellous, Piero?'

'Not as marvellous as all that,' I corrected. 'Think of upstairs. Your showroom should be extended. Why not a winch?'

Adriana glanced quickly at Piero. 'Upstairs?' I looked at them, suddenly more alert. You can't help wondering, can you?

'The lifting problem,' Piero snapped, which is all very well if you're willing to be snapped at. I wasn't.

'There is no lifting problem, Piero. I could build a winch for practically nothing.'

A winch was part of the rip, so to me there was no

question. Piero glared, nearly as determined as me. 'You keep out of this, Lovejoy.'

'I'll have to think about it, Lovejoy.' Adriana's tone was finality itself.

I watched them return to the showroom. What the hell was upstairs?

Anyhow, I began sketching rough plans for the rent table. I'd got Anna to collect the photographs so I should have more precise dimensions to go on. The amount of wood in a rent table is relatively huge. I'd already expected that, but the final estimate made me gasp.

Especially when I multiplied it by two.

Locking up that day, Piero caught me staring up at the rear of the building. The wall looked solid, and the drop was vertical.

'It looks on, Piero,' I offered, to break the awful silence. 'See – take a drop from above the top window – '

'Lovejoy,' he interrupted, quiet and dangerous, 'when we need extra storage space Signora Albanese will rent it. Okay?'

I shrugged. 'Just remember I tried to save us money, that's all.' Let him guess.

Fabio was inside the showroom entrance, smiling and listening. He said nothing, which was another odd thing because he was practically obsessional about money. Its roof was within reach of the lower upstairs window which was near the drainpipe . . . '

I got my usual paper from Adriana, with a restaurant's name and address for that evening, and tried it on as usual, asking her for the money so I could eat where I liked. As usual she said no, but avoided looking at me. Usually she managed at least a withering glare at that point. Still, I didn't mind watching her nosh for an hour or so, if that was the rule.

I departed, whistling.

Until then I thought I'd seen all possible kinds of

cramped antique shops. But I'd never seen one with space left begging.

The problem was getting time to study the Vatican, among other things, because it was only open for a limited period each day. What with that and the Easter rush looming, Anna and I were on a tight schedule.

One thing I had to admit: as a caser Anna was brilliant. She recognized most of the guards, where they lived, their shifts, relatives. She was good at distances, too. Never guessed worse than five per cent error in every measurement – length of corridors, heights of walls, thickness of brickwork. Marvellous. More than once I foolishly found myself telling her she was great, but nipped it in the bud. A rip's no time for friendship. Just because we were living together was no reason to become close.

I started to get up as soon as she did, and even began tidying the room up while she put on her make-up to become Old Anna. The old thing really was endearing once she reappeared, but the actual process of watching that beautiful young bird transmute inch by inch made me feel physically ill. I asked her once what had given her the idea, and got a surprise. She laughed, really laughed, for the first time.

'An old woman isn't an obvious predator,' she said, smiling her head off. 'A young one is.'

'You don't like me doing this, Lovejoy,' Old Anna croaked that day, on her way out. 'Once the rip's done I'll be able to stop. We'll have our villa.'

'Villa?' Presumably she meant Carlo.

'It's what I'm saving for.'

So she still thought we were going to make a fortune from the rip. Her place was utterly frugal, and she ate only sparingly. No clothes to speak of. Never seemed to go out. She lived on a shoestring. Well, nothing wrong with optimism.

I called her back. 'Here. Anna. One thing.' I'd practised the casual air. 'Am I still being followed?'

'No,' she said levelly, in her young voice. 'Not since that man got injured. The night you went for a walk by the river.'

'Thank heavens for that,' I said with innocent relief. 'Have a good day.'

'*Ciao*, Enrico.'

By the end of that week I was ticking off my progress. Enough wood to make two rent tables – much of it matured, bought from various idiots who had ruined antiques by making them into something of greater apparent value. Workshop fully functional. Vatican nearly sussed out enough.

'And I'll need two tables.' I'd told Anna. 'The sort you see in cafeterias, the typical modern *tavola calda* table. Tubular steel and all that.'

She promised to take me round a couple of supply firms at the weekend to see which I liked. She counted on her fingers. 'You need a white plastic collar, two silk ropes, a disposable razor, a pencil torch. A new tie. An ambulance. Squares of cloth. That it?'

'Oh. And a pharmacopœia.'

'A *what*?'

'A book of common drugs. But a proper one – not a granny's home guide.'

She looked doubtful. 'That might take a day or so, Lovejoy.'

'I want an out-of-date one, 1930s or 1940s.'

'Are you kidding me?'

'I never have yet, love. If you can't get one, I'll join the library.'

That stung. It was a slur on her expertise as a thief. Her lips thinned. 'I've never missed yet, Lovejoy.'

I waited till she reached the door, then said, 'And a hand grenade.'

'Okay.' She didn't even pause. The door closed with a slam. Like I said, a real pro.

Chapter Seventeen

I waited until Anna's breathing had evened out. She had quickly become used to my reading till all hours, though at first she played hell about the light. Now she just let me read.

The trouble was we were becoming acutely conscious of each other. At least, I was of her, and a few times I saw her regarding me with an odd look. We'd become very reserved in a curious sort of way. I was worn out being polite. Still, we both understood the reason we were together: the rip, the whole rip and nothing but the rip. That's what I told myself.

I let myself out in my bare feet. She had given me a key the second day. The only risk was the couple of groups who lived upstairs, one small family right at the top and an elderly couple who worked as caretakers to the furniture place next door. It felt clear. In the alley I donned my socks and shoes and set off down the glittering, dark alleys.

A few minutes later I was on the workshop roof. It was easy enough. People forgot about roofs and floors when protecting places. Torch in my left pocket so I could cling with my right hand, and I began to climb, only partly paralysed with fear.

Some kind of gauze, a little separated, covered the window. When I think of it now it was lucky they were so preoccupied in that great oval bed. Bonny and plushily expensive, but modern crap, of course. Like the expensive Axminster carpet and the velvet drapery. And the splendid wall mirrors. And the oak panelling. It was a tasteful and elegantly appointed bedroom, and it was being put to proper use. Gold light shone from a Garian porcelain bedside lamp. Piero lay beside Adriana, hands behind his head as he talked at the ceiling. She lay on her side facing me, eyes closed. They seemed to be having words. Clinging there, my impressions were indelible: a glass with a small demi-lune of drink, a woman's satin robe over a chairback. The mirrors. The tight set of Adriana's mouth. Her lovely skin shining golden.

I realized with a sudden shock her eyes had opened and fixed on the window. She did not move. I froze, breaking into a sweat. My face was only a foot from the glass. I drew it slowly back and sank gently down below the level of the sill, hoping she hadn't seen me.

A few shaky minutes later I was tiptoeing into my pad. Anna gave me the fright of my life.

'Welcome home, Lovejoy,' her voice said, not a bit sleepy. 'You found her little love nest?' I could swear she was smiling. The little bitch had known about it all the time. She could have saved me all that bother.

'Well, yes.'

As I lay down, knackered after my pointless exertions she put her geriatric voice on, for devilment. 'Signor Peci's been the pretty Signora's stud for some time now. She likes them strong and handsome, Enrico. In case you're interested.'

'Don't call me Enrico.'

She cackled and I heard her turn over. I lay there sickened. Why I should feel like that I don't know, but at least now Piero's resistance to my winch was finally explained. No wonder he'd gone pale around the gills. I'd suggested turning his private knocking-shop into a store room for reproduction 'antiques'. There'd be no question of the decision Adriana would make – after giving my scheme a token consideration, for the sake of appearances.

'Poor Lovejoy.' I heard her mattress creak as she

huddled down to sleep. 'You've a worse surprise to come.'

'What do you mean?' I tried again, getting mad. 'Anna. *What* surprise?'

She wouldn't say any more. I lay there wondering why it was suddenly so important to me and finally decided it was because Adriana's Emporium was the one place with everything I needed for the rip. Satisfied with my logic, I eventually rolled over to sleep.

'*Cretino*,' Anna murmured.

Chapter Eighteen

The Holy Father blessed sixty thousand of us on that
Palm Sunday. He spoke vehemently of the cross of
faith and our responsibility. Not all life could be at our
own behest or lived at the whim of desire, it seemed.

How right he was.

I applauded with the rest when he waved a cream-
coloured frond in farewell. It was great to be part of
a happy crowd. Anna thought so too, for she was busily
working the dip in the thick tourist clusters round the
fountains.

During the early part of the day, when the Holy
Father was celebrating Mass on St Peter's steps, I
reached my final decision. The well-guarded Arch of
Bells was out. Its pace of life was too casual, far too
intimate. Also the giant Portone di Bronzo was out.
I'd glimpsed inside when somebody was admitted for
an audience. The habit those vigilant Swiss Guards had
of standing on the steps ready to move either way was
most disconcerting.

St Anne's gate was not too bad, for all it had distressed me when I first clapped eyes on it. I decided
that was our exit line. Anna had been incredulous.

'You decide the way *out* first, Lovejoy? When you
haven't even got in?'

'In is no problem.'

She was furious. 'Might your one and only partner
know why?'

I grinned at her. 'They'll invite me in, love.' I got
my own back by refusing to say any more.

During the mass exodus from the Square later I

missed Anna, though I observed some disturbance over near the Vatican City post office. A policeman stopped me near the Cancello di Sant' Anna, giving me a momentary infarct.

'That your auntie over there in the police car?'

'Eh?'

'That old lady. She's been pickpocketing.'

Everybody was looking. 'Er, yes. Good heavens!' I pushed through the crowd towards the car. A tired policeman in the front seat was smoking a cigarette. Anna was hunched shamefacedly in the back, putting on an act of dizziness.

'This old bag – ' the cop began.

'Auntie!' I cried in relief. 'Where've you been?'

' – causes us more trouble than the rest of Rome.'

'I've been looking everywhere for you!'

'Now, signor.' The copper with me tapped my shoulder. 'Now. We tire of her. Understand? You take her in hand, or else . . .'

'I will! I promise!'

'If you looked after her properly she wouldn't need to steal.'

'You are right, signor,' I said, all humble. With my hand on my breast and my heart seething with murderous intentions towards Anna I smiled apologetically.

'We warn you,' the boss cop said, wearily exhaling smoke into my face like he was doing me favours. 'You are responsible in future. Okay?'

They took my name and address and let us off with a warning. I even had to sign for the silly old bitch. I grabbed Anna and backed off into the crowd, bowing and scraping to the cops as I went. All the way I said nothing, dragging Anna home in a blaze of white-hot fury, and once there it happened without any conscious decision. I didn't even give her time to have a shower. I gave her a damned good shaking, and called her all the names under the sun for risking the rip and getting us booked like that.

She took it in silence, struggling a bit at first and sobbing a little.

'I'm sorry, Lovejoy,' she snuffled after I'd nearly calmed down.

'So you ought to be,' I snapped. 'You're now a registered felon on the cops' frigging books.'

'I'll make it up – '

'There's no time.' As I said it my heart was in my boots. I felt ill at the thought.

'I'll ditch old Anna, build another character – '

'The fucking rip's next week, you silly cow!'

'Next week?' Stricken, she raised a tear-streaked face. 'We must put it off – '

'Rips can't be postponed. They're cancelled, or done. Silly bitch.'

'But, Lovejoy – '

Then I nicked her handbag – why change a profitable habit? – and slammed out into the alley. The trouble with allies is they try to help, and nothing is more trouble than that. Within an hour I'd got plastered on white plonk, and that evening was thankful it was Sunday. I could barely totter to the restaurant whose name Adriana had written down.

I worked so hard planing and chiselling that I could see wood wherever I looked.

I'd better explain. A rent table is not your usual rectangle or flapped circle, nothing like that. Think of a mushroom, a top on a pedestal. It was used for what its name says, collecting rent from the peasantry. The serfs' coins went on to a decorated centre, which sinks like Sweeney Todd's chair and drops the gelt into the pedestal below. Some are oval. Arcellano's was angled, with drawers all round. It stands to reason that *every* drawer can't be rectangular, or they would have no space to enter. Slices of cake are wedge-shaped for the same reason. So some of the drawers have to be phoney for the exterior to look right.

I was using wood cannibalized from cheap furniture about thirty years old, plus a few panels quite a bit older. Incidentally, when you are forging furniture don't turn your nose up at chipboard. It's a hell of a weight but it's cheap, it veneers like a dream, and it won't warp in central heating. Very few whole-thickness woods have all those merits.

As my plan called for two rent tables I was wood from floor to ceiling. A lucky find was a supply of beeswax and turpentine at the furniture makers next door to Anna's place, and a reasonable range of wood varnishes from the main Corso. The adhesives you can get nowadays are great, but a few have one terrible drawback – a characteristic stink – so those have to be avoided. I'd also need a controlled temperature of 68° Fahrenheit or so to do all this glueing and varnishing, and as I'm very keen on knowing what the relative humidity is playing at around furniture, another battle with Adriana was obviously called for. The trouble was Piero would say the opposite to whatever I proposed. Him having the monarch's ear, so to speak.

During an afternoon break Anna conducted me to a couple of furniture warehouses. The tables I finally decided I liked were crummy and modern enough to break your heart.

Anna noticed quick as a flash and burbled, 'Why, Enrico! They're exactly like the ones in – '

I trod neatly on her foot and ordered three, for delivery next afternoon. 'They're just the thing I need in the workshop, Auntie,' I explained loudly.

On the way home Anna demanded, 'Has the beautiful signora said you could buy them on her account?'

'Not yet.'

'But you expect she will agree?'

'Yes,' I lied, looking Anna straight in the eye. 'They're expensive, Lovejoy.'

'They're for the rip,' I said coldly. 'What's expense between friends?'

She saw sense. 'Why did you tell the man to deliver the tables at four o'clock? The Emporium's closed – '

'Anna, love,' I told her wearily. 'Shut it.' She was driving me mad. 'And you forgot your voice, you silly bitch.' Old Anna had twice spoken with the mellifluous voice of a young woman. I'd had to kick her into the right gear.

She gave me a mouthful. 'It's working with a selfish brute like you!' But I could tell she was shaken.

It was in this happy mood of fellowship we parted, Anna furiously plunging into the nearest crowd of tourists and me slamming off to the workshop for another few hours' beavering.

Mondays are always busy with customers. Several times I was interrupted by Fabio to try the tray dodge, which began to get on my nerves. It seemed every few minutes. Still, whoever pays the piper. Whether it was the row with Anna or the knowledge of Piero's special, erm, position with regard to Adriana I honestly don't know. But by closing time I was thoroughly cheesed off. When Adriana called me in to hand me my restaurant chit I refused to accept it.

'No, thank you, signora.'

Piero was bolting the back yard. Fabio was checking the window grilles.

'Where will you eat, Lovejoy?' Her frigging trump card.

'I'll manage.'

She flamed. 'Like you did the other night, I suppose. With that fat tourist?'

So she knew of that. Good old Fabio. Or Piero. Or yet another of Arcellano's goons? Christ.

'She wasn't fat.'

'And you naturally know for absolute certain *how* fat!'

I'd never seen her so pale and angry. It was one of

those days. Everything was in a bloody mess at the Emporium and I didn't even know if Anna and I were still speaking.

'Signora,' I said, because I was fuming too, 'all my childhood I had food tickets on the charity. I'll have no more. Please decide what you think I've earned. Give me any cheap antique you think will come near it. I'll manage the way I always have. Antiques is my game. Greed appears to be no different in Rome than anywhere else.'

I left her to make the choice and went out to help with the locking up, though one of the others always checked them after me again anyway.

We did our reporting session as usual, me last. I told her I'd ordered *two* modern cafeteria-type tables that afternoon and told the suppliers to bill the Emporium.

Fabio started up instantly. 'Of all the nerve.'

'They were needed for glue tables in the workshop.'

'Will there be any further expenses, Lovejoy? I mean, this is your last requirement?'

'No. An old box iron, but I can make one of these.'

'Very well. But in future ask first. Is that understood?'

I drew breath to explain that there was very little future left, but Fabio broke in with an exasperated 'Oh!' so I turned to go, writing the whole bloody thing off, when Adriana said, 'Lovejoy. Here, please.'

Please? She was holding out a sealed envelope between her fingers, avoiding my eye by the trick of paying attention to Fabio's complaints. I hesitated, but took it and went to shut the workshop windows.

I opened the envelope. A posh monogrammed card was inside. It read,

Signora Adriana Albanese requests the pleasure of Signor Lovejoy's company this evening at supper in the Gold Season Restaurant, Rome.
Eight-thirty for nine o'clock.

I had the sense to put it in my jacket pocket before I turned round. Piero was waiting there in the doorway.

'All done, Lovejoy?' he said without inflection. It could have meant anything.

I said, 'Nearly.' And left.

I felt a real scruff in the Gold Season. The carpet absorbed me up to my ankles. The walls were discreetly illuminated along their entire lengths, gold light warming the restaurant as far as the crystal fountain in the centre.

Needless to say, an incoming tramp flashing a card and being given an ostentatiously hysterical welcome by the senior captain caused no little stir. You can't help feeling a right duckegg sometimes. Even people in the alcoves looked up to see the fuss.

I was given a dry sherry as if I'd asked for it. The offered smokes I declined. I was nervous as hell, though I'd washed. The invitation presumably meant I was to dine with the Albaneses, rather than in some quiet corner. But what did one talk about with a bloke like Signor Albanese? And I'm a clumsy sod. I was sure to drop everything or knock his wineglass all over his precious papers. Every portent indicated a really swinging time. I sat miserably listening to the gentle background music and trying to work out things to say.

There are times when even portents get things wrong. This was one of them. A second sherry had just arrived to make me hungrier still. I could hardly remember the pizza I had had at two o'clock. I'd just decided that the invitation had been some kind of elaborate joke when a cough alerted me, one of those directional look-out-we're-here coughs waiters use. I looked up, and there was Adriana, being ushered towards my table.

I stumbled to my feet, nudging the bloody table so the glasses tinkled dangerously. Calm hands steadied it and trained voices murmured apologies for the habitual clumsiness of serfs, as if it had been them and not me.

'Good evening, signora,' I mumbled.

'Good evening, Lovejoy.'

They say Queen Victoria is the only person in history never to check that a chair was available before sitting down. (One always was, of course.) Well, Adriana did it too, sinking elegantly in the sure conviction that enough kulaks were around to spring forward with a chair. She was blinding. Her dress was a simple sheath thing in green with a scooped collar. The emerald on her breast seemed out of place at first until she raised her arms to the table and the gold bracelets picked up the emerald's gold setting. Her emerald earrings shed a million lights. I'd never seen anything so exquisite before. The waiters hurtled about to bring her sherry.

I had to tell her. 'Look, signora. I'm letting you down, being here.'

She said coolly, 'I invited you, Lovejoy.'

'I know. But you're. . . perfect. Just look at me.'

'Appearances are unimportant, no?'

'That is untrue, signora. As your husband will agree.'

'Signor Albanese will not be able to join us this evening. He's unavoidably detained.'

Until then I'd assumed he was merely telling the chauffeur where to park that purple Rolls. 'Oh. I'm sorry.' Unsuccessfully I tried to suppress my overwhelming relief.

'You're very kind.' While she accepted the sherry I wondered if I detected a certain dryness in her tone but decided I couldn't have. 'Lovejoy. I saw Signor Gallinari over the weekend.'

The bloke who'd sold us the lovely Jacobean piece. 'You didn't tell him I'm on your staff?'

'Yes. He remembered you.'

I pulled a face. 'Pity. He has two luscious early Wedgwoods, both underpriced.' We couldn't pull the same lift twice. Gallinari wasn't that dim. A lift is persuading somebody to sell an antique ridiculously cheap. Dealers are always on guard against other dealers.

Her brown eyes flicked up at me, seeming big as saucers. 'He called you *that young man who loves things*.' Lustrous. That's the word. 'You rather surprised him, Lovejoy.'

'How?'

'When I said you . . . assist me, he expressed astonishment that you had not asked for a special deal.'

'I don't do milkers.' A milker is a trade trick. You claim you've had to pay more than the real purchase price. Had I done a milker, Gallinari would have given me two invoices, a genuine and a phoney one. The loser would have been Adriana. 'Is that what Piero and Fabio expected, too?'

'Of course. And I.'

'Look.' I cleared my throat. Even a perfect woman can be dim. 'Antiques are valuable to me even if they aren't mine. They're not just hard currency. They are love. Some people – kids in slums, men and women slaving in intolerable conditions, dying as they worked – solidified love, welded it into things they made. When you think of it, it's magical. There's nothing more valuable than that.'

'There's feeling.' She was watching me again.

'No there's not.' That sort of yap riles me. 'Feeling isn't love.'

She waved away a hovering waiter. 'What are they, then?'

'Feelings are feelings. Nothing else.'

She was nonplussed. Women hate the cold light of truth. I saw a milliard doubts flicker across her face, to and fro like dappling sun on a stream. She said slowly, staring past me, 'I'm not used to this kind of discussion. You'll have to explain . . .'

'Look,' I said apologetically. 'Erm, sorry about this, but could we possibly, erm . . . ?'

'Oh, certainly!'

She ordered, and mercifully the grub started coming. I just lasted out. Apart from the prawn cocktail being so natty it was practically microscopic, the grub was lovely. I fell on it, desperately trying to maintain a light chitchat till each next lot appeared. The signora kept it coming, thank God. By the time the second lot of dessert rolled up I had slowed to a steady noshing rhythm and only then noticed that conversation had ceased at the adjacent tables. A good number of diners were watching us – well, me. Adriana had hardly eaten a thing. I reddened and glanced up at her but she only smiled.

'I would like your opinion,' she said smoothly, 'on those profiteroles. They are supposed to have quite a name for them here . . .'

'Oh, er,' I stammered, wondering if I ought to pretend I was full from politeness. Adriana overrode my embarrassment by interrogating the captain on the cream and insisting on inspecting it herself. Not knowing what the hell profiteroles were I was a bit lost and waited till all our fates were decided. They turned out to be little chocolate things that tended to vanish when you bit.

You have to admire a woman like her. Instead of being mortified by this shabby moron whaling his way through platefuls, she blossomed and funnily enough raised her voice, almost showing off. She seemed to take a curious delight in supervising what was going on. I suspected afterwards she was just covering up so I wouldn't feel bad on her account, though at the time I was just a bit surprised because I'd never seen her so animated. If I hadn't known I was a proven liability I'd almost have believed she was enjoying being with me. Like I say, women are odd. Over coffee I tried to apologize in case I'd put her off her grub. I'd just been so hungry.

She smiled. 'Not in the least.'

'You never have much.' As I said it I realized the mistake. It meant I'd ogled her every mouthful whenever she dined. 'Sorry.'

'Don't apologize. I never really enjoy mealtimes.'

A message to cut and run? 'Erm, I think I'd better be getting along . . .'

'I've ordered coffee,' she commanded. 'I'd like you to try our famous liqueur. *Sambuca* isn't to everyone's palate, but I'm told . . .'

She insisted we finish the wine and asked where I was living.

I said, 'Over in a small street near the Castel Sant' Angelo,' but I was trying to work it out. If Piero had followed me to that hotel when I'd visited that lady tourist, and reported back to Adriana, why didn't she know where I lived?

'Is it satisfactory?'

'It's free.' Another mistake, possibly implying resentment at being fastened on her financial chain. Her colour heightened, I could have kicked myself. 'I meant it's okay.'

She gathered her handbag then, in a glitter of emerald and gold. Dinner was over. Minions panted up, quivering. She said, 'I'm afraid I shall have to ask you to drive.'

'Me? That big thing?'

'No. Something much smaller. The Rolls is . . . in use. Can you manage . . . ?'

She meant was I tipsy.

An army of waiters leapt to drag our chairs away. We processed out of the restaurant, Adriana sweeping ahead and me following.

The car was the same longish low job. Adriana passed me the keys. All fingers and thumbs, I made a pig's ear of opening the doors, and once in I took a fortnight finding the controls. Adriana said nothing, just laid her head back on the headrest and closed her eyes until we got going. Then she opened her eyes and from then on simply directed, telling me only left or right and saying nothing else.

It came on to rain after some twenty minutes. We were on a major carriageway. Quite a lot of traffic was about though it thinned as we turned off on to a smaller road. I had no idea where we were. She never said where we were heading, though when the city ended and the countryside seemed to rise, and the road with it, I began to wonder. Possibly they had two houses, and her husband had some business out of the city.

Our drive through the rain took maybe an hour or just a little less. We pulled in to the gateway of a villa. It was lit by an outside ornamental lantern so presumably somebody was home and waiting up for her. Lights of a couple of other villas were visible not too far off. I couldn't see for rain and dark, but gained an impression of palms and paths leading off a patio into a garden.

I waited, thinking, now what do we do? It was a hell of a way back, and by now so late I doubted if a taxi would make the journey out this far.

'You'll have to come in,' she said. 'No sense in sitting here.'

We ran up the few marble steps into the shelter of the porch. Dashing in the rain always makes me smile. I noticed she used keys instead of ringing. I stood feeling full of doubts while she clicked the door open and went in shaking her hair like they do. She had hall lights on before she realized I was still dithering in the porch. Her shoulders drooped as if with exasperation.

'Lovejoy.' She didn't even turn round.

'Yes, signora?'

'You now come *in*.'

'Erm, thank you.' I stepped inside. She still hadn't turned.

'And *now* you close the door behind you.'

'Right.' I did as she said, feeling a twerp. 'Look,

signora,' I said doubtfully. 'About my, erm, getting back . . .'

She turned then. I couldn't tell whether she was laughing or crying. 'Lovejoy,' she said. 'I don't believe you're real.'

She said the same thing again during the night. It must have been about three o'clock in the morning. I was across in the bathroom. She came from the bedroom and stood wobbling sleepily in the doorway.

'Lovejoy. What are you doing?'

'Washing my socks.' I'd done my singlet and underpants and was hanging them on the heated rails.

'You are *what*?'

'I've only one lot.' It was all right for her. I'd never seen her in the same clothes twice. A set of heated drying pipes was not to be sneezed at. 'Finished.'

She came against me, apparently snuffling with laughter. I was glad, because I was stark naked. So was she for that matter, but nude women don't look stupid like we do. A woman like her could make a man forget Maria.

'I told Fabio to get you fitted out.'

'He must have forgotten.'

'I'll make sure he remembers.'

'Mind, signora,' I warned. 'My hands are wet.'

It was then she said it again. 'Lovejoy,' she breathed against my neck, her hands about me. 'I don't believe you're real.'

Her saying that was getting on my nerves. 'What are you on about?'

'I mean you call me Adriana now. Come back to bed.'

She meant *cretino*.

Chapter Nineteen

Next morning was a right scramble. It shouldn't have been, but for some reason Adriana was anxious to make a proper breakfast for us, warbling in the kitchen with me gaping at the loveliest of views over a valley. I had her point the places out on the map and was delighted to learn we were near the Tivoli Fountains at the Villa D'Este. She said we would go one day.

She drove quite expertly and probably twice as well as me. Women are mostly better drivers than us. I've noticed that. I was thankful, because there was a snarl-up on the main road into the city. We had delayed getting off the bed as well, which didn't help. She dropped me with money for a taxi.

Anna had not left for the day's work. We had a brief skirmish, but that was practically par for the course nowadays. She was at her make-up when I came in and she rounded on me. Of course I had no reason to feel guilty but women always put you in the wrong.

'I suppose you've been with that posh whore? The grand signora.'

'No,' I lied. 'If you must know I've been looking around.'

'The rip?' she breathed, unbending.

'Yes.'

'I'm glad, Lovejoy.' She gave a half-smile. 'One of us messing it up's bad enough.'

She was apologizing for that business with the police. I felt a heel but quickly suppressed it. There were too many people not on my side for me to go over and join them.

'I want you to do something. Can you get hold of a camera? They took theirs back.' And asked all sorts of awkward questions when I couldn't produce any photographs.

'I'll get one.'

I warned, 'Legitimate, no stealing. Make sure you get a film that fits. Have somebody do it for you if you're uncertain. Then photograph the Colosseum.'

'*All* of it?'

'No. Go in to the right. The terrace ends about half way round, where the ancient Romans had a sort of elevator. There are great blocks of stone – '

'I know the place. Where the masons work?'

'Photograph the stones, the recess, everything.' I didn't say that was where Marcello died. 'From every angle you can think of. It's vital, so do it properly.'

'I'll do it, Lovejoy.' She looked at me through the mirror, doing her mouth. 'And thanks.'

'What for?' I'd just given her a monumental load of work to do, one my life would depend on.

'Just thanks.' I let it go. I don't understand birds sometimes.

She came to close the door after me. 'Lovejoy. I've had news. Carlo comes out of hospital tomorrow.'

'About time,' I said as levelly as I could. It had had to come. 'Tell him I want the ambulance on standby in three days. 'Morning, Anna.'

''Morning, Lovejoy.'

I started making the winch that morning.

Maybe my timing was a bit unfortunate, knowing what I now knew of Piero and Adriana, but I was on a tight schedule. You can't keep Vaticans waiting. So while I was drying out some glued pieces after weighting them down I went into the yard to measure up for the beam, a plain girder with a pulley.

'What are you doing, Lovejoy? Who said you could start on that?'

Good old Piero had come to check on me. He did this about twice an hour usually. Never said much, just gave a long glance, then went back in. This time he was inquisitive and suspicious.

'Well, nobody, but – '

'You were told your winch idea's off. Listen.' He came closer, casual as anything. I glimpsed Fabio's delighted face at the rear window. 'Your job here is to *take* orders. Understand?'

'I know that. But it's daft to waste – '

'Piero.'

Adriana was standing at the top of the showroom's back steps. An entirely new outfit. Lemon was today's colour, a graceful suit and chiffon scarf. No gold, just enough silver to bend the bullion market. Her hair was lustrous. She looked straight out of Imperial Rome, a real blinder.

'Eh?' I realized she had asked a question, what was going on? 'Oh. I thought I'd start measuring up – '

'For a winch for the top floor,' Piero said. He never took his eyes off me. If Adriana hadn't arrived we'd have been having harsher words than this.

I shrugged. 'If we can't use it for upstairs, it'll do for the showroom. A kid could use it to lift the heaviest furniture right into the ground-floor showroom. For God's sake,' I said, making out I was getting tired of it. 'Even the ancient Romans had lifting devices. Go to the Colosseum. The mason there lifted those great blocks all day long with one finger, and we hump wardrobes and cabinets up and down those stupid steps, into the loading yard. Daft.'

'Then he can make it for the showroom,' Adriana told the middle distance. 'Will it be safe?'

'Perfectly.' I smiled at her but not at Piero.

And I thought, like hell it will.

Fabio spent a contented morning after that, pouring oil on troubled fires. He took great pleasure in calling me into the showroom, innocently asking my advice on this or that antique. Twice I told him the stuff he was asking about was gunge, modern fakery, and each time he simpered with pleasure. It was only when I saw Piero's thunderous expression that I realized what game Fabio was playing. They were 'antiques' Piero had bought in. Hey ho.

Adriana spent her time being exquisitely beautiful in the office and taking customers around. We were quite busy. I was brought up to play the tray dodge again, once with Piero and once – at some considerable distance – with Adriana.

The influx always fell off about half past twelve, and it was then I really got going. Instead of working feverishly in ten-minute dashes I could tear into my Chippendale with a single mind. Of course they didn't look like tables, and if things went smoothly they wouldn't for quite some time. Piero came into the workshop about one o'clock. I was pedalling like a maniac at the spindle lathe, running a polisher into action, when I felt him there. I let the spindle creak to a halt, thinking that this was it. I gave him a disarming grin, friendly old Lovejoy.

'You rang?'

'Those bits the rent table for Adriana?'

'Yes. Want to see?'

'Not really.' He was quite casual again, in full control. I think it was then I understood what a dangerous opponent he could be. Give me somebody berserk, every time. 'There seems a lot of pieces for just one table.'

'I'm making the occasional duplicate piece,' I explained casually. 'It's called templating. Then if the signora finds it sells quickly, I can easily make another. Saves working it all out every time.'

'What I mean is, Lovejoy, you're not making separates, are you? One for the signora, one for yourself? Because I wouldn't like that, Lovejoy.' He spoke like a boss.

'No,' I said, thinking I was getting quite good at lying. I'd lied my head off all morning and it felt marvellous. 'I promise you, Piero. Everything here belongs to the signora.'

'You know, Lovejoy,' he said thoughtfully, inspecting me. 'There's something wrong with you, isn't there?'

I didn't like this. Piero the ape I could handle. Piero the thinker was an unknown quantity. 'Wrong?'

'You bend too easy. Yet I get the impression you're just not bendable. And all this honesty.'

I shrugged uncomfortably. I don't like being looked into. 'Everybody's different.'

'And your gig here. Working on spec, when you're a natural at the antiques game.'

'Scratching bread, same as the rest.'

'Maybe, Lovejoy.' He was still quite calm as he left, but he said it again. 'Maybe.'

When we started to break at two o'clock I received a type-written message. In an envelope with just my name on the front: *Lovejoy*. It read:

Lovejoy,
    Please phone the number below, two-thirty.
It was a Rome number.

I asked Fabio, 'Who delivered this?'

'It was with the rest of the post.'

'No postmark?'

'Just as I passed it to you, Lovejoy.' He grinned wickedly. 'Some handsome admirer you haven't told us about?'

I was on tenterhooks wondering, so I made sure I broke off on time. On the way out Adriana spoke to me as I was dismissed – turning approximately in my direction but speaking a mile over my head.

'Lovejoy. Your lunch arrangements are altered.'

I'd forgotten my nosh money. 'They are?'

'Yes. I've phoned an account in, at the pizzeria across the street and the trattoria next to it.'

'Er, thank you, signora.'

'For one,' she said absently. I felt the barb: no hungry partners share your dinners, Lovejoy.

'Of course, signora.'

I made my farewells and hurried to the trattoria where they let me use their phone. My hands were shaking as I dialled. A bored bird announced a hotel's name quite openly.

'Look,' I said with some puzzlement. 'My name's Lovejoy. I was asked to phone this number at two-thirty.'

'It's not that yet.' She was bored and belligerent. 'I'll put you through but don't blame me.'

It was Arcellano all right. I felt my flesh creep as soon as I heard the poisonous bastard. He asked, 'How's my old friend?'

'I haven't a bean,' I complained. 'I'm having to work on tick.'

He gave his cat-cough chuckle but I'll bet without a proper smile. 'Exactly as I like it, Lovejoy. Here's my instruction. As soon as you've completed our trans-action, you will ring this phone number, in Bonn. The very instant. You'll be told where to deliver the item. Do you understand?'

'Yes.'

'And Lovejoy. No more accidents with cars.'

'What do you mean?' I was all innocent.

The phone went dead. I wrote down the number he'd given me and had a sombre meal.

I left the trattoria thinking resentfully that half of the people in Rome now seemed to be my bosses. I had Anna bellyaching that everything I did was wrong. I had Adriana telling me where and when I could eat, and now who to sleep with. There was Piero fighting me every inch of the way. Fabio was stirring it. And

Arcellano, probably having me watched now even as I walked through the Piazza Navona towards Anna's.

It was then that I got the other half. A familiar motor was waiting as I emerged on the south side of the Navona. Familiar because you don't get many of them that ghastly purple colour. The chauffeur stood out as I crossed over.

'Signor.'

Like a fool, I was smiling as I got in, but the thing was empty. I sat, puzzled. Adriana had said nothing about sending her car for me.

We rolled like a mobile cathedral into the river road. I listened carefully. There was not a cheep out of the clock.

'Where are we going?' I asked the driver, peering out at the car roofs. I'd never been this high without a ladder. 'Look. I have to be back at work – '

'One moment, signor.'

That was all I got from him. The interior of the car was carpeted and there were more cupboards around than I had in my cottage. It was lovely. With my B movie memory I tried the door handle at a traffic light. It wasn't locked, so I wasn't going to be gassed. Only Adriana, probably, wanting to talk.

We were only a few minutes reaching the block of apartments. Not too tall a building, and very discreet. The ground floor was occupied by a suite of offices, some kind of property development company by the looks of things. I'm thick sometimes. I was still smiling in anticipation when I realized the place was Signor Albanese's, not Adriana's.

A suave young bloke showed me in. Signor Albanese was reading documents behind a rosewood desk. I trudged the mile between the door and the chair. He had more sense than keep me waiting by pretending preoccupation, and looked up immediately with a smile that told me once again it was not my day.

'There you are,' he said, smiling at the secretary to

bring a sherry. 'You are much younger than I'd imagined, Lovejoy. I put you in the mid forties.'

'Some of us never make it.'

He smiled and invited me into the chair.

'You can leave us, Ernesto.'

'I'm afraid I don't have much time,' I said.

'I know. You must be back at the Emporium fairly soon.' He nodded as though that side of things was of the slightest importance.

I sussed him. He was a calm, immaculate sort. You immediately received the impression that nothing could possibly take this man by surprise. It was a troublesome world, clearly, but controllable. His thinning hair was flattened, his suit brand new. Behind all that cleanliness and order he was tough, and in charge.

'About your presence in Rome, Lovejoy.' He raised a podgy palm to arrest my run of falsehoods. 'No fabrications, please. Save those for others. You are, I believe, a divvie?'

'Yes.'

'An impressive attribute.' A pause. 'For one so poor.'

'My stuff was stolen. I got dipped.'

'So you say.'

'It's the truth. I'm earning my wages in antiques. Signora Albanese decided the deal, not me.'

'I heard. But that still leaves a gap in your story, no?'

'Not that I'm aware of.'

'Perhaps I should explain, then. You come here, ostensibly as a tourist. You are relieved of your wallet. So you gravitate to a job in an antique shop, simply to earn your fare home.'

'That's it.'

He continued smoothly, 'I am reliably informed that your country's authorities have an enviable record in establishing administrative systems the world over. I am further informed that they can cope with a stranded tourist.'

'I never thought of it.'

He leant forward, shaking his head.

'Lovejoy. I swear to you. I do not intend to destroy you, or any plans you might have. And whatever you say will go no further. But I must know. Do you understand?'

I was getting sick of people uttering threats at me and then demanding if I understood. They'd all been at it today and it was getting on my wick.

'No, I don't understand.'

'You were merely one of the crowd,' he said gently. 'At first, that is. Until now. When you and Adriana . . . ' He paused to make certain it sank in. 'Naturally my wish for Adriana is that she enjoys a stable relationship. I condone it. And, until now, that which has existed between Adriana and Piero Peci has been eminently suitable. I am naturally very concerned when Adriana shows signs of changing her arrangements.'

I was lost. It was all too liberated for me to take in at one go. 'You mean I'm sacked? Or I'm not to see Adriana?'

'Not at all. Some relationship, of the kind Piero has previously provided, is essential. All I want to know is what your game is.'

I drew breath. He didn't mind Adriana having another bloke, even if it was in the plural, and all he wanted was for me to be frank about my presence in Rome? I began to get a headache.

'It's . . . ' I hung my head, as if in shame. What the hell could I tell him? Tinker always says you should get your lies in first. Second and you're sunk. I started to talk, praying something would come. 'It's . . . somebody I've met.'

'Adriana?'

'No.' That road might be even more dangerous. 'I

admit I have some motive for staying . . . ' *Anna*! Anna! I burbled, 'I . . . I want to stay for a while, at least until I've worked things out. She . . . she isn't free. She has obligations. I'm not at liberty . . .'

'Somebody else? Not Adriana?' There was a dry rasp. I looked up. The blighter was laughing, heaving up and down in his chair. 'So. It isn't really Adriana at all? By acquiescing to Adriana you were merely demonstrating unfailing obedience to your employer?'

'Well, if you put it like that . . .'

He took off his specs and wiped his eyes. I didn't think it was all that funny but he was rolling in the aisles.

'I'm sorry, Lovejoy,' he said, wiping his eyes with his glasses lifted on to his forehead. 'Very remiss of me. But if you only understood the context . . .'

'Is that all?' I rose, trying for a bit of dignity. It can be useful in the right place.

'My abject apologies, signor,' he said, still falling about. He came with me to the door. 'But Adriana playing second fiddle to some other woman is delicious.'

I went frosty. 'Can I go now?'

'The car will be at the entrance for you. Don't be too offended, Lovejoy. Let's say it's our little secret, shall we?'

'Look, signor.' I had to get one thing straight. 'What if the signora says I'm to dine with her again, and . . . . ?'

'Be her guest, Lovejoy.' He smiled and patted my arm.

'After all, everybody's different. And you are merely . . . what's the expression? . . . scratching bread, same as the rest. Isn't that so?'

'Yes,' I said, wondering where I'd heard those words spoken recently.

I was returning in the Rolls, wondering about the rum world we live in, when I remembered where I'd heard those words before recently. And who spoke them.

It was me, to Piero. Word for word. My headache got worse. Well, whatever they were all up to, Piero, Adriana, the signor, and Fabio, the rip had to go ahead.

I made the driver drop me near the Emporium, seeing it was getting on for four o'clock. The three cafeteria tables were delivered on time, to my satisfaction. I'd told Adriana two, and instead had ordered three. I was very, very pleased, because two from three leaves one. Smiling at last, I covered them with a sheet of plastic and walked home to see Anna.

Chapter Twenty

In the heat of the day the Colosseum induces a curiously offensive languor, inducing scores of cats to live there. God knows where the Italians get all their moggies, but it's by the gross. I'd never seen so many. Anna came with me, still in her old gear and occasionally conning a few lire from stray tourists. And she was in a bitter mood. 'You tell me what magnificent photos I took,' she complained, 'then waste our rest time wandering about these old stones.' And her photographs really were great, every nook from every angle. Real skill. I like talent like that. But you really need to get the feel of the place you might die in, I always say, and you can't get that from photographs.

There was hardly anybody in, just us and a straggle of Scandinavians. Anna kept asking me why we were looking at the same recess over and over again. Finally she got on my nerves and I told her to shut it. That did it. Nothing's quieter than a bird in sulk.

The recess was the stonemason's place. Presumably the animals for Rome's great circuses had been fed into the great arena through this kind of entrance. What I liked about it was that it stood just below a great mason's hoist, complete with block and tackle, and with an almost-completed block of stone in the centre of the sandy flooring. Obviously, from the tools and the stone chips, scattered around, the workers were still at it. Before long they would be ready to haul the missing stone into place.

But what I really liked most was that the recess was

at least forty-odd feet deep, and had smooth walls impossible to climb.

'Why are you smiling, Enrico?'

'Don't call me Enrico.' I asked her, 'What would happen if somebody were to get himself trapped in that recess?'

'He'd have to stay till people lifted him out. But nobody could get trapped down there.'

'Why not?'

'Don't you see?' Scornfully she pointed across to the opposite wall below us. 'He could just walk out, couldn't he? That great stone's missing. *Cretino*!'

I shaded my eyes at the great beam overhead. 'But if that unfinished stone were to fall into that hole . . . ?'

'*Then* he'd be trapped!' She took my arm. I was still gaping skywards. 'Enrico? I don't like you when you're like this.'

'You don't like me anyway,' I reminded her acidly. I'd slept in the same room for what felt like a lifetime, and we were as chaste as Abelard and Heloise – different reasons, of course.

'It'd be an open-air prison.' I realized I was smiling at thoughts of Arcellano.

'Enrico.' Her eyes looked at me, enormous with a deep beauty. 'What has this place to do with the rip?'

'Don't call me Enrico.' I was feeling a lot more confident as we left. The arena was after all just one great maze made up of those stone blocks. If anything went wrong I'd be off like a scared rabbit, being the fastest coward ever recorded. And in my time I've been chased by experts. Yes, I was pleased – fool that I was. Nothing could go wrong. So I thought.

During the rest of our spare time I either pored over the photographs, went over Anna's Vatican Museum measurements, or intently read the pharmacopœia. In this last Anna had excelled herself, having an epileptiform seizure in the huge bookshop on the corner of the Leone IV and nicking the pharmacopœia while people ran about for water. She kept asking what I wanted it for but I shoved her away and said it was rude to read over other people's shoulders.

'I've indigestion,' I told her snappishly.

'You eat like a horse when that cow of a signora feeds with you at those expensive restaurants!'

'She hardly eats anything,' I corrected.

'Only people! In her grand villa!'

Which told me a lot. For one, Anna obviously didn't trust me. For another, she had some means of knowing where we dined each evening, and about my visit to Adriana's villa.

Now we'd done the Colosseum I needed a little money and a chance to finish in the workshop. Then it would only be a question of checking the van. But first we had to welcome the great man himself.

Carlo came home like a wounded hero, groaning in a taxi, over-acting and being brave but in pain. Sickening. It was all the same to me, but you couldn't help being really peeved at the fuss Anna made over him, snatching everybody else's cushions to make sure he was comfortable. For once she'd bought in a load of provisions and made him a tantalizing mound of unrecognizable food. He managed to force it all down, the greedy pig, while I sweated my guts out over the photographs and sketches. I've never seen anybody look so sorry for himself, the pillock.

No use asking Anna for a loan after the argument we'd just had, though I wouldn't need much. I'd have to work on Adriana, which was a nuisance because being a bird she'd be as mistrustful as Anna. But there was another problem, just as serious and far more urgent. What did Lovejoy do now hubby was home? So far there hadn't been a single bad vibe – not more than usual, anyway – but it had to be faced.

'Look,' I began when Carlo mournfully started on his second bottle of wine. (Naturally, I'd been offered none.) 'Do you think Carlo's up to it?' As is the way with invalids present I spoke over Carlo's head to Anna.

'Of course he is.'

Carlo straightened up briskly. 'You questioning my ability, Lovejoy? You can't do without me.' Well, I'd been told that by indispensible allies, and they'd been just as wrong as Carlo.

Nastily I demanded, 'Has he ever done anything before?'

'Tell him, Carlo.'

He got up to stride the room, obviously full of beans. Clearly a good recovery. 'I've ripped off every film crew which has ever come to Rome.'

'Great,' I said drily. That meant pinching a plug or a bulb and selling it back to the cameramen. 'Anything with cars?'

'I can drive faster – '

'No,' I told Anna flatly. 'You tell him he's to drive like a fifty-year-old, not Fangio. Get that into his thick skull or it's off.'

Anna smiled, but I could tell she was annoyed. 'It's not off, Lovejoy. You know it. I know it. Carlo will do anything you say.'

'He'd better.' I moved towards the door.

'Hey,' Carlo called, now mirror boxing and admiring himself. 'You've not said what the plan is.'

'If we get it right, Carlo, you'll never know.'

'You going back to work, Lovejoy?' from Anna.

'Yes.' I hesitated to give Anna time to follow me into the gloomy passageway. 'Erm, what's the arrangement for tonight, Anna?'

'Arrangement?' she was honestly puzzled.

'Well, now your bloke's back . . .'

She pealed laughter and clapped hands. 'You mean . . . *Carlo*?'

'Yes,' I said irritably. 'What's the joke?' Women like Anna nark me.

'He's my brother.' She fell about some more. 'He sleeps on the folding camp bed.'

'Oh, right.' I felt even more of a nerk and backed out into the alley. 'See you tonight, then.'

'*Ciao*,' she called, slamming the door on me. '*Cretino*!' I heard her laughter as I walked the uneven alley towards the Castel.

That same day I had luck, which was important. By nightfall I had become practically independent in Adriana's business. A trustee instead of a convict.

The antiques game's the queerest on earth. Some days – weeks, months, even years – you come across nothing worth a second glance. Then they roll in, and everywhere you look there is some genuine wonderment, preening its lovely feathers and shrieking to be bought.

We hit a purple patch. Adriana had reluctantly agreed to visiting a small antiques bazaar about a mile away. I'd felt vibes almost like never before while passing on a bus. The dazzling spiritual glow from beyond Piazza Argentina all but blinded me. I was almost certain I'd glimpsed a monk's chest – neither a chest nor for a monk – being unloaded in a small street. The funny thing was I could have sworn I'd seen its photograph in one of Adriana's catalogues where a great deal of miscellaneous items, arranged as job lots, had been listed. (This in itself is a serious mistake and argues a cataloguer too idle or inexperienced.) I persuaded Adriana to come and see if they had picked up any of these items as well as the monk's chest. It turned out like Christmas.

It was a small quickie business run by three lads and their birds, you know the kind of place, everything for speed. They had bought indiscriminately, and hadn't even unpacked the smaller stuff. So eager to display their larger pieces, they let me go through and buy four small cardboard boxes of stuff practically without doing much more than unwrap a couple of top items in each. I made out I was in a great hurry, wanting stuff to trade for period reproductions in Turin the very next morning. It was a steal. Of course it cost Adriana more than the same pieces would have done had she attended the auction itself, but that was okay.

Adriana waited round the corner in Piero's car with him while I did the deal. She'd collected enough money for me to buy outright, and I came haring across the Piazza Argentina practically crowing with delight. I was so chuffed I nearly downed a fat bloke ambling across the road. The youngsters had been hugely pleased – we always say the first profit is the best, and best means fastest – but I'll bet they weren't as pleased as me. I swear I'd felt the clamouring of the eighteenth-century malachite green decorative jewellery inside among all those newspapers, and nobody could help feeling that ringing emanation from the Chien Lung agate-tiled silver box. The only William IV lead funereal marker I've ever bought was among them – and you know what's happened to the price of those. Ten years ago these flat lead pieces were thrown out with the beer bottles. Practically everything was worthwhile, and some pieces – like the little box of early model French soldiers – would pay for the rest.

She took the receipt while I hugged the stuff to me on the way back to the Emporium. Unbelievably, there was a travelling dealer waiting with Fabio. He was a pleasant but tatty little Milanese bloke and had with him a collection of miniature early furniture, probably used for display in some furniture maker's in the 1830s. We call these geezers 'sweepers' in the trade because they do 'sweeps' through the country trying to gather up anything and everything which could be regarded as antique. They're the blokes who come knocking at your door on dark nights. (Take my tip: *always* send them packing. No bigger crowd of rogues exists on earth, and I should know. I was one for years.) The

BBC and Sotheby's do 'sweeps' too – respectable ones, and at least as honourably, I'm sure.

I urged Adriana to buy the stuff. When the sweeper had gone we all looked at each other. It was only half past six, and I'd made the Emporium a fortune.

'We overpaid the sweeper,' Piero said sourly, the miserable sod.

I wasn't having that. 'We'll make twice the cost on his stuff.'

'Of course, we still have to sell them,' Fabio said waspishly, another ray of sunshine. 'And as for buying those little balls – '

I'd bought two balls of compressed feathers wedged inside a small fraying leather case the size of a shaving stick.

'We paid the price of two beers,' I said gently. 'We'll sell them for the price of a car. They're early golf balls. Rare as hen's teeth. I'll bet you – '

'You haven't a bean to bet with, Lovejoy,' Fabio countered waspishly, sweeping back to his accounts.

I felt myself go red but Adriana said quickly, 'You were very astute, Lovejoy. Thank you.'

'Not at all, signora.' I hadn't meant to sound bitter but it came out different from what I'd intended. The workshop was clearly the place for me, though I was itching to go through the rest of the job lots to see what other brilliant stuff we'd got.

Time was getting short, though Adriana's rent table was coming along fast. It would soon be finished and good as new. Better still, good as old. One difficulty was not having the sketches of the Vatican Museum's period piece with me, but I'm not that daft. If Piero or Fabio found drawings like that they'd smell a rat. So I worked in the old way, from notches cut in sticks. Every morning at Anna's I tied the sticks to my calf inside my trouser leg. Once I was at the workshop an extra stick or two went unnoticed.

Another difficulty was assembly. The reproduction

rent table I was making for Adriana to put on display had to be ready fairly soon or they'd be wondering what the hell I was doing down here, especially after they'd all commented, each in his pleasant little way, on my working speed. So I did a zillion test assemblies of every drawer and every joint, and never put it all together. The outer surfaces of her table I copied precisely using light plywood but giving them the same kinds of finish. These were the pieces I'd told Piero were my patterns for copying.

Like hell they were.

Somehow I made room for the two cafeteria tables, scattering bits of wood about on them to show how useful they were being. The third one I left out in the yard, allegedly ready to be returned.

A further stroke of luck came about thirty minutes before we closed for the night. Signor Gallinari phoned us to say he was ready for swapping – we were doing a trade of chairs to make up complete period dining sets. Piero and Fabio went off in the van grumbling and sulky. I immediately put the metal saw across the tubular steel tips of one of the cafeteria table's legs. I put the four tips in my pocket, wrapped in a hankie so as not to clink, and stepped off to look. Nobody could tell. I was whistling happily and splitting some thin dowelling when Adriana came in.

'Here, Lovejoy.' She held out an envelope.

'Thank you, signora.' It was thicker than usual.

'Open it, please.'

There was money inside, besides the invitation card. I drew breath. I needed money badly, but not that bad.

'No, thank you, signora.' I kept the card and held out the notes.

'Why not?'

'We've agreed what the rules are, signora.'

She avoided my eyes. 'It gives you the choice, Lovejoy. Where to dine, what to do in the evenings.'

I tried to make light of the whole thing. 'With all this gelt I might streak off.'

'No, Lovejoy.' She sounded listless. 'Not you. You do what you want. You're here for your own reasons.'

So she'd realized too. 'But signora – '

'No more, Lovejoy. Please.' All the day's successes were forgotten. 'No more hypocrisy. I don't ask why you stay. From now on you won't be forced into anything. I'll see you are paid money each day.'

Her eyes were wet. I was lost. 'What about Fabio? He'll realize . . .'

'I'll find some way. Take it out of the petty cash. He won't know.'

That seemed odd, almost as if she was apprehensive about Fabio. She was the boss, after all, and Fabio was only a hireling, like me.

'Am I to be at the restaurant?'

'Only if you wish.'

I hesitated while Adriana dabbed at her eyes. Women get me mad because you never know where you are. 'Did Signor Albanese say anything? He had me taken to his office.' She looked merely resigned as I told her about it, word for word. 'I made up some cock-and-bull story about having fallen for another bird and wanting to stay here to work it out.'

'What woman?' she asked immediately.

I had a hard time convincing her there was no such woman, that she was a figment invented on the spur of the moment. 'The signor thought it hilarious.'

'I see,' she said, finally convinced. It was more than I did.

'The only thing is, he seemed to know that, erm, you and I, erm, at your villa . . .'

The others came back at that moment, so we got no further.

When we locked up later Piero was unusually affable while Adriana was still there, and walked with me as far as the corner. I wondered if this was it. There were plenty of people about, but he was such a bloody size.

'Lovejoy.' He'd made certain the purple Rolls had floated off. 'Time for you to go away, no?' He tried a wintry smile. It wasn't a patch on Arcellano's, but he was quite patient, and that disturbed me because calm fighters always do. They've seen it all before.

'Why now, especially?'

'Before, I didn't mind you too much. You were . . . incidental.' He meant insignificant, the pillock. 'But now, Adriana begins to take you seriously. You're a good antiques man, the best I've seen.' He shrugged. 'A divvie's special. Okay – so you're good for her business. But I won't be displaced by a bum that's planning some crazy rip, and using her for camouflage.'

I gave a hollow laugh. 'Rip? You're off your head. It's my hobby.'

'You joke.' He nodded gravely, eyeing me. 'Though everything you do is serious, Lovejoy. Deadly serious. You're a driven man. So I'll make a deal: go tomorrow.'

'Where to?'

'Anywhere, Lovejoy. Name the place and you'll receive money, a passport and ticket.'

'And what's my part of the deal?'

'I save you from gaol, Lovejoy.' He picked his teeth, wrinkling his eyes against the fading sun. 'I've got your fingerprints, your photograph. Fabio will provide evidence of pilfering. The Rome police are serious about antiques, Lovejoy. Whatever the rip they'll have you. You've got till tomorrow. *Ciao*.'

I watched him go, working it out. Now I had to leave, to stay, to do the rip, not to do the rip, chat up Adriana, leave her alone . . .

And that evening we dined together in the Gold Season, just the three of us: me and Adriana, and her husband. I felt between the devil and the deep blue sea because I was now sure I was being followed.

The fat bloke I'd nearly knocked down in the Piazza Argentina was shown to a corner table five minutes after we arrived. A different digit, but definitely Arcellano's finger.

That wasn't all. After a couple of hours' nosh and onesided chat – Signor Albanese was in fine form, with Adriana unresponsive and me demented – we rose and departed, and this time a Jaguar waited for Adriana. Beside it was the purple Rolls, with a familiar figure standing peevishly by, handbag on the swing.

Adriana resolved all doubts by passing me her keys quite openly. 'Drive, please, Lovejoy.'

'Erm – '

Signor Albanese gave me effusive thanks for my company and said he would not rest until we dined so pleasantly once again.

'Come *on* Emilio!' Fabio shouted petulantly. 'I've waited hours!'

'I'm hurrying!' Albanese called.

I stood while Adriana slid into the Jaguar. Emilio Albanese waved to us once and joined Fabio at the Rolls. I watched it glide away before getting in beside Adriana. I drew breath to say something and then thought better of it. Adriana was looking away. Evidently that was the other surprise Anna had promised me, the night I learned about Piero and Adriana. Piero and Adriana because of Signor Albanese and Fabio? And now Lovejoy and Adriana because of . . . ? I gave it up.

'To the villa, darling,' Adriana said. She sounded a hundred years old.

Chapter Twenty-one

It had been an uptight morning, with Fabio and Piero giving smouldering glances at the clock to warn me I should be gone by nightfall. I trotted home to Anna's eating pizza on the hoof.

I could tell Carlo was already there from the blaring transistor echoing pop music down the alley. Sure enough he was dancing sinuously before the mirror, admiring himself while Anna was removing her make-up. Ominously, he looked sloshed. Three empty wine bottles projected from the waste basket.

'Get your knickers on, troops,' I said from the door. 'And turn that bloody thing off.'

'Miserable man.' Carlo glared sullenly at me while Anna flicked the tranny, and slumped on his camp bed, obviously ready for a hard afternoon's kip.

I said, 'It starts, lad,' and toed him beneath the canvas. 'Up.'

'What does?' Carlo propped up on an elbow.

I leaned down, smiling. 'The rip, comrade. Now.'

'This instant?' from Anna, suddenly pale, her lovely face rimmed by those theatrical bulbs.

'Finish your make-up, Granny,' I said heartlessly. 'Carlo's going to show me the ambulance van.'

'It's ready,' he was saying, insolently starting to lie down again, when I tipped him out and heeled his knife hand. The knife fell clear. 'He thinks I'm a kid,' he complained, staggering up.

'Kid, no. Stupid and drunk, yes.' I yanked him into the corridor. 'Anna. You be here at four.'

The van was in the smallest garage in the world half

a mile from St John Lateran. We got the Metro, Carlo paying – obviously in blood – and leering at women. That journey was a record: he only combed his hair a couple of dozen times. Pests don't come more pestilential than Carlo. He was doing his spy theatrical all the way out of the Metro and crossing the road. We got more attention than Garibaldi's entry. I still don't believe it – he gave eight significant raps on the garage door, looking cloak-and-dagger as he hissed a secret code word through the gaping slats, even though the door was half off. Bloody fool. Wearily I pushed it open and stepped through while Carlo was still at it. He swaggered after me undismayed, narrowly failing to light a cigarette. That was because I took his matches and fags off him and dropped them underfoot. He was standing next to a petrol pump and a drum of waste oil.

'Patrizio.' Carlo leaned against the garage wall, flicking a coin. The nerk was unbelievable.

A tubby cheerful bloke in trousers and singlet emerged from the engine of a derelict one-tonner. He was glad to see me and smeared me with oil in an effusive greeting.

'Patrizio, this is the boss,' Carlo rasped, his eyes hooded. He missed his coin which plopped into an oil puddle.

'Ah, Signor! You like her, eh?'

'Like who?' I looked about.

'You want the van tomorrow, no?' Patrizio slammed a hand on the ancient relic – it nearly fell apart – and grinned enthusiastically. 'Big rip, eh?'

I swallowed carefully. There wasn't another vehicle in the place. '*That*?'

'Sure!' Carlo thrust out his lower lip. 'Me and Patrizio done a deal. She'll do a hundred, boss.' Carlo screwed the words out the corner of his mouth in a crude American accent.

Stricken, I walked around the van. Patrizio came,

exclaiming and extolling with enthusiasm. It had obviously done service in the Western Desert, World War II graffiti and all. Now, the old banger was having a hard time standing upright. 'Fine, eh?'

'No, Patrizio. Carlo must have misunderstood.'

Patrizio's thought winged instantly to money. 'Cheap, Lovejoy.'

I sighed. He knew my name. Carlo had probably given him my address as well.

'Carlo,' I said. 'Keep watch outside.'

'Sure, boss.' The duckegg hunched his jacket collar up and sidled out, tripping over an immense air hose as he did so. He slammed the door so a plank fell out, and stood outside pretending to chew gum.

'Now,' I said carefully, giving Patrizio one of my special looks. 'I need a professional driver, and a pro van.'

Patrizio was no fool. He glanced at the garage door and shrugged. 'Apologies, signor. I thought – '

' – I'd be a fool, too?' I smiled, quite liking him. 'Be frank and there's no harm done.'

'Tomorrow, no?'

'Tomorrow, yes.'

He nodded, gauging me. 'You need my boy Valerio.'

'What's he like?'

Another mile-high shrug. 'I'm his father, signor.'

'You'll need uniforms, Patrizio. Possible?'

'Certain. But if it's tomorrow the van'll have to be . . . obtained, not fabricated.'

'Do it. One thing.' I shrugged, at least an inch. The best I've ever been able to manage. 'It'll have to be a flat fee.'

Patrizio looked at me as if into the teeth of a gale. 'Never heard of a straight-price rip, Lovejoy.'

'You have now.'

'And Carlo? Anna will be furious if he's left out.'

'I'll deal with Anna.'

He grinned and slapped my hand. 'Good luck, Lovejoy. You get your van. Where and when?'

I'd met a pro at last. Smiling with relief, I told him.

Back home Anna was incredulous. 'Carlo dropped? He can't be!'

'You want him so badly?'

She nodded. She was wearing a young print dress and was all ready for me when I returned a few minutes after four. I'd sent Carlo to count the traffic at the traffic lights on the Leone IV, telling him it was our getaway route, the burke.

'Please, Lovejoy. I know what he is, a child still. But he is all I have.' She was ashamed.

I recognized the symptoms from my own career, and relented. 'I've got him a part, love.'

Her face lit, like sunrise. 'You have?' She flung her arms round me wildly. 'Oh, thank you, Lovejoy! Thank you!'

'A vital one,' I said into her hair. 'I'll see he's useful.'

I was thinking, by the time she realized exactly *how* vital, I'd be a thousand miles away from Rome and in the clear. Like I say, sometimes I'm just too thick for words, but you can't be right all the time.

On the way to the Emporium for my late stint I popped into the church on the Borgo San Spirito. It's one of the churches still burning honest-to-God candles instead of those gruesome candle-shaped electric sticks they have in Rome nowadays which for a hundred lire give you a few minutes of electron-powered devotional flicker.

Feeling vaguely embarrassed by the novelty I lit five candles, stuck them in the holders and knelt down. I won't tell you everything I said, but I promised God I'd take Arcellano alive. Then, mumbo-jumbo done with, I emerged blinking at the sun – and saw Anna across the road and waved. To my relief, she was smiling and nodding, so I knew the clever girl had got it, that dark old-fashioned brownish bottle from the chemist's shop by the Via del Mascherino. All systems go.

That evening Adriana and I stayed at the Emporium. It was the oddest sensation, climbing the forbidden stairs and seeing Adriana move about the bedroom as if we'd been together there all our lives. Adriana tried to act casual but I saw her hand tremble as she hung up her stole and I realized that bringing me here was a big thing for her. Another worry.

She insisted on making us both coffee and bringing it over to me. She'd taken my jacket and sat me on the couch, promising to show me around once I'd become accustomed to the idea of being alone with a rapacious woman. I smiled to show I too was solemnly concentrating on lightness of heart.

'New locks,' I observed.

'The stair door? Yes. There are so many thefts nowadays, darling.' She swept her hair from her face. 'I thought it was wiser.'

Which meant that Piero's key was now obsolete.

'Adriana. Will you get in trouble?'

She concentrated on not spilling the cream. 'With Emilio? Hardly. You saw, Lovejoy. Him and that creature Fabio. It's beyond a woman's control.'

'Piero, then? He's the sort to play hell.'

She only had one lamp lit, that lovely minareted Garian case which dappled gold about the room. Her face was silhouetted in a deep bronze fire. She was sitting beside my chair, looking away. I'd never seen anything so wondrous in all my life as that miracle of line and form. Sorrow enveloped me. What a mess it all was, the whole fucking rip.

She said rather sadly, 'He can be got rid of.' The words were so matter-of-fact I hardly took them in at the time, especially as she continued talking with her head on my knee and her breast against me. 'Are you married, Lovejoy?'

That took my by surprise. 'Rescued.'

406

Her eyes deflected, all casual. 'A dragon?'

I thought a bit. 'A pretty laser.'

'So sometimes you too plan badly.' She continued, 'How could I have known about you, Lovejoy? You weren't here.' I suppressed exasperation at the bitterness in her voice. I hadn't known about her, either. Nor that Marcello would be murdered. 'A woman needs a man.' She turned quickly to loan me a half-smile, an on-account sort of expression. 'Not as badly as a man needs a woman. You've taught me that, Lovejoy. With you it's one hundred per cent yourself. The rest is incidental.' She indicated the apartment vaguely. 'This. The money, the firm. With Piero it was a percentage. And the others were the same.'

I returned her defiant look trying to smile. It was a hell of an effort. She was so lovely.

'People make allowances for men.' Bravely she explained, 'A woman taking a lover is a hedonistic bitch. A rich gentleman is merely a roué, a gay old dog. And it's women do the damage – at least, in Rome it is. They're on to you like wolves.'

'What now?' I asked after a pause.

'Now?' She raised her lovely head and smiled. 'You've come at last, Lovejoy.' She smiled gently and reached back to ruffle my neck. 'I don't care what you've done in the past, darling. I take you as you are. And you'll please forgive the measures I've taken while enduring the long, terrible waiting.'

Until then I'd been absolutely determined to go back to Anna's divan. Honestly, I really had. The trouble is, women can be very assertive. I'd be well-balanced and even-tempered all of the time if it weren't for them. So I stayed. I swear it wasn't anything in the way of a deal between Adriana and me. Honestly it wasn't. Adriana in her mind had simply given Piero the push, that was all there was to it. I knew divorce from Emilio was out of the question for Adriana. I sighed inwardly. I'd have to give Anna the excuse that I was working on the rip. Anyway, this couldn't last.

What a mess it all seemed. I'd have stopped to work it all out, but now there was no time left anywhere. The rip was upon us. Here. Now.

Chapter Twenty-two

Teaching Carlo the rip was like talking to a frigging wall.

'Repeat it,' I said wearily for the umpteenth time.

'Lissern you guys,' Carlo ground out, flicking ash into his own coffee by mistake. 'This is the plan, see?' He did a Cagney hunch-up and chewed gum. 'We cruise into the saloon – '

'We walk casually into the cafeteria,' I corrected.

' – Get a shot of bourbon – '

'Wine and cream cake.'

' – And wait for the Big Wheel's signal – '

'And read a newspaper until I say.'

'All rightee!' he said grimly, grinding out his cheroot – *cheroot*, for God's sake. I ask you. 'Get your holster on, boss, and let's *go*!'

'Not till two o'clock this afternoon. And leave your knife here.' So help me, he'd got a knife long as a sword especially for the occasion.

'Right, boss. High noon.'

He burned his thumb trying a one-handed strike for another cheroot. The goon was actually wearing a white tie with a black shirt and a black suit with shoulders a mile wide. In the cold light of early morning he was utterly unreal. I could have throttled him.

'You've warned Valerio and Patrizio, Anna?'

Anna patiently passed him some butter for his burn and lit his cheroot at the gas-ring. 'Yes, Lovejoy.'

'You got me the phone number?'

'Here.' She'd printed it carefully on the face of a postage stamp, a good touch. I smiled approval at her.

'They'll be waiting from one o'clock. If the rip aborts they'll go on stand-by until seven.'

'You've done well, Anna.' I shoved Carlo's elbows off the table and checked once again.

'Bottle.' The brown bottle Anna had stolen from the chemist's stood among the Colosseum photographs I had neatly arranged in rows. 'Photographs. Measurements written out. Suit. Shirt and tie. Case. New shoes. Towel. Gloves. Hygienic sealing tape.' We went over the entire contents, krypton lamp, coat hook, tubes of adhesive, the lot. My own toolbag felt heavy as lead. 'Thanks, love.'

The measurements were for the winch. We'd tried the dark sober suit an hour before and it fitted me pretty well. I hadn't worn a suit since my missus left home. It felt decidedly odd. Anna had lifted it from that elegant gentlemen's outfitters on the Viale Giulio Cesare. The new shoes pinched a bit, but on the whole she had stolen with uncanny accuracy. I thought uneasily, maybe she watches me as closely as I watch her. I waited while she packed everything neatly into the black rectangular briefcase.

'Now – breakfast.'

Anna brought out a cloth and began to lay the table. A dozen mental re-runs later I scented the fragrant aroma of frying bacon. I looked across questioningly but she did not meet my eye as she cracked some eggs on the side of the pan. Breakfast was usually a roll in a paper bag, and mostly Carlo got to it first. I was looking at the floor when she served it up with a mound of bread and butter.

'What's all this?' Carlo demanded, for once shaken out of his acting career.

'You'll both need a big breakfast inside you!' Anna rasped. 'The rip starts today – or hadn't you heard? *Cretino*?'

She slammed an immense meal in front of each of us, and even made tea specially. Hearing somebody else called that instead of me made it a breakfast to remember. Carlo went out in a sulk, so I had his as well.

Piero spotted my little case the instant I stepped in the Emporium that morning and grinned all over his face. I tried to look defeated.

'Going anywhere, Lovejoy?'

'I have to visit somebody. I only came in to clear up loose ends, Piero. I don't want any trouble.'

'Okay.' Nonchalantly he threw me the keys to the workshop. 'Finish what you can, then piss off for good.'

I've never really been able to whine, not really convincingly, but I did my best. 'Look, Piero. About that passport . . .'

'You'll have it tonight.'

Thank Christ. I pulled a face. 'Er, the signora hasn't paid me . . .'

He sneered, his lip curling. No, honestly. It really did curl. I'd never seen a lip curl with scorn before in my whole life. I stared admiringly and only remembered in the nick of time that I was supposed to be a hopeless scrounger. 'You'll get your fare,' Piero promised scathingly. 'And enough to get drunk on the way home. Now work.'

'Please don't say anything to the signora – '

He grinned again. 'I can handle her.' I could have hit him.

By the time Fabio swept in I was working like a mad thing, quietly and efficiently testing the strength of my plywood mock-up. The base of a rent table's essentially a modified cylinder, with tangential walls showing lovely wood patterns. Now, a table top's always easiest to falsify, so don't trust it when you're buying antiques. Also, remember that a table is a flat surface or it's nothing, which means its top is always the first to suffer should drinks be spilled or serving maids have catastrophes with smoothing irons. Luckily, I was in the enviable position of forging a table whose major surface would be covered by a Presidential cage of synthetic sprawling birds.

But the pedestal base would be in clear view the entire length of that gallery. It had to look genuine, solid and *old*.

Tip: polyurethane varnishes *are* superb and polyurethane hardglazes *look* superb, but only true beeswaxes *feel* absolutely correct. Antique dealers dress a falsely veneered surface by varnish, then by beeswax which is given a microscopic craquelure by rapid drying. This is done effectively only in two ways: in front of a fan or by a chemical desiccant such as sodium hydroxide in a sealed container. I'd applied both, placing the workshop's fan heater on 'cold' during the day and stuffing the folding veneered plywood into a plastic bag with the crystals overnight. There's always plenty of these crystals in an antique shop – even honest dealers (should there be any left) use it for putting that golden gleam on oak. Like I say, it's getting so you can't trust anybody these days.

With my heart in my mouth on that day I checked Piero was fully occupied, and extracted the veneered plywood. It was beautiful, its gleaming surface now dulled by drying. Microscopic examination would reveal minute cracks in the waxed surface, such as are normally associated with ageing. The corners and intersections were more obviously peeling than the rest, but I helped this artefact along with a little crushed carbon from a piece of drawing charcoal (use Winsor and Newton if you can get it) blown on to a piece of chamois leather and rubbed gently along the edges.

I still had the thin top sections and hinged edges to slot under the cafeteria table, but when Adriana sent to tell me I was to stop for coffee the collapsible pedestal was folded out of the way under the work bench.

I was well into machining the metal support rods which would give it strength. Two hours to go.

I was on time. My heart was banging.

Dead at one o'clock Patrizio came for the cafeteria table in his wheezy World War II van. He arrived with the characteristic boredom of the vannie, smoking laconically and humping the steel and formica job on his shoulder without a word. Piero came to see I wasn't flogging a Regency piece.

'Get a receipt, Lovejoy,' he ordered.

'You,' I shot back, getting on with my job.

Patrizio gave Piero a don't-interrupt-me look and drove off leaving Piero looking foolish, to my delight. That was my last smile for a long, long time.

We closed at quarter to two, me strolling unbelievably casual into St Peter's Square exactly at two.

Valerio was a chip off Patrizio's block all right. He was a square thickset young bloke. I'd told his dad no drinks, no smokes. Valerio was obediently sitting picking his teeth and reading the *Osservatore Romano* on the end of the lines of chairs set out between the fountains.

'You want a seat?' He made to rise. Daft, really. There were four hundred empty places.

'No,' I said, mouth dry and voice no more than a croak. 'I have an urgent appointment.'

He eyed me curiously. I eyed him. It was the first time we'd met. Anna had suggested this ludicrous interchange because security forces everywhere had these directional microphones. He nodded imperceptibly. My words meant the rip was on.

'Then go well,' Valerio said.

'Ta.' I walked past him on legs suddenly made of uncontrollable rubber and headed for the loo to the left of St Peter's façade. The Vatican post office was doing a roaring trade. Old Anna was being bothersome among a crowd of amused Americans near the great basilica steps. From the corner of my eye I glimpsed her sudden querulous departure. Judging by the burst of laughter she had made some crack. Her job now was to find Carlo and hurtle him in to the loos after me.

The two usual women attendants were sitting at a little white table by the door. They ignored me. As long as I remembered to throw a hundred-lire coin into their plate as I left I'd remain an invisible passing tourist. Once in a cubicle I frantically started stripping off my clothes, hands shaking. I was sweating like a pig. My shirt and jacket were drenched, the sleeves clinging to me from damp. I cursed and wrestled in the confined space, a couple of times blundering against the door so noisily I forced myself to slow down. Hurry slowly. Good advice for anyone, as long as they're not frightened out of their skulls.

I dressed in my new sober gear. Make sure the handkerchief's showing from your top pocket, Lovejoy, Anna had said. It's a man's equivalent of white gloves in a woman, she'd said, trying to smile brightly, and I'd promised. Shoes cleaned, and in a plastic bag so as not to soil the clothes. Money – what there was – shifted into the new navy suit. Shirt. Sober tie, monogrammed imaginatively but with careful ambiguity. Cuff-links. Surprisingly, as I flopped on the lavatory pan to lace my shoes, a note on a stolen card. It read, 'Good luck, darling *cretino*,' and was signed with three cross-kisses. The card was for a silver wedding. I had to smile, even the shaky state I was in. Obviously she'd had difficulty finding a card with an appropriate good-luck-nicking-the-Pontiff's-antique motto.

I stood with the customary stiffness of a man in a strange new suit, and checked over the discards. Items into the briefcase, one by one. A moment's stillness. A quick listen. Deep breaths for control. Hundred-lire coin in my right jacket pocket for the women attendants, a tug on the handle to flush the loo – I'd tried to squeeze out a drop but every sphincter I possessed was on the gripe – and out, walking with purpose.

One old man leaving, tapping his stick. Two German youths combing hair and talking loudly, about to depart. And Carlo, nodding and winking and chewing gum and rolling a cowboy's cigarette one-handed, doing it all wrong. Sweating worse than ever, I ignored him and went to wash my hands.

From the handbasins the women attendants were talking just out of sight. I ran the water, peering through the mirror towards the entrance. The German lads left, still talking. The old geezer was gone. All the cubicle doors were open. Nobody.

I pulled a third-bottle out of my pocket and swiftly unscrewed the cap. 'Carlo.'

'Yeah, boss?' He slid over, gum-chewing and shoulder-hunching. His hand was thrust deep into his jacket pocket. He now sported a white trilby pulled down over one eye just to prove to the world's armies of Swiss Guards that he really was a genuine hundred-per-cent gangster on the prod. With virtually uncontrollable hands I poured him a capful of the dark rum. No good doing things by halves. His eyes widened delightedly. No acting this time, I noticed wryly.

I whispered, 'Cheers, Carlo,' and tilted the bottle, my tongue in its neck to stop any leaking into my mouth.

'But you said – '

'Shhh! Old custom,' I told him, gasping to good effect as if stunned by the booze.

'To the death, Captain!' He swigged it back, the poor sod. His eyes bled tears and he gasped, 'A superb shot o' old red-eye!'

'Er, yes.' I screwed the cap on and slipped the bottle into the case. Still nobody. 'You have fifteen minutes, Carlo.'

'Sure, boss. Ready? Willco!'

The poor goon slunk out, hunching and glancing, his

collar up. The two women rolled eyes to each other showing exasperation at the young. Carlo looked a right carnival, but he no longer mattered much – as long as he made the Museum cafeteria at speed.

Coin casually in the dish, and I was out into the warmth of St Peter's great square, a picture of the professional gentleman scanning the sights of Rome. There is no real short cut to the Vatican Museum doorway, so it meant making a brisk diagonal under the Colonnade, down the Angelica, round the Risorgimento and along. I was panicking in case there was a queue.

Seven minutes to reach the slope where I could see three coaches reversing into the slip by the Museum doorway. I lost all decorum as I hurried up the street to reach the entrance before the scores of Dutchmen poured out, and only slowing down once I was certain I would be ahead of them.

An elderly lady sold me some violets from the low wall near the entrance. I paid, leaving my briefcase to be swiftly covered by her shawl. Anna squeezed my hand as she gave me the change. While buying my ticket I realized she had short-changed me by five hundred lire, but that was only her joke. Anyway, I was almost smiling as I made my way up that spectacular staircase. Three violets were our signal that Carlo had made it ahead of me by three minutes. A rose would have been the signal to abort, that Carlo had failed to show.

Anna had said you couldn't reach the cafeteria from the Museum entrance in less than four minutes. I had argued and argued but she'd remained adamant, and now I was glad she'd been so stubborn. The small corridors between the decorated chapels were crammed with schoolchildren. Teachers herded classes to and fro. I blundered among them in a lather, trying to keep up a steady count in my mind so I could keep on schedule but finding to my horror I was starting over and over again at one, two, three . . .

Worse, the bloody cafeteria was bulging though its self-service line was moving forward fairly quickly. I looked anxiously for Carlo. He was near the front, almost at the till by now and sandwiched between two strapping blondes. Apart from Carlo, I was the only person there not in jeans and tee shirt. If I'd known I wouldn't have worried about looking exactly right. My spirits hardly rose, but at least they crept cautiously out of hiding an inch or two.

We shuffled forward. I collared a couple of wrapped sandwiches and moved with the rest, sliding my tray along the chromed rails. Carlo carried his tray to a newly-cleared table by the picture windows which over-looked the garden terrace. He sat and immediately started wolfing his cream cakes.

'Move along, please.'

'Er, sorry.' The worrying thing was Carlo had three glasses of wine, not one. The two blondes were watching him with conspicuous amusement from a table across the aisle. Yoghurt-and-soup queens. Mer-cifully he was too busy stuffing his face to respond to them. I shuffled on, nervously paid up and tried to get a seat facing Carlo but a sprinting Aussie beat me to it, so I started on my sandwiches with my ears exquisitely tuned, listening for sudden activity at Carlo's table behind me two aisles away. Old Anna came through the cafeteria, on the cadge. She plumped opposite me, doing her exhaustion bit and openly nicking one of my sandwiches. I chuckled affably to show my good-humoured acceptance of the old dear, especially when I felt my heavy briefcase slide on to my feet. Idly I checked that everybody was too preoccupied to notice, and edged it beneath my chair. Anna gave me a roguish wink and departed, chewing gummily on my sandwich. By now I trusted her enough to know my briefcase would be emblazoned by a Department of Health sticker. But that Carlo . . .

Ten minutes later I was beginning to wonder if I'd poisoned him all wrong. There was no sound other than the usual cafeteria din. He must have had a stomach like a dustbin liner because at least a third of the rum which I'd given him was a mixture of jalap and colocynth, the most drastic purgatives known to the old nineteenth-century doctors – and they were experts in drastic purgatives, if nothing else.

It happened just as I was about to chuck it in and abort the whole thing. A chair crashed over behind me. Somebody exclaimed in alarm. Casually, I glanced round in time to see Carlo streak through the doorway into the loo across the other side of the cafeteria.

The eddies created by Carlo's passage had not stilled when I moved purposefully among the tables and into the men's loo. Ominous noises came from one of the cubicles. A worried man was hastening out.

'I think somebody's ill in there,' he said. 'You think I should go for help?'

'I'm a doctor,' I said calmly in the best American accent my Italian could stand. 'Wait until I see . . .'

'Oooh. Lovejoy – ' Carlo's voice moaned from the cubicle as I glanced in. I could have murdered the fool, giving out my name, except I was worried that maybe I had. He sounded in a terrible state.

'That must be his name,' I pronounced glibly to the man. 'Signor. I want you to stand just inside this entrance. Let nobody in. I don't like the look of him.'

'Yes, *Dottore*.'

'Don't you worry, Signor Lovejoy,' I called loudly to Carlo in the poisonously brisk voice. 'I'll have you safely in hospital in no time at all.'

I strode purposefully out into the cafeteria and headed round the queue of people at the paypoint. I had the full attention of the customers. A lady emerged

418

from behind the line of servers. She wore the harrowed look of a superior longing for obscurity.

'Good day, Signora – Manageress? I'm Doctor Valentine.'

Her eyes widened. 'Is anything wrong?' She'd glimpsed the sticker on my briefcase.

'Have you an office, please?'

'There's nothing wrong, is there?' she pleaded over her shoulder, leading the way behind the terrace of stainless steel and bright cookers.

'Nothing that cannot be efficiently handled, signora.' I kept my Americanese variation of Italian going. 'A man's been taken ill after eating your cream cakes – '

'They are perfectly fresh – '

'Of course. I know that.' I smiled bleakly to keep some threat in the words. She trotted ahead into a neat pastel-blue office. Her name was on the door stamped in white on brown plastic. Signora Faranada was a pretty thing, understandably distrait but the most attractive manageress I'd yet seen in the whole Vatican. If I hadn't been terrified out of my wits I'd have chatted her up. She pulled the door to. 'Signora,' I said, instantly becoming terse. 'He is very sick. It looks like Petulengro's.'

'Petulengro's? A *disease*?'

I reached for the telephone, laconic and casual the way doctors always are when putting the boot into suffering innocents. 'You've heard of Legionnaires'? Similar thing.'

'Legionnaires' Disease?' she moaned. 'Oh my *God*! But – '

'Nothing that can't be handled quietly and efficiently,' I reassured with my wintry smile. 'You're lucky. I was just calling on you – courtesy visit. I'm from Communicable Diseases, Atlanta, USA. Currently with World Health, on loan to the Rome Ministry. Here.' I passed her the receiver as if disgusted with the slowness. 'Get me an outside line.'

She frantically spun the dial.

'The Vatican has its own children's clinic and physicians. Am I right?'

'Yes, Doctor.'

Impatiently I dialled the number as if I knew it by heart, reading it off Anna's postage stamp I had stuck to my left wrist. 'But no resident epidemiologist expert in communicable diseases, right?' I barked the question, the old lawyer's tricks of two knowns followed by an unknown, all to be answered with the same word.

She hesitated. 'I don't think so, doctor – '

I turned away impatiently. Valerio came on the other end. A sweat of relief started to trickle down my collar. 'Doctor Valentine. Get me the epidemic section – fast.'

'Epidemic!' moaned Signora Faranada.

'Hello?' I made a conciliatory gesture to the lady as I spoke commandingly into the phone. 'Hello, Aldo? Great! There's a rather problematic issue here – Vatican Museum. Cafeteria. Looks like a case of Petulengro's . . . No. Only one, a man. I've got him under control in the toilets . . . Of *course* I applied emergency treatment, brought him round . . . No. The place looks really superbly clean. . . .'

'We scour and disinfect every half-day,' Signora Faranada bleated, tugging my sleeve.

'Sure, Aldo.' I laughed reassuringly, the expert all casual in the presence of somebody else's catastrophe. 'No, I agree. We can't take chances . . . Look, Aldo. Can I leave it to your to . . . ? Fine . . . No, no sirens. Quietly does it . . . The least noise the better. No sense in being alarmist . . . ' I smiled and nodded at Signora Faranada. 'So you'll send an ambulance . . . ? Good . . . No. I'm sure the manageress can handle that . . . Agreed?'

I slammed down the phone.

'I'll get back to take charge,' I told the lady. 'I've arranged hospital transport.' I stilled her protests with a raised hand. 'Infectious diseases are always sent to a special unit because they are, erm, infectious.' I smiled a cut-rate Arcellano smile. 'You know how patients just love to sue places these days, I don't doubt.'

'Sue?' she gasped, the poor thing.

'It won't come to that,' I said smoothly. 'I promise.'

'What must I do?'

'Do you have a rear entrance to the cafeteria, where the ambulance can pull up?' She nodded anxiously and reached towards the top filing drawer. 'The gate will need notifying,' I said, ticking off the items. 'Aldo – that's Doctor Cattin of the Public Health Division – said St Anne's Gate. Is that acceptable?'

'Yes, yes. I'll telephone – ' She clutched feverishly for the phone.

'And the table. It may be contaminated. For taking specimens, and disinfection.'

'I'll see it's brought round – '

I snapped, 'Tell everyone it's in need of repair, wobbling or something. Use your discretion.'

'Yes, yes. Discretion,' she gasped, dialling frantically.

'Get your duty security man. I'll need that terrace quietly sealed from the public. It overlooks the drive-in, correct?'

'Yes! Yes! I'll get him right away – '

'Do you have a store room?'

She was gasping. 'Yes. By the loading bay.'

'Good. And I'll seal the lavatory cubicle until it's proven clear. Don't worry.' I rounded on her like I'd seen on the movies. 'Do as I say and people'll hardly notice. You have a beautiful clean restaurant here. We don't want to attract attention – '

'Thank you, Doctor!'

She was in a worse state than I was when I left and strode commandingly through the cafeteria. I cautioned Carlo's relieved custodian to silence and thanked him for waiting. Carlo looked so bad I grew really frightened but there was nothing I could do.

The duty security officer was a stout Turin chap with the intriguing name of Russomanno. He was delighted at the whole thing and determined to be pompous, thank God, and proudly showed me the tiny loading bay. Signora Faranada wanted instructions so I told her to parcel up Carlo's table and the utensils he had used in sealed plastic. She dashed off up the steps.

I glanced about. There were occasional faces peering from the Vatican Museum windows overlooking the tiny roadway and the loading bay, but with an ambulance backed in all sight of the loading steps leading into the rear of the cafeteria would be blocked off. From the other side walkers on the upper terrace could see over.

'I wanted that terrace cleared,' I said tersely.

'It's entrance will be closed immediately, *Dottore*.'

An ambulance was trundling slowly down the narrow thoroughfare. Time the security man went. 'You'll have the numbers of diners checked, of course?'

'Of course, Doctor.' He looked quite blank.

I smiled, nodding. 'Forgive me. I forgot I was dealing with a professional. Rest assured my team will be discreet and swift.'

The stout man puffed up the steps as Valerio reversed the ambulance – a full-blown, genuine ambulance – smoothly up to the loading bay. Patrizio sported a moustache, to my alarm. Did ambulance men wear them? Both he and Valerio wore some kind of dark blue uniform. Valerio's peaked cap bore an impressive but anonymous badge.

We had one nasty moment when I couldn't yank the door of the store room open, but Patrizio's hand gently pushed me aside and turned the handle.

'The table, Lovejoy.'

My work of art – still apparently nothing more than ordinary steel-and-formica cafeteria furniture, though with a thicker top than usual – was wedged between the two stretcher slots. I stood on the steps ready to use delaying tactics should the manageress come fluttering down to do some ground-level panicking. Valerio and Patrizio carried my table into the store. I mopped my forehead.

'Let's go. Bring the stretcher.'

Eight minutes later Carlo was inside the ambulance with Captain Russomanno standing proudly on the running board. Poor Carlo was ashen and almost comatose. Anna would go for me if I'd really killed him. With him went the table at which he had been sitting, his plates and drinking glasses.

I trudged upstairs, nodding confidentially towards the worried Signora Faranada to show everything was in hand. 'I'll seal off that one toilet cubicle,' I said in an undertone. 'It might be contaminated. The rest of the loo can be used with safety. Then I'll slip out. I'll return tomorrow. Just tell your staff to continue as normal.'

'Very well. Doctor, I am so grateful – '

I smiled nobly, wishing there was more time for this sort of thing. She was lovely.

'Only my job, signora,' I said, smiling. 'If only I met such charming people every day – '

The cafeteria was full as ever. I melted among the crowd and made my way over to the loos. Inside my grand case I had tape labelled 'Hygiene. Sealed by Order' to seal the cubicle.

And in the sealed cubicle would be me, sitting silently waiting for the closing hour. The ambulance by now would be rolling into the Via Porta Angelica.

For the rest of my team the rip was practically over. For me it had only just begun.

Chapter Twenty-three

I sat in the loo, that powerful creative location, thinking and listening.

Sealing the outside of the cubicle door with that impressively worded sticky tape had been a simple matter. I had written 'Out of Order' on a piece of cafeteria notepaper and stuck it to the door then climbed inelegantly over and dropped inside. There was enough of a hubbub in the cafeteria to convince me the manageress would assume I'd slipped out as I'd promised. Now, short of some nosey-parker peering in, I was safe.

People came and went in gusts of noise from the cafeteria. I heard all the languages under the sun. I learned a dozen new jokes, but only one was even vaguely amusing and anyway I always forget the endings. There was a two-inch gap under the cubicle door, so at the faintest sound of approaching customers I sat with my knees hunched and toolbag on my lap, just in case. Once I actually dozed, probably reaction to the state of abject terror in which I'd lived all day.

Somebody wiser than me – or even more scared – once said hell was other people, or something. Sitting in the foetal position there on one of His Holiness's loos was the loneliest place I'd ever been in my life. I'd have loved to go out for a minute, just for a cup of coffee, with normal happy people all around and noise and light reassuring me that everything was as it should be. But there was no chance of that. While blokes came and peed and chatted and were replaced by others I sat miserably on, convinced it was the end of the world. Hell, I couldn't even have a pee myself in case of noise.

The trouble was Arcellano. Even though I was tormented by visions of Adriana worrying herself sick about my sudden absence it was Arcellano's vicious face which kept recurring. Throughout those long moments, while I waited for the Vatican City to quieten, the evil that was Arcellano seemed to dominate my mind whichever way it turned. What maddened me was how little choice poor old Lovejoy had in all this. There's just no way round the bastards of this world. If they conscript you into their army, you're a draftee for life.

Unless . . .

Sitting there in utmost privacy, I gulped audibly and shook my head. None of that. No sinister thoughts of revenge, no creeping desires to fight back as savagely as Arcellano himself, because I'm a peaceable bloke at heart. I've always believed (and I really do mean it) that *Homo sapiens* is a higher being, noble and even God-like in his innate purity and benevolence. Okay. Occasionally you do come up against evil. When that happens the natural inclination is to grab the biggest howitzer you can find and let fly, but that's all wrong. Maybe it was the gentle atmosphere which was getting to me, but there in the loo I vowed fair play for Arcellano. I nearly moved myself to tears. Maria would love me for it. Anna would lash me up a lovely unhealthy breakfast of polysaturated fats for it. And Adriana would forgive me everything for it. Noble and even God-like in my innate purity and benevolence, I dreamed on about my final confrontation with Arcellano and his pair of psychopathic killers. I would be smiling, persuasive, kind.

But as I sat on, hunched and fretting and dozing, some little gremlin in my head kept sniggering and saying, I'll be frigging kind all right. You see if I'm not.

As long as my homemade winch was strong enough.

Eventually the cafeteria noise settled to a steady muffled banging as the servers gave the counters an end-of-day scouring. It was poisonously familiar. I'd dish-washed often enough to recognize that sound anywhere. Twenty minutes later some heavy-footed bloke stopped by the loo, presumably the security, banging the doors of the other cubicles back and giving my door an experimental rap. I heard him spinning the stopcock on the ascending water main, obviously a security man of the most careful and pestilential kind. His footfalls receded and the outer door went again.

I listened to my sanctum's silence, holding my breath as I did so. Presumably I was now alone and the whole loo empty. Just in case I counted slowly to a hundred and listened again. Nothing. I did another hundred. Nothing, not a sound.

You feel better with your feet on the floor instead of dangling. I lowered them carefully, put my briefcase down and slowly stretched. A quick peer underneath the door made me feel even better – no nasty boots waiting motionless for poor unsuspecting intruders to emerge whistling. I was alone.

Nobody's had more practice than me at being scared witless. The trouble is, every time's the worst. With the caution born of a lifetime's cowardice, I gauged the time. Anna said the security shift of eight officers signed on at seven o'clock. The international football came on the television at half-eight, a live screening from West Germany which meant two untroubled spells of forty-five minutes, briefly intersected by that worrisome fifteen-minute interval. Some conscientious nuisance could trot out of the telly room for a quick listen for burglars in that gap. I couldn't repress a surge of irritation at weak-kneed footballers actually needing a rest between halves. Soft sods. When I was a kid we simply switched ends and carried on. You get no help when you need it.

I'd planned a couple of hours' calm reflection at this point, but being calm doesn't work for some blokes and I'm one of them. I just can't see the point of serenity. My inner peace lasted three minutes. After that I sat and sweated.

Anna had assured me that the Vatican Secret Police were mythical. There's no such body. Security guards, yes. Secret cloak-and-dagger artists, no. I'd believed her. Alone in the gathering gloom, I wasn't so convinced.

In fact I was shaking as I peered into the deserted cafeteria. Empty places are really weird. Not bad in themselves, but you're used to seeing them filled with people, aren't you.

The cafeteria was spotless, shining and neat. And silent. Long curtains were drawn across the long curved picture windows. Through them a weak light diffused, presumably the floodlights which played along the Stradone di Giardini, the low road which runs straight as a die between the four hundred metre stretch of the Museum and the Vatican gardens. The central security possessed eighty closed-circuit TV monitors arranged in banks five screen high before a control console. They needed light. I *had* to trust Anna's map of the security electronics.

Slowly I stepped out into the cafeteria, feeling curiously exposed though I made no noise, almost as if I were performing on a stage with some vast silent audience watching my every move. Absurd.

The downstairs store room was locked, which meant an irritating ten-second delay while I pressed my plastic comb through the crack. A quick lick to stick my suction-pad coat-hook on the door, a series of rapid push-and-pull motions, and the lock snicked back. The delay was minuscule but worrying. That it was locked meant some bloody guard was doing his stuff, and that was bad news. I wanted them all cheering and booing in that staff telly room between the Museo Paolino and the Sala Rotunda.

No windows in the store room, thank God. I locked the door, took the thin towel from my toolbag, rolled it into a sausage and wedged it along the door's base to prevent light leaks. My krypton bulb beamed round the room. Two spare batteries weighing a ton were the heaviest items in my toolbag, nearly, but I couldn't risk working blind for a single second. They'd be worth the effort before the night was out. A rectangular black cloth to hold the tools, a swift unpacking, jacket on the floor and I was off.

My cafeteria table on which I'd laboured so much was the same as all the rest, except that its top was thicker, and an X-shaped strut reinforced the tubular steel legs. A security man might pass it over at a glance as an average modern nosh bar table. To me it meant ripping the Vatican.

I inverted the table and levered off the gruesome shiny edging strips. The main section I wanted was held on the underside by eight mirror brackets with their flat-headed screws. For one frightening second I thought I'd forgotten my favourite screwdriver, but I'm always like that when I've a job on. It was there all the time, beside the hand drill. The wooden section was only a series of oblique triangles. To fold a polygonal surface you can only hinge it along three lines. (Experienced forgers will already know this. You beginners can work it out.) I'd done this by linen hinges, for flatness, and now I unfolded the wood. It was a lovely Andaman surface. Some call it 'Padouk' wood, a rich rosewood-like Burmese wood which has been with us since the eighteenth century. Now I took my prepared rectangular blocks and made a quick swirl of the resin adhesives. I hate these modern synthetics, but a lovely old-fashioned smelly gluepot was a wistful

428

dream in these crummy circumstances. I laid the
inverted polygonal disc on the floor and glued the little
blocks across the linen hinges, which had now served
their purpose. In thirty minutes the disc would be rigid,
and would become the 'Chippendale' rent table's top.

Meanwhile I unplugged the tips of the four hollow
legs and from two drew out the slender steel rods
carefully packed inside. The tissue paper could stay in,
to save telltale mess. From the other two legs I shook
out a dozen pieces of quartered wooden doweling. The
glued blocks had holes to take the rods which slipped
in easily, to my relief, though I'd rehearsed this a
million times. The polygonal rent table top was now
reinforced.

The cafeteria table's steel legs themselves and my
added cross-strut came apart once the screws and clasps
were undone, which only shows what modern rubbish
stuff is nowadays. I had long ago dissected away the
thin formica layer back in Adriana's workshop. Now I
simply pulled it off and leaned it against the wall behind
some stacked chairs.

That gave me the cafeteria table's rectangular chipboard top. One of my most difficult pieces of work had
been cutting the rectangle into four so that it could
become an elongated cube. The tubular steel legs
would hold it rigid enough to carry practically any
weight. They already had screwholes, made three days
ago with a noisy electric drill. I'd veneered the exterior,
of course, but the travelling had done it no good and
I wasted time worrying about the shine. Anyway, the
top central spot would be covered by that monstrous
case of stuffed doves. The pedestal's lock keyhole was
phoney but looked good.

The real rent table upstairs had a base plinth as deep
as the drawers – always a good sign in an antique of
this kind, because the plinths got deeper as fashions
changed, the narrower the plinth, the earlier your
antique. This place of honour was reserved for the last

bit of chipboard which I screwed along the base. It was only stained African white wood and the colour was too dark compared with the thing upstairs, but it was the best I could do.

The metal X-shaped strut I placed across the centre of the polygon. By now the adhesive was setting well. I turned the huge wooden polygon the right way up and screwed it to the strut through the six holes I'd stencilled there. Solid and lovely.

Sweating badly in that confined airless room, I found my jacket and carefully removed the six tiny circles of Andaman veneer from the top pocket. I'd pencilled a number on the underside of each to show which screw-hole it came from. A touch of synthetic glue, and the shiny screws were covered precisely by the matching veneer.

I was having to hurry now. The false drawer fronts were the weak spots. If people fingered underneath the edge of my table, nosey sods, they would realize the game instantly, because there'd be only a sharp edge instead of a lovely smooth underface. I'd have to risk that. Once the rip was over they could laugh their heads off at my folding copy – because a million miles off I'd be laughing too.

The drawer fronts had come fitted easily between the undersurface of the cafeteria table's top and the folded polygonal section, being only veneered three-ply. My pieces of quartered doweling rods came in handy now to hold the drawer façades completely rigid. It had to be glue, though my heart ached for a small brass hammer and a supply of fixing pins. I hate doing a job by halves.

So, in total silence, I completed the table margin with rotten modern adhesives and stood the polygonal top on its façade of drawers to set firm.

Looking at it, I was quite proud. It looked really great, even in the harsh beam of a krypton torch. Once the gleaming top was plonked on the pedestal it would be indistinguishable from the real thing, unless you looked underneath or pulled it to bits. The only good thing you could say about it was that it was twice as sound as the jerry-built modern crap they sell nowadays.

I must have taken about an hour. I was on schedule. Time.

Chapter Twenty-four

The Vatican places great faith – charmingly quaint, really – in the reliability of mankind. As I say, it takes all sorts. There are the pilot lights at each of the corridor intersections, set high by each of the main doorways. They indicate the security time clocks where the patrolling guards clock in. No hidden infra-red sensitor beams, unless you include the sets indiscreetly built into the walls near the Viale Vaticano entrance and between the Cappella Sistina and St Peter's itself. You mustn't know about them because they're secret. And the secret cameras which connect with the screen-outs in the security room which I mentioned can be seen quite clearly from the galleries. They're not quite archaic, but striving hard for obsolescence. They're about as secret as Mount Palomar. Anna had mapped out the camera blind spots, and I had them by heart. Anna had reported that there were more magic rays to trap unwary burglars at St Anne's Gate. Big deal. That's the trouble with museums. They're crazy about entrances.

Nervous as a cat, I locked the store-room door with a horrible loud click and walked in silence up the stairs to Signora Faranada's office. There were two risks: a wandering guard, and some unexpectedly simple alarm system like a bell on a door.

The office door came apart at a waggle of my comb. The top filing-cabinet drawer was locked, but they all have that fatal flaw of a spring-loaded catch, and old Joe Bramah showed civilization the way round that in the 1880s, so I hardly paused. The box inside was

unlocked, and held the set of master keys the manageress had used earlier in the day. I was worried about
the light from my pencil-torch and did all I could to
shield it. The trouble was, I was going into places
where windows would be a constant risk. The Vatican
has more windows than a mill.

Outside the signora's office a narrow corridor ran
about ten yards to end at a door. The fourth key
worked. With my hand clutching the rest of the bunch
to avoid jingling, I turned the lock. My stupid heart
was banging loud enough to wake the dead as I pulled
the door open and waited a second for the alarms and
sirens to sound off. Dead silence. A brief dizziness
swirled in me. God knows how long I'd held my breath.
Unsteadily I clung to the door a moment to recover
and had to close my eyes for about a fortnight until
the nausea passed.

I stepped out nervously. I knew where I was. To
understand the layout of the Vatican Museum you have
to think of a huge letter H, except that now with the
new wing it has a double crosspiece with the great
library between the two struts. From Anna's drawings
I was somewhere underneath the Paoline Room and
the Biblioteca. One floor up and across, and I would
be in my favourite gallery beside my least favourite
museum showpiece. To the right and along.

Stairs are the ultimate risk. You can peer down a
corridor, count doors, watch for shadows at the far
end. But staircases are a swine because you can't see
who's having a crafty smoke in cupboardy alcoves
beneath.

I reached the top stair on hands and knees. I
squirmed flat and squinted at right angles down the
long gallery. The ranged series of long rectangular windows, the slanting shadows from the outside lights in
the grounds, all there in frozen gloom. And no glow
of a cigarette.

Opposite the faint white blobs of the odious stuffed

doves the shadows thickened. That would be the blue-and-gold double cupboards, full of stored early Christian figurines. Happily, ancient cupboards with natty antique locks. They sound and look impregnable, but believe it or not they were my one stroke of luck.

I eeled out into the main chamber a yard or two. Not much light from the Stradone. Mercifully no curtains at the long gallery's windows, not since that time ten Popes ago when His Holiness had done his nut and the drapery was retired in disgrace, which served them right for mixing maroon and blue. Nothing moved. Better still, *felt* right. Silence everywhere and that precious feeling of loneness. The football was probably midway through the second half by now, maybe twenty minutes before the security round. Yet . . . there was something wrong. Nothing to stop me, but definitely a wrong vibe somewhere. Still, no time now for imagination.

I got up and practically sprinted back the way I had come, flitting along the camera blind lines, snicking past Signora Faranada's office and through the cafeteria. I reached the store room excited and a little breathless, but it felt good. Really great. Except . . . again there was something vaguely wrong, but I couldn't put my finger on it. The rip was on. Scramble, Lovejoy, and worry about vibes when celebrating afterwards.

Inside my bag were two slender coils of silk rope. It costs a fortune – at least, it would have if Anna hadn't nicked it. Both were exactly the right length. The longer one stretched double, over and under my great polygonal table top so it lay on my shoulders like a set of clumsy wings. A top loop to put round my forehead. Indian style, leaving my hands free, and my pedestal easily carried by the smaller length of rope slung over my shoulder. Clumsy, but with care not to bump I could do it. My toolbag I looped on my wrist.

Creeping along in the semidark hunched under my

tabletop like a tortoise, pausing for breath at corners and manoeuvering my pieces slowly round them, I switched between panic and exasperation. Shuffling along the gallery towards those pale blurs, I was pouring sweat and burning at the unfairness of it all.

It took about ten minutes and seemed a month. Close to, the stupid white birds' glass case was a good landmark. Wheezing with the strain, I lowered the pedestal and then slipped the table top off my back. The relief made my head swim and I had to shift, and fast. My bag of tools.

Looking along the gallery to check, I slid across to the cupboards which stand on the Stradone side of the chamber. There are six double ones, each about six feet wide, though other galleries have as many as twelve. Two minutes to pick the lock and I creaked one cupboard door open.

'Jesus,' I muttered. My pencil torch revealed scores of small terracotta figurines staring back at me. Lovely and nearly priceless, but in the circumstances a real bloody nuisance. Feverishly I began lifting them haphazardly from the middle shelf and stowing them on the other shelves. God knows how long it had taken the curators to arrange them. I thrust them anywhere, scooping their labels up and rammed them towards the back of the lowest shelf. That feeling of sickly confidence had evaporated in my sweat. Now this whole dig felt bad and that depressing sense of wrongness enveloped me, but I'd no idea why. I began to feel I was being watched from somewhere further down the long silent chamber, which was impossible. I knew that. But I was starting to shake. Maybe it was all those unnerving terracotta eyes.

My sense of time deserted me. I don't know how long it took to clear the middle shelf, six long feet of valuable early Christian figurines. I'd been quite prepared to saw out any middle divider to give me room to lie down, but the cupboards are without vertical divisions, as sensible cupboards ought to be. I hate those modern coffin shapes they call cupboards nowadays.

By the time I'd cleared the shelf I was close to babbling with fear, feeling invisible avenging angels closing ominously about me. Without looking about, I slid across to that glass-cased monstrosity and lifted it clumsily to the floor. There was a nasty moment when my foot entangled itself in my carrying ropes. I rammed the two lengths into my toolbag out of the way and carried my pedestal over to the cleared shelf. End on and pushed to the shelf's extremity, it still gave me room to lie down – as long as my feet were stuffed down the hollow pedestal's interior.

I made myself stare down the gallery. No sign of movement. My confidence began to creep back when something intruded into my consciousness. In the distance I could hear motor-horns in regular cacophony. For one horrible second they suggested police sirens. My mouth went dry from fright till I recognized it. *Dah-dah-dadadadadada-dah-dah*. The universal rhythm of the soccer fan's applause. I turned to jelly. This was it. The televised match from West Germany must be over, and jubilant fans were parading Rome on their way to a celebratory beer-up. Lucky I'd heard the racket, but how long had it been going on? Was *that* what felt so wrong? No chance of calm now. My worksheet to protect Arcellano's rent table, then three wobbly goes to lift my phoney antique table top on top. My measurements were too generous if anything. I'd allowed three extra inches, which turned out plenty. A little sliding adjustment of my phoney top, and I could replace that glass case of doves. In a sweat of relief I stepped back. Done. Only an expert would realise that the precious table had widened slightly. There was no other visible difference. I was supremely confident of my veneer. I'd sold worse to experts.

Lying down on a shelf is harder than it sounds. Why I'd chosen the middle shelf when the lowest one was so much more logical I don't know. I was mad with myself. Probably some daft idea of peering through the lock to see the security guards pass. Even that was lunatic, because I'd have needed an eye in my belly-button. Stupid, stupid. I was in a hell of a state by the time I'd slotted myself along the shelf, breathless and tired. The toolbag fitted in the crook of my knees. I lifted the pedestal up and shoved my feet down inside it. A blue cotton thread from my pocket, wetted and threaded through the keyhole, enabled me to pull the door gently to.

And there I was, safely shelved among the precious early Christian figurines. The important thing now was not to nod off and start snoring. I'd never felt so knackered in my life, but it was going perfectly.

Which raised the important question of why it felt so frigging *wrong*.

The security guards came an hour later.

I'd dozed fitfully, jerking awake and imagining a million noises. The cupboard was unbearably stuffy. I'd allowed for a mere fifteen minutes on the shelf. The temptation recurred to open the door briefly for air but I never change a winning team. And by all possible estimates I was undoubtedly winning. I'd made my replica. I'd smuggled it into the Vatican. I'd fiddled myself in. I'd left no traces. Not a fingerprint, not a mark. All I needed now was for the security guards to hurtle past, leaving me five precious uninter-rupted minutes to somehow lower the true antique down to the Stradone. Heavy as it was, from there I would simply carry it across to the loading bay steps and conceal it in the store room among the cafeteria tables. I hadn't quite worked this bit out, trusting to Patrizio to pull a switch with the ambulance again, but you can't think of everything. And the security blokes knew their cafeteria table was due to be returned once it was proved contamination-free.

There were two of them, talking in undertones about the big match. Two-one, apparently. A last-minute decider after untold agonies, the opposition as unsportsmanlike as ever. The usual crap.

Luckily they were disagreeing about the team choice, a famous Milan striker having been dropped – unaccountable stupidity or the wisdom of ages, depending on your viewpoint. They passed, muttering arguments. I was worried because their shoes hardly made a sound on the luscious antique flooring, which proves how basically unpleasant these security people actually are. There's no cause for suspicion that bad.

I listened them out of earshot. Anna maintained they went one way first, then retraced the route at the next circuit. We'd argued time and time again over this. I kept telling her it was too good to be true. She called me a cretin. Twice I'd done the entire circuit myself, among tourists. Pausing a full minute at the position of each time-clock and walking at security guard pace, the whole route took forty-six minutes dead. I waited at least that long in the confined space, horizontal and running sweat. Inevitably their meal would come between circuits.

It took longer to climb out of the cupboard than it had getting in. My legs were stiff as hell. Grunting at the effort I had to re-educate my muscles before I could even put my foot down. I practically whined with pain as pins-and-needles tingled up my legs. The feeling had never got that high before.

I lifted my pedestal out, having the wit to recover my blue cotton thread and leaving the cupboard door unlocked in case I suddenly needed to hide. No sign of lurking guards. I was about to start across the gallery to assemble my phoney 'antique' when I froze. I knew what was wrong. In fact, *I'd known all along*. Only my

438

abject terror had prevented me from appreciating the unpleasant truth.

I slipped across the gallery and reached underneath to touch the wood of the precious piece of Chippendale. Not a single chime of ecstasy. I tried again. And again.

Arcellano's genuine antique table now wasn't.

Being a divvie's not as easy as it sounds. It's hard work. Okay, so you *know* without understanding how it is you know. You're absolutely certain that Grandad's old clock is a genuine Jerome, and not a modern copy. You know you are one hundred per cent right, that the rough old timepiece is actually made by that great Yank whose shelf-clocks popularized brass (instead of wooden) movements and whose clocks are now worth a fortune. (Tip: look for Jeromes in East Anglia. It's where genuine examples are commonest found. God knows why.) But all this inner certainty only helps as long as you *let* it. You can stay an ignoramus, if you're determined. It takes hard work to learn who's making today's best Jerome forgeries, and how many genuine pieces Jerome himself exported from Bristol, Connecticut, to England between 1821 and 1860, and memorize information on his contemporary rivals. You can be an ignorant divvie, and I should know. In that terrible moment nobody was more of an ignoramus than me. I'd been fooled.

I'd been sent to nick a bloody dud.

I felt my face drain of blood. I stood there like a fool, holding my useless bag of tools and licking my lips, looking about for a trillion Vatican Guards to spring out of the shadows and nail me. A frame. A set-up. Hunted. I was hunted. In an instant I was transformed from a clever supercool burglar about to pull off the greatest rip of all time to a nerk who'd been had.

In a sudden panic I began slipping down the gallery

towards the marble staircase. And just as abruptly paused. A good steady listen into the dark silence. Nothing. A quick kneel to press an ear to the flooring. Nothing. I sat back on my heels, thinking quickly.

Whether the Museum's 'antique' was valuable or not, I hadn't been rumbled. At least, not yet – and not by the guards. There might still be a score of police waiting outside to nab me, but the fact remained I was still in the Vatican without a single clamouring alarm bell. A memory came – of a day, among crowds of sprinting tourist groups, I'd stood in this very gallery before that 'antique' and been stunned by the clamour and radiance emitted by the loveliest pristine *genuine* Chippendale I'd ever seen in my life.

Which meant someone else had already done what I'd intended, nicked the genuine item and substituted a dud. In the antiques game we call it 'doing a lady', after the cardgame of dummying queens. For maybe another minute I remained there, trying to flog my poor old tired cortex into action.

How long had I got? Say an hour for their break, plus five minutes for starting the reverse circuit. Sixty-five minutes. Take away twenty minutes for shifting the phoney table. Say forty, forty-five at the outside. I managed a swallow. I'd need luck, and every ounce of skill I possessed. I flitted silently back towards those gruesome doves, undoing the toolbag as I went, with cold murder in my heart.

Chapter Twenty-five

I woke with a muffled squeal of terror, instantly stifled by the even greater fright which swamped me as I realized where I was. I'd fallen off the lavatory, knocking my head against the wall. The clatter of trays and the sound of vacuum-cleaners close by was almost deafening. How long had they been on the go, for heaven's sake? A trace of blood from my chin worried me for a second. Then I remembered. I was in the Vatican Museum cafeteria's loo, for the moment safely ensconced in a cubicle, sealed. I'd pulled off the rip, but the Museum's Chippendale was a fraud.

Blearily I remembered I had shaved in the early hours according to plan by means of the disposable mini-razor. Blisters wept painfully on my right palm where I'd gouged and slaved to dismember Arcellano's supposedly precious antique Chippendale in the long gallery. Sitting on the loo I smiled at the memory, weak with relief. I'd never been so vicious with any piece of furniture before, modern or otherwise. With a complete disregard for the ridiculous copy that his supposed Chippendale was, I'd unscrewed what could be unscrewed and sawed what couldn't, using a fine-gauge metal saw for stealth. Three times – actually at the pedestal joins – I'd levered off the supporting brackets using my work-cloth to dampen the creaking as the modern toothplates lifted away, and then gathered the sawdust under the pedestal. My entire concern had been speed. Arcellano's 'antique' was a piece of crap, and I treated it accordingly. I'd gone to all this trouble to nick it, so I swore it would get duly nicked.

But as for respecting it any longer. . . As far as I'm concerned, a bad forgery's the ultimate insult.

Leaving my own – much superior – mock-up proudly looking every inch a thoroughbred, I did two journeys with the disarticulated pieces of Arcellano's table. The top surface was heavy as hell, almost uncontrollable, waggling from side to side on my bowed back, and once I accidentally clouted it on the bannister with a loud echoing thump that made me freeze, despairing that I'd finally blown it. Nobody came and, in a state of collapse, I finally tottered into Signora Faranada's corridor almost unbelievingly. It took me almost half an hour to recover enough to get the pieces down into the store room.

For the rest of the night, way into the early hours, I slogged quietly in that airless room inhaling its stale cloying aroma and steadily whittling Arcellano's phoney but solid pieces into sections. I settled after a lot of sluggish thought to use two of the modern cafeteria tables, and simply sawed the 'Chippendale' into sections for screwing underneath one of the cafeteria jobs. That left the drawers and pedestal and a few angled pieces from the surface. These I arranged like bits of a child's jigsaw beneath a second table. I used the spare sheet of formica, which I'd earlier left in the room against the wall, to hold the pieces against the underside in a kind of concealed sandwich. The only odd thing was that the two tables both had formica surfaces top and bottom. I covered both by my one plastic sheet and reeled back to the safe haven of the loo.

I listened to the cafeteria kitchen preparing for the ten o'clock rush, gathering my resources for the last act. At ten past ten, as Signora Faranada's staff coped with the influx, I would make my way out of the cafeteria under cover of the queue. The two sedentary guards permanently stationed at the staircase leading to the

Gallery of the Candelabras would be questioned at ten-fifteen by Dr Valentine in his grotesque American-accented Italian. He would be professional as ever – clean collar, new tie, smart briefcase – but would have missed his way while taking the cafeteria manageress a good report. Could the guard please phone ahead to announce his arrival . . . ?

Signora Faranada would of course be delighted. In the flush of victory, she'd be only too happy to arrange that Captain Russomanno issue a transit permit for her own table to be returned from the health laboratories. I could ask to use her phone to summon Valerio from my 'department'. Anything to get shot of me and the suggestion of contamination, to wind up the whole problem. And I would promise the fullest report to the tiny Vatican emergency clinic.

Wearily muttering my plans to myself for the last time, I smiled. I would promise her a special certificate, a clean bill of health, if not more. She had a lovely mouth.

At eleven-thirty that morning I walked wearily out of the Vatican Museum into the Viale Vaticano. It was straight ahead, across the road, down the street shops towards the market. My face felt white. My nape prickled and my hands were tingling. I could hardly move my legs for shaking.

There was a public phone in a store entrance on the Via Candia. I dialled, but not the number Arcellano had given me. I kept missing the hole from nerves. I cupped the mouthpiece and asked the Vatican City switchboard – nuns run it – for the boss priest in Security. They kept trying to give me a captain and I kept refusing, telling the switchboard it was a matter of life and death. I've always wanted to say that, but not in these circumstances. It took three feeds of the coin box. I had to trust somebody, for God's sake.

'Very well. I'll put you through.'

As the clicks went I wondered what the hell you call them. Monsignor? Sir?

'Hello?' a distinguished voice intoned gravely.

'Er, hello, ah, Reverend. I want to speak to the, er, bishop in charge of the Vatican City security.'

'Cardinal Arcellano speaking.'

I closed my eyes and put my forehead against the cool wall for a moment before asking him could he please repeat that.

Five minutes later, my mind numb from the shock, I made it across the Via Candia, turned right among the barrow stalls displaying shoes and leather goods. Immediately on the left is the best bar in Rome. I reeled in, went through to the back and sat.

The girl brought me a glass of white wine and a *cappuccino*.

'And one for that old lady,' I told her, nodding towards the far corner.

'*Grazie*, Signor,' old Anna wheezed.

'*Prego*, Signora,' I said back. It was our signal we'd pulled the rip.

I'd never seen tears in Anna's eyes before. Women always surprise me. But then so does everyone else.

That afternoon I did two things, bushed as I was. Anna and I became lovers, and I phoned Adriana. I realized at the time one thing was stupid and the other profoundly wise. To this day I don't know which was which.

Chapter Twenty-six

Piero came on the line. There was no time left for mucking about, so I owned it was Lovejoy wanting to speak to Adriana.

'Where are you? If you're still in Rome – '

'Sod off, lackey,' I said, bone weary. 'Get her.'

'Lovejoy?' Adriana sounded breathless, not as furious as I'd expected.

'It's me, love. Listen. I've been held up.'

'Darling. Are you all right? Do you need – ?'

'Nothing. I'll contact you tomorrow. I have to see you.'

'Darling. Just tell me where and I'll come . . . '

There was more of this. In a daze I broke off and floated home to Anna's. Adriana was lovely in that spectacular Roman way I was coming to worship. And when she rose up so fragrantly to meet me swathed in the opulent creamy linen of her bedroom –

'You fucking swine!' Anna went at me, spitting and scratching.

'Eh?' I ducked among the furniture. 'What are you on about – ?'

'You poisoned Carlo! *Cretino*! Assassin!'

Poisoned? I moaned. Don't say I'd got the dose wrong, not after all this. She raged after me. 'He's in hospital again!'

'Put that knife down, you old lunatic!'

I had to belt her before she would stop. She sobbed uncontrollably on the couch. I was so utterly tired, but credible lies were called for. My strong suit.

'It wasn't me, love,' I said. 'He'd had a whole pint

of Scotch and threw up. I merely turned it to my advantage.'

'Is that true, Lovejoy?' she sniffed. With her aged make-up running uncontrollably she looked horrible.

'Honest,' I lied. 'Cross my heart and hope to – er, honest.'

'Poor Carlo.'

Well, quite. I argued persuasively, 'You know what he's like, Anna. By tomorrow he'll believe he pulled off the whole rip single-handed.'

'That's true.' She dabbed her face, making things twice as bad. 'Only . . . Lovejoy. If you didn't dose Carlo with that stuff, what was it for?'

'Last-minute varnish,' I lied. There was no answer to that. 'It's my secret,' I said as coldly as possible, to freeze her off. 'We're allies, Anna, but if I let on to you exactly how . . .'

The dear bird jumped to a woman's favourite conclusion in the pause and breathed, 'You are afraid that would be the end of our partnership?'

'Not really *afraid*,' I said nobly. In fact my greatest craving was to get shut of this maddening old crone and her goonish brother.

'I see,' she said, looking at me in a new way.

I cleared my throat after a year's uncomfortable silence. 'I'd, er, better have a lie down,' I said eventually. 'I've more night work ahead.'

She rose then and crossed to the dressing-table. 'Shower while I make up your bed.'

When I came tottering blearily back her alcove curtains were pulled aside. My couch wasn't made up at all. Uncaring, I reeled towards it, clutching my towel round my middle.

'Here, Lovejoy.' I felt her guiding touch on my arm and collapsed on her bed. She looked down at me, her make-up gone and only her lovely young face hovering. 'You'll sleep better here than on that old couch. Are you very tired?'

'Done in.' My vision blacked. 'What are you doing?' My towel had gone and a smooth lissom body was moving alongside my exhausted hairy neck.

'You need keeping warm, Lovejoy.'

Actually I didn't, but when your hostess offers you tea it's rude to refuse. And as it turned out I wasn't as tired as all that.

'That you, Arcellano?'

'Where the hell have you been, Lovejoy?'

It was my old friend all right. 'Pulling the rip.'

That shut him up, for about ten seconds. 'You what?'

'You heard.'

Another pause, then much quieter: 'Lovejoy. Are you serious or drunk?'

'Serious.'

'But it's impossible.'

'*Was.*' We both listened to heavy breathing.

'So you'll deliver – '*But he was uncertain*!

I cut in. 'No, Arcellano. No nice long trips to Bonn. I deliver here, in Rome.'

'You're off your head.'

'In the Colosseum. Exactly at sunrise. No sooner, no later.'

'Lovejoy.' His sibilant voice made my skin crawl. 'Lovejoy. If you're planning to work a fixer, I'll have you crisped. You do understand?'

'Perfectly,' I told him. 'And if I find you skulking in ambush when I arrive at the Colosseum, Arcellano, I'll take to the hills.' I put a whine of anxiety into my voice. 'I want no trouble.'

'Very well, Lovejoy,' that voice purred. 'I'll be there.'

'Alone, Arcellano. Agreed?'

'Agreed.'

I walked the half mile to Patrizio's garage. I had remembered to bring the keys to Adriana's workshop so Valerio and I could nick the winch and bring it over

447

in his van. I walked quickly. It was already dark, and I still had work to do.

Chapter Twenty-seven

As the first sun ray touched the high rim a cool breeze wafted through the Colosseum's gaunt stone honeycomb. Fawns and dark browns started stuffing the blackness out of sight among the pits and arches. A pale midnight blue appeared above the jagged edge of the great interior. All around me the huge crescents were thrown into relief.

I sat there like a nerk, daintily at breakfast on top of one of the great masonry teeth which protruded from the floor of the vast arena. Even the most suspicious-minded crook could see I was alone, unaided and completely vulnerable.

I had been there an hour, perched on my stone block. Anna's white tablecloth fluttered indolently in the stirring air. My elbows on the coffee table and the coffee almost gone. What dregs were left in the cup were now stone cold. I was only saving them for effect.

Getting the table up had almost proved too much for me and Valerio. Patrizio and Anna had sussed out the entire Colosseum at four a.m., reporting all clear in whispers. Apart from one sleeping old drunk and the inevitable prowling cats, the place was empty. I made Patrizio and Anna promise to leave once I was in position. Anna was all for staying and taking on the universe with me. I refused to explain, saying it was all part of the rip. I felt utterly alone.

The sky lightened. Rectangles of pastel blue began to appear, stencilled out of the enormous brown stone rim above me. I shivered, half wanting the sun to reach down into the enormous bowl and warm me but too frightened to wish really hard. When it rose, Arcellano would come. Some murderers come alone. Others come with a band of assassins. I knew which sort Arcellano was.

A distant bus revved up and chugged out into the streets. First sound of the day. A few moments later a car came close, changed gear, droned away to silence. Near by a cat stretched, scaring me to death by suddenly being there. I calmed myself as best I could by rehearsing my movements. Arcellano would send his goons to go over the Colosseum inch by inch. I'm not that dim. With a little luck – and the speed which my terror would lend me – I'd be off out of the whole frigging mess with the speed of light. I looked down and along the sandy ground across to my left. There, half the arena's width away, was the spot where Marcello's broken body had lain. My eyes lifted, as casually as if I were idly waiting, to where my pulley and beam overhung the stonemason's area. The massive stone block which hung suspended there did not even stir in the cool shifting air. I swallowed. It represented safety, but the bloody thing looked miles away. I'd have to run that far, dodging among the vast blocks.

I was becoming worried. Time was getting on. I let my gaze move inch by inch round the scagged interior. No sign. No movement. Only one of the cats coughing gently in the gloom directly ahead. The place was dappling swiftly. And the sky blueing, and gold touching the stonework. Soon, visitors would be waking to start the day and there was no way I could cajole Arcellano into a rerun of this meeting . . .

That cat coughed again. And I remembered the sound. Too late.

Against the weakening shadows a pale shape was emerging. About as tall as a man, a big man, with a fawn overcoat draped elegantly over his shoulders. And he was laughing. The laugh was short and dry, unvoiced barks like a coughing cat. I glanced involun-

450

tarily towards the long sandy run towards my recess. The pale shape saw my glance and began to drift that way. I thought, Oh Gawd.

I took a sip of coffee dregs to wet my throat and called, 'Is that you, Arcellano?' The cup rattled in its saucer.

'Charming tableau, Lovejoy.'

'Coffee, or have you had breakfast?' It was the best I could do. Everything I possessed had got the wobbles.

'You're allowed one cigarette, Lovejoy. Before execution.'

'Don't be daft, Arcellano. You owe me. I pulled the rip.'

'Wrong, Lovejoy. My men checked. The Chippendale's still there.'

I lifted the edge of the tablecloth to show the pedestal and the rent table's unmistakable edge. 'It's here, friend. Your antique from the Vatican. The one now in the Museum gallery is a forgery. I made it.'

He thought about that before speaking. 'Then why no alarms yesterday?'

'Because I made a *good* forgery. Go and check. I'll wait here.'

That cat cough laugh really sounded then, maybe a whole minute. He wiped his eyes, but all the time he was drifting to my left along the terracing. I had to look upwards at a slight angle to see him.

'You bastard, Lovejoy,' he called down. 'How?'

I explained the outline. All the time he was drifting, drifting in the direction I had glanced earlier. The swine suspected that was where I'd try to make my escape. He paused, leaning on the iron tourist rail. I could see him clearly now. With every second the day was rushing into brightness.

'You clever bastard.' He honestly sounded full of admiration. 'The old fiddle switch to rip the Vatican. I might have known. A bluff on a bluff.'

'It was nothing,' I said, all modest.

451

'They said you were really something, Lovejoy.' He was chuckling. 'Robbery without alarms. The only way it can be done. Congratulations.'

I thought, Here goes. 'Thank you,' I said with careful loudness. 'Captain.'

I moved my trembling legs ready to leap off the stool and run.

He paused, tilted his head. 'Captain? What are you talking about, Lovejoy?' He waited. I tried not to glance again at the million miles of sand which stretched between the recess and me.

'You're a senior officer of the Vatican Security guard, Arcellano.'

'You're insane.'

'You thought up this rip to test the Vatican's security. On the quiet.' I let that sink in. 'So you had a grotty copy made of the Chippendale original. This is that copy.'

'So where's the real piece?'

'You have it stashed away.'

'And why should I go to all that trouble?'

I smiled, the thing I least felt like doing. 'If I succeeded in pulling the rip, you naturally assumed there'd be a gap left in the gallery's exhibits. Then you could put the real Chippendale back. Nobody would then know there'd been a rip at all.'

'And if you failed?'

'Then I'd be nabbed,' I said evenly. 'By you. Your men would have me in clink.'

'Doubtless telling tales, no?'

'Yes, but an improbable tale people would laugh at. You gave yourself away, Captain.'

'Really?' The bastard was too calm by far. I could feel his two goons smiling in the morning shadows behind me and tried not to look round, to concentrate on this murdering bastard who had now resumed his oh-so-casual stroll round the terrace towards my only escape route. 'Really, Lovejoy? How?'

452

'A clever geezer like you would naturally want to protect his interests, in case things went wrong,' I said. 'Captain Blood put an end to the straight-lift caper, nicking the Crown Jewels from the Tower of London in 1671. Substituting the dud showed your hand.'

'But why should I bother, Lovejoy?'

'Because you had the greatest prize of all in mind – a method, Captain. If I succeeded, you'd know how it could be done.'

He was smiling, the fucking swine, thinking he'd won. 'And you've given it to me, Lovejoy. A method which can be repeated times out of number.' He grinned. 'I'm indebted. Now I can drain the whole Vatican, item by item. I thank you. Sincerely.'

'But you murdered Marcello, Captain.'

'Well.' He spread his hands. 'He started asking around about Cardinal Arcellano.'

'That was my fault,' I cut in. 'I knew no other name for you except that. I should have realized as soon as Marcello sounded suddenly so different, full of urgency.'

'Silly of me to use the honoured Cardinal's name at that little auction. It seemed just a joke at the time.'

'It misfired, Captain. You had to kill Marcello because of it. Am I correct?'

'Near enough. But it's over, Lovejoy. Once that table's out of sight all your evidence has gone, right?'

'You've forgotten one thing, Captain.'

He snapped his fingers. The stockier of his gorillas stepped out of the terrace shadows. A second appeared far over to my left. My exit run was now overlooked by them both. Arcellano made some light quip to the goon, the pleasant way his sort do before knocking somebody off. He turned back to me, a picture of mayhem in classy suiting. His voice was suddenly flint hard. 'If you mean payment, Lovejoy, you'll get paid – well paid.'

I said shakily, sweat stinging my eyes and my voice

quavering, 'I don't mean that. You're under arrest, Captain.'

It should have come out crisp as a western gun-fighter's threat. It came out a feeble warble.

His famous non-smile was back. 'I'm . . . *what*?'

'You heard, piss-head.'

A car droned by. It didn't stop. Yet this was the moment Russomanno and his Keystone Kops should have come bursting in with lovely protecting howitzers. There was silence. A cat yawned extravagantly. Arcellano was glancing about swiftly. His two goons had reached inside their jackets. With innate skill they backed against the supporting pillars, fading from the daylight into shadow.

'*Get him!*'

I flung myself sideways, dropping to the ground, and was off, keening with fright. I ran like a stag down the narrow avenue of tall stones, hunched and babbling imprecations, begging for my life. Instinctively I weaved, ducking in and out among the colossal rectangles and scuffing the sand. If only I'd trained. Something plucked the air by my head, clipping stone chips from the masonry. My face stung. A bang, echoing. I heard Arcellano screaming instructions. I could hear footsteps along the terrace.

Frantic now, I cringed behind an upright slab as a piece of stone exploded at eye level ahead of me. Three cracks sounded. More stone chips. I moaned in terror. The bastards were everywhere. It was all wrong. Arcellano should have come down to this level so I could imprison him by my ingenious falling block in that recess up ahead, for the police to arrest at leisure. I ducked into view, saw Arcellano on the terrace, hurled myself back into cover. Two more gunshots, one from behind and to the side. My leg went funny. Bleating with terror I tottered forward, weaving among the standing stones as fast as my sudden limp would allow. I whined, 'Please, please . . . '

'Halt! Halt!'
'*Get him!*'

Along the stone avenue, with shots going everywhere and people shouting. I glimpsed Arcellano
directly against the metal railing. He swung over ahead
of me and dropped lightly to the sand, to my level at
last. But he carried a shiny slate blue length in his
hand. For a big man he moved like a dancer, soft and
easy. I moaned in terror at the sight. He was only
twenty yards off and floating like the hunter he was,
his teeth bared in a silent hiss. I'd never been so frigging scared of anything or anybody. I limped to the
right. More shouts and a small fusillade of echoing
shots. Somebody screamed. It wasn't me, thank God.

'Lovejoy!' some lunatic yelled, as if I wasn't out of
my skull with horror.

Gasping, I lumbered along the arena wall and across
the straight avenue of standing stones. The bastard was
gliding away from me, looking from side to side. I
must have made a noise, maybe scraped on a stone or
something, because he spun instantly and the blue
thing in his hand flashed. The air near me warmed and
splinters flicked blood splashes from my face. I tumbled
to one side, scrabbled lopsidedly across to the far side
where my chain hung. The only place I could go was
my recess. My own bloody prison.

The space was the size of a large room. Masonry
tools lay scattered. Chisels, hammers, mallets and set-
squares, some as Valerio and I had dropped them
during the dark hours. Too late to think of using those
now. I made it to the coil of chain and gave it a yank
to set it firm on the pulley. My throat was raw with
fright. Somebody shouted again up on the terraces. I
heard rather than saw Arcellano step towards the gap
through which I'd come. I flicked the chain once,
released it and stepped aside as the dull rumbling
began.

Arcellano came into the space. The fucking gun looked enormous.

'Okay, Arcellano,' I yelled, though he was only a few feet off. 'I surrender! I'll say it was me!'

'Too late, Lovejoy.' He was smiling now. 'You're resisting arrest, you see.' He raised his voice and shouted, 'The table, Maria! Just push it off that stone. It'll smash.'

'Who?' I asked dully. He'd said Maria.

The gun lifted. My belly squeezed. He glanced up then. Maybe it was the sudden swiftness of the rectangular shadow, maybe the rumbling of the descending block. I don't know. It was all in an instant. But he glanced up and froze, appalled at the sight of the massive block plummeting towards him. He hesitated, started to step back.

'Forward!' I screeched. 'Step forward, man!'

He halted, then leant towards me into the space left for the great stone, his eyes on mine. It was only then that I realized I'd told him wrong. I'd said forward when I actually meant to shout back. Either way I'd have been safe, but somehow my mind got the words wrong. It was unintentional. I swear it. Honestly, I never meant him to suffer like he did. The great stone settled into its allotted area with a faint scrape and hiss, pressing Arcellano's broad shoulders down and crushing blood into his face, and forcing the very life out of his mouth. His eyes popped in a spurt of blood that sprayed over my face. His face puced, swelled, burst out of its expression in a splatter of blood. The gun in his hand cracked once, sending splinters round the confined area. Needles drove into my neck and thigh but what the hell.

Maria. He'd shouted instructions to *Maria*. His woman, Maria. To push the table, my evidence, off the central stone and break it to smithereens. I suddenly remembered why the table was up there on the stone, and drew a great breath.

'Maria!'

The name echoed round the Colosseum. 'Maria!' No sound but a distant shout – man's voice – and rapid footsteps.

I screeched. 'Maria! Don't touch the table. Please! For Chrissakes, leave it – '

Her dear voice came clear as a bell over the great arena. 'It's no good, Lovejoy.' Then those terrible words I'd give anything to forget. 'Get rid of him, darling.' Her voice had a finality I'd hoped never to hear. '*Do it*!'

She wasn't talking to me. She meant this dead thing under the stone. She obviously couldn't see – hadn't seen – the block fall on her man Arcellano. Frantic, I drew breath to scream a warning, but she was telling her man to do it. To kill me. Me, who loved her.

And I uttered no sound.

I slumped to the sand. It was all happening too fast. Dully I heard footsteps, people running. I sat against the wall of the recess, staring at that horrid mess of Arcellano's popped face squeezed bloodily from between the giant stones. His arm protruded in a great purple sausage. The other arm was nowhere to be seen. Tears streamed down my face, for what or why I don't know to this day.

The explosion came exactly four seconds after I heard the table crash to the ground. The whiplash crack of the handgrenade's plug against the stonework sounded near my head. I didn't even flinch. They always say, don't they, that the plug of a grenade seeks out the thrower. Maria did not even have time to scream before she died.

I don't know how long I was there, sitting in the sand of that accidental prison. The first thing I remember is a face grinning over the edge up there against the blue sky and saying into the scream of sirens, 'What is it? Filming?'

457

It was the drunk, wakened by the war. 'Yes,' I told him.

'Where are the cameras?'

'Hidden.'

I saw him fumble and bring out a tiny bronze disc. 'Want to buy a genuine ancient Roman coin?'

I squinted up against the light. The same old acid patina, two days old. 'It's phoney. You've used too much acid to get the verdigris.'

He mumbled, nodding. 'I told my mate that. He's a know-all.'

He made to withdraw. 'Hey,' I said. 'Want to buy a genuine antique?'

Somebody up there was yelling everybody to freeze because this was the police, that the place was surrounded. Sirens were going, car doors slamming. Now it was all done for them.

Typical.

Chapter Twenty-eight

No airport's pretty.

They gave me my green boarding-card after an hour's wait. It's always a relief because it means you are going to get aboard and some other poor nerk's going to be left behind. The passengers I was with were a cheerful, talkative crowd. I sat to one side trying not to remember the inquest, the harsh post-mortem evidence given over the verdict on my lovely Maria and on Menotti, her murderous lover. In the official hearing I had been gently reproved by Cardinal Arcellano for calling Menotti 'Arcellano', but explained I'd known him by no other name. The Cardinal was a quiet little bloke with a mind like a computer. He'd been understanding, even compassionate, when I'd given evidence about the killer Menotti's attempt to finish me. On the way out of the hearing I'd tried to avoid saying a farewell. He got in my way and told me he'd pray for my peace of mind. I'd said thanks and passed on by. I don't know what people are on about half the time.

'Signor Lovejoy?' An air-terminal policeman stood there, all phoney boredom.

'Yes?'

'Would you come this way, please.'

'But my flight's nearly called – '

'Only a moment, signor.'

Obviously a slight passport difficulty, easily resolved. I got my bag and followed him to the manager's office, trying to exude a sense of confidence towards the other passengers. I even swaggered, for show.

There were four policemen in the office, including a captain. He had his thumbs in his belt.

'You are Lovejoy?'

'Yes. If it's this passport, I can explain . . .'

'You know this old lady?'

A photo of Anna in her pickpocketing clobber. 'Yes.'

'Your aunt, I believe?'

I thought swiftly. 'Er, not exactly. You see – '

'You lodge at this address with her?'

'Well, er . . . ' The signature on the form was oddly familiar. It was my handwriting. That time Anna got nicked by the Via Porto Angelica. No wonder two of these cops looked familiar. The two in the car, who'd made me sign to get Anna off the hook.

'Yes or no, signor?' That phoney boredom again. I'd rather have hate. It's safer. 'And this is your signature?'

I swallowed, took a chance. 'Well, yes.'

'You went surety for this old lady?'

'Not really,' I burbled. 'It wasn't meant to be taken seriously – '

'You signed a police form *frivolously?*' The officer swelled ominously. 'Intending to default, slip the country, leaving your aged aunt – ?'

I said desperately, 'She's only twenty-odd, for Christ's sake. It's all make-up – '

He smiled a wintry smile. 'She told us to expect all sorts of ludicrous explanations, signor.' He dropped another photograph on the desk. 'You recognize this antique shop?'

'Yes. It's . . . ' I hesitated. My job there was illegal. No work permit.

'Albanese Antiques Emporium, signor?'

'Yes.' I had a headache. It worsened abruptly as he reached for the phone and dialled without looking the number up.

The police stood about with the terrible patience of

their kind. I noticed two were now between me and the door.

'*Pronto*, signora! Yes, we have him . . . At the airport.' He listened attentively, full of importance. 'Yes, signora.' He turned, placing the receiver on his chest in token of confidentiality. 'Signor Lovejoy. You are in default of a contract of employment with Signora Albanese, no?'

'No!' I cried desperately. My bloody flight number was being announced. 'Listen! I never had any legal . . . er . . .'

The captain's eyebrows rose in mild surprise. 'You are saying, signor?'

'Erm . . .' Adriana had me either way.

'Having given surety for a vagrant,' the captain said affably, '*without* gainful employment?'

'No.'

'Then you've defaulted, signor.' He lit a cigar one-handed. It was clearly his trick. Carlo should have seen him.

'Let me speak to her.' Furious, I snatched the receiver from him. 'Adriana? Now you look here! This is Lovejoy –'

'Hello, darling.' She sounded quite pleasant, even chatty. 'Speaking from police custody, I believe.'

I deflated. 'Er, yes. Only temporarily. Some crazy mistake. I want you to tell them that –'

'That you have a job, darling, and are not a vagrant?'

'Yes, that's it!' I cried eagerly. My flight number was blipping on the monitor screen in the corner of the room.

'But, *darling*! There's this slight matter of those tables, the ones you wrongfully purchased on my account.'

I thought. 'Is there?'

'Yes, darling,' she cooed, sweet as a dove. The police were staring patiently at the ceiling as Adriana went blithely on, 'And I'm in such a mess here. A load of

461

antiques being delivered tomorrow, ready for the new season. Such problems.'

I waited, but so did she. 'So?' I said weakly.

'Well, darling. You know how much more expert you are at this sort of thing . . .'

I swear there were tears in my eyes as I watched that monitor screen. I tried for a last-ditch stand against the unfairness of all womankind.

'Okay, then. But I want a good rate of pay.'

'You'll work for your keep, Lovejoy.'

I yelped. 'For *nothing*?' I eyed the police, wondering if oppressed antique dealers got a discount from the judges in Rome for murdering their tyrannical employers.

'You'll receive, shall we say, payment . . . in kind, Lovejoy.' I could tell the sadistic bitch was falling about with delight at the other end. 'The most intimate kind, of course. In fact, I shall insist on delivering it personally. Think of yourself,' she added sweetly, 'as providing an essential service.'

The captain blew smoke. He slid an employment form across the desk to me in silence.

I read it swiftly, my face red. 'Erm, Adriana.'

'Darling?'

'Listen,' I croaked hopelessly, 'I, er, have this police form to fill in.'

'Do it, dearest. I'll come for you directly.'

'Erm, there's this space. *Nature of occupation.* I can't write – '

'Hired consort?' She was rolling in the aisles, though her voice was sugar.

'What shall I put?'

There was a pause, then a smile crept back into her voice, and she said, 'I know, Lovejoy. Apprentice.'

I thought, I'll kill her, but said, 'I can't put that. They'll assume – '

' – The truth, Lovejoy?'

The phone went dead, purring anonymity. I looked

at the receiver for a long minute before replacing it carefully on its rest. The tannoy announced my Alitalia flight, final call.

'Your elderly aunt is waiting for you outside, signor,' the police captain said. He too was carefully out of smiles. I glanced about, frantic.

The four cops inhaled, ready for the dust-up. Brokenly I thought of Adriana streaking out to collect me, of Anna prowling outside the door. The trouble with women is they win so bloody often.

The captain demanded, 'I take it you are staying a while, signor?'

'Yes Captain.' Bitterly I pulled the form towards me and wrote *Apprentice* in the space provided. I said, 'I may not survive, but I'll definitely be staying.'

THE TARTAN RINGERS

ring'er: a person or thing
very like another
Dictionary definition

Chapter One

This story starts with criminal passion in a shed. It descends into sordid corruption. But all along just remember one thing: love and antiques are the same. Hatred and evil are their opposite. I'm an antique dealer, in bad with the law, and I should know.

There's nothing antique dealers hate worse than fog and rain. Ellen agreed.

Three o'clock in the morning on a foggy rainy bypass Ellen was tired – only the same as anybody else daft enough to be awake at this ungodly hour, but women are very self-centred.

'How much longer, Lovejoy?' she moaned.

'Couple of minutes.' I'd been saying this since midnight.

We were in Ben's hut. He's the vigilant nightwatchman hired to watch for thieves who habitually steal the roadmenders' gear. He's never caught any because he mostly kips in front of the portable telly his daughter bought him last Easter. Me and Ellen had made love and the old bloke hadn't even stirred from his glowing stove.

'I'll get into trouble,' Ellen whimpered.

I quaked. 'Er, your bloke isn't . . . ?'

'Of course not. I've got a meeting tomorrow. That old bitch from the vicarage has a filthy mind.'

Ellen's husband is heap big medicine, being a Customs officer. Mercifully a kind Chancellor had sent him to patrol the coasts and keep a lookout for dark deeds. Meanwhile my own particular dark deed was thrombosing in the fog while Ben snored his old head off and me and Ellen swilled his rotten tea. Who'd be an antique dealer? I ask you.

'What *are* we waiting for, a fake, Lovejoy?'

'A reproduction bureau,' I corrected coldly.

Ellen shivered, a lovely sight even when she's indianed in a moth-eaten blanket. 'Why couldn't they send it by train?'

She'd reached the repetitive stage. I sighed wearily. Women get like this. They believe that if they say something often enough it becomes true. 'Nobody in their right mind sends antiques by proper transport. The whole bloody kingdom uses a night lorry.' For a few quid on the side, of course.

'But isn't that illegal?' the poor little innocent asked, turning her beautiful blue eyes on me. Old Ben broke wind, as if in criticism.

'It's safer, and surer.' Most antique dealers have their barkers down on the bypass all over the country collecting and loading up. This fraudulent system has the merit of being beyond the reach of tax.

Huddled over the brazier, we waited dozily for the signal from out in the rain-soaked night. I thought of her and me.

Men are amateurs; women are professionals. And that's in everything: love, life, greed, hate, all the emotions. And why? Because we blokes have animal souls. Oh, I don't deny that every so often some bird thinks she's educated us out of being primitive, but it's only imagination. Women never seem to realize this. Like now.

'We could be somewhere warm, Lovejoy,' Ellen's blanket muttered. 'You make the best fake antiques. Everybody says so. What's the point of sending to Caithness?'

'Shhh.' I said. Old Ben's principal asset is that he's bent. He often helps with loading, especially when German buyers are scouring soggy East Anglia spend-

468

ing like drunks. His conscience only costs a pint, but I still didn't want him learning too much. I whispered, 'Nobody local'll know it's a fake, see? I'll sell it as genuine.'

'Matthew will be cross if he finds out, Lovejoy.'

See what I mean? She ignores the fact that she's literally shacked up with a grubby antique dealer riddled with lust and perishing cold. See how they shift the blame?

'Your husband can get knotted.'

'That's not a very nice thing to – '

Ben stirred, woke, spat expertly into the stove's grille. 'It's here, Lovejoy. Far side.'

There are two lay-bys down the road. They're about a mile apart. I shrugged. The lorry should have been coming from the other direction but I knew better than argue. These old roadmen have a third ear. 'Best get going, then.'

'Can we go, Lovejoy?' Ellen asked hopefully.

'No. I need your car.' It has a roof-rack. Ben's hut always holds ropes and tools for neffie schemes like this. 'Drive into Colchester, then back here and into the lay-by this side. I'll be waiting.'

'But it's foggy! Can't I just – ?'

'No. The bloody lorry's stopped on the wrong side.'

'Stupid man.' She cast off the blanket with a whimper.

'Cheers, Ben,' I said, and opened the hut door.

'Here, Lovejoy.' Ben was listening, past me into the blackness. 'There's two engines in the lay-by.'

Silly old sod, I thought, and stepped out as Ellen's car pulled away up the gravelly path. God, but the night was opaque. The way down the long slope to the road was familiar. There isn't quite a footpath. You find bearings by hawthorns and brambles. Usually there's enough light from passing cars and the distant town's sky glow. Tonight there was only this horrible graveyard opalescence.

Ellen had thoughtlessly forgotten to bring a torch. Typical. I skittered down, brambles plucking at me, until the level road surface jarred my heel. No traffic sounds, so presumably safe to cross.

Listening nervously, I loped over, climbed the central crash barrier and thankfully made the opposite verge. Left turn, keep within reach of the grassy slope for safety, and plod until the road margin indented the steep bank. Then a huge car started at me of a sudden, roared off, all in one instant. I had a vague swirly image of two figures, one familiar, then silence. Bloody fools could have killed me.

The wagon when I came upon it looked enormous. Oddly, its lights were dowsed. I almost walked into its radiator in the damned fog. The heat-stink of the cooling engine drifted at me.

'Hello?' Fog muffles sounds, doesn't it? My call hardly went a yard. No answer. 'You there, mate?'

The cab's door was ajar. I swung myself into the driver's seat, feeling at altitude. A fumble for the keys, there sure enough, and a half-twist for beam headlights. The dashboard's fluorescence cast a ghostly apparition on the windscreen, losing me a heartbeat till I realized it was my own nervy face. A square white card was lodged in the corner of the thick glass. I turned the card over. A black capital L. My signal, so this was the right wagon. But stillness is stillness, and there was a lot of it about. The size of these night haulers is daunting. I levered down, leaving the lights on. A car swished by steady and fast heading for the coast. The driver was probably having a pee, or gone looking for me.

'Hello,' I called. My voice warbled. I cleared my throat, called again as unconvincingly. No sound. I walked the length of the vehicle. It seemed all wheels. The rear doors were unlocked, one leaf swinging ponderously open at a pull. Interior lights came on, like in a fridge. Empty.

'Hello?' I shouted. The place was giving me the spooks. Now, the one thing a night haulier never does is leave his wagon. Gulp.

A car crawled into the lay-by, spotlighted me in its beams, Ellen to the rescue at two miles an hour. 'Darling?'

I walked round and got in, trying hard to disguise my relief. 'Where the hell have you been?'

'Charming,' she said bitterly. 'It's hundreds of miles to the Marks Tey turn-off. Where's your cupboard?'

'It's four miles. And it's a bureau. Gone.'

'Then ask the driver, dear.'

'He's gone, too.' I peered uneasily into that black-grey smirch.

'How *very* thoughtless. I'll give him a piece of my mind.'

You have to forget logic with Ellen. She was moved to aggro, actually starting to get out to bollock a van-ished lorry-driver, when I stopped her. 'No, love,' I said piously. 'I've kept you out in this awful weather long enough. It's time I considered your feelings.'

'Darling,' she said mistily. 'You're so sweet.'

True, but I'd better get rid of her sharpish after dawn because Liz was due about ten with a genuine pair of mid-Victorian nipple jewels, sapphires set in diamonds. I joked nervously as we pulled out. 'Promise not to ravish me again.'

'Very well, dear,' she said seriously. 'look, Lovejoy. The lorry's left its light on. It'll waste its electricity.'

'How careless,' I said uneasily. 'No, love. Don't stop.'

Next morning I had three jobs. First was Liz, chatty antiques dealeress from Dragonsdale that I was conn-ing into selling me those lovely nipple drops – think of earrings with bigger loops for dangling pendant-like from the pierced nipples of interesting Victorian ladies. Liz had found a set with their accompanying large gold

471

sleepers. I'd been banking on profit from the bureau to afford them.

My second and third jobs were easy, now I was broke. Two lithophanes of erotic couples, and a pride of tortoiseshell seamstress scissors, 1840, were in the auction. I'd hate seeing them sold to some flush swine, but I could no more keep away than fly.

Ellen fried me a good nosh. She brings supplies because I'm always strapped, and leaves little labelled packets in the fridge – 'Boil 10 Mins In Slightly Salted Water' and all that. I never do it, because it always goes wrong. I got shot of her at a safe nine o'clock. She always wants to strip the bed and hang sheets on the line, God knows why. What good are they waving in the breeze? I lied that I'd do it, to make her trip home to Ipswich less of a rush. She said I was an angel. Modestly I waved her off, concealing my relief, and got down to sussing out The Missing Bureau Problem.

First, however, remember this ratio: five to one. Not a Grand National bet, but the number of phoney/fake/reproduction bureaux to the genuine. Five times as many fakes as genuine. And that's here, in rural East Anglia where habits – and furniture, and paintings and porcelain – don't change. I have figures for most antiques. Jewellery is eight to one; pearls twenty; pre-Victorian oil paintings three fakes to one genuine. So, all in all, the odds are heavily against the honest buyer and heavily in favour of the crook.

It stands to reason that you're on a loser. The dice of honesty are loaded against you, the poor unsuspecting customer.

Lately, though, I'd been having a bad patch. Even though I'm a very special type of antique dealer – tell you more in a minute – it was pathetic. Sometimes, antiques vanish like snow off a duck. Buyers evaporate. Collectors get a collective 'flu. Money zooms into the Inland Revenue's coffers untouched by human hand. In other trades things never become utterly hopeless.

472

I mean to say, a farmer at least still has the good earth if his crop fails, and doctors can always look forward to a really great epidemic if their patients strike a depressingly healthy patch. But in the antiques game there's nothing. An antique dealer with no antiques feels a right prune. A hungry prune, because when you're broke the Chancellor simply refuses dole. No, subtract antiques from the great equation of life and all is zero.

Well, nearly zero.

Because there's fakes. And frauds. And counterfeits, reproductions, marriages, twinners, naughties, copies . . . I finally found my note about the bureau in a heap of paper clippings that makes my tatty armchair a hell of comfort:

'Jo: Teddy repro b. split m/u, Inv. T. fix Thurs. M.'

Roughly translated, an Edwardian period reproduction bureau was available. I'd agreed to divide the mark-up (i.e. my hoped-for profit) with the sender, who would ship it from Inverness, a collecting centre for the four northernmost counties by these night wagons. I'd told Tinker to fix delivery for the previous night. Jo – Josephine – had been my original contact. Tinker's my old barker, my message ferret.

I'd better try to catch Jo, then get to the town Arcade where antiques and dealers congregate.

For a second, guilt tugged. I glanced around. The cottage's interior was a mess: books, newspaper cuttings, a mouldering heap of unpaid bills, the divan bed I'd promised Ellen I'd make. I opened the door, masterful with guilt. I was actually smiling from the relief of having triumphed over housework, when my jubilation ended.

''Morning, Lovejoy.' Liz Sandwell stood there in the tiny flagged porch. Pretty as a picture. The trouble is her live-in boyfriend's one of those strength-through-

473

joy fanatics who gasp their way through our rain-soaked countryside and finish up where they started. A tough rugby player.

''Morning, love,' I said brightly, slamming the door to edge on past.

'Well? Did it arrive?'

Blankly I stared at her. 'Eh?' I never know what the hell women are on about half the time.

'The money. From your Uncle Percy.'

'Ah.' Evidently one of my less memorable myths. Swiftly I switched to heartfelt grief. 'No, love. Uncle Percy's just sent a telegram. He's ill and needs me.'

Concern leapt into her eyes. 'Oh, how terrible, Lovejoy. Are you very close?'

Not as close as I'll be to that burke of a wagoneer who lost my bureau and disappeared, I thought grimly, but said brokenly, 'Yes. Can we postpone the deal over the nipple jewels, love? Only I'm hurrying to town to borrow the fare to, er, Llangollen.'

Liz took instant charge. 'Let me run you to the station, Lovejoy. How much is it? You can't shilly-shally at times like this.' A warm-hearted, lovable lass is Liz. Where the hell's Llangollen, I wondered, getting into her car. Let's hope it's a fair distance. Then with that money I'd have enough to split-purchase Margaret Dainty's Belleek porcelain trelliswork basket – no harp-and-greyhound mark, so post–1891, but lovely . . .

A few minutes later I was mouthing gibberish at a puzzled railway clerk while watching the reflection of Liz's departing car in the glass. She'd lent me a real handful of notes.

''Ere, mate. You going any bloody where or not?' A soldier in the queue behind me was growing impatient.

'Sorry, sorry.' Liz'd gone. I stepped aside. 'I can't leave Nellie and the little uns,' I said nobly.

Twenty minutes later the bus dropped me outside Jo's school. It was playtime.

Chapter Two

The playground was a screaming turmoil. Through the railings I said to a snot-riddled urchin, 'If I give you a million zlotniks, will you give Miss Ross a message?'

'Piss off, Lovejoy.'

I sighed, and looked about. Most of the little psychopaths are from my village and believe I'm a bum. 'Lottie,' I called. One of the tinier girls skipped closer, pigtails flying with each bounce. I used to babysit her.

'Salt, mustard, vinegar, pepper,' she chanted breathlessly.

'I'm going to elope with Miss Ross,' I said. 'Say I'm here.'

Lottie bounced off, chanting. I sat and waited while the playground roared on. Five minutes and Jo came, red-faced and embarrassed. She's a lovely slender faun of a woman, mid-twenties. Infants flocked round, staring.

'Lovejoy! What on earth?'

'Aren't you escaping, miss?' a kiddy asked disappointedly.

'Certainly not! And get away the lot of you!'

They dispersed with that silent scorn only infants can attain, Lottie explaining, 'I told you he tells lies.'

'That bureau, love.' I had the scrap of paper out.

'You interrupt school and make me a laughing-stock just to ask stupid questions?'

Women are always narked. You just have to ride out the storm. I nodded. 'Yes, love. Only it didn't arrive.' She'd given me the original address, an Inverness box number.

'Well, I can't help that, can I?'

'Why did you tell me instead of some other dealer, Jo?'

Momentarily she coloured deeper. 'You happen to be the first antique dealer I thought of.'

I turned to go, and said loudly, 'Pretend to start teaching, darling, then slip out. I'll be waiting – '

'Shhh, you fool.' She was trying not to laugh. A police car pulled alongside the kerb. Two Old Bill descended. The children fell silent and gathered at the railings.

'You Lovejoy?' one peeler said.

'Give over, John.' I've known Constable Doble ten years. Every Friday night I beat him at darts.

'You're under arrest,' he said. 'Get in.'

'For anything in particular?'

'Murder of a night driver,' he said. 'In particular.'

Jo gasped. Thinking quickly, I passed her the note. 'To Tinker, please, Jo.' The children's faces solemnly followed me as I crossed to the car.

Lottie called, 'I'm sorry you didn't escape like you planned, Lovejoy.' Another nail in my coffin.

'Ta, chuck,' I called back, best I could do with my throat dry.

The other bobby was already scribbling this new evidence as we drove off. Education gets everywhere these days, doesn't it.

Gaols have been great literary stimulants. John Bunyan or Oscar Wilde would have used the next dozen days to dash off a masterpiece. Me, I simply languished. Twice I was dragged out to stand before Arthur. He's our famous magistrate. He writes little stage plays about ghost trains and doubles as Judge Lynch. I was remanded in custody. I didn't claim my two witnesses because Ben's lies are notorious, and fornicating with a Royal Customs officer's wife while illegally transporting a fake antique might not stand up as a character reference.

Maslow came to see me on the first day.

'Your fingerprints are all over the wagon, Lovejoy,' he told me. 'The man was found dead a hundred yards up the bank.'

'Ah,' I said, baffled. Maslow's not a bad old stick for a troop leader, but there's only a limited amount of truth police inspectors can take. 'That explains why I couldn't find him. I wanted to give him a message.'

'At that hour in the morning? In the fog? On a lonely road?' He was beginning to glare and breathe funny. 'Ben the roadmender said he hadn't seen you, Lovejoy.'

Thank you, Ben. 'I walked to the lay-by. When I got there the driver had gone. I looked about the wagon, wondered if he was, erm . . .'

Maslow nodded, and left. Three local prostitutes work the lay-bys. Night hauliers find solace for the loneliness of the long distance wagoneer in the privacy of their own vehicles.

Three days elapsed before reassuring rumours filtered in. The driver, a big Brummie, had put up a struggle before being bludgeoned. Needless to say the peelers had taken my clothes, scraped my fingernails. The screw told me this news between bowls of porridge and atrocious jokes.

It was Monday evening before a wonderful sound floated in through the bars of my cell. I brightened, listened as a long cough began, swelled and shuddered the walls. The cough rumbled closer. I ran to the bars grinning all over my face.

'That you, Tinker?' I yelled. 'In here.'

'Wotcher, Lovejoy.'

In he came. Small, shambling, in a grimy old beret and tattered army greatcoat. An aroma of stale booze and feet wafted in as he subsided wheezing on the bunk.

'Never been in this one,' he croaked. A connoisseur of gaols. 'Did we do it, Lovejoy?'

That plural warmed me. Tinker's not much to look at, but any ally counts one. Since my arrest I'd been solo. 'No.'

'Fank Gawd,' he said, rolling a grotty cigarette in mittened fingers. 'They've been at me three frigging days. Yon Scotch tart got the paper to me in time.'

I nodded. That had warned him to disclose nothing. He gave another cough. I waited. They seem to start somewhere out to sea, like thunder. 'You'll get sprung, Lovejoy. That bird you wuz shagging in Ben's hut's seeing the Commissioner.'

I sank back, eyes closed in relief. Tinker lit up, coughing. Ellen had come to give me an alibi. 'Learn anything?'

'About the bureau? Aye. Word is that frigging Dobson creep's had it away, to frigging Amsterdam, Antwerp, one of them places through the Hook. Twinned it.'

'Jesus.' An antique which is made into two of itself is 'twinned' in the trade. If half of a piece is truly genuine antique, it becomes very difficult to dismiss it as a fake. And of course you get twice the profit. If Tinker's information was true, the only piece of evidence which could pin the killer had been destroyed as effectively as if they'd burned it to ashes. Dobson is a barker, like Tinker. He works with a pleasant youngish bloke we call Dutchie. Oddly, I thought of that familiar face in that great old car. Had it been Dutchie? Indistinct, but . . .

'How'd you know?'

'Seen down the hangars, two nights back.'

My bad luck, I thought bitterly. Anybody with stolen antiques takes them to a disused wartime airfield near here. No questions are asked down at the hangars. Jade, jewellery, silver, porcelain, complete suites of furniture, I've seen stuff change hands a dozen times an hour. Always at night. No way of backtracking there.

'Here, Lovejoy,' Tinker was grinning toothily in his fag smoke. 'If you'd not been shagging that Excise officer's missus they'd be topping you.' He really fell about at the thought of my being hanged, cackling through his brown fangs.

'They don't hang people now, stupid sod,' I said icily.

'Maslow always said he'd make you an exception, Lovejoy.' He was still rolling in the aisles, coughing himself apoplectic, when his visiting time was up and they shelled him out.

They released me on two counts. One, the big Midlander had fought his murderers, and I was unmarked. And two, a respectable lady testified that, marooned with a stalled engine on the main A12 during the night of the great fog, she had been assisted by a stranger who started her motor and drove her to safety. As a gesture of appreciation, she had insisted on driving him to his home, a thatched cottage in a little village nearby.

'How could the lady see your cottage, thatch and all, in the pitch fog, Lovejoy?' Maslow asked evenly, with that threatening peace police manage so effortlessly. 'And how come you'd forgotten the entire incident?'

'I couldn't compromise a lady,' I explained nobly.

'One day, Lovejoy. One day.'

Deliberately I let the office door slam on him. I waggled my fingers at the desk sergeant.

He too warned, 'One day, Lovejoy. One day.'

'Great phrase you police've got there, Ernie,' I said. 'Stick at it. Might make a full sentence one day.'

And I left happily. In fact, super-happily, because in my languishment the penny had dropped in my cavernous skull. You never twin a fake, right? All that extra skilled labour is only worthwhile if the original

piece in a *genuine* antique. The driver had been done
for a valuable piece, not a cheap reproduction.

Now things made sense I began hurrying.

Chapter Three

Our ancestors liked to be thought fine, moral folk. Same as us, eh? Flesh being flesh and spirits being weak, they rarely made it. In fact they were as hopeless at sanctity as we are. Sadly, it bothered them more, but they were better at pretending. Look at lithophanes, for example, that I was currently angling after.

You've seen how light transluces through a lampshade? If you're a craftsman you can make porcelain thin enough to show translucency in exactly the same way. Lithophanes are small plaques of super-slender porcelain in which you see a picture when you hold them up to the light. However, naughtiness crept in to the Victorian designs. Not all the pictures hidden in the antique porcelain are pretty trees and hillsides. They are often lascivious ladies in mid-frolic, doing scandalous things with sexual abandon. Nowadays collectors pay through the nose for erotic lithophanes – purely for the art, you understand.

Tinker was in the White Hart soaking the day's calories and coughing so well that people had given up trying to listen to the jukebox. It's where our local antique dealers gather and pretend to celebrate between failures.

'Wotcher, Lovejoy.' He jerked his chin. Ted the barman nodded and drew two pints. I paid. It's Tinker's principal method of claiming his salary from me. I've gone hungry before now to get him sloshed, because a barker's vital. He can winkle and cheat with abandon. Antique dealers must be circumspect.

'Wotcher, Tinker.' I forked out. I bought us a bar

pasty in the euphoria of freedom. 'News of the bureau? Dutchie?'

'Nar. I got you Dobson.' He indicated with his eyes the tall lone figure at the bar's end. Even in a crowd the thin silent barker somehow stood apart.

Dobson's a sombre one-off. For a start, he's the only bloke I know in the trade who doesn't have a nickname. And he never says much, just hangs around listening, vigilant. Folk say he carries a knife and once did time. He looks fresh from an alley war. On the other hand I like Dutchie, a genial bloke with a word for the cat. He appears out of nowhere once every Preston Guild. He comes like a comet, handles the deals Dobson's lined up for him, then vanishes for a fortnight or so. But Dobson unsettles me. A few minutes later I was asking Dobson where his wally Dutchie was.

He never answers immediately, in case there's another way out. 'Gone on the ferry. Dunno where.'

Fair enough. 'See anything of a bureau, the night that wagon driver got done?'

'No. Sorry.' Nothing here for an inquisitive dealer fresh out of clink.

'Was Dutchie around that night?'

He shrugged after a long lag phase. Nothing. I rejoined Tinker, back to hungry reality. So I'd lost a fortune. I couldn't afford to lose still more by inactivity. 'The lithophanes, Tinker.'

'Them little pot flaps?' Tinker's way of describing artistic genius. 'Three-Wheel.'

'Three-Wheel Archie? Great. Come on, Tinker.'

He wailed, 'But I haven't had me dinner, Lovejoy.'

Fuming, I gave him two of my three remaining notes, which left me just enough to breathe. 'See me tonight, then. The Three Cups.' The sly old burke was cackling with glee as I left.

From the call-box outside I phoned Ellen to beg a lift. The glass was shattered so I had to stand in the rain and shout over the whistling gale. Unbelievably, she put down the receiver the instant she recognized my voice. Bloody nerve. Next week she'd prove to me, by complex female reasoning, that her refusal to speak was a precaution to help me in some way.

A call to the Infant School earned another rebuff, this time from Jo. A bad day for loyalty. A stranger gave me a lift in his car to within a mile of Archie's place, and told me all about astronomy.

Three-Wheel Archie gets his nickname from a tricycle he rides. He grew up in an orphanage somewhere near Whitechapel. When I say grew up, I mean his head and features did, but the rest of him sort of lagged behind. Mind you, with most of us others it's the opposite, isn't it; relatively big over all but very little brain. Archie ended up a thickset titch who walks with a low swagger. He deals in engines, mechanicals, and watches, and lives alone down the estuary. I like him.

He was cleaning his dazzling new motor-car when I arrived. It lives grandly in a brick-built garage, cavity insulation, dehumidifier, air-conditioner, the lot. He'd run it out on polished lino. He lives in the near-derelict cottage adjoining.

'Sprung, eh, Lovejoy?' he panted, sprawled on the bonnet polishing like mad. 'No way a soft bugger like you could clobber a big Brummie to death. The Old Bill are stupid.'

'I've come about the lithophanes.' I walked round his car, admiring. 'Posher than ever. How old now?'

'Ten next September thirtieth. She's Libra.'

'Er, great. Still going okay?' It has one mile on the clock, in and out of the garage once a fortnight. Five yards a month mounts up.

'Brilliant, Lovejoy,' he said proudly, sliding chute-wise down to the ground carrying his sponges. 'Glass?'

'Ta, Archie.' When I said new, I used the term loosely. Archie's one ambition from birth was owning a saloon car. He bought it a decade gone, and built for it that luxurious garage. Of course he's so dwarf he can't reach the pedals to drive the damned thing, but he loves it. He runs the engine every week, has engineers in to service it. Once, a local dealer laughed at Archie for having a new/old car he couldn't drive. Archie's never spoken to him since. Nor have I.

'Here, Lovejoy.' He gave me some homemade wine. 'Last autumn's blackberry.'

'Mmmmh.' I smacked my lips. Dreadful.

'The lithophanes'll cost you, Lovejoy.' We sat on packing cases beside the glittering vehicle.

'Archie. If you wanted an antique bureau twinned up, who'd you get to do it?'

'You, Lovejoy, on that rare occasion you're not dicking some bint. Otherwise Tipper Noone at Melford. He's done lovely stuff lately.'

'I mean a rush job.'

'So do I.' Archie drained his glass. He knew what I was asking, the crafty devil. 'Somebody said Tipper did one a few days back, for shipping to the Continent.'

I sighed. That's the trouble with East Anglia. Most is coast, inlets with busy little ships steaming to and fro. And continentals spend like lunatics when they've a mind.

'I'm the one who told Tinker, Lovejoy.'

Useless. That was as far as we'd got before a car pulled in and Jo descended. I introduced Archie to her. He rose, shook hands gravely. I knew she'd behave properly, thank God.

'Good of you to come, Jo.' I was mystified.

She stood in the mucky yard, hands plunged into the pockets of her floppy coat. Her collar was up, framing her face. Women stand with elegance, don't they, one foot slightly averted so they're all one lovely composite shape.

'Won't you sit down?' Archie offered her a crate. She sat without a trace of hesitancy. I really like Miss

Josephine Ross. More, she gravely accepted a glass of
Archie's wine and said reflectively that it was possibly
a little too dry, like her father's recipe. Archie adored
her.

'Don't let me interrupt, Lovejoy,' she said, smiling.
'I only wanted to say sorry, cutting you off on the
phone just because you'd been . . . seeing the police.
It was mean of me.' Her colour was high. 'We shouldn't
be swayed by public stigma.'

'Don't mix metaphors,' I said, to get us off ethics.
'Give me a lift and I'll forgive you.'

Me and Archie settled the deal over the lithophanes
while Jo admired the car, wisely not touching it. She
had quickly registered the difference between Archie's
grotty residence and the opulent garage, but said
nothing. Archie came to see us off. The swine wouldn't
let me have the lithos on approval.

'Four wheels on your motor,' Jo said. 'Why Three
Wheel?'

'Come on, Jo.' I got in her car irritably.

'Tell her, Lovejoy.' Archie was grinning, saw I
wouldn't budge, and walked over to a shed. He pulled
the door open to reveal a beautiful tricycle with an
elegant canopy.

'How lovely, Archie!' Jo exclaimed. 'Do you ride
it?'

'Makes me mobile, Miss Ross. Courtesy of Lovejoy,
five years ago now.'

She looked at me. 'Really.'

'Can we go?' I called wearily. 'Bloody time-wasters.'

Archie waved to us. By the time we left the yard he
was already buffing the car's hubs. We drove a couple
of miles before she said anything. 'Lovejoy?'

She wanted to prattle about Archie, but I wasn't
having any. 'You only gave me the box number for
that bureau, Jo,' I said. 'Is there more?'

She took a while to answer. 'Very well,' she said

finally. 'Grammar apart, Lovejoy, you'll have to sing for your supper.'

It was Jo's free afternoon. She stayed and I made tea for her. Ellen had washed up, so I had clean cups. I made some sandwiches and cut their crusts off to make natty triangles. A bit thick, but all the more nourishing. The tomatoes had gone pappy so I blotted them on newspaper first. I felt posh serving up, like the Savoy chef. I had to use a towel for a tablecloth because I can never find anything when Ellen's tidied.

'I'm impressed, Lovejoy,' Jo said, smiling.

'Ta,' I said modestly. I knew she would be. I can really lay on the elegance when I want. I'd even found the teapot lid.

She wore a beige twin set, tweed skirt, but mainly a black opal ring, Edwardian setting, heavy and gold. Beautiful.

'It was my friend I was at school with, Shona. We've kept up correspondence.' She coloured, proving rumour right: a farm manager, a passionate holiday affair, and her coming to a teaching job in East Anglia to be near his fertile acres.

Shona was a teacher in Caithness, which is almost as far north as you can go. In a recent letter Shona had mentioned selling some furniture. By pure chance, Jo said, carefully avoiding my gaze, my name entered the correspondence.

'It was soon after I'd met you at the Castle show,' she explained. Farmer Bob had been away. Jo and I had met on that local gala day – everybody goes to our Castle's flower displays. We saw quite a bit of each other for a fortnight until her favourite yokel homeward plodded his weary way.

'You told Shona I was a divvie?'

'I may have mentioned it. In passing.' She spoke offhandedly. 'Maybe. I can't remember. Shona insisted on selling through a box number. I passed it on to you. You wrote, and . . . and now that poor driver . . .'

My mind wouldn't stop nudging me, but I'd have scared her off if I'd started a serious interrogation.

'Wasn't it lucky, you meeting that woman in the fog?' Jo said, too casual. She'd reached the suspicion bit, about Ellen.

'A fluke,' I agreed.

'You deserved it, Lovejoy,' she said, smiling. 'For giving Archie that grand tricycle.'

'It isn't his fault his legs can't reach the car throttle.'

'Of course not.' Still smiling, she put her fingers to my face. We were suddenly close.

My hopes of examining the true worth of Farmer Bob's black opal engagement ring were dashed when Jo found her hand on a pair of Ellen's stockings. They'd treacherously crept out from behind a cushion. She was up and vehement in a flash.

'Lovejoy! And to think that I was about to . . . *oh*!'

'Honestly, Jo. They're my sister's . . . 'Trala trala. Good night, nurse, with Jo storming out in a ferocious temper and me shouting invented explanations after her.

Women really get me down sometimes. They're so unreasonable. You'd think they'd learn sense, having nothing else to do all day. I watched her car burn off up the lane, then went in disconsolately.

The sight of her unfinished grub cheered me up and I sat down to finish it. My spirits began soaring. Where one valuable antique came from there was bound to be more, right? And if the sender was dim enough to send a pricey article thinking it a mock-up, I was in for a windfall.

Give Jo a day to come round, wheedle Shona's address off her, then hit the high road. Or the low road. I'm not proud.

Between mouthfuls I burst into song.

Chapter Four

Jill was at Gimbert's infamous auction rooms. This emporium of wonderment and infamy is lodged between a row of ancient cottages, a ruined priory, two pubs and a church. She was inspecting the assorted junk in her time-honoured way, which is carrying a microscopic poodle and trailing a knackered seaman. Jill's tastes are catholic, as they say. She wears furs, grotesque hats, rings, brooches, pearls, the lot. I like her. She saw me pushing through the dross and screamed.

'Lovejoy *darling*!' She drenched my face with a kiss. Quickly I pulled away. Her embrace is a dead risk. Either the poodle gnaws your earhole or you stink like a boutique. 'How clever to escape from gaol! Meet . . . the name, lover?'

'Dave,' the young sailor said.

'Dave,' Jill repeated, trying to lock the name in. She always forgets. 'Dave's just into port, aren't you, honey?' In or out is her only criterion.

'Yes.' Dave was bemused, like all Jill's Jolly Jacks. Coastal ships docking at our town's minuscule port take turns lending Jill nautical manpower. The names change, to protect the innocents. I've never met the same one twice. Tinker says they don't dare land again.

'Hello, er, Dave,' I said heartily. 'Jill. You sometimes commission Tipper Noone?'

'Not lately, Lovejoy. I've been absolutely *rushed* off my feet!' Big Frank from Suffolk, silver dealer among the Regency ware, snickered at the unfortunate turn of phrase. A couple of other dealers up-ending furniture

488

politely disguised their guffaws as coughs. 'Dobson gave him a twinner, Patrick said.'

Tinker's tale was beginning to sound true, despite Dobson's reticence.

'Ta, Jill. Tell him to bell me, eh?'

I evaded another soak, gnaw, and scenting by eeling among heavy suites of 1910 furniture to where Patrick stood. He always looks crazy to me – crocodile handbag, silken bishop sleeves and enough mascara to black your boots – but he's a hardline dealer. I was swiftly getting narked. This bloody drudgery's Tinker's job.

'Hiyer, Pat. Where's Lily?' Lily's a married woman who loves Patrick while her husband's away and sometimes when he isn't. I'd say more but it's too complicated and I'd get it wrong.

'Patrick,' he corrected. 'That stupid bitch brought the wrong cheque-book, Lovejoy! Can you *imagine*?' He swore extravagantly in falsetto. 'I made her go right home!'

'That's the spirit, Pat. Look. Where's Tipper Noone?'

'To each his own, dear heart. You won't find him in my boudoir.' He boomed – well, trilled – a gay laugh.

'Don't help, then,' I said evenly. 'See if I care.'

Other dealers sieving through the gunge on display paused at the implied threat. Even Patrick abated somewhat.

I may not be much to look at, but among antique dealers I'm special. Very few dealers know anything about antiques. In fact most are simply Oscar-minus actors highly skilled at concealing their monumental ignorance. Try one out, if you don't believe me. Offer an antique dealer a Rembrandt – he'll hum and ha and won't offer you more than eighty quid. It isn't because he's miserly. It's because he can't tell an Old Master from an oil slick, which is why you can still pick up fortunes hidden among loads of old tat.

Ignorance being endemic, it follows that antique

dealers need somebody to help them, not only with reading and writing, but also with *knowing* antiques. I don't mean somebody who's simply read the right books. I mean somebody whose inner sense tells if that fifteenth-century Book Of Hours is a brilliant sequence of illumination from the unsullied monks of Lindisfarne, or a newspaper and starch. Easy? Yes, for somebody like me, who quivers and trembles when that Roman oil lamp radiates its honest ancient little soul's vibes out into the universe, or when that antique Chinese jewelled fingernail cover emanates gleams under the auctioneer's naked bulb.

The people distributed in Gimbert's showrooms had paused with alert interest because I'm the only divvie for many long leagues. I'm gormless with money and women, which is why I'm always broke, but I'm the only one of us who isn't gormless with antiques.

Patrick's venom is legendary. But if I called his antiques fakes he too would be broke. Mostly I'm honest because special gifts aren't for monkeying about with. So, wisely, he turned sulky and pulled his mauve silk lace gloves on.

'Don't be *nasty*, Lovejoy. I positively sweated *blood* arranging for Tipper to give me an estimate for mending a Chippendale fret. He didn't turn up, did he, Lily?' Patrick's admirer had just breathlessly returned proudly bearing her cheque-book.

'Tipper? Yes. Here you are, darling.'

Patrick dropped the cheque-book, demanding icily, 'Do I have to carry everything, silly bitch?'

Lily was picking it up, saying, 'Sorry, sweethear . . .' as I left. They're both on a loser, but neither thinks so. It's hard proving people are wrong when they're doing what they want.

There on the pavement stood Antioch. He's a slim, quiet bloke. A friend, thank God. (You'll see later why I'm glad on that point.) He waits motionless, never lolls. He's the contact man for the night wagoneers. As I hesitated, he nodded hello.

'How do, Antioch,' I said, nervous. 'Look. That driver.'

'You're asking around, Lovejoy?' he said quietly.

'Aye. No luck so far.'

'You find out who did for him, don't do anything. Understand?'

'You know me, Antioch,' I said heartily. 'Scared of my own shadow.'

He looked into me. 'Just tell me who, Lovejoy.'

'Right, right.' I watched him go, my nape chilled.

Then I phoned Jo, trying to sound urgent. 'The police, Jo.' There was a background din. Some school. 'They pulled me in for questioning but I didn't let on about your involvement, love.'

'My involvement?' she said faintly.

'I'm just reassuring you, in case you were anxious. I've said nothing.' Pause, for her to say nice of me. Not a word. I'd have to be even nicer. 'And I'm sorry the jumble sale stuff made you mad. I've not had a minute to clear up since – '

'What jumble sale stuff?'

'Those women's clothes lying about. Old Kate brings them. I collect for the, er, hospital charity. Next time you come it'll be tidy. Honest.'

'Oh.' Uncertainty at last. Belief might not be far behind.

I gasped indignantly. 'Jo! You didn't think those underclothes were . . .'

We agreed on the Tudor Halt restaurant, six o'clock. A bit posh for me, but I'd scrape the gelt together somehow. And Jo might give me a lift home afterwards, during which dot dot dot to the sound of the waves upon the shore, with any luck.

I don't blackwash people, because what's the use? All reputation is just whitewash carefully applied. So for

491

me gossip, the sole means of communication among antique dealers, is valueless unless it's filtered by an expert.

Tinker, my only employee, is that all-time gossip-filtering expert. He was hard at work becoming paralytic in the Ship tavern when I arrived. I wheedled Sandra the barmaid into letting me slate his next few pints. She blames me for having stood her up once, and makes me earn my badges back every now and then. Women never forget what you owe. On the other hand they're great at forgetting repayments. Swings and roundabouts.

'Ta, Sand,' I said. 'Don't give him more than six.'

Tinker cackled. I leant away as his alcoholic fetor wafted past and moved him away from the bar. He was with a group of barkers boozily trading rumour. I kept my voice low. The barkers had shut up and were oh-so-casually inclining their ears at an eavesdropping angle.

'Tinker. Where the hell's Tipper Noone? Gimbert's viewing today and he's not showed.'

'Not been in the Arcade more'n a week.' He drained his glass. I sprinted for a refill.

'Listen. Here's what I think, Tinker. That bureau we had shipped down was nicked. The driver protested, and got done. They owffed it to the hangars. It changed hands a few times as usual. Then – '

' – Dutchie got Tipper Noone to twin it, shipped it out.' Tinker nodded. 'Benjie bought it, then Nacker Hardie, then Alison Verney, but nobody remembers how it first come.'

He'd done well to find all that out. 'Tipper's a home bird,' I reminded.

He said nothing, stared at his empty glass. Sprint, smile at Sandra, refill. Resume. 'Aye. Never goes anywhere, doesn't Tipper. But he's not in the Eastern Hundreds any more.' This was making me uneasy.

Tinker suddenly looked sober, a novel but alarming

sight. 'It's bad news.' His rheumy old eyes were on me. 'Are we in trouble, Lovejoy?'

'Yes,' Maslow said, sitting down beside me. There was a faint stir in the taproom smog. I looked across. The mob of barkers had vanished as if by magic.

'Another false arrest, Maslow?'

He grinned from behind his pipe. The match tufted flame so bright I turned away. 'False arrest isn't trouble, Lovejoy. Trouble's the body of a man washed ashore off the estuary.'

I drew breath to ask the question but Tinker was clobbering my arm with his glass. I took the clumsy hint and rose for another refill.

'Some boating accident?' I said sympathetically, returning after telling myself to watch my big mouth. Sometimes Tinker's worth his weight in gold.

'Possibly, Lovejoy.' Distastefully Maslow watched Tinker slurp the ale. 'You know, you repel me, Dill. A dosshouse fusilier. I'm sick of the sight of tramps like you.'

Tinker said humbly, 'Yes, Mr Maslow.'

'Tinker's the best barker in the business,' I said. Maslow narks me.

'And you, Lovejoy. Pillock. You could have made something of yourself. Instead you haunt junkshops, shag your way through women's handbags. You're pathetic, you know that? You're too cuntstruck, Lovejoy.' He was really motoring now, glaring and practically yelling. 'You two burkes – '

'Get stuffed, Maslow.' I can bawl as good as him. 'You frigging peelers should be out there finding who drowned poor bloody Tipper Noone instead of . . . ' I paused, aghast.

Tinker groaned, head in his hands. Maslow smiled.

'How did you know the body was Tipper Noone, Lovejoy?' he asked gently. 'Fancy a ride to the station?'

Chapter Five

They let me go, shaken but not stirred, about four that afternoon. I'd seen poor Tipper's horrendous mortal remains. A fishing line had entangled his legs. His head was stove in, but Maslow said the pathologists never learn anything from drowners. Tipper must have been in the water some days. His drifting dinghy was found a couple of miles out to sea. I'd been in clink at the time, a fact I mentioned every chance I got.

'You see, Lovejoy,' Maslow said staring morosely at the traffic from the police steps. 'This isn't a game, is it? And you're deep in because as soon as you're sprung from one problem you're asking after a furniture-restorer who lo and behold comes bobbing in without a boat.' He added his pipe's carcinogens to the lead-soaked traffic pollution. 'You're no killer, Lovejoy, not really. You fancy yourself, but you're brim full of cowardice, cant and crap. O' course you didn't do for Tipper. Never believed you did. Any more than I believe that Tipper accidentally drowned.'

He wouldn't let me reply, just reamed his pipe like they do. Pipe-smoking's a job.

'I'm telling you all this by way of warning, Lovejoy. Witnesses are a public's protection of innocence. Consequently they're at risk. They tend to get eliminated. Now you're tied in with the wagoneer's death and Tipper's. So stay in the company of friends, close to that Customs officer's pretty wife, or Mrs Dainty, or yon Scotch lass, or – '

'Here,' I said defensively. I didn't know he knew.

'And stay off the bypass. Stop contrabranding old wardrobes till I clear this up. Okay?'

Which is why I spent an anxious hour in the library with a gazeteer, and the next hour divvying for Francie to earn some money to feed Jo to get Shona's address to leave the district. A process of elimination was going on, and I wanted out.

Francie's rarely around, but always is, if you follow. She travels with her husband and sixty-seven others. They're a fairground, the sort with roundabouts, roll-a-pennies, sideshows and a Giant Caterpillar that whirls round and covers you over for a quick snog. They've even a Galactic Wheel and a Ghost Train. It's marvellous, lights and action and people. I like fairgrounds, always have. Francie collects antiques on the side, eroding the whole enterprise's meagre profits year after year. I used to make smiles with Francie before she went a-gipsy-roving.

The place they land is Castle Heath, a greensward where centuries ago some baddies shot some heroes to death, or the other way round. They come like night-thieving arabs, suddenly there in full swing. It's one of the most exciting scenes to see an early-morning fairground with wagons and tents and fanciful structures. I love their colours, for the same reason I love them on canal boats; they are the brilliance of an earlier century showing through modern grot.

Francie welcomed me as always as I shouted at the steps and climbed into her caravan, which is to say with hardly a glance. In her tribe it's an insult to dawdle at the door. She immediately put the kettle on.

'How do, love.' I bussed her and quickly sat down uninvited, another must. 'How's it among the oppressed nomads?'

'How is it among the static fascists, darling?'

'Bloody grim. Better for seeing thee, though.'

'So you got off.' That always makes me blink. The

fair only arrived a day ago, but here she was knowing everything.

An infant came in, looking vaguely familiar, fetched a toffee out of the fridge.

'Is this good for your teeth?' I demanded, obediently unwrapping it for her.

'Ta.' The kiddie left to join six others milling about outside. Fairground children are always so business-like.

'Yours, Francie?'

She didn't look up. 'Mmmmh. And you got off today from Tipper Noone's accident, Lovejoy. Two out of two.'

That explained the familiar feeling I'd got from look-ing at the little girl. Family likeness. 'Eh? Oh, aye. I'm a master of escapology.' She came and sat on the bunk seat, facing me so our eyeballs practically touched. Odd that I'd never seen her kiddie before, though I'd been to her caravan a few times. Shy, I suppose.

'Still trying to fit two days into one, Lovejoy? Still hopeless with women, with money?'

'Don't talk daft.' The kettle was whistling. She rose to see to it. Women are always narked when they find somebody who understands them better than they know themselves. And as for being useless, they should bloody well talk. 'You got much to divvie?'

'Maybe.'

These caravans are modern trailers, windows and bunks in tiers, a kitchen at one end. Francie's is small, but mirrors cunningly exaggerate the space she has. Tables fold out of walls, all that. She saw me looking.

'Fancy the life yet, Lovejoy?'

'Among the wraggle-taggle gipsies O? When the Mounties are after me, happen I will.'

She was bringing out the stuff while we spoke.

'Over there,' I told her, nodding at the table across from where I sat. A reasonable light falling semi-obliquely across my field of view. Francie knows the drill.

'Yes, love,' she said. 'I'll be quiet.'

Eyes closed, I relaxed and waited until she told me, 'Right, Lovejoy.' I faced the heap of items and began reaching, touching, stroking, listening, feeling.

It seems daft to say things actually speak, doesn't it, but they do, they do. Correction: antiques speak, and do it with a resonance that tremors through your very being. Gunge – and I do mean everything modern – is inert, lifeless. It deserves to remain so. The explanation is that you can't trick Nature. Humanity gets back exactly what it puts in. Passionate learning plus artistic creativity are what made little Tintoretto a bobby-dazzler instead of simply a paintmixer for his dad. Look at a great oil painting, and then at the front cover of a magazine. Just as many colours, maybe the same size and even the same subject. But there's a difference.

The caravan's interior was hot. I lifted objects, peered, sniffed, fondled, laid them aside and went on to the next.

Feeling – I mean touch – is the great modern omission. People dance apart. Even old lovers merely wave hello. It was different when I was little. You got a thick ear for not remembering to kiss even your most wrinkled auntie. Folk embraced, patted, impinged. Human contact was in. Nowadays everybody intones catch phrases proving we're hooked on togetherness, yet we run from contact. Talk loudly enough of love, and you conceal from yourself the terrible fact that you've forgotten the human act of loving. That wondrous joy of loving is everything, everything . . .

Headache. God, it was terrible. The interior was suffocating, the watery sun blinding. I felt old, drained, weary. There were three objects left on the table. The caravan's floor was littered with junk. Francie was sitting with her little girl watching me.

'You talk to yourself,' the little girl said.

'Shut your teeth and brew up.' I didn't need criticism from a neonate.

'Are those genuine, Lovejoy?' Francie asked.

'Yes.' Pulling myself together I priced them. 'This tatty watercolour's not much to look at, Francie, but it's worth a bit.' No known artist admittedly, and a crudely drawn row of Georgian shops. 'Mid-eighteenth century. He's painted the three balls on the pawn-broker's sign blue. They didn't change to brassy gold until modern times.'

The little girl said, 'Mam said you'll mend my doggie bell.'

I tried to sip the tea but it was scalding. Francie remembered, quickly rose to cool it by pouring it into a bowl.

The doggie bell was a bell-shaped silver fox's head. 'It's a cup, sweetheart. Posh people drink from them before, er, going riding.' Ritual drinks are still taken when the unspeakable pursue the inedible. These mar-vellously embellished cups are the best thing that ever came from fox-hunting. 'Don't let anybody stick a clap-per in it, for Gawd's sake.' The AB and GB initials were probably the Burrows, a rare husband-and-wife team of silversmiths in old London. Francie would have the sense to look them up. The trouble is that now-adays people make them into 'nice' things. I've seen a silver beagle-head stirrup cup, 1780 or so, made – with great skill – into an eggtimer. Cleverdaft, my old granny used to call such folk. Leave beauty alone, I always say. Sometimes.

'Is the dolly's house yours too?' It was a white por-celain cottage, two storeys. Coloured porcelain flowers adorned it. Antique dealers the world over call them Rockingham, but you never see these little white cot-tages marked.

'No. Daddy found it. Mam'll sell it.'

Daddy is Dan, nice bloke if you like swarthy and tough. He does a motorbike act, Wall of Death.

'Tell Daddy to ask a lot of money, love. It's a pastille burner.' I showed her the recess which led to the cottage's hexagonal chimney. 'You put a perfume cone underneath, and the chimney smokes a lovely scent all day long. Mam will light it for you. People called them Staffordshire fumiers. This is a lovely one, 1830.'

'Is Staffordshire near Penrith, or Edinburgh?'

'Er, that way on, love.'

'We're going there.'

Those were the three. Betty and I chatted while Francie sorted the crud. A few good collectibles lay among the discards – fairly recent wooden household implements people call treen (cheap but soaring); a few Edwardian photos but none of the most highly-sought kind (military, industrial, fashion and streets); a recently made pair of miniature wainscot chairs six inches tall (very fashionable to collect these small repros).

'You did well, Francie. Got any grub?'

She made me some nosh, then walked me to the war memorial with Betty. She'd worked out ten per cent of my estimates and insisted on giving me a part of it.

'I'll post the rest, Lovejoy. Buy an overcoat.'

'Er, good idea.' It was coming on to rain. I left them there, crossing among the traffic. They stood side by side. Betty had a little yellow umbrella up. I acted the goat a bit, turning and waving umpteen times till she was laughing. It was fooling about that saved me.

The traffic had become a sullen and glistening queue like it always does in drizzle. I was moving across the traffic lights, on red, when I did another half-step back, turned to wave. It happened all in a second. The nearest car's engine boomed. Its side edged my calves and tipped me over. I heard Francie yelp. My trouser leg tore. Its tyres squealing, the bloody saloon streaked across against the red light and swung down East Hill.

'Here,' I yelled indignantly. 'See that silly sod?'

The lights changed to green. The traffic moved. Witnesses dispersed in the worsening weather. I grinned back at Francie. 'I'm all right, love,' I called cheerily. 'Lucky, eh?'

If I hadn't been fooling about to make Betty laugh I'd have been . . . Keeping up a brave smile for Francie's benefit, I made the opposite pavement and walked on before looking across the road to where Francie and Betty stood by the war memorial. I waved once, then the museum cut them off from sight. Only then did I start the shakes and lose my idiot grin. Luck's great stuff, but it's not stuff you can depend on.

Chapter Six

Everybody lusts, but differently. And it seems to me that lust's main function is the pursuit of what you haven't got. So nuns in their lonesome beds may not all crave similarly. Likewise, me and Jo were panting after different prey when we met at the Tudor Halt. I was super-consciously nervous about having luckily stayed alive. Tonight I'd be the perfect lady's man.

She was especially pretty, wearing a dark silk shawl and a late Victorian Neapolitan mosaic brooch, neat and minute. Her hair was ringletty, her face oval. Her lovely eyes had dark lashes ten feet long. She glanced about, amused.

'You chose this place because of some antique, Lovejoy. I know you. And I've lost sleep achieving this Regency look.'

'It's not. Honest.'

We bickered all through supper. Lovely candlelit grub in the nooky old joint, with a beautiful woman shimmering opposite. You can't spend your time better, almost. I enjoyed her company even though I was sussing out the other diners, checking that Karl's waitresses hadn't transmuted into thinly-disguised mafiosi. Jo explained what the meal was – posh grub comes hidden under sauce – but knows me well enough to gloss over the grue. Finally I got Karl to bring me a cigar so they'd bring me one of the antique smoker's companions. Jo laughed and clapped her hands.

'I knew it, Lovejoy!'

Found out. My face was red. This restaurant has an entire dozen of these lovely creations. Tonight I'd

501

drawn the silver figure of a frog leaning on a toadstool. Remove the frog's head and there's a spirit reservoir. Decorative holes sprout spills for lighting your cigar with a grand flourish. Antique dealers often advertise them as 'silver ornaments, incomplete', thinking they've bits missing. Wrong. Buy them even though they're little more than a century old, which isn't much. You can still talk them off a dealer for an average week's wage.

Jo and I left the nosh-house holding hands. Karl's an old Hanover man whose wry good night was as good as a body search. For six years he's refused to sell me the smokers' companions. But one day . . .

'You love those old things, Lovejoy, don't you?'

'Yes. Same reason as I love you older women.'

'Cheek.'

She came in for a coffee, and told me enough about her friend Shona. Enough for me to find her, I mean.

'You think it's worth phoning her, love?'

'It would only worry her, Lovejoy. And her bureau was probably insured . . .'

Shona McGunn, I listed mentally. Teacher. Near Dubneath, Caithness. Single. House owner, etcetera.

Jo stayed a long, long while. I was on my very best super-romantic behaviour, really gallant. As the fire died into embers and pitch night began I suffered fantasies about noises outside. Twice I got up to peer nervously into the darkness. Once, too, Jo laughed when something scratched in my thatched roof, probably a bat or some night creature. Jo's jokey question if my cottage was haunted didn't help either. I'm thankful my garden's an obstacle course of weeds and brambles.

Hiding my nervousness, I became frantically adoring and, I prayed, adorable. That night I really earned survival. I was the world's most ardent lover. I became a raconteur, the wittiest humourist, sensitive and worshipping. And, it turned out, the most wide-awake

502

sleeper. Not a bloody wink all the dark hours from worry while Jo softly breathed. All right I'm a coward, but that car business . . . Anyway, cowards last longer, even if knackered.

'Lovejoy,' Jo whispered as the curtain gained its grey dawn rims. 'I must go. Will you see me tonight?'

'Anything you say, er, darling,' I said fervently. After all, maybe I owed her my life, having used her as a night shield against the predators. 'Er, sorry about those, er, marks.' Her arms wore bruised fingerprints.

'Silly. I'll come at nine,' she said mistily. 'We must talk seriously. About us. And Bob.'

This sounded bad news. 'Of course, love,' I said sincerely.

Cautiously I saw her off into the palish world. I waited until the milk float clattered along the lane, then, calming in the comparative safety of dawn, I fried some bread for breakfast.

That evening, ostentatiously carrying no suitcase, I caught Jacko's rickety lorry into town.

Once, I saw a famous comedian die – not meaning he got no laughs, but as in death – on the stage. The newspapers trumpeted that he'd 'gone as he would have wished'. Never. Death is the worst option, and I was going to give it up for Lent. The police would only ballock me if I asked their help because they always do. Flight was the best policy, and where else but to pretty Shona McGunn? And the prospect of that treasure mine of antiques.

An hour of flitting from alleyway to ginnel in town, from doorway to cranny, and I left the place underneath a friendly driver's tarpaulin bucketing along the A604. He dropped me off at a Sudbury tavern where I stayed until closing time. I stole a white towel during my sojourn there, and was down on the bypass by midnight among the windblown rubbish cutting letters from the towel with a penknife. When held, a passing motorist could see the name FRANCIE quite clearly.

503

Then, soaked to the skin, I crouched miserably in the shelter of the hedge and waited with my improvised sign. God, I was tired.

The fairground cavalcade came through three hours after midnight. Clapped out, I creaked erect, and held up my sign against the driving rain. The seventh vehicle was Francie's. I was among friends.

'Fairs are creatures of habit,' Francie told me as she drove northward through worsening weather. Husband Dan was driving the big wagon which carried his Wall of Death sideshow. Little Betty was asleep in a specially-made bunk in Francie's vehicle. She handled it with reflex skill, towing her caravan. Unless there was a hold-up along the Great North Road somewhere, they'd be pitching in Penrith in time to catch the early-evening crowds. The fair did the same every year.

'Penrith's always worth two evenings,' she explained. 'We call pitches two-ers, fourers, sixers, according to how many days.' She'd put the heater full on to dry me out. 'I guessed you were in trouble, Lovejoy. Dan was all for seeking that saloon car that tried to run you down when I told him. He was mad at me, not taking its number.'

Not imagination, then. I cheered up. Even a murder risk becomes easier to cope with when you know it's really there. 'Look, sunshine. I can't exactly pay for the ride, but I'm good value. Any ideas how I can fund this excursion?'

She was a full minute replying. 'I'll think of a way, Lovejoy.'

I took a further minute. 'Ta, love,' I said.

That day I slogged harder than I'd ever done. Illusion's my main problem. In fact it's the one main problem for us all, because illusion does us down. It's true: blokes are narked that their bosses turn out to have feet of clay. Birds go sour realizing their lover isn't exactly the handsome film star they'd imagined. Sometimes an illusion becomes an essential part of life; I've told you about Lily loving Patrick. She pretends that his womanlike behaviour is just a passing phase. Illusion. It catches you out.

My own illusion in joining the fairground was multiple wrongth. I'd assumed that a travelling fair is jolly, colourful, gay – wrong. It's a million laughs a minute – mistake. Being with Francie meant free journeying . . . Oh dear. Very wrong.

We hit the pitch mid-afternoon, a big grassy field rimmed by hedges. I was woken by Betty shaking me and saying to come and help. The fair had to be up by seven. After only a cup of tea I slogged with a gorilla called Big Chas and his mate Ern erecting broadwalks and canvases, hauling generators and winching struts and wooden walls. I fetched and carried. Francie wrapped my hands in oily cloths to keep me going. As the fairground took shape I began to peter out so they put me on netting the dodgem cars. God did great making mankind, but He was all thumbs when He came to antique dealers. I felt useless.

By seven o'clock parts of the fairground were in action. Customers were strolling among us. Lights came on as generators throbbed. The sideshows were first off, rifle stands, darts for goldfish, chestnuts, hot dogs, an eastern phantasy show with burning torches and seductively moving bellies, quoits for ringing mystery prizes, the whole gamut. Then children's carousels, opening hopefully to tinny organolium music nine-ish. Dodgems, the caterpillar, the Giant Wheel, and the Great Cavalry Ride (wooden horses) began about eleven.

'By-laws make us close at midnight,' Big Chas rumbled when I scraped enough breath to ask if we ever packed in for slumber. He was grinning at me with poisonous good cheer, the̽ moron. He and Ern were

505

pestilentially happy, singing hymns while we worked. 'Quite a decent crowd, Lovejoy, eh?'

Meek with exhaustion and self-pity, I reeled obediently on, toting dat barge and liftin' dat bale among the fairground's bright pandemonium. Once Betty brought me a bowl of mushy peas when I was half way up a perilous wooden structure trying to bolt some huge planks to something else, God knows what, among a tangle of great wet ropes. The din of these music engines sounds positively melodious from a distance, but you try dangling among their pipes screwing bits together and you're deafened and blinded. That Big Chas and Ern were alongside happily warbling *Sankey's Sacred Songs and Solos* did little to ease my bitterness.

Oddly, you miss hell when it stops. I was spread on a rain-soaked canvas a million miles up in the night sky near Andromeda when silence struck so suddenly I nearly slid off from shock. Blearily I looked around. Our Zoom Star had stopped careering through its demented ellipse. Whole banks of bulbs plunged painfully into dark. Quietness returned to the land. Thank God for by-laws.

'Finish that rope and we're done, Lovejoy,' Ern called up, flashing a krypton lamp and warbling, *'Lead, kindly light, amid th'encircling gloom.'* Bloody maniac.

A few minutes later I clambered down. Betty was standing there, neat and prim under her frilly yellow umbrella. 'It's dinner-time. I came for you, Lovejoy.'

'Shouldn't you be in bed?'

She pulled my hand. I stumbled down the trampled lanes between the booths to Francie's caravan. It seemed full of steam. Dan was wolfing a Matterhorn of spaghetti, his elbows flying. Try as I might, I couldn't quite see how he managed his with that enormous moustache. We said hello. Francie dished up for me, and a littler mound for Betty who prattled all during dinner, telling Dan and Francie how well I'd done.

'Lovejoy's trouble should soon be over, Dan,' Francie said. 'He'll sleep in the wagon.'

'What job'll you do, Lovejoy?' Dan managed between yards of spaghetti. I was narked. Had I been resting?

'I shouldn't put him selling tickets,' Betty said. 'He swears all the time.'

'Shut it, you,' I said coldly.

'Big Chas said he's not much use,' the little pest reported.

'I'm the world's greatest antique dealer,' I informed her.

'You're hiding from the bobbies. Daddy said.'

Dan thought all this was hilarious, the nut, and fell about laughing. 'Do the Wall of Death with me!' Another roll in the aisles. I quite like Dan, ever since he got me that tricycle for Three-Wheel, but you can go off people.

'Stop it all of you,' from Francie.

So, amid Death-Riders and Sky Bursters, I was relegated to collecting pennies rolled down a groove in a wooden peg.

Big Chas and Ern laughed themselves stuporose when they heard I was second string on the roll-a-penny. Dan kept guffawing as he did his bikes. Ashamed, trying to look like a gruff-voiced lumberjack, I helped with the boards on his Wall of Death.

At noon I thought, Sod it, slipped away and phoned Tinker at the White Hart, cascading coins into the greedy slot. Mercifully he'd managed to get only slightly paralytic in the first hour. His cough quivered the receiver. I held it a mile away till his voice recovered.

'Where the hell you been, Lovejoy? Everybody's asking.'

'Who?' I badly wanted to know. That was half the

point of being with this wagon train to Utah or wherever.

'Helen. Margaret. That Customs bloke's bird with
the big tits. Jill, the slag. Three-Wheel Archie. Liz
Sandwell, wouldn't mind stuffin' her. That poofy bleeder's tart Lily.' He means Patrick. 'And yon Scotch bint,
arse and legs.'

'Charmingly put, Tinker.' Very little wheat in all this
chaff. 'What'd Archie want?'

'Dunno. Wouldn't say.' He waxed indignant. 'Interrupted our dominoes down the George, the burke.'

Archie dicing with death there. 'Dutchie back yet?'

'Nar. Don't like his neffie barker, that Dobson.'

'Yeh, yeh.' Tinker's likes and dislikes can get you
down. I thought a minute, the delay costing another
fortune in the coinbox. I heard a gust of renewed
hubbub as the taproom door swung. Voices shouted
hello, one falsetto. That'd be Patrick making his
entrance.

'Tinker. Tell Archie I say to pass the message on.
I'll ring the Spread Eagle after midnight.' I added with
brutal calm, 'And get going or it's no beer money.'

That set him coughing from worry so I hung up.
Leaving the phone, I had an idea. Why not look around
for antiques where I was, treat it like an antiques sweep
through the countryside? That at least might pay my
way and rescue me from the dreaded roll-a-penny.

I walked back to the fairground whistling.

Chapter Seven

I'm one of those whose mind is ablaze in the dawn. It fires again going on for midnight. In between, though, my intellect becomes a rubbishy zero. During the daytime I just walk among mankind for the sake of appearances. It is very necessary, because in our dark East Anglian villages they start sharpening up long oaken stakes if a neighbour seems too nocturnally inclined. This afternoon, however, I was a ball of fire.

Betty ran me an errand, three dozen large sheets of yellow paper and a box of crayons. Between customers I made strikingly inept posters. There were six arguments with folk convinced their coins had rolled to victory; I gave in and paid up, to the derision of the entire fairground. By five o'clock I'd done thirty posters. Francie took over with Betty while I literally ran about the town stapling my posters to telegraph poles and bus shelters. I got so carried away I even paid a baker's shop my last quid to put one in their window. It read:

AT THE FAIRGROUND NOW!!!
CHRISTYS AND SOTHEBIES
JOINT OFFICIAL GENUINE
ANTIQUE ROADSHOW!!!

Expert Free Appraisal of Household Objects,
Paintings, Pottery, Furniture, Jewellery, Other Items!
All Valuations Free
As Seen On TV.

Then underneath, in the neatest painting I could manage:

This Genuine Antique Roadshow is Guaranteed
By The Trade Descriptions Act
By Parliamentary Law.

By six-thirty I was breathlessly noshing Francie's fry-up in her caravan with Dan and Betty. They were curious and asking me what I was up to, which made me maddeningly evasive. Francie got quite irritated.

The posters were quite legal, in that fraudulent way Law permits. Near-skating, I'd carefully misspelled the names of the two great London auction houses. The correct name of the BBC's so-called spontaneous antiques sweep uses the plural: 'Antiques'. Copyright. Make it singular, and it becomes legal. The Trade Descriptions Act simply covers trade, and I'd do the valuations free. At least my own particular roadshow really would be spontaneous, not a put-up job like all the rest. It was basically the old saying about the Mountain and Mahomet. I'd have to move on with the fair, so I wouldn't have time to scout the area for junk. Now, the countryside would bring their junk to me.

And they did.

Funny, but that first night I was really nervous. Francie pressed my trousers and jacket, and gave me one of Dan's least gaudy shirts. A maroon silken scrap poking from my top pocket as an artistic touch. My hair got semi-straightened and painfully I scraped my nails with a borrowed emery. I was neat, an all-time first. Francie bought me some new modern sponge impregnated with shoe-polishing wax to do my shoes. I was delighted, because Cherry Blossom thought that ancient idea up long before the modern fairground was born. Nice to see old friends.

Dan found me a corner in the peas-and-spuds tent,

and Big Chas and Ern erected a section of green canvas. To the sound of roaring generators and in the fug of black peas I set up my borrowed rickety trestle and switched on Francie's Anglepoise lamp. Dan's best cufflinks gleaming at my wrists, my frayed jacket cuffs inturned and my scrubbed face frowning with sincere honesty, I was ready for the world.

Dross, when it comes in a deluge, isn't really dross. It's really something else, like snow. Look at snow one way and it's a nuisance, blocking roads and flooding your socks. Look at it another, and it's brilliant crystals spun into magical mini-webs up there in the heavens. If nobody's looking I always try to catch a snowflake on my tongue, outer space's holy communion . . . Where was I?

In this tent, waiting. A whole hour.

Another hour. Eight o'clock.

And a half. I was tormented by the aroma of black peas but determined not to spoil my grand image of the London expert.

Nine-oh-five, and in she came, an old lady with the inevitable brooch. I drew breath. One thing I've learned in this mad game is that sinning with a smile somehow detoxifies the transgression enough to make people want to join in.

'Come in, love,' I said, with a smile. She was the first of the horde that came between then and the midnight closing.

For a start, they brought jars of buttons and boxes of foreign coins. Every house has a jamjar full. God knows why. They fetched christening clothes and mysteriously ornate lenses. They wheeled in complex wooden garden structures. They carried in rusting machinery too heavy to stand on my table. They brought tiny pieces of jewellery, rings, bits of pendants that made my heart weep for the loneliness of it, opera glasses, stair-rod fittings, scent bottles, glass inkwells, old umbrellas . . . Dross is snowflakes. I was in paradise. Until, that is, Francie took a hand. Women have very decided views on paradise, thinking it bad for morale. In days when I was a terrified believer, women saints never seemed up to much. They didn't deliver the goods.

'Ladies and gentlemen,' Francie announced suddenly, appearing brightly. 'Our resident antiques expert will be having his break now, for twenty minutes only. Until resumption, please avail yourself of the fairground's refreshments at reasonable prices . . . ' The queue groaned.

'Wait, Francie,' I began, but she gripped my arm and said with that steel, 'This way, sir.' I was hauled out. 'My caravan,' she whispered as we left the tent for the light-starred fairground night.

'Look, Francie,' I said, peeved. 'Can't you wait? And hadn't you better check Dan's not around?'

She tutted angrily. 'Not *that*, Lovejoy.'

Abducted by a desirable bird, yet not for rape? Could this be?

There was quite a delegation in the caravan. Dan, Big Chas but for once not singing hymns, Sidoli, Calamity Sadie the black-rooted blonde from the Wild West Show, Big Jon the Eastern Slave Spectacular's eunuch with the bad teeth, and silent sexy lone Joan the Devil Rider who crewed the Ghost Train. And Sidoli's two unshaven henchmen.

I entered, smiling and pleased they'd gone to all this trouble to express their thanks for my efforts. Dan rose, jabbed furiously at me with a finger like a rail.

'What the frigging hell do you think you're frigging playing at, Lovejoy?'

My grin felt like biscuitware. This was no congratulation party. I'd been summoned before the Supreme Soviet.

'Lovejoy the crowd-puller,' I said, narked.

That made him worse. 'Explain, Francie.'

512

'Priced and advised on twenty-eight items,' Francie said.

'Grass,' I accused, quite pleasant.

'Sod the list, Dan,' Sidoli said. He had one of those stiletto-and-alcove accents: Sowed dee leest Dane.

'There was some very collectible stuff,' I defended, narked. 'One bird brought a near-undetectable Sisley copy. And a millefiore glass bowl, 1870. It'll fetch – '

'Fetch!' Dan barked. He was having a hard time not clouting me. He was still in his spangled waistcoat from his death ride, all hair and brawn. 'Fetch? Who for, Lovejoy?'

'For . . . ' Ah. They were worried about the money. 'For the punters,' I admitted.

'Any ideas on making it pay us?' Big Chas asked, and sang a phrase, '*Each other's wants may we supply . . .*'

'Shut that row, Chas,' from Sidoli, obviously first pecker.

I said, 'Is that what's bothering you?'

Sidoli's face darkened. 'Don't bait me, Lovejoy.' Dan came between us, placating but clearly worried. I realized that to the fairground I was his and Francie's responsibility.

Francie spoke up. 'Sid. Lovejoy's quite serious. He doesn't think much to money. It's old things. Antiques.'

They all stared at me as though I'd just dropped from Saturn. Joan's eyes penetrated my anxiety. I'd never seen such grey eyes. Steady, still. Ethereal almost.

'Not care for money?' Sidoli said. 'He crazy? He's making it on the side.' Own eee say-ert, in his exotic syllables.

'Let Lovejoy talk. Please,' Francie pleaded.

'I feel on trial, Francie. What's the charge?'

Francie said, 'If some of the things you valued were so desirable, Lovejoy, say why you didn't buy them.'

There was silence. Then I said, ashamed, 'Because I'm broke, love.'

I'd gone red. Dan looked at Francie, who glared a typical female told-you-so. Sidoli drew breath for more threats, said nothing. Glances exchanged. Despairingly I decided to help.

'There was a silver Taureg ring I could have got for a couple of quid,' I said. It's hard to suppress enthusiasm. I found myself rattling on, smiling at the memory. 'An original Waterman fountain pen, the very first sort – the bloke would have let us have it for a go on the rifles. A pair of silver-and-glass cosmetic powder cylinders, late Victorian. They come in pairs, one for powdering each glove, see? And . . .'

Sidoli raised a hand. 'Shtope, Luffyoy.' Lovejoy stopped.

In the painful silence that ensued we were all thinking, some of us thoughts quite different from the rest. Everybody shuffled, eyes avoiding mine. Except for that level pair belonging to Joan.

'How many items could you've made something on, Lovejoy?' Dan said eventually. The assembled company leaned forward.

'Sooner or later? Ten. Three if you mean at the next reasonable-sized town.' I spend my life being ashamed of myself. It's another of my unpaid full-time jobs.

Sidoli gave a low moan. Calamity Sadie uttered one grievous sob. The rest exhaled despair and gin fumes.

Francie spoke to the row of sombre faces. I swear three of them were in surgical shock. She said quietly, 'I told you he was honest, even if he is stupid. You wouldn't listen.'

'Here,' I began indignantly, but Sidoli's hand lifted to shtope me.

Big Chas had cheered up. '*So we must hymns of welcome sing In strains of holy joy.*'

'Are you sure that's right?' I asked Chas. 'Isn't it: *And we . . . ?*'

514

Big Chas frowned. 'You sure, Lovejoy? It's the *Inst-antis adventum Deum*, isn't it, where – '

'Ask Ern,' I said helpfully. 'It's *Hymns Ancient and Modern.*'

'He's off his frigging head,' Sidoli screamed. 'Right! That does it! Francie, you pick a helper to put up the money and rig a punter system.'

Francie examined the faces. 'Big Chas,' she decided.

'No,' Sidoli ruled. 'Enough hymns in this fair-ground.' Eeen eess foyergron.

'I will,' Joan said quietly. Her first words all that session. Maybe all year.

'Right,' Sidoli said brokenly. He had his face in his hands. 'Now get him out.' Dan jerked his head. I left.

Within half an hour the new system was operating perfectly. By that is meant that the poor public were being robbed blind. Situation normal.

In case you ever take your Sheraton cabinet to one, here are the hallmarks of the Great Antique Roadshow Con Trick:

You are put into a queue and given a number ('to make sure of your place . . . '). The 'expert' values your great-grandad's Crimean War medals, and off you go. Maybe he'll even scribble the valuation on your number. As you leave, you'll be approached by some-body apparently from the public – in the queue, just arriving, just leaving – who will say that his uncle/bro-ther/auntie/grandad just happens to collect medals. And he'll offer you about a quarter of the valuation marked on your number. 'Good heavens,' you cry, recoiling. 'Certainly not! They're worth four times that!' With great reluctance, the chap ups his offer, and finally in considerable distress offers you the sum named by the expert. You'd be a fool to refuse, right? Because the great London expert's just valued them, right? So you sell your grandad's medals and go on your way rejoicing, with the gelt.

And the passer-by takes the medals, grinning all over

his crooked face. Why the grin? Because he's the so-called expert's partner. The 'expert' of course grossly undervalued your medals. To make it worth their while, the average mark-down (i.e. underestimate) must be what crooks call 'thirties'. That is, they'll never pay more than thirty per cent of the current auctionable value, not for anything. Anything higher than that is going dangerously close to a fair market price, you see.

Francie used Betty, in a little coloured stumper's booth, to give out the numbered tickets. She herself scraped the punters, as the saying is, with two young-sters hastily borrowed from the electric generators. Joan, as she'd promised, put up the money, silently fetching the bundle of notes from her caravan in a grocery basket. She gave me her transfixing stare from those opal-grey eyes, and returned to her Devil Riding. I said thank-you, nodded to Betty on her perch and we were off.

Some things ruin pride. I told myself this crookery was all in a good cause, the preservation of Lovejoy Antiques, Inc. That and safely heading north to meet Shona McGunn. But I didn't feel pleased with myself and my progress any more. Like I said not long since, everybody lusts. I only wish we knew what for.

Chapter Eight

I'm not the only fraud in and around antiques. Look at names, for instance.

'Dresden china' is really a descriptive term. The truth is there never was a porcelain factory at Dresden. The famed Royal Saxony porcelain factory started in 1709 was a distance away, at Meissen. The patron was King Augustus the Strong, whose domain took in Poland and Saxony, which is why the so-called 'Dresden' mark is actually his AR Augustus Rex monogram. There's a further truth, too: they weren't up to much at the beginning, mostly copying styles and adopting colours from the more sophisticated Chinese. This is why the early stuff looks eastern – robes on the figures, stiff-looking mandarins and clumsy attendants. Artistically they're dud, not a patch on the later stuff. But it goes big among collectors and dealers because it's rare. The modern dementia for rarity's a pathetic revelation of how little we know. I mean, this pen's rare because I made it myself from hawthorn, not another like it in the world, but it's still not worth a bent groat. Cynics say 'Dresden china firstly copied Chinese, secondly Venetian, and after that anybody,' but it's harsh criticism because once Joachim Kändler arrived about 1730 they really took off. His figures are lively original objects you never tire of: pretty ladies in fardingales and yellow-lined cloaks, hussars, dancers.

The night we left Penrith I sat mesmerized long after the fairground closed and the folk had all gone. I'd bought a broken porcelain figure of a Harlequin. He was seated on a white stump in his chequered costume

517

and grinning mask. Black cap in one hand, the other to hold what had once been a jug, now broken off and lost. A junk bloke had lugged in a great wooden box of assorted porcelains and slammed it on the table.

'Fifty quid the lot, mister,' he said. 'Good and bad.'

'For a flyer, yes.'

Without looking, I'd humped the box to the floor, got Francie to pay him. My chest was clamouring like Easter Sunday. Something pure and thrillingly antique lurked down among the clag. It was the Harlequin, when I looked. Harlequins are the most vigorous of Kändler's porcelains, these and dancing ladies and waist-coated gentlemen. They were often in pairs, but one swallow does make a summer.

'The show's pulling up, Lovejoy.' Carol and Mike ran the peas-and-mash booth, a noisy homely couple with their six spherical children. Carol had an idea it might advertise her grub if the antiques expert was seen dining off her elegant edibles. 'There's a bowl and a brew-up for you.'

'Oh. Right. Ta.'

As the crews fell on the fairground and began dismantling it, I had the pasty and peas while evaluating the haul. A piteously worn slender wedding-ring with the thick broad gold band that Victorians called the Keeper Ring, to be worn distal to the wedding-ring and prevent its loss. There was an old love-letter some young woman had told me was her granny's, and that she needed money for her baby . . . Her boyfriend, a flashy nerk with gold teeth and a giant motorbike, had waited outside. I'd paid up without a second thought.

'Lovejoy.' Francie was there, with Joan. And Sidoli, and his two stalwart lads off the electric generators. They still hadn't shaved. 'Sid wants to know what the take is.'

'Take?' I said blankly. 'You mean gelt? Nowt.'

'No money?' Sidoli's lads seethed, leaned in.

'Let him tell you, Sid,' Francie said. 'I've seen Lovejoy work before.'

'What you pay for this?' Sidoli hinted to the letter.

I shrugged. 'Fiver. Can't remember.'

Sidoli paled. 'Can't even remember?'

'He's been had,' the slinkiest lad said. He held a length of metal rod. 'It was a bird, crying poverty. She was dressed to the nines. With a bike bloke in leather. Stank of booze, both of them. She told Lovejoy the tale. He paid her, not a word. They went off laughing.'

'You're a trusting sod, Mr Sidoli.' I'm not keen on sarcasm, but it has its uses. This time it stopped him signalling his two nephews to annihilate me. 'No need to read the letter. Just glance. It's in two alphabets. Called "messenger writing" – a letter within a letter. Sort of secret code. The young couple who brought it had made the story up, granny's love-letter and all that. Messenger writing of that style was popular during the Great Civil War – sieges, politics, family conflicts, elopements, heaven-knows-what. The subject will determine the price. But 1642, or I'm not me.'

'How much about?' Sidoli asked.

'Twenty quid, maybe more.'

'The percentage'll reduce the loss, Sid,' Francie encouraged.

'Sooner or later,' Sidoli moaned. 'That's what this idiot said. His very words.' His voice rose to a scream. 'The loss is *tonight*! It rains two days people stay home and don't come to the fair! And he's got a box of old pots.'

'Francie told me about your loss rate,' I said, rising and stretching. 'You can forget it this pitch.' That stilled the galaxy. 'One of those "old pots" will cover you this stop.'

'Jesus,' Sidoli gasped. 'Is true?' Eeass threw?

'Yes, Sid,' Francie said. 'Lovejoy'll be right.'

Joan spoke. 'Profit or not, it's my stake, Sid,' she announced quietly. 'I have the say. Give him a week.'

Sidoli was staring into the box with awe. 'One of these is worth . . . ? Which?'

Big Chas came and shouted, 'Hey. Nobody striking the show or are you going to stand gossiping all night?' And he sang, '*Through the night of doubt and sorrow, Onward goes the pilgrim band*. . . .'

'Coming,' I said, peering out at the rain past him. I felt all in, drew breath and stepped out to join the gang, leaving Sidoli to stew in his own explanations.

We finished bottling up, as they call it, about five in the morning. I spelled Dan and Francie alternately, one hour in three off for a juddery slumber in Francie's wagon. Ern normally spelled Dan but this stop he and Big Chas were among the rear gang who would clear the generators and heavy machinery and haul on after us by eleven.

Our next pitch was near one of the Lancashire mill towns. I was relieved as we bowled in, because it meant grub and a kip before the rearguard arrived and we'd have to start erecting the fair all over again. After Francie's fry-up I went straight out and did my poster stint.

When I returned, the cauliflower sky mercifully clearing into a geographical blue, the camp was still. Everybody was kipping. I made my way over the heath to the wagon hoping my blanket hadn't got damp during the journey, when somebody called my name quietly. Joan was sitting on her caravan steps.

'Coffee, Lovejoy?'

I hesitated. 'Well, ta, but I was hoping to sleep my head.'

Joan's grey stare did not waver. There's room for that.' She rose and opened her door.

'Well, actually, Joan,' I began, but she'd already gone inside, so there was nothing else for it. It's churlish to refuse an offer that's kindly meant, isn't it? My old Gran used to say that. 'Well, if you're sure . . . '

No answer again, so I stepped inside saying, 'Just a cup, then.'

All that month we zigzagged up the country, moving from industrial towns to moorland markets. It was a slog. One heaven-sent pitch was six whole days long, the rest only three or four. The distances were less tiring than striking and pitching, because once you're on the road that's it.

As fairs go, I learned, we were quite a respectable size. Some deal which Sidoli had pulled off meant we stuck to the eastern slice of the country except for parts of Lancashire and bits of the north. I did well and started sending stuff down to auction houses in the south. Of course I used the long-distance night hauliers in the road caffs, mentioning Antioch's name. Some items I sold locally practically the next day, sometimes in the same town. One I sold to a town museum. It was only a dented lid off an enamel needlecase, but the curators went mad when they saw it: a Louis XVI piece showing a sacrificing nymph. They immediately identified it as Degault from its *en grisaille* appearance (just think grey). It had chimed at me from inside a leather-covered snuff-box – some Victorian goon had ruined a valuable antique needlecase to make a dud. I ask you. God knows what they'd done with the case's body, but there's a fortune going begging near Preston if anybody's interested.

By the third stop, tenth day or so, the profit was trickling in. Antique dealers live in a kind of monetary para-world, always owing or being owed by others. It became nothing unusual for a dealer to wander in, ask around for me, and then shell out a bundle of notes in payment for some item a colleague had received in the south a couple of nights earlier. Often they'd take away one of my items just purchased from the never-ending queue of punters. I always took a quick sale, following the old maxim. First profit's best, so go for it.

Halfway through the month the income became a stream, and Sidoli offered me a regular pitch. And more. His percentage was the standard fee from stall-holders plus a tenth of the take. For this he did book-ings, the pitches, argued shut-out arrangements with other fairmasters, dealt with the local councils and hotly denied liability when people blamed us for any-thing. Or, indeed, everything. He brought three old silent geezers in dark crumpled suits who only tippled the wine and listened, and his two menacing nephews.

We talked all one long cold night in Joan's caravan, them smoking cigars in my face and poisoning me with cheap red wine. His two nephews bent metal pipes in the background, nodding encouragingly. But I declined. I had a job on, I explained. This made every-body frown, which terrified me into useful lies.

'It's a matter of honour, you see.'

'Ah,' said Sidoli, interested. 'You kill someone, no?'

'No,' I explained. 'I've certain obligations . . .'

'Ah.' He beamed at this and to my alarm signalled for another bottle. He was desperately inquisitive but I tried to seem noble and up-tight and he went all understanding. 'But after you have shot this pig and all his brothers, and his father – assuming he had one . . . ?' The nephews chuckled, light-heartedly bent more pipes.

'After,' I promised, 'it'll be different.'

'Excellent!' He poured more wine. 'Lovejoy, I have heard of your police record. Very formidable.'

'Er, that's all lies.'

'*Certo*,' Sidoli agreed politely. 'Police. The Law. Judges. All are complete liars. Now.' He leaned for-ward. It was the Joseph Wright lamplit scene straight out of the Tate Gallery. 'My fair will pitch the Edin-burgh Festival.'

I looked at him blankly. 'Are we allowed?' Francie'd told me the arrangement: our fair stopped short and our rival Bissolotti did the Festival.

'Ah,' Sidoli said, doing that slow shrugging chair-bound wriggle Mediterranean folk manage to perfection. 'Well, yes. I did promise. But, Lovejoy, it's a question of money.'

This sounded like more bad news. 'Er, Mr Sidoli. Won't the other mob be, er, furious?'

He spread his hands in pious expiation. 'Is it my fault if Bissolotti lacks Christian charity?'

'No,' his nephews said. In the pause the three mute mourners shook their heads. We were absolved.

'Er, well, no,' I concurred obediently. 'But – '

'No buts, Lovejoy.' He patted my hand. 'I misjudged you. I thought you a man of no honesty, a man only interested in those pots. Woman's things. Now,' he smiled proudly, 'I hear you are a multiple killer, who fooled even Scotland Yard. You slew a lorry-driver. With your own hands in an ocean you drown an enemy. It is an honour to have so great a murderer, when we fight Bissolotti. His people are animals.'

Some lunatic scientist once proved that headaches are actually useful. He should share mine.

'Eliminate Bissolotti,' a nephew prophesied.

'More wine, Lovejoy?' Sidoli invited. 'I say nothing about you in Joan's caravan.' He smiled fondly. 'And call me Sid.' Cow-all meey Seed.

'Thanks, Seed,' I said. Out of the frigging frying-pan into Armageddon. Headache time.

Chapter Nine

Better explain Sidoli's crack about Joan before going on.

Joan was the most reserved bird I've ever met. Even for a sensitive bloke like me she was a puzzle: thirty-two or so, smallish, hair permanently fading from mousey, face unremarkable in daylight and eyes that lovely grey. She'd be what other women call plain, except the first night I saw her by candlelight, and then I knew. Her beauty hit me like a physical blow.

We'd pitched that night after Joan gave me tea and a lie-down, me working with Big Chas and Ern. Joan had asked if I wanted to use one of the spare bunks in her caravan. I checked with Francie, who said it'd be fine. Betty asked if Joan would be my mummy now. Dan fell about and slapped his thighs. After the midnight dowsing I went over to Joan's caravan and knocked. She called me to come in.

For her devil-riding on the Ghost Train she wears a crash helmet with horns and a bone-and-spangle costume, bat wings and a forked tail. Sparks shoot from her head and her suit belches coloured smoke and radiates a green fluorescence. Because of this she always has her hair in a tight bun and flattened on her head. It was the only way I'd seen her.

The caravan was in darkness, except for slits of wavering yellow light showing from behind a cross curtain. Hesitantly I called, 'Joan?' and she said to come through. Making plenty of noise in case – she might after all be shacking up with Big Chas or somebody – I coughed and pulled the curtain slowly aside. The sight caught at my breath. Her face was looking obliquely back at me from the dressing mirror. A single white candle in an old pewter candlestick, the only illumination, stood to one side. Her hair, enormously long, hung down her back to her narrow waist. It was now a lustrous brown, even russet. Her skin was smooth, her lashes long and dark. She wore an old lace nightdress – some would have said wrong by reason of its age, but not me. In the mirror's frame she was a living Gainsborough.

'Sorry about the light,' she said.

'Eh?' I thought: it spoke.

'My father was strong on the right light for make-up,' she said calmly, doing something to her face with folded tissues from a jar.

'You're beautiful,' I heard myself say, to my alarm.

Her so-grey gaze returned to the mirror for a quizzical second, then she nodded slightly. 'If the beholder says so, Lovejoy.'

That was the start of what Sidoli meant. From then on I, well, lived in Joan's caravan. Francie still scraped the queue from my Christys and Sothebies Great Official Genuine Antique Roadshow, and Joan still banked it. But henceforth Joan also banked me as well. I owned up to little Betty that, yes, Joan and me were family.

The night before we hit Edinburgh was the week working up to the Festival. The city was already bubbling, teeming with actors spilling over into street theatre. We pitched a mile or so south of the centre. All the world and his wife had turned up. Bands, orchestras, dancers, artists, poets, jugglers, the lot. You had to have your wits about you or you found yourself frantically hip-hopping among bedecked morris teams. Sidoli was beside himself with glee. 'Bissolotti is late!' he exulted, frantically exhorting us to greater speed as we threw the fair into one glittering noisy mass.

By now Sidoli's advance agent – a near-legendary figure called Romeo who got ballocked every time our cavalcade rested long enough for Sidoli to reach a telephone – had learned of my Roadshow, and was papering the towns for me two days before we hove in. This made life much easier.

Tinker did his part of the antiques scam, fixing sales, and organizing transport through Antioch. He was getting a regular screw through money drafts – essential, because he can't even remember his name when he sobers up. Get him sloshed and instantly he's the Memory Man. It was my plan to jump ship at Edinburgh, preferably before Bissolotti's 'animals' cruised in and wanted their rightful share of the Festival crowds. Also, Maslow would be very, very cross indeed if I blackened his district's reputation up here among the dour Provosts of jolly old Edinburgh. Sidoli had as good as admitted that he himself would take any blame, but from vast experience I knew only too well who'd carry the can.

So my plan was to do a moonlight as soon as I'd done one night's pitch, then head off north to net Shona McGunn. In any case, this was as far north as the fair would travel. For me it had outlived its usefulness.

I found a phone in a pub near the little green and reached Tinker contentedly imbibing his daily swill in the White Hart. He sounded mournful.

'Lovejoy? Here, where the bleedin' 'ell are you?'

'Mind your own business.' I was a bit sharp with him. The White Hart's never without a mob of dealers. All along I'd been ultra careful, not wanting neffie people following me with unkindness in their hearts. I wanted no baddies lurking to catch me when I leapt from the fairground. 'Ready? Here's the list of stuff I'm sending during the night. Most to Brum and London; a few bits and pieces to you.'

'Yeh, Lovejoy, but – '

'Shut it and listen.' Patiently I read him my list, adding which dealers to try and minimum prices to accept. 'Right?'

'No, Lovejoy.' The old burke sounded really down. 'It's Three-Wheel. Remember?'

For a second I had to rack my brains. Of course. I'd told Tinker to phone me Archie's message. It seemed so long ago. Days, weeks even. I felt a hand close on my chest.

'They did his motor, Lovejoy.'

'Oh, Jesus.'

'Smashed it to smithereens. Windows, bodywork, set fire to the inside. Some boat geezer down the estuary saw the smoke and wirelessed the fire brigade.' Long pause, me mechanically feeding the slot coins. 'Lovejoy?'

'How's Archie?'

'Knocked down on his trike hurrying home. He wuz at the auction when they brung the news. But he's only a little bleeder. He rolled clear, scooted through the hedge. Says he saw nothing. Not bad hurt.'

'Did the Old Bill have any luck?'

He snorted. 'Them idle sods. Archie's trike's a write-off, Lovejoy. Sorry, like. Archie says now he never had any message for you at all.'

'Any chance of finding out what his news was?'

'You think I'm not trying?' He was very aggrieved. 'You're a grumpy swine, Lovejoy. I'm sweating my balls off while you're . . .'

We slang-matched abuse for another costly minute before going over the payment – part into Sidoli's num- bered account, part into Joan's with my commission. I told him to pass the word to Jo somehow that I'd be trying to reach her during the early hours.

'She won't talk with you, Lovejoy,' he was warning me as I rang off. I'd had enough of people explaining why everybody else was even more narked than me. I felt it was time I began to be justifiably narked instead, and decided to work out a scheme.

My scheme was temporarily interrupted by World War III. The Bissolotti convoys arrived that night.

Joan's Ghost Train wasn't due to open until the following noon, as was usual with the bigger rides. They drank too much electricity, needed extravagant cabling up. And Joan, being nominally without a feller, so to speak, depended on the main fairground: she paid her percentage to the fairmaster and received help with striking and pitching from Sidoli's mob, hefty blokes. All except Big Chas, and Ern, his toothy walnut-faced mate, seemed to be Sidoli's nephews, and dined at Mrs Sidoli's tent.

After fixing the antiques shipments with Tinker I went to Joan's caravan. She had some stew thing frying or whatever it does. She was a good cook. Once, some days previously, I'd asked her what was worrying her. She'd smiled beatifically and said seriously, 'Would you hate lentil soup?' which made me realize you can be somebody's lover for a million years and never really know her.

'Wotcher, love,' I said, coming in. 'Sid's ordered no break tonight. We're to open at eight in the morning.'

'Big Chas and Ern will be on the Caterpillar in an hour, Lovejoy.'

'Eh? That's back to front.' We normally got the Little Giant Wheel and the generators centred first after the sideshows.

'Sid's ordered.' She placed an aromatic dish for me and sat watching as I made to dine. I waited a bit. She was alongside me, elbows on the table, grey eyes and soft skin shining in the candlelight, like the first time I'd . . .

'Here, love. Are you not having any?'

'Not yet.' She sprinkled pepper on my grub,

watching me nosh. This was typical Joan, guessing condiments for you.

'And you're not in your working clothes,' I observed, mouth full. 'You seem . . .'

'Ready for bed,' she completed. She was smiling but not in a way I liked.

'What's up, chuck?' I said.

She gave that curt nod at my hands. It was a gesture I recognized and had come to love. It meant: Carry on, my reply will be along in a minute. Obediently I did, but sussing out the caravan. Joan's home. It was her place. Where the outside wheels had stopped for the night didn't matter. Inside, the candlelight, the soft furnishings, the old photos of her parents who'd started the Ghost Train, the romance books she read in quiet times . . . I stilled, waited. This feeling is one I mistrust. In antiques there are enough terrible risks without heartache.

'You're leaving tonight, Lovejoy, aren't you?'

How women do it beats me. I'd not said a word. 'Maybe, love. I've a job on.'

That abrupt nod. 'On the door mantel,' she said quietly. 'I've guessed how much you're due. Not wanting to ask Francie direct.'

There was an envelope on the shelf over the speer. 'Look, Joan, love,' I tried uncomfortably, but she shushed me with her other characteristic gesture, a tiny handshake with a blink.

'Don't, Lovejoy.' Her eyes climbed from the table to mine. 'I've no illusions. Life is a lone business, isn't it. Nobody's permanent. We're like places.'

Places? 'Will you tell Sidoli?' That'd stop my flight for certain.

'There's no way of keeping a . . . partner if he's going anyway. Even the best affair is only half a film. You get the movie up to the interval.'

I could have clouted her for making me feel bad. Women always blame me. Why should I be the one who ends up with this rotten bloody sense of being ashamed? She put her hand on mind gingerly.

'Don't feel like that, darling. It's nobody's fault.'

I pulled my hand away. 'I wasn't feeling like anything,' I said bluntly. 'Silly cow.'

She smiled properly then. Her eyes were wet. 'No, Lovejoy. Of course not.' She rose, took my hand, pulled me to the curtained alcove.

'Look, love,' I said weakly. 'There won't be time . . .'

She slipped a breast into my hand, then slowly raised her arms to shed her gown. 'Yes there is, Lovejoy,' she said quietly. 'It's tomorrow there won't be time.'

Past one o'clock on a cold frosty morning, fed, loved, and enriched in material ways, I left Joan's caravan and started work with Big Chas and Ern hauling the cables for the generators.

'You're late, Lovejoy,' Ern said, grinning. We worked by paraffin lamps until the electric's set. 'I worried you'd miss the scrap.'

'Scrap?' I ragged up my hands, took hold of the cable.

Big Chas sang piously astride the generator, '*Mighty are your enemies, Hard the battle ye must fight.*'

Over the other side of the green strange wagons were pulling in. Even the vehicles looked sullen, hateful, as their engines revved and their headlights swathed us.

'Bissolotti?' I croaked nervously, thinking: Hell fire. The new convoy was forming a crescent. The green was on a slope, and we were below them. Even as I paused to look, another set of headlights rummaged the darkness to our right. 'Hell, there's a lot of them.'

'Big mob, Bissolotti's,' Chas agreed cheerfully. 'What weapons do you usually use in a rumble, Lovejoy?'

My legs, mainly, I thought shakily. Or a Jaguar. I'm not proud.

530

'I heard he's a gun man,' Ern said.

Those lunatics were actually pleased at the notion of an all-out battle with Bissolotti's. I felt sick. This wasn't my scene. A peaceful fairground, yes. But a military column tearing to a private El Alamein, a thousand times no. Soon I'd go for say a pee, and vanish.

For about an hour we worked on. Every few minutes I sussed out the growing arc of lights about the green. Bissolotti's wagons began to pitch. We were only a hundred yards apart.

'They're pitching,' I said apprehensively to Ern.

'Aye, Lovejoy,' he called laconically.

'Will we share the pitch?' I was hopeful.

Big Chas roared with laughter from somewhere under the Caterpillar's railed wheels. 'Lovejoy's worried there'll be no rumble,' the idiot bellowed.

'Don't worry, Lovejoy,' Ern said consolingly and carolled, '*Ye that are men now serve him, Against unnumbered foes . . .*' Big Chas joined in the hymn. I worked on, sane in a world of lunatics.

They hadn't finished that particular hymn when negotiations began between the two fairmasters. Bissolotti with ten blokes met Sidoli near where we worked. Our fairmaster also had ten nephews. They stood in two cagey crescents, the bosses talking vehemently for quite a time before our lot returned, chatting animatedly.

'Ready, Lovejoy?' Sidoli called. Ray-dee, Luff-yoyee? He'd caught a glimpse of me on the Caterpillar bolting the hub's canopy roof. 'You get your wish!'

'Great,' I called back. That one wobbly word took three swallows.

'Come on, then,' Big Chas said. '*Fight the good fight.*'

Men were gathering into small groups from our wagons. The pitch was falling silent as the hammering and clattering ceased. Our people were talking. Groups formed. Tactics were being discussed. It was eerily

531

happy, and here was I frightened out of my skin. Madness. Sidoli was among a cluster of paraffin lanterns lecturing strategy. Heads nodded. Some maniac was dishing out steel rods. I thought: For God's *sake*.

'Just finish this, Chas.'

'Won't let a scrap interrupt work, eh?'

He and Ern left to join the nearest group, laughing and shaking their heads. 'He's a cool bugger,' Ern said admiringly.

'Good night, lads,' I muttered. I checked the scene once more, then slid off the wood on the dark side, nearest the enemy camp. 'And good luck with the war.'

Across the damp grass the Bissolotti mob's lanterns were wavering as their men assembled. Behind, our own lamps showed where clusters of blokes were being positioned. I crouched indecisively near a pile of wooden façades from the Caterpillar. What were the rules for a rumble? From what little I'd learned, fairs were pretty orderly along timehonoured lines. Maybe they were as set in their ways when it came to all-out warfare. Apprehensively I darted a few yards towards the Bissolotti vehicles, then hesitated. Surely the thing was to avoid both gangs, never mind the wagons?

Our own pitch was a circular lay-out on the green's down slope. Ahead and above stood the Bissolotti crescent, all flickering lamps and din. A wall, terraced houses and some sort of iron railing formed the perimeter where streets began. There were three exits for vehicles, but for an enterprising slum-trained coward spiked railings were hardly an obstacle.

Suddenly the lights in the Bissolotti camp vanished.

In ours, there arose a subdued murmur, then somebody called a nervous order and the glims dowsed here and there until Sidoli's pitch was black. I heard Sidoli yell. A hubble of voices responded, one panicky shout stilled by a threat. We'd been caught napping. Only a sort of air-pallor from the nearby street let you see a damned thing. I went clammy, cursing myself for not having escaped sooner. If it hadn't been for Joan's loving farewell I'd be miles away by now. Bloody women. No wonder I'm always in a mess.

Somebody shouted, 'Fan out, lads,' and somebody else shouted, 'No. Two lots. Over there . . . ' Then a third, 'Bunch up. Get in line . . . ' So much for Sidoli's confidence. His men were a shambles. I began to move instinctively to my right. I'd once been in a real army and recognized only too well the authentic hallmarks of disorder. Time Lovejoy was gone.

I froze in mid-slink. Nearby there was a steady touch of movement. The night air somehow pressed on my face. A hoary old sergeant – a survivor – once told me, 'Never effing mind what you frigging see,' he'd said. 'Survivors *feel*.' So I felt, lay down with my head towards the Bissolotti camp, and stayed still.

A line of men crept past and over me. One boot squelched an inch from my hand. I swear it. The guilty thought came that a true friend would behave like a Roman goose and cackle the alarm. Not me. As soon as the silent line of assaulters had passed I rose and moved tangentially right. No more than forty slunk paces and I came against a giant wagon. I felt my way along its flank. My heart was throbbing. I'd not breathed for a week.

The wagon's side seemed to go on forever and I cursed Sidoli for a lying swine. He'd represented Bissolotti's as a small vulgar outfit. If they could afford massive new transformer-generators like this supersize it was no cardboard cut-out job. And the chug of new Bissolotti arrivals in the next street showed that enemy reinforcements were at hand.

Smoke. Cigarette smoke. And nearby. Somebody was probably cupping the fag into his palm the way convicts and soldiers do. I'd nearly eeled into them in my fright. I edged beneath the enormous generator wagon and crawled out under the other side. Even then I nearly brained myself by standing up. My shoulder caught on the cab's open door.

'How much longer?' a man's voice muttered.

'Five minutes. Then we shout the rest up.'

Hell fire, I thought. There must have been thirty or so in that assault line. Plus those vehicles I'd heard nearby. Sidoli's fair – not to mention me – was caught between two aggressive mobs. A classic pincer movement. I almost moaned in terror. As soon as the rumble started Bissolotti's would switch on every light they possessed. I'd be spotlighted like a prisoner against a wall. That explained the Bissolotti tactic, of lining his wagons facing down the slope towards our pitch.

This wasn't for me. I lay down and wriggled under the vehicle's vast bulk. The next wagon was smaller, probably a slab carrier, to transport the wooden façades. I heard two more men muttering by the tailboards, found the driver's cab of the slabber, and lifted myself up. Somebody said, 'What's that?' as I slipped the gear lever into neutral and the handbrake off. I dropped and crept behind my transformer wagon's quadrupled rear wheels and wormed towards the front. The slab lorry creaked. Its bulk drifted past.

'Christ. It's moving.' Somebody ran past, grunting with exertion as he tried to swing into the cab. A man shouted for a torch. Two men cursed. 'Over here! Over here!'

I was up and into the transformer's cabin. A flashlight jumped the gloom. The slab lorry was trundling slowly down the slope, three blokes clinging to its sides and one man already in the cab struggling with the wheel.

Headlights sprang. The green showed brilliantly. I snicked my wagon's gear and the handbrake, then saw there were no bloody keys. As my vast wagon began to glide down the slope I fumbled desperately with the dashboard, failed to find the wires, crouched and fiddled. The sodding vehicle went faster. I fiddled faster. Somebody yelled. Boots clashed on the door. I dived, clobbered a bloke's face and he fell off. Something clanged on the truck. Glass shattered. Men were yelling, running, throwing. I finally shorted the wires with my teeth as the giant vehicle juddered and careered down the slope. The engine boomed. I struggled up, cast the headlights and gave an appalled moan.

It was like a battlefield. The slab carrier had caught some of Bissolotti's assault men on the green. Two lay strewn. A third was pinned against the Caterpillar's gearing where the lorry's front had nuzzled itself to rest. Blokes were tearing about here, there, everywhere. I gunned the engine. Two strange faces appeared, one on the windscreen, I yelled at him in terror, drove crazily to shake him off. They vanished. I jolted round the field, slammed back through the Bissolotti convoy and glimpsed a street lamp in the distance.

Putting the big wagon at the narrow street took courage, or terror. I remember bawling in panic as the wagon thundered through and out into a brightly peaceful main road. A line of waiting fairground lorries to my right, so swing left to traffic lights, green so on through, to anywhere. Behind was death in that ludicrous war zone.

It's hard suddenly pretending everything is normal, but I did my best, stuck up in that tall cab and trying to look like I knew what I was driving, where I was going. It was an interminable cruise in a puzzled Edinburgh, until I found a road that finally promised north by following the arrows. I was forty miles away before I stopped shaking.

Telling myself I'd done it, I relaxed and let the road decide what happened next, meekly following the headlights to my fate.

Quiet old life, antiques.

Chapter Ten

Before I invented sex, when the world was flat and weather constant, I had all sorts of ideas. Cycling round the entire country in a record-breaking week; going for gold in mountaineering; discovering uncharted continents; rescuing damosels. A lad does a lot of this daft imagining, never grows out of his dreams. Girls do, but don't ever realize that the male is often miles away in his silly head being anointed king of a lost tribe in the Andes or whatnot. Women never learn to see blokes as we actually are, namely incurable dream-spinning romantics, because early in what passes for development women trade perception for appearances. The bird learns that her bloke could only go for Olympic Gold in flower-arranging. She starts assuming he's only what he seems – a portly geezer wheezing when tying his shoe. The point I'm making is that people aren't merely things. Never mind what politicians say. You can gaze at stones and tarmac, rivers and fence-posts, with complete dispassion if you want. They're no big deal. But you have to *think* when you look at people. You have to. If you don't, you become a robot.

One of my old dreams was knowing every town in the Kingdom, so that if some stranger mentioned a tiny village in, say, the Shetlands, I would casually say, 'Ah, yes. Population eighty-one. Stands on the tributary of . . . ' I failed geography at school. Dubneath was therefore a mystery.

The big transformer wagon's petrol ran dangerously low in Clackmannon, though when I got out and inspected its container drums they showed half full.

Perhaps you had to switch to reserve? Anyhow I decided to ditch it, before daylight revealed me in all my glory as the non-secret thief of the known world's largest fairground transformer-generator. I entered Fife, and drove across Kinross in a stealthy manner in the least inconspicuous of vehicles, with BISSOLOTTI THE FAIRGROUND FOR THE WORLD gaudy on its side. I started admiring myself. After all, it takes skill to nick a thing this big.

Ten miles outside Perth my brain had another megarhythm. Mentally shelving a niggling reminder that my previous brainwave had nearly got me killed in a night riot, I knew I'd now got a winner. Find a reasonably-sized transport caff, park my giant wagon, and get a lift into Perth where trains and buses lived, and zoom to find the enigmatic Shona McGunn. No road map in my nicked wagon, of course. Typical.

By dawn I was noshing among the hunched leather shoulders of the night hauliers in a caff near Perth, rather sad at thoughts of leaving my monster.

A walk of three miles along the road when the lorry convoy had departed, and I became a poor motorist whose car had broken down. A kindly motorist gave me a lift to the Perth turn-off, and I got a bus into that lovely city just as the shops opened.

Pausing only to sell a Hudson's Bay Co. folding rusty penknife pistol that I'd kept back from Francie – flat horn sides, percussion, two blades – for a giveaway price which still rankles (these 1860–70 collectibles go for twice the average weekly wage nowadays), I phoned the police, anonymously reporting that a Sidoli wagon was ditched in the night caff. Then I got on the train and dozed. I'd got a cold pasty and some rotten crumbly cake I couldn't control. They fetch tea down the corridor just as you're on your last legs, so I eventually made it, though weakening fast.

Painful thoughts of Three-Wheel came to me while I nodded on the journey. And Joan's grey eyes and long-term philosophy – maybe she was the one bird whose perception had made it? And Jo. And Tinker would be bewildered, with a score of deals waving uncompleted in the breeze. And poor dead Tipper Noone under the coroner's hammer. And yon driver, poor bloke. Naturally, a twinge of fear came with the haze. I'd started the journey north towards Caithness with a whole fairground full of tough allies, and ended it with two fairs bulging with enemies: Sidoli's for leaving them in the lurch, and Bissolotti's for, er, borrowing their vehicle.

Not much of a social record, you might say. But I felt that all in all I was entitled to pride. So far I'd reached Sutherland. I was in one piece, and being alive is always a plus. I had money in my pocket, and was heading for a mine of antiques, those precious wonderments whose very existence is proof of something more than the brute Man. And good old Shona knew where they were.

The last part of the journey was by bus. Our little local trains have been abolished in the interest of greater efficiency, so now nobody can get anywhere except by public yak. Dubneath's version of the yak was a bus carrying smiley basket-toting women and distant-eyed men. Before we bowled into minuscule Dubneath I'd revealed all, grilled by the clever interrogation of a pally little rotund lady. I confided that I was a visiting writer. Not going anywhere in particular, just travelling. And I might look up some possible ancestors . . . Oh, my own name, yes. That's what I wrote my poetry under. What name would that be? 'Oh, sorry, love,' I said absently. 'McGunn's the name. Ian McGunn.' Cunning, no?

It was the last bus that day. I was put down in Dubneath. The sea was there in the late evening. It earned a word of praise from me, which pleased my companion, though the little town was poorly lit and somnolent. Bonny place in full day, I supposed. My plump pal was going on to Lybster further up the coast, but she said there was an inn in Dubneath. 'Where,' she added darkly, 'folk drink.' We both agreed, tut-tut, sin gets everywhere these days. She'd told me that McGunn was not an uncommon name hereabouts. I said fancy that, and waved the bus off into the night.

The tavern, replete with drinkers, instantly recognized me as a fellow sinner and agreed to put me up. I'd bought a cheap cardboardy case in Perth, plus a skimp of clean clothes, so I could portray respectability. I was so thrilled at myself I offered to pay in advance. A huge meal, and I tottered exhausted to bed in a long narrow room.

Came daylight, I saw that it was Sunday. In that part of the world they go big on the Sabbath. Nothing happens. By that I mean nil. Even the bloody seagulls didn't seem to fly, except a couple of backsliders that revelled unrepentantly in the clear air squawking their silly heads off. I walked down the quay, examined the sea. Yep, still there, all the way out to the skyline. Back to the tavern, two streets from the edge of the known world.

The surrounding countryside was uncomfortably close. As long as it stayed loomingly over there and didn't ride into town to take over I'd be happy. The shops were closed. The harbour boats looked at prayer. A few people emerged blinking into daylight, hurried away bowed as if under curfew.

I walked down the quay, Dubneath's vortex. Two old geezers were there, eyeing the sky. A lone kid fished off a wall. I bade the blokes good morning; they said good morning. A riot. I sat on the harbour wall. Got off after a minute, and walked the streets of the metropolis.

And back.

About eleven a saloon car of baffled tourists –

French registration – whined miserably through. It was all happening today in Dubneath.

High noon, and a man strode out with a spyglass, notebook, knees showing above elasticated socks. God, I was overjoyed to see him. We spoke. He was disappointed that I wasn't a bird watcher. I was disappointed that he was. We parted, him off into the countryside, smiling in happy anticipation. You get these nutters in East Anglia too.

The tavern creaked awake. By that I mean they served up at dinner-time, after which Dubneath plunged back into the twilight zone. Of interest: a few badges glass-framed in the taproom, wartime memories now worth enough to redecorate the downstairs rooms; a brass racehorse doorstep of Crowley & Co, Manchester, about 1860 – go for these if you're wanting cheap Victoriana with class – and by the bar mirrors a trio of little matchstrikers. Go for these too: many pubs have them left over from times when every smoker used unboxed matches. You can get them for a song because pubs hardly change, and people have forgotten what they're for. The most desirable are German porcelain figurines by Conte and Boehme. A good one, with a humorous inscription, will keep you in luxury for a week. Three should pay for a modest Continental holiday.

'You know about those?' I couldn't help explaining their value to the taverner, a husky bloke called George MacNeish.

'Is that a fact,' he said.

'They're highly sought-after, you see.'

'Aye, but I like the wee things.'

My heart warmed to him. I'm always pleased to hear this. I offered him a drink, but no. The Sabbath.

A few hours later as I was strolling somewhere, or back, merely waiting for the world to reopen, George called me from the inn steps.

'There's a body to meet you, Ian.' He waved towards

the quay. I felt pleased. A kindness shown, a kindness sown. Swiftly remembering that I was temporarily Ian McGunn, I waved thanks and went down the stone harbour front. A youngish bloke was sitting on the wall. His pipe was unlit. The Sabbath again, I supposed knowingly.

'How do.' I stood a second. 'I'm Ian McGunn.'

'Hello,' he said, smiling. 'Jamie Innes.'

'Not angling,' I observed, glad.

'Not on Sunday.' He grinned, blue eyes from a tanned young leather face. 'You?'

'No. Fish never did me any harm.'

'Hunter? Deer? Nature-watcher?' He ran down a list of lethality, earning a constant headshake.

'Ah, well. Poetry. One slim volume, a few here and there in obscure journals.' How obscure only I knew.

'I'm not a very educated man,' he confessed. 'But at least I can tell Shona I met you first.'

Shona? 'Shona?' I said as blankly as I'm able.

'We're engaged. She's a McGunn. She'll be pleased to meet you, seeing you've possible relatives here.' He rose and invited me to accompany him by tilting his head. 'You were saying on the bus. Old May Grimmond from Lybster's a cousin to Mrs Ross who keeps the shop, who's related to George MacNeish at the inn, who . . .'

Until that moment I'd assumed that the Highlands were a large underpopulated expanse of differing counties. Illusions again. Now I could see a strain of blood ties ran strongly round somnolent old Dubneath. What worried me was that here I suddenly was, Ian McGunn, urgently needing an entire clan's genealogy, addresses and photographs.

We walked a few hundred yards before Jamie stopped outside a terraced cottage and pushed open a wooden gate. The cottage door was pulled, and a melodious voice said, 'Welcome, Ian McGunn! You'll stay for tea.'

'Shona,' Jamie introduced. 'That beast's Ranter.' A dog the size of a horse stared at me with less than ecstasy.

'Er, hello,' I said. The impression was swirling blue, gold, yellow, and a smile. The bird, not the dog. 'I, er, trust I'm not inconveniencing . . .'

'Come in, man. Us here waiting and you so long to call I've to send Jamie Innes combing the town seeking you out wandering all the county before setting foot in the house . . .'

Gasp. 'Erm, thanks, er, Shona . . . ' I honestly believe that a woman meeting a man only takes him in piece by piece – eyes, height, age, smile, face. But a man's different. We take in the complete woman at one swallow. That's why particular points – remembering the colour of her eyes, for instance – aren't really important to a man. It's also why women get very narked, because they assume we use their scoring system. I couldn't keep my eyes off Shona, and struggled to keep from being too obvious. She was lovely.

The cottage was prepared for action. Linen table-cloth-plates just so. The most formal tea-table you ever did see, while Shona swung her long bright hair and spun herself fetching the teapot and piles of sandwiches. She told Ranter to wait outside. It left calmly, giving me a warning glance.

'And what's this about you in a common lodging like that MacNeish's tavern no more than a pub and you not even bothering to knock on a door – ' etcetera.

'Give the man a chance, Shona,' Jamie pleaded.

'Aye, well, if he's come through the south he'll only be used to them Edinburgh folk . . .'

Jamie winked. 'We blame Edinburgh for giving us all a bad reputation. There's a joke. Edinburgh folk tell callers: Welcome – you'll have *had* your tea!'

'What did that MacNeish give you for your dinner, Ian?' Shona demanded from the kitchen.

And we were off into womanchat. By sheer skill I

managed to keep off my relatives for the whole visit. Shona was lovely in that spectacular way some woman are. Jamie Innes obviously worshipped her, laughing appreciatively at her stories of the schoolchildren even though I'm sure he must have heard them all before.

Getting on for six Shona rose to shoo Jamie away and summoned me to walk her out.

'Time for chapel,' she commanded. 'The Innes clan being famous heathens, Jamie doesn't go so you'll walk me down, Ian.'

'Er, if you wish.'

'And while we do,' she said, bright with anticipation, 'I'll exchange tales of the McGunns with you.'

'Shouldn't I go with Jamie . . . ?' I tried desperately.

Jamie said, 'But I'm outnumbered, Ian. You McGunns use unfair tactics.'

We parted at the gate. Jamie turning up the road leaving me and Shona to start towards the chapel by the waterfront. She slipped her hand through my arm. There was a low rumble behind us, Ranter stalking. Its eyes were almost on a level with mine. A stair-carpet of a tongue.

'Take no notice of the beast, Ian,' she said happily. 'Now we can have a really good gossip.'

'Gossip?' That was it. My heart sank. I invented desperately. 'Well, er, I think my grandad came from Stirling . . .'

'Not that, silly.' She was laughing prettily at me. 'What I really want to know is, are you and Jo lovers, Lovejoy?'

Chapter Eleven

That stopped me. She was rolling in the aisles laughing.

'Your face!'

Women really nark me. 'You're sly.'

'Oh, whist, man! I guessed when I heard you'd been telling George MacNeish about his old things. And you couldn't take your eyes off my old father's mulls.'

These are peculiarly Scottish containers for snuff, made of horns, silver, sometimes bone or stone. It's easy to pay too much for these, because usually they've bits missing. The complete ones have a decorative chain holding tiny tools – a mallet, scoop, prong – also of silver, and of course it's these that have casually been nicked or lost. Mulls come in two sorts, the larger table mull with castors for use after posh dinners, or the personal mull. Antique dealers invent wrong names, being too thick to learn the right ones, and call the portable sort a 'baby' mull, it being small. I'd never even seen a matching pair of snuff mulls before. But Shona had such on her mantelpiece, lovely horn and silver shapes with all the accoutrements. I'd only given clandestine glances, but should have remembered that women can always recognize a drool.

She was enjoying herself. 'Handed down. Family.'

'From about 1800,' I said with a moan of craving.

She fell about. 'Well you can't have them,' she said at last, recovering. 'Jo said you're a terror for old things.'

'Jo said I was coming?'

'Yes. She's been ringing every couple of days.' Shona

544

grimaced at me. 'That's why I suspect you and she of . . .'

'None of your nosey business.'

She hugged herself as they do. 'I like you, Lovejoy. Secretly, I'm glad you won't tell.'

'Only women gossip about lovers.'

She thought a bit before beginning an argument about diarists. I was too impatient to listen. 'Where did you get the bureau from?'

'The one Jo said got lost? Oh, a place I know.'

'A place with antiques?' I asked evenly. I'm not devious like other people. I honestly say exactly what I mean practically always.

She gave me a look, women being of a suspicious nature. 'Very well,' she said at last, some decision made. 'You'll come up to Tachnadray with me tomorrow.'

Tachnadray? I said great, never having heard the name. For the sake of propriety off she went to kirk and I went to read Untracht's monograph on jewellery. Each to his own religion.

That evening I had a demure supper ritual in the hotel lounge served by Mrs MacNeish. It was like a barn. Dead fish and stag heads on wall-plaques and sepia photographs of ancient shooting parties proudly dangling dead birds. I'd have to send somebody up here to buy these exhibits on a commission job. Someone else. I'm not a queasy bloke; I just can't rejoice in extinction. Mary MacNeish laid up for major surgery. I'd never seen so much crockery and cutlery in my life. I told her cheerfully, 'Just met Shona.'

'Aye, I heard,' Mrs MacNeish said.

We bantered a bit while I tried to keep my knees together and hold off the slab cake till the starting gun. Politeness is a killer. Also, something wasn't quite right. In the woman's prattle a discordant note was sounding. You can always tell. The publican's wife was open-faced and friendly, but she was having her work cut out to stay so when Shona was mentioned. Yet Shona was pally and really something to see. I wondered if it was me, and like a fool put it out of my mind.

During the gluttony I had the sense not to mention Tachnadray, and eventually returned to reading Untracht's methods of inlaying silver strips in English box-wood bracelet carving.

Maybe for once I should have thought deeply instead.

Next day I consulted the Register of Electors. They're those cobwebbed, yellowing, string-hung pages of local names in every village post-office-cum-stores. Pretending idleness – nothing new – I found that Tachnadray listed umpteen McGunns, plus one ectopic: plain James Wheeler. Yet even here somebody had inked in the McGunn surname, converting him to clan. Odd, that. Amending electoral rolls is illegal, even if you changed your name lawfully. I checked its date: printed twenty years previously, and that ink had faded. I wondered if Lovejoy McGunn sounded better than Ian, then decided to let ill alone.

Shona brought Jamie's van about ten o'clock. She drove as fitted her personality, with good-humoured extravagance, and asked if MacNeish's pub was comfortable.

'Grand parlour,' I said. 'Are those places only used for funerals? It felt like the dust covers were just off.'

Shona laughed. 'In the Highlands the best room's always kept for occasions, Lovejoy.'

'Tachnadray got one too?'

She sobered swiftly. 'How much do you know, Lovejoy?' We turned uphill inland.

'This Tachnadray's where the antique came from?'

'Yes.' She faced me defiantly. Odd. Defiance is for enemies. 'I arranged it.'

'But down in East Anglia we'd been told to expect

546

a reproduction.' I cleared my throat, not wanting to seem a crook. 'You see, if a genuine antique had showed up we, er, might have only paid you for a repro.'

'And claimed that a reproduction had been delivered.' Shona nodded, getting the point quicker than I really wanted. 'And then, Lovejoy?'

'Then?' I said blankly. 'Well, I'd have flogged your genuine antique.'

She was so patient. 'And *then*, Lovejoy?'

'I'd have come here to . . . ' I slowed, nodding.

' . . . To find who was stupid enough to sell off expensive antiques thinking them reproductions.' She gave me a satisfied smile. 'You've found her. It's me. It was bait, Lovejoy.'

Expensive bait. 'But why?' We'd gone half a mile and already the houses had vanished. We were on an upland moor and still climbing, the van labouring and coughing.

'Because I need a divvie. Jo had mentioned you. I'd heard of one in Carlisle, but it's so difficult to trust anyone in antiques, isn't it?'

'Sometimes, love,' I agreed piously. 'Why didn't you tell Jo to ask me up without all this?'

'It hadn't to be me that procured you, Lovejoy. You had to wander in on your own. You pretending to be a McGunn simply made it easier for me.'

Therefore she wanted ignorance, which meant I'd have to get a move on to suss her game out. Antiques were at stake. If I allowed her to distract me they'd slip through my fingers. It happens to me every time when women are around. 'I'm part of your plot?'

'A plot for survival. We McGunns are a lost tribe, Lovejoy.'

'Here. I thought you'd given up pretending – '

'Be quiet and listen!' she blazed it out fiercely.

For a few minutes she drove, winding us away from the coast into bleak countryside. Rocks, gullies, a little rivulet or two, heather and a few trees having a desperate time. There was even a big-bellied bird noshing some heather. Funny life for a pigeon, I thought, though whatever turns pigeons on in Caithness . . . Shona cooled enough for her sermon.

'You picked an august name, Lovejoy. We McGunns are Picts, inhabitants here long before the rest of these . . . people came.' She meant anybody else was a serf. 'Yet now we're dispossessed. The Highland clearances of two centuries gone, the clan rivalries, everything in history has been against us.'

The sky was grey, cloudy. A distant grey house glided along the horizon. Wuthering Heights. A small lorry drove past us towards Dubneath. Shona beeped her horn in reflex salutation. A few sheep watched us, hoping for a lift to civilization. I hid a yawn. Nice place if you were an elk.

'We were driven to the coastal villages,' she continued. 'People who've heard of Armenians, the Jews and Tasmanians would think you mad if you classed us with the likes of them.' She shot me a hard glance, waggling the wheel the way women do for nothing. 'Wouldn't they?'

I thought a bit. For all I knew she might be a nut. 'Well, yes,' I said. 'But it's life. Families come and go. Names peter out, get revived.'

'In 1821 we tried,' she said bitterly. 'The Clan McGunn formed a society – like those Gordons and Grants.' She spoke with hate. 'But our last clan chief died and we were finished.'

'And you'll reunite the clan and march on Rome.'

'No,' she said, choking down an impulse to chuck me through the windscreen. 'But the loyals among us must share some feeling of . . . pride.'

Odd word, I thought, I'll bet that sentence was surprised when it ended like that. 'By giving away what genuine antiques you've got left? Slinging them on the first lorry heading south?'

548

'You'll see, Lovejoy.'

For a while she drove us angrily on into ever bleaker countryside without speaking. Just as I was wondering if she'd brought any nosh she screeched us to a jolting stop above a chiselled glen. There was a muddy-looking lake off to the right, seemingly on a tilt. Can lakes actually slope like that? Trees, clearly unwelcome tourists, clustered around a large gable-and-turret building of grey stone. Ranked windows and disguised chimneys, a long drive with drystone walling, and a bare flagpole. It could have been uninhabited except that the main door stood open and somebody was standing waiting in shadow at the top of the steps. I thought it was a woman. A man with a wheelbarrow near outhouses stood peering up the hillside at our van.

'Tachnadray, Lovejoy. Isn't it beautiful?'

'The architect read *Jane Eyre*.'

'During your visit, Lovejoy,' Shona said after a moment with careful coolth, 'you'll refrain from sly digs. Understood?'

'Not really, love,' I said, opening the van door and sliding down to stretch my legs. It was time me and Cousin Shona got a few things straight before hitting the old homestead. 'I've gone to a lot of bother to get here. Right now I could be out of your hair, and home in peace. I sympathize with your diaspora, but we Lovejoys never had a posh dynasty.'

'So?'

'Explain why you're Pretty Miss Welcome down in Dubneath, and Boadicea as soon as we see that phoney Victorian castle. And,' I went on as she drew furious breath, 'why you think you have the right to ballock me as soon as we're out of Jamie's earshot.'

She said quietly, 'So it's money you want.'

'Or antiques. Or both.'

'Very well, Lovejoy. You'll be paid.' Pause. 'Enough.'

A minute's reflection, and I nodded. We rolled as I

got in. She nearly took my toes off with the wheel. Our relationship was deteriorating fast.

'The . . . owner of Tachnadray agreed with my idea of having copies of the antiques made and selling them. We have two men doing it.' She turned us between two tall stone gateposts bearing carved coats-of-arms. 'I believe we – Tachnadray – are being defrauded.'

Such disloyalty, I thought, but didn't say. 'And I'm to prove your suspicions?'

'Much, much more, Lovejoy.' She'd recovered her smile. However daft her dreams, she really seemed to come alive again in Tachnadray. She'd recovered all her sparkling good humour as soon as we made the glen. 'You're to prove who's doing it.'

'Here, love,' I said uneasily. 'You're not wanting anybody buried at midnight in the crypt, are you? Because hunting's not my game – '

'Here we are, Lovejoy,' she said gaily, stopping the van below the steps. 'Tachnadray.'

The woman waiting in the shadows of the main door stepped forward into view. She walked with grave composure to the top step and stood to welcome us. I got out and went forward. For half a step I was a bit uncertain. After that there was no question. Between the two women the air had thickened with utter hatred. It's not fair that hunters last longest, or that prey wear out fastest. Somebody should change the rules. Quickly I stepped to one side, put on my most sincere smile and went bravely up the steps. This new woman couldn't give me a bigger pack of lies than Shona.

Chapter Twelve

Caithness is one of those places you think of as perfect, full of plain wisdom, isn't it. The simple life: dawn porridge, down to the trickling burn to brew up the day's malt whisky or whatever, then highland reels all evening. Idyllic. Instead, here I was ascending these wide steps, grinning hopefully at the elegant older woman smiling down at me, with a lovely bird like Shona smiling away at my side, and me wishing I was in battledress being fired at. It had felt safer.

''Morning,' I said pleasantly. 'I'm . . . ' Who the hell was I?

'Ian McGunn, Michelle,' Shona introduced in her lovely brogue. 'We stopped to admire the klett.'

'Isn't it a lovely view, Ian? Welcome to Tachnadray.'

Klett? 'Thanks. Yes. Lovely, er, klett.'

'Do come in.'

'Ian's the one I spoke about, Michelle.' Shona walked ahead with her, ever so pally. Neither tried to stab the other, with visible restraint. 'A furniture craftsman. He trained at the London College.'

'Oh.' Michelle placed her dark eyes on me. 'You're going to be marvellously useful, Ian.'

French? Belgian? Her accent matched her dark hair, wavy and lusciously thick. She seemed about fifty. She wore that Continental dressiness which our women only manage on Derby Day. I blame those rotten hats the Royal Family keep wearing.

'Eh?' Somebody'd mentioned antiques.

'Duncan will show you later on. I'll arrange it.' Mich-

551

elle rotated those deep eyes. 'But we'll expect excellent output, Ian. We can't afford passengers.'

Shona drew breath. Evidently multo double meanings were hidden therein for somebody not me. Between the two women I felt as nervous as a Christmas nut.

The house was a giant of a place, with those lovely Victorian wooden panels nobody does properly any more, and even the glass bowls chained over each hanging ceiling light. They've become a fantastic source of profit – nowadays builders clearing old housing estates let you have them, five for a quid. They're collectors' items. Tip: look in 'redevelopments' (as our psychopathic town planners now term vandalism). I once got a small cast-iron staircase, circular, with the Darby Ironworks stamp on and everything, thrown in because I took sixty glass light bowls off a builder's hands while he battered a priceless 1695 building to smithereens in East Anglia for a car park. I'd dined in superb elegance for six months on the profit . . .

'Ian McGunn, darling,' Michelle announced, showing me into the tallest sitting-room on earth.

The girl paused a second – surely not for effect? – and spun her wheelchair. I honestly gasped. She was the loveliest creature I'd ever seen. About sixteen. Limpid eyes, pale skin with that translucency you instinctively want to chew. She was so slight in her lace blouse. A tartan blanket covered her legs. Pearl earrings, a beautiful black velvet choker with a central silver locket, probably late Victorian, and hair pale as her face. She honestly did seem lit from within.

'Come in, Ian McGunn,' she said. 'I'm Elaine.'

'Elaine's – ' Shona started, but the girl silenced her with an abrupt gesture and propelled herself forward.

'Don't listen to Shona's old clan nonsense,' she instructed. 'Somebody get us coffee, to convince this refugee from East Anglia that we're civilized in the north. I'll show him the house.'

Lame people always disconcert me. I never know what to do – help? push the handles? let them get on with it? It's a problem. Not only that, but here was the boss all right. I began to long for this Duncan to crash the party.

'Don't worry, Ian,' Elaine said, spotting the difficulty. 'Trail somewhere I can get a good look at you.' She smiled mischievously. 'This leg thing is permanent, I'm afraid, but I manage most things. It's only temporary disableds need assistance.'

'Ta.'

'You're English,' she said, like giving absolution. I followed her from the room, heading down a panelled corridor. 'And you bought some of our reproductions?' The furniture we were passing was all reproduction. I listened to my chest, hoping for a dong of antique sincerity, but no. Not a genuine antique in sight, though some of the work was really quite skilled.

'Er, one. Through a friend.'

Michelle had disappeared. Shona was walking by Elaine. She caught my eye and nodded. I was doing all right so far. Unhappily I met Elaine's delectable eyes in a hanging mirror. She was smiling, a naughty girl enjoying interplay. I sighed. Even peaceful women are trouble enough. Bravely I followed on down the longest corridor in the world.

Once, I went into an Eastern Bloc capital city. It was in the dark hours. The opera house was perfection, all brilliance and glamour. At half time, I strolled out to clear my brain of all that recitative, and realized with a shock that the lovely old street was a giant façade. Literally, the house fronts were shored-up replicas with only rubble behind. Since then I've never believed in appearances. The same sense of shock overcame me as Elaine turned to me and asked, 'Well, Ian?' We'd finished the penny tour.

'Er, yes. Lovely house,' I said lamely. Apart from two ante-rooms and the sitting-room the entire place was bare. Not merely relatively bare, note, but completely empty. Some bygone gas-mantle fittings remained, but with newfangled electricity points hung on. And it was only in the main hall and reception place that the great old house kept up the pretence of past grandeur with any conviction. Uneasily I got the point. An unexpected visitor could be welcomed, even entertained, and be sent on his way praising the manor house's majesty, without realizing he'd been deceived. No living face behind the death mask. I felt sick. All this way, all that fairground shambles, and not a sniff of antiques. What little furniture the house possessed was simply heavy Victorian.

Barren. A wilderness where I'd expected a harvest. She'd told me that upstairs the west wing still housed a considerable store of valuable antiques. 'That's why it's closed off,' she'd said. Odd, really, because I'd not felt a single chime. And upstairs was clearly one place she couldn't get to, not on her own in a wheelchair. How neat.

We returned to find Duncan waiting. I was glad. Elaine introduced us pleasantly enough. 'Duncan, meet Ian. No prizes for guessing surnames.' She looked at me while saying this, that mischief smile again.

'Wotcher, Duncan.'

'Welcome, Ian.' He was a chunky, elderly bloke, his compact form slow but full of that sedate dynamism the born worker possesses. I realized that he must be the man who produced the reproductions. So who was Michelle? Elaine chipped in.

'You'll be wondering who Michelle is, Ian.' She emitted that beautiful smile and said, 'Michelle is Mrs Duncan McGunn. And our voice of sanity.'

'Then there's two of us,' I said companionably.

'Indeed? A cup of welcome, and we'll let you start work. Duncan needs all the help he can get.' She lit Duncan with a glance. 'You've guessed right, man. Ian no has the Gaelic.'

The way she spoke the words made it a skit. Duncan managed a wry grin, though the beautiful lass's mockery obviously stung.

'I'll give the man a wee dram, then. It's our own malt.' He meant whisky.

'Er, ta, Duncan, but coffee'll do.'

That halted the gaiety, except that Elaine fell about. In fact she laughed so much that tears rolled down her cheeks and she had to be helped to a hankie. Mentioning coffee had never seemed hilarious to me before, but each to his own giggle. I waited patiently for the girl to recover. Michelle was taking all this in her stride, Elaine merely a mischievous child. It was Shona whose cheeks showed bright red spots of suppressed fury. Our hostess was getting to her, and delighting in her success.

'Er, what's the joke, love?' I asked to clear the air.

'A Scot, Ian! One of the clan. One of us. Preferring coffee to our own malt! Isn't that an absolute scream, Shona?'

'Well, no,' I said to save Shona. There were clues here if only I could spot them. 'I'm not big on spirits.'

'Sure you'll not prefer tea?' Elaine gasped.

'Please,' I said politely. 'If it's no bother.'

Another winner. During the ensuing paroxysms Michelle gave Duncan the bent eye for us to withdraw to let the three of them get on with it.

Duncan's genteel exit line was, 'I'll show Ian the workshop. We'll be a minute or two.' I followed, really quite happy.

We walked out by the front steps towards the out-buildings near where the red-haired man with the wheelbarrow had stood peering. Nobody else about now, though.

'What was so funny, Duncan?'

For a little he said nothing. We passed between two silent stone buildings, leaving the carefully tended forecourt.

'Well y'see, Ian,' he said finally, 'it pleases Miss Elaine to needle Shona about Scottishness.'

'And everybody else about their own particular fancy, eh?'

'Maybe,' he said drily. 'Yon's my wee factory.' We paused outside a low stone barn, slate roof tethered by large flat slabs against winter storms.

'Is that what Elaine needles you about?' I asked.

'O' course.' His honesty was disarming. I began to like Duncan McGunn. 'And my Michelle about being Belgian.'

'The question is why,' I prompted.

'Not so, Ian.' He did things to a padlock to let us in. 'The question is what will Miss Elaine find irks you, isn't it?' I didn't think much to what he said. I wish now I had, honest to God.

The place's interior was a hundred feet by forty, give or take, and daylit from a couple of long slender windows running much of the length. Its scent was exquisite to a born faker – oils, varnishes, sawn woods, glues, sweat. Duncan's current opus stood on a low metal bench.

'Sheraton copy,' I said. I could tell I was grinning from the sound in my voice. 'Where'd you get it?'

Cagey silence. I didn't blame him. No trader gives his sources away. It was a battered Victorian chest of drawers imitating Sheraton. Three big drawers below two 'half' drawers, with slightly curved short legs. Some nerk had given each drawer wooden bulb handles. The Bramah locks were a giveaway because that locksmithing genius wasn't around in 1786, the pretended age of this poor relic. I walked around it, pleased to be back in the real world.

'You'll reduce it, of course?'

He filled a pipe slowly. 'How?'

'It looks pretty well made.' I pulled a drawer and inverted it to check the wear and patination of age. Some wicked modern fakers add these small convincing details. It's terrible to buy a piece like this, only to find once you've got it home that it's phoney. We have a saying in this rottenest game, that you can never make anything good from a bad fake. But this was some skilled Victorian carpenter's forged 'Sheraton'. It had once glowed, been really quite stylish.

'Any ideas?' Duncan asked.

All right. He'd a right to expect proof I knew what I was on about. 'Only one,' I said, and tapped its top. 'Lose the two smaller drawers. Settle for the bottom three. They'll need cutting down in size, of course. Replace the handles with brass reproductions. Leave the Bramah locks; when you advertise it admit quite openly that they're later additions.'

'Aye, but if a buyer looks at the base he'll see where the curved front's been cut through the middle.'

'Then don't sell it to a sceptic, Duncan.' I'd given him the best recipe and he knew it.

'Fancy your chances?' he said. A challenge.

'Yes.' We got chatting then about some good 'reproductions', as I politely termed them, which I'd seen fetched through East Anglia. It turned out that he'd forged a Hepplewhite pot-cupboard I'd bought and sold on to Dortmund (think of a box with tall straight unadorned tapering legs).

'So you made that torchère I bought last autumn?'

'Aye.'

'God. Was it worth it? It must have cost the earth.'

He sighed, nodding. 'It did, Ian. Days and days of work. But it convinced reluctant buyers that somebody up here could do the job as well as most.'

'Well done.' I love a craftsman. The tall torchère had had a tripod appearance – three elegant mahogany legs, with three slender central supports up to an everting triple for the six-sided tray, that would hold the household's oil lamp. Some antiques are too expensive to fake commercially. The decorative torchère is one, because there are plenty of cheap pole screens about

– genuine antiques, too – which fakers can buy to make them out of. 'Pity you killed a Queen Anne pole screen to build it, though.'

'How'd you spot that?'

I checked myself in time. 'Oh, the mulling top and bottom ran different ways, I think.'

'Did they now,' he said evenly, faithless sod.

'Mmmh.' Quite honestly I couldn't remember. It had been the sad little bleat of the genuine mauled antique that had brought tears to my eyes.

'One thing, Duncan. I thought clans hall lairds. Isn't a chieftainess unusual?'

'The Laird James passed away a few years since.'

Aha. I'd save that bit up. Had plain James Wheeler become The McGunn? Maybe he married into the position. Well, it happens in business empires. Why not?

A bell clonked on the wall. I was glad to see it was an original spring-suspended clapperbell and not some shrill electric foolishness.

'Time to join the ladies,' he said, making for the door. He added scathingly, 'For tea.'

'I've nowt against your whisky, Duncan.' I went with him.

I felt three goals down.

Before Shona drove me back to Dubneath for my things, we settled my job amicably. This means I listened to Elaine and agreed with whatever she said. My terms were a fraction of the profit and all found – free nosh and bed in a stableman's loft among the outbuildings. They showed me a bare cube with a single bed, a cupboard, and one uncurtained window with a view of the barren fells. Great if you're Heathcliff waiting for Cathy, but I played along. Duncan was there too, ruefully swigging what he conveyed was his first and last non-alcoholic drink.

'We're assuming Ian proves capable, Miss Elaine,' he put in gently. That caffeine was getting to his brain.

'*Are* you capable, Ian?' Elaine asked innocently, looking across at Shona, a tease. Shona turned aside, busied herself with the sugar for Duncan.

'Your bills for plastic wood will take a turn for the better, Elaine,' I said. Duncan had the grace to laugh at the jibe. Plastic wood's the poor forger's friend.

They came out to see us off, talking casually. I turned to admire the house's clinging splendour, and saw the big ginger-headed bloke among the outbuildings. He was kilted, strong and stridey. Just as long as he was on our side.

'I can trust Robert,' Elaine said to answer my thought.

'Thank God for that.' I climbed into the van. 'Back before evening, then?'

'Ian.' Michelle came to my window as Shona hung back saying so-long to Elaine. Duncan was already off, anxious to be at work. His wife spoke softly, perfume wafting in. 'I'm so relieved you're here. It's time all was . . . resolved.' Her fingers, probably accidentally, rested on mine. But the pressure and that faint scratch of her nails down my hand was communication. I swallowed, too near her large eyes to think straight. What was she saying?

'Oh, er, ta. I'll do what I can.'

'We'll make sure you *exceed* your potential, Ian,' Elaine called. She rippled her fingers in a child's wave. She must have hearing like a bat.

Shona marched up, flung in and revved noisily. She hadn't liked seeing Michelle speaking to me in confidence. She reversed at speed with a crash of gears, but Michelle anticipated the manœuvre and glided away in time.

We made Dubneath at a record run with Shona not speaking a word. Disembarking, I was jubilant at how things had gone. I was in. My thin disguise was holding.

559

I was blood cousin umpteen times removed to this barmy load of clannites. Very soon I'd have the lion's share of a sound antique fakery scheme, at least. Stupidly overconfident, I decided to buy some curtain material before phoning Tinker.

Now the bad news, as they say.

Chapter Thirteen

The best about little towns is that most things are crammed into a few shops. I found the drapery/general/ household stores by spotting the only building in Dubneath with more than two parked cars. Women are the trouble, though. They immediately sensed I was curtain-hunting and started eyeing the swatches. The stores lady, Mrs Innes, hung about itching to decide for me.

'A pastel,' I hazarded, playing it close.

'You'll be Ian McGunn,' she said, smiling. 'That converted loft's a draughty old place.'

So much for secrecy. How the hell did they do it? 'You shouldn't know that. Naughty girl.'

She laughed, colouring. 'I meant, Joseph was always complaining. No wonder the poor man drank.'

'Joseph?'

Instantly she changed tack. 'And that pokey little window. You'll only get one pattern if you choose a large floral.'

'Boss me about and I'll go elsewhere.'

'You can't. The Wick bus left an hour gone.'

Her brass measuring rod was screwed to the counter. She fell about when I offered her eight quid for it and laughingly told other customers how I'd started to buy her out. I settled on a bright oriental print, bamboos and japonicas, and ballocked Mrs Innes for not knowing the window's dimensions. We parted friends. I crossed to the tavern.

Joseph? Who had been my predecessor at Tachnadray. Something had driven the 'poor man' to drink.

Not the draught, that's for sure. I didn't like the sound of all this.

I told Mary MacNeish I'd be leaving. By purest coincidence she already happened to have me booked out.

'You guessed,' I said drily. If they introduce gossip at the next Olympics we're a cert. Dubneath'll get the Gold.

'Eat your fill before you go, Ian.' It was the mildest of mild cautions, a very natural expression. So why the Mayday hint? 'Tachnadray's bonnie but can chill a man's marrow.'

'I'll be slinking back for your pasties, Mary.'

'I'll be pleased.'

On the spur of the moment I tried a flyer. 'Don't suppose it'll be easy taking good old Joseph's place. Is he around? Like a word with him.'

She was shocked that I knew, and the cake-stand just made it to the table. Her face suddenly went abstract, as women's do for concealment. 'Now what did I do with that butterdish . . . ?' she said vaguely, and that was as far as I got.

Margaret finally landed Tinker for me in Fat Bert's nooky shop in the Arcade. I'd wasted a fortune trying different pubs. Absurdly, I was really pleased to hear his long rasp.

'Where the bleedin' hell you got to, Lovejoy?' he gravelled out, wheezing. ''Ere, mate. We in trouble?'

'Shut it, Tinker.' Maybe he was only three-quarters sloshed, I thought hopefully. I hate to chuck money away on incoherence. 'You sober?'

''And on me 'eart, Lovejoy. Not a drop all bleedin' day.'

'Listen. That driver who got topped. His name Joseph Something?'

'Dunno, Lovejoy.'

'Find out from Antioch. I'll ring tomorrow. Any news?'

'Nar, Lovejoy. That bleeder's still round the Hook.'
He meant Dutchie hadn't returned on the Hook of
Holland ferryboat. 'But there's some Eyties hangin'
round.'

'Italians?' My soul dampened.

'Aye. Millie's youngster Terry reckons they wuz
circus rousters or summert. Two big buggers. They
come soon after that tart.' Millie's a barmaid. Terry
runs pub messages, bets for the two-thirty at Epsom
and that. Terry'd know, if anybody would.

'Tinker.' I'd not had a headache all day. 'Which
tart?'

'The one you used to shag down Friday Wood
before – '

'Tinker.'

' – before that little blondie you had went for that
shoeshop manageress you fancied in the White Hart – '

That's what I need, I thought bitterly, hearing Fat
Bert roaring laughing in the background while Margaret lectured the stupid pair of them. Friends. 'Clear
them out, Tinker.'

Mutter, mutter. 'They've pissed orf, Lovejoy.'
Tinker's drunken idea of subtlety. 'You remember her,
lovely arse – '

'What did she want?' I'd already identified Francie.

'She come in hell of a hurry, after midnight. Said
nothing, only asked where you'd got to. Her nipper
told me it'd been in bed on a train.'

All children are 'it' to Tinker. Betty Blabbermouth,
my erstwhile helper at the Great Antique Road Show.
Francie must have hoofed into East Anglia on a night
express, and reached Tinker a few millisecs before
Sidoli's killer squad came a-hunting. I swallowed. In
spite of Joan, Francie still felt something for me and
had rushed to warn.

Well, I didn't have to be Sherlock Holmes to reason
that various folk were cross, simply because I'd injured
a few blokes, damaged a wagon or two, shambled a

fairground's livelihood and nicked their vastly expensive generator. And now they wanted repayment in notes of the realm, my blood or other equivalent currency. I quavered, cleared my throat.

'Sure there was no message?'

'Only she'd be at the Edinburgh Tattoo.' A long pause. 'It's north of Selkirk,' he added helpfully.

Francie's way of saying steer clear of Edinburgh until that vast military Tattoo closed the Festival? Well, I was already in Edinburgh's black books, and there must be enough guns in two fairgrounds to make a jury think that one accidental shooting of a no-good scruff like me was a permissible average . . . No. Francie's message was a very, very useful hint indeed.

'News from Jo?'

'That teacher bint? She visits Three-Wheel Archie.'

A glass clinked, Tinker finding Fat Bert's reserve bottle.

'And, Lovejoy. There's money from your sweep. We made a killin'. Margaret says as she'll send your slice to a post office if you'll say where the bleedin' 'ell you – '

Click and burr. I didn't want anybody knowing my address after that lot. Escape's like murder, a private business. I stood indecisively, then walked out of the tavern into Dubneath's cool watery day for a deep ponder. Life's got so many risks, you're lucky to get out of this world alive. Wherever I looked, enemies lurked. Back home in East Anglia fairground heavies dangled ominously in the trees. The long roads between Caithness and my village were filled with irritated night drivers whose colleague had got done in. I strolled down Dubneath's empty wharf to examine the vacant harbour.

Hell is people, somebody once said. He forgot to add that so's Heaven. The more I thought about it, the safer Tachnadray's claustrophobic solitude seemed.

Two hours I walked about the somnolent town. For

ten minutes I stood with Dubneath's one layabout and watched the traffic lights change, really heady excitement. A tiny school loosed about four o'clock, pretty children much tidier than East Anglia's, with twisty curling accents. I thought longingly of Jo, a lump in my throat. And of Joan. And Francie. And Ellen. And, a startling pang, little Betty. I felt deprived of all life. Maybe it wouldn't be too long.

Dubneath was static. Not even a shrimp-boat a-coming. The wind was rising, wetting my eyes. I tried the obstinate child's trick of staring into the breeze until your eyelids give up of their own accord. Of course, I'd have to lie low. That much was plain. I didn't relish this on-the-run bit, even though it's the only rational course for a coward. It tends to throw you willynilly into weird folks' company. Like that lot up in Tachnadray.

Six o'clock I went for my last meal – no blindfold or cigarette – at the MacNeish pub.

Providentially, the television was on in the snug, a pleasant girl giving out the news. I caught the last of it: ' . . . the theft of a vehicle from an Edinburgh fairground. Six men are in hospital, two of them critical. A police spokesman today deplored the increasing violence . . .'

The surface of my beer trembled. The glass rim chattered on my teeth and I saw George MacNeish glance slowly along the bar from where he was wiping up. I tried to make my momentary quake resemble thirst.

'Nice drop, George.'

' . . . search moved north. The vehicle was found abandoned but undamaged at a roadside halt frequented by long-distance . . .' She read it so chirpily, holiday camp bingo. I went to do the best I could with Mary's calories.

Seven o'clock Jamie brought his van. Shona, he said, was tired. I left the tavern clutching my curtain material, a hermit to the wilderness. It could always make bandages.

'Can we stop at the, er, klett, Jamie?' I said as we trundled inland. 'Lovely view.'

'You're keen on our bonnie countryside?' Jamie waxed enthusiastic, changing gears. 'There's grand scenery beyond that wee loch . . .'

Ten points on the creep chart, Lovejoy. The trouble was I'd painted myself into a corner. Crooks in East Anglia trying to do me in. Maslow would put two and two together when the Police Report stimulated his aggressive minibrain, and hasten into Edinburgh to help his neffie brother peelers. All the travelling folk on the bloody island were out. And here I was at the very tip. Hardly possible to run any further. That's the trouble with being innocent. You get hunted by cops *and* robbers. Even the worst crooks on earth only get chased by one lot. No wonder people turn to crime.

Chapter Fourteen

Houses are fascinating, aren't they? The house at Tachnadray was superbly positioned for light, setting and appearance. Grudgingly, during the first few days of labour on Duncan's Sheraton lookalike, I came to admire the place. Catch it any angle and you get an eyeful. The old architect might have had delusions of grandeur, but he'd got it exactly right. Pretty as a picture, was Tachnadray. It brings a lump to my throat just to remember how it all was, in my serene encounter with the clan-and-county set. The surrounding moorland somehow seemed arranged for the purpose of setting off the great mansion's style. Hardly 'antique' in the truest sense of the word, pre–1836, but lovely all the same. The creation of an artist.

Very quickly I learned that routines were almost Teutonic in Tachnadray. The first afternoon I wandered across the grand forecourt to chuck some crumbs into the stone fountain. Goldfish sailed in its depths. I'm always sorry for fish because they have a hard life, no entertainment or anything and scared of every shadow. I'd saved a bit of russell roll and was busy shredding it into the water livening up their wet world when my own dry world was suddenly inverted. I do mean this. It honestly spun a hundred and eighty degrees and I was crumbing the atmosphere.

'What the fuck you doin'?' a cavern rumbled in my ear. Giant hands had clutched my shoulder and spine and tipped me upside down.

'Feeding the fish,' I yelped. 'Please.'

'Who the fuck said you could?' the cavern boomed.

'Down, Robert.' Elaine to my rescue. Wheels crunched gravel. *'Down!'* Like you say to a dog. Then something in a language I didn't understand, slidey smooth.

The world clouted my left knee. He'd simply dropped me.

Groggily I clambered upright. My trouser leg was ripped. The big kilted man stood skywards over me. Another McGunn, I supposed wearily, making yet more instantaneous assumptions about good old Cousin Ian. He marched off on his great hairy legs. A knife hilt protruded from his stocking.

'You came just in time, love.' I was wheezing. 'I'd have put him in hospital.'

She laughed, applauding. Robert turned his maned head, but kept going.

'Don't mind Robert, Ian. He's big for the cause.' She wrinkled her face at the scudding clouds. 'Rain soon. The anglers'll be out as far as Yarrow Water.'

A distant clanking tapped the air, Duncan calling work on the iron rod which hung by the workshop door.

'My free hour's up, Elaine,' I said, but hesitated before sprinting back to the treadmill.

'Another time, Ian,' she said. 'Not on your first day. Turn me round, please.'

'Chieftainesses of distinguished clans shouldn't have to ask.'

She glared up at me. 'Oh yes we should!'

Some women have a terrifying knack of seeming to move their faces suddenly nearer you without stirring a muscle. They do it in love or in fury. I've noticed that. Elaine was the best at it I'd ever encountered. The images of physical love and the poor paralysed girl juxtaposed in my mind.

'Penny for your thoughts, Ian,' Elaine said slyly as I obediently set off along the drive to Duncan's workshop.

'Just how fascinating people's faces are,' I lied. 'I'm good at faces.'

'Women's especially?'

'Mind your own business.'

She was back to laughing then, swaying in her wheelchair. It was one of those oddish moments when the environment conspires. She was there beside the fountain. The sky behind her had darkened. Thunder rumbled. Yet a watery sun picked up the grey-yellow gravel, her white blouse, the colours of the old tartan. Lovely enough to mesmerize. Lucky I'm not easy to manipulate, or a girl this lovely could have me eating out of her hand. A terrible desire rose within me. My body's a hostage to hormones, but with a lass who couldn't walk –

'Actually,' she said, as we parted, 'we cripples have different ways of making . . . music, Lovejoy.' Another super-correct guess what I'd really been thinking about.

She left me so preoccupied that I hardly noticed Duncan playing hell with me for skiving instead of getting the bureau's drawers undone. Elaine was disturbing. Weirdly swift to guess what you were thinking – far too swift for my liking. Only supposition of course. I don't believe in telepathy or whatever it's called. But I didn't like this idea of not being alone in my own head.

Duncan put me at the old piece. He watched me like a hawk as I tapped and listened and set about marking the wood components. I'd got some self-adhesive labels from the Innes stores in Dubneath.

'A waste of money, Ian,' Duncan disapproved.

'Oh?' I cracked back sardonically. 'So you're the daft faker who pencils his illegal intentions all over the finished product, eh?'

He surrendered with a chuckle and lit his pipe to watch. He'd had to concede. Simplest tip on earth: when you're thinking of buying antique furniture take a glance at its inner surfaces. There you might see measurements indicating the faker's reduction factor – inches cut off, even types of wood to be used.

'One goon I know in Newcastle even writes it on in felt-tip,' I told Duncan. 'I ask you.'

'You know a lot, for a wandering cousin.'

Caught. 'Ah,' I stammered. 'We had to learn all that. At the London College.'

'Very thorough. Have you a family, Ian?'

'No. Except now you lot. My erstwhile spouse found my transparent honesty too much to cope with.'

Duncan helped me to up-end the bureau. The base was in a better state than I'd hoped.

'You should use Newcastle, Duncan,' I panted, struggling to tilt it on a block support. 'Handy for Liverpool, without being too direct.'

'Aye, we tried . . . ' He ahemed and reamed his pipe. I'd caught him, but absently worked on. *Aye, we tried and failed*, is what he'd been about to say. He'd discovered, like many antiques fakers, that there are folk pathways in dirty deals. New dirt's distrusted. Old schemes have a kind of inbuilt security. That's why a woman chooses a particular colour, fancies a special perfume: it swept Cecil off his feet, so why not Paul? It's the reason crooks stick to a particular *modus operandi* even when they know it hallmarks their particular chain of robberies. And a painter faking Cotman's genius, like Big Frank's mate Johnnie does in Suffolk, would rather polish off a dozen *Greta Bridge* phonies and sell them to that same fence in Hamburg than paint different ones every time.

Clue: Tachnadray's fakes had only one outlet, and that was through my own stamping-ground, East Anglia. Which meant also I could easily find out how much Duncan's replicas had made lately. I whistled, irritably searching for tools on the bench.

'No wonder you got rid of Joseph,' I grumbled. 'Messy sod. I'll rearrange this lot when I've a minute.'

Duncan stilled. 'Joseph?'

Unconcerned, I began rearranging the tools into some sort of order. 'I knew a bloke once was so bloody untidy that – '

'As long as you do better than he did, Lovejoy.' Duncan went down to the other end of the workshop to mix varnish. An unpleasant reprimand, that, with its hint of threat.

Come to think of it, where *was* this Joseph? I decided I'd better find out. Tactfully as ever, of course. That's my way.

It was three days before I had a chance of talking to Elaine without being up-ended by Robert the Brute. Which doesn't mean they had passed uneventfully. Duncan and me'd argued non-stop about our next opus. I favoured faking a series of small Georgian tables from scratch; Duncan stuck out for modifying – 'putting back' in the antique-fakery slang – some tired Victorian bureau, very much as we were doing now. It was evidently his thing. And we had burdensome mealtimes with Elaine teasing us all, over Michelle's table. Her grub was Frenchified, by which I mean tangy of taste but ethereal. We had supper-time visits from Shona, and a couple of flying visits from Jamie who dropped us some materials in his van. This, plus a shepherd bringing two sheepdogs to prove they were topnotchers, was it. I quickly got the hang of life at Tachnadray, or thought I had.

But getting the hang of a scene doesn't mean tranquillity. It can mean just the opposite. There were just enough worry points to disturb my beauty sleep. Like, Michelle and Shona smiling their hundred-per-cent hatred smiles. Like, everybody knowing about Joseph but nobody saying. Like, Tachnadray's pose as a glamorous laird's mansion complete with loyal retainers yet having barely enough furniture to dress out two rooms, a stage-set in a ghost palace. Like, Duncan's lone wilting attempts to provide the crumbling estate with an income. When at my noon break Elaine called me over to meet the shepherd's wriggly black-and-white dogs I thought: Here's quite an opportunity.

'Er, great,' I said, trying to sound full of admiration.

The shepherd grinned, said something in Gaelic. The dogs gave each other a sardonic glance as if saying, Here's another idiot townie who hasn't a clue.

'They like you, Ian,' the shepherd said. 'But they think you'll no be a countryman. I'm Hector.'

We nodded. Another cousin. Were I the genuine article I'd feel safe up here, even from Sidoli's vengeance-seeking mob of circus hands prowling the Lowlands.

'They're right, Hector,' I said. 'What do they do?'

'Best working pair north of Glasgow.' He waited, then explained, 'Sheep, Ian. Tessie's four, Joey two.'

'You bullies.' The dogs grinned and waggled round me, noses pointing up.

We talked about dogs for a minute while Elaine did one of her prolonged smiling stares at me. I felt her attention like a sunlamp, and listened while Hector listed his dogs' excellences. Dogs are all right but doggy folk are real bores, aren't they? Hector was confident about some sheepdog trials.

'How do you train them?' I asked. 'And what do you feed them on?' Much I cared, but Hector was loving all this in his grim Presbyterian way.

'You must come over and see them do an' out-run or two,' he said. 'It's but a short step. Mornings I walk to check the cottage – '

Elaine interrupted brightly, 'Och away, Hector. Can't you see Cousin Ian's not really interested in your ould dogs?'

'True,' I said, maybe a little too quickly.

We all parted friends, me patting the dogs and seeing them off but thinking, The cottage, eh? Immediately Hector was out of earshot, Elaine said, spinning her wheelchair to accompany me back towards the house,

572

'The cottage is an empty crofter's place on the fells. We use it for winter shelter. There's quite a few about.'

It's that sort of nimble guesswork that makes you give up trying to out-think a female. I plodded along pushing her until she told me to walk beside her.

'Tachnadray must have been a lovely estate once, Elaine.'

'But . . . ?' she prompted.

'It could be developed. Tourists. Fishing. Build huts for nature cranks. Camp sites. Tours round the baronial hall.'

She halted. Thinking I'd struck oil, I enthused, 'Have your own Highland Gathering. Tents, pipers, dances, folk song evenings, original tartan kilts, Ye Olde Clan McGunn whisky-making kits. McGunn brand genuine Scottish bagpipes – '

'And breed hordes of McGunns? Repopulate the Highlands?'

She spoke with such quiet sibilance you had to strive to hear the venom. We'd stopped, her luminescent face white with anger.

'Well, er, not all of it.'

The nervous quip failed. She motioned me to sit on the wall and listen.

'Fall off a horse and lose the power of your legs, Ian. Myths are never the same again. They stand out with a certain clarity.' She laughed, an ugly spitting ejaculation I wouldn't like to hear again. 'So we should join the great Folklore Industry? It's the road to insanity. A social mania.'

I said, narked, 'I was only trying to help. A little profit – '

She pointed a finger at me. 'Don't interrupt. Just pay heed. Original tartan? There's no such thing. Listen: three centuries ago The Grant ordered his entire clan into his standard tartan.' She put on a cruel brogue to mock the words. 'And his own family turned up wearing a dozen different. You see? It's all fraud.'

'But tartan's – '

'A French word, Ian. "Tartaine" is a material, nothing to do with patterns. But then the *Irish* were great cloth weavers. The bagpipes? – the only invention ever to come out of Egypt. Scotch poetry? – our earliest indigenous one is in Welsh, for God's sake. The kilt? – invented by Thomas Rawlanson, an English iron-smelter in 1730. 'All tartans indigenous to our Scotch clans? – nonsense; there's even an authentic Johore tartan. Didn't you know? With a royal imprimatur, too!'

'I wish I hadn't come to see your bloody dogs.'

'We rhapsodize about Robert the Bruce and his spider, conveniently forgetting that he was an Anglo-Norman whose favourite method of murder was a stab in the back while the victim was unarmed and at prayer. Ask John the Red, whom he killed in the Franciscan church at Dumfries. And our fantastic Bonnie Prince Charlie? – a drunken Pole who thieved every penny his loyal followers possessed. And our famous Rabbie Burns.' She rolled her r's cruelly to mock. 'Don't tell anyone – his famous dialect is pure Anglo-Saxon. Nothing wrong with that, of course, unless you pretend it's a pure something else. When adherents trump up clan loyalties and urge me to "develop my clan's potential", I begin to ask what they're *really* after. You understand?'

'You mean what I'd get out of it? Twenty per cent – '

'Twenty per cent's out of the question.' She'd actually said her first three words in time with my last. Did she guess every bloody thing I thought? 'Five.'

'You mean bugger.'

She laughed, clapping her hands, and that terrible vehemence was gone as suddenly as it had come. At an imperious wag of her finger I trundled her obediently towards the ramp. Michelle emerged to see Elaine back in.

'Duncan's sounding for you, Ian,' Michelle called.

574

'What else is new?' I said irritably.

Elaine laughed. 'I've been telling Ian that we owe our tartans to Lowland machinery makers,' she announced. 'I think he's really upset.' She called after me: 'Still, Ian. At least our patron saint is real. Your English one's pure imagination.'

'Sensible bloke,' I said with feeling. 'If I were him I'd stay that way.'

Her musical laughter followed like a hound on my heels.

Chapter Fifteen

That evening I struck out of my mental cocoon. It was definitely becoming time to rock the boat. Over a frothy frozen thing which tasted of lemons, I asked about Robert. I badly wanted a phone but wasn't even sure if Tachnadray had one.

'It's a question of money, folks,' I announced, mostly to Elaine. 'We ought to get Robert in to help us.'

Shona looked up quickly but it was Michelle who countered. 'He's no furniture man, Ian.'

'He's a pair of hands, love,' I corrected, thinking: So Michelle wants Robert kept out of Duncan's hair. Does Shona?

'No,' said Elaine as Duncan drew breath to chip in. 'Robert's already got too much to do.'

Duncan subsided. Happily I clocked up another fact: Robert was busily occupied, on Elaine's orders.

'Money,' I said. 'There's a lesson here. Me and Duncan have laboured long and hard, and finished the "antique" piece this afternoon. It's good, but now we're stuck. We must start looking for wood, materials, decide on the next – '

'You can't start one till the first's finished, Ian,' Elaine said.

'Wrong. It's bad fakery, Elaine.' I leant forward on the mahogany, eager from certainty. 'Even genuine workshops work by overlapping. Sheraton, Chippendale, Ince, Mayhew, Lock. Do one at a time and you end in the workhouse.'

'It's dangerous, Elaine,' Michelle said. Shona gave her a look, normally not this quiet.

'Ian's inclined to be bull-at-a-gate,' Duncan added.
I don't like being apologized for and said so.

'Let him speak.' Elaine was in a lace blouse with a
blue velvet neck ribbon. Some pudgy lady serf was
helping tonight. New to me, but she was clearly a
Tachnadray veteran and called Elaine 'pet', to Michelle's evident annoyance. 'I've already disappointed
Ian once today. He wants to make us an olde worlde
Disneyland.'

'How much does running the estate cost?' I asked,
ignoring Duncan's warning frown to go easy. 'Say it's
X, for rates, wages, food, heating, clothes. And what's
the income? Say it's Y, from Duncan's reproductions,
sheep, crops – do you grow crops?' I enthused into
their silence, 'It's Mr Micawber's famous problem:
happiness is where X is less than Y. What's wrong with
not being broke?'

Duncan cleared his throat. 'Like you, Ian?'

'Touché,' I said, beaming. 'We hire a promotions
man for plans to make the estate solvent.' I gazed
round at them all. 'It'd take one single phone call.'

'I won't have Tachnadray a mere tourist stop.' Elaine
had spoken. 'I couldn't have dinner ogled by tourists
at so many dollars a head.'

'It's degrading for a noble house,' Shona said.

'Not even a Clan McGunn coat-of-arms on head-
scarves, wooden plaques?' I pleaded. 'Pride's expensive. Christ's sake, Elaine. Have you never seen a
Manchester mill on the go? For a percentage they'd do
thousands a bloody day – tea towels, travelling bags,
all in McGunn tartan. Cups, mugs, silver brooches,
Tachnadray deer. And Duncan's workshop'd turn out
phoney shields – ' I was in agony. 'Can't you see?'

'No.' Elaine calmly pronounced over my distress,
and with utter serenity gestured the serf to pour coffee.
'I'm becoming rather tired of your schemes, Ian.'

One last try. 'Then it's your dreaded Tachnadray
secret.'

Everybody stilled, even the beverage-toting peasant.

'Secret?' Michelle made a too-casual search for sugar, which anyway was within easy reach.

'What secret?' It wasn't until Duncan demanded point blank, his voice harsh and his pipe like a clutched weapon that the penny dropped and I thought in sudden jubilation, God, there really *is* something.

'Wine,' I explained, cerebrating at speed.

'Establishing a vineyard,' from dear innocent Michelle, 'takes centuries.' She'd dressed in lovely harebell blue.

'So we don't,' I explained, thinking: Give me strength. 'We never even see the bloody wine, see? A vineyard simply bottles us up Tachnadray Special. Prints new labels, ships it to a distributor.'

'Outsiders!' Shona spat.

'No, Ian.' Another royal imperative. 'Too longterm.'

'Then you don't need money,' I concluded with angry finality. For a second I thought I'd over-acted, but not for Michelle.

'You're wrong, Ian. We're in dire straits.' She really did say it, dire straits, straight out of her English lessons.

'Michelle,' Duncan warned, too late.

I said, acting driven to the brink, 'Then we sell up.'

Outrage. Horror. The lackey almost dropped the coffee-pot. Duncan almost swallowed his pipe. Michelle gave a Gallic squeal of turmoil-powered indignation. Shona paled. Even Elaine's smile wilted somewhat, a case of needle reversed. Robert would have inverted me in the nearest soufflé.

'At an auction. Here, in Tachnadray.' It was my turn to smile now. 'We sell every damned thing. Even,' I said, choosing my words carefully, 'even some things we haven't got.'

Well, what works for Sidoli's travelling fairground can work for Tachnadray's immobile gentility, right? Elaine looked and said nothing. The rest tried to argue me into the ground. They hadn't bothered to listen to a word I'd said, so I just noshed, nodded, muttered 'You've got a point there' sort of responses, and started working out the scale of the operation. Barefaced robbery, lies and immoral usury are the tools of the work world's greatest auction firms. They'd be just as useful in Tachnadray.

Because of Elaine's telepathic swiftness in mind-guessing, I carefully didn't think of my other scam, which was to find this oh-so-unimportant cottage and raid the damned thing.

Theft, I often say to myself, is often in a good cause. It's especially beneficial when it happens to somebody else. Oh, I don't mean the great Woburn Abbey silver haul, though even that netted mind-bending reward money when those two workers found the cache in that Bedfordshire waterpumping station. Somebody always does well out of it, even when theft goes wrong. One problem is Finance Law, the great rip-off of modern times. Those lucky enough to be in on it – police, lawyers, estate agents – are of course all for it and want us, the oppressed majority, to join in their hearty approval. We don't. Reason? Because the Law costs us a fortune. All we can do is try to exist in spite of it.

That evening, aware now of the strong differences of opinion around the table, we separated with Elaine saying she'd 'take advice' and that we'd have a conference about it all in a day or so. Money was obviously Tachnadray's old battleground where Shona and Michelle fought daily. Very serious stuff. Solvency's a perennial laugh, though a rather moaning sort of laugh, at Lovejoy Antiques, Inc. But I've always managed by having friends I can rely on, borrow from, or otherwise sponge off, and Tachnadray only had this gaggle of clan innocents.

Up in my converted garret I easily worked out the

solution, how to hold an important auction sale of the many valuable antiques we hadn't got. The idea wasn't new, but the actual sin would have to be. In immorality freshness is always important, like in fruit. I shelved it, and settled down to examine the Ordnance Survey map I'd brought. This cottage Hector had mentioned was niggling.

Scattered thinly among the colours and contours of the uplands round Tachnadray were black rectangles which indicated buildings. The mansion was clearly marked. I'd work outwards, and start with the cottage on the valley road. I'd noticed it standing maybe a mile beyond the end of the drive.

Which is how I wasted a couple of hours that night, stumbling along the driveway in virtual pitch darkness and trudging the Dubneath track to find a miniature collapsed ruin. Some giant bird – at least, I hope it was only a bird – swished past my head and frightened me to death as I felt the fallen stones of the old crofter's cottage. Maybe the gatehouse, a retainer's place from the estate's grander days? Nothing there, anyway. The bird mooed and swished me again, so I cleared off. One bare porch light was always left burning, on Elaine's instruction, so returning was less problematic. I just followed that lovely civilized glimmer down below, and made it safely.

A cross mark on the map to show which building I'd investigated – leaving about a dozen isolated buildings within about a five-mile radius of Tachnadray – and I was ready for bed. Nobody had followed me, I thought. I was quite confident.

Some people have a politician's mind. They're always highly dangerous because politicians, remember, have a vested interest in doom. Robert was like that. I mean, just because I was up early next morning and strolling a couple of miles across the uplands he decided to follow, obviously longing for me to turn out to be a traitor. Me! I ask you.

There was a light drizzle on a long breeze. It was only when I turned to shake the water off my mac hood that I saw the suspicious swine. He was perhaps a mile off, but covering the ground at a hell of a lick, his enormous hairy red head topped by a bonnet and nodding like a horse does at each pace.

He saw my pause and stopped. Casually I went on, giving a glance back down the hillside. He started up after me again. I paused. He halted. I moved, and he came on.

No use continuing in these circumstances, so I made a curve along the hill's contour and fetched up on the Dubneath track about a mile from where I'd started. Robert, by then higher up the hill, realized my intention and stopped to watch me without any attempt at concealment. He simply held the skyline looking down. I gave the hearty wave of the dedicated dawn-rambler, and cheerily whistled my way back to the big house for breakfast.

The building I'd wanted to inspect was over the hill's shoulder, about two miles off. Robert was proving a nuisance, especially as it was his terrain, but I couldn't get it out of my mind that if I found that cottage I'd find Joseph. Predecessors are always a nuisance in any job. Predecessors who prove elusive and taboo are even more disturbing.

'Och, the poor wee thing,' Mrs Buchan said, noisily brewing up. She was the serf-factotum, red-faced, plump and breathless. I watched fascinated amid the din. All kitchens look like pandemonium to me, but Tachnadray's was special. It was a vast long hall, sort of Somersetshire-ninepin-bowling-alley shaped but with huge iron ranges along one side. Mrs Buchan rushed everywhere. I'd asked about Elaine.

'Can't the doctors do anything?'

'Don't ye think they've tried, you daft man?' Mrs Buchan sang, trotting her large mass from table to oven with raw bread. 'It was that horse. A stupid great lummock. I'm against horses, always was. But do people listen?'

'Why aren't you a McGunn, Buchan?'

The far door opened and Robert entered. He sat without a word. With me at one end of the long table and the red-bearded giant glowering at the other we were a gift for a passing jokester.

''Morning, Robert. Breakfast presently.' She sprinted to the copper porridge pan, panting, 'I am. Before Buchan wed me. My two bairns are away in London.'

'Sinners.'

The joke fell flat. 'Aye,' she wheezed over the frying bacon, 'I pray for them night and day.'

'I walked out this morning,' I said hopefully as the porridge came.

'Aye. You were seen.'

The laconic shut-out. I bent to my spoon. 'I thought I saw Hector walking Tessie and Joey.'

'No, man. He'd be away in the opposite direction, on the . . . ' Mrs Buchan's voice trailed off as Robert's massive hulk emitted a warning rumble.

'Lovely dogs,' I said casually, reaching for hot new bread.

Eating always cheers me up. And happiness brings luck, though folk mistakenly assume it's the other way round. Nice knowing that the cottage Hector inspected every morning lay in the opposite direction to the place I'd just tried to reach. Progress in Tachnadray.

Duncan told me when I reported for work that Elaine had called a meeting tomorrow morning. I'd have to get a move on with Plan X.

Chapter Sixteen

You must have played that imagination game where you can have any woman (or man, *mutatis mutandis*) on earth? And 'have' in any way you like? It used to be my big favourite until matters got out of hand, over this bird called Wilhelmina. She was a drama student and lived on Natural Earth-Friendly Pulses, which means beans. It ended in tragedy when, in the throes of orgasm, somebody (she claimed it was me) uttered a strange bird's name. She played merry hell and stormed out in a rage. Naturally I missed her almost until the pubs opened, and felt the chill wind of economics because she'd paid the mortgage. Still, I got used to food again. God, those bloody beans. But the point of mentioning that dream game of yippee is, Shona was beginning to figure in my imagination. Disloyal to Jamie, of course, to think hopefully of Shona rapturously savaging my defenceless body. Only a heel would lust like that. Her great dog Ranter was the deterrent.

Duncan gave me permission to go into Dubneath that morning, to see what was available in a small lumber yard. It sounds quick and easy. In fact I had to walk four miles on the track to a cairn of stones and wait there on the bare hillside for a lorry to come by at half past ten. It was on time, driven by a warped old geezer called Mac whose one utterance was, 'Aye,' in various tones of disbelief. Oddly, I was almost certain I'd seen Robert stalking the upland stones while I'd waited, but looking more intently only seemed to make him vanish actually on the hillside. Clever, that.

I got the lorryman to drop me on the outskirts of the megalopolis and walked in.

The lumber yard was soporific. A neat rectangle of sloped planks, a barrow, a wooden shed with a corrugated roof. A few pieces of second-hand furniture were covered by a lean-to on the side opposite the double gate. I shouted a couple of times, wandered a bit. The only rescuable items were a heavy rosewood desk, eastern, and a Wellington chest whose top and side panels had split badly. Beggars can't be choosers. I scribbled a note, offering for the two, and wedged it in the shed door saying I'd call back.

It was too early to phone Tinker, or call on Shona – I wasn't going to risk that great silent dog without protection – so I went to see George MacNeish. He was doing out the saloon bar with Mary. They seemed honestly pleased to see me.

I pretended to stagger to a stool. 'I'm in hell. No houses anywhere, and all the grub's French.'

'That'll be Michelle,' Mary said, smiling. 'But Gladys Buchan'll start you off right each day.'

'She tries.' I closed the door because two old anglers in tweedy plus-fours were chatting in the parlour. 'Look, folks. Who and where is this Joseph?'

The smiles faded. After a moment of still-life I said, 'I can't go out and ask Mrs Innes. Everybody in Tachnadray shuts up if I mention him. It's getting on my nerves.'

George was about to say something when Mary put in one breath ahead. 'It's no business of ours, Ian. Maybe you've been too long in the soft south. Up here family feelings are best not touched.'

'Seems daft to me. Okay, he drank. Is that enough to launch a bloke into oblivion? And where's the harm telling me?'

George deliberately chose his words. 'Joseph is a McGunn, so he's rightly your clan's responsibility, not ours. But to settle your mind: Joseph worked up at

584

Tachnadray, yes. And left under a cloud. That's all. Now stop your asking, and stay mute like a canny man.'

'There!' I said with evident pleasure. 'Wasn't painful, was it? And look how relieved you've made me. Just for that I'll drag your wife down into her kitchen, bolt the door and force her to warm up some of her rotten old mouldy pasties.'

Their expressions lifted and amid smiling prattle Mary started for the kitchen. I don't know which of us was the more relieved as normality reasserted itself.

'Typical McGunn,' George mock-grumbled. 'Always thieving.'

'Shut your face, MacNeish. Or I'll take up golf and thrash you at your own game. Here, missus,' I said, slamming the kitchen door after me. 'What's this about the soft south? I'll have you know I work bloody hard down there . . .'

My heart felt sick, though I cleared Mary's grub quick enough and kept up the rabbiting. The MacNeishes had been generous enough to give me a warning when I'd left for Tachnadray, but now I needed to know something definite they'd handed me a load of codswallop. I didn't believe that about Joseph leaving under a cloud. He was still around, and I badly needed to find him.

By eleven o'clock I was at the great Innes emporium, smiling as I entered and hoping to find it empty of customers. It was, but a glance at Mrs Innes's closed face made it apparent there'd be no joy there. She'd been warned. I put on a show of buying a few things – staples, resin, electric torch, stout twine, wood stain – and asked about the lumber man.

'Why, ye stupid man!' she exclaimed, clearly glad to be on safe ground. 'He's at the pier loading his uncle's boat.'

'Wrong, Innes. There's only Jamie there.' I'd looked

towards the water as I'd left the tavern. He'd been loading a small motor ketch, the only activity.

'Aye. It's him.'

'Jamie owns the lumber yard?' The only supplier of obsolescent furniture, the antique faker's raw material, was Shona McGunn's Jamie. My brain sighed an exhausted sigh.

'Of course, Ian. Didn't Mary McGunn tell ye that?'

'Mary McGunn?' I only knew one Mary in Dubneath.

'Mary MacNeish.' Mrs Innes was bagging up black currants. Her eyes held mine. *It's the best I can do*, her careful gaze said, as she joked, 'You McGunns are all too wrapped up in your silly selves . . .'

'Will ye no be resenting that slur from an Innes, Ian?' Shona came in the shop doorway behind me, smiling, her great dog beside her. It was enormous with the light behind it. 'The Inneses are great misjudgers.'

'Glad you came, Beautiful,' I said, joining the spirit of the thing. 'While Jamie's busy have we got time to sneak off?'

Shona laughed. Ranter grinned. 'For coffee, Ian?'

'I've had nothing all morning.'

'Oooh, the lies in the man!' Mrs Innes exclaimed after us. 'He's full of Mary's cooking!'

My least favourite headache returned as I walked along the narrow pavement with Shona and her pooch. It comes from fear, which is generated by a terrible realization of ignorance. Mrs Innes had tried a second time to warn me, in her way. I'd just been too slow to appreciate it. There was only one ally left, and that was Shona. After all, I thought, glancing sideways at her lovely bright face, she was the one who'd brought me up here. She alone knew who I was, and kept the secret. She alone had promised me a fair share. And she alone was on my side, however erratic her personality. This clan-loyalty business could surely be safely forgotten, except among the elderly gossipmongers of Dubneath.

I'd only been allowed back into town when Shona was free. I must have accidentally slipped her by alighting on the outskirts instead of being fetched directly into Dubneath's centre. She must have gone hunting me after realizing I'd gone missing. Still, an ally is an ally. I wanted to get Tinker because I badly needed things done. In the meantime I'd have to rely on the one natural asset we all possess. Perfidy.

'Darling,' I said at her gate. 'Won't the neighbours talk?'

'No,' she said evenly, 'providing you're quiet.'

Ranter came in and watched me make myself at home, as the saying is. It was quite unnerving. As matters progressed from the possible to the inevitable, I had to ask Shona to send the dog out. Amused, Shona compromised by ordering it into the little front garden, and led me upstairs after latching the door. After that it was all smooth sailing. If my brain had been functioning, I'd have still talked myself into making love to Shona on the grounds that the worst I could expect was betrayal. After some of the women I've known it would be a small price. I'm fully trained in disaster. As it was, my intellect had hibernated at the first hint of forthcoming ecstasy. I don't know how sociologists manage all that dispassion they brag about. Women only make me think hooray. With my own brand of logic going full steam, the mere act of lying dazed and sweat-stuck to Shona afterwards was somehow proof that we were more fervent allies than ever.

'Who's the crook, love?' I said, drifting from oblivion to somnolence. Women are always awake when I come to. How do they do it?

'That's my question, Lovejoy.' She lay aside, somehow. The pillow had fluffed up between us making it hard to breathe.

'It's not Elaine, that's for sure. Nor Duncan. He's a naturally nice bloke.'

'Is he a good . . . antiques faker?'

'Not bad. Certainly not in the same league as some.'

'Michelle?' Her voice was in exact neutral, oho.

'Your pal?' I was unsure. Michelle was one of those lovely succulent women who should be eaten whole with mint. I've always been vulnerable. 'Dunno. What's her motive? Money?'

'That. And Elaine.' Shona's hatred showed now. Her throat thickened. 'Michelle's an intruder. A spider. She'll take anything she can. Men are blind, Lovejoy.'

'Oh aye,' I said drily. Fascism gets everywhere, even into lovers' beds. 'So Michelle and Duncan are your guess. Not Robert?'

She still spoke muffled. 'Robert does as he's told.'

'Which leaves Hector, but he's too busy with his dogs and sheep. And Jamie. Lucky that he runs the woodyard, eh?'

'Essential.'

There are two sorts of pests: women who never leave you alone after loving, forever inspecting your morphology and asking questions, and women who mentally move out and lie there, eyes closed, disowning the nerk they've drained to exhaustion. Shona was clearly of the second category, hunched away in the bed, making me feel a right hitch-hiker.

'Look, Shona.' I pulled her over to face me. 'Michelle couldn't pull a scam on her own. Duncan knows so little about the antiques game that he doesn't even suss out alternative routes, different fences. He's a craftsman, but no crook.'

'What are you saying, Lovejoy?' she said towards the window.

'There's been no crime.'

Which raised her, bedclothes pulled modestly over her breasts. 'No crime? Of course there's been a crime!

We've been selling furniture and paintings to keep Tachnadray together ever since I can remember. For less and less money!'

'You'd only a limited number to start with. You've simply run out of originals.'

'*We*'ve never relied on lies, Lovejoy! That's *your* trick!'

Well, she'd a right to be angry. She was the only person I'd ever met who'd passed a genuine antique as a fake. I spend my life doing the opposite.

'The point is, love,' I said along the pillow into her lovely furious eyes, 'there's no antiques worth mentioning left at Tachnadray. It's empty. That genuine bureau you sent down was Tachnadray's swan song.'

'How do you know, Lovejoy?' It was a whisper.

'The house feels dry, all wrong. It's got a few sticks, and that's it.'

'You really can tell,' she said with wonder.

'Afraid so, love.' I watched her beautiful blues well up. 'The stuff left in Tachnadray isn't worth a dealer's petrol for the journey. You made the wrong assumption. You couldn't understand why so little money was coming in when one or two reproduction pieces were being sent off every month. And poor old Duncan is slogging his guts out to make enough copies, fakes, repros to keep Tachnadray fed. He and Michelle were too tender-hearted to tell Elaine the truth.'

I was up and dressing, keeping an eye out for that bloody great dog. If it ever learned I'd made Shona cry I'd be a chewed heap.

'Where are you going, Lovejoy?'

'Tachnadray. Elaine's called a gathering tomorrow. I've to speak the plan out.' A naked man looks grotesque, so I was glad to be covered. Shona lay there, eyes dulled, pretty. Nakedness looks good on a woman. 'I can offer a reasonable scam, Shona. Only one-off, but it'd bring in a hell of a lot of gelt. If Elaine accepts, I'll stay and do it. If not, there's nothing to keep me here.'

'You'd leave? Because there's no antiques?'

'I can knock up fakes anywhere, love. It doesn't have to be in Tachnadray.'

For a few moments I dithered. I never know what to say when leaving a woman's bedroom. You can't just give a sincere grin and a thanks, love, can you? And women are too distrusting to believe dud promises.

'Will Ranter let me pass?'

She smiled, cold, I thought. She uttered the slow words like a thumbs-down to an arena. 'This once, darling.'

I gave her a sincere grin. 'Thanks, love,' I said, and left.

Chapter Seventeen

'Shut your gums, Tinker,' I said into the phone, frantic lest Mac's lorry left without me on the home run.

The gabby old sod was woozier than ever. He was in the Rose at Peldon, sloshed out of his mind. The Rose is a pub by the sea marshes, always heaving full of antique dealers.

'Eh, Lovejoy?' he bawled. The background noise was Grand National Day. 'I'm lissnin'.'

'A month from now I'm doing a paper job. A mansion.'

'Us? Paperin' a stately home?' Tinker yelled, coughing between syllables.

The distant pub's racket silenced as if by magic. Some lunatic talking football was instantly throttled.

'Start enrolling the dealers, Tinker. Pass their names on to Margaret.'

'Is it secret?' he howled to the universe. Jesus.

'Not any more,' I said wearily. 'Tell Margaret she can chit and chop for me. And get Antioch Dodd to collect the pots. Got that?' 'Pots' are lorries, from rhyming slang: pots and pans, vans. It'd be quite a convoy. Chits are IOUs and receipts, chops the stamps of approval. It meant I'd honour whatever deals Margaret decided for me. I might murder her afterwards if she guessed wrong, of course, but fair's fair.

'Right, Lovejoy. How much do we need?'

Tachnadray was say, sixty rooms of which two were still respectably furnished. The rest stood bare. A quarter of the rooms would have been servants' quarters, say about nine.

'About fifty rooms, Tinker, assorted, but I split half and half.' In its heyday half would have been bed-rooms, retiring-rooms, and half reception rooms, libraries, smoking-rooms and that.

'Fifty? Bloody hell. Where is it?'

'Never you mind. I'll phone down every fourth day.'

'Wait, wait! Lovejoy! Who's to reff the stuff?' Reff as in referee, to gain some slight assurance of authen-ticity for the antiques – real or fake'd hardly matter much – as they were loaded up.

'Who've you got there?' I could imagine two-score dealers frozen in the pub, listening breathless at this news of the biggest scam to hit East Anglia all year.

'Here? Well there's Harry Bateman, Liz Sandwell, Helen, Big Frank from Suffolk, Sven, Mannie, Jill . . . ' His rubbled croak became inaudible in instan-taneous pandemonium. The silly nerks had erupted, grabbed for the receiver to bawl their names and shout-ing offers, percentages, splits on the knock, part deals –

Click. Burr. I get fed up with other people's greed when I've enough of my own.

It was coming on to rain when finally Mac's lorry hove in. Somehow he'd heard, God knows how, of the furniture I'd left pencilled notes for at the lumber yard. They were on his wagon under a tarpaulin in the back.

Robert met us at the crossroads, pushing a handcart. Mute, he transferred the two pieces without my assist-ance. I called thanks to Mac and in the driving rain followed the giant's form along to Tachnadray. I felt a spare tool at a wedding.

This next bit's about crooked money, and how you – repeat, *you* – will sooner or later be robbed blind. There's no escape, so if you're of a nervous disposition I'd skip it.

A 'paper job', a.k.a. 'papering a house', is one of the commonest antiques tricks in the world. And make no mistake, everybody in the game tries it. Since the Great Antiques Boom, however, it has come to be a speciality of the world's poshest auction houses. It works thus:

A householder dies, alas. In the ten seconds which elapse between the crusty old colonel's last breath and his widow phoning the insurance company, several dealers will call offering to sell the colonel's personal effects. The widow sorts out what she wants to take to her daughter's and signs a contract with a respectable auctioneer.

Now an auctioneer can do two things. Either all the auctionable stuff is vanned off by the auctioneer's respectable vannies (they will be called assistants in the written contract) to the respectable auctioneer's premises, or else the contents – furniture, cutlery, linen, carpets, the colonel's campaign medals, paintings, porcelain – will be left *in situ*, and the house opened for a grand auction.

You can imagine that the final printed catalogue might look a bit 'thin', as we say, if old colonel, R.I.P., didn't have much. But oh how nice it would be, thinks our respectable auctioneer wistfully, if the deceased had a couple of handsome almost-Chippendale tallboys, or an oil painting possibly almost nearly attributable to Turner or Vermeer. How sad a respectable auctioneer's life is, he sighs.

Happily, sin slithers in to help out. Within hours of that respectable auctioneer's naughty daydream, would you believe it but the house's contents begin to swell, multiply, increase, until finally on auction day the colonel's antiques overflow into the garden, where the respectable auctioneer has thoughtfully hired numerous elegant marquees for the purpose. Isn't life great? Soon it gets greater.

The cataloguer's erudition helps the thing along. She (cataloguers are normally female; more careful, you see) will say of some neffie portrait of a bog-eyed clergyman: ' . . . once attributed to the immortal Gainsborough . . . ' or some such. The fact that the daub was created in an alcoholic stupor by an incompetent forger now doing life on Dartmoor is regarded as a mere quibble, because the words *as written* are actually true. So Law condones the fraud: the portrait *was* once so attributed – by a crooked forger. See how it works?

Just as theatres are 'papered' – i.e. crammed by the actors' friends, who are given free tickets – so auctioneers swell their offerings at house auctions.

Innocent souls might ask: 'But what's the point? Who gains?' To answer this, best simply buy any item at such a sale, then try to sell it. An old Lowestoft jug, say. First, offer it just as it is. To your alarm antique shops don't want to know. Dealers spurn you and your jug. They see a dozen a day, so what's one more? Tomorrow, however, take along the auctioneer's lovely catalogue. You can now show the dealer your jug's handsome picture and precise printed description. He'll be over the moon. Of course he'll still haggle over the price. The point is *he'll want your jug*. You've made a sale. Good, eh?

The reason he now wants it is that magic thing called provenance. He can ascribe your jug, truthfully, as 'from the famous sale at Nijninovgorod House . . . ' and show your catalogue as proof. Appearance, condition, and provenance – they're the three great selling points in horses, cattle, bloodstock. And, oddly enough, people. Why not in antiques too?

Paper jobs are highly popular in the antiques game, because everybody profits: dealers, public, buyers, cataloguers, auctioneers, the colonel's widow, the bloke who prints the catalogue . . . The only slight hiccough in it all is that it's fraudulent. It *has* to be. Why? Because if every house was ramjam packed full of delectable antiques there'd be no demand. It'd be like everybody suddenly being millionaires. So the 'sets' of dining chairs aren't sets at all; they're made up from here, there and everywhere. Vases reputedly brought back from Japan in 1890 were actually fired in Wapping last week. The delicate Chinese porcelain pillows weren't shipped home from Canton last century: they were a job lot in a Hong Kong package tour this Easter. The colonel's campaign medals will be sold – and sold, and sold, and sold, for entire sets will be put together by every dealer in the country and sold as the colonel's one genuine set. Which explains why the printed catalogues for important house auction sales are always sold out instantly – to market twenty sets of medals you need twenty catalogues, right? It's cast-iron profit. It's today's favourite crime. All you need is a posh address, and you can make a fortune. The customers get diddled, but so?

That's the paper job. All you need is care, skill, and a team.

After dinner I retired to formulate my paper job, promising Elaine to reveal it in all its glory at the morning gathering. Then, in the cascading rain, I went out for a sly walk. The death simply wasn't my fault. Honest.

The drive to the main gate was the only orthodox way off the Tachnadray estate. Stone walls rimmed the thirty or so acres of paddocks, outbuildings, lawns, with a few straggly hawthorn hedges infilling the tumbled drystone stretches. Behind the great house, vegetable gardens were busily reverting to weeds. Glass cloches sprawled higgledy-piggledy. Greenhouses shed panes. Huts flaked planks. Even the outbuildings had joined the disintegration wholesale and gone toothy by extruding stones. I'd asked Duncan why he didn't grow stuff, market some produce. He'd waxed sarcastic: 'I'll get a dozen retainers in on it immediately.' The poor bloke was doing his best.

Hell of a place to hide, I grumbled inwardly as I

drifted through the dark garden. Soon after Mrs Buchan had blundered by admitting that Hector's dawn patrol was on the hillside opposite to the main gateway, I'd sussed out a cracked path between lines of old bleached canes. It made stealth clumsy and full of din, but what could I do? The map showed a fairly smooth slope, then a few upland folds. And, in grand solitude two miles off, a cottage marked *Shooters* in a narrow gully.

Climbing the wall was easy, and quieter. Torch in my pocket, I began the long slow climb up the fellside, walking bent and pressing my hands on my knees. The ground was soaked to squelching over my shoes. It made me slip on rocks projecting underfoot. Heather started kicking back at each pace, whipping my legs. There was no moon. How the hell had highwaymen managed? I did my best to follow the direction I'd planned, but within minutes I was using my torch to find the first gale-torn hawthorn and check its position against the faint glow of light from the house below. There were two leaning crags which would be my markers to aim off at a forty-degree angle to the right. The cottage was more or less a mile from there.

Common sense told that *Shooters* wasn't Hector's home. If it had been, why did he need to walk out there? The shepherd had innocently assumed that, being a McGunn, I was in on the cottage thing. Maybe *Shooters*, I hoped with spirits rising, was in fact a great Victorian shooting lodge and it was there that Duncan/Robert/Michelle or whoever had salted away the missing antiques from Tachnadray, if any.

Maybe nine o'clock when I set out. That made it getting on for ten when I made the first leaning crag. Odd, but I was starting to understand how the night-walkers had managed. It's quite easy, really. Once you get used to being away from civilization's buildings and lights, night resolves into distinct components. Ground underfoot stays pitch black, but the sky's dark intensity lessens somewhat. Tall stones and trees condense the sky's consistency, so that though you still can't actually see them as such, you can somehow perceive that they're there in your path. Tachnadray's light was more distant, but seemed almost blinding from the hilltop. I stopped looking at it because it lessened my night vision.

From the crags the ground descended and took me out of direct view of Tachnadray for the first time. Even so, I wasn't too worried. The faint sky shine from that direction was enough to show me the hilltop's sky interface. Ever so often I cricked over on the stones that littered the fells, so I developed a trick of walking with knees bent, using short steps, not putting my heels down first. It intrigued me. I'd adopted Robert's curious gait. A new way of looking, and a new way of walking, all in one go. I felt a real discoverer.

In fact I was so busy praising myself that I was stuck when a building thickened the darkness to my left. I'd actually come upon *Shooters*. A disappointingly small edifice. A pointless low wall ran from it for a short distance. Something to do with cattle? A snowbreak to halt fell drifts in blizzards? I felt my way along it, stepping carefully in case tins or bottles or other fellwalkers' debris lurked in wait.

Derelict? There was no sound. I halted, listened. In the distance a short deep bark sounded, curt and businesslike. I dismissed it. Hector's dogs probably wouldn't be out at this hour. I'd heard Duncan talk of red deer. Perhaps a stag calling its herd, maybe scenting me and resenting intrusion on its patch?

Risking, I took my flashlight and moved off a few silent yards. If somebody saw me I wanted a head start. I wasn't in good enough shape to sprint the two boulder-riddled miles to Tachnadray without breaking my neck, so I'd have to do a short dash and hide among the outcrops. Escape by subterfuge is really my thing, but it's easier in towns than out here in all this loneliness. I crouched.

Flash. The beam swept, hit buildings, dowsed into blackness again. In that instant of brilliance, my eyes beheld a child's drawing two-storey cottage, symmetrical and unadorned. The windows were wood-shuttered. Slate roof. Single chimney. A bare building on a barren hillside. What the hell was I doing out here, I asked myself irritably. One upper-floor shutter had stood slightly ajar, I'd noticed. I thought over the image in my mind. The obvious thing was to wait a minute in case my beam had disturbed an inhabitant, then creep up and simply try the door. For all I knew I might be stalking an empty house.

As I felt around me for a couple of decent-shaped stones I heard again that deer's bark. Closer, and only once, but now out beyond the cottage. I actually chuckled to myself. If only that apprehensive stag knew how little it had to fear from me it would get back between the sheets and nod off. God's creatures are gormless. No wonder. God was a beginner at creation.

It's a fallacy to assume that burglars can't climb a wall without a ladder. A burglar can climb anything, because even a blank wall offers ledges, pipes, rectifying studs, cistern overflows. You might say that such feeble supports might not support a burglar's full weight – and you'd be right. But they'd support a quarter of a burglar's weight, and that's all he needs because he can do the bolus trick, the town burglar's favourite.

This evolved from sailing ships, I've been told. Others say it's what Argentina's cowboys do to hobble bulls. The stones make the cord whiptangle anything hit. I've even seen it used to put a rope round untouchable scalding steam pipes along a mill ceiling. You take a piece of strong twine a yard long, and tie stones at the ends. This is the bolus. Then fasten a long length at the midpoint, and coil that length on the ground beside you. Take the midpoint of your bolus between finger and thumb of your left hand, and hold one tied stone in your right. Then start swinging the other dangling stone in a circle. Clockwise or anticlockwise doesn't matter. Once it's going, you simply fling the opposite stone in the opposite direction, and you'll find you are holding a piece of string by its middle with two stones whirling round in opposite directions. Naked tassle-dancers do it in night clubs from their breasts – er, I mean I've heard they do. To keep the bolus spinning, you simply move your hand up and down.

You lean, fling the bolus with a slow overarm cast. The best is that if you miss the chimney you simply reel it in again, or cut your cord and make another bolus. This actually happened. I missed the chimney stack twice. I tried pulling on the twine but the bolus must have caught on something on the far side of the cottage roof. It's usually the guttering or a cistern overflow pipe. I bit through the nylon, let its free end whip away into the night air, and chewed away another one-yard length. By feel, I'd still got enough to stretch from roof to ground, and I was in no haste.

Mostly, I (I really mean burglars who go in for this sort of thing) prefer elongated waisted stones because they hold the string better. City burglars use spark plugs, partly to assume innocence if they're caught. I only took a minute finding a decent heavy pair of stones out in all this horrible countryside, and I was in action, for another go. I reached for my coiled twine.

And stopped.

Almost beyond hearing, I could just make out a faint yell. 'Run! Run!' Quite like a yell heard through glass.

Baffled, I strained to hear. Run? Run where? And why? I actually got up and turned this way and that, head tilted to catch the gnat's whine of a shout, before it dawned. It was inside the cottage. Somebody was yelling for somebody to run. If I hadn't been thick I'd have guessed, but I've a zillion untrained neurones. I was quite unconcerned, merely puzzled.

My beam cut the night. And something moved, far over to my right beyond the low wall.

Robert stood there. He looked gigantic in the solid glare from my torch. With him on a leash stood Ranter, its eyes two brilliants against jet. That bark had been no deer. Dogs bark.

'Hello,' I called feebly. 'I was just out for . . .'

Robert fiddled with the huge animal's neck. Nervously I backed away a pace. Robert stepped aside, a whole dark space between him and the giant hound. He raised an arm and pointed at me. His kilt flapped once in the night breeze.

'Run! Run!' the little insect screamed inside the cottage.

Frightened, I backed off. Run? Somebody was warning me – *me* – to run. Christ. From what? From . . .

The giant figure held its biblical pose in my torchlight.

'*Kill*,' Robert said. He turned and walked away. I turned and ran like hell.

Chapter Eighteen

For a second or two I thought the damned animal wasn't coming after me. I fled across the slope I'd climbed, my torchlight flickering ahead on shining angles of granite projecting from the heather. Maybe I even imagined I was going at a speed Ranter couldn't match.

Then I heard it, breathing like a train. It slobbered as it ran, a flopping sound as its feet landed. It didn't dash like a greyhound or scamper like a beagle. It simply loped. In that first terror-stricken moment when I'd seen it start, its apparently casual movement said it all. What's the hurry? its graceful mass announced as it hunched up to start the pursuit. It's not a race – it's a hunt. Sooner or later, it seemed to say, the quarry'll tire, weaken, flake out, and then . . . I was moaning as I ran. If I'd had breath enough I'd have whimpered, prayed, screamed, anything.

Ahead a roaring sound. I'd say I headed for it except that that expression makes my progress sound like a ramble. Reality was different. I was scrambling, stumbling, gasping, across the stony hillside slope, trying to hold my torch out ahead for sight, anything to keep ahead of that dreadful slapping which proved the bloody monster was gaining.

It could have been only a minute when a roar opened the ground ahead, and I tumbled over an edge. I fell maybe ten feet, more, found myself in swirling water and floundered forward, anything to keep going.

A waterfall. Some sort of gully, with a narrow freshet of water. I'd kept hold of my torch. I splashed across, climbed a tall projecting slabbed rock dividing the swirling course. Maybe I could get to the top, sit there and somehow stop it climbing up after me. A stone, a cobble. I realized I'd got my new untried bolus still in my hands, stuffed it in my jacket pocket and hauled a cobble up out of the onrush.

A flop, flop, behind. Here it came. With a slither Ranter appeared at the margin I'd fallen over and without a pause came bounding on. I saw him hit the water with a ploosh, force his way up to the base of my rock, and try to leap up. I flung my cobble and hit the bugger. He leaped to one side, and halted. I squatted up on my pinnacle, sick from breathlessness and fright.

He looked at me, transfixed in my beam. Ranter's appearance arrested me. He honestly appeared noble. The strain of chasing hardly showed. He'd cornered me. His teeth would be along in a minute to perform massacre. It was all so serene, this hunting business.

So that's what a hunter-killer looks like, I thought dementedly. His stance was one of attention, of cool certainty. His tongue lolled. His flanks shone. What I hated most was that he was *thinking*. I honestly mean it. The murderous beast was actually cerebrating, its great head swinging as it took in the geography of the gully and the pouring beck, calmly working out how to catch and kill the shivering bloke perched ludicrously up there.

Directly upwards from the water my angular granite projected, its faces a mixture of smooth and rough, but on the whole vertical, thank God. The side I'd climbed up had barely a fingerhold. I'd done well to haul myself up. I prayed fervent gratitude that I had hands and Ranter hadn't any means of clutching.

Its head swung, marcasite eyes glittering. I whimpered. It took no notice and benignly continued inspecting my slab. Don't worry, its urbane manner informed me; this is only a job. I'll get you in a minute.

Above all, be patient. I moaned. The bloody beast was a real pro.

We were maybe thirty feet apart. The animal – it wasn't good old Ranter any longer; executioners don't have names – backed, tried to get space for a run, changed its mind.

My torchlight couldn't be helping it. I kept the beam trained on its face. Not much of a dazzle, but what else could I do? I found a single loose stone flake, chucked it. The murderer leaned its head an inch and the stone flew by, clattered down the rock wall. It didn't even blink. For a daft second I thought of persuasion. I said, 'Ranter. Good dog.' It gave me a glance of withering scorn. In fact, so compelling was its thorough examination of the stream's narrow gully that I did it too. We were a weird partnership, quarry and hunter.

Downstream no hope that I could see, the spate frothing on a mincing-machine of large stones. The gully's sides slanted outwards from the granite bed. My beam flicked, returned to the dog, flicked away for a quick glance, back. I didn't want the beast doing anything sly while I was being conned into studying the terrain.

The monster moved, one of those sudden tensions as if about to leap sideways. I yelped in fright. It stayed, splay-footed. I followed its gaze, used my torch to see what it had worked out. The sides of my slab were ripped vertically by ancient geologic forces. A man could just about climb up there but no dog. So? I shone back at Ranter. And it was smiling, its stare fixed above me.

Above? I shone upwards and nearly peed myself in terror. There was an overhang. Barely seven yards above my head the gully's side leaned in to form a shelf. Ranter could get me. I'd had it. Any creature on earth could get up there, look down on me. Then leap and . . . and . . . I whimpered.

The hound gave one last calculating stare, gauged the distance from the ledge to me, then splashed off downstream bounding from rock to rock with that casual, lethal grace. A mad hope swept into me – suddenly Shona had missed him and whistled one of those dog-whistles to call him off.

But no. The overhang was from the side opposite. No way to cross upstream, so it was doing the sensible thing. Downstream where the gully flattened it could easily lope upslope to gain the plateau, then reach the projecting granite and leap . . . I've made it sound like miles. It was maybe a couple of hundred yards, at most. I wondered if there was time to make a run for it . . . But it had nearly caught me when I'd had a start. And now I was knackered. I'm not proud of what I did then. I blubbered and wailed, yelled for help. And did nothing.

Wearily I discarded my jacket, some lunatic notion of wrapping it round my forearm for a last futile aquatic wrestle. It rattled. I felt in my pocket. Two stones. I pulled them out, still tied at opposite ends of the strong twine.

My bolus. That gave me . . . well, one go. The flopping sounded. I set one stone swinging, set the other going, and stood upright with the thing humming vibrantly in my right grip. Up and down, faster. Eyes on the tip of the overhang, I shone the torch there. It was only when I saw his great head loom above the overhang that I realized my stupidity. Too close. My perch was maybe a square yard wide. Any hit would bring me down with him.

He looked. For a millisec I saw puzzlement in his eyes as I leaned away, the bolus whirring. His head nodded up and down in time with my oscillating hand. Perhaps he could hear the string thrumming even over the torrent's din. Then his brow cleared. That humming cord in the man's hand was irrelevant. Orders were orders. He was to hunt and kill, string or no strings. He gathered and leapt down on me.

My arm came from behind. I was already in mid-throw when he left the lip. The bolus met and tangled. The stones were still whipping round and round him as I flung myself forward to avoid his hurtling mass. Foam pressed into my mouth and I was tumbling over, over. Stones slammed my legs, bum, head, shoulder. Noise deafened me. I rolled, engulfed and retching, too dazed to struggle or wonder which way was up. I was drowning. I lashed out, flailed at everything else not me. I was dying.

Except the pandemonium was now somewhere else, with me no longer part of it. I retched. Air. I was in air, not in the water. I breathed, vomited half of the torrent back where it belonged, breathed and crawled. A vertical stone stopped my crawl. I lay there, done for and too terrified to struggle further in case that damned hound heard me and came for me again. I lay, half hiding, half resting. I must have dozed a few minutes I suppose, not much more.

Something pressed against my feet. Something floating, pushing. Perhaps a log? I withdrew my legs, shoved them out.

Still there. It was being moved by the onrush. It was therefore inert. I reached out, scrabbled a cobble up from beneath me and lobbed it at the nudging thing by my feet. Thud. Not a splash, or a sharp crack of stone on stone. A thick bump.

Laboriously I raised myself, extended a hand. Fur. I recoiled in panic, started away. But it hadn't growled. I felt. A huge paw. A great head. A metal-studded collar. And, tethering its forepaws to its neck in a stranglehold, twine. One of the stones seemed to have struck its eye. It was my hunter, my personal executioner.

You can only retch a few times, they say, then the body gives up. True.

Countryside is supposed to increase insight, make poets. That's a laugh. Countryside does nothing but dull your wits. My mind was so addled that I actually started towards where I imagined *Shooters* to be before I said hey, and sat down for a think. It had emitted none of those chiming vibes, so it was no antiques cache. Whoever was in there had warned me, 'Run, run!' An ally. And trapped. Could I spring them? Perhaps, but would I get him/her as far as Dubneath before the clan caught up? Hardly, the state I was in and burdened by a possible ex-prisoner. And I already knew Hector checked the cottage each dawn.

No. The thing to do was turn up at tomorrow morning's gathering and suss out the reaction to my sudden reappearance. So, typically stupid, I started in the reverse direction, then got lost.

An hour wasted wearying myself even more. See what I mean about countryside? Finally I followed the tumbling water downhill, going slowly and feeling my way. I was perished. No jacket, no torch, wet through, exhausted. The Tachnadray track crossed a stone bridge over a wide fast stream, probably the same water, about a mile from the gateway. I must have been travelling a good hour before I walked into the bridge arch and almost knocked my silly head off. I'll never make a countryman if I live the rest of my life.

Which is why I had a fluke, coming at Tachnadray from that direction. Not as daft as all that, I was on the drive's verge for silence, and moved on the grass round the big house, to reach my pad. There was a light showing beneath the curtain. I thanked my inexpert needlework that had left a wide gap. I slid to the wall and waited.

Shona and Robert came downstairs. The light was off now, but I could hear them clearly. I almost stepped out to warn her.

'Nothing but the map,' Robert rumbled.

'That's proof enough,' Shona said. Her voice was

teasing, provocative. 'Ranter should be here now, lazy beast. Doubtless enjoying himself chasing something.' They both laughed. She gave in. 'Come, then, man. Let's lay your head.'

They walked together past the end of the workshop, over to the far outbuilding near the perimeter wall. There was no risk of being overheard. Duncan and Michelle slept in the big house, as did Elaine. Hector was miles off. Mrs Buchan slept downstairs in the cook's flat.

A light showed briefly. Robert having his head laid, doubtless. I stood unmoving for quite some time. Shona was a busy, busy girl. Sex as a reward for complicity. The idea wasn't new. What worried me was its use as an assassin's weapon.

Feeling a hundred years old, I crossed quietly to my garret, went in and locked the door. I had a bath in the dark and lay thinking until dawn blew the fright from the eastern lift. I wish I'd told Shona I'd had a headache in her cottage.

Chapter Nineteen

"Morning,' I said brightly to the gathering.

"Morning, Ian,' Duncan gave back affably, pipe ready to stink us out. Michelle was in powder blue, her neat skirt stencilling her waist. She wore a light necklet – not necklace – of a single silver band with a central amethyst, say 1900. Risky, but stunning. Oh, and she too replied an easy good morning. Robert was silent, glaring. Shona, already pale and worn, whitened even more. She knew what my arrival – indeed, my existence – meant. Old Mac was there, to my surprise. And Hector, waving a cheery greeting. Mary MacNeish sat beside Elaine, who today seemed excitable, less transparent than usual.

'Good morning, Ian,' the boss said. 'We were beginning to wonder where you were.'

'Stopped off for a quick snack, love.' Also, I'd actually been to check that my finished fake antique had already gone from Duncan's workshop. I was very pleased at discovering that.

'I've heard about your wee snacks,' Elaine reprimanded drily. 'Mrs Buchan calls you Dustbin.'

'Bloody nerve.' She always pretends she likes my appetite. 'I'll take my custom elsewhere if there's criticism. She's not the only pasty-maker in Caithness, is she, Mary?'

If Mary MacNeish expected me to be staggered at seeing her revealed as a McGunn she was disappointed.

Elaine began. 'Listen, all. Ian suggests we pretend to sell up Tachnadray.' She held a fragile hand to shush the murmurs. 'I've summoned you to judge the merits.

You all know our difficulties. Income's too little to keep the seat of our clan intact. At best we'll last a twelvemonth. Then it's the bailiffs and a boarding-house –

'Never!' Robert growled, fists clenched, glaring.

'Whist, man! We have some reserve antiques still – '

My cue. I rose, ahemming. We were arranged round the hall on a right mixture of chairs and benches. I had no notes, standing at my customary hands-in-pocket slouch. The cultural shock had been too much for us all. Truth time.

'Sorry, Elaine. There's no reserve antiques.' I spoke apologetically, but why? 'Not a groatsworth.'

'That's quite wrong.' Elaine held out her hand imperiously. 'The list, Duncan.'

Duncan's gaze was fixed on the floor. He made no move as I went on, 'The list is phoney, love. Duncan and the rest made it up, probably to reassure you. They gave you some cock-and-bull story about the upper west wing being exactly right for storing the remainder of your antiques.'

Everybody tried to talk at once. Elaine cut the babble with a quiet, 'Go on, Ian.'

'Tachnadray is broke *now*, not next year. So, with the last genuine antique gone – '

'Well I mind that day,' Mac suddenly reminisced through his stubble. 'Aye. Me and Cousin Peter from Thurso took it. Your father's grand four-poster, Miss Elaine – '

'Shut up, you old fool,' Duncan said. 'The past is past.'

'It's a familiar story,' I went on. 'Youngsters drift to the cities, a few adherents cling to the past. We've empty villages in East Anglia for the same reason. Tachnadray's marsupialized. It's a rock pool inhabited by crustaceans and sea-anemones – yourselves – after the tide's ebbed.'

'Is this true?' Elaine demanded quietly. Nobody

answered. She gazed at each in turn, waiting calmly until heads raised to meet her penetrating stare. She even gave me one. Suddenly I was the only honest crook on the campus. 'Continue.'

'There's only one way out now. We pull a paper job.'

They listened, doubts to the fore, while I explained the rudiments. Duncan's pipe went out. Michelle was enthralled, leaning forward and clearly excited by the whole thing. Robert sank into deeper caverns of hatred. Shona was still getting used to my resurrection.

'We start the papering with a pawnbroker.' Murmurs began, thunder from Robert, but I was fed up with their criticism and raised my voice. 'Not to use. To buy from. Pawnbroking law changes, when items exceed fifty quid. The trick is to find a pawnbroker who'll value even the Crown Jewels at forty-nine ninety-nine. In other words, the meanest. We take his stock – rings, necklaces, clothes – '

'And pretend they are Tachnadray's heirlooms?' Elaine asked. 'Isn't that rather hard on the widows and orphans?'

'Yes.' My answer led into a vale of silence. I was a dicey Sherpa in treacherous mountains.

'Will that be sufficient?' Elaine must have been painfully aware of the outraged glances from the others.

'No. We'll need more. But pawnbroking's gone downhill these sixty years. There's only a couple of hundred left in the entire land, which narrows our choice. We'll want an entire convoy of antiques from somewhere, especially furniture. I've already started raising the dealers.'

'And told them *here*?' Shona was on her feet, furious.

'Don't be daft.'

She subsided. Twice she'd absently reached out a hand as if about to pat a loyal hound. Both times she'd looked about, distressed. More grief was on the way, poor lass.

'I've one problem, how to bring the antiques in. It'll be a sizeable convoy.'

They waited. Elaine waited. And so did I, examining their expectant faces.

'Well?' Elaine's telepathy trick had gone on the blink.

'Air, road, or sea?' I asked. 'Same as usual?'

And Old Mac, bless him, said, 'Och, yon sounds a terrible lot for a . . . ' Hector shut him up by a double nudge.

' . . . For a wee ketch like Jamie's,' I finished for him, nodding. 'And your old lorry, Mac. I'd better organize a road convoy. The airport at Wick's too obvious.'

Elaine was smiling. 'Congratulations, Ian. We can't be blamed for trying to conceal our method of delivery. I hope you don't think us too immoral. The fewer people know, the better.'

'Is it agreed, then?'

'Yes.' Elaine's pronouncement gained no applause. The atmosphere smouldered with resentment. 'How long does this . . . papering take?'

'A month. First, we need a compliant printer.'

'Hamish in Wick is clan,' Elaine said.

'Next, I'll need a secure helper. Can I choose?'

'Of course,' said the young clan leader, and everybody looked expectantly at Shona.

Shona spoke first. 'I can start any time.' She gave me her special bedroom smile.

'Thanks,' I said, beaming most sincerely. 'But no, ta. Ready, Michelle?'

We were given an office in the empty west wing. Hector and a couple of men fetched some rough-and-ready rubbish for us to use as furniture. Michelle was awarded a desk: a folding baize-topped card table.

They found a lop-sided canvas chair from somewhere, and, unbelievably, for me a discarded car seat nailed to a stool. An elderly lady appeared from nowhere and contributed a brass oil lamp. Elaine ordered herself carried upstairs by Robert to inspect our progress.

'I'm ashamed this is the best Tachnadray can offer, Ian.' She directed Robert as an infant does its dad, by yanking on his nape hairs. She held a fistful of mane.

'I've done nowt yet, love. Got some carrier pigeons?'

'The phone was . . . discontinued. I'm sorry. Mrs Buchan will gong your mealtimes. I've sent for writing paper.'

Just then it arrived, two incomplete schoolbooks and half a letterpad, and a bottle with an ounce of ink dregs. Michelle was pink with embarrassment. Even Elaine, who was anti-prestige, looked uncomfortable. But to me rubbish is about par.

'One thing, Elaine. I'll want to ask questions occasionally. If Robert assaults me every time we'll get nowhere.'

'Robert,' promised our chieftainess, 'will not hurt you. Ask away.'

'Question one: nearest telephone?'

'Dubneath.'

'Two: nearest stores which'll give us credit?'

'Innes in Dubneath.'

'No, love. I've had to pay for everything there.'

'We never shop in Wick,' Elaine said, aloof but mortified.

Lucky old Wick, I thought. 'Then I'll break with tradition. Three: transport. Old Mac's lorry, I suppose?'

Elaine hesitated. 'There's the laird's car. It's old.'

Laird? Presumably her late dad. 'Tell Old Mac to siphon petrol out of his wagon, enough for a run to Wick. I'll manage after that. And four,' I added as Robert became fidgety at my peremptory manner, 'I must be given a free hand. Okay?'

An instant's thought, then Elaine's see-through gaze turned on Michelle. 'Very well. You, Michelle, will be responsible for his movements. Entirely. You do understand?'

'Yes, Miss Elaine.'

I didn't, though the threat was evident to all. Michelle and I stood and watched the redhaired giant clump down the corridor. I reached out and shook Michelle's hand. She was puzzled.

'Yes, Ian? What . . . ?'

'Welcome to the antiques game, love,' I said. 'It's murderous, packed with deceit, wonderful. We begin, you and I, by making a promise to each other. I tell you everything I'm doing, and you do the same for me. Deal?'

That took a minute to decide. She nodded at last, and smiled, but with that familiar despair hidden in her face. It occurred to me that she was as imprisoned as Joseph, in her way. Interesting thought, no? I laughed as she flapped her hand helplessly at the room.

'It's ridiculous,' she said. 'All we've done is put some scraps in a bare room, and you're grinning all over your face. Why?'

A window-pane had lost a corner. Putty flaked the sills. Patches of damp showed at two fungus-hung corners. Plaster had fragmented here and there, exposing laths and bricks, and powdered mortar lay in heaps ready for a dustpan, if we ever acquired one. An old wall cupboard had lost its doors, its wallpaper blebbing in the recess. Three cavities showed where somebody had wrenched out the gas fittings. How very thorough, I thought. Laird James Wheeler McGunn must have been harder up than me, even. The floor lino was reduced to a torn patch.

'Showbusiness time, Michelle,' I said. 'Start.'

'Start what? How?' She was lost.

'We pretend to drive to Wick, but finish up in the opposite direction.'

'But, Ian . . . ' she said uncertainly.

'Sod Ian,' I told her. 'My nickname's Lovejoy. Ready, steady, go.'

Chapter Twenty

The laird's car was familiar. I'd last seen it on a foggy night a wagoneer had died. I said nothing. It was a Mawdslay 17 h.p., that collectors call The Sweet Seventeen.

We drove beside Dubneath Water, my least favourite river, to gain the coast road north from Dubneath towards Clyth Ness. Using the louring mass of Ben Cheilt for guide, we forked left and made the inn at Achavanish with the huge old motor clattering away. It seemed glad to be out for a run. Certainly it hadn't seemed to notice the road's pitch, and took steep hills with hardly a change of note. I phoned from the inn, and got Tinker at Margaret's nook in the Arcade.

Margaret was relieved. 'Oh, thank goodness you've phoned, Lovejoy. It's practically civil war here. The Eastern Hundreds are a madhouse. Everybody wants to know percentages – '

'Don't we all?' I said with feeling. 'Put Tinker on.' I covered the mouthpiece and told Michelle, poised with the inn's notepaper, 'List what I say.'

Tinker's cough vibrated Caithness. 'Wotcher, Lovejoy. Gawd, you started summink, mate – '

'Shut it. Get Tubby Turner, that pawnbroker. I'll accept maybe three dozen items well over the pawn limit as long as they're in period. Plus a hundred separates under limit, and half a dozen baskets.'

'Gawd, Tubby'll go mental. You know what he's like.' His cough bubbled and croaked.

Michelle had stopped writing. 'But you said that there's a legal limit to what pawnbrokers – '

My digit raised in warning. She wrote.

'Listen, Tinker. Tell Alan the printer that he's had four hundred sale catalogues nicked.'

'Whose?'

'Catalogues for this sale. Now give me names, Tinker.'

'Right, Lovejoy. Helen wants in. She says you owe her.'

Only I knew how much. Plus there was the money side. She'd have to come in. Why is it women are born with so many advantages in life? Nothing to do all day, and all known privileges. 'Right-oh. Helen in.'

'Them two poofs. Sandy or Mel.'

'*Or* Mel? Not both?' The exotic couple had never parted since they'd become, in Sandy's gushy phrase, a real Darby and Joan. Tinker hates them. They're fast aggressive antique dealers, though, and that's what I needed.

'They had a scrap over some menu.'

How can you fight over a menu? 'All right. Sandy or Mel.'

'Next's Big Frank from Suffolk.'

That meant I could safely forget Regency and William IV silverware, thank God. It can be a nightmare. If only the Yanks had worked out a proper five-character hallmarking system . . .

'Is he out of trouble, Tinker?'

'Him? Some hopes. His second ex-wife's come.' Bad news for the latest wife, currently seventh, because his bigamies started with Number Two. But that meant he'd accept a lower percentage. 'Big Frank in.'

'Sven.'

'Not Sven.' His stuff's always got a leg missing.

'Margaret, Lovejoy?' Tinker knows about me and Margaret.

'Margaret, in. She'll reff. Next?'

'Liz Sandwell from Dragonsdale?'

'In, but not with Harry Bateman.' Tinker cackled. There'd been sordid rumours.

'Then Hymie. Says you owes him, that pearl scam . . . '

'How come I owe everybody when it's me that's bloody broke?' Tinker cackled himself into a coughing fit. For the first time in his life the antique dealers would be falling over themselves to buy him beer.

Next Lily. And Mannie of caftan and cowbell fame, dealer in antique timepieces. And Jill for porcelain, as long as she didn't bring her poodle and wandering matelots. And Brad because I needed flintlocks. And Long Tom Church for musical instruments. And Janice who never smiles, for late antique jewellery . . .

While Michelle tidied her lists I telephoned a general stores in Thurso, and asked to speak to the manager. I decided to become a Cockney trying to talk posh, Harrods-on-Woolworth.

'This is Sinclair, sir,' I announced gravely, which arrested Michelle's flowing pen. 'Butler to the laird, who is come to stay at Tachan Water. Local purveyors are not to my required standard. I am consequently obliged to send the laird's motor with his man Barnthwaite and the housekeeper. They are empowered to purchase. An invoice note is necessary for each item, if you please. They will arrive two hours from now.'

Michelle was aghast as I rang off. 'You said you were somebody else!'

'So?'

'And you told Elaine's gathering we'd only have cheap antiques. You've just ordered three dozen that could cost thousands. Don't deny it!'

'All right,' I concurred amiably. 'Got money for grub? Driving always makes me peckish.'

'But you've not long had breakfast – '

'Stop arguing, woman, and read me that list. Incidentally,' I said as we boarded the motor, 'do the mean buggers ever let you visit Joseph?'

That shut her. She took a long time to speak. 'What's going on, Ian?' she said.

'How the hell do I know?' I grumbled. I hate being famished on a journey.

'No,' Michelle finally answered, listlessly letting the wind buffet her hair as we lammed off north-west. 'I've asked. And Duncan tried to go on strike once. Hopeless.'

'The rotten sods. That'd annoy me, if he were my son.'

'There's nothing we can do. Not after he'd betrayed Tachnadray.'

The immense bonnet nudged the winding slope, with me trying to hold her below thirty m.p.h. 'Look, Michelle. Betrayal's too big a word. You betray countries and kings, not a bloody house with a few ageing retainers. Your Joseph tried to make a few quid on the side by selling Tachnadray's last antique bureau. It isn't the end of the world. I don't know anybody who hasn't had a go.' Feeling my way still, but not doing too badly. 'Never mind, love. We'll see what we can do for Joseph, eh?'

Her eyes filled. She looked away and rummaged for a hankie in her handbag. What on earth do women keep in them? It took a fortnight before she was snivelling right.

'There's no way out, Ian. We just had to protect Joseph after the incident. Robert saved him from being caught.'

'Check your list,' I said with a cheery smile. 'Take your mind off things.'

Thurso's a lovely old place. Ferries from the north wend to the islands. Its size and bustle surprised me; North Sea oil, I suppose, or innate vigour. Folk might say it's not up to much, but for me Thurso will always get a medal. It was there that the whole thing fell into place.

Mr McDuff was pleasantly young, very impressed by our motor. I'd parked it outside in full view, surreptitiously asking Michelle who I was supposed to be.

'You told him Barnthwaite.' She sat, clearly having none of it. I yanked her out, maintaining a charming smile and gripping her arm bloodless.

'Smile, love,' I said through my smile. 'You're Mrs MacHenry until I say otherwise, or it's gaol for the pair of us.'

I introduced myself to Mr McDuff while Mrs Mac-Henry made her selections. We were told that a separate invoice would have to be signed for every order. I sighed, said Mr Sinclair the butler was a stickler for inventories.

It was after we'd loaded up that light dawned. The stores lad carried out the victuals, groceries, wines and whatnot, while Michelle and I went to sign. Mr McDuff had the invoices all ready and offered me them. I frowned.

'No, sir,' I corrected. 'I'm never empowered to sign. The laird's housekeeper does it, Mrs MacHenry.'

He ahemed, hating being caught out in protocol. He'd rather have died. 'Of course,' he exclaimed, passing her the pen.

Now, one of the most surprising facts of life is that women make bad crooks. Which, when you think about it, is really weird. I mean, they're born deceivers. Right from birth they're talented fibbers and con-women. And their entire lives are a testimony to pretence. Yet how often do you hear of a really dazzling robbery executed by a bird? No. Birds go for the drip-feed: a zillion minor transgressions, debts created wholesale because trillions of housewives skilfully delay paying today's electricity bill. Individually, nothing. Totalled, a genuine migraine for Lloyd's of London. It explains a lot about the structure of society.

Which is the reason I'd warned Michelle every second breath that she wasn't to forget her true identity, Mrs MacHenry. And even as she took the manager's pen to sign I watched her, heart beating, in case she absently signed 'Michelle McGunn'. That was how I saw her face when I mentioned the laird. For that fleeting moment, she suffered anguish. But it all passed smoothly, and we left for Tarrant's.

This was a mine of stuff. Brass, woods, sheet metals, resins, glues, studs, tools. Aladdin's cave. I'd had the forethought to ask Mr McDuff's opinion of ship-chandlers in Thurso. A phone call from Mr Tarrant to McDuff established our credibility, which sadly nowadays means mere credit-worthiness. Sign of the times, that the word for trustworthy now relates only to money.

'The laird doesn't hold with plastic cards,' I told Mr Tarrant. 'He settles in money, though it'd make it so much simpler for us, wouldn't it, Mrs MacHenry? He won't listen.'

'True,' Michelle sighed. By then, to my relief, she'd stopped that awful inner weeping which started at McDuff's stores when I'd called her the laird's.

We got a ton of invaluable materials, promised to call in four days for more stuff, and departed. Luckily Michelle had enough money for us to buy pasties from the market. I pulled in south-east on the A882 for us to nosh.

Michelle gave a rather hysterical giggle, gazing at the car's contents. We'd had to buy a roof-rack to load the stuff.

'We've committed a robbery,' she said, laughing.

'Scrub that plural, love,' I corrected. 'You signed, remember? In fact, we've got to call in at Dubneath police station and tell all.'

She laughed so much that she finally started to cry. I'm not much use at consolation, so I had her pasty to save it going cold. We weren't so credit-worthy that we could afford to chuck good stuff to waste. It was faith we lacked. Anyway there was no time left now for any of this malarky. It was splashdown.

The first splash occurred at the police station, where I spoke to the one bobby in charge.

'It's rather a serious problem,' I said. 'We wish to report a theft.' Which widened Michelle's eyes even further. She was already frantic, thinking we'd come to surrender over the groceries.

Michelle groaned. I admonished her, 'Please, Mrs McGunn. Do keep calm. The police are here to help in these cases.'

The bobby swelled with understanding and eagle-eyed vigilance. We got Michelle a chair while I explained, in strictest confidence, about the secret auction at Tachnadray.

'Naturally,' I said, leaning anxiously over the constabulary desk, 'Miss Elaine wants this information kept confidential. I employed a printer in East Anglia. I've just heard that all four hundred printed catalogues were stolen in Suffolk.'

The sergeant put his pen down. 'Only catalogues?'

'*Only*?' I bleated, aghast. 'Advance notice to antique dealers is valuable information. We hope to restrict the sale to a limited number of trusted collectors.'

'And?' He resumed writing, without enthusiasm.

'So we want a twenty-four hour police guard, please.'

He stopped writing. 'A what?'

'Round-the-clock surveillance. Now – ' I waxed enthusiastic – 'the way I see it is a road block, and a helicopter – '

'Sir,' the sergeant said wearily, 'do you know the size of our area? And the number of officers with which we're expected to run it?'

'But surely you see the implications for the sale?'

He sighed. 'Consider a moment, sir. These book-lets.'

'Catalogues,' I corrected, frosty.

'Catalogues. Where would they have gone to?'

'Well, I ordered them posted to collectors as far as Germany, America – '

'And the material in them . . . ?'

'Descriptions of antiques for auction at Tachnadray.'

He put his pen away. 'Well, sir. Naturally we're only too anxious to assist Tachnadray Hall, but auctions are quite legal. And for people to come and buy's quite legal too. How they hear about it's their own business. The only problem is the loss – you say by theft – of your catalogues. That's a concern for the Suffolk division. Naturally, if you have any problems about admission on the day . . .'

Polite, but undoubtedly the sailor's elbow. Showing profound disappointment with Dubneath's constabulary, I extracted a promise of complete silence on the matter, then left huffily. Michelle was already bewildered into obedience, so my dragging her into the MacNeishes' tavern to use the phone produced no demur, not even when I feverishly phoned the local *Tachan Times and Argus*, the district's *Pravda*, to issue a denial.

'This is Ian McGunn,' I told the reporter sternly. 'There is absolutely *no* truth in rumours that we attach the slightest importance to the outrageous theft of sale catalogues on their way to Tachnadray.' The girl squealed to hold on please, evidently scrabbling to snap her Marconi Patent Office Wax-Cylinder Voice Recorder into action. 'Furthermore,' I went on, 'we deplore the inability of the police to respond to requests for total surveillance, and demand that you omit any mention of this . . .'

We did the same denial for six other newspapers, including the *Glasgow Herald*. Mary hadn't baked that day, having been up at the Hall, so no pasties. I had to make do with a batch of over-sweet Chorley cakes and a left-over cheese and onion pie before we hit the road to Tachnadray.

'Anybody in the clan a crooked auctioneer, love?' I said through a mouthful.

Michelle smiled, thinking I was joking. 'Ian. How do you remember everything we're doing? Including all your lies to Sergeant Kerr?'

I said piously, 'I didn't lie, love.'

She gasped a pure innocent gasp, her hair fluffing in the breeze. I was beginning to like Michelle. 'There really *was* a theft? Our catalogues really were stolen? How dreadful!'

'Well, it actually doesn't happen till tonight.'

'But how can that possibly – ?'

'Shut it, love.' Liking her didn't mean all this explaining wasn't giving me a headache. 'And don't admit I know about Joseph. They already know I know, but still don't.'

She gave a heartfelt sigh. 'Hasn't it been a day?'

She didn't know it yet, but the poor lass should've saved her heartfelt sighs. She'd soon need every one she could get.

Chapter Twenty-one

Just as you can't outdo the Maltese for doorknockers or the Swiss for cuckoo clocks, so you can't beat Caithness for conviction. Once Tachnadray had declared for crime, it became Fighter Command in a 1940 film, furiously active yet meticulous. Maybe it was their first delicious taste of scamming that gingered everybody up. I don't know. Within three days it came alive.

At my seminary school they used to set us a perennial problem: given the choice, whether to disbelieve in God or His absence. I never knew how to answer. Similarly, I'm never quite sure whether it's crime or sanctity which offers the least painful compromise for the human race. I've experimented with both, and found little difference. Now, I think perhaps sin has the edge, because it at least provides a decent income. So maybe it was the hope of solvency which spurred Elaine's retainers on.

At my request Elaine had spread word. Any old objects relating to the clan, or to any McGunn, Tachnadray, Caithness or indeed the Highlands, were badly needed at Tachnadray. Anyone wanting to sell the same should communicate with Michelle McGunn at Tachnadray forthwith. They actually started coming in by that first afternoon. How the hell did news travel? I tried asking an old woman who came trogging up carrying an infantry officer's telescope – leather-cased, War Office stamp and arrows – and she merely smiled, 'Och, I heard,' which was as far as I got.

Our peaceful scene had a visit from a police car asking if everything was all right. I started my favourite spiel requesting road blocks, helicopters . . . They drove off in haste. A Glasgow paper'd run a spread showing Alan pointing to bits of broken windscreen on the Ipswich bypass – the result of my phoned instruction to Tinker. Decadent youth, exploited by international financiers, was apparently to blame. More coverage – as the media nowadays term falsehood – was on the way. A TV crew was turned away. That sat sullenly on the hillside until Robert mustered a sortie to persuade.

And the letters came in.

That second day, Michelle was thrilled, rushing to find me in the workshop and holding all three. 'And one's from London!' she cried, beside herself. 'From a collector!'

'Get notepaper printed, love,' I said. I was busily engraving Elaine's coat-of-arms on a mid-nineteenth-century pipe box, silver. It's murder by hand, but more artistic than the modified dental drills most forgers use. I felt bad about it for the box's sake, but murder asserts priorities.

'Notepaper? Think of the expense, Ian!'

'All right, love.' I regoggled and resumed my engraving. 'Only don't come wailing I didn't warn you.'

'Michelle.' Duncan was fretting out some wood sections I'd marked. 'Do as Ian says. Get young Hamish along today.'

'Very well.' Michelle was still doubtful. 'But I can't see why we'd waste money printing grand notepaper when I can just as easily write our address longhand.'

Duncan didn't glance at me. 'We've never done anything like this before, and Ian has.'

Hamish McGunn, printer, came on a bicycle about teatime, fingers black and face pale. He looked subnourished, Charles Dickens in the blacking factory. Michelle brought him across, still in a huff from being told off. She fetched tea in mugs and a bowl of barmcakes with margarine. No jam, and it served us right.

'Ian wants notepaper printed,' she said, angrily offering the nosh so fast you had to make a dive.

'Embossed,' I said, 'if you've got that thermal process. Tachnadray's coat-of-arms left, and address. Put Michelle as "Auction Secretary". And our phone number.'

'Tachnadray isn't on the phone,' Michelle said.

Hamish wrote on unheeding, squarish writing, hard pencil.

'And then do a flyer sheet. The colours are yours, but choose discreet posh.' I gave him a crumpled paper. 'That's the wording. A thousand of each by tomorrow noon.' I grinned inside as his head raised. 'Ten days Michelle'll give you the full catalogue. Two thousand, about sixty pages. There'll be one score colour plates and three score black-and-white.'

'Ay, there's just the question, Ian,' Hamish said, embarrassed.

'The money in seven days. But – ' I raised a handy maul in threat – 'use Linotron Baskerville or Bembo and the deal's off. We've got educated folk coming. Okay?'

He left laughing, pedalling like the clappers.

Michelle stuck to her guns. 'Tachnadray's no longer on the phone.' Poor lass, it was all becoming too much.

'A Telecom van'll be here soon, love.' I gave her my most innocent gaze. 'Could you direct them to Dr Lamont's office please?'

'Dr Lamont?' She stood helplessly.

'Doctors get priority with phones.'

'But is there really a Dr Lamont – ?'

A kilted man staggering under a bookcase from Mac's lorry shouted, 'Michelle. A telephone man's here asking . . . ' She left at a stumbling run.

'Honestly,' I said to the silent Duncan as we resumed work. 'Women. Set them a hand's turn and they go to pieces. Notice there was no jam?'

The whole of Tachnadray was silent. It was ten-thirty, long past nightfall. Michelle, lustrous as a grisaille-glass Early English cathedral window at sunset, had met me as instructed in our lonely office. Our only light was candles and an oil lamp.

'Ready?' I asked huskily.

'Yes,' she said. Her face glowed, her eyes danced.

Cunning to the last, I dialled and passed the receiver. 'Our first phone call from Tachnadray.'

'This is the house auction secretary speaking,' she said. 'Could I please have, ah, Tinker?'

I egged her on. 'Don't forget the room.'

'Tinker? This is Mrs Michelle, auction secretary. You will please transfer to a separate extension in a room away from noise.' An alarmed expression, her hand on the mouthpiece. 'He says he can't, Ian. It sounds like a . . .'

'It *is* a pub. Tell the boozy old devil to take his beer and Ted can shoot refills through the hatch.'

'He's going,' Michelle whispered. 'What a dreadful cough.'

'You're doing great.'

'He said where's Lovejoy. That's the name you – '

Tinker's cough ground out as I took the receiver. 'Tinker? 'Course the scam's on. Listen: make sure you remember this bird's voice, d'y'hear? She'll be doing the phoning every night. She's new so talk slow, understand? And a new pub every night. Treble Tile tomorrow, same time. Make sure she gets the number.'

'Bird indeed,' Michelle muttered.

'And Tinker. I've decided on the auctioneer. Tee up Trembler.'

'Bleedin' 'ell,' Tinker croaked. 'Asking for trouble?'

I lost my rag. 'Do as your bloody told,' I yelled. 'Everybody's flaming boss until it's time to pick up the tab – '

'Awreet, Lovejoy. I'll find him. But Aussie's free and Flintstone's out of clink – '

'*Trembler*!' I bawled, then, smiling, passed Michelle the receiver. 'Off you go, love. Good luck. Tell Tinker to glam Trembler up. And get a typewriter.'

'Glam? A typewriter? Where from?' she was asking, round-eyed, as I took my leave with a candle to light my way. I didn't reply. Where from, indeed. Did I have to think of everything? I went to see if there was blood on the laird's old car.

The monster motor was housed in a drystone coach-house behind Duncan's workshop. Before knocking off as night fell I'd trailed a cable from the window while Duncan had a final smoke at the door, his closing ritual safe from our volatile solvents. I'd left the switch down.

The cable stretched to the coach-house, explaining its length. Robert padlocked the double doors on the motor's return, always good for a laugh. I opened the door, trailed the cable in after me, pulled the leaf shut. A bulb from my pocket, and I started searching.

Say, forty minutes later, and defeat. No blood that I could see. Blood's russet after a few minutes, then brown, then black. It was a common enough art stain in its time, and you can tell the shade. Therefore, Joseph, who was Michelle and Duncan's son, who'd 'betrayed Tachnadray' and was now kept imprisoned at *Shooters*, had returned without being bludgeoned. Persuaded? Drugged? Gunpoint? I gave up. Lots of puzzles in clan country. Not a lot of explanations.

Two dozen letters next morning, proving my denials to the world's press were working a treat. Michelle drumming her fingers saying things like, 'Where's that Hamish got to?' Mrs Buchan gave me a three-plate breakfast and some scruffy young lass zoomed coffee to our office.

'I like your new nail varnish, Michelle. Women don't use enough make-up.'

'Thank you,' she said. She was narked because the

coffee bird was talkative. 'Shouldn't we make a start? There's so much to do.'

And there was. I'd nicked a few old fruit boxes, into which she sorted the letters by postmark. I was pleased. I like evidence of suspicion. It means people are thinking.

'Haven't you got little feet?' I said. 'Has everybody got titchie plates in Belgium?'

'Tinker's list is completely erratic,' she began, ignoring this banter. 'I tried to make him dictate items according to the dealers. He was most abusive.'

'Tut-tut.' I apologized for Tinker, struggling for sobriety. 'You'll have to crossfile, love.'

'And he doesn't seem to know you as . . . as Ian McGunn, Ian. Only by that absurd nickname.' She wasn't looking up. We'd never been closer. I said nothing. She shrugged and began, 'First, then. A tortoiseshell – '

'No, love. Give everything a number starting at one zero zero zero, or you'll make mistakes. Documentary errors run at four per cent among auctioneers.'

'Number one thousand, then. A tortoiseshell armorial stencil, from Three-Wheel Archie. Then a word: quatrefoil.'

I almost welled up. Putting him first was Tinker's way of saying everything was normal between me and Three-Wheel, that he was back on my side. I coughed, and covered up my embarrassment by explaining, 'Quatrefoil's the code you'll use for secretly pricing Archie's items. No letter recurs; ten letters, see? Q is one, U is two, so on to L which is nought. It's called steganography. You can use the letters to denote any amount of money.' Craftsmen serving noble houses cut coat-of-arms designs in tortoiseshell for ease of repainting armorials on coaches, chests, even furniture. Women used them for embroidery.

'Secret pricing? What a cheat!'

'You know anybody who doesn't cheat?' I asked drily. She reddened and read on.

'Number thousand and one. A nineteenth-century button die from Helen, eight sides; she thinks the Howard family crest. Sutherland. Another code?'

'Yes. Helen always uses "Sutherland" as her price code. But refuse it, love. Too many wrong crests'll reveal it's a papering job. Pity.'

A button die's valuable because you can strike genuine silver buttons on it till the cows come home. A bit of sewing then converts any period garment into Lord Howard of Effingham's, with great (but illicit) profit.

'One thousand and two. Fob seal, glass intaglio on gold, Chester 1867. Big Frank . . .'

Hamish came at nine-thirty, looking even younger still. He was hesitant, definitely guarded.

'Noticed something amiss, Hamish?' I joked.

'It's this: Sotheby's "Standard Conditions of Sale" Apply Throughout.' He showed me a copy. 'As long as it's in order.' I reassured him a mite, and he went down to unload. His bike pulled a tiny homemade cart, a packing case on pram wheels. I went to the window to watch him in the forecourt. What a lot of people.

'Michelle. How many McGunns are there?'

'Thirty-two, but very scattered.'

More than I'd supposed. Yet if you counted them all over the Kingdom . . . ?

'I mean retainers, pensioners, employees at Tachnadray.' Hamish below was hanging a wooden tray round his neck to carry those obsessively neat brick-like parcels printers make. 'What *is* a retainer, love? Is Hamish one?'

'Somebody on a croft belonging, that sort of thing.'

'Tied to Tachnadray by loyalty and economics?'

Michelle hesitated, unhappy at the way my questions were heading. 'Yes. But nobody would express it in those terms. Not nowadays.'

' 'Course not, love.' I gave her a sincere smile.

Still looking down, as Michelle, with ill-disguised relief, recommenced her list checking, and Hamish clumped up the stairs with the stationery, I couldn't help thinking: thirty-two, probably, not counting infants. Say, twenty houses or so. Which is quite a lot of hidey-holes.

At noon I decided to drive into Thurso with Elaine, leaving Michelle replying to the letters and sending out flyers in envelopes. She still hadn't got a typewriter. I'd refused her baffled excuse that there simply wasn't one. 'Don't plead unavailability,' I commanded.

'But, Ian – '

'Look, Michelle,' I'd said kindly, tucking a Scotch plaid rug round Elaine's knees. 'We've reached the stage where talking's done. We need action.'

She blazed up at that. I think she really only wanted to come for a ride. 'Action, is it! Then what about postage stamps? By tea-time we'll have scores of letters to post and no money – '

'A post office franking machine arrives today, love.'

The post office supplies a little printing gadget which marks your envelopes. It's the only postage you can get on tick. You pay only when the man comes to read its meter.

'And,' I concluded, 'two letters'll arrive, neither with enough postage. You'll have to pay a few coppers to the postie.'

Michelle listened, nodded, didn't wave us off. First time in her life she'd ever shut up. Swinging us out of the gate, I asked Elaine to issue an order to the vestigial remnants of the clan.

'Not you too, Ian!' she exclaimed. 'I've noticed it creeping into your bones. You're careful to say "Scottish" instead of Scotch now, even when "Scotch" is correct. Soon you'll be fighting drunk at football matches. You'll believe our stupid tribal myths.' She was watching Tachnadray recede in the wing mirror. I said nothing, making my unresponsiveness an invitation.

She began to speak on, quiet and intense. 'That lunacy killed my father. He drank himself to death. Failing to become the legend of the Scottish clan chief. You know something?' She gave me a woman's no-smile smile. 'He had a stroke the day after two immigrant Pakistanis registered a Clan MacKhan tartan. What could *that* possibly have mattered?'

'Shona thinks you're a heretic. Paradox, eh? Clan Chieftainess as iconoclast.' The giant Mawdslay's tyres made a crackling sound on the track. I could do with these vintage motors, but everything seems on the outside almost out of reach with you perched high as a pope in a palanquin.

'Wasn't William IV the best socialist of his time?' she shot back. 'Pride's for those with money to burn. Pomp and circumstance reduced Tachnadray to penury. The carriages – we had six, matched horses – went, the grooms, liveried servants. And Father entertaining, hosting the County Show, silver everywhere, guests by special trains we couldn't pay for. Shooting parties. Mother gave up early, passed away when I was two. I saw the whole film round, the dozen pipers on our battlements. One enormous sham. You know what? Father even had battlements built, because Tachnadray had none.'

Her bitterness was getting to me. I knew all about tribal ferocities, having seen Sidoli's war with Bissolotti.

'Why not simply take the gelt from whoever wants to pay you? Everybody else does. An ancient lairdship's marketable – '

'Because,' she said. The little girl's defiant silencer.

I wasn't having that. 'Because Shona's mob won't let you?' It was my pennyworth. I'd wrestled the great Mawdslay as far as Dubneath Water before she answered.

'Whose side are you on, Ian? Tradition's?' The last word was spat out with hatred.

Well, I couldn't really say until I'd visited her mother's grave, but I gave her my best fill-in. 'The prettiest bird's.'

'Me?' She was smiling.

'Bullseye.' So far I'd counted two men watching on skylines, plus Robert.

'Then I've a problem for you.' A pulse beat, then, 'I'm still a virgin, Lovejoy. Which means I require information about sex techniques . . . Why're we stopping?'

'*What* did you say?'

'It's a golden opportunity. There's no one else I can ask. Tell me. Do women mostly make love on their sides sometimes, with their leg over the man? Only, with my handicap – '

The lumbering Mawdslay, slightly shocked, resumed its journey. 'Look, love,' I said anxiously.

'Don't go all coy, Ian.' She was quite reasonable. 'I read once that sexual intercourse . . .'

Shona's van caught us up by the first houses. She'd been following us, naughty girl. And Jamie was waiting in Dubneath's market square. All smiling friendliness, but very definitely there.

Chapter Twenty-two

Shona's presence in Dubneath put the kibosh on any further interrogation – me of Elaine about crookdom, Elaine of me about sex. Elaine had to visit the one bank, and Shona seemed determined to accompany her. Innocently I said I'd sightsee, happy to be squeezed out. Shona's furrowed brow cleared at that. Jamie went off down the harbour after we'd lifted Elaine's wheelchair to get her mobile. I walked to the chapel, slow and idle.

Reverend Ruthven was a pleasant balding man who told me, 'Two things, Ian. I'm a pastor, not a vicar. And secondly, I'm the exception that proves the rule.' He had to explain that Ruthvens were addicted to assassination over a long and bloody history. 'I'm probably the first peaceable Ruthven on earth!'

'Lineage seems a right pest.'

He sighed. 'It can be, Ian, heaven knows. Come. I expect you're here to see the McGunns. A fated clan, if I may say so.'

'Fated? Everybody's fated. Why McGunns especially?'

'Conflict dooms life. They say your very name is Norse, *gunnr*, meaning war. Etymological pill, of course. But the war between those wretched Sinclairs and the Sutherland Gordons crushed the poor McGunn clan. It's a wonder there's any of you left. The Gordons are a rapacious breed.'

He took me among the chapel's gravestones, and pointed out Elaine's mother's. And the laird's headstone, coat-of-arms on marble, a little way off. James Wheeler McGunn.

'Elaine was telling me about her mother, Pastor. How very sad.' I shook my head sorrowfully as if I knew so much.

'Aye, Ian. Isn't that life all over? Unable to come to terms with The McGunn's fanaticism. Clan was everything to the poor man. Driven. It's often the way, with converts. Reasoning erodes. Jesuits call it a state of erroneous conscience.'

'I understand.' I was very knowing, and lied, 'My mother and she used to correspond, until matters . . .'

We both sighed. Pastor Ruthven determined to exonerate Elaine's mother. 'Then you'll know how hard The McGunn took it. Women tend to blame themselves in those circumstances.'

'And needlessly.' I was busy working out in what circumstances.

After that it was sundry graves, the chapel foundation stone, a list of former pastors, gold lettering on stained mahogany, before I decided it was time to go. 'You'll have had your bite, Ian . . . ?' An Edinburgh man. He said to call again. I promised to, but wouldn't need. How come Ruthven likened James Wheeler McGunn to a 'convert', when he in fact was The McGunn?

Shona, Elaine and me sat down for a nosh at the MacNeish tavern. Mary told me that two letters had come addressed to me, care of Michelle, with only half the requisite postage. Elaine looked across. I went all innocent and said my friends were sometimes careless. My granny actually taught me the trick: registered letters hint at riskily valuable contents. But skimp the ordinary postage and the postman'll beat a path to your door to recover that outstanding penny. It's cheaper than registration and far more reliable.

'Just think, Mary,' I told her through a mouthful.

'Soon we McGunns'll be able to start paying for these tuppenny pasties of yours.'

She blazed up at that. 'Twopence? I'll have you know, Ian McGunn, that my cooking's worth more than – ' etcetera, etcetera. A pleasant meal, with me prattling away and inspecting Elaine's and Shona's respective faces. Faces are fascinating, but I've already told you that.

Shona followed the Mawdslay back. I was determined to tell Elaine about attribution. Elaine was determined to ask about sex.

'When you buy a painting at auction,' I said firmly, 'you'll lose your life savings if you simply believe what's written in the catalogue. Never mind that it clearly states: "Giotto, *St Peter Blessing the Penitents*". That only means a work of the school of Giotto, by a student or merely some ninth-rate artist who painted in Giotto's style, and that the date's completely uncertain. In other words, it could be by the world's worst forger. Now,' I waxed enthusiastically, holding the booming engine in up the fell road, 'if the catalogue gives the artist's initials as well – '

'About sex,' Elaine interrupted.

' – then you're on safer ground. It means the painting is of the artist's period, though *only possibly* his work, in whole or in part – '

'Have you ever raped anyone, Ian?'

'What you look for,' I shouted desperately, 'is the artist's complete name. That means it's really by Giotto himself – '

'Who decides that sex will happen?' Elaine pondered. 'Does it hurt very much the first time?'

'Knock it off, love,' I begged, hot under the collar.

'How does it end? I mean, do you both simply get tired?'

'You need your bum smacked, miss.' Me, with sternness my next failure.

'Spanking,' said this devil seriously. 'A sado-masochistic ritualization enjoyed by ninety-one per cent of women. A Salford survey – '

Good old Salford, still hard at it. See what I mean about women? If they find they've a problem, their inborn knack makes it yours. No wonder they live so much longer. One day, I promised myself, savagely bumping the Mawdslay along the stone track, I'll think up some privileges for myself. Then watch out, everybody.

'Why ask me, love?' I pleaded.

'You look lived-in, troublesome. You're sexually inclined. I can tell.' She was quite candid. 'Tell me. I'd like to know how it's actually *done*. I mean, a man's so heavy. Does the woman bear his weight? And how does a man's *thing* feel? I imagine something rubbery. Is this correct?'

'Please.' I was broken. 'I've one of my heads.'

'How did she know your address?' Michelle was in a high old rage, holding two letters out.

'Eh?' I'd come bolting upstairs for protection, leaving Robert to unload Elaine.

'A woman's writing. And you knew these letters were coming because you said – '

'Mmmmh,' I said absently. 'Is Elaine Aries?' I don't even know what Aries is.

'Libra. September.' Like Three-Wheel's motor.

Thanks, I said inwardly, and opened the letter. Margaret could be trusted not to give my location away. She'd sent me the list of Trembler's usual team, putting asterisks beside those who'd been in police trouble lately. That was all, and best wishes with one discreet cross. The other envelope, much thicker, held a mass of newspaper cuttings, notes, annotated catalogues and police notices. I'd told her to get them from my cottage.

Supper-time, the safety of numbers. I informed

Elaine that our auctioneer would be arriving in a week's time, by air from Edinburgh to Wick's tiny airport, and could I have the car to meet him, please. She said of course, sweet and demure. Her grilling had really drained me. Still anxious about her telepathy trick, I didn't let it enter my mind that Trembler would of course come by road, and to Inverness, not Wick.

Late that night I pulled another sly trick, though I hated creeping back to our office in that draughty old deserted west wing. It was made for Draculas and spooks. I spent a long time on the phone talking to Doc. He's a genealogist, been one of my poorer customers, lace bobbins, some three years. He was delighted to be given a difficult problem, tracing a complex family tree. I dictated the dates from the gravestones, and what I knew about Elaine's family. I bribed him to secrecy. He demanded, and I promised, an Isle of Man lover's bobbin I hadn't yet got. See how friends take advantage?

Inspection time. We'd had a run of three days' warm clemency. Weather helps fakers, or, as I decided we should start labelling ourselves, reproducers and copyists. This meant that stains worked better. Sunshine is an excellent ageing factor. And we could move the McGunn clan's assembled items unafraid of drizzle. Elaine was nervous, for once keeping her thoughts above her umbilicus, as we trooped down to see the three days' worth.

'They've stopped coming in, Ian.' Her tone said therefore this was it, everything her retainers could raise. Pathetic.

It was unfortunate that Michelle had chosen the Great Hall. Our voices echoed. The long stained-glass windows accentuated the space. I'd nigh on thirty rooms and halls in a stately home to fill. This piteous heap was two journeys of Drummer's donkey-cart.

My dismay must have communicated itself to the

others. I looked round, slowly, wanting faces. They were observing me in total silence. Hector, stoic and relaxed, with Tessie and Joey eeling round his feet. Robert's eyes gleamed hatred from that mass of red hair. Shona silent and dogless, whose heart must be beating faster because she more than anyone here realized it was crunch hour. Elaine, mortified in spite of herself. Duncan frankly ashamed. Mary MacNeish ticking off which neighbours'd contributed what. Mac patient, waiting orders. My annunciatory cough made us all shuffle.

'Not much, folks,' I said. 'Is it?'

Silence.

'Is it?' Still no answer. 'How many retainers, Elaine? Thirty or so? And they raise twelve mass-produced pieces of furniture, earliest date 1911.'

'You may have noticed,' Elaine said, pale, 'that my people are not well off. And Tachnadray is not Edinburgh Castle.' She had a right to anger, but insufficient reasons.

'True. But why not?'

Shona glanced at Robert. 'What does that mean?' she demanded.

'I mean that it was. Once.' I walked towards them, vaguely embarrassed by their being in a facing line, a barrister at somebody's trial. 'It's really quite simple. The clan centre, a great house. The laird tried to uphold . . . tradition. So debts mounted. The estate folded. Produce faltered, finally dwindled to a few flocks of sheep – '

'Here, mon,' Hector blurted. Sadly I waved him down.

'I know, Hector. Nobody could've done better, I'm sure. You must have slogged, winning cups at the Gatherings, doing what you could with damn-all help. Robert, too.' The man's head rose ominously. 'Probably the most loyal seneschal on the planet. You all

639

tried. But people were paid off, and the laird finally passed the torch on to Miss Elaine.'

The end of the faces. I started a reverse stroll. Elaine in her wheelchair was the centre of the group. It was a Victorian clan tableau, proud before the magnesium flashlight struck their likenesses for the mantelpiece. All it needed was a dead tiger and bearers. And, in this case, a mantelpiece.

'So you hit on a scheme. I guessed wrong earlier, and none of you corrected me. Because there wasn't a bleep of an antique in the west wing, I assumed there weren't any left. That they'd all been sold to pay Tachnadray's way. But they hadn't, had they?'

'What does he mean?' Elaine demanded of the world.

'That there's really quite a bit left. Right, everybody? Look,' I said, halting in the photographer's position. 'I needn't stay here. I can push off, leave you to it. You must at least help. Out with it, troops.'

Silence. Elaine's ferocity glowed, the radiance almost blinding. She was realizing she'd been had, completely, by this ultra-loyal mob of serfs.

'All right, I'll say it for you. You dispersed the remaining antiques among yourselves. When Elaine sent word for everybody to chip in any relevant saleables they had, you very carefully fetched only junk, and are keeping the authentic Tachnadray furniture, silver, God-knows-what, concealed.' I could have told how Shona, realizing I'd begun to suspect, bribed me with herself, failed, then sent Robert to hunt me to my death on the dark moor. I'd have been a fellwalker, carelessly falling down some crevasse. They'd have all told the police the same tale, and cocooned Elaine from the truth. Again.

'Bring it out, folks,' I said. 'Tachnadray needs you.'

'Duncan.' Elaine didn't even turn her head.

'It's true, Miss Elaine.' Duncan shuffled out of the line to address her, full face. He made to rummage for tobacco, put his pipe away, coughed uneasily. Nobody else spoke. 'We indeed did that.'

'I ordered everything sold!' Elaine said.

'You did, Miss Elaine. But it was selling out the McGunn heritage, despoiling your own – ' he choked on the word – 'birthright.' Well he might, poor man.

'Permit me,' I interrupted. 'Bring the genuine stuff to the auction. You needn't lose it.'

Elaine rolled her wheelchair out, spun it with her back to me. 'All of you. Go now. Tell the others. Bring everything – every-*thing*! – back. Forthwith.' A sudden queen.

They dispersed slowly, looking back at the blazing girl. While they were still within earshot she pronounced loudly, 'And on behalf of us all, Ian, I apologize for your shabby treatment.'

'Then can I go places on my own?' I asked swiftly. 'Without being confined, or Robert skulking on some distant hill?'

'Granted,' she said regally. 'Wheel me outside. And get rid of that rubbish. It's defacing the Hall.'

'Ah, well.' I pushed. 'Old tat's useful in the workshop.'

That night I rang Tinker and told him to get Trembler up to the railway hotel in Inverness soonest. Antioch had nearly three dozen wagons ready, which news wobbled me. More would be loading up by dawn. It seemed only a few hours since I'd arrived at Tachnadray with all the time in the world. Now it seemed there wasn't any left at all.

Chapter Twenty-three

Trembler came down the stairs holding on to the banister like a beginner drunk. He's of a tallish lazaroid thinness, forever dabbing his trembling lips with a snuff stained hankie. I like Trembler. Always tries to keep up appearances, wears a waistcoat, though stained with last night's excesses, and polishes his shoes. He tottered across the foyer from couch to armchair, from pillar to recliner, exactly as street children play stepping-stones. He knew I'd be in the hotel nosh bar. A porter helped him down the three steps.

'Wotcher, Trembler.'

'Lovejoy.' Shaking badly, he made the opposite chair and pulled my tea towards him. It slopped over the saucer as he sucked tremulously at the rim. His quivering upper lip was dyed snuff gold. Looking at this gaunt wreck, I wondered uneasily if Tinker was right. He looked a decrepit nonagenarian.

'Had a good night, Trembler?'

'Splendid.' His rheumy eyes closed as a server clattered cups. 'What day is it?' he whispered.

'You've a few days before the off, Trembler.'

'Right.' He opened his eyes, willpower alone.

'Grub's in front of you.'

Everything I could think of, including waffles, porridge, eggs in a slick fry-up, all on a hot plate. He focused and nearly keeled over. 'Jesus, Lovejoy.'

People began looking across to see where the noise was coming from as soon as he started. His cutlery fibrillated, his crockery clattered. He sounded like a foundry. Once he actually did tremble himself off his chair trying to pick up a fallen spoon. A kindly waitress came to ask if my father was all right.

'Yes, ta, love.' I gave her a soul-deep smile. 'He improves with the day.' I didn't tell her Trembler's age. He's thirty-one. Wine and women have transformed him. Trembler recovered enough to lust feebly after her. Luckily his vision peters out at ten paces, a spent arrow, so to speak.

'How much do I know, Lovejoy?'

Funny how glad hearing your own name makes you. 'It's a weird place, Trembler. Near derelict. They keep three rooms to impress visitors. The owner's a lady, seventeen, in a wheelchair. There's a few retainers still. All are suspect. So far I've a heap of rubbish which I'm transforming into saleables.'

Trembler nodded his understanding, as far as I could tell. He quakes so much normally it's difficult to distinguish a nod in his version of immobility.

'Where'll you get the stuff, Lovejoy?' he quavered.

'Tinker's organizing a convoy.' I hesitated, giving him time for the unpleasant bit. He managed to slop half a yolk-dripping egg into his mouth. I looked away, queasy. 'I want no whizzers who're in trouble, Trembler. Sorry.'

Normally an auctioneer, crooked or straight, has the final say on staff. Whizzers are those blokes – scoundrels to a man – who hump antiques about. An auctioneer's whizzers stay with him for life, part of his team, so I was asking for heresy.

'I heard it was special, Lovejoy.' He resumed his idea of eating, with distaste.

'Margaret sent me the list.' I passed it over. 'You've only two who're holy enough for this, Trembler. Agreed?'

'A sad reflection on modern morality.'

It's amazing what good grub and a job'll do for a man. Before my very eyes Trembler was filling out. His eyes were clearing, dawn mist from an estuary autumn. He drank another pint of tea. I gave him more, sent for another ton of toast, marmalade. Years were starting to fall from him with every mouthful. Even his voice, the querulous whine of an ancient, was becoming the measured and tuneful instrument of a Fellow of the Institute of Chartered Auctioneers. I watched admiringly. He only looked fifty now. A couple more breakfasts and he'd be down to a sprightly forty, maybe make thirty-five.

'So far, Lovejoy, you've told me nothing.' He dabbed his mouth with a napkin, rearranged the condiments, crockery. All really good signs. 'Are you bringing in valuers?'

My laugh made people smile across the tables. 'Who on earth can afford five guineas per cent, Trembler?' Valuing is robbery, money for jam – indeed, for not even jam. He's the bloke who comes to value your precious old table, guesses a guestimate (always wrong) and *you* pay *him* a huge percentage of that guess, for nothing. No, never let a stranger into your home, especially if he's a valuer. They are the antiques game's equivalent of politicians. 'There's some pinning to be done.'

He smiled. 'Thought as much. Who's the mark?'

'Are,' I corrected. 'Tell you nearer the day.'

'Pinning' is a noble art practised by auctioneers ever since time began. It means manipulating the bidding so as to land a particular lot on a poor unsuspecting member of the public who doesn't want it. When the Emperor Caligula auctioned off his dud antiques – he'd wasted a fortune buying forgeries – he ordered his auctioneer to pin Aponius Saturnimus. This rich Roman had nodded off during the bidding. He woke up poor.

'And I want a phone bank. Two.'

'Right-ho.' He knew I meant false ones, because otherwise I'd have asked the phone people. Big bidders phone live bids in as the auction progresses.

'About the money, Trembler.'

He shed another two years. 'I've put this hotel on my credit card, Lovejoy.' He carries only phoney credit cards, but he was trying to help me by deferring the cost of his stay.

'Good lad. You stay here and enjoy the . . . facilities. Now, Trembler, when I call, there's to be no delay. Get it? Ten minutes' notice, you move out. There's a code word. It's Lovejoy.'

'Your name's the codeword?' He was puzzled.

'That's because I'm under an alias; Ian McGunn.'

He repeated it to prove he was back among thinking men. 'One thing, Lovejoy. Can I bring my own tallyman?'

'No, Trembler. Sorry.' Trembler always picks some gorgeous tart without a brain in her head. I saw him once at an auction near Southwold where he'd hired a bird who actually couldn't count or write. Talk about a shambles. 'I've already got you a tally woman. She'll need training in, the day previous.'

He brightened. The deal done, we had another breakfast each to celebrate, seeing it was getting on for coffee-time. Then I rang Doc the genealogist and had my suspicions confirmed. Couple of good bookshops in Inverness. I got some paperback reprints for Duncan's benefit.

Michelle was working flat out now. Letters were coming in so fast the postie had graduated to a van. She was becoming conscious of the pressure. Each night we phoned up the list of antiques *et al* from Tinker. Next morning we sifted through them, and next night she'd tell Tinker which I'd accepted and which were refused. Tinker gave her nightmares: 'He doesn't seem to make any notes!' she complained. I'd go, 'Mmmh.'

There was a growing body of cards filed in old shoeboxes, a card for each collector writing in, and a spare list of antiques for which people, mostly genuine collectors, were writing urgently wanting special lists. These are almost always coins, medals, hand weapons, clothes or paintings. Then there was the catalogue file, the biggest. Michelle tried talking me out of one card per antique, thinking she'd discovered a quicker way. She tried the wheedle, even the vamp, to no avail. I made her stick to my scheme. I also made her keep an *nth* file, of those antiques which I'd told her to reject. She again played hell. 'What's the point of recording details of antiques we'll never see – ?'

I clapped a hand over her mouth. This was the alluring lady who'd so joyously rushed to find me when the first letters came. Now we were inundated she was falling behind and inventing ever-dafter ways of ballsing up the documentation. A born administrator.

'You, Michelle, are attractive, desirable, and rapidly becoming a pest for other reasons, too. Get help if you like, but do as I say. And hurry up.' I let go. I had to sort the last of Tachnadray's genuine stuff out in the Great Hall. 'I've a job for you to do, later.'

This time the items arranged at the far end of the Great Hall were superb. Among them I recognized Shona's – well, Elaine's – double snuff mull. Some things make you smile. The silver wasn't plentiful. One triumph was a bullet-shaped teapot. Not a lot of people admire the shape ('bullet' meaning spherical as an old lead bullet), which is a ball with a straight spout. The lid completes the roundness, with a mundane finial topping the lid off. They were made from the late 1700s for sixty years. The engraved decoration of these characteristically Scottish teapots is one pattern carried round the join of lid and body. It sat among the rest glowing like, well, like Elaine smiling. Edward Lothian of Edinburgh, 1746, before the fluted spout came in. There was also a silver centrepiece. These so-called épergnes (it's posh to give things French names) usually weigh a lot, so you're safe buying one by weight alone, never mind the artistry. This was 1898, Edinburgh, a dreadful hotchpotch of thistles, tartan hatching, drooping highlanders, wounded stags. It was ghastly. It'd bring in a fortune.

The furniture was dominated by a genuine Thomas Chippendale library table. It was practically a cousin of the mahogany one at Coombe Abbey, mid-eighteenth century, solid and vast. I honestly laughed with delight and clapped. You see so many rubbishy copies that an original blows your mind. Five Hepplewhite-design chairs (where was the sixth?) with shield backs and an urn-pattern centre splat were showing their class. A few good Victorian copies of the lighter Sheraton-style chair were ranged along one wall. In the catalogue I'd call them something like 'Louis Seize à l'anglais', as Tom Sheraton designs were termed in Paris at the time. Only I'd be sure to put it in quotation marks, which would legalize my careful misattribution. It'd give Trembler a chuckle.

Predictably, the porcelain was anything. The retainers had clearly preserved what impressed them most. They'd gone for knobs and colours, hoarding with knobs on, so to speak. A few times they'd guessed right. A royal blue Doulton vase, marked 'FB 1884', indicated that factory's famous deaf creator whose wares Queen Victoria herself so admired. It might not bring much, but it'd 'thicken' the rest. A lone Chelsea red anchor plate in the Kakiemon style – here vaguely parrot-looking birds, brown and blue figures on white and flowers – would bring half the price of a car, properly auctioned. I loved it, and said hello, smiling at the thrilling little bong it made in my chest. The stilt-marks were there, and those pretty telltale speckles in the painting. The rest were mundane. Sadly, sober George the Fifth stuff. Not one Art Deco piece among them. That set me thinking.

The paintings were ridiculous recent portrait travesties, some modern body's really bad idea of what a gen-yoo-wine Highland chief would have been wearing. Talk about fancy dress. These daft-posh portraits are so toffee-nosed they beome pantomime. The one painting I did take note of was a little scene of Tachnadray, done with skill in, of all things, milk casein paint. These rarities give themselves away by their very matt foreground. (Be careful with them; they watersplash easily.) You let skim milk go sour, and dry the curd out to a powder. Then you make a paste of it with dilute ammonia (the eleventh-century monks used urine) and it's this which you mix with powder paint. 'Pity you're very new, though,' I told it. The painter had varnished it to make it resemble an oil painting. This is quite needless, because casein is tough old stuff. You can even polish the final work to give it a marvellous lightness. It's brittle, though, so you paint on rigid board . . . I found myself frowning at the painting. Two figures were seated on the lawn, quite like statues. Modern dress, so there was no intent to antiquize.

A wheelchair's tyres whispered. 'What now, Ian?'

'I think some painters must have frigging good eyesight, love. This casein-painting's too minute for words.' Casually I replaced it. 'Pity it's practically new.'

'Is it any good?' She was oh so detached.

'High quality. The artist still about?'

'Me.'

I nodded, not surprised. Now I knew it all. 'You're a natural, love. Who taught you about casein paint?' No answer, so under her steady stare I decided to swim with the tide. 'Your dad? Or Michelle?'

'Yes. Michelle.'

'And egg tempera? You've a great career ahead of you, love. Copy a few medieval manuscripts for me and – '

'Stop that!' Michelle came in. 'I'll not have you inveigling Miss Elaine into your deceitful ways!'

With Elaine laughing, really honestly falling about,

I escaped into Duncan's workshop for my stint with the panelling. Michelle had come a fraction too late.

Later that day Mrs Buchan brought up two candidates to help Michelle in the office. One was a plump lass, fawnish hair, beneath a ton of trendy bangles and ear-rings, lovely eyes. The other was Mrs Moncreiffe, an elderly twig scented with lavender and mothballs.

Michelle chose the twig.

About ten o'clock I was working my way through a bottle of white wine in my garret, racking my two neurones to see if I'd forgotten anything, when the stairs creaked. Michelle came in with a woman's pur-poseful complicity, placing her back to the door edge and closing it with hands behind her. This manœuvre keeps the woman's face towards the occupant. They have these natural skills.

'Come in,' I said. 'Have a seat.'

'I . . . I just wanted to say that the catalogue's up to date.' She made to perch on the bed, rose quickly at the implications. I gave her my chair and flopped horizontal. 'We only have this evening's list to do. Mrs Moncreiffe has proved a godsend.'

'I'm glad. Out with it, love.'

'How many more days before . . . '

'Soon.' I didn't want to be tied. 'Michelle. Your son Joseph sent down an original antique, didn't he? Shona sent Robert after it in the Mawdslay, Tachnadray's one car.'

'Yes.' Her voice was a whisper.

'I don't know quite what happened, but Joseph was fetched back. He's hidden at *Shooters*, because he's supposed to have killed that driver. Dispute over the money, was it?'

Michelle nodded bravely. 'They . . . assumed so.' I watched admiringly. Women lie with such conviction.

'Tough for you, love. Torn loyalty and all that.'

'You're . . . you're really nothing to do with that London college, are you?'

'No.' I pretended anger. 'Have you been phoning people?'

'No, no. I just . . . surmise, that's all.' She regarded her twisting hands for a moment. 'You're not police. And you talk to things. You're a bit mad, yet . . . '

'Thank God for that 'yet''.' I gave her a sincere smile. 'Don't worry, love. I'm on Elaine's side. I'll honestly do the best I can when the time comes.'

She nodded and stood, watching me. 'I wish,' she got out eventually, 'we'd met in other circumstances. Better ones.'

'We practically did.' I shooed her out. 'I've got to think. Do Tinker's call on your own tonight, love.'

Eleven o'clock I went with a krypton handlamp and a small jeweller's loupe to look at the painting. It had gone. That told me as much as if I'd studied it for a fortnight in Agnew's viewing room. One of the two figures gazing so soulfully in the painting had been Michelle. The other had been a man slightly older, but not Duncan. He'd looked in charge, attired in chieftain's dress.

Which called for a long think to midnight. To one o'clock. To one-thirty. More deep thoughts for another hour.

Tinker was still swilling at the pub by the old flour mill. I told him to phone Trembler early tomorrow morning and just say, 'Lovejoy.'

'Right,' he croaked, anxious. 'Here, Lovejoy. When do we come? Antioch keeps asking. There's frigging trucks everywhere – '

'Now,' I said, throat dry. 'Roll it, Tinker.' I lowered the receiver on his relieved cackle.

Chapter Twenty-four

Economy's always scared me. Or do I mean economics? Maybe both, if they're not the same thing. I mean, when you hear that Brazil is a trillion zlotniks in the red the average bloke switches off. Mistakes which are beyond one man's own redemption simply go off the scale, as far as I'm concerned. Maybe that was why I'd run from Sidoli's rumble. Plus cowardice, of course.

The books I'd got from Inverness, paperback reruns, showed Duncan a few more possibilities. He was hard to persuade.

'This pedestal sideboard from London's *Encyclopaedia* of 1833,' I told his disbelief. 'Plain as anything, simple. Never mind that architects call it cabinet-maker Gothic – '

'Make it? Out of new wood?'

'Out of that.' A wardrobe, slanted and damp-warped, leant tiredly in the workshop. 'By suppertime.'

'What about those great pedestals?'

'The design's only like a strut across two bricks,' I pointed out. 'So cut those old stairs Robert's trying to mend in the east wing. The wood's good. The pieces are almost the right size, for God's sake.'

We settled that after argument. Two new lads had come to help Duncan, relatives of relatives. One was a motor mechanic, the other a school-leaver. That gave me the idea. Motors mean metal, which means brass rails, which with old stair wood means running sideboards.

'Make a pair of running sideboards. They're straight in period, Duncan. All it is, three shelves each with a brass rail surround, on a vertical support at each end. Put it on wooden feet instead of castors, French polish to show it's original, and it'll look straight 1830.'

Grumbling, I did a quick sketch. Sometimes I think it'd be quicker to do every frigging thing myself. 'Finish all three of these by sevenish, then I can age them sharpish.'

'All this haste's not my usual behaviour,' Duncan said.

'Times,' I said irritably, 'are changing at Tachnadray.'

Honestly. You sweat blood trying to rescue people, and what thanks do you get?

Michelle's first lesson in the perils of auctioneering. Explaining an auction's difficult enough. Explaining a crooked one to an unsullied soul like Michelle was nearly impossible. We were in the Great Hall.

'Auctioneers speak distinctly, slowly, in this country, love. It's in America they talk speedy gibberish.'

For the purpose I was the auctioneer, she the tally girl with piles of paper. She listened so solemnly I started smiling. Older women are such good company.

'There's a word we use: stream. Always keep a catalogue in front of you clipped open, no matter what. The cards from which you compiled the catalogue are in your desk. Those two, the catalogue and cards are your stream. Right?'

'Maybe I should have the cards on my desk,' she mused.

'You think so?' Casually I leant my elbow over so one card pile fell to the floor. 'See? A customer could accidentally do that, and steal a few cards while pretending to help as you picked them up. Then he'd know what we paid.'

'But that's unfair!' she flamed.

'Look, Michelle.' I knelt to recover the scattered cards. 'The people coming are all sorts. Some'll be ordinary folk who've struggled to get a day off from the factory. Others will come in private planes. But they'll all share one terrible, grim attribute: they will do anything for what we've got. They'll beg, bribe, steal.' God give me strength and protect me from innocence. I rose, dusted my knees. 'Cards,' I reminded her, 'in the desk. Catalogue on top.'

'Now I'm a customer.' I swaggered up. She got herself settled, pencilled a note. 'I ask, Where'll the stream be at twelve-thirty, missus?'

She thought. 'You're asking what lot number the auction will have reached by then?'

'Well done.'

'But how do we actually *sell* things?'

'Say I'm the auctioneer. Tally girl's on the left, always, except in Sotheby's book sales, where they know no better. Not real gentlemen, see.' I chuckled at the old trade slight. 'I call out, Lot Fifty-One, Nail-sea-type Glass Handbell – '

'No. Fifty-One is a gentleman's Wedgwood 1790 stock pin, blue-dip jasper with a George Stubbs horse in white relief – '

'Michelle,' I said, broken. 'I'm *pretending*.'

'Oh. Sorry.'

'The auctioneer calls out the catalogue number, Lot Whatever, and then says, Who'll start me off? or something. The bids commence, and finally Trembler calls, Going, going, gone! or Once, twice, gone! depending on how he feels. Once he bangs a hammer, that's it. He'll also say a name – Smith of Birmingham, say. It's your job to instantly write out a call chit. It's the bill, really. Lot Fifty-One, two hundred quid, Smith. So you get that chit across to Mr Smith quick as a flash. That entitles Smith to pay Mrs Moncreiffe. Her only job is to accept payment, stamp the call chit Paid In Full, and tick her list.'

'Must I provide Mr Trembler with a hammer?'

'No, love. Auctioneers always have their own. Trembler's isn't a real gavel. It's only a decorated wooden reel his sister's lad made him.'

'How sweet.' She smiled, scribbling like the clappers.

Apologetically I cleared my throat for the difficult bit. 'Er, now, Michelle, love. There's a few rules.'

'Never issue a call chit unless I'm sure?' she offered knowingly.

'Eh? Oh yes. Good, good.' This was going to be more difficult than I'd supposed. 'Ahem, sometimes, love, you might not actually hear some of the bids. If so, you mustn't mention it. Trembler will see them, because . . . ' I tried to find concealing words. Because he'd be making them up, 'taking bids off the wall'. 'Because, he's had special training, see? Bidders have secret signs arranged with Trembler beforehand. It's silly, but that's how they like doing it. They're all rivals.'

I ahemed again. 'And there's another thing. There'll be two telephones against the windows. People will be telephoning bids in for particular lots. The, er, assistants bidding from the phones are treated as genuine – er, sorry, I meant as if bidders were genuinely here.'

'Telephonists to receive call chits,' Michelle mouthed, pencil flying.

'I'll draft call chits with you when Trembler arrives. One last thing, love. Never, never contradict Trembler. Never look doubtful. Never interrupt.'

'What if I think he's made a mistake?'

I took her face in my hands. 'Especially not then, love.'

She moved back, looking. 'All this is honest, isn't it?'

'Michelle,' I said, offended. 'Trembler's a fellow of a Royal Institute. We've already certified that Sotheby's and Christie's rules govern every lot. We've certified compliance with Parliament's published stat-

utes.' I gave a bitter laugh, almost overdoing it. 'If our
auction isn't legal, it won't be for want of trying.'

Michelle stood to embrace me, misty. 'I didn't mean
anything, really I didn't.'

'Am I interrupting?' Shona, silhouetted in the door
light.

'Sealing a bargain.' I thought I was so smooth.

'A . . . gentleman's just arrived in Dubneath, calling
himself Cheviot Yale. He told Mary he's for Tachnadray. He's just waiting, saying nothing.' She was still
being accusing. 'His name sounds made up. Is it?'

'No.' I'd not felt so happy for a long time. 'That's
the name he was born with. People call him Trembler.'

No way of stopping it now.

The Caithness National Bank manager was delighted
with us. A big-eared man with a harf-harf laugh he
made political use of during Trembler's curt exposition.
Trembler was doing the con with his episcopalian
voice, always a winner.

'In requesting a separate account,' he intoned, 'I
don't wish to impute criticism of the Mistress of Tachnadray.'

'Of course not, sir.' On the desk lay Trembler's
personal card and personal bank account number at
the august Glyn Mills of Whitehall, London. Even
when starving Trembler keeps that precious account in
credit. It doesn't have much in it, but the reputation
of an eight-year solvency in Whitehall is worth its
weight in gold. Trembler gave a cadaverous smile
straight out of midwinter.

'In my profession,' he said grimly, 'it falls to me
sadly to participate in the demise of reputations of
many noble families. Normally, it would be regarded as
natural to use the lady's own account. But international
collectors and dealers from London – ' Trembler
tutted; the banker shook his head at the notion of
wicked money-grabbers – 'are of a certain disposition.

They demand,' Trembler chanted reproachfully, 'financial immediacy. The young Mistress's authority would carry little weight.'

'Sad. Very sad.' The banker's portly frame swelled, exhaled a sigh of sympathy.

'Mr McGunn here tried to persuade me to agree for the auction sale to be administered via the Tachnadray account in Dubneath.' Trembler paused for the manager to shoot me a glance of hatred. I smiled weakly. 'I insisted on coming here. Tomorrow morning, first thing, a number of small sums will be paid into the new account.'

'Very praiseworthy,' the banker smirked.

'One cheque will then be soon drawn on it. A small credit balance will remain. I will require a late-night teller on auction day to accept much larger sums.'

'Certainly, sir!' The man was positively beaming.

'I will require a special deposit rate of interest.'

The beam faded. 'Sir?'

'It will be a relatively vast sum.' Trembler didn't so much as get up as ascend, pulling on his gloves. 'Possibly the largest your . . . branch has ever handled. I would be throwing money away not to demand the interest. Have the cheque-book ready within the hour, please.'

We left, Trembler striding and using his walking cane so vigorously I had to trot beside the lanky nerk. You have to hand it to crooks like Trembler; always put on a great show.

'Here, Trembler,' I said. 'Notice that geezer's name? Only, I heard they were all assassins once.'

'Ruthven? Garn.'

'No, honest. Local vicar told me. Incidentally, Trembler. What do you think of openly cataloguing a couple of fakes in the sale? Reinforce confidence in the rest of the stuff . . .'

We went to celebrate. I promised Trembler his advance money and asked if he could manage until tomorrow. He said all right, which only shows how good friends help out. He really can't do without exotic women and drink. Same as the rest of us; he's just more honest. He orders the birds from a series of private Soho addresses. They're very discreet, but not cheap.

As we drank, me a lager, him a bathful of scotch, I stared out over Thurso harbour.

Antique dealers would now be booking the night-rider trains from King's Cross. The London boyos would have their cars serviced tomorrow for the long run north. Phones would be humming between paired antique businesses. Syndicates would be hunched over pub tables, testing the water. Auction rings would be forming, dissolving, reforming, illegal to a man.

And the convoy this very minute'd be rumbling on the great North Road, coming steady, a long line of weatherstained wagons carrying the beauty and greed of mankind. Soon they would swing left over the Pennines, then haul northwards for the motorway to Carlisle. Then they'd come Glasgow, Inverness . . . My mouth was suddenly dry. 'Have another,' I offered. 'Against the cold.'

Chapter Twenty-five

Nothing an antique dealer hates worse than fog and rain. Me and Michelle were for once agreed.

At three o'clock in the morning in a foggy rainy lay-by, it seemed to me that the wheel had come full circle. We were in the giant Mawdslay on the main A9 which runs northward from Bonar Bridge. Forty miles to Tachnadray. Not long since, it'd been Ellen and me in old Tom's hut, while a man had died bloodily outside. Then the disaster over Three-Wheel Archie, my escape with the travelling fair, my panicked flight from the fight between the rival fairground gangs . . . I've spent half my windswept life recently on night roads. I shivered. These old motors sieve the air. Michelle's breathing had evened. I nudged her awake.

'Watch for the lights.'

'Will they come? Only, Mr Tinker doesn't seem very reliable.'

I wiped the windscreen. Not a light out there. Nothing moved. 'He's the best barker in the business. Anyway, Antioch's running it.'

'Tell me about Antioch.'

'Eh?' I said suspiciously, but she was only trying to make up. 'Antioch and me's old mates. He was a Gurkha officer.'

'You know so many different sorts of people.'

'Everybody's into antiques, love.'

'Can't be.' She was smiling in the darkness. 'I'm not, for instance.'

'Aren't you?' I said evenly, which shut her up.

There came first a faint row of dot lights. Ten

minutes later the convoy approached, a slow switching queue of lorries revving on the incline, the ground shaking as they came. Even in the night it was impressive. I heard Michelle gasp. I stood out, collar up against the drizzle, and held up the krypton lamp. Characteristically, the lead wagon merely flashed, slowed to a crawl. I smiled, recognizing Antioch's trademark. The double blink went down the whole convoy. The last lorry pulled out, overtook at a roar into the lay-by.

'There are so many!' Michelle was beside me, shoulder up to ward weather away.

'Love, if I could have done it by correspondence,' I said, going forward to greet Antioch in the din of the passing lorries. He saw me, waved at the column. It churned on past.

'Lovejoy.' We both had our backs against the roar.

'Wotcher, Antioch. Any trouble?'

He grinned. He enjoys all this, driving about in all weathers. He loves nothing better than a catastrophe, a breakdown, a flash flood washing a roadbridge. You feel you want to arrange an avalanche for the frigging lunatic.

'Police query near Carlisle, but I'd the consignment notes. A caff dust-up with some yobbos. Peaceful.'

'Antioch. About your drivers.'

'We'll unload, then can you feed them? I've compo rations but they'll need more before daylight.'

'Yes.' I'd already warned Mrs Buchan, who'd been delighted at my threat of dozens of voracious appetites. 'Then?'

'We'll run to Aberdeen, the oil terminals.'

'Your destination's a place called Tachnadray.' He likes directions military style, eastings and westings and that. I'd forgotten how, so I chucked in my own map with Tachnadray ringed. He shone his light, grinned and shook his head. His lorry's cabin door was open. Michelle was looking in.

'There's a tramp inside,' she said reprovingly to Antioch.

The ragged figure coughed, a long gravelly howl which silenced the roars of the last lorries passing us. Michelle clutched my arm. Recognition had struck.

It opened one bleary eye. 'Gawd, Lovejoy. Where the bleedin' 'ell?'

'Hiyer, Tinker. Go back to sleep. We're nearly there.'

Antioch climbed into the cabin, revved and joined the convoy's tail. I stood, smiling, watching the red lights wind into the fog.

Michelle got her voice back. 'He's . . . he's *horrible*!'

'Please don't criticize Tinker.' We made for the Mawdslay. 'He's the only bloke who trusts me. A lot depends on him. Me. Tachnadray. Joseph. And,' I added, 'maybe you.'

Ten o'clock on a cold wet morning. At eight we'd waved off the empty convoy, and I was just back from depositing a mixed bag of cheques, money orders and notes into the National Caithness. Me and Trembler had drawn Antioch's draft. He'd set off following the convoy. There'd been enough to give Antioch's drivers a bonus. Michelle had opposed this, exclaiming that it left hardly any. I didn't listen. You have to pay cash on the nail sometimes, and this was one of them. She was still at it when we found Tinker happily trying out Mrs Buchan's homebrewed hooch in the long kitchen.

'Giving away all that money!' Michelle was grumbling.

'Listen, love,' I said. Trembler strode past, discarding his gloves ready for his third breakfast. 'How many men would you say Antioch brought?'

'Forty-six,' Mrs Buchan called, in her element. The tubby lady had two crones and no fewer than four youngsters all milling obediently to her orders. 'Like the old days! You poor English, starving to death.' She wagged a spoon to threaten me. 'This poor auldie's never tasted a drop of homebrew in his life. The crime of it.'

Tinker raised suffering eyes long enough to wink.

'Forty-six,' I repeated. 'Look around.' The kitchen was like a battlefield. 'They aren't choirboys, love. What would have happened if they hadn't been paid? After loading, driving the convoy the length of the country? They'd have torn the place apart.'

Michelle shivered. 'It's all so violent. I mean . . . ' She was bemused at the scale of things. 'Suddenly it seems, well, out of our hands.'

'It is, love. We're half way down the ski slope. No way of strolling back to the start, not now.' I patted her shoulder kindly. 'Have some nosh, love. We've a lot to do.'

She stared. 'But we haven't slept a wink. And everything is here. Isn't that the end of it?'

Tinker guffawed, his mouth open to show partly-noshed toast and beans. Trembler tutted and asked for more eggs, bacon, and perhaps just six more slices of fried liver, please. The women rushed, pleased.

A lass laid a place and poured tea as I said, 'It's the start, love.'

Michelle sank in the chair, pale.

''Ere, Lovejoy,' Tinker said. 'Notice yon Belfast geezer, tenth truck, fetched them frigging Brummy gasoliers?' The gaslight chandeliers had delighted me, genuine Ratcliffe and Tyler sets of three-lighters, 1874, with sundry wallbrackets for the extra singles. They are valuable collectibles now, especially pre-Victorian versions. Tinker was falling about, cackling. 'He got done at the sessions. Selling tourists *parking tickets*! Magistrate went berserk.'

Trembler joined in the reminiscing. 'Nice to see Antioch Dodd again,' he said. 'We last met when I auctioned that old mill down Stoke way. Antioch owffed it on canal barges. Even pulled a special police guard . . .'

Michelle was shaky, superwhelmed by all this criminology. Mrs Buchan on the other hand was oblivious, keeping her assorted team busy. Aren't women different? They're a funny lot. We talked on, preparing for the grind ahead.

By midday Trembler had made up his mind. All fixtures and fittings were to be assembled in the corridors for security, but I was downcast.

'What's the matter?' Michelle had left Mrs Moncreiffe in the office bombing out the checklist.

'It's not elegant.' I'd had visions of using the retainers – four more by now – to maybe redecorate the house. 'But Trembler's right. Bidders have sticky fingers.'

Trembler drew an outline plan on an improvised blackboard. He likes to talk to everybody at once. We were called to the Great Hall, crowded in among the furniture. Schooltime.

'This is where I'll hold the auction itself.' He pointed with his cane. 'There are all sorts of problems: security, money, catering, a bar, parking cars. But the most difficult is people. You'll all have a number. Anybody who hasn't memorized everybody's number by tomorrow must leave Tachnadray until the sale's over.'

People shuffled, looked askance, nodded. Tinker snored. He was on an early Georgian day bed, canebacked. I guessed it was from Jake Endacot's shop in Frinton.

'Hector, you've got dogs. Patrol outside, and check cars in. One of you men will photograph, obviously as possible, every car arriving. One or two people might complain or turn away. Let them. Remember, these people are mostly townies. They don't know sheepdogs are harmless.'

Two of the girls nudged when Robert glared my way.

More knew of Shona's missing dog than I'd thought. It still hadn't been mentioned openly.

'You will be in two groups.' Trembler notices everything, pretending not to. He'd have spotted those meaningful nudges. He'd ask me about it later. 'One group will help with the auction itself. The others will be stationed at a doorway, a corridor's end, wherever. *Stay there.* No matter what – a lady customer fainting, a man having a heart attack, a sudden shout for help, a customer telling you that Miss Elaine, me, or, er, Ian wants you urgently – *stay there.*' We all paused while Tinker coughed a majestic mansion-shaker of a cough. It faded like distant thunder. Trembler resumed. 'And nothing must be taken away. Suppose a bidder in fine clothes comes up to you with a receipt bearing my signature, saying they've got special permission to remove their lot an hour early. What do you do? You stop them. They'll be thieves, robbers, crooks who make a superb living.' He smiled his necrotizing smile. 'My rules never change: stay at your post. No exceptions. Everything, sold or unsold, stays until five o'clock. Then a bell sounds, and it's all over.'

'Sir,' one red-haired girl piped up. I liked her, our coffee lass. 'What if we need . . . ?'

'There'll be a floater. One of you circulates, takes the place of each of you in turn, for ten minutes at a time. Your list will give the order in which you'll have a break. And when your break time comes, you *must* take it. No deviation.' He did his wintry smile. I watched it enviously. 'We have a rehearsal. It's called Viewing Day, which is Tuesday. Wednesday is Sale Day. Last point: take no bribes, accept no explanations, and *don't talk* to people. If they insist on talking, simply smile past them.'

Robert had been fidgeting. Now he rumbled. 'If you're so clever spotting the thieves, why not bar them? It's stupid, mon.'

'Then we'd bar all. They're all crooks.' Trembler

looked down his nose at Robert, who flushed in fury. 'Rich Swiss, showy Yanks, suave Parisians, pedantic Germans, cool Londoners. The lot. Remember they work in groups. They'll lower jewellery, even furniture, out of a window to friends outside. They'll try all sorts.'

'But we know this place,' Duncan protested.

'Not you. Once, a lady carried an oil painting *in*. The guard let her pass. A minute later she left with her picture, saying it was the wrong room after all. They discovered she'd arrived with a worthless fake, and swapped it for an Impressionist painting worth a king's ransom. No. Do as you're told, and we'll profit. Do what you think is best, and we'll be rooked hook, line and sinker.'

Robert was still glowering, so I chipped in. 'Mr Yale is right. It's obvious you have no idea of the forces we're up against.' I hesitated, but Elaine nodded me to continue. 'The best experts in the country are on Tachnadray's side. They're me, Mr Yale, and Tinker there. Tachnadray's crammed with valuables. Your job is to contain them until the money's in. That's all there is to it.'

Trembler tapped the board. 'Those who will obey my orders without question, please rise.'

Slowly, in ones and twos, they stood. Elaine spoke once, sharply, when Robert rose. He remained standing determinedly. She nodded to Trembler.

'Very well,' Trembler said, smiling. 'Mrs Michelle will issue your numbers. From now you'll wear them. And remember one vital truth: it's Tachnadray versus all comers. Everybody understand?' He had to insist on a reply before they sheepishly concurred. He gave a warm smile as they shuffled out. 'The game starts now.'

I called, 'Mrs Buchan has coffee and baps for everybody downstairs.' She fled with a squawk, driving two girls before. I hadn't warned her. 'Then back here for Mr Yale to allocate your groups.'

Tinker woke at the third rough shake. We were a tired quartet, but we started a quick tour of the house.

'It's not bad, Lovejoy,' Trembler said. The furniture was parcelled, as auctioneers say, meaning arranged in categories.

'It's bleedin' great,' Tinker corrected indignantly. They were both seeking my approval. I said nothing, though I sympathized. It's always a difficult time when the scammer, he who arranges the entire ploy, does the appraisal. 'We wus runnin' about like blue-arsed flies. I give more bleedin' scrip out than the friggin' Budget. Christ, in one afternoon – '

'Shut it, Tinker.' I walked quickly, the three of them in my wake.

Trembler had opted for the ground floor. Ropes were tied across each staircase and crude notices forbade entry. We'd have more imposing barriers by View Day. Heavy furniture stood along one wall of every corridor. Light stuff and assorted massive beds were in the larger drawing-rooms with musical instruments. The library was half full of books; books are most trouble when rigging an auction because booksellers want the highest mark-ups. That's why country house sales always lack books. It isn't because squires don't read.

'Frigging booksellers.' Tinker hawked phlegm. I raised a finger. He went to the window and spat out.

Porcelain, cutlery, decorative ceramics were in the east wing. We clumped, steps echoing, the length of the corridor and worked backwards to the Great Hall. Fireplaces, fire tigers, gasoliers, pole screens, in one room. Conservatory furniture and garden items in another. The big east drawing-room, once a light bath-house green, was now hung with sixty or more paintings.

'Thought that was in France,' I remarked in surprise. A Victorian lady in a pale lavender dress admiring a flower.

'Should've been,' Tinker grumbled. 'More frigging trouble than a square dick.' Barkers are addicted to pessimism for the same reasons as Opposition politicians: there's more mileage in it.

Farm implements, machinery, carts, outside in the bay between the densely overgrown rose-beds and the east windows. 'Good old Antioch,' I praised. They were arranged in a kind of Boer lager. The presence of a steam ploughing engine explained the bulky carrier in mid-convoy.

'Fair old lot, that, lads,' I said.

'Ta, Lovejoy.' Tinker smirking's a horrible sight, but the old soak deserved praise.

The jewellery was in one strip, a grotesque higgledy-piggledy array spread as it had arrived, in bags, trays, boxes, on wobbly trestle tables. Tinker grumbled at the trouble the roomful had caused him. He hates jewellery. 'Fiddly little buggers.'

'Shouldn't we be examining each piece?' Michelle exclaimed.

'Please, missus,' Trembler said.

'Aye,' Tinker added, 'gabby cow.'

The glass was in the east wing's smoking-room. The smaller withdrawing-room held the first miscellany.

'You described the laird as "that well-known collector",' Trembler said. 'So you'd want the collectibles separated?'

'Right.'

A room of bronzes, statuettes, sculptures. Two of silver. One of arms and armour. I left them chatting in the Great Hall as the retainers returned. Michelle seemed rather put out, par for the course, as I went outside and sat on the steps.

When preparing for a divvying job, I can never keep track of time. It must have been nearly an hour when Trembler emptied the whole house of people, Elaine and all. They came out in twos and threes, giving quizzing glances my way, one or two talking softly.

Robert carried Elaine. She waved. Tinker stood waiting behind me, gruffly shutting Michelle up when she started to speak. Some things must be done in quiet. Women never learn. He knows this sort of thing can't be hurried. Trembler strolled past with a 'All yours, Tinker,' and got a wheezed, 'Fanks fer noffin'.' Silence. The great crammed house paused.

Afternoon moor light plays oddly on the rims of high fells. I'd often noticed it as a kid. For quite a while I'd been watching the hues discolour and blend. According to the map, some Pictish houses stood over to the south beyond the loch. I'd love a visit in peacetime. Miles north-westerly, Joseph languished alone. Behind me a bottle clinked. A gurgle, wheeze, a retching cough. Michelle tutted. A cloud slightly darkened the moor, fawns umbered, ochres into russet.

Maybe it was an omen. I rose and dusted my knees off for nothing. My big moment. Just me and antiques. Probably all I'm good for, showing off to nobody.

'Let's go,' I said.

Chapter Twenty-six

The tapestry was hung beside the stair foot. I'd heard
Tinker say to Michelle, 'Shut it, missus. Just friggin'
scribble,' but I was no longer listening.

Sometimes the best plan is its absence. Like, I never
know how I'm going to divvy. Setting about examining
an antique is as individual as making love. Even people
who know a little (which excludes all known experts,
museum curators, and antique dealers) approach the
task differently. There's a geezer in Manchester who
goes through a whole superstitious ritual, knocking
wood, hex signs, the lot. Another, a Kendal bird good
with amber, always sits on the floor even if she's in
public. Me, I just touch and listen. No particular order,
no magic incantation.

Single antiques are easy, in a way, because meeting
any one is like meeting a woman. The love quantum
is immediately apparent. Encounter two together and
immediately there's difficulty. They react on each other
so a man's bemused. The only way he can recognize
that inner essence is by concentrating on one, to the
utter exclusion of the other. Society calls it rudeness.
In divvying antiques it's essential. The trouble is the
process is so seductively pleasing that it sucks time
from the day. I mean, here was I with hundreds, maybe
thousands, of alleged antiques to divvy, and I couldn't
resist touching this tapestry, the first thing I'd clapped
eyes on stepping through the porch.

'Hello, Jean,' I said to it, mist blurring the figures.
Jean Bérain, Frenchman, once turned fashion upside
down. He and his son struck eighteenth-century nerves

by depicting naked courtesans reclining provocatively wearing the haunches and legs of a lion. You see Sèvres porcelain with similar figures. It became quite the thing for a famous beauty to have herself erotically depicted thus, like Peg Woffington the famous actress, for example. 'Long time no see.' I touched the lovely tapestry's texture. Warm. The feeling was heat, an exalting swirl of energy to the chime of melodious bells. I found myself starting to move, slowly at first, then quicker, quicker still, all else forgotten in a wondrous hedonistic spree. Distantly, Tinker's emphysematous croak was there, 'Hundred ern free, no; eight six nine, yeah,' but only for a while.

Battles do it. Orgies do it. Mysticism is said to do it. And women. Maybe it's true. The experience of beauty leads to a temporary death from recognizing its unattainability. I've never been in a trance as far as I know. I often wonder if it's the same as recovering from these other things. If so, I don't envy mediums. Certainly, coming out of one of these divvying sessions is appalling.

There was light intruding everywhere. My head was splitting. People talking in murmurs. A long leathery cough. A bottle, glugging. Somebody spluttered, murmured, 'Gawd.' A woman's voice thin as a reedpipe played out on the water. She was asking about something with numbers. I must have slept.

Headaches are a woman's best friend. They're not mine. The kitchen, shimmering. Mrs Buchan peeling something, one of her scullions doing mysteries on a cake's top. Another minion teasing about hair done different.

This end of the long table was fenced with beer and bottles. The talk was going on, that cough, her still counting. I drew breath.

'Help us up, Tinker.'

Hands hauled, propped. The place swam for a few seconds. I swigged the tea and stared at my hands until the world tidied itself up. Tinker scornfully refuted the women's suggested medications, clove inhalations, feet up, sal volatile. 'He needs a coupler pints, obstinate bleeder,' Tinker said.

'Shut it,' I got out, and winced at his cackling laugh.

'He's back. Wotcher, Lovejoy.'

'All right?'

'Aye, great. Missus, brew up. He'll be dry as a bone any mo.'

Michelle was there, weary. I told her she looked like I felt and got a wan smile. Trembler reached across to pat my shoulder.

'Beautiful, beautiful. A few questions when you're ready.'

That cheered me up. Auctioneers lust in percentages. Trembler was thinking ahead. As I recovered coherence, he began slowly introducing particular antiques into the conversation.

'That bronze cat, Lovejoy. What've you got, lady?'

'One Five Oh Seven.' Michelle's papers rustled as she worked her clipboard. 'It's one of six from Boy Tony, Winchester. Six reproduction metal sculptures, 1850, Birmingham.'

'As one's genuine Egyptian, we should delete it, Lovejoy.'

'And?' I prompted. Exquisite tea, strong enough to plough.

Trembler shrugged. 'I incline to Phillips, London.'

'No.' I'm never sad vetoing a deal between auctioneers. Once you've decided that money's the name of the game, all is clarity. 'No. Make out an addendum list. Have Hamish print it, free issue on the door. Say that One Five Oh Seven's now only five repro bronzes, that one's been withdrawn. Bronze cat, Egyptian, resembling Säite period 644–525 BC. And tell Boy we'll split the mark-up one to two.'

'But why take it out of the auction?' Michelle asked.

Trembler answered for me. 'If six cheap reproductions are listed, and one is specially withdrawn, it's as good as announcing that somebody's realized it is genuine. From ten quid it leaps to maybe ten, twenty thousand. Lovejoy says we ask for a third of that difference. The addendum sheet's the first thing dealers look at. Bronze collectors will pay on the nail.'

'Will Mr Boy, er, Tony agree to share?'

'Lady,' Trembler said gently. 'He sent off six grubby old doorstops hoping for a few quid. And gets a fortune. Wouldn't you agree to fork out the expenses?'

'Sod the explanations,' I interrupted. 'How far'd I get?'

'Did it all, mate.' Tinker was pouring himself another pint of beer. From the tomato sauce on his mittens he must have had a meal or two while waiting for me to rouse. 'Lady here hardly kept up.'

'I got all of it,' Michelle said, glaring at Tinker.

'Kiss, then,' I ordered. 'Chance of a bite, Mrs Buchan?'

'I beg your pardon!' Michelle exclaimed indignantly, then quietened when she saw Trembler and Tinker marking an X on each of her pages. I did the same. God, I felt stiff. Something happens to your muscles. I saw her staring and smiled.

'A St Andrew's cross used to be put at the bottom of legal documents as a sign of honesty. That's why it's still a valid mark from people who can't write. It degenerated over the centuries into a love kiss. We use it in its original sense.'

'Truth and honesty!' Tinker laughed so much one of the girls had to bang his back to stop him choking to death.

'The dolls, Lovejoy.'

'For heaven's sake split them into single lots, Trembler. Who the hell boxed them into one?'

'Bleedin' toys,' Tinker grumbled. My answer.

'That tall French bride doll's the one to milk on the day, Trembler, but there are some good German bisques. Incidentally, d'you reckon that mohair wig character doll's by Marque? One went at Theriault's for over twenty thousand . . . ' We chatted as my grub came. Tinker was by then really enjoying himself. The girls pretended to refuse his request for another jug of Mrs Buchan's homebrew, liking the scruffy old devil. The divvying had been a real success for him, because the stuff was exactly what I'd asked for. By dusk he'd be justifiably drunk in celebration.

Trembler and me went on, Tinker spraying us all with mouthfuls as he put in an occasional word and Michelle making notes. The set of wooden decoy ducks, retain as likely in this area. The collection of twenty-six fans, accept. The sixty pieces of lace, retain but split into different-sized lots. And the William Morris furniture look-alikes, put into one motif room. The alleged early Viennese Meerschaum pipe was a fake, but leave in because some collector might be daft enough . . .

Late that same night Michelle came across me in the conservatory.

'What are you reading?'

'A real cliffhanger.' I held out the book. '*Dame Wiggins and her Seven Wonderful Cats*. I like Kate Greenaway. Can't help wondering if she had an affair with George Weatherby. Co-authors and all that.' She sat opposite me, composed, hands clasped.

'Yonks ago – ' she used the slang self-consciously – 'I'd have said you looked ridiculous sitting in that old bath-chair. Now it seems so natural, you reading an old book by candlelight when there are comfortable chairs, new books, electric light, television.'

'It's pleasanter, love.'

'Is it always like that?' She meant divvying.

'Not long back I divvied a few things for a fairground. Took it in my stride. This was a bit of a marathon.'

'And payment, Lovejoy?' First time she'd used my name.

'Money? You fixed the percentage.' I shrugged. 'It never sticks to my fingers. A woman I knew says it's because deep down I hate the stuff. Pay me in Roman denarii, love.'

She showed no inclination to go. Well, in for a penny, in for a pound. I said, 'You must be very proud of Elaine. Sad that James Wheeler didn't live to see how she turned out.'

Women who delay a reply are usually opting for truth. It's unnerving, like all rarities. Michelle's face was pale when finally it lifted.

'I suspected you'd guessed, Lovejoy.' She looked away for the crunch. 'He took his . . . wife to the Continent. I went as a companion.'

'Because you were pregnant with Elaine.' Good planning. 'The wife condoned everything?'

'Of course.' She was faintly surprised at my astonishment. 'The importance of a clan heir overrode everything. Duncan didn't know. He stayed to help Robert run Tachnadray.'

'All these dark secrets put you in my power,' I threatened. 'Now I'll exploit you rotten.'

She smiled at that, really smiled. 'Anyone else, yes. But not you, Lovejoy.'

She rose, hesitated as if seeking something, then bent over and put her warm dry mouth to mine.

'Thank you, Lovejoy.'

'Don't say thanks yet, love,' I said sadly. 'Unless you know what's coming.'

Her eyes, so close to mine, showed doubt an instant before her woman's resolve abolished it. She decided I meant gain.

'Duncan won't expect me for an hour,' she said evenly. Her perfume was light and fresh. New to me, irritatingly. It's one of my vanities that I can guess scents. 'I was on my way to leave this list in your room.'

'See you there, then,' I said, just as evenly as her.

'Don't be too long, Lovejoy.' Her voice was a murmur.

I watched her recede from sight in the gold glow, then returned for a quick minute to Dame Wiggins. One of the Wonderful Cats would land in the gunge if it didn't watch out. Like Dutchie and Dobson. Except they'd only two lives between them. A cat's got nine. Right?

Chapter Twenty-seven

One of the worst feelings in the world must be when you throw a party and nobody comes. I mean, that Bible character who dragged in the halt, lame and blind has my entire sympathy. I began to get cold feet, though all portents were for go. Letters were still arriving. We'd had three calls from Mr Ruthven, banker, ecstatic because nearly fifty firms or unknowns had transferred sums to the Caithness National out of the blue. Pastor Ruthven, notable non-assassin, blessed our enterprise. The phone was constantly trilling, bloody nuisance. Mrs Moncreiffe had her hair done.

Outside was like Highland Games day. Yellow ribbons on metal hooks fenced the tracks all the way from the bridge over Dubneath Water to Tachnadray. Robert and his men, now a staunch six, had put night-glitters on the ribbons, good thinking, and had laboriously mowed a spare field. Five hundred cars and eight coaches, he said. A man was sacked for blabbing in the MacNeishes' pub; drummed out of the Brownies, lost his badge, and got mysteriously convicted and clinked for a week's remand by magistrate Angus McGunn.

A trailer arrived from Thurso carrying a kind of collapsible canvas cloister. Mrs Buchan blew up, learning that Trembler was making inquiries among Inverness caterers, but I quashed her campaign when one caterer undertook to run a grub-and-tea tent and give us a flat fee. I agreed the same for a bar, plus a percentage. The catalogues were fetching in six times the print-

675

ing costs. Hamish, maniacal by now, was doing a colour catalogue of fifty-one pages with a 'research index', meaning notes, by Mr Cheviot Yale, Auctioneer and Fellow of this and that. The coloured versions were for sale at the door, at astronomic cost to the buyer. Trembler prophesied they'd sell all right. A firm from Inverness brought a score of portable loos for an extortionate fee. They looked space-age, there on the grass, white and clinical. The local St John Ambulance undertook to send a couple of Medical Aid people, in case.

The estate had never seen days like it, not since the laird's spending sprees. Mrs Buchan's kitchen was going non-stop. Duncan finished his last piece, a pedestal case. This is the 1820 notion of a filing cabinet, with five hinged leather-covered cardboard boxes in a tier. It sounds rubbish but with its lockable mahogany frame it looked grand. I explained how to age it with dilute bleach and a warm stove. Duncan's products, a round dozen by now, would go into the auction as extra lots on the addendum.

It felt like a holiday. Trembler went off south for a well-earned, er, rest after ordering two of his exotic ladies from a Soho number. Tinker was paralytic, but messily filling out in the kitchen. It was there I roused him while Mrs Buchan's merry minions were screaming laughing over laundry in the adjoining wash-house. He came to blearily, hand crooked for a glass.

'Noisy bleeders,' he groused while I poured. Mrs Buchan's latest offering was like tar. He slurped, shook the foundations with a cough, focused. 'Yeah, Lovejoy.'

'Dutchie and Dobson.' I waited for his cortex to reassemble in the alcohol fog. 'Dutchie back from the Continent?'

'Never.' He hawked, spat into the fire.

'You sure? Our local dealers say you can set your clock by Dutchie's reappearances.'

'Not this time, Lovejoy.'

'Tinker. I reckon Dobson did that driver, and Tipper Noone. Watch out for Dutchie and Dobson.'

'Fine chance, Lovejoy,' he croaked witheringly. 'Them bastards are too lurky.'

They'd both be here. I already knew that. The only question remaining was their attitude towards me. I was pretty confident Dutchie wouldn't – maybe couldn't – harm me. But that cunning silent knife-carrier Dobson . . . I hunched up and sipped Tinker's ale for warmth. What's the expression, an angel walking over your grave? I thought, some angel.

View Day's always a let-down, with added tension, same as any rehearsal. Everybody was keyed up. Trembler returned looking like nothing on earth but steadying as the day wore on. Tinker spent the morning 'seein' the bar's put proper', meaning sponging ale. Michelle checked the numbers, and fought Trembler over sticky labels on the oil paintings. I kept out of it. Robert and Duncan drilled the retainers twice. No hitches.

They came. First a group of three cars, hesitantly following the signs. They'd driven from Eastbourne. Then a minibus from George MacNeish's tavern with the six overnighters we already knew about. Duncan's men had erected signs everywhere. Nobody had an excuse for 'accidentally' getting themselves lost. Our people were on station in doorways, corridors and one on each of the seven staircases. Five hawkeyed men simply stood on the grass staring at the big house, Hector with Tessie and Joey spelling them in sequence every twenty minutes. One thing was plain to even the casual viewer: security was Tachnadray's thing.

Our viewing was timed for eleven a.m. to four in the afternoon. The trickle was a steady flow by noon. By one it was a crowd. Two o'clock and the nosh tent was crammed, the bar tent actually bulging at the seams. A coach arrived. The car park was half full, and filling. But throughout I kept a low profile. From the west wing's upstairs corridors I could see the main doorway. I had a pile of sandwiches against starvation and a trannie against boredom in case Dutchie and Dobson didn't show. I sat on the window-ledge watching.

There was only one way for them to enter the house, and that was up the balustraded steps. And one way out, the same. As people arrived, I counted with one of those electronic counters. Like watching an ants' nest in high summer. I recognized many, smiling or scowling as I remembered their individual propensities.

Lonely business. Twice Michelle sent a breathless girl – we had two of these runners, not really enough – with some query, quite mundane. It occurred to me that maybe Michelle was checking on me, rather than proving she was on the ball. Once Tinker came coughing up, carrying me a pint of ale. At least, he nearly did. The beer slopped so much on the stairs he didn't think it worthwhile to finish the ascent, so he drank it and called up that he'd go back and get me another. 'Another?' I yelled down. 'I haven't had the bloody first yet.' He clumped off, muttering. That's friends for you. I mean, I thought from my perch by the leaded window, Michelle was really too attractive, but cuckolding Duncan, whom I liked, hadn't been my fault. She'd realized how good and sincere I am deep down. That's what did it. Finer qualities always go over big with women . . .

Dobson walked from the covered way. He paused to scan the still kilted figures of Duncan's five watchers. Undecided, he strolled round the east wing. I smiled. Sure enough, he returned. Hamish's big cousin Charles, No 17, was posted there with his shepherd's crook and his noisy eight-year-old son. Dobson moved more purposefully, round the west wing. I waited while the viewers, now a teeming throng, poured about. And back he came, now surly and fuming. It was Hector's sister's lad Andy on that corner with his border collie. Dobson turned, shook his head slowly. No go, he was telling somebody.

My blood chilled. An overcoated man, bulky and still, was standing among the crowd. He raised his hand to his hat, and five – *five*, for Christ's sake; there's only one of me – others joined him. They came and ascended the steps with Dobson's lanky morose figure striding behind. I swallowed. Well, I tried to. These were hard nuts, Continentals from the Hook. Ferrymen, as Tinker calls them. Pros, the heavies with which our gentle occupation abounds.

They left after two hours, into the nosh tent. At four Duncan's bell started ringing. At four-thirty the last cars left, carrying the caterers. A lady dealer, one of the Brighton familiars, was winkled out of the loos by a dog. Five o'clock and Duncan's men raised an arm, Robert's numbers each holding a plaid flag from the windows. Michelle came out and signalled jubilantly up to me, smiling all over her face. I opened the window and yelled to stand down, everybody. One or two applauded, all delighted. Trembler had one small item missing, a fake Stuart drinking glass. Cheap at the price, but Trembler went mad. Tinker complained the beer tent hadn't allowed the statutory twelve minutes' drinking-up period, and went to fill the aching void with Mrs Buchan's brew. Other people haven't his bad chest. Elaine was thrilled and joined us all in the kitchen for a celebration.

'A perfect View Day!' she exclaimed, congratulating Trembler in the hubbub. 'Absolutely right!'

Nearly, I thought, as the retainers talked, grinning in the flush of success. Almost nearly. But I grinned yes, wasn't it great, well done. All there was left to do now was leave my promised panic message on Antioch Dodd's answer phone and wait for the dawn to bring Dobson's vicious army and the holocaust.

Chapter Twenty-eight

Auction Day.

The Great Hall at Tachnadray was crowded. Seats were in rows, three hundred. Dealers, collectors, and even other auctioneers, plus a few stray human beings were cramming in. The talk was deafening. Michelle was lovely though pale on her podium with little Mrs Moncreiffe in place behind her neat blocks of forms. To the auctioneer's far left two solemn lasses waited at telephones. Retainers were stationed at the exit and by each window down the length of the hall. Trembler's two shop-soiled whizzers had arrived overnight. With the eidetic memory of their kind, they hastened once round the entire stock, then went to the beer tent to take on fuel, bored. I entered as Trembler checked the time, made for his podium. He looked great, really presentable posh.

''Morning, Lovejoy,' somebody said.

''Morning, Jodie.'

'How did a scruff like you get a commission like this?'

She was smiling as she jibed. Jodie Blane's a bottle-blonde who does business with those clandestine dealers who're forever in and out of Newcastle. She's genuine watercolours and Regency silver. She says.

'Me? Influential friend of the family.'

We laughed. I said I thought I'd just seen Dutchie. She said no, that I must be mistaken because she'd heard Dutchie was in Brussels. I asked from whom, and sure enough she replied Dobson. Surprise, surprise. Elaine wheeled in, emitting the ephemeral radiance of the love-child and smiling up at Trembler. Oho, I thought, moving on in the press. Trembler gavelled, and we were off. His two whizzers appeared from nowhere, one in each aisle.

'Good day, ladies and gentlemen. Welcome to Tachnadray. Please refer to the conditions of sale. No buyer's premium – ' a few ironic handclaps met his wintriest smile – 'but otherwise Sotheby's rules apply. Note that the auctioneers deny responsibility . . . ' Jeers and catcalls, some laughter. In the buzz Trembler summarized all the other escape clauses, making sure we could get away with murder, and went straight in. It'd be a long sale. He begged for haste in the bidding.

'Lot One. De Wint: "Dovecot, Derbyshire", watercolour'.

'Showing here, sir!' cried a whizzer.

'Who'll start me off? Two hundred?' Trembler intoned, then in surprise responded to a nod from the furthest telephone girl. All phoney. Last Sunday he'd drilled her till she cried. He feigned a bid beyond me, also off the wall, and finally knocked the painting down to the telephone girl. She called the buyer's name: 'Gallery Four, sir.' The fourth private gallery registered incognito with the auction. It indicated big secretive buying interests. The audience's faces hardened, and settled down for blast-off. The phoney telephone wires dangled out of sight below the girls' desks, of course. It didn't matter, because the De Wint watercolour was also dud. Elaine had done it, under my guidance. But it had keyed the audience up to a spending mentality. Trembler's a real artist. I stepped into the corridor.

'Hector. All the men in position?'

'Aye. Why?'

The dogs panted, grinning up at me. 'One bloke yesterday tried sussing out the two wings. Ever seen him before?'

Hector tried to grin. 'No, Lovejoy. Should I have?'

'No. Any extra men we can use?'

'No variation,' he said. 'Your own rules, mon.' So no extra man guarding the cottage.

I bit my lip anxiously. 'Watch out for the blighter. Tall, thin. Looks sour.'

'Aye, I mind him. Dinna fash.' He laughed, thinking I believed him about Dobson.

Apologetically I grinned and left, hands in pockets and pausing for a last look at one of my favourites, a Joe Knibb bracket clock. Simple rectangular, 1720, and worth a fortune. 'Tara, darlin,' I said to its lovely face, and walked out just as I was. Tinker was in the beer tent as I'd instructed. I didn't glance his way, nor he mine. At the corner of the east wing Andy waited with his energetic collie. Why are dogs never still?

'Going well in there, is it?' he asked. Great how the retainers had committed themselves.

'Aye, Andy. Don't let yon dog nod off' And I strolled on past, through the unkempt garden. Under a crumpled greenhouse's door stone lay the two-pound hammer and cold chisel. Heavy, but Joseph was probably bolted in and I'd need something for the door.

Then I trotted away from Tachnadray. I'd miss it.

Distances contract during daytime. I've often noticed that. Maybe it's because you know where you're putting your feet. I had the sense to follow Dubneath Water from the bridge, moving on the stones and eventually climbing up where I'd been baulked by Ranter. The guard was standing on the skyline a half mile off, facing the house in a patriarchal pose. From there he could see the cars and all the activity. No dog, thank God.

Somewhat muckily I climbed out of the watercourse and moved left, getting the cottage between us before I made a direct move towards it. The main door was on the side facing the distant guard, as was that unlatched shutter. The rear door my side was virtually rusted in place. Using the chisel, I levered off the bolt, and did the old lock with my belt buckle. A push on the Suffolk latch, and I was in. Must, rust, dust. Just to make sure, I peered into the two downstairs rooms, a parlour and a kitchen. Unused for years. Grime was trodden shiny on the middle of the stairs. A trannie played pop music above my head. I went up, a bit scared – well, not really scared as such. More worried. Maybe I'd got it wrong.

But I hadn't. Joseph was sitting in the upstairs room with that shutter ajar. They hadn't even allowed the poor bugger a light, perhaps in case he signalled. He stood, jaw dropping and stared at me in the doorway with my hammer and chisel. One hand was manacled to the wall, a long chain, and his ankles were chained to a granite cube. He could move, but he'd be noticed in company.

'Dear God,' he said faintly, his face drained.

'Wotcher, Dutchie.'

'I didn't kill the driver. Honest, Lovejoy. Please.'

'I know you didn't, silly burke.' I tested the wall chain. With that broken I could at least get him away.

'Lovejoy . . . ' His voice broke. 'Is there a chance?'

'Let's make one,' I said, and started on the damned thing.

I was past caring by now. He had a towel which I used to muffle the blows. The cold chisel through the wall link with me banging the two-pounder on it in great sideways swings. When the wall insert did go it nearly took my eye out, whizzing past my forehead and pitting the wall opposite.

Dutchie carried his chains over his shoulder, me humping his granite cube. We left *Shooters* and crawled to the gully. We must have looked a sight by the time we reached the bridge. Dutchie was exhausted. I shoved him so he was in the dry under the arch, and heaved myself up to join him. He tried to gasp what the hell were we doing but I shut him and whispered that our own private express service would be along shortly.

Cars were still passing overhead heading towards Tachnadray, but only intermittently. One of them would be Dobson and his five sociopaths.

It was three o'clock in the afternoon before that ancient engine came thumping down the track and arrested humming on the bridge. Even then I didn't make a move until a gravelly cough temporarily muted the racket.

'Come on, Dutchie.' I tugged on his chain. We struggled up the bank. Tinker gaped from the Mawdslay.

'Bleedin' hell, Lovejoy. That Dutchie you got there?'

'Shut it.' I dumped the granite block in. 'Drive. South.'

He blasphemed at the gears. ''Ere, Lovejoy. Why's Dutchie in chains?' We slammed forward, skidding wheels spraying earth. 'Can we stop at a pub?'

Chapter Twenty-nine

We ran into Dubneath, veered south and started the long run. In the first few miles we hardly spoke, except for me once.

'Give over hammering, Dutchie. The frigging floor'll fall out.'

'But I'm chained,' he bleated.

Aren't we all, I thought wearily. I'd lost all track of who I was being loyal to. The shyly elegant Michelle; the lovely Elaine inheriting the sins of her fathers, *sic*; teacher Jo; Shona the priestess-oracle of a McGunn renaissance; or this lout with whom I was now lumbered.

There hadn't been much choice of direction. North or east meant splash. West was back to Tachnadray. Within ten miles Tinker drove me mad, complaining about the signs.

'Kyle of what?' he grumbled. 'Strath of Kildonan? Here, Lovejoy. Funny bleedin' names up here.'

'Give us that wheel,' I said irritably. We changed places. Cackling joyously, he fetched out a bottle, the old devil.

'Give Dutchie a swallow,' I told him.

He coughed long and harsh, giving himself time to think up an excuse. 'Dutchie shouldn't,' he wheezed, with rheumy old eyes streaming. 'On account of his chains.'

'*Tinker.*' For half a groat I'd have slung them both out. I was sick of the lot of them. Everybody was safe except me, heading back into danger.

Morosely Tinker passed his bottle to Dutchie, whose

glugs made Tinker squirm in distress. He decided to get at me for enforcing charity at his ale's expense.

'There wuz only two of them burkes with Dobson,' he said.

'You sure?' I felt my nape prickle. I'd banked on all five, plus Dobson, turning up at the auction. Dobson must have guessed I'd make a sly run for it.

'I waited, Lovejoy. They went in. Eyes all round their heads.'

'Dobson's here?' Dutchie sounded pale in the rear seat.

'With five goons. Tough lot.'

Dutchie groaned. 'We've had it, then. They'll be on the road waiting for us, Lovejoy.'

'That's the spirit,' I said bitterly.

'Will . . . they all be safe at Tachnadray?' He sounded like a bloke on his deathbed.

'You mean your mother and dad? Certainly. I've got Trembler up. There's a big auction on the estate. Paper job.'

Tinker belched, hawked. 'Mam and dad?'

'Michelle and Duncan,' I explained.

'Dutchie's?' His eyes widened. 'You mean that bird you – ?'

'Shut it.' Tinker always knows more about my affairs than I'd like. 'And your sister is fine.' Still nothing following in the rear mirror.

That took a minute to sink in, but he tried. 'You know about that, then, Lovejoy.'

'Only guessed. She did a painting, your mother Michelle and the laird. Pastor Ruthven gave part of the game away. The laird's wife couldn't conceive and he became obsessed with providing an heir for the crumbling clan. Dynasty delusion.'

'He was always like that. Ever since . . .'

'Ever since he arrived as plain James Wheeler.' I adjusted the mirror to watch Dutchie's face. 'Even had his name changed to McGunn, by deed poll. I had it checked. Which makes Elaine Michelle's daughter. You're Elaine's half-brother.'

'Elaine and me always got on, in spite of all.'

Tinker's brain buzzed. 'Then what she have you chained up for, Dutchie?'

I answered for him. 'Remember that bureau? The night of the fog, when the driver got topped? Dutchie was trying to nick it. You were hoping to make a killing of a different sort, eh, Dutchie?'

Tinker put his mouth near my ear to whisper hoarsely, 'Lovejoy. If Dutchie kilt the driver, what you give him that frigging hammer for?'

'Dobson clobbered the driver.' I kept checking my accuracy on Dutchie's face. 'When me and Ellen reached the wagon the bureau had been offloaded. Dobson organized the twinning job knowing its value. Maybe the driver also realized, so Dobson did him, poor sod. Dobson told Robert that Dutchie'd shared in the killing. With the fog lifting during the night, Robert drove Dutchie to Tachnadray. Dobson had to do in Tipper Noone, who'd done the twinning. He knew it was Dobson.'

Dutchie said, 'Robert came up just as Dobson clobbered me because I wouldn't go along with the driver's killing. I'd been unloading while he killed him.'

Tinker cackled. 'Bet Robert got an eyeful. Lovejoy was in Ben's hut shagging that Ellen. Biggest bristols you ever – '

'*Tinker.*' One day I'll replace the garrulous burke by a Cambridge MA. I'm always making these vows, never fulfil them.

'There was no hiding place except Tachnadray,' Dutchie said. He sounded really depressed.

'Because one of Dobson's goons is from Michelle's home town in Belgium. The Continental connection, eh?' I should have realized a million years ago, if only from Michelle's accent. And Dutchie's nickname: any-

687

body from the Low Countries is called that indiscriminately in East Anglia. Thick as ever.

Dutchie was telling Tinker.' . . . friend of my mother's side.'

The old drunk was delighted. 'Hey!' he exclaimed. 'I know it! Nice little place. I blew a bridge there. Up to me balls in water. Lovely little Norman arch it had – '

'One more word from you, Tinker,' I warned him. He shut up. 'Tell me if I'm right, Dutchie. Duncan and Michelle hid you at *Shooters*. You tried to escape, thinking you'd turn yourself in and tell the truth. Elaine supposed they were protecting you against yourself.'

'I tried telling them.'

I said, readjusting the mirror, 'Shona discovered my identity because I opened my big mouth about antiques. She claimed then to have deliberately sent a real antique to entice me to Tachnadray. Like a prat, I believed her. Here, Tinker, take a glance. Is that motor the one which Dobson and the goons had at Tachnadray?'

'Eh?' He screwed his eyes, peered. 'No.'

'It could have overtaken us twice, and hasn't.' I'd noticed it a mile since. 'It has the legs on us.'

Dutchie sounded almost in tears. 'There's no way out, Lovejoy.'

'Optimist.' The trouble with some people is they're not big enough cowards. Anyway, they didn't want Dutchie any more. They wanted me. 'There's nowt they can do until we pass Dingwall. We're going to double back north for a bit. The A890 to Achnashellach.'

'Funny frigging names round here.' Tinker started a prolonged cough, phlegm and spittle over the side. If his chest would mend we'd be ten miles faster.

The big blue Mercedes stayed on our tail. I took on petrol in Dingwall, as Antioch had told me to do, then left the Inverness Road and pretended to try to shake them off by over-desperate demonstration driving.

The day was fading. The road grew thinner and traffic lessened. An occasional car overtook us and a lorry or two passed going east, but that was about it. We left the security of towns as we hurried west. Countryside is rotten old stuff, lonely and ominous. The Government really should do something. I was as worried what was happening up ahead as much as by that bulky saloon dogging me, and kept staring into the middle distance on every rise. The skies abruptly lowered on us, and a drizzle started. The Mawdslay was a tough old thing, booming up each slope with ease, but steering it through the twisting dips was hell. It had a will of its own. Tinker started snoring.

As we ran on and the day ended there was nothing but hills, and woods and lakes to the left. Dutchie started some lunatic suggestion: drop him off and he would nip down an incline, granite block and all. 'I could reach the Strath Bran railway.'

'Ta, Dutchie, but don't be daft.' He was only trying to help. Bravery's more stupid than cowardice.

Tinker coughed himself awake and also made a contribution. 'Here, Dutchie. How'd you manage to go for a – ?'

'The chain was long enough.' Dutchie rattled it as proof.

We were a couple of miles past the chapel near Bran when we saw the man mending a motorbike by a lantern, thank Christ. He didn't watch us drive past, made no move. I was beginning to worry I'd missed him.

'Hang on, lads,' I said, and cracked on speed. The old giant roared, fast as I could go in the darkening rain.

'Here, Dutchie,' Tinker was rabbiting on. 'What percentage d'you give that Dobson . . . ?'

Here I was sweating, grappling with the controls,

689

and this pair sitting yapping like at a tea-party. The road curved, left to right. Down, then uphill. A slow bend, the Mercedes coming fast, its headlights on full beam. It'd be soon. I yelped, cornering too fast, wrestled up straight, cursing.

The tall lorry swept past in the opposite direction. I saw the Mercedes waver as its driver realized. A horn blared. The crash sounded actually in the Mawdslay and for one crazy instant I thought: Hell, it's us they've got in spite of everything, before sense reasserted itself. I was still driving, unimpeded. Something burst. Air rushed along over the Mawdslay, blew on my ears. I slowed. Only the lorry's tail-lights in the rear-view mirror, nothing moving.

'Gawd Almighty,' Tinker croaked. 'See that?'

Head out of the window, I crawled in slow reverse to where the man was standing by his lorry. I disembarked and stood looking over the edge of the camber.

'Ta, Antioch. All right?'

He heaved a sigh, tutting. 'No gumption, some people. If he'd braked, he might have got out of it.'

A car was ablaze down below among a haircut of young trees. Even as I watched another bit of it woomphed. The air stank oil, rubber. A big bloke arrived on a motorbike, somehow folded it and lobbed it into Antioch's lorry's tailboard with ease. He nodded at the fire on the hillside below, as if acknowledging the inevitable. 'Well,' he said in a singy Ulster voice, 'they shouldn't go round killing drivers, should they?'

'Six in it, eh?' I asked Antioch.

'No. Three. They're using a band radio. They've a rover block on the A87.'

'What's best, Antioch?' Three from six leaves three.

'No smoking, O'Flaherty,' Antioch said absently. The man put away his cigarettes. He had the envious tranquillity of the professional. I'm only glad I'm not that tranquil. 'Look, Lovejoy. I can see you safe part way, say Glasgow?'

'I've a better idea, Antioch,' I said. Lovejoy Knowall. 'They'll suspect I won't touch Edinburgh.' I didn't give reasons. 'Will you put us that way on?'

'Right. I've things to do here, so O'Flaherty'll see you as far as Perth. Then it's motorway.'

The rain was worsening, but it made no difference to the fire below. A lorry chugged past. O'Flaherty waved.

With difficulty I turned the Mawdslay and followed O'Flaherty's lorry. Antioch gave a distant nod as we passed. Aren't people funny? He supports an orphanage in Affetside, then he goes and does a thing like that and stays cool. I kept having to clench my teeth to stop them chattering.

Dutchie's voice wasn't all that steady, either. 'Where to now, Lovejoy?'

'Down the middle, to Edinburgh.'

Past Balmoral. We could always pop in and check that the royal gardeners were growing enough flowers under the old Queen Mum's roses. She was murder on ground-cover plants.

Chapter Thirty

There's not a lot of northerly roads into Edinburgh. Unless you've a hang-glider, this means two accident-prone motorways. O'Flaherty pulled into a lay-by south of Perth, still not smoking as he shook my hand.

'Get them bastards, Lovejoy,' he said.

'Me?' I was amazed. 'I'm not like that. Honest.'

'To be sure. But the driver they topped was my mate.' He was so wistful as he said, 'I wanted Antioch to let me drive the pusher. Good luck.' I waved him off.

Assassins are pretty cool, and often misunderstood. I've often noticed that. I was trying to evade the blighters, not find them. Which worried me, thinking about Mr Sidoli and the travelling funfair. Except Edinburgh's Festival was still in mid-orgy. Which meant Sidoli and Bissolotti would presumably still be hurdy-gurdying grimly on that green. But, my hope-glands flicked into my mind, where can you hide a Lovejoy best, but in a lovely throng? I shelved the terrible fact that any solution would be only temporary. Dobson & Co. had my home territory sewn up. The north was done for, now I'd sprung Dutchie. Edinburgh was limbo, but a satisfactorily crowded one.

'We'll leave you in the motor, Dutchie,' I decided. 'A cutting file and you'll be free as air.'

'We're splitting up?' he asked.

'About Tipper Noone,' I said, concentrating hard on the long strings of motorway lights. I had to be sure. Now that Michelle and me had come together, maybe I was feeling like his dad or something equally barmy.

'Tipper ships for us, Lovejoy. Repros through the Hook.'

Does? No past tenses for poor old Tipper, RIP? Dutchie, for all his gormlessness, was looking better and better. I drew breath to exploit Dutchie's unawareness, but Tinker said helpfully, 'Your pal Tipper's snuffed it.' So much for tact.

The A90 had most traffic, so I bombed in on that while Tinker cheerfully narrated Tipper's tale to the stricken Dutchie. Parking the motor would be a nightmare . . . Too late I noticed the bloody toll bridge. Too tired for any more vigilance, I was in the queue and the man asking for the gelt. He could see Dutchie quite clearly, manacles, chains, block. No hidey nooks in a tourer.

'Fringe?' he said, nodding at Dutchie.

'Eh?'

'Your show.' He shook his head sadly. 'The council should provide proper places for the Fringe Festival. It's a disgrace'.

'Ta. We'll manage.' I tried to look brave but wounded.

'Good luck.'

And we were through. Fringe? 'What was he on about, Dutchie?'

Dutchie chuckled. His first ever. 'He thought we were performers. The Fringe Festival's unpaid art. It makes its way. Streets, bars, even bus stops, living rough.'

I cheered up. We were along Queensferry Road. Civilization and people – God, the people – lights, traffic. 'Shout if there's an ironmonger's.' Suddenly it was simple. I could buy a cutting file without fear. Part of our show's props. See how easy towns are, compared to countryside?

Signs directed us a different way than I'd intended. Older buildings, denser mobs, louder talk, songs, turmoil. I didn't want the old crate trapped in some sequinned cul-de-sac.

'There's a pub, Lovejoy.' Tinker had dried into restlessness.

We were down to trotting pace. I didn't fancy this at all. I wanted a zoom through the fleshpots, a rapid file session to lighten our load, then to go to earth while Tinker and Dutchie caught the Flying Scot south to safety. I'd follow later when I'd convinced our pursuers I'd escaped. But sedate traffic in a glare of road lights can be inspected quite easily – as indeed the pedestrians were doing, openly admiring our Mawdslay.

'Tinker. Got your medals?' A brainwave. The cunning old devil always carries them, and a mouth organ, to do a bit of busking if he's short of a pint and I'm not around.

He obeyed, smoothing them in place. A cluster of stilt-walkers followed us, striding and waving. A couple of girls in Red Indian costumes danced carrying buckets. A jazz band led by a pink donkey, I assure you, stomped jubilantly beside us, one of the players drumming on our side panel, a deafening racket. At a traffic light, me grinning weakly and trying to hum along to show we honestly were fringe people too, a lass in a straw boater stuck her head next to mine and screamed, 'Seen a gondola?'

'Er, no, love.'

'Soddation.' She climbed into the passenger seat. Tinker cackled. She seemed to wear little, black mesh stockings and bands of snakeskin. 'You can drop me off. You in the procession?' She lit a cigarette. Where the hell had she kept that? 'Or marching?'

'Well, er, you can see how we're fixed.'

'Ah.' She gazed round, eyes narrowing as she took in Dutchie's slavehood. 'Good, good. Rejection of imperialistic chauvinisms. The medals are genius.'

'Me wounds still hurt, dear.' Tinker started a shuddering cough. Sympathy always starts him cadging.

'Shut it, Tinker.' No exits down the side streets. All one way now, with the multicoloured mob a long winding tide. Police grinning, waving. A Caribbean dustbin band bonged to our right. A non-band of chalk-faced mimers played non-instruments alongside. Jesus. We were in a parade. My head was spinning. 'Lads, look for a way out.'

'I agree,' the girl groused. 'No political motivation. They're hooked on happiness. Perverts.'

I'd no idea what she was on about, but I made concurring mutters and simply drove in the worsening press. It was pandemonium. In front were handcarts, a lorryload of Scotch bagpipers. All the shops were lit bright as day. Pirates dangled from lamp-posts, singing that chorus from *Faust*. A girl wearing a dog on her hat reclined on our bonnet with a weary sigh and popped a bottle of beer on a headlamp. Tinker whimpered. The dog looked fed up. Two ballet dancers danced outside a shoe shop, *Jewels of the Madonna* but I couldn't be sure because of the other bands. Applause. A youth dragged a floreate piano into the swelling parade, making placatory gestures to me to hold back while he made it. Wearily I waved him on. That said it all – Lovejoy, hot-rodding to escape, overtaken by a pianoforte. A poet declaimed from a girl's shoulders. She was dressed as a skeleton and clutched an anchor.

'See what I mean?' Our girl was bitter. 'A waste of political potential.' She suddenly burst out laughing. The Mawdslay stank sweetly from her smoking. Oh dear. And Dobson's gaunt face among the pavement mobs.

'Lovejoy.'

'I see him, Dutchie.'

He was hurrying along the pavement, quickening when we could make a yard or two, dawdling in each hiatus. One overcoated bloke was with him. As long as we stayed with the carnival . . . A group of tumblers formed a sudden arch. The parade trundled beneath, to cheers. Our snakeskin girl sang tunelessly, head back.

'This bint's taking tablets,' Tinker croaked, disapproving. To him anybody stoned on drugs is 'taking tablets'.

Ahead a regular thumping sounded. A brass band. Correction: a military band, getting closer. Pipes. A cluster of actors froze an instant, took three paces, froze, dressed as vegetables. A pea pod, a cabbage, a possible lentil, a flute-playing celery. Fireworks lit the sky, hitherto the only turn unstoned. A bobby waved us on, veering towards somewhere distantly tall. The thumping of drums at long range. Our pink donkey's jazzy band bopped past as we got stuck behind the piano. I felt clammy. No sign of Dobson and his goon, but one bloke was stock-still on the pavement, keeping his eyes on us even when jostled. Depression and fear fought for my panic-stricken spirit.

'There's no bleedin' notes in that piano,' Tinker said.

'It's Jan The Judge,' our snakeskin said, happy herself now. 'He plays silence. The performance is in its nothingness.'

'What happens if he don't turn up?' Tinker was puzzling.

'Lovejoy. It's the tattoo.' Dutchie pointed. Searchlights swept the night. Pipers lined the battlements. A fusillade crackled.

Slower and slower. The parade was practically static now. Sweat poured off me. The Mawdslay, inch a minute, was trapped. Exactly as I hadn't wanted, there was no way for us to go. Behind us bands jigged, actors twisted and danced. Both sides were thronged with acts and noise. Giant puppets milled. Above us stilted actors and balloons. Something shattered the windscreen. Nobody noticed except me.

'Hey, your gondola!' I grabbed the girl, now floppylimbed and crooning. 'Scatter, lads.' I was crouching below the dashboard, yelling. 'Tinker, hop it. Dutchie, stay among a band.' I hauled the lass sideways. More glass cracked. The Mawdslay trembled. The bloody donkey trod on my foot. Its band swayed past.

'Where?' She stood up, peering.

'Over there,' I yelled, fetching her down on me by a yank of her arm. The shots came from ahead but obliquely, so I spoiled a few syncopations by shoving my way through to the pavement. I couldn't even do that right. I had to step over three actors in evening dress in the gutter. A placard announced that they were the Drunken Theatre of Leigh. I tugged the snakeskin girl along, some protection. You penetrate crowds fastest hunched over and butting along at waist height. The trouble is you can't see. After a hundred yards a doorway, people shoving inside with such a tidal rip I got crushed along.

Brilliantly lit, wall labels and pseudo-Victorian illumination. Red plush, chandeliers. We were in a foyer. Cinema? Theatre? Thickset men in dinner-jackets on the door directing us, me included.

'No, mate,' I said, breathless in my terror sweat. 'You see, me and my bird are – '

He practically lifted me aside. 'Dressing-room there, laddie. She in the Supper Room? The Music Hall shares the same accommodation.'

'Where?' My girl's question was audible. A bell sounded two pulses. People began to hurry carrying half-finished drinks. A theatre's two-minute bell.

Applause burst out upstairs, amid catcalls. A xylophone began. I pulled the door. Two girls were just leaving, all spangles and scales. 'Jesus,' one said, disgusted. 'Not more? There's not room to swing a cat.'

'Sorry, love.'

The room was empty but looked ransacked. A ring of tired bulbs around a mirror, a lipsticked notice pleading for tidiness. Graffiti criticized somebody called the Dud Prospect Company for nicking make-up. My ears worked out what was the problem, finally got there. Silence. My adrenals gave a joyous squirt and relaxed: safety and solitude. I sat at the mirror.

'Right, love,' I said. Hopeless. 'Do me.'

'What?' She squinted over my shoulder. 'Are you on soon?'

'Five minutes.' I swept all the Leichner sticks and pots closer. 'Do the lot.'

'Bastard apolitical theatre managers.' She started me.

For the first time ever I didn't feel much of a clown. No clown's clobber, of course, except gloves and a weird hat. I'd sliced the fingers so they dangled, and scalped the topper into a lid. My face was chalk-white. Red nose, scarlet lips, lines about my eyes. I looked like nothing on earth. She'd done a rubbishy job, but I was grateful as I left, promising to send along any passing gondolas and vote something-or-other. She was carolling drowsily to her reflection, another smoke helping the mood. I turned my jacket inside out, and nicked some baggy trousers. Being noticeable was the one chance.

One of the evening-suited bouncers said, 'Hey. Other way,' but I kept going, down the foyer and out. The carnival was flowing on, over and round the Mawdslay. It stood there forlorn. No sign of Tinker or Dutchie. An overcoated man moved against the flow, finding refuge behind a pillar-box. I capered clumsily into the mob and drew a squad of ghosts trotting with a fife band. A jig. How the hell do you do a jig? I moved faster, advancing up the parade. I even caught up with my stilt walkers, jazz band, the silent piano man.

A policeman pointed me to one side. 'I reckon you're late, son.'

Thank God, I thought, prancing out of the stream.

And saw Big Chas. And Ern. And Mr Sidoli's two terrible nephews. They were in carnival gear, flashing bow ties and waistcoats, striped shirts, bowlers.

'No,' I bleated in anguish. The bobby'd thought I was something to do with the fairground. Even as I whined and ran the familiar sonorous pipes of merry-go-rounds sounded.

'*Lovejoy*.' I heard Big Chas's bellow.

I fled then, down across the parade so terrified that cries of outrage arose even from those fellow thespians who'd assumed I was an act. I needed darkness now as never before. If the gunshots from Dobson's two goons had seemed part of the proceedings, a clown being knifed would seem a merry encore. I hurtled into a small parked van, wrenching the door open and scrabbling through. Two first-aid men wearing that Maltese Cross uniform were playing cards. I waited breathlessly, gathered myself to hurtle out of the front sliding door.

'All right, son?' one asked placidly, gathering the cards. 'An act, is it?'

'As long as he's not another Russian.' He gave me a grandfather's smile. 'No offence, laddie. They only come over here to do Dostoevsky and defect.'

'Aye. Always the second week – '

I swung the door out and dived. Somebody grabbed, shouted. Some lunatics applauded. 'How real!' a woman cooed as I scooted past, bowling a bloke in armour over. God, he hurt. Another carrying a tray went flying. I sprinted flat out, hat gone and trousers cutting my speed, elbows out and head down. I charged, panicked into blindness, among a mob of redcoated soldiers. They were having a smoke, instruments held any old how, in a huge arched tunnel with sparse lights shedding hardly a glimmer. I floundered among them. A few laughed. There was floodlight ahead, a roaring up there, possibly a crowd. Well it couldn't be worse. Here, nark it, Coco,' a trumpeter said, and got a roar by adding, 'Thought it was Lieutenant Hartford.'

A gateway and an obstruction, for all the world like a portcullis. I rushed at it, bleating, demented. An order was barked behind in the tunnel, and I'd reached as far as I could go. I was gaping into an arena filled with bands. Jesus, the Household Cavalry were in there, searchlights shimmering on a mass of instruments and horses' ornamentation. Lancers rode down one side. I could see tiers of faces round the vast arena. I moaned, turned back. Out there I'd be trapped like a fish in a bowl.

The soldiers formed up, marching easily past, some grinning. The drum major glared, abused me from the side of his mouth. The portcullis creaked. Applause and an announcement over the roar. The back-marker strode past, boots in time and the familiar double-tap of the big drum calling the instruments into noise. Gone. The entrance tunnel was empty. I couldn't follow the band into the arena, so I turned. Best if I tried to get to George Street. Those Assembly Rooms . . .

I stopped. My moan echoed down the tunnel towards the exit. Dobson stood there, pointing. Two goons, overcoated neat as Sunday, appeared and stood with him.

'Help!' I screamed, turning to run. And halted. Round the side of the arena gateway stepped Sidoli's nephews. Two more henchmen dropped from the tunnel archway, crouched a second then straightened to stand with the Sidolis. Big Chas walked between them. Five in a row. Both ends of the tunnel were plugged. I was trapped.

'Now, lads,' I pleaded, swallowing with an audible gulp. Blubbering and screaming were non-negotiable. 'Too many people have been hurt in all this . . . ' The fairground men trudged towards me.

Dobson called, 'He's ours, tykes.'

'Ours,' a Sidoli said. The tunnel echoed, 'Ow-erss, owerss.' He was Sidoli's nephew all right.

No side doors in the tunnel's wall. I stood, dithering. Big Chas's line was maybe twenty yards away and coming steadily. Dobson's pair had pulled out stubby blunt weapons. I thought: Oh Christ. A war with me in the middle.

'Stop right there, Chas,' I said wearily. 'You were good to me. You've no shooters, like them. It's my own mess.'

And I walked towards Dobson. My only chance, really. And it bought me a couple of seconds. It bought me much more than that, as it happened. I moved on trembling pins towards my end. At least I now only had one army against me instead of two. More favourable odds, if doom wasn't a certainty.

'No!' a Sidoli shouted. 'Noh,' the tunnel yelled angrily.

Dobson backed smiling out of the tunnel entrance to where I'd first cannoned into the Guards band, his goon with him. I came on. They were in a perfect line. A stern warning cry, 'Loof-yoy! No!' behind me.

If I'd known it would have ended like this, in a grotty tunnel, I'd have marched out into the arena with the band and hared up through the crowd somehow –

An engine gunned, roared. It seemed to fill the tunnel with its noise. I hesitated, found myself halted, gaping, as a slab lorry ran across the arch of pallor, and simply swept Dobson and the two overcoats from view. And from the face of the earth. All in an instant time stopped. To me, forever Dobson and the two nerks froze in a grotesque array, legs and arms any old how, in an airborne bundle with that fairground slab wagon revving past. They're in that lethal tableau yet in my mind. Dobson's expression gets me most, in the candle hours. It's more a sort of let's-talk-because-there's-always-tomorrow sort of expectation on his face. But maybe I'm wrong because it was pretty

701

gloomy, and Ern didn't have any lights on as he crashed the wagon into and over Dobson and his nerks.

Footsteps alongside. I closed my eyes, waiting.

Big Chas's hand fell on my shoulder. 'Lovejoy,' he said, friendly, and sang, '*Hear thy guardian angel say: "Thou art in the midst of foes: Watch and pray!"* '

'I'm doing that, Chas,' I said.

Mr Sidoli was overjoyed to see me; I wasn't sure why. They gave me a glass of his special Barolo while I waited. I'd expected death. Unbelievably I was left alone on the steps, though everybody I remembered came up and shook my hand. The fairground seemed to have grown. There was no sign of Bissolotti's rival fair. Instead, a marquee boasted a dynamic art show, periodically lasering the darkness with a sky advert.

Francie rushed up to say everybody was proud of me. Her whizz kid was temporarily running the Antique Road Show. Like Tom the cabin boy, I smiled and said nothing, simply waited for this oddly happy bubble to burst.

It was twenty to midnight when I was called inside. Mr Sidoli was in tears. His silent parliament was all around, celebrating and half sloshed.

'Loof-yoy,' he said, scraping my face with his moustache and dabbing his eyes. 'What can I say?'

'Well, er.' Starting to hope's always a bad sign.

'First,' he declaimed, 'you bravely seize, Bissolotti's main generator, and crush his treacherous sneak attack.' He glowered. Everybody halted the rejoicing to glower. 'And restrained yourself so strongly that you only destroyed three men.'

Scattered applause. 'Bravo, bravo!'

'Destroyed? Ah, how actually destroyed . . . ?'

His face fell. 'Not totally, but never mind, Loof-yoy. Another occasion, *si*?' Laughter all round. 'Then you cleverly tell the police it is my generator so I can collect it and hold Bissolotti to ransom.'

702

This time I took a bow. The nephews burst into song.

'And at the arena you bravely tried to spare my nephews then the risk when they go to help you, knowing how close to my heart . . . ' He sobbed into a hankie the size of a bath towel. Everybody sniffled, coughed, drank. I even felt myself fill up.

'And you walk forward into certain death!'

I was gripped in powerful arms. Ern and Chas sang a martial hymn. Fists thumped my back.

When you think of it, I really had been quite courageous. In fact, very brave. Not many blokes have faced two mobs down. It must be something about my gimlet eyes. You must admit that some blokes have this terrific quality, and others don't.

Joan was watching in her usual silence. Her eyes met mine. Well, I thought, suddenly on the defensive. I'd been almost nearly brave, hadn't I? I mean, honestly? Joan smiled, right into my eyes, silly cow. She's the sort of woman who can easily nark a bloke. I'd often noticed that.

They'd have finished the auction in Tachnadray.

It was three o'clock in the morning before I remembered Tinker. Sidoli's lads found him paralytic drunk busking in George Street, Dutchie doing a political chain dance round his political granite block. Tinker said we'd all go halves. His beret was full of coins, enough for a boozy breakfast for us all.

Chapter Thirty-one

Countryside. No rain, no fog. And, at Tachnadray, no longer only one way out. Me, Duncan and Trembler were talking outside the workshop. They'd taken on half-a-dozen apprentices. From the quality of their work I wouldn't have paid them tea-money, but Duncan said they'd learn.

'Make sure you spread them about this time.' I meant the reproductions they were going to mass-produce. 'One each to East Anglia, Newcastle, Liverpool, Glasgow, Bristol and Southampton. Stick to one route and you're in the clag.'

'We've had enough trouble,' Duncan said with feeling.

'You didn't have any,' I pointed out nastily. After all, I was the hero. 'Okay, your son was a hostage, but safe. He's a McGunn.'

'There's no trouble for you now, Lovejoy, eh? I mean, those two men, and the others?'

'Tipper Noone? And the driver? No. Whatever the police find won't matter a bit. Dobson and his killers are dead.'

The vehicle was fixed by Ern, a spontaneous case of brake failure. The police could enjoy themselves speculating on the guns found on two of the deceased. I, of course, wasn't within miles. I sprouted alibis, Sidoli's doing.

'Wotcher, love,' I said to Elaine.

Elaine had a new automatic wheelchair. I said it wasn't as good as the old garden machine we'd sold at the auction. She'd bickered back that I didn't have to sit in it.

'Lovejoy,' she said, in that tuneful propositioning voice women use when they're going to sell you a pup. 'How'd you like to become a partner?'

'If that is a proposal of marriage, you're too plain.'

'Stop fooling. In Tachnadray.'

'It's not me, love. Trembler here will. It's time somebody took him in hand.'

That's what we'd been heading towards all along. Elaine turned her sea-bed opalescent eyes on Trembler. 'Will you, Cheviot?'

'He's been on about nothing else,' I said irritably. 'He's trying to work out how to word it. Nerk.'

Trembler tried to start a solemn contractual conversation. 'I'll have to think – '

'Me and Tinker did a draft contract for you after breakfast. And,' I added, 'my percentage of the auction profits you can split three ways – Tachnadray, and the families of the driver and Tipper Noone. How's that?' As soon as I'd made the offer I groaned. Still, easy come, easy go.

'Is Lovejoy serious?' Elaine asked.

'I'll do a list of exploitations. Pottery, prints, pressed flowers of Tachnadray, tartan novelties, photographs of the ancestral home. And you'll sell inch-square plots to tourists, fortune at a time, each with a great Sale Deed in Gothic Latin lettering, a sealing-wax blob on a ribbon. Postage extra. And "coin" tokens in fifteenth-century denominations. It's where greatness lies.'

'There's something scary about all this, Lovejoy.' But Elaine's eyes were shining.

You have to laugh. For the first time in her life she'd challenged the outside world, and won victory. Now she wanted the thrill of the contest over and over. There'd be no stopping Tachnadray now, especially with Trembler on the team.

'I'll come and check on you every autumn, Cheviot.'

It was the end of an era. There'd be a sudden drop (I nearly said tumble) in Soho's sexploitation shares tonight.

They had moved away when Elaine paused. 'Oh, Lovejoy. Can I ask something?'

I walked over. Trembler moved politely out of earshot. Her eyes were radiantly lovely looking up at me.

'Lovejoy. Did you and Michelle?'

'Eh? Did we what?'

She blushed, a lovely rose pink. 'You *know*.'

'No.' I was puzzled. Then my brow cleared. 'You can't mean . . . ?' I was mixed furious and hurt. '*Elaine!* How can you ask that, after . . . after . . . you and me . . .'

'Shhh,' she said. 'I'm sorry.' My back was towards the workshop. 'I honestly didn't mean anything, darling. And thank you.' She blew a mouth and left smiling, beckoning to Trembler.

Duncan and I watched them go.

'She'll take him in hand, Duncan.'

'Aye.'

Michelle was there in the car, waiting to drive me to Inverness for the train home. I'd already said my goodbyes. Mrs Buchan had wept uncontrollably at the simultaneous loss of two prize appetites. I'd restored her to normal apoplexy by saying I had to get home because her pasties weren't a patch on East Anglia's. Mrs Moncreiffe was also sad: 'It was all so naughty, wasn't it?' she said, tittering. Tinker hates tittery women. Dutchie would be down again before long. I'd said so-long to Hector, his two dogs and the others. Robert hadn't looked up from shoeing a horse. I kept out of range in case he lobbed the anvil at me in farewell.

'Duncan. You'll say cheerio to Shona for me?'

'Aye. I will.' He knocked out his pipe, cleared his throat. Something was coming. 'She's always been

706

headstrong, Lovejoy. She shared all the clan obsessions. Don't blame her.'

'I don't,' I said, with my sincerest gaze. 'But the road Elaine's taking is healthier. More open. More people.'

'Aye.' He sighed. 'My sympathy's with Jamie. It'll be a sorry union between that pair.'

'One thing, Duncan.' I pointed to the east wing, by far the weaker of the two. 'Ever thought of having a fire? Accidental, of course. Just before a sale, like that Norfolk business in the mid-'seventies . . .'

'Och, away wi' ye.'

He was laughing, as I was, as we left.

'Are you sad to be going, Lovejoy?' Michelle had waved to Duncan, said she'd be straight back after she'd dropped me.

'Not really. No antiques up here, is there?'

She gave a tight smile. After we'd reached that wretched bridge and were cruising on the metalled road instead of shaking the teeth out of our heads on the bumpy track, she shot me a glance.

'Lovejoy. Did you ever . . . you know, with Elaine?'

'I *knew* you thought that.' I spoke with indignation. 'I could see the bloody question coming. Look, love.' Bitterness now. 'If that's the best your vaunted woman's intuition can do I'd trade it in for guesswork.'

'Did you?' She slowed, to inspect my eyes.

'No,' I said levelly, with my innocent stare. I never try for piety because it never works. 'And if you count the tableware you'll find it complete. Anything else?'

'I was only – '

'Because I'm a bit scruffy and don't share your blue blood I'm the perennial villain. Is that it?' I was looking out at the moors, quite a tragic figure really, I thought.

'I'm sorry, Lovejoy. But you must realize – '

'You and the laird, okay. I did realize, eventually. But your main problem with Elaine is Trembler – forgive me, Cheviot Yale, Esquire – not me.'

She pulled at my hand. 'Don't be angry, darling. It's only natural anxiety. I didn't mean to offend . . .'

We were three hours reaching Inverness. I forget what took us so long. Anyhow, before saying goodbye Michelle promised in spite of all my protests to accompany Dutchie on the runs to East Anglia with the reproduction antiques. She looked shy, new, voluptuous.

'You don't want me, love,' I said, thinking of Francie, Joan, Ellen, and Jo who would be desperate to hear how I'd got on. 'I'm even bad at hindsight.'

'Next month to the day, darling,' she said. 'I'll stay with you a whole week. I'm dying to see your cottage, and nobody need know. Here. For you.' She gave me a parcel, quite heavy. I know you're not supposed to, but I can't help palpating presents to guess what's inside. She saw me and laughed. My chest was bonging a definite chime.

The Mawdslay had gone before I remembered. I'd promised Ellen I'd stay on her houseboat down the Blackwater for a few days about then. And Sidoli's fairground was through on its run south in that week. And Jo had hinted she'd have three half-term days to spare. And I'd Margaret to thank. And Helen. Oh God. Why is it that trouble always follows me, and never anybody else?

On the train I unwrapped Michelle's parcel. The lovely pair of snuff mulls shone as the fading light patched and unpatched the carriage windows. The milky silver gleamed in time with the train wheels, and then blurred. Bloody women. No matter how you try they always get you at a disadvantage, don't they.

One day I'll give everything up, I honestly will. As soon as I find out how.